ARE YOU SURE ABOUT THIS?

Chris Keating asked himself. *If this works, it changes everything. All the dreams of the First Landers, overthrown in an instant. Contact with Earth. Marseguro a colony, not an independent world . . . no more Selkies,* he reminded himself. *No more second-class "landings," becoming more second-class every year as the Selkies breed like the animals they are. No more men like my father being murdered by the Selkie masters. A chance to return to Earth, where real humans belong . . . a chance to find something better to do with my life than cataloging algae samples and scrubbing growth tanks.*

Chris remembered the Selkies throwing him off the pier just to watch him flounder, just to humiliate him, just to mock him.

He remembered his father, lost at sea.

He remembered his mother, dying in a hospital long cut off from the latest medical advances.

He remembered her words to him, just yesterday morning . . .

"The Selkies murdered him . . . and now they're killing me . . . they'll kill you, too, my boy . . ."

He blinked hard twice. "Not me," he said, and flicked the switch on the Emergency Interstellar Transmitter. . . .

THE HELIX
WAR

**DAW Science Fiction Titles by
Edward Willett:**

THE HELIX WAR
Omnibus:

Marseguro   *Terra Insegura*

LOST IN TRANSLATION

THE HELIX WAR

MARSEGURO

TERRA INSEGURA

Edward Willett

DAW BOOKS, INC.

DONALD A. WOLLHEIM, FOUNDER

375 Hudson Street, New York, NY 10014

ELIZABETH R. WOLLHEIM
SHEILA E. GILBERT
PUBLISHERS

www.dawbooks.com

First Printing, April 2012
1 2 3 4 5 6 7 8 9

AUTHOR'S NOTE

The omnibus edition of *Marseguro* and *Terra Insegura* you hold in your hands is about seven hundred pages in length, contains some 250,000 words . . . and began with two sentences I tossed off one September morning in 2005 at Robert J. Sawyer's course in writing science fiction at the Banff Centre in Banff, Alberta.

That morning's class began with Rob asking us to write, cold, in five minutes, the opening to a story. I wrote: "Emily streaked through the phosphorescent sea, her wake a comet-tail of pale green light, her close-cropped turquoise hair surrounded by a glowing pink aurora. The water racing through her gill-slits smelled of blood."

Over that week I tried to turn that opening into a short story, but as I followed my usual story-building procedure of self-interrogation—"Why does Emily have gills? Why is there blood in the water? What is she fleeing?"—I kept coming up with answers I couldn't cram into a short story. And so when the time came to propose a new book to Sheila Gilbert, my editor at DAW, to follow *Lost in Translation*, those answers begat *Marseguro*, which in turn begat *Terra Insegura*, which has now begat this omnibus volume, *The Helix War*.

It's quite astonishing to me that all this sprang from that simple writing exercise. It's even more astonishing to me—but hugely gratifying!—that *Marseguro* went on to win the Prix Aurora Award (Canada's equivalent to the Hugo Award) for Best Long-Form Work in English at the World Science Fiction Convention in Montreal in 2009. *Terra Insegura* was a finalist for the award the following year.

It's also been gratifying to see the response from readers to these two works. I hope that with the publication of *The Helix War*, many new readers will have the opportunity to enjoy these novels.

Normally, that's where I'd wrap up a note like this, but I do want to add one more thing: that night in Montreal when *Marseguro* won the Aurora Award, I was so flabbergasted that I forgot to thank the two most important people in my life.

So to my wife, Margaret Anne, and my daughter, Alice, thank you a million times over for your love and support. It's kind of weird having a husband and father who makes up entire worlds out of thin air, I know. But remember this: I have never created, and never will create, anything as wonderful as our family. Thank you, thank you, thank you.

And, gentle reader, thank you, as well.

Edward Willett
Regina, Saskatchewan
November 7, 2011

MARSEGURO

For my big brothers, Jim and Dwight: if not for all those science fiction books they brought into the house, I never would have started reading and writing the stuff.

Acknowledgments

This book began with a single sentence, written in September 2005, as an exercise in Robert J. Sawyer's class in writing science fiction, part of the Writing With Style program at the Banff Centre. Thanks, Rob!

Heartfelt thanks to my editor, Sheila Gilbert, whose insightful comments and questions helped make this a much better book than it would otherwise have been. Any remaining failings are entirely my own.

Finally, special thanks to the staff of Second Cup in the Cornwall Centre, Regina, Saskatchewan, where most of this book was written, fueled by icepresso Chillers.

Chapter 1

THE MAIN PIER of Hansen's Harbor stank, but that was only one reason Chris Keating hated it.

He stood in the early spring sun, shivering, glaring down the three-hundred-meter-long, fifty-meter-wide stretch of preformed bioplast planks. The pier looked secure, but Chris knew better. Some of that stink came from the salt water. Some of it came from the alcohol-fueled engine of the catamaran-sub *SeaSkimmer*, idling at the end of the pier. Some of it came from rotting seaweed. But some of it, Chris knew, came from the slowly decomposing bioplast itself. To him it always stank of anaerobic decay, the smell of swamps and stagnant ponds. One day—he *knew* it—one of the pier's massive posts would give way, and the whole structure would collapse, flipping everything and everyone on it into the deep, cold water of New Botany Bay, where they would drown like his father drowned, lost at sea, when he was four.

One day. Maybe even today, while *he* was on the pier.

Chris shivered again. He hadn't expected to come down to the pier today, and his white shirt and pants were made of thin cloth designed for comfort in the warm, humid environs of the genesculpting lab's algae room, not for keeping out the wind currently whipping up whitecaps on the bay's blue-green water. But Dr. Stanless had radioed half an hour ago for someone to come help unload the samples he'd collected from the algae fields off Slick Rock, and the only someone who could be spared had been Chris.

He hadn't dared refuse. No one on Marseguro knew his shameful secret except his mother, and she wasn't likely to tell.

He clenched his fists when he thought of her. He'd visited her in the hospital on his way to work that morning. She'd looked so frail, lying in that hospital bed hooked up to the machinery that kept her alive—not at all like the strong woman he remembered from childhood, the woman who had single-handedly raised him after his father's death . . . and single-handedly made sure he knew the truth that lay behind that "accident."

She'd been conscious this morning, an unusual occurrence since the last stroke. She could speak, after a fashion. Most of what she said made little sense, and usually she hardly seemed to know he was in the room, but this morning had been different.

She'd squeezed his hand with astonishing strength for someone at death's door. "Selkies!" she'd hissed, her eyes focused on his face with a feverish intensity he well-remembered but hadn't seen in six months. "They killed your father. They're killing me! They'll kill you, too, if they find out . . . if they know. . . ."

"Shhh!" Chris had shot a look over his shoulder, though he knew he'd been left alone. Still, you could never be *certain* the Selkies weren't listening. . . .

"He hated the sea. They *made* him go on that boat. The Selkies all came back. The landlings all died."

Chris almost reached out and put his hand over her mouth. These were things they only talked about in their own home, never in public, never where someone else might hear.

"They knew . . . they must have found out he Believed . . . he never wanted to be here at all . . . never wanted to be on the *Rivers of Babylon* . . . Hansen kidnapped him . . . the Selkies murdered him . . . and now they're killing me . . ." Her wide eyes suddenly filled with tears. "They'll kill you, too, my little boy . . . my little . . ." Her eyes fluttered closed.

Chris had eased his hand away from her and stood up, shaking. He'd had to take half a dozen deep breaths before he felt calm enough to walk out of the hospital, and it took all his strength not to look over his shoulder to see who might be watching him go.

"It's not just the Selkies," his mother had told him over and over. "Most of the landlings are on their side. A very few of us know the truth. A very few of us cling to the Body Purified. But we can never let on . . . or they'll kill us.

"Like they killed your father."

Chris looked at the alarmingly narrow ribbon of bioplast stretching from the shore into the bay, and the balefully glittering water all around it. *God, I hate this planet.* But he couldn't let on, or the secret Selkie cabal his mother had told him *really* ruled Marseguro would know he had inherited his family's dangerous beliefs, and eliminate him as they had eliminated his father.

Maybe they've already decided to. Maybe this errand is a setup, carefully arranged to provide an opportunity for another "accident". . . .

He shook his head. *Don't be paranoid,* he told himself. If the Selkies wanted to kill him, he'd simply disappear. Hardly anyone would notice. Even fewer would care.

No, the errand was just what it seemed to be. And though he hated his job almost as much as he hated the pier—and the planet—everyone on Marseguro had to work, and if he quit at the genesculpting lab he'd be stuck scaling hulls or filling potholes with a Council make-work crew, doing jobs bots could do better and faster.

Gathering his courage and holding it tight like the teddy bear he'd carried everywhere until his tenth birthday, he set off down the pier.

Halfway to the *SeaSkimmer,* the Selkies swarmed him.

They soared out of the bay like dolphins, trailing drops of water that flashed silver in the sun. Their broad, bare webbed feet slapped down on the bioplast with the sound of fish being poured from a net. There were at least a dozen, male and female, all adolescents or young adults, all wearing the water resistance-lessening skinsuits the Selkies favored, vibrant reds and purples and greens and yellows personalized with lightning bolts and starships, Earth dolphins and Marseguroite squigglefish, flames and starscapes and abstract designs that made their owners hard to look at. They surrounded him in a whirlwind of color, and he stopped dead. They laughed and chirped in their own language, one landlings could neither understand nor speak, since they lacked the Selkies' modified vocal apparatus and enhanced hearing.

"What do you want?" Chris could barely squeeze the words out through a throat gone tight with fear. His heart pounded in his chest, a caged animal frantically throwing itself against the bars of its prison. *"What do you want?"*

They ignored him, circling him like Earth sharks were said to circle their prey, chanting—not in Selkie, but in English. He suddenly realized *what* they were chanting: just a silly poem, but one that almost loosened his bowels. "Eeny-meeny-miny-mink, tip a landling in the drink, watch him splash and watch him sink, eeny-meeny-miny-mink." Oversized eyes stared at him, transparent nictitating eyelids sliding sideways across giant green irises.

He knew this "game." He'd known it since childhood. He'd seen Selkies "play" it on other young landlings. He'd always managed to avoid it.

Until now.

The Selkies rushed him, laughing. Strong hands seized him. He felt his feet leave the ground, then he was horizontal, held high above short-cropped hair, pink and violet, green and blue, and shaved pates tattooed to match the skinsuits. They were carrying him, running with him. He screamed, then he was flying through the air, the horizon flipping, the pier suddenly above him . . .

. . . and then he hit the water. Its cold embrace enveloped him. He sank, kicked desperately, managed to get his head into the air, grabbed a precious breath, sank again, and couldn't find the surface. His clothes pulled at him, sucking him down. He floundered, striking out blindly. He couldn't see, couldn't breathe, couldn't think through the heart-stopping terror. *I'm going to die!* his mind shrieked, then shrieked again, a mantra he couldn't stop, running through his head over and over. *I'm going to die! I'm going to die! I'm going to die!*

Something grabbed him. He struck out at it in panic, his body no longer under his control, but the thing was stronger than he was. Against his will it pulled him deeper and deeper into the . . .

. . . then his head broke water and he sucked in a lungful of air, coughing and choking as spray came with it, and he realized he'd been pulled up to the surface, not down into the deeps, and maybe, just maybe, he wouldn't drown after all.

Hands reached for him again, but this time they pulled him up, lifted him out of the water, laid him on the pier. Prostrate, eyes closed, cheek pressed against the reeking wet bioplast, he coughed out the last of the water. Selkies chirped and squealed around him, then a shadow fell across his face and he opened his eyes to see one, a girl, crouching down and looking at him. Her zebra-striped yellow skinsuit, practically painted on, left little of her lithe body to the imagination. She had violet hair and the same green eyes as every other Selkie . . . and she looked familiar. He wasn't sure why. "Are you all right?" she said. "I'm so sorry. We never thought . . ."

Chris closed his eyes, shame and anger choking him in equal measure. He couldn't talk. He wouldn't give them the satisfaction of hearing his voice break. He pushed himself up onto all fours, then stood shakily, ignoring the girl's proffered hand.

"We didn't know," said another Selkie, a boy with a red-and-blue spiral tattooed into his shaved head and wearing a skinsuit covered with iridescent scales. He looked vaguely familiar, too. "We didn't know you couldn't—"

"Chris? Is that you?" A burly, bearded, and bald-headed nonmod pushed his way through the now sheepish-looking crowd of Selkies. Behind Dr. Stanless, Chris glimpsed the rest of the crew of the *SeaSkimmer,* nonmods and Selkies alike, gawking like bystanders at an accident. "Are you all right? What happened?"

Selkie kids at the edge of the crowd began melting away. Three slipped into the bay, barely raising a splash. But the tattooed boy and violet-haired girl stood their ground. "It was just a prank," the boy said. "We were celebrating the end of school. We didn't mean anything by it . . ."

"We didn't know he couldn't swim," the girl said.

"We didn't know *anybody* couldn't swim," the boy said.

Chris felt himself flush. The shame and fury had reached the surface.

Dr. Stanless glared at the Selkies. "It was a stupid prank. It's one thing to pull it on one of your friends, but grabbing a stranger and throwing him into the bay . . ."

"He's not exactly a stranger," the boy said. "We went to landschool together." He glanced at Chris. "Don't you remember? I'm John Duval."

Chris still hadn't spoken. The world seemed preternaturally bright and clear around him, as though the air had turned to diamond. At the sound of John Duval's name, it grew harder and brighter yet.

John Duval. The Selkie boy who had bullied him from the time they were both eight Earth years old until they were thirteen, and Duval had gone off to seaschool. Tripped him in the cafeteria. Pulled down his trunks in the swimming pool, then swam off with them, leaving him naked and shamed in the water, begging someone to bring him a towel while the other kids laughed at him. . . .

He looked at the girl. Emily Wood. He remembered her, too. Remembered her standing with the other girls pointing and laughing.

How could *they* not know he didn't know how to swim? The teacher had forced him into the pool that day, told him he had to overcome his fear of what had happened to his father. He'd been too little, too scared, not to give in. His mother had always told him if he didn't conform, didn't hide the truth, something bad would happen to him . . . but he'd never forgotten the shame, never forgotten that early proof that Selkies couldn't be trusted. "They're not real humans," his mother had said. "They're monsters." Before that, he'd wondered. After that . . .

He'd never gone back into the pool. And the teacher, once she'd realized what had happened, had never made him.

They knew, he thought. *They knew. It's a warning. I'm being warned. The Selkies . . . the secret cabal . . . they suspect me, suspect I'm like my father . . . they're letting me know what will happen to me if I cross them. . . .*

He shivered as the sea breeze flowed over his wet body. *I'm all alone,* he thought. *Mom was the only one I could talk to, and now . . .*

Something clicked into place inside him, as though a switch had been thrown, and the heat of his anger vanished. Instead, he felt as if he had been doused in water even colder than that of the bay, water that froze into certainty his determination to do something that, until that moment, he had only toyed with on his blackest days.

He didn't say a word to John Duval and Emily Wood. To Dr. Stanless he said, "I hate to ask, sir, but may I have a few days off?"

Dr. Stanless blinked, then frowned. "I understand you're upset, Chris, but it was just a soaking."

"It's not that, sir." Not *precisely*. "It's . . . my mother." Again, partly true.

"Oh." Dr. Stanless knew all about Chris' mother, of course. "Oh, I see. Of course. Take as long as you need."

"A week or two at most," Chris said. "Thank you, sir."

With all the dignity he could muster, letting his gaze slide past the shamefaced Selkies as if they weren't there, he turned his back on the sea and walked inland.

He didn't look back.

Emily watched Chris Keating walk away, and felt her face burn. The prank that had seemed so harmless just an hour before when her waterdance class had streamed out of the Hansen's Harbor Seaschool for the last time now seemed incredibly cruel and stupid. They'd recognized Chris as one of their old landschool classmates, thought he'd get the joke, laugh along with them. . . .

She glanced at John. He stood with his head bowed, biting his lower lip.

"I hope you two are ashamed of yourselves," Dr. Stanless said. "Chris is one of my best lab assistants. A nice quiet kid. He was on his way to help me unload algae samples when you jumped him. Now who's going to help? You two?"

Put like that, they really didn't have a choice, and in fact, Emily thought a few minutes later as she helped pull slimy, stinking buckets of multicolored goo from the hold of the *SeaSkimmer*, she didn't really mind. It was the least she could do to make amends . . .

. . . *although Dr. Stanless isn't really the one you need to make amends to,* she told herself. She shook her head. She could barely remember Chris Keating as a kid; they'd never had much to do with each other. In fact, she couldn't really remember Chris Keating having much to do with anyone. *We should have known he'd react badly. It's our fault, not his. Dr. Stanless is right. It was a stupid thing to do, and it would have been just as stupid even if Chris* did *know how to swim.*

Except how could you live on a planet more than ninety percent water-covered, with fellow citizens genetically

modified to breathe both air and water, and *not* know how
to swim? She shook her head again. *Well, it takes all kinds
of genes to make a genome,* as her mother liked to say.

An hour later they'd loaded the last of the algae tubs
onto the rollerbot, and it had trundled off toward the labs.
Dr. Stanless, his arms splattered with stinking slime, grinned
as he watched the samples roll away. "Some fascinating
specimens there," he said. "I can't wait to get at them in the
lab." He stretched his arms above his head, yawning hugely,
then turned to where Emily and John stood side by side,
every bit as splattered and stinking as he was. "A nasty job,
but thank you for it." His eyebrows drew together and he
gave them each a hard stare. "And I hope you've learned a
lesson."

They both nodded. Dr. Stanless held his severe look for
a moment, then broke into a grin. "All right. Get out of
here. You're probably feeling dry."

"Thank you, Doctor Stanless," Emily said.

"Yeah, thanks," John echoed, and they jumped off the
pier together.

With a shiver of relief and pleasure, Emily welcomed
the embrace of the water. Muscles landlings didn't even
have tightened the passages to her lungs and squeezed her
nostrils closed. At the same time, the tight-clamped gill slits
on either side of her neck relaxed and opened wide. She
wriggled her long, webbed toes and with a flick of her feet
dove deeper into the bay. Like all Selkies, she could function perfectly well on land, certainly better than landlings
could function in the water, but only for a few hours. When
forced to stay on land for extended periods, the Selkies
wore special water-filled landsuits that kept their gills and
skin wet. Without moisture, tissues modified for life beneath the waves began to dry out. Discomfort would eventually turn to pain . . . and then to lingering, agonizing
death. Emily shuddered, and swam a quick figure-eight
loop-the-loop to shake the horrible image from her mind.

John swam up beside her, the high-pitched chirps of his
underwater laugh tickling her ears. "Feeling frisky?" he
said, though no landling would have heard more than a few
clicks.

"Not the way you mean it," Emily retorted. A notorious
tailchaser, John Duval had worked his way through most of

the seaschool's female population, but hadn't yet managed to land her (so to speak). A quick fling in the foam wasn't what she wanted, or she would have had it by now, from John or any one of a dozen boys. *That's one thing Selkies and landlings have in common,* she thought, flicking her feet in John's face as she turned and swam deeper into the waters of the bay, toward the strings of lights that glowed below, marking the "streets" of the underwater portion of Hansen's Harbor. *All the males can think about is sex.*

Of course, that was partly due to the work of Victor Hansen, the genius genesculptor who had created the Selkie race and shepherded them safely to Marseguro forty years—almost fifty Earth years—ago. He'd wanted them to "be fruitful and multiply," so he'd made sure to build in a healthy interest in sex.

Emily had the same basic genome as every other Selkie and a perfectly healthy interest in sex to go with it, thank you very much—but she had a mind as well as a body, and she'd long ago decided not to take that plunge until she felt mentally and emotionally ready for it. And when she did, it would be with someone for whom it was more than just a splashy game with all the depth of the shallows off Whitesea Point.

For now, she had other things on her mind. She'd finished seaschool. In a month, she would start specialization training. She knew what she wanted to specialize in . . . but she hadn't told her parents yet.

She was pretty sure they wouldn't like it.

John followed her deeper. "I wasn't making a pass."

Emily laughed. "You're *always* making a pass."

"Not this time! I know better. I was just making conversation."

"Sure you were." They'd reached the bottom of the bay. Dome-shaped and cylindrical structures rose from the sandy seafloor on either side, connected by water-filled tubes, heated swimways that freed people from having to wear skinsuits indoors. Emily put a little extra kick into her swimming, but John easily kept up.

"What's your hurry?" he said. "The rest of the class is probably still over at Freddy Fish's. And they've got an hour's head start at drinking. We'll have to hurry to catch up."

Emily sighed, and stopped swimming, holding her position with gentle kicks and arm waves. John stopped next to her and stared, his eyes, so much larger than a landling's, glowing green as they reflected the light of the streetlamp behind her. "I can't come to Freddy's now," she said. "We're late, remember? I have to go have dinner with my parents."

"They'll understand . . ." John began, but Emily shook her head.

"I doubt it. I'm going to tell them my specialization plans."

John's mouth opened in a silent "Oh."

"My mother the eminent practical geneticist and my father the noted underwater construction engineer are unlikely to be thrilled with my decision to pursue a career in the arts," Emily went on. "You know how much trouble I had just convincing them to let me *take* the waterdance class."

"No wonder you were so willing to haul stinking buckets of algae," John said.

"It was probably more fun than what I've got to do next," Emily admitted. But then she grinned. "However, I do have an ally."

John shook his head. "No way. I'm not coming with you to help you do *that*."

"I didn't mean you," Emily said, while mentally adding another line to her secret list of *Reasons John Duval is Never Getting Any From Me.* "Amy has an announcement, too."

"Let me guess. She's decided to marry a landling."

Emily laughed. "Nothing that drastic. But after two years out of seaschool, she's finally chosen her specialization, too . . . amphibian opera."

"Music?" John stared, and then burst out laughing and flipped head over heels in a swirl of bubbles. "Oh, I almost wish I could be there."

"You can still come if you want to," Emily said sweetly.

"No, no, no." John flicked hands and feet, backing away from her. "No way. I'm off to Freddy's. But I can't wait to hear how it all turns out."

He spun and swam off. Emily watched his wriggling legs and butt fade into the green gloom. *Might be fun . . .* she thought, and then shook her head. *No. There are better Selkie in the sea.*

Anyway, there was no hurry for all of *that*. First things first.

First, she had to face the Selkies whose genomes had blended to make her everything she was today.

That being the case, she thought, you'd think they'd be happier about the outcome.

She jackknifed, kicked, and swam off in a new direction.

Chapter 2

CHRIS KEATING STRODE up through the streets of Hansen's Harbor to the old concrete building that housed his dingy one-bedroom apartment. The building dated from the first wave of construction at the site of what eventually became known as Hansen's Harbor. Flat-roofed, utilitarian, it stood three stories high and housed two other tenants besides Chris. He'd never exchanged more than five words with either of them.

Once inside he stripped off his still-wet pants, shirt, and underwear, rolled them into a sodden ball, and dumped them into the clothesbot for washing, drying, and folding. Next, he took a long, hot shower, only stepping out when he could no longer even imagine he smelled the stink of the pier, the bay, and the Selkies who had attacked him.

He ran a comb through his collar-length sandy brown hair, checked on the still-disappointing growth of his wispy beard, then padded into the bedroom. He liked hiking and until his mother had gone into the hospital this last time had headed inland whenever he had a couple of days off, camping there out of sight and smell of the sea. The last time had been weeks ago, but his pack stood ready, leaning against the closet wall.

He tugged on underwear, then his favorite worn-but-waterproof hiking pants, shirt, and jacket, shoved his feet into his toughest, most comfortable boots, then went into the kitchen and pulled out enough prepackaged camp rations to last him for a week. They were made mostly of algae and seaweed, and tasted like it, but what wasn't made of algae and seaweed on this flooded excuse for a planet?

From a cupboard by the door where he kept odds and ends, he pulled out a short crowbar. He stuffed it into his pack.

The last thing he picked up before heading out the door was his multiplayer. He left the stack of music and vidchips on his bedside table. Since his mother's stroke, he'd only been listening to one thing: the ancient, precious chip his grandfather had given his father before shipping him off to the Moon in the hope he'd survive the impending destruction of Earth.

Chris had listened to it before, of course, but its contents had become more meaningful as he faced the dreadful truth that his mother would soon be gone, leaving him completely alone among the monsters of Marseguro. The chip was his lifeline to Earth, to a planet free of Selkies or any other genesculpted abominations.

His grandparents' faith had been weak, he thought, not for the first time. Had it been stronger, his grandfather would have known that the Avatar would successfully Purify the Earth, and that God would repent of Its threatened destruction of the planet. Had his grandfather truly Believed, he would not have secretly paid to have Chris' father, then just eight years old, smuggled to the Moon along with another family and their young daughter . . . and his father would not have been one of the refugees, forced to live on the dry-docked *Rivers of Babylon* by the overtaxed Lunar government, who had failed to get off the ship before Victor Hansen and his followers flung it into space ahead of the oncoming Earth fleet.

Very few of the people trapped aboard were Believers. Of those who were, only one man made the mistake of admitting it. Hansen's followers had thrown the man out of the air lock before the ship crossed the orbit of Mars.

The other Believers had kept quiet, and pretended to be as relieved to be free of the Body Purified as Hansen's followers were. They'd kept on keeping quiet even after they landed on Marseguro. But in the privacy of their homes they'd clung desperately to their beliefs, and so Chris' father, and his mother—the small girl whose family Chris' grandfather had also sent to the Moon, and given the care of his son—had grown up immersed in the truth. Even if they hadn't fallen in love, they would have married, Chris believed. How could either of them have polluted themselves with a moddie-lover?

Chris didn't even know the names of the other original Believers, didn't know if they had clung to their Belief, didn't know if any of the other children of his generation were secretly of the Body. Belief, as his grandfather had demonstrated, could be a fickle thing.

He sometimes hated his grandfather for that reason. *If only he had truly Believed, I would have been born on Earth . . . and everything would have been different.*

Chris locked the door of his apartment behind him and looked up and down the street, empty this time of day: the only buildings on it were clones of the one he'd just exited, and the people that lived there (all landlings like him, of course; Selkies lived in underwater habitats) were either at their low-paying Council-prescribed jobs or asleep because they worked nights.

Nobody to see him leave, then. Just the way he wanted it.

He turned left, then left again down the just-wide-enough-to-pass-through space between his building and the next. A paved alley ran behind both buildings: every night, the sanitation workers—some of whom were probably his sleeping neighbors—drove along it, collecting refuse, most of which they delivered to the microfactories ringing the south side of the bay as feedstock for the fabricators.

On the other side of the alley, rock-strewn ground, barren except for the occasional low purplish-red needlebush and patches of scraggly blue-green notgrass, rose steeply to a ridge crowned with the open-umbrella-shaped treelike plants dubbed bumbershoots. Following a path up the slope he himself had worn, Chris climbed until he stood beneath one of those plants. There, for the first time, he stopped and looked back.

Hansen's Harbor stretched left and right, curving around the semicircular shore of New Botany Bay, sheltered and surrounded by the ridge he'd climbed. Many of the buildings, especially those farthest from the water, were gray concrete like his own; others sported the violent colors favored by the Selkies. To his left, the microfactories lay haphazardly scattered across the ridge slope like squat black building blocks dropped by some careless giant. Taller structures of glass and black or dark red stone, the homes and offices of well-to-do landlings, rose at the water's edge. The very tallest buildings stood in the water itself, with eight or nine stories above water and another four or five below. To Earth eyes, Chris suspected, the city would have looked half-flooded—but no Earth eyes had ever seen it.

Maybe I can change that. He turned inland. There, ridge after ridge marched toward the horizon, each taller than the next, until the towering, snow-capped mountains no one had ever climbed took over. Massive waves, unimpeded in their sweep around the planet except by this one small continent, crashed against the sheer cliffs on the far side of those peaks, which also broke the backs of the powerful storms that roared across the world ocean. In the relatively calm water and atmosphere in the mountains' lee, Victor Hansen's creations and the nonmodded humans who had accompanied them to Marseguro had carved out a place to live.

If you can call it living.

The trail Chris had made plunged down through native forest to join a larger, paved two-lane road running parallel to the ridge. That highway connected Hansen's Harbor to Marseguro's other eight settlements: tiny Parawing and Roger's Harbor and slightly larger Beachcliff and Outtamyway to the north, and Rock Bottom, Good Beaching and Firstdip, Marseguro's second-largest town, to the south. Only landlings ever used the road; the Selkies preferred traveling by sub or "sputa" (an acronym for Self-Propelled Underwater Towing Apparatus), an unlovely word for a form of travel that terrified Chris just to think about. Some goods rolled along the road in giant transbots, but boats could make the trip just as effectively *and* carry greater quantities of cargo. On those rare occasions when a medical or other emergency necessitated speedy travel, one of the colony's half-dozen aircraft could be called into service.

Chris wished he could call one into service right then, because stuck on his own two feet his destination lay two days away; but since what he had in mind would undoubtedly have gotten him thrown into Hansen's Harbor's tiny Criminal Detention Center, he could hardly file an application for the use of community transportation. Instead, he picked his way down the ridge through the bumbershoots and stickypines and turned left, walking south toward the town of Firstdip, a journey which would take him the rest of the day, if that were where he was going . . . which it wasn't. His real goal was a fork in the road just shy of the Firstdip turnoff, a fork that would take him farther inland.

As he walked, he fished out his multiplayer, unclipped and unfolded the earset, and thumbed the play button.

The male reader's accent sounded strange to Marseguroite ears, like that of all Earth people in the old vid and audchips Hansen's Hijackers (Chris' private term for the original colonists) had brought with them. But a mere half century wasn't enough time for English—Hansen's language, and thus the language of Marseguro—to drift to the point where it couldn't be understood.

"The Wisdom of the Avatar of God," the voice intoned, "presented for the edification and enlightenment of the Body Purified, that all who are within the Body might know the Truth, and be well-armed against the lies of those who are without. Prologue: The Miracle. Hear the words of the Avatar." The reader paused. "In 2178, through the might of God Itself, the Earth experienced a miracle . . . a miracle I foresaw."

Chris had heard those words more times than he could count, but they never failed to give him goose bumps. Even now he felt his arms and the back of his neck tingling, though he'd begun to sweat in the jacket that had seemed just right when he first stepped outside. He pulled off the jacket and tied it around his waist, rubbed his arms vigorously—but kept listening to the resonant voice.

"The asteroid on a collision course with the planet should have destroyed most of the biosphere. There was no hope of a reprieve. None . . ."

". . . no hope of reprieve. None."

You can say that again, Richard Hansen thought, shifting his weight from one sore hipbone to one slightly less sore on the unforgiving polished oak of the pew. Salvation Day services had just begun, and although bets had been laid, down in the Body Security office, over just how long the reading from *The Wisdom of the Avatar of God* would go on this year, even the most optimistic—who had not been Richard—had predicted the entire first chapter at a minimum. And today Richard had particular reason to want the service to be short.

Of course, he had no say in the matter.

"Those who could—the rich, the politicians, the religious leaders—had already fled the Earth for the Moon, for Mars, for the Belt, for the moons of Jupiter and Saturn, for New Mars and Bon Mot and the other handful of young colonies among the stars. Those who could not—the poor, the working people, the deluded but faithful flocks of the blind and useless pastors and popes, imams and ayatollahs, sages and seers and ministers and monks—waited to die . . ."

The Messenger, a sallow-faced Lesser Deacon with pale blond hair and the most pitiful excuse for a goatee Richard had ever seen, spoke in a singsong, slightly nasal voice, a close approximation of chalk squeaking on a blackboard. Richard had heard of people who claimed to get goose bumps when they heard *The Wisdom of the Avatar of God* read, but he doubted this was quite what they meant.

He tried, as he always did, to imagine what it must have been like, after the scientists proclaimed the planet's death sentence. The World Government, formed at the end of the twenty-first century as the Terror Wars finally stumbled to their bloody conclusion in an orgy of ethnic cleansing, bombings, and poison attacks, had tried to keep the news secret—but no secrets could be kept in those days of instantaneous data transfer and brainwebs.

"Cities burned. Countries crumbled. Hundreds of thousands died," the Messenger said. Stained glass windows behind the pulpit purported to show those events, although the hundreds of thousands were represented by half a dozen figures in a variety of extremely unnatural poses. *Well, you probably can't do much better with stained glass,* Richard thought. It might have been the height of medieval special effects, but it was hardly full-sensory vurt. Not for the first time, he wondered what had been in Avatar Harold the First's background that had made him model the House of the Body—and all the lesser Meeting Halls—after Gothic cathedrals, especially considering he had claimed to hate all established religions equally. *Couldn't he have gone in for padded seats and a concession stand?* Richard thought. *Maybe a vidscreen? If you wanted to distance yourself from religion and were reaching into the past for inspiration anyway, an early twenty-first-century movie house would have been just the ticket, by all historical accounts* . . .

"But one group of people remained steadfast in the face of terror and catastrophe," the Messenger went on. Passion—or something—seemed to have gripped him as he read the words of The Avatar. Unfortunately, it squeezed his voice even higher. "They moved through the chaos, calm and unafraid, giving aid and succor, promising that all was not lost, that the oncoming asteroid need not destroy the Earth." The reader paused. What *The Wisdom of the Avatar of God* did not spell out, but Richard knew because of his somewhat privileged position within Body Security, was that those early followers of the Avatar had also moved through the corridors of power of the World Government, bribing, assassinating, coercing, convincing, paving the way for the Avatar's rise to power. You had to admire their faith, Richard thought. Everyone else thought the end was near, but *they* believed in a future—a future they intended to control.

"Thus spake the Avatar," the Messenger intoned, the ritual insertion Messengers used when reading from the Great Work whenever they came to a first-person passage, to ensure that listeners understood that what followed were the Avatar's words, not their own. "They were my followers, the Body Purified, the faithful whom I had prepared for the Edge Times for twenty years, for I knew . . . I *knew*, with the certainty that only one who has heard the Whisper of God can know . . . that the asteroid was coming, long before the so-called men of science detected its approach."

As a child, Richard *had* felt a thrill every time he heard *that* passage read. The truth of it could not be denied. The Avatar *had* had advance knowledge of the approach of the Fist of God. Where else could that knowledge have come from but God Itself?

"Those 'scientists' fled, too, those who could. Nothing could stop the asteroid, they said. It was too big, too fast. No power within humanity's grasp could deflect it, or alter Earth's doom." Richard's eyes moved to the next stained glass window, where the asteroid loomed, although the artist, either through scientific ignorance or simply for effect, had surrounded it with blood-red flames that it most certainly had not displayed.

"And they were right. No power within humanity's grasp *could* have stopped it. But what is impossible for humanity is as nothing for God. 'We must show God we repent,' I told my followers, as God had instructed me to tell them. 'We must show God that we will cleanse the planet of the evil that has fouled it, that we will purify humanity, the Body of God. If we do this, God will repent of Its decision to destroy us all. If we do this, humanity will regain its future.'

"Some laughed. Some mocked. Some turned their backs on me and rejected my message. But some remained faithful. And it was they who took the actions that convinced God humanity deserved another chance."

And now they neared the part that Richard had particularly loved as a child, imagining himself as one of the selfless heroes of the Purification . . . and a part he had grown to dread as an adult, since the day he discovered his family's not-so-secret shame. He shifted again on the unforgiving pew.

"It was they who burned the unnatural crops and the evildoers who had defiled Earth's God-given soil with them, they who bombed the genesculpting laboratories, they who slew the genesculptors, and they who hunted down and eradicated the genesculptors' abominable creations, the foul results of their blasphemous defacement of God's Holy Human Genome. Many of those first Holy Warriors of the Body died in battles with inhuman monsters created by scientists blinded by greed and hubris. But the battles were won. Earth was Purified."

Scientists blinded by greed and hubris, Richard thought. *Like Grandfather Victor.* He kept his gaze resolutely ahead, looking at the next stained glass window in the row, showing the burning labs and the battles with genemodded humans who looked remarkably like the demons of—again—medieval religious iconography. He always felt like everyone in the House was sneaking glances at him when that passage was read. It was no secret—hadn't been since his father's death—that he was the grandson of Victor Hansen, the man who had successfully fled in a starship full of genemodded humans just before the Moon fell to the Avatar's forces.

Richard had never known his mother; his father had told him she had died in childbirth. He did his duty, raising Richard in a stern and rather distant fashion, as though obeying orders rather than because he felt any strong familial connection to the boy.

And then, one day in Richard's thirteenth year, two decades ago now, his father had gone to the roof of a very tall building, taken off all his clothes, and thrown himself naked onto the very hard pavement directly in front of the groundcar carrying the man the Council of the Faithful had just elected and proclaimed the new Avatar, Andrew the First.

He'd left no explanation for his actions: no suicide note, no political rant, no video.

Richard had his own theory: that his father, a minor functionary in the Deaconate of Food Allotment, had been driven into suicidal depression by the way he had been consistently shunted into the nether realms of the Body Purified hierarchy, where his career and his life had stagnated.

It couldn't have been easy on him, losing his wife so soon after their marriage. Richard had never even seen a picture of her, and his father would answer no questions about her, beyond the bare-bones facts of her death; the topic seemed to pain him deeply. In-laws? Cousins? Uncles? Aunts? None that Richard had ever learned about. Just his father and him . . . and now, just him.

On his darkest nights, Richard suspected the Body Purified had eliminated all other relatives of Victor Hansen. Though if so, he had no idea why they would have let his father and him live.

He kept his gaze forward. Maybe people were looking at him, maybe they weren't. He wasn't sure which would be worse.

The Messenger somehow managed to raise his voice even higher, to the point where he sounded like a five-year-old sawing the E string of a toy violin. "The Holy Warriors killed or drove all the moddies from the planet and with them as many of the lesser abominations as they could identify—drunks and drug users, homosexuals and adulterers, pedophiles, and the priests and imams and shamans and sages of all the false religions that have too long held sway over the minds of the ignorant."

At last, the Messenger paused, but only to interject another, "Thus spake the Avatar." Alas, when he continued, his voice remained at the same painful pitch.

"Then one night, just days prior to what the scientists and politicians and religious leaders had told us would be the end of the world, God spoke to me a second time, in a dream. 'You have done well, my servant,' It said. 'I have repented of my decision to destroy your world. But I will still deliver a powerful rebuke. Warn your followers to take shelter. Then, when the rain of fire has passed, emerge and lead the world into a new age.'

"I gave the orders. The Body Purified descended into the shelters I had ordered built beneath our places of worship and training. From deep beneath the surface, we watched the Miracle occur on the vidscreens providing our only link to the surface.

"Within the orbit of the Moon, another asteroid, miraculously unseen until that moment, slammed into the oncoming killer, slapping it out of the way like an annoying fly."

The stained-glass artist had certainly outdone himself depicting *that* amazing occurrence, Richard had to admit. That window rose directly above him to the right, though, and if he did more than glance at it he'd get a crick in his neck. Instead, he dared to look around the House again. Two thousand people, all looking in his direction—but up, at the window. Not looking at him at all.

Not anymore, he thought, fully aware he was being paranoid. But then, he knew that "they" really *were* out to get him, if you defined "them" as the Body Purified hierarchy. He could never be trusted until he had proved his loyalty.

Soon, he thought. *Soon.*

He'd worried the problem so long it had even begun to seep into his dreams. Recently he'd been waking from nightmares in which he was Victor Hansen, desperately loading followers and monstrous creations alike into ships fleeing Earth's imminent destruction. Odd he'd never dreamed of the final flight from the Moon, though . . . perhaps his imagination couldn't extend that far.

Well, if what he'd just discovered panned out, he might be able to put paid to those nightmares forever. Although . . .

He shook his head and tried to refocus his attention on the Lesser Deacon instead of worrying about his own state of mind.

"The asteroid missed the Earth," that worthy continued. "But though God spared us from total destruction, It delivered a stern rebuke, just as It had promised.

"Small pieces of both asteroids streaked into Earth's atmosphere. Some burned up. Some blasted through the ionosphere, and kept going. Some fell into harmless orbits. One, as I fully expected, destroyed *Orbital Orleans,* the space station infamous for its licentiousness and debauchery even among the most godless people of Earth—and crawling with moddies who 'entertained' the patrons of that devil's palace in unspeakable ways.

"That alone was a powerful sign that I and the Body Purified had done the will of God. But the most powerful sign of all was that, though the rocks that made it through the atmosphere destroyed a dozen cities, raised tsunamis that scoured whole islands and coastlands clean of life, and killed tens of millions," (Richard didn't even attempt to crane his neck to see *that* window), "not one—*not one*—of the members of the Body Purified who heeded my call to the shelters died.

"And thus when we emerged we had the supplies, the knowledge, the training, and the inclination" (*and the bribed and cowed government leaders,* Richard thought) "to impose order on chaos, law on lawlessness, and most importantly, godliness on godlessness.

"Thus did the whole world, for the first time in its long, sordid history, fall at last under the sway of God.

"The Day of Destruction proclaimed by the scientists had become The Day of Salvation, a new beginning for all of humankind.

"Praise God, for It is good, and Its mercy endures for as long as humanity does Its will!"

And then, to Richard's pleased astonishment, the Messenger stopped speaking. He gestured at the girlchoir seated below his elevated pulpit, and a hundred preadolescent children rose and launched into "The Path to God Leads through Destruction," the closing hymn. Richard rose, shaking his head. *Phil wins the pool again,* he thought. *He must be blackmailing the Messenger.*

Not that the service was over yet. The Order of Worship ended with what the Body called the Penitents' Parade and ordinary people called the Parade of Fools.

They came in now, a larger contingent than usual, maybe two hundred in all, escorted by Holy Warriors wearing snow-white dress uniforms highlighted by black piping and looped silver chains. The prisoners wore dark-brown Penitents' Robes, marked with the symbols of their guilt: crosses for the Christians, crescents for the Muslims, Stars of David for the Jews, lotus leaves for the Buddhists, pink ribbons for the homosexuals, old dollar signs for the thieves and interest chargers, and—

Richard blinked. He'd never actually seen anyone wearing the double helix that marked a moddie before. From the reaction of those sitting near him, he guessed they hadn't, either. People craned their necks, trying to get a better look. The robe hid any obvious modification. Of course, it might be something relatively minor and invisible, like enhanced hearing, or extra-sensitive taste buds, something that had shown up in one of the random genome scans Body Security regularly—

Fast as a striking snake, the moddie moved. It ducked behind a Holy Warrior, vaulted the rail separating the stage from the audience, and landed beside the Messenger, still standing at the pulpit. It grabbed his arms and twisted one behind his back until he shrieked like a rabbit in the jaws of a fox. The moddie's hood fell back, revealing a young girl, hair and skin white as the Warriors' uniforms, lips red as blood. Her eyes had the slitted pupils of a cat. She looked wrong, evil, horrible . . .

. . . and yet somehow, to Richard, *familiar*.

She opened her mouth, revealing sharply pointed canines, and screamed, "Free—"

But who or what she wanted freed, no one ever heard. A puff of black, greasy smoke burst from her chest and back. Her voice choked off and she collapsed, the smoke swirling as she fell.

Her body continued to smoke as two Holy Warriors leaped over the railing and dragged her away. The Messenger, now almost as white as the moddie, clutched the pulpit and said, "Behold the . . ." His voice faltered and he had to swallow before beginning again. "Behold those who have been God's Enemies, those whose very existence threatens us all, for God's forbearance on the Day of Salvation was not unconditional, and was not for all time. We must continue in the ways of God, as set forth by Its chosen vessel, the Avatar, or God will unleash Its wrath on us again, and next time there will be no salvation.

"Those such as these—" he pointed to the Penitents standing before the pulpit, and his voice rose to a shriek as fury found its way through the terror that had gripped him a moment before, "—and that!" He pointed after the Holy Warriors departing with the smoking corpse of the moddie, "Deserve death! But the Avatar is merciful and has interceded with God on their behalf. Today these Penitents—those that still live—" he smiled at his own joke, "—begin five years of service to the Body. If they truly repent of their foolishness and embrace the Avatar's Wisdom, they may yet find forgiveness and enjoy the mercy of God. Praise the Avatar!"

"Praise the Avatar," the audience intoned. Not one of the thousands jammed into the House of the Body had made a sound during the drama with the moddie—Richard especially. Most of them had probably seen sudden death before—the Holy Warriors were big believers in summary punishment—and drawing attention to yourself at such a moment could end with *you* being in a Penitent's Robe at the next service.

And Richard, burdened with his family history and also trying to understand how a creature he'd never seen before—had never even imagined—could have seemed so familiar, like an old friend, when he saw it for the first time, had more reason than most to avoid drawing attention to himself.

A dream, he thought. *I must have seen it in a dream . . .*

But if he'd never seen one in real life, how could that be possible?

"Praise God!" the Messenger said.

"Praise God!" the congregation repeated.

"The service is ended," the Messenger said. "Go in Purity and serve the Body."

"We will serve the Body," the audience replied. They watched in silence as the remaining Penitents were led out of the building to the transports waiting to take them to the Body's Penitent-manned mines and farms and factories and lumber camps, then made their own hushed way to the exits.

With everyone else, Richard filed out of the House of the Body (every teenager independently dubbed it "the bawdy house"). He looked up at the single spire that towered above the entrance, pointing the way to God Itself. High above, six Holy Warrior airfighters roared across the city, white contrails slashing the sky like the claws of God Itself. Richard watched them until they were out of sight. As a kid, he'd wanted to be a Holy Warrior, but his father wouldn't let him enter the Junior Jihad program at school . . . and then, by so effectively and publicly removing himself from Richard's life, had ensured Richard could *never* be accepted.

Or so he had thought. But . . .

Shamed and furious after his father's suicide, Richard had promised even then, barely into his teens, that he would clear the family's name within the Body, though of course he had no realistic way of doing so. In fact, as he served out his final few years as an adolescent within the strict confines of Home and School for Orphaned Boys No. 381, he had fully expected to be barred from any service within the Body. It had therefore shocked him deeply to be summoned, the day before his graduation, by the Deacon in charge of the school, and informed that he had been selected for service within Body Security. After four years of training in data analysis and electronic communications, he had entered Body Security at the lowest possible point, as a data-mining drudge in the Sub-Deaconate of Planetary Communication Oversight.

To his own surprise, he had discovered he both enjoyed and excelled at the work. He had a knack for netting and landing important information swimming in the flood of data that passed through the Planetary Communication Oversight office every day. He'd quickly risen to the rank of junior analyst, then analyst, and within five years had become a second-level assistant to Archdeacon Samuel Cheveldeoff himself . . .

. . . and then he rose no farther, and for three years

watched as others with neither his talent nor his dedication leapfrogged over him into positions of greater and greater authority.

And then, late on Richard's thirtieth birthday (which he celebrated by working late, as he celebrated most birthdays), Cheveldeoff summoned him to his office.

A summons from Cheveldeoff seldom meant good news, and something just a bit more solid than rumor strongly suggested that occasionally those whom Cheveldeoff summoned were never seen again. Heart in his mouth, Richard took the elevator down to Cheveldeoff's deeply buried office. No one staffed the receptionist's desk in the dark-red waiting area, and the double oak doors stood open, revealing Cheveldeoff at his desk.

Not for the first time, Richard thought Cheveldeoff looked like an artillery shell. He was bald, broad-shouldered, thick-necked, and surprisingly short when he stood up—which he didn't, for Richard. Eyes like polished mahogany glinted beneath bushy eyebrows the color and texture of steel wool. "Come in," Cheveldeoff said. "Sit down."

Obscurely relieved he hadn't been told to close the door, despite the emptiness of the antechamber outside, Richard followed Cheveldeoff's orders, as did everyone with any sense. "I'm going to explain your predicament to you," Cheveldeoff said, and did, directly, frankly, brutally: Richard, being "the grandson of a traitor and the son of embarrassment," had advanced as far within the hierarchy as he ever would.

Unless . . .

"You have two options, as I see it," Cheveldeoff said. "You can quit the Service of the Body and find an ordinary civilian job. As you are certainly aware, however, we will watch you closely for the rest of your life.

"Or, you can prove that you are to be trusted . . . that you are not tainted by the evil of your grandfather or the weakness of your father. I'll even tell you how you can do it." He leaned forward, hard brown eyes locked on Richard's. "Find the planet to which your grandfather dragged his misbegotten brood of malformed monstrosities. If they're out there, we want them. And if we find them, and you helped us, well . . . then Bob's your uncle, the sky's the limit, you're sitting in the catbird seat, you're God's favorite mortal." He leaned back and smiled, or at least showed his teeth. "Hell, you might even get my job . . . after I retire, of course."

And so Richard Hansen had been handed the quest— the completely hopeless quest, he suspected, but he knew well enough that Cheveldeoff's "two options" had been nothing of the kind—that, should he fulfill it, would redeem him and his family in the eyes of the Body Purified, and by extension, all of unmodified humanity.

He glanced at his watch. And if he didn't hurry, he'd be late delivering his latest report on that quest.

He increased his pace down the broad boulevard leading from the House of the Body to the headquarters of Body Security, at the heart of the City of God (once known as Kansas City, though no one who had lived there before the Day of Salvation would have recognized any part of it; the original had been largely pulverized, then burned, by the nearby impact of one of the larger chunks of the asteroid, and the remaining ruins had been scraped away and used as feedstock for microfactories).

For two years, Richard had been reporting to Cheveldeoff at monthly meetings. At the very first one, Cheveldeoff had surprised him by bringing out a chessboard. "You play, of course," Cheveldeoff said. It hadn't been a question, and Richard could hardly be surprised that the Archdeacon of Body Security knew of his predilection for the game. He hadn't really been surprised to discover that Cheveldeoff excelled at it, either. Richard, no slouch himself, always put up a good fight, but hadn't won once.

He sometimes wondered what would happen if he did.

Two years. Hard to believe. When he'd taken on the challenge of finding his grandfather's pet moddies, he hadn't realized just how thoroughly Victor Hansen had disappeared. He'd assumed the moddies would have maintained some kind of contact with other colonies settled from Earth, so he had begun his search on New Scotland, recently Purified and brought under the oversight of the Avatar. But though he had scanned and searched and combed through current and archived intercepted communications using every tool at the disposal of the Ministry, he had found nothing to point him to Grandpa's secret hideout . . .

. . . until yesterday.

He looked up at the cloudless sky and grinned. Today, he had a surprise for his chess partner.

Samuel Cheveldeoff finished setting up the ancient hand-carved ebony-and-ivory chess set, and glanced at the loudly ticking image of a clock on one of the vidwalls, currently displaying his favorite wallpaper: the interior of a nineteenth century Italian villa. The images of rich furnishings and Old Master paintings gave his Spartan office warmth it generally lacked. Richard Hansen should arrive within minutes.

Cheveldeoff sat back in his chair and glanced at another vidwall, temporarily switched from displaying the villa to showing the rapidly emptying interior of the House of the Body. The automated defense systems in the House had made short work of the moddie who had attacked the Messenger, but Cheveldeoff still felt unhappy about the incident. If the moddie had gone the other way, into the crowd, there would have been casualties, and it looked bad for the Body to lose worshippers on the holiest day of the year. The Avatar . . . he grimaced; no, not the Avatar, but the Avatar's Right Hand . . . would not be pleased.

"Message from the Holy Office," the computer suddenly said, as if on cue. "Your presence is required in the Holy Office at 1900. No rescheduling permitted."

Cheveldeoff clenched his jaw for a moment; then forced himself to relax it. Much as he would have liked to tell the Right Hand what he could do with his meeting, the stakes were too high. The Avatar, felled by a mysterious stroke . . . and though Cheveldeoff suspected the Right Hand suspected *him*, he had had nothing to do with it . . . lay alive but vegetative in his private hospital. The prize Cheveldeoff had been working for all his life was in play—but the Avatar had been struck down too soon. He could not be certain he had enough votes on the Council of the Faithful. His main rival, Ashok Shridhar, Archdeacon of Finance, controlled the purse strings of the Body—and purse strings could easily become puppet strings.

If the Avatar's illness had been brought on by something other than his own penchant for debauchery, it could mean Shridhar *was* confident he had enough votes among the Council members.

Well, Cheveldeoff could not outbribe the Archdeacon of Finance, but he suspected he could outblackmail him.

In the meantime, though the Right Hand officially remained above all such maneuverings for succession, and would serve whomever God in Its wisdom appointed through the deliberations of the Council, in this situation the Right Hand essentially *was* the Avatar, and until the real Avatar died or recovered, Cheveldeoff dared not cross him. The Right Hand could bring his own weight to bear on certain Council members, for he knew everything that had happened in the Avatar's Dwelling, behind the screen of discreet silence even Cheveldeoff had never been able to pierce. Cheveldeoff had heard rumors of some of the activities certain Councillors had enjoyed in the company of the Avatar, but he had no proof. He suspected the Right Hand had pictures, video, and gene samples.

Enough waffling. "Computer, accept meeting request from the Holy Office."

"Meeting accepted," said the computer.

My turn, Cheveldeoff thought. "Computer, request meeting with Grand Deacon Ellers. Topic: the poor performance of the Holy Warriors at today's Salvation Day service in the Central Meeting Hall. Time: tomorrow, 7 a.m." He grinned savagely. "No rescheduling permitted."

"Meeting request sent," the computer said. A pause. "Meeting accepted."

Cheveldeoff nodded to himself. An early morning meeting that forced Ellers to clear his schedule for Cheveldeoff's convenience should powerfully remind the new commander of the Holy Warriors that, since the primary function of the Holy Warriors was to keep the Body secure from enemies both internal and external, the Holy Warriors served Body Security.

Or, to put it another way, they served *him.* Ellers, whom Cheveldeoff knew from his agents on the Grand Deacon's staff would prefer that Shridhar be the next Avatar, needed to be very clear on that point, because Cheveldeoff intended to ensure, by any and all means, that the Holy Warriors *continued* to serve him, in case the coming succession battle moved from the Council chamber into the streets.

The sound of a faraway doorbell rang through the room, and the computer said, "Archdeacon, Richard Hansen to see you. Identity confirmed."

"Computer, all walls to Villa Two," Cheveldeoff said, and the image of the interior of the House of the Body disappeared, replaced by ceiling-high windows framing a sun-drenched view of vineyards and olive trees. "Computer, open door."

A door in the villa apparently opened, and Richard Hansen came in. The ultramodern blood-red vestibule behind him clashed visually with the wood and marble of the wallpaper for a moment, then the door closed.

"Come in, Richard, come in," Cheveldeoff said. "I believe it's your turn to play white."

"Good afternoon, Archdeacon," Richard Hansen said. He crossed the matte-finish black floor and sat down across from Cheveldeoff. Without another word, he moved, pawn to king four, and the game began.

Cheveldeoff played with half his brain. Though a decent enough player, Hansen couldn't really challenge Cheveldeoff, who could have been a Grand Master if he had cared to pursue it. Cheveldeoff enjoyed their games, but not because of the chess. The real reason he brought Hansen in week after week was that the man fascinated him.

As well he should. Richard Hansen had been Samuel Cheveldeoff's pet project for a quarter of a century, ever since Cheveldeoff had taken command of Body Security (at the remarkably young age of thirty) and had first been briefed on the long-term experiments already underway with Victor Hansen's "son" and "grandson."

I wonder if he knows just how much he looks like a young Victor Hansen? Cheveldeoff thought, studying Richard as Richard studied the board. *Probably not.* The Body strictly controlled all information about Victor Hansen, including images. And Peter Hansen, Richard's "father," had certainly not been provided with a stock of images of Victor Hansen to keep around the home.

Even if Richard Hansen were to see a photograph of Victor Hansen at the same age, Cheveldeoff doubted he would put two and two together. After all, many grandsons looked like their grandfathers. Cheveldeoff's own grandfather had been not that dissimilar from himself.

But Richard Hansen, though he would never know it, was an exact duplicate of Victor Hansen at his age—because Richard Hansen, as only about ten people on the planet knew, was not Victor Hansen's grandson at all.

He was Victor Hansen's clone.

Cheveldeoff moved. "Bishop to Knight Five. Check." Hansen bent to the board, giving Cheveldeoff a few more minutes for reflection.

When that old sinner Victor Hansen had stolen the *Rivers of Babylon* and fled the solar system, he had left behind undercover operatives to cover his tracks. In the chaos and confusion that had followed the Day of Salvation and the ensuing meteor storms, they had had no difficulty clearing the Stellar Survey databases of any trace of any research Hansen might have conducted into possible destinations—and Cheveldeoff, like every head of Body Security before him, had no doubt Hansen had had a specific destination in mind before he fled.

Hansen's followers didn't remain undercover for long. Betrayed for money by someone they had trusted a little too much, interrogated by the Body, they had provided a great deal of information about Hansen and his plans—though not, unfortunately, his ultimate destination.

And one thing they had revealed was that Hansen hadn't been content to leave behind a few loyal followers. He had also left *himself* behind, in the form of five frozen cloned embryos, only awaiting implantation.

Victor Hansen had been long-divorced by the time he fled for Luna. Officially, the split had been vicious, and his wife had become a loyal member of the Body . . . but that, the Hansen loyalists revealed, had all been a ruse. In fact, Hansen's ex-wife had remained fiercely loyal to him, and he had left the clones in her care.

Physically, the clones were all identical to Victor Hansen. But in their brains . . .

According to Hansen's agents, each of the clones carried within them modified genes that somehow (Cheveldeoff didn't pretend to understand how) would at some unknown point in their lives provide them with unlearned knowledge about Hansen's plans. Hansen's followers said Hansen did not believe the Body's reign would last more than a few years, and he hoped his clones would be able to reconnect his hidden moddie "children" with humanity at some point.

More: just about the last thing Hansen's loyalists had revealed, before they succumbed to the side effects of their questioning, was that Hansen's implanted gene-bombs were expected to do more than just rewrite the clones' memories: they would at least partially rewrite the clones' personalities as well, making them mental as well as physical copies of Victor Hansen.

The man must have thought he was God Itself, Cheveldeoff thought.

Shortly after the interrogations ended, the Body-controlled media reported that Victor Hansen's ex-wife had taken her own life, leaving behind a suicide note that explained she could no longer live with the shame of her former relationship with the evil genesculptor *extraordinaire.*

With her disposed of, the Body had turned its attention to Hansen's clones. Two had been implanted almost at once in surrogate mothers. One had developed abnormalities in the womb and been aborted. The other, however, throve. Given the name Peter Hansen, raised in a Body orphanage and told his mother had died when he was an infant, he had been guided by Cheveldeoff's predecessor into a noncritical job in a minor bureaucracy while the Body waited for the Hansen gene-bomb to explode, at which point he would be interrogated to learn the coordinates of the planet Victor Hansen had fled to. A simple plan, but one that had gone badly awry shortly after Cheveldeoff took over Body Security, when Peter Hansen had decided the best way to celebrate the ascension of a new Avatar was by naked base jumping without a parachute.

Victor Hansen's gene-bomb, it appeared, could have unanticipated side effects.

Cheveldeoff had therefore decided to take a different approach with the third clone, already a teenager, which had been implanted in Peter Hansen's (carefully selected) wife, who had then tragically "died" in childbirth. (In fact, she had died shortly after childbirth, in a sealed room not far from where Peter Hansen already grieved for her—Cheveldeoff's predecessor had not liked loose ends any more than he did.) He directed the clone into Body Security itself.

The geneticists (such as they were; in a society that outlawed genetic modification except within strict guidelines closely supervised by the Body Purified, the best and brightest did not choose genetics as a career) had persuaded him they had a gene therapy that would blunt most of the gene-bomb's personality rewrite. They were *almost* sure it wouldn't interfere with the transfer of "memories" about the destination of the *Rivers of Babylon*.

Cheveldeoff had agreed to the experiment. During an otherwise routine vaccination, Richard Hansen received protection against more than he knew. And then, as Richard approached the age when the gene-bomb should detonate, Cheveldeoff had posed him the very question they hoped the gene-bomb would provide the answer to: "Where did Victor Hansen take his moddies?" And ever since he had kept Richard close at hand and closely watched, waiting to see what would happen.

"So," said Cheveldeoff, several moves into the game he already knew he would win, "how goes the great moddie hunt?"

Richard frowned at the board. *How does he do that?* he wondered. *I'm already struggling. No matter what I do, he's a move—or three!—ahead.*

But Cheveldeoff's question made him smile. "It's going well," he said, looking up from the game, which patently wasn't.

Cheveldeoff's bushy iron-colored eyebrows lifted like caterpillars trying to crawl up onto his shaved skull. "You have news?"

"I do." Richard's smile widened to a grin. "I have a vector."

The Archdeacon sat up straight in his chair, more reaction than Richard had ever seen from him. "Tell me!"

First, Richard moved, advancing a pawn to protect an exposed knight. Cheveldeoff countered without even looking at the board, and Richard suddenly found himself forced to choose between sacrificing a bishop and a rook. Richard studied the board. He didn't like what he saw. "I've concentrated for years on a handful of possible routes the

Rivers of Babylon might have taken," he said, his hand hesitating over first the bishop, then the rook. "All very logical, all based on the fragmentary records we have of the ship's flight out of the solar system. But last week I decided to take a different tack. I had . . . a hunch. I took a look at some data I'd never bothered with before, because they'd been recorded a quarter of a way around the orbit of Uranus from the last known position of the *Rivers of Babylon*."

Yeah, call it a hunch, Richard thought. *Whatever you do, don't call it what it was—a sudden flood of complete certainty that if he looked at those long-ignored records, he would find something. Because if you call it that, you'll have to admit you don't know what the hell is going on inside your own head these days.*

He moved the rook. Cheveldeoff took his bishop. Richard studied the board again. The situation had *not* improved. "The records are stored on the far side of the Moon, but they're raw data files downloaded from an old automated deep-space station, ironically one of the ones that first saw the Fist of God approaching. They hadn't been completely ignored—some analyst studied them immediately after Hansen escaped. But the micro-nuke that destroyed *Sterling Heights* at the moment of departure fried electronics all over the far side, and for several months after a lot of data that came in from deep space was lost or scrambled while equipment was being repaired or replaced. I doubt the analysts of fifty years ago could retrieve anything." He needed the rook more than the bishop, he decided, and pulled it back a rank to safety. "But technology has advanced. My algorithms identified a great deal more data from that deep-space station tucked away in odd corners of the database than those old analysts knew existed." He attempted to threaten Cheveldeoff's king with the rook he'd saved on his last move.

Cheveldeoff blocked the rook with a pawn-protected knight and with the same move opened up a new line of attack from his bishop on Richard's remaining rook. "Go on."

"That space station had picked up something, I could tell that right away, but the signal was almost nonexistent. It took several days of tweaking to filter out the noise burying it, but by yesterday, the computer and I agreed: the space station had recorded—and located in space—the electromagnetic footprint of a Cornwall branespace engine spinning up. The *Rivers of Babylon* must have changed course just before it left the system. Combining the data from the deep-space station with the final observation of the *Rivers of Babylon*'s position within the system gave me . . ." He slid his queen forward, on the theory that the best defense was a strong offense. "Check."

Cheveldeoff blocked with his bishop, without a second's pause. "A vector!"

"A vector." Richard shook his head. The queen move had been an act of desperation. He couldn't sustain the attack. He had to move her back and concentrate on defense again . . . or resign, and he wasn't quite ready to do that. He pulled the piece back toward his side of the board. "It's not enough to tell us where the moddie planet is . . . if it exists . . . but at least it narrows the field of search. All we need now is one unexplained burst of electromagnetic energy, one anomaly reported by some fortune-seeking scout ship . . ."

"And we'll finally be able to Purify the worst abominations the genesculptors ever created," Cheveldeoff said. "And just maybe save the human race from the wrath of God. Excellent news, Richard!" His own queen slashed across the board. "Check. Mate in three."

What? Richard stared at the board. *How did I miss that?* Well, he could see it now readily enough. He reached out and tipped over his king. "Good game, sir."

"I eagerly await the next," Cheveldeoff said, getting to his feet and thus signaling the end of the audience. But he held out his hand, and he'd never done that before. "Good work, Richard," he said as Richard took it. He held it a moment longer than necessary for a handshake, and looked Richard in the eyes. It wasn't a comfortable look; Cheveldeoff's eyes had a way of boring into his head and leaving him with a vague sense of dread, even when he was being congratulated. "If this pans out, the sky's the limit for you." He released Richard's hand. "Now get out of here. Go home. Relax. It's Salvation Day!"

"Yes, sir." With relief (not an unusual emotion when leaving Cheveldeoff's office) and a certain euphoria (which certainly *was*), Richard made his way up from the bowels of Body Security HQ. He emerged onto the front steps and paused to look back along the boulevard, paved with blue tile, lined with white stone sidewalks and white stone buildings, to the needle-sharp spire of the House of the Body pointing the way to the heavens. It pointed the way to God Itself, but now, Richard thought, maybe it also pointed the way to his future . . . a future where the Hansen name was no longer anathema, a future where he could finally get everything he deserved.

He shook his head. *Well, that was pretentious,* he told himself, and headed down the steps toward the undertube station that would take him home. He couldn't help grinning. *But that doesn't mean it's not true.*

Chapter 3

THE FIRST CHAPTER of *The Wisdom of the Avatar of God* ended with "Praise God!" and Chris grinned as he always did, remembering an old Selkie joke about the Avatar that ended with the punch line, "Praise God! That's *not* a request." But today, his grin died quickly. *I shouldn't make fun of the Avatar*, he thought. *Some things are not a laughing matter.* And though there was no one on Marseguro to report him to the Purity Watchers—and no Purity Watchers, either—there might be soon enough.

Best to Purify himself *before* that day arrived.

"Chapter Two," said the reader. "Why the Body Must Be Purified If Humanity Is to Survive." Chris kept walking, and kept listening.

Two hours later, well into Chapter Five, "On the Evils of Historical Religion," he came to a fork in the road. One path was broad and led along the coast to Firstdip, curving out of sight around a hill. The other, though still paved, was narrow and led inland. A small green sign pointed the way: "Landing Valley."

Chris directed his feet along the narrower path. The symbolism, though rooted in a long-banned religion, was not lost on him: if all went well, this straight and narrow way would indeed lead to life, a new life for him and all the other nonmods—"normals," as he now dared think of them—being gradually drowned, symbolically and sometimes literally (in the case of his father) by the Selkies.

He spent the night in a gully beneath a rock overhang that provided shelter from the regular-as-clockwork midnight downpour of the Marseguro interior. Very little of the planet's flora ran to anything tall enough or grand enough to be dubbed a tree, and the species that did—such as the bumbershoots and stickypines—lived only within a kilometer or two of the coast. Nevertheless, even here, certain of the native fernlike bushes grew to almost the height of a smallish man, and enough of those grew thickly enough at the north end of the gully to block the chilly wind that accompanied the rain. With his pocket heater and ultralight sleeping bag, he was comfortable enough.

In the morning, after a quick breakfast of something that was supposed to taste like bacon and eggs but Chris very much doubted really did (because if bacon and eggs had really tasted like that, why would anyone have ever eaten them?) Chris packed up and hit the trail. As the orange rays of the sun cleared the ridges, mist rose from the wet pavement, swirling around him as he walked.

Today he chose to walk in silence. He doubted even an Archdeacon could listen to the Avatar's book every day. It was too rich, like eating bubblesquid *pâté* for breakfast, lunch, and supper. And too infuriating.

The last time he had come this way, he had been one of a company of two-dozen ten-year-olds, Emily Wood and John Duval among them. They had been on the traditional field trip to the Landing Site, and they hadn't been walking. Instead, they'd been riding in big-wheeled electric cars with sealed, humidified interiors designed to keep the Selkies' skin from drying out, never mind how uncomfortable it made the nonmods. "It's only for a short time," the teacher said when he complained. "You'll live."

This morning the air held at least as much humidity as those car interiors had, so much he was almost surprised it didn't trigger his fear of water. Sometimes Chris dreamed about living somewhere dry. The closest thing Marseguro had to a desert was a high plateau in the mountains where it only rained or snowed three or four times a year, but the only way to get there was by air and you had to have a pressing scientific reason to make the trip. Suspecting mold had started growing on your skin didn't count.

After an hour, the road's gentle slope steepened, and it began to wind up the side of the ridge between pink boulders and purplish bushes. Chris walked faster. If he remembered right, once he crested the top . . .

There. Landing Valley, broad and flat as a table: the ideal place to set down a starship.

Very little remained of the *Rivers of Babylon* after all these years. The settlers had stripped the electronics and most of the metal out of her to build Firstdip which, after decades, Chris had always thought, *still* looked like a refugees' shantytown. But the First Landers hadn't been entirely focused on the immediate needs of survival. They'd left one section of the ship undisturbed, as a kind of monument, and it glinted below him in the afternoon sun, a short, stubby cylinder of silvery metal, ten meters wide and a hundred in diameter, set on its side so that it towered over the site: a cross section of the hull taken from the holds, showing the heavy shielding that had protected the Selkie children in their water-filled tanks from radiation through the long trip to the edge of Earth's solar system, through branespace (not that radiation was a problem *there*) and then in from the edges of this system to Marseguro. Years later, a museum and interpretative center had been set up in a low building next to the hull section.

None of that interested Chris. He descended into the valley and strode past both the museum and the hull section without a glance, heading instead for the dark opening in the steep red rock of the far valley wall, maybe three hundred meters farther. He remembered asking the teacher about it during the field trip.

"It's a cave," she'd said. "The First Landers lived in there for a while, even dug out some extra rooms. It's just used for storage now . . . a lot of mothballed equipment. Stuff the First Landers thought might be needed in the future, or if the microfactories failed."

"Like what?"

"Spare parts, survival rations, communications equipment, things like that," she'd said vaguely. "An emergency beacon, I think. Maybe someday we'll want to talk to the rest of humanity again. After the Body Purified is gone. Now hurry up and catch up with the rest of the group. I think there's gelato!"

Chris couldn't remember if he'd had gelato that day, but he'd never forgotten the cave. He'd longed to explore it even then, but of course children weren't allowed in, and

nobody ever came here except on school field trips or for
significant Landing Day anniversaries—the next would be
the fortieth, still half a year away.

They're probably planning something really special, Chris
thought. *Well, it will certainly be special if* this *works out.*

He reached into his pack and pulled out his flashlight
and crowbar. He didn't expect much in the way of security,
but surely the entrance would at least be locked: and so it
was. The mouth of the cave had been closed off with a wall
of cement blocks, which held a metal door, painted in peel-
ing blue. A rusty hasp, secured by an equally rusty padlock,
held the door closed. The crowbar made quick work of the
hasp, and a moment later Chris flicked on the flashlight and
stepped out of the just-starting-to-warm-up day into a
dank, dark chill.

He had no idea how far into the hillside the cave and its
additional rooms reached, or how long he might have to
search, but in fact he found the equipment he wanted in the
first natural chamber, just inside the cement-block wall,
where it could be easily retrieved if needed. The First Landers had only wanted some place out of the rain; they weren't
trying to hide anything. Why would they? They believed
everyone on the *Rivers of Babylon* was united in purpose,
had all thrown in their lot with this do-or-die quest to found
a world safe from the Body Purified, a new home for a new,
improved breed of human . . . *and their unimproved slaves,*
Chris thought. *Us.*

Just the day before, he'd heard once more the Avatar's
unanswerable question: "What good are normal humans to
superhuman monsters? They'll come to despise us, then enslave us, then eradicate us."

The death of Chris' father was proof enough the Avatar
was right. Chris shook his head. "Not me," he growled.

He found the equipment he wanted, clearly marked. No
inkling that it should be secured or at least left unlabeled
had apparently ever crossed anyone's mind. *Some superhu-
mans,* Chris thought, pushing the white packing crate toward the door. The scraping of plastic on stone echoed
back from the cave walls with the sound of a knife on a
grindstone. As Chris pulled the crate into the light, the text
that he had previously only seen in the circle of illumination from his flashlight became clear: EMERGENCY IN-

TERSTELLAR NULL-BRANE BEACON, and below that, an identification number, and a small panel of instructions. He read them over carefully. Among other things, they told him to make note of the ID number on the case, as he would need it to activate the beacon. He pulled his clunky old datapad from the backpack and stored the number, then turned his attention to getting the beacon out of the cave.

It weighed too much to lift. That meant he'd have to drag it, and that meant he couldn't place it where he really wanted to, one valley over. Not that it was all that likely anyone would stumble over it wherever he put it, given how infrequently people came to Landing Valley, but still . . .

Well, he didn't have any choice. And he could at least hide it a bit.

He tugged and pushed and pulled the crate away from the cave mouth, downslope but off to one side, away from the hull section and the museum, forcing it through a screen of two-meter-tall needlebushes into an open space on the other side. Sucking the back of his badly scratched left hand, he used his right to press the two green buttons on the front of the case. Something clicked and the crate's lid sprang open, revealing the top of a silver cylinder about half a meter in diameter, featuring an alphanumeric keypad and, inside a transparent cover, a green-lit switch.

For the first time, Chris hesitated. *Are you sure about this?* he thought. *If this works, it changes everything. All the dreams of the First Landers, overthrown in an instant. Contact with Earth. Marseguro a colony, not an independent world . . .*

. . . no more Selkies, he reminded himself. *No more second-class "landlings," becoming more second-class every year as the Selkies breed like the animals they are. No more men like my father being murdered by the Selkie masters. A chance to return to Earth, where real humans belong . . . a chance to find something better to do with my life than cataloging algae samples and scrubbing growth tanks.*

He remembered John Duval stealing his trunks, Emily Wood laughing at him, both of them and all their inhuman friends throwing him off the pier just to watch him flounder, just to humiliate him, just to mock him.

He remembered his father, lost at sea.

He remembered his mother, dying in a hospital long cut off from the latest medical advances.

He remembered her words to him, just yesterday morning . . .

"The Selkies murdered him . . . and now they're killing me . . . they'll kill you, too, my little boy . . ."

He blinked hard twice. "Not me," he said again, and flicked the switch.

The transmitter beeped. "Please enter identification number," a male voice said. Chris consulted his datapad, and carefully entered the string of digits and letters. "Thank you," said the voice. "Please step back a minimum of three meters. Transmitter deployment begins in five seconds . . ." (Chris hastily retreated the suggested distance) ". . . four . . . three . . . two . . . one."

The cylinder suddenly got longer, the top rising out of the packing case, which itself sprouted three mechanical spider legs, each of which budded and grew three smaller fingerlike appendages that dug into the ground and gripped. The top of the cylinder, now twice as tall as Chris, split open. A delicate dish-shaped antenna blossomed. The voice spoke again. "This transmitter contains a high-energy battery equivalent in power to a small fission reactor," it said. "This level of energy is necessary to transmit a null-brane pulse of sufficient strength to be detected by any starships within this transmitter's range. Diagnostics indicate that this battery is in good operating condition; however, this transmitter's internal clock indicates that fifty-two Earth years have passed since the last regularly scheduled maintenance of this battery. This increases the possibility of catastrophic battery failure to an estimated one in ten. Such a failure, should it occur, will explosively release energy equivalent in force to two Hiroshima-sized nuclear weapons. Do you wish to proceed with activation?" A panel slid open at the base of the cylinder, revealing a green button and a red button. "Please press the green button, located on the right, if you wish to proceed. Press the red button, located on the left, to cancel."

This time, Chris didn't hesitate. If the battery failed, he'd hardly notice, and at least he would have made a statement they couldn't ignore back in Hansen's Harbor. He strode forward and pressed the green button.

"Activation complete," the transmitter said. "Automated distress signal will be transmitted until battery power is exhausted, in approximately five Earth years. Transmission begins in thirty seconds . . . twenty-nine . . . twenty-eight . . . twenty-seven . . ."

Chris looked up at the sky. He couldn't be sure anyone would pick up the signal, even in five years . . . but at least he had done something. At least he wasn't just a passive victim this time, as he had been on the pier, in the pool, so many other times . . .

. . . like his father had been . . . like his mother . . .

". . . ten . . . nine . . . eight . . . seven . . . six . . . five . . . four . . . three . . . two . . . one . . . transmission begins."

The transmitter did not blow up. In fact, nothing visible happened at all. Chris stared up at the sky for another long moment, then began packing up for the trip home. He'd clean up as many traces of his visit as he could before he left the site—brush away the scrape marks the crate had left in the dirt leading from the cave, do his best to make the padlock look undisturbed. Then it would be back to Hansen's Harbor, back to the algae tanks, back to the bedside of the remnant of his mother, back to being alternately ignored and tormented. Everything would seem just the same to everyone else, but not to him.

The thing he had dreamed of doing for years, he had actually done at last.

Now he would wait, and nurse his secret hope.

The meeting with her parents didn't go at all as Emily had anticipated.

She'd suggested Coriolis for dinner. Since it was a celebration for the end of school, her parents had agreed, even though Coriolis was probably the most expensive restaurant above or below the waves of New Botany Bay. Eating out was one of the activities both Selkies and landlings could enjoy together, since Victor Hansen's modifications had not extended to making Selkies underwater eaters. Who wanted a belly full of seawater? They might be able to breathe underwater, but Selkies were still humans, not dolphins or seals. As well, even though Selkies could communicate underwater, their language, being so new, lacked the richness of English. Conversation in air was both a pleasure and, sometimes, a necessity.

So Coriolis and similar establishments had air. But they also had water. In fact, Coriolis had just about any combination of the two elements anyone could want. There were submerged-seating areas that looked like pictures Emily had seen of swim-up bars on Earth, rooms that were not only nonsubmerged but dehumidified for the comfort of landlings, other rooms that were nonsubmerged but regularly humidified by a fine mist of water vapor (available in a variety of scents from floral to savory), and two-level rooms that allowed Selkies to sit submerged and landlings to sit high and dry.

Emily's parents were waiting for her in a small private submerged-seating room. She swam up into the room from below and surfaced, then ran her fingers through her short violet hair and over her face to clear away the water. "Hi," she said.

"Hi, yourself," said her mother, and Emily instantly knew she was in trouble.

Dr. Carla Christianson-Wood was in her late thirties, local years, which put her in her mid-forties in Earth years. Her hair, much longer than Emily's, remained more blonde than gray, and unlike her daughter and most of the rest of the younger generation, she had never dyed it.

Dr. Christianson-Wood's mother, Dr. Alice Christianson, had been one of the first-generation Selkies on board the *Rivers of Babylon,* and had studied genetics with Victor Hansen himself. Dr. Christianson-Wood, like her mother before her, had focused her research energies on viruses—specifically, the differences between the local equivalent to viruses, which fortunately, as predicted by Victor Hansen's scientific team before the *Rivers of Babylon* landed, were incapable of infecting Earth-evolved life, and the viruses the settlers had brought with them from Earth. "There is some concern that Marseguroite and Earth viruses could exchange genetic information and produce something really nasty that neither we nor Marseguro life would have any immunity to," she'd told Emily once. "We need to know if that's possible and what to do about it if it is." Most of her work was funded by the Planetary Council, Marseguro's elected government, such as it was—with most residents of the planet spread along the coast in widely separated villages, most government was pretty strictly local in nature. However, the Planetary Council did collect taxes to support projects of planetary interest, including an investigation branch that helped local authorities solve crimes, a handful of prisons (almost empty) for people convicted of those crimes, and various research and construction projects.

But somehow, Emily doubted the chill in her mother's voice had anything to do with her research. "Is something wrong?" she asked, but she already knew: her mother had heard about what had happened on the pier.

"What were you thinking?" Dr. Christianson-Wood demanded, confirming Emily's suspicion. "Swarming a nonmod? Dumping him in the bay? Especially one who couldn't swim?"

"We didn't know he couldn't swim," Emily protested, even though she knew it was a pitiful defense. "Every other landling—"

"Nonmod," her mother interjected. "I don't like the term 'landling.' It's disrespectful."

"Every other *nonmod* I've ever met has learned to swim. Why would you live on Marseguro and *not* learn to swim?"

"It's not like he has any choice where he lives," her father said, speaking for the first time. With his bristling beard and bushy eyebrows, Peterson Wood looked a little bit like ancient Earth representations of King Neptune, although he wore a sedate black skinsuit rather than going around bare-chested. One of the leading underwater engineers of the planet, he had helped build Coriolis and the majority of the other buildings constructed within the last twenty years in the waters of New Botany Bay.

"And whether he could swim or not was hardly the point," her mother said. "Throwing someone off the pier is assault, Emily. He could have pressed charges. He still could. And then what would happen to your school career?"

"School career?" said a new voice behind Emily. "Emily, you were going to wait until I got here!"

Oh, no, Emily thought as her two-years-older sister

Amy slipped into the water beside her. *I've got to stop her from—*

But it was far too late for that. With her usual knack for saying the wrong thing at the wrong time, Amy said, "Well, if Emily's told you, I guess I'd better tell you, too. I've finally made up my mind. I'm not going into the sciences, either. I'm going to be a singer. Amphibian opera."

Their parents stiffened. "What do you mean, singer?" said their father.

"What do you mean, *either*?" said their mother, gaze slicing from Amy to Emily.

Not the way I intended to break the news, Emily thought. The waiter hadn't even come to take their drink orders yet. "I intended to tell you . . . later," she said, shooting a glance at Amy, who had the decency to look stricken. "I've been thinking about my specialization training and I've . . . I've decided to go into underwater dance." There, it was out.

Her parents stared from one to the other of their daughters, then looked at each other, and then, to her astonishment, burst out laughing. "Opera? Dance?" her mother said. "How long have you two been planning this?"

Amy began to grin. "Well, it was Emily's idea. I thought you'd understand, but she said . . ."

Emily's eyes narrowed. "No, Amy, you don't get it." She glared at her mother. "They think it's a joke."

"But a very good one," her father assured her. "Underwater dancing. Amphibian opera, for God's sake!" He burst out laughing again. "Please."

Amy's grin had faded before it fully formed. "But . . . we're not joking." She looked at Emily. "At least . . . I'm not."

"I'm not, either," Emily said. "Mom, Dad, I know you want us to go into the sciences. Mom, I know you want a third-generation geneticist in the family. But that's just not what I'm interested in. And Marseguro has come a long way since you chose your specialization. We've been here half a century now. It's time we focused on the arts a little bit more. Dr. Naborikov says that—"

Her parents' laughter had died as she spoke. Now their expressions hardened into anger. "Naborikov," her mother said. "I might have known. 'In the long run, the arts are more important to society than the sciences.' " She mimicked Naborikov's rounded vowels and clipped consonants perfectly. "As if the arts will help us survive on a hostile planet!"

"But that's just it," Emily retorted. "Marseguro *isn't* a hostile planet. After four decades, we *know* that. There are hardly any threats. Some nasty sea predators, but that's about it. You've said yourself there are no native diseases to worry about. Solar radiation? Not a problem. Hurricanes? Rogue waves? The mountains shelter us. Marseguro is a paradise."

"You sound like a Consolidationist," her mother said. She made the word sound like an insult. "We've barely begun to *really* colonize this planet. All our people, nonmods and Selkies, live within a few thousand square kilometers of each other, close to this one continent. The nonmods have barely penetrated the interior, and the Selkies have barely explored beyond the shelf. We may never live in the abyss, but there are shallows that we could make our own, a whole barely submerged continent where we could build underwater habitats—and maybe even anchor floating habitats for nonmods. The Council is already talking of building a prototype floathab as a test. But if the Consolidationists get their way, this tiny corner of the planet is all we'll ever inhabit."

"I'm not a Consolidationist," Emily said. "But I'm not an Expansionist either. Those are last generation's labels, Mother. Members of my generation just want freedom to live our lives the way we want. Some of us will go into the sciences. Some of us will help build new habitats. But not all of us." She gestured at Amy. "Not these two of us."

"You're being selfish and shortsighted," her father said, softly but forcefully. She knew that voice: he'd used it when she was a little girl and he was very angry with her but trying not to yell. "You have the brains and the grades to go into the hard sciences, and that means you have a duty to do so. A duty to improve life on this planet and help us spread across its surface. A duty to your ancestors, who fled tyranny to build a new life here. A duty to Victor Hansen, who created our race and led us to safety. Freedom!" Now his voice rose, though he still wasn't shouting—quite. "What kind of freedom will you have if the Holy Warriors find us all nicely bunched together for them to exterminate, amusing ourselves with waterdance and amphibian opera? You know your history. You know the Body Purified is still searching for us. All it takes is one scout to stumble on us, and—"

Emily shook her head, hard. "No, I *don't* know that the Body Purified is still looking for us. It's been fifty years on Earth. The Body Purified probably doesn't even exist anymore." She saw her parents' lips tighten but plunged ahead just the same. "All that crap they said they believed. Nobody could force a whole population to swallow that bunk for fifty years. It's insane."

"I'm going to have to have a word with the head of the Education Committee," her father growled. "They seem to have left Earth history off the curriculum. Fifty years is nothing. Empires based on myth and superstition have enslaved entire populations for *centuries.*"

"But not in the scientific era," Emily argued. "The neocaliphatists tried early last century. They couldn't do it."

"But they killed millions in the attempt," her mother said. "And that war went on longer than fifty years. Maybe the Body Purified is doomed to collapse—I hope so—but that doesn't help us if the Holy Warriors show up in orbit. We can't rest. We have to work, to build, to expand—"

Emily shook her head. "I'm not willing to live my whole life in fear of something that will probably never happen. I want to create, entertain, communicate, move people. I want—"

"You want to be a self-centered, naïve, shortsighted eighteen-year-old," her father said. He looked at Amy. "And twenty-year-old." Amy said nothing, leaving the argument to Emily, as she tended to do when family disagreements broke out. "I understand that. Perfectly natural. But just because I understand it doesn't mean I can condone it.

"And there's another thing, Emily." He leaned forward and shook an accusing finger at her. "Underwater dance is Selkie-only."

"Well, of course it is," she said impatiently. "You can't expect landlings to do it. Even with scuba gear they're about as clumsy as—"

"It's exclusionary," her father said flatly. "It can't be enjoyed by *nonmods.*" He emphasized the word. "It's not helping to unify Marseguro society, it's driving a wedge down the middle of it. It's just another example of the kind of mind-set that's creeping into the younger generation of Selkies . . . the same mind-set that led you and your friends to think throwing some poor nonmod off the pier was the height of harmless humor.

"It's a mind-set that will destroy Marseguro if it isn't checked. There are no second-class citizens on Marseguro. We're modified humans, but we're still human, and modified doesn't mean 'better.' That's as bad in its own way as the Body Purified's doctrine that moddies are subhuman at best, nonhuman at worst. Pursuing Selkie-only 'arts' like underwater dancing is counterproductive and antisocial, and I won't have a daughter of mine lending credence to it." He turned his attention to Amy. "And amphibian opera is no better. Nonmods may be able to appreciate the above-water part of the performance, but not the underwater part. They can't even hear most of it.

"No. You are both free to pursue your artistic endeavors, of course—your mother and I enjoy and encourage your creative efforts, you know that—but pursue them as your sole careers? Out of the question. Our society is not large enough or well-established enough to allow our best and brightest to fritter away their talents on frivolities of any kind, much less frivolities that exclude half our population."

Emily felt her face flush. She'd always blushed easily. Her father used to call her a Selkie thermometer, teasing that he could measure her anger or embarrassment by how high the red wash of blood rose in her face. She hoped he remembered, because if she were a thermometer, she was sure the top of her head would have burst by now. "Do you have any idea how pretentious you sound, Dad?" she said, keeping her voice at a reasonably normal volume, but only with an effort. "We aren't a totalitarian state, remember? Society doesn't get a say in what I do with my life, as long as I don't hurt anybody else. And just because you're my father doesn't mean you get a say, either.

"And don't give me that bottomgunk about 'excluding half our population.' To begin with, last I heard, the *landlings*," she emphasized *her* term for the nonmods, "made up less than a quarter of the population, and that's falling all the time. So why shouldn't there be some arts designed for the majority? The landlings are free to create arts that Selkies can't appreciate—I don't mind a bit. Why should they care what Selkies are doing out in the wet where they can barely function anyway?" She pushed herself away from the table in a welter of foam. "You're just trying to make me feel guilty, and I'm not buying into it. I *don't* feel guilty. And I don't think you're grasping the reality of this conversation, either. I'm not *asking* your permission to specialize in waterdance. I'm *telling* you that's what I'm doing. Subject closed. And I'm out of here. Have a nice dinner." She whirled, intending to make a grand exit by plunging straight down through the underwater access, flicking her webbed feet in her parents' faces, but the waiter had chosen that moment to come in through the half-dry access and stood chest-deep in the water right behind her with two floating trays of appetizers her parents must have ordered before she swam in. She stared at him; he stared at her. "Excuse me, miss—" he began.

"Freeze off," she snarled at him. She ducked past him, tipping a tray of unidentifiable tidbits into the water as she did so, and dove out of sight just as her father and mother said, "Now see here!" and "You listen to me!" in a perfect melding of stereotypical parental outrage.

The water cut off their words. She swam toward the glowing globe that marked the exit into the swimways, trailing bubbles, furious with her parents and equally furious with herself for having lost her temper.

"Emily, wait!" someone chirped in Selkie. Almost at the exit, she backwatered and flipped to see Amy undulating toward her. Her sister stopped and floated a few feet away. "I'm sorry," she said. "I didn't mean to surprise them like that. I thought you'd already told them."

You didn't think at all, Emily thought. *You never do.* But that was Amy, and Emily doubted she would ever change. "Not your fault. They would have reacted the same no matter how we broached the subject. They're so . . ." She couldn't find a word in Selkie—or English, either—and finally settled for ". . . . conservative."

"They'll come around?" Amy said, but she added the double click at the end that turned it into a question.

"Sure," Emily said. "We're their only daughters. What are they going to do, disown us?" *They* were *awfully mad,* she thought uneasily. *But they wouldn't really* . . . "The worst thing is that I stormed out before the food came. And I'm starving. I spent an hour hauling algae sample buckets out of the hold of a ship before I came."

Amy blinked. "Why?"

Emily shook her head, a gesture that still meant the same for Selkies as for landlings. "Never mind. A bunch of my friends are probably still at Freddy Fish's. How about a weedtickler burger?"

Amy nodded. "Sounds good to me."

"Let's go." Emily flipped again and dove through the exit. "We'll talk to Mom and Dad later," she chirped. "After they've cooled down."

They will *cool down,* she thought.

Won't they?

Chapter 4

SAMUEL CHEVELDEOFF ARRIVED in the ante-chamber of the Holy Office precisely at 1900 hours. It was twice the size of the waiting area for his own office, far more lavishly decorated, with ancient and priceless paintings and sculptures—and empty of staff or supplicants.

No witnesses, Cheveldeoff thought. He didn't think the Right Hand intended to have him arrested, though certainly the Chosen Elite, Holy Warriors loyal only to the Avatar, would have no compunction carrying out such an order. His own loyalists wouldn't stand for it, and at the tricky time of succession, that just might trigger a ruinous civil war that nobody wanted . . . at least, not yet.

No. The Right Hand simply wanted this meeting to be private.

Cheveldeoff planted himself in front of the massive black doors leading into the Holy Office, folded his arms, and waited to be admitted. He half-expected to be held outside for a lengthy period of time, just to emphasize that his otherwise massive authority meant nothing here, but in fact the doors opened less than a minute after he entered the antechamber.

The Right Hand himself greeted him. A slender man with short-cropped gray hair and a neatly trimmed mustache, Karl Rasmusson smiled and held out his hand. "Come in, come in, Sam. Good to see you."

"Karl," Cheveldeoff acknowledged, shaking hands. He felt off-balance; he'd expected a frosty reception. *What's going on?* It was his job to know the answer to that question, and right now, he didn't.

Rasmusson led him, not to the Avatar's imposing desk

in its semicircular, vidscreen-lined niche at the far end of the colonnaded-and-vaulted room, but to a side area with a simple table of polished stone set between two couches covered with buttery black leather. "Drink?" Rasmusson asked, going to the small bar set against the wall.

"Soda and lime," Cheveldeoff said. He wanted his wits sharp.

Rasmusson fixed the drink, poured a glass of white wine for himself, and came back to the table. "I've been wanting to talk to you in private for some time now, Sam," the Right Hand said, handing Cheveldeoff his drink.

Cheveldeoff sipped it. *Here it comes,* he thought.

Rasmusson sat down on the opposite couch, leaned back, and took an appreciative sip of his wine. "I've decided to back you in the upcoming election."

Cheveldeoff had trained himself for decades not to react to sudden surprises like that, so he didn't choke on his soda—quite. He swallowed hard, though, before setting the glass down. Then he leaned forward and locked eyes with Rasmusson. "Why?"

Rasmusson looked away, took another sip of wine, set it on the table, and finally met his gaze again. "Because I do not believe it is God's will that Ashok Shridhar become Avatar at this time."

Cheveldeoff waited to see if Rasmusson would add to that. When he didn't, he repeated, "Why?"

Rasmusson smiled slightly. "I have my reasons. They relate to you only tangentially, however, and therefore I will not share them. In any event, I did not ask you here merely to tell you you have my—entirely unofficial, of course— support. I asked you here to tell you that merely having my support is not enough to guarantee your election."

Cheveldeoff couldn't help it; he blinked. Then he sat back in the couch. "But my count—"

"Your estimate is flawed," the Right Hand said. "Shridhar's influence reaches farther than you know. Six of those who have told you they will support you will actually, come the vote, support Shridhar. I believe I can . . . persuade . . . perhaps two of those to return to your fold, and believe I can turn two currently in Shridhar's camp in your favor without him being aware of it—well, until the vote, of course. But if you will do the math . . ."

Cheveldeoff already had. The Council of the Faithful had twenty-four members. He had been certain of the support of ten of them, and had thought Shridhar had the solid support of nine, leaving five undecided. But according to Rasmusson, he had only four certain votes. The Right Hand promised him another four, putting him only at eight. Shridhar would have eleven. "The undecideds?"

"Are still undecided. But I believe three, possibly four, are leaning toward Shridhar."

Cheveldeoff felt a familiar sensation: cold rage. "What do you want me to do?" he growled.

"I want you to win the election," Rasmusson said. "But to do so, you need a major success, something that will shift Councillors to your side through fear that the people will erupt in the regions they personally supervise if you are not elected. In short, Sam, you need to become a hero—a Julius Caesar, if you will." The Right Hand sipped more wine. "The question is, how."

Cheveldeoff grimaced. It was all very well to tell him to come up with a major success, but if he could do that on demand, he would have done it already, wouldn't he?

Every continent had its hot spot. The Middle East was the worst, of course, but parts of China were almost as bad and even sections of the Rockies were complete no-go zones for Holy Warriors at the moment. "Central America has quieted down," he pointed out. *Mainly because hardly anyone is left alive down there,* he thought, but didn't add. The Right Hand had personally approved that particular pacification program, after all.

"It has," the Right Hand agreed. "But if you'll forgive my saying so, a quiet Central America is unlikely to impress anyone much beyond the few Neo-Incans who still survive down there." He put his now-empty wineglass down and leaned forward, hands folded, elbows on knees. His eyes narrowed. "If we cannot have a security victory—and things do not look any better for such a victory among the colonies, do they . . . ?" He paused.

"No," Cheveldeoff admitted after a moment. The Holy Warriors had so far barely penetrated the New Mars system, where the residents appeared to have built a highly effective space navy and system defense grid, and several ships had been heavily damaged in the attempt. As well, fresh fighting had just broken out thirty light-years in the other direction from Earth on Tuin, which had theoretically been Purified for a decade. "Our space forces are spread thin right now. Even to refocus their energies on one of the remaining colonies on the Unpurified list would take months."

"So I thought," Rasmusson said. "So, if we cannot have a security victory, I believe we need a propaganda victory. I believe we need to 'discover,' try, and execute . . . the clone of Victor Hansen."

Cheveldeoff stiffened. "No!" he said. "We've worked too many years—"

"With nothing to show for it," the Right Hand snapped, his geniality suddenly discarded like the camouflaged cloak Cheveldeoff had always known it to be. "The first clone went mad. This one has done nothing, and most likely will go as mad as his 'father' when Hansen's gene-bomb goes off.

"He'll be worse than useless then, so I say we use him while we still can: grab him, try him, shoot him—openly, publicly, with full-press media coverage—and make sure you get the credit. And with that credit . . . the votes you need to become the third Avatar: Samuel the First."

Cheveldeoff sat very still. He didn't object to having Hansen arrested if it furthered his own ends . . . but he did object to throwing away years of investment with nothing to show for it. Especially at the very moment that investment might be about to pay a dividend.

He hadn't intended to tell the Right Hand what Hansen had told him just hours earlier. Information was power, and by instinct, he kept as much of it to himself as possible. But now . . .

He cleared his throat. "It's possible . . . just barely possible . . . that I might be able to offer up something rather more grand than a late-blooming clone of Victor Hansen." He had looked down at the thick red carpet while he thought; now he looked up and locked eyes with Rasmusson again. "I may be able to offer you Hansen's Selkies themselves . . . a whole planet of moddies to be Purified."

Rasmusson had worked at least as long as Cheveldeoff to learn to hide his reactions, but three quick blinks betrayed him. "Tell me more."

Cheveldeoff obliged.

*   *   *

Richard Hansen hadn't expected much to change after his meeting with Cheveldeoff. Sure, he had a vector, but one half a century old. All it really meant was that he had doubled the amount of data he had to search through, though at least it was *different* data. . . .

But something did change. The morning after his meeting with Cheveldeoff, he descended to his barely-tall-enough-to-stand-up office in the basement only to find movers stripping everything out of it. For a moment he thought he'd been fired, but then his supervisor explained. "You've been bumped out of here," he said. John Riedl knew all about Hansen's dubious ancestry and had seldom missed an opportunity to belittle his underling for it. Now, it appeared, he didn't dare, which probably explained why his already hollow-cheeked face looked very much like that of someone sucking a lemon. "Cheveldeoff's orders. New office. Three floors up. Follow your stuff." To Richard's astonishment, he offered his hand, and too bemused to do otherwise, Richard took it. "Good luck." Reidl then dropped Richard's hand like wet garbage and disappeared into his office.

Richard took his advice. By late morning he was ensconced in the central office in a suite of rooms, into which his new staff—staff!—members were being installed. By then, at least, he had a better idea of what was going on, though he still couldn't believe it.

Cheveldeoff had left him a private vidmail. "Congratulations," the Archdeacon said in it, and actually smiled. "I have decided your breakthrough warrants full-scale exploration. You and your new staff are to sift through every scrap of data you can find pertaining to the sectors of space lying along the vector you identified. I am confident that if the Selkies are out there, you'll find them. I'll expect weekly reports. Good luck." Then, almost as an afterthought, "Oh, and you are hereby promoted to the rank of Deacon, Third Rank. Your pay will be adjusted accordingly. Again, congratulations."

And that was that. It took a week to get the new staff settled in, assign tasks, begin refining search algorithms; more days before really serious analysis could take place. And then . . .

. . . nothing. Three weeks of nothing, so far. And Chev-eldeoff, at their last meeting, had made it very clear to Richard that "nothing" was not an acceptable outcome in exchange for the huge amount of manpower and money Body Security had invested in him. "Time is of the essence," Cheveldeoff said. "To both of us."

Exactly what he meant by that he didn't explain, and Richard certainly wasn't going to ask.

He yawned hugely and stretched. Three o'clock in the morning, and he was the only one in the office. Why hadn't they found anything? How had Grandpa Hansen managed to hide his tracks so thoroughly? *Someone* must have stumbled on them in all these years. . . .

He knew they were out there. He couldn't explain how he knew it, but he had no doubt that the Selkies' planet lay somewhere within the cone of space suggested by the vector. Sometimes it seemed to him that the planet's location was on the tip of his tongue, like someone's name he couldn't quite place . . . but that was nuts. And yet . . .

He rubbed his forehead. He hadn't been sleeping well: more bizarre dreams in which he took the role of Victor Hansen. Just last night he'd spent a large portion of one dream giving a lecture on genesculpting to a large audience in some vaguely tropical location. In the dream he'd known exactly what he'd been talking about. When he'd woken up, what little he could remember of what his dream self had said in the lecture meant nothing to him.

And as if that weren't bad enough, he'd also been having headaches recently. Tonight he had a doozy. *Time to call it quits. I'm not accomplishing anything.*

The computer had just proffered a new star map. Richard leaned forward, intending to close down his workstation . . . but then he stopped. Something, some thought or feeling he couldn't quite grasp, made him peer more closely at the star map. An old Class A star centered it. He looked at the coordinates. No . . . those weren't quite right. . . .

He tapped keys, adjusting the string of numbers. No . . . no . . .

Pain stabbed his head so sharply it frightened him, then quickly subsided. Those numbers . . . looked *right,* in a way he couldn't explain.

This is crazy, he thought. But the star that *now* centered the display had codes beside it that cross-referenced to the databases they'd been searching. The codes indicated that the algorithm only rated the connection as "of potential interest," but it couldn't hurt to look.

"Computer," he said. "Display details of data associated with star at coordinates . . ." He read them off.

The screen changed. He rubbed tired eyes that didn't want to focus, then squinted at the small print. Apparently an automated freighter several light-years from the star in question had picked up a weak signal from its direction. The signal had not triggered any particular action on the freighter's part, since it did not match any current distress codes. In fact, if the freighter hadn't been an ancient piece of crap, still running its original communications equipment, it might not have picked up the signal at all: it arrived as a crude null-brane pulse in a region of the branefield no one had used for communications for a couple of decades. The freighter's computer had flagged the signal as random noise, but logged it nevertheless.

"Computer, download signal, analyze per standard search parameters."

Richard still didn't expect anything. He certainly didn't expect what flashed up on screen almost instantly: PARAMETERS MET. ESTIMATED PROBABILITY 100 PERCENT.

"Parameters met," the computer said redundantly. "Estimated probability 100 percent."

For a long moment, Richard just stared; then he remembered to breathe. His heart raced. *Calm down,* he told himself. *It's not the first hit you've seen, and they've all been false alarms so far.*

Which was true, but he'd never seen, or *expected* to see, a probability estimated at one hundred percent. In fact, the way he'd written the search parameters, he wouldn't have expected to see a rating like that unless—

"Computer, display intercepted message."

It appeared on his screen, and his heart skipped one beat, then another, then raced even faster.

—unless a transmission came from the Rivers of Babylon herself.

He opened his mouth to tell the computer to contact Cheveldeoff, then closed it again without speaking. *Double-*

check, he thought. *Triple-check. You don't want to wake up the Archdeacon of Body Security only to find out you've been duped by some interstellar con man.*

Not that he thought that likely: you didn't set off something with the transmission power of a ship emergency beacon just for laughs. But he ran the checks anyway. It took him another half hour, and by the time he finished, his heart no longer pounded in his ears, but his excitement soared. Everything matched: the bizarre branefield frequency, the encrypted header attached to the message, even the slightly unfocused quality of the transmission, exactly what the computer predicted a signal generated by fifty-year-old equipment *should* look like.

And it had originated from the very star whose coordinates he had somehow intuited, a star he might never have looked at closely if not for that strange sense of *knowing* he should look there.

I don't believe in ESP. I don't believe in magic. And neither does Cheveldeoff.

He doesn't need to know how I found the star.

"Computer," he said at last. "Contact Archdeacon Cheveldeoff. Priority call."

The opening chords of Beethoven's Fifth Symphony woke Cheveldeoff from a sound sleep. He answered the vidcall prepared to bite off the head of whomever had thought anything short of armed revolution worth waking him at that ungodly hour, but when Richard Hansen told him what he thought he had discovered, Cheveldeoff's sleep inertia vanished. Two hours later, he sat in his office at the same table he and Hansen played chess on every month, *sans* chessboard. Three of the walls displayed the Italian villa interior, but the fourth showed a block of repeating text, accompanied by graphs and lists of numbers providing technical details of the transmission's properties.

Hansen looked rumpled and bleary-eyed: he obviously hadn't been to bed at all. He'd been waiting for Cheveldeoff in the antechamber when Cheveldeoff arrived, and hadn't even sat down before launching into an explanation of what they were looking at. "The signal wasn't strong enough to reach Earth itself," he said, pointing to a series of numbers that meant nothing to Cheveldeoff. "A freighterbot en route from Stableford to Freerock picked it up. It recorded it and logged it, but didn't flag it as anything interesting. When it sent its next data dump to its owners on Freerock, our listening buoy intercepted it."

He's leaving something out, Cheveldeoff thought. *I wonder . . .*

"What made you look at it, then, if it wasn't flagged?"

Hansen looked uncomfortable. "Desperation, I guess. We haven't found anything in any of the obvious places to look, so I just decided to dig a little deeper."

"So it was a hunch."

"I guess you could call it that."

"Interesting," Cheveldeoff said, and meant it. *The genebomb's gone off . . . but he hasn't gone mad.*

Not yet, anyway.

"There's no doubt this originated from Hansen's ship?"

Hansen shook his head. "None. I've checked it every possible way, and everything matches."

Cheveldeoff looked at the text of the message, which was less than informative: STARSHIP *RIVERS OF BABYLON* REQUESTS ASSISTANCE. THIS BEACON WILL RUN CONTINUOUSLY. STARSHIP *RIVERS OF BABYLON* REQUESTS ASSISTANCE. THIS BEACON WILL RUN CONTINUOUSLY. . . . "How long has this beacon been active?"

"That's the strange thing," Hansen admitted. He pointed at another of the analysis fields. "According to the message header, the beacon was activated less than a week ago."

Cheveldeoff lifted an eyebrow. "They've been sitting out there for fifty years and suddenly decided to call for help?"

"Maybe," Hansen said. "Maybe somebody tripped the beacon by accident. After fifty years, they might not even have known what it was. They could be living in primitive conditions. They might not even be technological anymore."

Cheveldeoff nodded. "Hmmm." He read the message again. "So we know they're out there. But can you pinpoint where?"

"I already have." Cheveldeoff had long ago given Hansen limited voice access rights to his office computer so he could display any files he needed Cheveldeoff to see. Now Hansen raised his voice. "Computer, display image Hansen Two."

The display changed to a standard star map. A red circle highlighted a Class M star at its center. "According to the freighterbot, the transmission originated here."

Cheveldeoff leaned forward. "What do we know about that system?"

"Nothing," Hansen said. "And that's weird, because everything around it was surveyed long ago, before the Purification and the Day of Salvation, in the first few years of branespace travel. I can tell you, at a minimum, the number, sizes, and orbits of every planet in every system within fifty light-years of this one. But there's no indication this system was ever surveyed."

"Or else the system was surveyed, but somebody tampered with the computer records," Cheveldeoff said. A surge of excitement raced through him. *My God, he may actually have found them . . .*

. . . and I may have just been handed my key to the Holy Office. I'll be the man who completed the Purification.

Beyond what it would do for *him,* Purifying the human race by destroying abominations like Hansen's moddies was a sacred duty, part of the constant battle to please God Itself, so that It did not again turn Its wrath against humanity. Cheveldeoff believed in that doctrine, of course—the miracle of Salvation Day left little room for nonbelief—but as Archdeacon of Body Security he also had more secular concerns, and it was the prospect of finally and forcefully demonstrating the futility of rebellion that excited him most, never mind the welcome boost it would give his own ambitions. He knew full well that Victor Hansen's thus-far successful hijacking and flight had inspired and continued to inspire would-be revolutionaries of all stripes. Purifying Hansen's secret planet would be a graphic demonstration that "You can run, but you can't hide," and could well lead to the rolling up of any number of the minor rebellions constantly simmering just beneath the surface of their rigidly controlled society. For every true revolutionary there were others balanced on a knife edge of uncertainty and fear, and the destruction of Hansen's Hijackers might well push them into turning on their compatriots to save their own skins from a suddenly seemingly omnipotent Body Security. "Richard, you're a genius," Cheveldeoff said. "Computer, record message to Grand Deacon Ellers."

"Ready," the computer said.

"Computer, message follows: Grand Deacon, report to my office at 0700 hours with whatever additional staff you need to plan the Purification of a rogue human colony. Message ends. Computer, send."

"Sent," the computer confirmed.

Cheveldeoff smiled at Richard. "If this pans out, Richard, I think we can safely say you've desmirched the escutcheon of your family."

"It will pan out, sir," Hansen said. "I'm sure of it." He cleared his throat. "Sir . . ." He paused. "Sir, request permission to accompany the Holy Warriors on their Purification mission."

Cheveldeoff looked into the projected flames of the Italian villa's fireplace, thinking. Hansen waited silently, watching him. *Well, why not?* Cheveldeoff thought. *If the gene-bomb really has gone off, and the gene therapy keeps him sane, he may have more "hunches" that will serve us well. If Victor Hansen's mad scheme works out fully and he becomes a mental as well as physical copy of Hansen, then he'll be even more valuable as an intelligence asset already in custody and available for interrogation. And if he simply becomes unstable, like his "father" . . . well, what better place to dispose of him quietly than within a combat force in a war zone?*

He looked up. "Permission granted. You will accompany the Holy Warriors as my personal observer."

Hansen's face lit up. "I'd like that, sir!"

So easy, Cheveldeoff thought. *People are so easily manipulated. An implied threat, an occasional treat . . . they're no different from dogs. And as Avatar . . . I'll have my hand on the leash. Earth will be pacified. I'll bring the colonies under control. And after that . . . well, it's a big galaxy. We can and will spread the human race to many more planets.*

God will be mollified. And even if It isn't, It will have lots of planets to choose from if It feels it needs to destroy one to get our attention.

"Good," he said out loud. "When Grand Deacon Ellers arrives, I'll introduce you. And feel free to make any suggestions you may have during the planning sessions, Richard. Your input will be invaluable."

"Yes, sir! And . . . thank you, sir."

"Grand Deacon Ellers will be here in less than three

hours, and you look like hell. Go get cleaned up, maybe take a nap, and I'll see you here at 0700."

"Yes, sir. Thank you again."

Cheveldeoff watched him leave, and thought again, *So easy.*

And then he activated his secure comm circuit to the Right Hand, who answered looking as if he'd been up for hours. *Probably a computer-generated image.*

"Yes?" said Rasmusson.

"We've got them," Cheveldeoff said. "Hansen came through." He explained succinctly. "Ellers is coming here at 0700 to begin planning."

Rasmusson (or his CG image) looked thoughtful. "You know that Ellers is secretly supporting Shridhar's bid for the Avatarship."

"I know," Cheveldeoff said. "But he's the Grand Deacon in command. There's no way to *not* involve him. And from my past dealings with him, I don't believe he will sabotage a mission as important as this for political reasons."

"I hope you're right, Archdeacon." The Right Hand nodded. "Well, this is excellent news. Keep me informed." He moved as if to switch off communications, then paused. "And move quickly, Sam. News of the Avatar's condition is leaking out. Just rumors, so far. We're countering with misinformation about a viral attack that has left him bedridden but still fully functional and in command. But we can't keep a lid on this forever. Eventually . . . within a few weeks, at most . . . we will have to pull the plug and convene the Council of the Faithful.

"Finish your business by then, Sam. Or start making your retirement plans . . . for somewhere far, far off Earth."

The screen went blank.

High stakes, Cheveldeoff thought, then smiled.

He'd always been a gambling man.

Richard left Cheveldeoff's office filled with elation. *At last!* he thought. *At last.* All his life, Victor Hansen's successful escape from the Body had hung around his neck like Jacob Marley's chains. Now he felt like Ebenezer Scrooge on the Christmas morning after the long, haunted night.

Not that anyone legally celebrated Christmas anymore, of course.

His elation persisted through the week of planning that followed, reinforced every time someone asked his opinion. Having the favor of Cheveldeoff, he discovered, made all the difference in the world. Even when they ultimately discounted his suggestions, people listened to them respectfully and explained why they thought they wouldn't work. But a few of his suggestions *were* followed. He'd made a study of his grandfather's abominations, and had already amassed much of the information about the Selkies' abilities that the Grand Deacon needed to know as he outfitted his troops and ship.

"They're not true merpeople," he explained during one session in Ellers' office, as he and the Grand Deacon looked at an image of one of the Selkies. Richard had studied it for years. Maybe that was why it no longer disgusted him as much as it once had. Green eyes without eyelashes, almost twice the size of normal human eyes, peered out beneath naked bony brows and a shaved skull in a face almost albino-white. The nose with its two slitlike nostrils made a barely-noticeable bump in that pale oval, and the ears were no more prominent. The mouth, oddly, appeared completely normal, and it seemed wrong that such an unmistakably human feature should appear in such an inhuman visage. And then there were the gills: three slits on each side of the neck, open in the photo, displaying a pink interior that made Richard think of . . . well, he didn't like to think about what it made him think of.

Alien . . . horrible . . . monstrous. Richard remembered thinking that about the Selkie. But somehow, today, he saw a kind of beauty in the strange face he'd never appreciated before. It wasn't a mutilated human being, after all, but a human-based creature designed—by his grandfather!—to live in an environment alien to normal humans.

An astonishing achievement, when you thought about it. *I wish we didn't have to . . .*

He cut that thought off. He couldn't think that, couldn't let a hint of those kinds of doubts infiltrate his thoughts. The Body did not allow doubt. God did not allow doubt. And while the Purity Watchers might not be able to read his thoughts . . . yet . . . God certainly could.

The Selkies were abominations. Their world had to be Purified. *End of story.*

But that stray thought worried him. Where had it come from?

He continued his mini-lecture. "They can't eat underwater, for example, and they need to drink fresh water just like a normal human. That means that although they may have underwater buildings—if they've got any technology to speak of at all after fifty years—those buildings must have breathable air in them. That means they're most likely to be located in shallow water close to shore, and to have some kind of air intake."

"Which means we can easily find most of them," Ellers said. "Excellent." A trim, gray-haired, square-jawed man, he was the very model of a modern Holy Warrior, like something off of a recruiting poster. He wore a light blue short-sleeved casual uniform. Beneath the skin of the inside of his left forearm, a nanodisplay crawled with ever-changing data. "Anything else?"

"They can function on land, but if they stay out of the water too long their skin and gills dehydrate. I understand that if their gills dry out, the pain is excruciating. Eventually, they die."

Ellers made another note. "Could be useful for interrogation," he said. "What about those big eyes of theirs?"

"Very good underwater vision," Richard said. "But they pay for it on land. They have a third eyelid that improves their vision underwater. On land, they sometimes close it to keep their eyes from drying out. It's transparent, but their vision suffers—they have difficulty seeing things at a distance. They have excellent night vision, at least over the short- to mid-range—much better than ours. On the other hand, a bright, sunny day is quite unpleasant for them; their eyes can't adjust."

"Hearing?" Ellers asked. "They don't seem to have much in the way of ears."

Richard nodded. "My grand—um, Dr. Hansen deliberately atrophied their ears, modifying them so they're more like dolphin ears. They hear much better than normal humans in the water, but worse on land, since their ears don't concentrate sound waves the way normal humans' do. However, they can hear well into what we'd consider the ultrasonic."

"Like dogs."

"Something like that."

"Sense of smell?"

"Probably unchanged. Their noses were modified so their nostrils can be tightly sealed for diving, but smell wasn't considered important for underwater life, so Dr. Hansen didn't make any other changes when he sculpted the genome."

"What about physical strength?"

"They're very strong. An average Selkie is as a strong as, say, a champion weight lifter. A strong Selkie is more like a gorilla or orangutan. Hand to hand, almost any human will be totally outmatched."

"Intelligence?" said Ellers.

Richard blinked. "They're human," he said. "Normal human distribution of IQs, I presume. I don't have any data on that."

Ellers grunted. "I wouldn't call them human," he said, and Richard felt a chill, remembering his almost admiring thoughts about the Selkies moments before. *What's wrong with me?* But Ellers dropped the subject. "Anything else you can think of that might help us plan?"

Richard had saved the best for last. "I've heard you have some kind of tracker device that's DNA-based," he said carefully. Common knowledge, really, but within the Body Purified, as he knew very well, quite a bit of knowledge was both common and restricted at the same time.

Ellers grunted agreement.

"I have a copy of the Selkie genome."

Ellers head jerked up. "Where did you get *that*?"

"It was in some old personal data files," he said. He hoped Ellers would jump to the logical conclusion that those old personal data files had belonged to Richard's grandfather. In fact, they had belonged to his father, who had hidden them very carefully, deeply encrypted, on his computer. Richard, looking through the family data for anything that might be useful to the coming campaign, had found the file, biometrically sealed, and on a whim had offered the computer some skin cells. To his astonishment, it had accepted his sacrifice and opened all of his father's sealed files to him.

There he had found the Selkie DNA, and a great many more of his grandfather's scientific notes. Tracing back,

Richard had discovered that his father had managed to retrieve them from encrypted data stores hidden inside public databases. Exactly how he had known how to access them, Richard didn't understand. From the time stamps, his father had accessed them just days before he had made his fatal leap from the skyscraper.

I should probably hand everything over to Cheveldeoff, he thought uneasily. *In fact, I know I should . . .*

But not yet. As Cheveldeoff himself said, knowledge was power. Knowledge you had that nobody else had was the most powerful of all.

That was rationalization, though, and deep down he knew it. The real reason he hadn't given any of the information he had found in his father's records to Cheveldeoff was that, in some strange way, it simply felt like it would be *wrong.* He didn't understand why, but there it was.

"That will be very helpful indeed," Ellers said. "Transmit it to me right away. We're building some special bots that should be able to take full advantage of it."

A few days later, early in the morning, Richard stepped through the door of his nondescript apartment in a nondescript building. He paused in the hallway to make sure the Godseye surveillance camera got a clear shot of him, then headed for the elevator, frowning.

He'd done everything he could to make the mission a success, but he'd almost fatally overstepped his authority at one point during a meeting between Ellers and Cheveldeoff to which he had been invited as Cheveldeoff's soon-to-be observer. Ellers planned to take a single ship, and Richard had wondered out loud if one would be enough. Ellers' response had been withering. "It's a Lebedoff-class multipurpose assault craft. It carries two hundred troopers plus their equipment, three fully armed assault craft and four unarmed cargo/personnel shuttles. It even has an Orbital Bombardment System. The moddies can't have much weaponry, and what they do have must be decades out of date. It's enough."

"They might have been armed by one of the colonies," Richard said, even while part of his brain yelled at him to *shut up.*

"Enough," Cheveldeoff growled. "Grand Deacon Ellers is the military commander. You're just a civilian observer. Your opinion has been noted."

Rebuked, Richard hadn't said anything more about it. *But I'd still feel better if we had a couple more ships with us,* he thought. Especially since he suspected the Grand Deacon would have preferred to have a couple more ships, too, but simply didn't have them. "News" accounts were heavily censored and widely thought to only incidentally correspond to the facts, but some of the messages Richard had monitored made him think that the New Martians were having rather more success keeping the main Holy Warrior fleet at bay than the Earth populace realized. As a Security analyst, Richard also knew, though very few other civilians would, that the bulk of Earth's remaining ships were en route to Tuin to deal with the new uprising there. And the system he'd pinpointed as the moddies' likely hiding place lay in a different direction than either of them.

Richard emerged from the elevator into the gray and dingy lobby. The Penitents, whose forced labor supposedly brought them closer to the Truth while benefiting society at the same time, were not the most diligent of workers, even when their overseers liberally applied the electric lash, but through the smeared and flyspecked windows, Richard could see the taxibot waiting in the predawn twilight.

He walked through the sliding doors, his large black suitcase following obediently like a well-trained dog. "Luggage, trunk," he said to it, and it rolled around to the front of the taxi, which obligingly opened its hood and extended a ramp like a black rubber tongue. The luggage rolled up into the trunk and the hood chomped down on it, the "tongue" slipping back inside at the same time. The side door swung up, and Richard climbed into the gray interior and settled on the cracked vinyl. The door closed, the electric motor in the back hummed, and the taxibot rolled away from the apartment building down wet, empty streets of potholed gray asphalt, very different from the sparkling blue tile of the Body Purified's walled city-within-a-city where Richard worked.

Richard could have counted on one hand the number of other vehicles he saw on the way to the spaceport. The City of God, like most large cities on the Purified Earth, had a dusk-to-dawn curfew, so only those with special clearance, like Richard this morning, were allowed out before sunrise. Most of the windows in the run-down office buildings they passed were dark, and there were few residential structures along their route, so the overall effect was of a city where all the people had somehow evaporated.

The illusion shattered as they turned a corner onto a long boulevard lined with walnut trees, and the spaceport came in sight. Brilliant lights struck reflections off the silvered sides of half a dozen ships in launch cradles and lit up the white sides of the support buildings like the midday sun. Richard leaned forward. He'd seen the spaceport all his life, but always from a distance; no one could get within a kilometer of it without good reason, and until today, he'd never had that reason.

Today, though, he'd not only be visiting it, he'd be departing . . . and departing Earth.

He'd never thought much about the possibility of leaving Earth; had never *dared* think much about it. Not that thinking about it was a crime, but talking about it, writing about it, or encouraging others to think, talk, or write about it *were,* because doing so encouraged people to entertain the possibility that there might be a better life somewhere than life on the Purified Earth, and theologically, that was heretical nonsense. The Body Purified was working toward making Earth perfect, to ensure that God would never again threaten the world with destruction from the heavens. Things therefore had to be better now than they had been yesterday, and would be better still tomorrow. The sole duty of humanity was to make the world into the paradise God Itself intended it to be. Leaving Earth would be abandoning that great calling. For most people, it could never be permitted.

But as of today, Richard was not "most people," and as his taxibot rolled through the main gate of the spaceport and he saw *BPS Sanctification* rising above its loading cradle like a giant beached whale of silver metal, he could think the unthinkable at last:

I wonder what's out there?

He smiled. Well, one thing he knew was out there was the planet where his grandfather's hubristic creations had gone to ground—or water, in their case. *They don't know what's coming.*

Five minutes later the taxibot rolled to a halt by a ramp leading up to the crew entry elevator in the landing cradle.

A Holy Warrior stood guard, somehow managing to look both bored and alert at the same time. He glanced at a wrist display on the forearm guard of his navy-blue body armor as Richard climbed out of the taxi and waited for his luggage to join him. Richard glanced up and saw the telltale bump of a Godseye camera housing above the door and knew he'd been scanned, vetted and—he assumed, since he wasn't being arrested—approved to board.

While his taxibot opened its mechanical mouth and extended its rubberized tongue for his luggage to roll down, Richard glanced right. Although one of the landing cradle's huge concrete buttresses blocked his view in that direction, he could hear the rumble of the heavy machinery hauling equipment up the much larger ramp to the giant elevators making trip after trip into the hold of *Sanctification*. The taxibot had brought him past some of that equipment, armored personnel carriers, boxes of ammunition and power packs, aerial bots and folded-wing ultralights, mysterious crates and boxes of uncertain origin and content, several boats, and at least three subs, two small, one fairly large. It all had to be secured for both takeoff and the zero-G conditions that would prevail in much of the ship thereafter. Much of it would be prestowed in the large transport shuttles that would take it to the planet's surface . . . after the assault craft had done their work, of course.

His luggage bumped against his leg as though impatient, and Richard turned his attention back to the crew-entry elevator. He climbed the ramp, luggage following a respectful meter behind. The guard gave him a slight nod, then turned his attention back to the expanse of pavement behind him.

Richard entered the elevator, the door closed behind him, and he began his ascent. *A journey of a hundred light-years begins with a single elevator ride,* he thought, and grinned. *And as long as we're thinking in clichés, "today is the first day of the rest of your life."*

If this mission went well, he expected the rest of his life to be much better than his life so far.

He'd dreamed again the night before that he was Victor Hansen. *Well, watch out, Grandpa,* he thought. *Little Ricky is coming for you.*

The funny thing was, even though he knew the old man

must have died long ago, Richard had the distinct feeling Grandpa Hansen would be waiting for him.

Three weeks after the disastrous dinner with her parents (who had not mentioned the evening again, but in that subtle-but-definite "we're not talking about this, but don't believe for a second it's over" way of not talking about it that parents had), Emily saw Chris Keating again for the first time since she'd almost drowned him.

She'd come to the Square to meet her friend Dahlia Schaefer. For weeks, they'd been talking about taking a trip to the Schaefer family's deep-water vacation habitat, but somehow they hadn't managed to buy all the supplies they'd needed. A store not far from the Square offered deep-water equipment, and so they'd agreed to visit it together.

Dahlia was late, not unusual for Dahlia, and Emily was early, not unusual for her; she seemed to be constitutionally unable to show up at the agreed-upon time for any appointment, for fear she'd be (unthinkably!) *late*. With time to kill, she'd ducked into the grandly named though in fact rather dinky Marseguro Planetary Museum for a few minutes.

Its dimly lit halls and brightly lit display cases always took her back to her days in landschool, those first six years when Selkies and landlings studied together. They'd made several field trips here. It hadn't changed: it remained, as it had always been, essentially a shrine to the man who had both created the Selkies and brought them and their landling comrades here—Victor Hansen. In fact, most of the museum's exhibits had been brought to Marseguro in his personal effects. So had about half the contents of the library next door, though all of the First Landers had contributed parts of their digital collections as well. The Old Earth section still dominated the Library, though new work by Marseguroites occupied an ever-growing space. *My generation will fill the place with homegrown music and art and literature,* Emily thought defiantly. *Whatever my parents think about people wasting their time on the arts.*

She wandered aimlessly around the museum. Photographs filled one room, images of Hansen on Earth before the asteroid threat brought the Body to power. Tall, black-haired, handsome, he smiled at the camera with confidence whether standing at a lectern, cutting a ribbon, or shaking hands with the President of United Europe. When he wasn't smiling, it was because the camera had caught him in impassioned speechifying, before the World Assembly, the Council of Scientific Advancement, the guests gathered at the Nobel prize ceremony.

Another room provided more background about Hansen. He'd always loved the water; among his effects had been a ship model, a Yankee Clipper, every piece of rigging impeccably strung in fine thread. Here, too, were the handful of hardcopy books he had brought with him: the Bible ("It's the story of God, isn't it?" she remembered John joking on one school trip to the museum. "Hansen thought it was all about *him*."), *Moby Dick,* a first edition of Darwin's *Origin of Species,* a signed copy of *The Double Helix* . . . and a children's book by Arthur Ransome, an early twentieth-century English author, called *We Didn't Mean to Go to Sea,* which Hansen supposedly included at the last minute as he made his plans to seize (with the approval of the Lunar government) the *Rivers of Babylon,* rebuild it, and get it into space before the Body attacked the Moon. "I loved that book as a kid," he'd said (according to the display text). "And the title appealed to my sense of humor, considering what I hoped to do."

Emily entered the next room. At its center, above a projector set on a pedestal, floated a holographic image of the *Rivers of Babylon* as it had been at launch. If she manipulated the projector's controls, she knew, she could peel the image like an onion, and see how its inner core, normally open to allow zero-G travel the length of the ship, had been bulkheaded and sealed and filled with water for the Selkie families fleeing Earth in Hansen's care. Diagrams and photographs around the room detailed the construction work, carried out under impossible deadlines. The Lunar government, which had sheltered so many refugees from Earth—moddies and nonmods alike—had refused to bow to the threats from the Avatar, firmly ensconced on Earth after the Day of Salvation. The Lunarites had provided the necessary materials and workers and had kept Hansen apprised of the massing of warships in Earth orbit.

Only the chaos on Earth in the aftermath of the Day of

Salvation had given Hansen and his work crews enough time to get the *Rivers of Babylon* ready. Most of his followers had been employees in his massive genesculpting business empire on Earth; other landlings who had joined them had been refugees, or Luna residents, who chose to throw their lot in with him rather than face life under the Body Purified.

A second ship, unmodified, had taken aboard many other refugees who intended to take their chances in the existing colonies.

Emily paused before the last display in the room, a large photograph of that other ship, *Sterling Heights.* The image, captured by the fleeing *Rivers of Babylon,* showed *Sterling Heights,* twice the size of *Rivers of Babylon,* breaking in two in a blossoming sphere of nuclear fire. An instant later there had been nothing left of it.

She shuddered, and decided she'd seen enough. Besides, Dahlia should have arrived by now . . . not that she minded making her friend wait, for a change.

She exited the museum into the Square. *Still no sign of Dahlia,* she thought, surveying it. A deliberately old-fashioned, white-cobblestoned space ringed by the museum, Government House, Town Hall, a couple of restaurants, a tea shop and the library, the Square's most famous attribute was the statue of Victor Hansen at its center, well-watered by a surrounding ring of fountains. Hansen held a model of the double helix of DNA in one hand and a globe of Marseguro in the other, and if his posture seemed a little off-balance and his face bore only a vague resemblance to the photos of Hansen prominently displayed in the nearby museum, well, the multipurpose microfactories they'd brought along hadn't been programmed for artwork and there hadn't been any great sculptors among the crew or passengers of the *Rivers of Babylon,* either.

But there might be in my generation, Emily thought. And then she looked past the statue and saw Chris Keating coming out of Town Hall.

She'd almost forgotten the incident on the pier, but seeing their victim brought it back and she felt her face turn red. For a moment she considered hiding, but then she stiffened both her spine and her resolve and strode to meet him. He had his eyes on a square of hardcopy and didn't see her until she was almost on top of him. When he did, he stopped dead.

"Hi," she said.

He looked so angry she thought for a second he wouldn't respond. But then, almost as though a switch had flicked inside his head, his expression changed. A little smile even flickered across his face—a secret smile, born of some internal amusement, she thought, not really directed at her. "Hello," he said.

"I wanted . . . I just . . ." She cleared her throat. "I saw you and came over to apologize."

"Really." The odd smile flickered again, but his voice remained cool.

"Yes, I . . . it was a stupid thing to do. As Dr. Stanless made clear to us." She grinned. "But in a way you got us back. We spent the next hour hauling out the algae samples you'd come to help with. What a smell!"

"I've never noticed." Still cool.

"Anyway, I just wanted to, um . . ." *I'm getting nothing here,* she thought. "Well . . . no hard feelings?" She winced a little at her own lameness.

"No feelings at all," Chris Keating replied.

Huh? What an odd way to phrase it . . .

"I'm, uh . . ." She cast around for some way to keep the conversation going, even though she really would have preferred it to end, and something said on the pier came back to her. "I'm sorry to hear your mother's been ill. How is she?"

"She died last week." She wouldn't have thought it possible, but Keating's voice grew even colder, and the strange little smile vanished completely.

"Oh, that's . . . uh . . ." Her voice trailed off. "I'm sorry," she finally said, again. *Sorry in so many ways,* she thought. *Sorry we pushed you in the water, and just about as sorry I came over to apologize for it.*

"So you've said. Several times." Keating gave her approximately the same look she'd use trying to figure out the origin of a slimy glob of floating sea trash. "Is there anything else?"

"No. I'll . . ." She tried a final smile. "I'll see you around?"

"For a while, maybe." Keating strode past her and on down the street.

Now what did *that* mean?

"Emily!" Dahlia's voice rang across the Square, and she turned to meet her friend, putting Chris Keating out of her mind.

The encounter with one of his Selkie attackers in the Square left Chris shaking with anger and disgust. At first he had rather enjoyed facing Emily Wood again, thinking of how little her apologies would mean when Earth answered his call. But when she dared to mention his mother . . . and then to pretend she actually cared what happened to a landling . . . the hypocrisy infuriated him. The Selkies had no true human feelings. They were nothing but intelligent animals, devolved and degraded from once-human stock. They could manipulate, mock, and mimic true human feelings, but they no more understood it than parrots understood the words they could repeat or monkeys understood the actions they could copy. So said . . . *had* said . . . his mother. More importantly, so said the Avatar.

But shame and guilt mingled with his anger. He'd felt secret relief when told his mother had died at last, and that shamed him, even though she had, in a very real way, died the day of her stroke. But what kind of son felt even an iota of relief at the death of his mother?

And mixed with that shame, the guilt: guilt that he had not triggered the emergency beacon years before, when he had first thought of it and his mother had still been alive. If he had acted then, instead of letting his fear for his personal safety get in the way, the Holy Warriors might have long since come to Marseguro—and brought with them the technology that could have helped his mother recover from her stroke, or even have prevented it altogether.

Now it's too late. He had traveled three blocks at a fast walk since leaving the Square, heading toward the genesculpting lab where he had recently resumed work, but now he stopped and sat down on an empty crate outside a survival supply store, the sort of place that sold deep-sea shelters to Selkies and tents to the few nonmods like himself who liked to travel into the interior. *What if they don't come at all?* It had been more than two weeks since he had triggered the beacon. He knew intellectually it could be months or even years before there would be a response, but knowing that and sustaining the hope he'd had when he first triggered the beacon were two different things. Already he'd begun to worry about what would happen the next time someone visited Landing Valley. Would they discover what he had done? Worse, would they figure out *he* had done it? He didn't think he'd left anything anyone could trace back to him, but there was no such thing as a perfect crime. . . .

He brought himself up short. *What I did was not a crime,* he upbraided himself. *It was my duty to humanity. The Selkies are monstrosities that should never have been created. And they're going to spread across this world like a plague, and someday back out into the universe, if they're not stopped.*

He couldn't believe he was the only normal human who felt the way he did, either, that he was the only second-or third-generation Believer, but he couldn't think of any way to discover others. There were too few nonmods and too many Selkies. Even broaching the subject would almost certainly bring him to the Council's attention and get him arrested. *More likely, it would get me killed,* he thought. The secret, all-Selkie cabal, the one that *really* ran things, didn't have to worry about niceties like a trial. They'd just arrange an accident, like the one that had killed his father.

Well, he didn't intend to be stuck in prison *or* dead when the Holy Warriors arrived and began the Purification Marseguro so richly deserved. He wanted to be free to greet them and then, and only then, reveal himself to be the hero—*hero,* not criminal—who had summoned them.

He heard voices coming along the street and his head jerked up. *Not again!* But there she came, Emily Wood herself, in her landling clothes (*slumming,* he thought), with another Selkie even sleeker and more self-satisfied looking, dressed in one of the barely-there two-strips-of-cloth skinsuits some Selkies had begun to favor, the dark skin of her exposed arms and legs and midriff glistening with moisture-preserving oil, her hair shaved down to peach fuzz and died bright pink. With their vestigial nubs for noses and ears, and their oversized, three-lidded eyes, both "girls" looked so alien to Chris at that moment that the bejeweled navel winking at him from the one girl's naked belly startled him: she looked like something that should have spawned from a drifting egg like a fish. Her body looked human enough, human enough he felt a stirring of desire at seeing it so wantonly displayed, but that stirring died in disgust. He knew plenty of nonmods had had sex with Selkies, who were notoriously oversexed, courtesy of Victor Hansen, and back in his horny adolescence he might have considered it himself, but now it seemed to him no better than bestiality.

They'll all be Purified, he thought. *The Selkies. The Selkie-lovers. All of them.*

Emily Wood looked up and saw him. The rage and depression that had left him shaking after they spoke in the Square had vanished, replaced by savage, sardonic amusement. He stood, smiled, nodded to her, and went on down the street toward the lab before she could again parrot her empty apologies.

Weeks, months, years: he could wait. His message would be heard, and then she really *would* be sorry.

They all would.

Chapter 5

RICHARD'S CABIN ABOARD *BPS Sanctification* had no windows, and though no doubt the bridge crew could choose from a multiplicity of video feeds showing the ship's exterior, he didn't have access to them on his little vidscreen. In fact, as he quickly discovered, he didn't have access to much of anything, including any part of the ship that wasn't either his cabin, the automated mess hall just down the corridor that he seemed to have entirely to himself, or the recreation room next door to the mess hall that it seemed he also had to himself, if you didn't count the image of the Avatar that appeared every hour on the hour in every holocube in the room to lead whomever happened to be present in the prayer *du jour*.

Despite being alone and apparently unobserved, Richard made a point of being in the rec room at least once every day at a designated prayer time. Just because he *thought* he was unobserved didn't mean he actually *was*. Given his family history, he doubted he'd spent more than a few hours of his entire life unobserved. If he hoped to change that with the success of this mission, it wouldn't do to give anyone any reason to doubt his devotion.

He didn't know what to expect from liftoff, but an automated announcement came on to tell him to strap himself into the chair/acceleration couch thoughtfully provided and to stow all loose items in the nearby drawers. During the launch, he felt very heavy for a few minutes, but not unbearably so. Another announcement urged him to stay strapped in "during spin-up of the habitat ring." For a few minutes he experienced weightlessness and barely managed to keep down his breakfast, but then weight returned, albeit not as much as usual: if he remembered right, the habitat ring spun up to about 0.9 G. Feeling both light and light-headed, he unstrapped when told it was safe to do so.

Some hours later, another announcement told him they had left Earth orbit, though he felt nothing unusual. About two days after that, there came another announcement that they had made the transition to branespace. Effectively, they'd left their own universe . . . and Richard hadn't felt a thing. He lay on the bed, staring at the blank ceiling, and thought that if people knew how boring space travel was, the Body Purified wouldn't have to outlaw talk about it.

Fortunately for his sanity, shortly after that announcement, his vidscreen beeped and lit with an image of Grand Deacon Ellers.

"Mr. Hansen," said the Grand Deacon. "I trust you've enjoyed your journey so far."

"I can't complain," Richard said—the literal truth. "I've been wondering if I'm really on the right ship, though. It seems pretty empty down here."

"I apologize for not speaking to you sooner," Ellers said. "There have been a great many demands on my time. In any event, security protocols are strict: nonmilitary personnel are restricted to isolated quarters during launch and the transition to branespace.

"Now, however, if you'd care to join me, I'd be happy to give you a tour of the ship. I'm sure you'll want to prepare a report for transmission to Archdeacon Cheveldeoff once we're back in normal space."

"I'm sure I will," Richard said.

"Excellent. I'll send an escort."

Twenty minutes later, after being guided through the ship's mazelike interior by a Holy Warrior who seemed to possess a profound aversion to small talk—or talk of any kind—Richard joined the Grand Deacon in a vidwalled briefing room. Three walls were blank, but the forth showed a schematic of an unfamiliar solar system.

"You made it, I see," Ellers said.

"Only with help." Richard nodded at his escort.

"Thank you, Chan. That will be all," Ellers told the silent Holy Warrior, who saluted and left.

"I'm glad I didn't have to find the way on my own," Richard said. "Who designed this ship? Escher?"

"It's a security feature," Ellers said. "Not only is the interior counterintuitive, many of the corridor/room combinations are mutable. Anyone attempting to take this ship by force is going to find it very difficult to reach any of its critical systems."

"I'm glad I didn't try to escape my comfortable little corner of it, then."

"You wouldn't have." Ellers indicated the system map on the vidwall. "I thought you might like to see this. Our branespace probe returned with this information just before we departed."

Richard took a closer look. The system had two Jupiter-plus gas giants in distant orbits, a couple of chunks of rock in close . . . and a fifth planet, third out from the star, right in the middle of what the diagram helpfully labeled the habitable zone.

"Some of this is conjecture—there may still be some undetected planets," Ellers said. "But there's no doubt that *that* planet," he pointed to the third from the star, "is our destination. The beacon whose transmission you uncovered is still yelling its message into space. The probe also detected low-strength radio signals. And," Ellers gave Richard a rare grin, "the probe is quite confident that that world is almost entirely covered in liquid water."

"A perfect Selkie world," Richard said. He thought for a moment how wonderful it would be to be able to breathe underwater and explore a vast world ocean . . . then shoved the thought down, almost in panic. *They're monsters,* he thought. *Not mythical merpeople.*

"Indeed," said Ellers. "Congratulations. I think there can no longer be any doubt that you have uncovered your grandfather's hideaway."

Richard took a deep breath. He felt huge relief—he'd been confident, but he hadn't been sure—but hard on its heels came a strange surge of . . . sadness? Panic? Anger?

Angst seemed to be the only word to describe it.

And again, he didn't know where it was coming from.

Ellers was still talking. ". . . take you on the grand tour. After that, you'll be free to come and go as you please, at least until we return to Earth." He rose and led the way to the door.

The tour took the better part of two hours. They even

ventured up to the ship's core, the central zero-G shaft. The
assault craft and transport shuttles were stored at the aft
end, but both ends boasted vast air locks. Should something
happen to the dock at one end of the ship, the core could be
evacuated of air and surviving vehicles could be flown the
length of the ship and out the other end. Surrounding the
central shaft toward the stern were the vast zero-G holds
filled with supplies and weapons. Anything that absolutely
required gravity was stored in smaller holds in the habitat
ring, the rotating torus where the crew lived and operated.
"It has a radius of around ninety meters," Ellers explained,
"and rotates at about three revolutions per minute. It's big
enough and slow enough that Coriolis forces aren't a problem. It would be difficult to keep troops in fighting trim if
we didn't have some kind of artificial gravity on board. The
branespace engineers keep claiming they're on the verge of
figuring out how to generate 'real' gravity, but they've been
saying that for twenty years now."

Richard discovered he had his own reason for appreciat-
ing the habitat ring's artificial gravity: neither he nor his
stomach very much enjoyed zero-G. He didn't throw up,
quite, but he was very glad to pull himself into the elevator
in the core and feel his weight gradually return as it eased
its way "down" — really, "out" — into the habitat ring.

The tour complete, Ellers led Richard to the bridge.
Here, at last, were exterior views of the ship, but since the
featureless void of branespace appeared in vidscreens as
pitch-black, they didn't hold much interest. Richard's eyes
were drawn instead to interior views that displayed some of
the places he'd just been shown, the holds filled with weapons and vehicles, the three assault craft, the training rooms
where the Holy Warriors practiced everything from knife
fighting to unarmed combat to light-weapons fire. In one
large simulator, a half-dozen Holy Warriors put a virtual
submarine through its paces. "It's very impressive," Richard said. "I feel sorry for the Selkies . . ." his voice trailed
off, and he hastily added ". . . almost."

"I don't," Ellers growled. "They're abominations and
they deserve what's coming." He grinned then, or at least
showed his teeth. Richard had a momentary and unsettling
sense of the skeleton lurking just below the thin layer of
skin and tissue that made a living human being. "And

what's coming is the Hand of God Itself, made flesh in the Holy Warriors of the Body."

Richard resisted the temptation to say "Oo-Rah," opting instead for, "What's our ETA?"

"Two weeks in branespace, two days in to the planet."

Richard looked back at the vidscreens of the Holy Warriors in training. "I've got a lot of time to kill," he said. "I was wondering . . ."

Two weeks and two days later Richard stood on the bridge again as *BPS Sanctification* entered orbit around the planet where they expected to find the Selkies. Looking at the screens displaying the planet's vast blue curve below them, he rubbed his left shoulder. After two weeks of long daily workouts, his instructor in the form of unarmed combat the Holy Warriors called "angel wrestling" had boosted the level of intensity a notch, and Richard had the bruises and strained muscles to show it. He'd had more luck with weapons training: much to his surprise, he'd turned out to be an excellent shot with both projectile and laser weapons. And at least now he knew which end to hold, should the need arise, and how to reload both.

He'd also managed to overcome his spacesickness . . . to a degree. He could function in zero-G as long as he didn't perform too many violent maneuvers. Gentle drifting—no problem. Zigzagging and jackknifing back and forth across the central shaft—upchuck city.

Although he had discovered that vomiting could actually be used as a crude—very crude—zero-G propulsion system.

Who knew?

The planet-wide ocean glittered below them, fluffy white clouds dotted across it, each trailing a deep blue drop shadow. It looked beautiful and innocuous, but *"Here There Be Monsters,"* Richard thought. The moment they had exited branespace two days before they had heard the powerful call of the emergency beacon. "STARSHIP *RIVERS OF BABYLON* REQUESTS ASSISTANCE. THIS BEACON WILL RUN CONTINUOUSLY. STARSHIP *RIVERS OF BABYLON* REQUESTS ASSISTANCE. THIS BEACON WILL RUN CONTINUOUSLY . . ."

All the way in they'd also been listening in on the planet's ordinary radio traffic. Accents were strange and references uncertain, but they'd overheard enough mentions of "Victor Hansen" and "Selkies" and "genesculpting" to make it clear to everyone that Richard's claim had been spectacularly upheld. Here at last was the secret hiding place of Victor Hansen's genemodded monsters.

They'd also learned what the residents called their watery home: Marseguro, Spanish and Portuguese for "safe sea."

I don't think so, Grandpa, Richard thought. He'd found himself talking to the long-dead genesculptor more and more in his head, and the weird thing was, it didn't feel like he was talking to himself.

At least the headaches and dreams had subsided during the trip.

Ship sensors had provided more and more detail about Marseguro as they had approached. Water covered all of it except for one largish island or minicontinent and a scattering of smaller ones, some little more than wave-pounded rocks. The ocean was kilometers deep everywhere except for one enormous area of much shallower water, where a continent seemed to be either rising or subsiding.

Human—*near-human,* Richard reminded himself—habitation appeared to be concentrated in a series of towns along the eastern shore of the continent island. (The north and south poles had been designated based on the planet's direction of spin, Earth's "sun-rises-in-the-east" paradigm having been taken as the norm—as indeed, according to Body Purified doctrine, it had to be.)

Twenty-four hours ago, a probe had been sent ahead of *Sanctification* to orbit the planet and collect more detailed readings. That data, now arriving in near real-time, confirmed what they had suspected since entering the system and finding no signs of space travel: civilization on Marseguro appeared focused almost entirely downward, into the ocean. The only artificial satellites ID'd themselves as being part of the complement of *Rivers of Babylon.* Their function seemed limited to providing global positioning information, over-the-horizon communications, and meteorological information. "They knew they might be pursued," Richard had mused out loud to Ellers as they neared the planet. "Why wouldn't they have at least a couple of early-warning sensor platforms?"

"They might have them and we can't see them," Ellers said. "If they were entirely passive, we'd have no way to recognize them as artificial." He shrugged. "But after fifty years, it doesn't matter. Our stealth technologies make us essentially invisible to anything but another Body ship. Whatever ancient sensors they might have hidden around the system couldn't possibly detect us. And even if by some miracle they did see us coming . . . what could they do about it? Fifty years isn't long enough to create the kind of technological and manufacturing capability it takes to build a ship that could challenge *Sanctification*. Their entire complement of microfactories would have to run flat-out for decades even to make a start, and they will have had other priorities. The most they could do if they spotted us would be to run and hide. And since no one is running or hiding . . ."

True enough, Richard thought now. The communications chatter remained mundane, talk of cultural events and sporting competitions and fishing grounds and, of course, what products were needed where, how soon the microfactories could produce them, and how much would be paid for them. It provided no hint that anyone below realized that Victor Hansen's pipe dream of escape from the Body Purified was about to become a nightmare.

Richard glanced at Ellers. The Grand Deacon held his head tilted slightly to the left, listening to the earbud he wore on that side, a tiny device that could also transmit his voice. "Well," Ellers said suddenly, in response to whatever he had heard, "I see no point in delay. Sound General Quarters. Pilots to their assault craft, drop teams to their shuttles. Attack to commence as scheduled, 0945 ship time."

Richard looked at the peaceful ocean passing far below them, then at the day/night terminator approaching. Soon they would swing through the planetary night. On the far side of Marseguro, the town they had learned was called Hansen's Harbor would just be moving into the light, most of its citizens, human and subhuman, still asleep.

They're in for a rude awakening. Grandpa, your dream is over.

He just wished he felt happier about it.

Sanctification swung into darkness.

*   *   *

"Is that it?" Dahlia asked as Emily tightened the final strap on the last of an inordinate number of bundles in the dolphin sub they'd rented. They were in the dry hold; the last food barrel had gone into the wet hold—which also made an excellent refrigerator—twenty minutes ago.

Emily stepped back and surveyed her handiwork. "I think so," she said. "Nothing to do but say good-bye." She checked the wall chronometer. "We're only an hour later getting away than I'd hoped. Not bad . . . well, not by your standards, anyway."

"Very funny," Dahlia said. "I still don't know why you insisted on leaving in the dark."

"I like the dark," Emily said. "It feels like you're in deep water the minute you undock. It's just more . . . romantic."

"I don't think of you in that way," Dahlia said dryly, and Emily laughed. Dahlia was the most heterosexual girl she knew, as any number of Selkie boys—and, she suspected, more than one landling one—would attest, generally with a blissful smile of reminiscence.

"I guess I'll just have to struggle on somehow," Emily said. "Come on, let's go see if my parents are awake."

They'd docked the sub on the bay side of the Woods' hab. They slipped into the water-filled lower half of the vehicle and swam through the open bottom hatch into the well-lit tunnel leading into the hab proper. Like most shallow-water Selkie habs, it was cylindrical, with the lower half filled with water and the upper half with air. (Deep-sea habitats tended to be spherical, for added structural strength.) Although they could sleep underwater if they had to, most Selkies preferred to sleep dry—albeit in very warm air with a relative humidity of 100 percent. And of course, they had to eat in the air. Socializing with landlings demanded an air-filled space as well, as did waste elimination. *We aren't merpeople, we're amphibipeople,* Emily thought, as she and Dahlia swam up past the wet sleeping, storage, and recreation rooms in the bottom of the hab. They emerged into the large round pool that was the central feature of the Woods' main room.

A broad deck furnished with comfortable chairs and sofas surrounded the pool. A higher, drier level contained the kitchen, the dry recreation room (filled with non-water-friendly electronics), and the level above, the top level, contained the bedrooms and bathrooms.

Treading water, Emily and Dahlia looked around the living room. The only light came from the series of blue-green panels just below the surface of the water around the edge of the pool. The wavering illumination reflected back from the curved metal beams that held up the dome of the roof and from the thick windows separating those beams. No light yet filtered down through the cold waters of New Botany Bay to herald the approach of dawn. "Still in bed, I guess," Emily said. "I'm surprised. Mom's usually an early riser."

"What about your dad?" Dahlia asked. She rubbed her hand over her pink peach-fuzz hair. "Mine would sleep till the middle of the afternoon every day if he could get away with it—then stay up until dawn every morning."

Emily laughed. "Dad would *prefer* to sleep in. But once Mom is up . . ." She looked up at the top level of the three tiers rising around them. "Well, I guess we'll let them sleep . . ."

"Didn't you say good-bye last night?" Dahlia said. "I did."

"Sort of." In fact, she and her parents still weren't exactly talking normally. Like a giant weight, the subject of her choice of specialization crushed all attempts at normal conversation. Mostly they grunted at each other or said things like, "Pass the salt." She couldn't help wondering, as she hesitated in the dark pool in the dark hab, whether her mother was deliberately putting off getting out of bed until she knew Emily had gone.

No sign of Amy, either, but she'd always been a late sleeper.

Well. Two weeks away—not just away, but completely cut off, with no way to communicate without launching an emergency transmitter buoy—ought to give both her and her parents time to think about what they would say to each other the next time they saw each other. Maybe they could manage more than grunts.

"Let's go," Emily said. She flared her gill slits and plunged back beneath the surface of the pool.

The transition from air breathing to water breathing always brought with it a surge of adrenaline, a "Help, I'm drowning!" reflex left over from their landling ancestry. She let the surge of energy carry her down the tube to the minisub. "Hey, wait for me!" Dahlia chirped at her heels.

Ten minutes later, they sat in the dolphin sub's cockpit. It could be operated flooded, but they'd chosen to keep it dry for this trip (except for regular skin-and-gill-moistening sprays of water) to make it easier to talk to each other. Emily had the con in the bay, where there were more subs, buildings, buoys, and boats to avoid. She turned on the bow light with the flick of a switch, hit another switch to disconnect and retract the umbilical, and one more to release the magnetic clamps holding them to the docking tube. The sub shuddered a little, then clanked and rocked as the hatch slid closed and dogged shut. The steering control, a simple wheel, operated like an airplane yoke—push it forward to descend, pull it back to rise. The computer adjusted ballast and buoyancy as required. *Child's play*, Emily thought, but Dahlia, after an unfortunate accident involving an underwater crane, three warning buoys, and a very surprised Selkie construction crew working on the new waterhockey arena, had decided to limit her sub driving to open water.

Emily shoved the throttle lever to one-quarter speed. The sub vibrated a little as the turbines spun up, then the water jets kicked in and they moved smoothly away into the underwater "street," a path reserved for vehicles that was kept clear of buildings and swimmers and delineated by lights at three levels: near the surface, on the bottom, and halfway between. Marseguro's equivalent of plankton formed green halos around the floating light globes. Occasionally a larger creature, one of the many species of what scientists called "flo," for "fish-like-organism," but ordinary people just called fish, appeared briefly in the lights, sweeping through the sphere of illumination, sucking up micro flora and fauna.

They didn't follow the street very long; a kilometer from the Woods' hab the buildings thinned out. Beyond lay only darkness, pierced by their own thin ray of light, a glowing blue-green pole of illumination along which they endlessly slid.

As they entered the uninhabited part of the bay and headed for open water, Emily saw a new light, filtering down from above, through the cockpit's transparent canopy. "Day's breaking," she said.

"Yeah?" Dahlia craned her neck back. "Guess so. Well, it doesn't matter where we're going." She turned back to

Emily and grinned. "Stick this thing where the sun don't shine, baby."

Emily laughed. "You've got it." She pushed the steering wheel down, and the faint light of the new day breaking over Hansen's Harbor vanished in the darkness above them.

Chapter 6

CHRIS KEATING WOKE to the gray light of dawn and the sound of thunder.

At least, he thought it was thunder. But as he lay in bed wondering blearily why the weather forecast the day before hadn't mentioned the possibility of a thunderstorm, he realized the "thunder" wasn't stopping. It went on and on, thump and rumble following each other in rapid succession. When a particularly loud bang caused the framed picture of him and his mother that hung over the desk to crash down into the cold remains of the previous night's snapperfish pizza, he sat up straight. When another, even louder boom rattled everything in the room, including his teeth, he staggered up and ran to the balcony, throwing the windows wide.

A blunt-nosed, delta-shaped craft bigger than the biggest surface ship on Marseguro roared overhead toward the harbor, so low he instinctively ducked. Flashes of light rippled along its leading edge, and explosions shook the town. Black smoke billowed up from beyond the buildings blocking his view of the bay. He looked up and down the street. On every balcony people in various stages of *dishabille* stood staring.

His momentary fear gave way to fierce, hot elation. *They've come. They've come!*

But the fear returned when another explosion shook his apartment so violently a large chunk of ceiling plaster dropped onto his recently vacated bed. *They're here, and I could get killed!*

He had to get out of the house. Better still, out of the city. He had faith the Holy Warriors would not target normal humans, but they probably wouldn't be too worried about collateral damage, either, considering the normals were mostly descendants of the traitors who had helped Victor Hansen steal a starship and escape Purification.

His hiking pack lay beside the door, where he had dumped it after he'd returned from his journey to Landing Valley. He couldn't run out naked—though he considered it for a moment as another explosion brought more of the ceiling down—so he took a moment to pull on the clothes he'd taken off and tossed on the floor the night before. Then he headed out, down the stairs in a headlong rush, then between the buildings and up into the hills. He started at a run that quickly changed to a jog and then a brisk, panting walk as the slope steepened.

I can't believe they're here! He'd resigned himself to a wait of months, even years, before his message received a response. But here they were. And such a response . . .

At the top of the hill, he turned to survey what he had wrought.

Black smoke poured up from flame-licked buildings along the water's edge. Half a dozen boats lay on their sides or upside down, hulls holed and smoking. He recognized one as Dr. Stanless' *SeaSkimmer*, and felt a momentary pang of guilt, quickly suppressed. *You can't make an omelet without breaking eggs,* he told himself, quoting the Avatar. Chris had never eaten an omelet or seen a chicken in the feathered flesh (Marseguroite "chicken," like "beef" and "pork"—pretty much everything but seafood—was vatmeat) but he understood the saying's meaning well enough, and now, as he surveyed the destruction he had helped bring about, he embraced it.

The pier where the Selkies had humiliated him had been reduced to two undamaged sections joined by a long line of half-submerged rubble, awash in the unusually troubled waters of New Botany Bay. In the bay itself, several structures had been hit. One or two had collapsed entirely; others burned enthusiastically, clouds of mingled smoke and steam rising into the clear morning sky, just turning pink as the sun neared the horizon.

For a moment, he thought the attack was over, then three of the black assault craft swept back over the pier, bursting through the pall of smoke that had hidden them from him. Missiles speared down into the city on shafts of fire. Orange flame blossomed. Seconds later the dull rolling WHUMPs of the explosions thudded into Chris' chest.

The assault craft banked, turned, came back for a second pass. This time one of the reaching missiles hit the genesculpting lab where just the day before Chris had been sequencing the new algae samples. Everything he'd worked on for the last two years disappeared in a bloom of red flame, a billow of black smoke, a rain of fragments, and a thump in his chest like a blow from a fist. Chris nodded approvingly. The more he'd listened to the Avatar, the more uncomfortable he'd become with his work in the lab. Genesculpting algae and *E. coli* to produce medicine and food seemed harmless enough, but it was just one short step from that to genesculpting humans and creating monstrosities like the Selkies, wasn't it?

He'd find a new job in the new regime.

The assault craft made one more pass, the wind of their passage swirling the smoke from the burning buildings into miniature sooty tornadoes. This time, dozens of small black objects fell from them, caught themselves, and zipped away across the city like the flying insects Chris knew only from old Earth vids. After that, one assault craft accelerated with a burst of flame and in seconds vanished north up the coast. The other two slowed and settled into the Square where Chris had talked with Emily Wood just a few days before. The blast from their landing jets toppled the statue of Victor Hansen—the sight made Chris grin—and blew the water out of the fountain pool. Both flanks of each of the shuttles slammed down onto the cobblestones. Soldiers in shining dark-blue body armor swarmed out, spreading out across the Square under the cover of constantly swinging weapons turrets on the assault craft.

Chris almost laughed out loud. Of course, they had no way of knowing what he could have told them: there were almost no weapons on Marseguro. Selkies had some powerful spear-and-dart-guns used to hunt or fight off some of the larger Marseguroite sea life. He had once heard that the Council kept six ancient automatic rifles—the *Rivers of Babylon*'s entire complement—locked up somewhere, but he'd never heard of anyone firing one. And no one had ever bothered to program a microfactory to manufacture firearms. After all, they were all one big happy family on Mar-seguro, and the best form of gun control, authorities and residents agreed, was no guns at all, for anyone. Even the Peaceforcers—all twelve of them—didn't have anything except a few stunners (though they could legally gain access to the Council's rifles if necessary), and he didn't see any sign of them attempting to use them on the armored soldiers, which would have been useless and probably swiftly fatal.

Too bad, Chris thought. *It might have been fun to watch.* He'd lost all respect for Peaceforce since his mother had explained to him that it existed solely to keep the oppressed landlings in their place, allowing the Selkies to enjoy and consolidate their undisputed and undeserved place atop the pinnacle of society.

The Holy Warriors had formed a perimeter around the Square. Two strange black vehicles shaped like stubby cylinders, with fins and bumps in odd places, rolled out of the assault craft on multiple wheels. The assault craft promptly lifted off again. One headed toward the harbor and settled there, but intervening buildings and thickening smoke prevented Chris from seeing any details. The other lit its jets and roared south.

He turned his attention back to the Square in time to see a group of soldiers disappear into Government House. One of the wheeled vehicles remained in front while its mate, accompanied by a couple of dozen troops, rolled off down a side street and out of Chris' view. The remaining Holy Warriors appeared to be searching the buildings around the Square. Chris suspected all except Government House and possibly Town Hall were empty this time of morning. Neither would have more than one or two people in it, and probably no one of any importance.

Aside from the symbolic value, why would they want to seize Government House? he thought, then answered his own question: *Planetary Communications. They have a message to get out.*

And I can help them do it.

He'd come up the hill intending to hide out in the interior until things settled down, but now he scrambled to his feet and headed down into the city again, a man with a new mission.

They need someone to help them take firm control. They need a native guide.

He squeezed between two buildings and emerged onto the main road to find that, out of his sight, the streets had filled with people, some running, though from where to where he couldn't guess, some standing in groups shouting at each other, some pushing carts of belongings, some supporting wounded friends or family. A father with a tear-streaked face went by, cradling a little boy in his arms, dead or alive, Chris couldn't tell. For the second time that morning, an unexpected pang of guilt stabbed at Chris' heart. *Couldn't they have been more careful? Why had they hurt normals?*

Eggs, he reminded himself. *Omelets.* And the sooner their liberators established firm control over the city—over the whole planet—the sooner the death and destruction would end.

Well, for normals, anyway.

He hurried on, against the tide of people streaming inland. He had almost reached the Square when someone grabbed his arm from behind.

He yelped and spun to find Dr. Stanless. The geneticist wore only torn and dirty pajama bottoms, and a nasty looking gash on his left shoulder had streaked one side of his body with blood. His right eye blazed at Chris; his left was black and swollen closed. "Chris!" he yelled. "Don't go down there! We've been invaded!"

As if on cue, four soldiers in dark blue body armor burst out of the doorway of the building to their left. Two seized Dr. Stanless, who struggled uselessly in their iron grip. Two seized Chris, who didn't resist at all. "Yes, Dr. Stanless, I know," he said, and smiled. He couldn't resist adding, "I called them." Dr. Stanless' face went slack with shock as the Holy Warriors hauled him away.

The two holding Chris tightened their grip on his arms. He grinned at them. "Didn't you hear what I said?" They exchanged looks. "Well, then, don't you think you'd better take me to whomever is in charge?"

They did, but to his indignation, they weren't gentle about it.

Richard watched the assault from the bridge of *Sanctification,* having been told in no uncertain terms by Grand Deacon Ellers that civilians were neither wanted nor permitted in the assault craft. After it became clear—as it did within minutes—that no organized resistance existed on Marseguro, he began to chafe under that restriction.

Not that he lacked information. The bridge's vidscreens displayed a constantly changing kaleidoscope of carnage, with feeds from cams on the assault craft, the armored personnel carriers, the helmets of the Holy Warriors, hovering reconbots and even the noses of smart missiles all vying for attention. But there were too many images, and too many voices, and vid, no matter how vivid, couldn't substitute for personal experience. Richard desperately wanted to go down on the ground and smell, hear, taste, and feel what was happening for himself. The desire was so strong it was almost a compulsion.

He put it down to his need to see for himself the long-delayed Purification of his grandfather's pet planet—and the long-delayed polishing of his own unfairly tarnished reputation.

He knew that the second wave of ships descending to the planet's surface would be supply shuttles. He'd heard they were a rough way to get through the atmosphere, but he was seriously beginning to wonder how he could talk his way onto one when he discovered he didn't have to.

He didn't pick out the message from Grand Deacon Ellers from the muted cacophony of voices all around. The first he knew of it was when a young man, pink-cheeked, blue-eyed and with the painfully erect bearing of a newly minted Holy Warrior, trotted around the second-level walkway that surrounded the main pit of the circular bridge and saluted. Richard felt his hand twitch in response but managed not to salute back. After weeks on *Sanctification,* he had to keep reminding himself he was a civilian observer, not a Holy Warrior. "Yes?"

"Grand Deacon Ellers' compliments, sir, and he requests your presence on the ground."

At last! Richard thought, but he maintained a studied calm. "Did he say why?"

"No, sir. Just that if you will take the next supply shuttle down, he'll provide an escort to take you to Government House."

"Government House?"

"That's what the moddies and traitors call it," the young man said. "Some kind of tribal headquarters."

"Very well," Richard said. "Thank you."

"You're welcome, sir!" The young man saluted again, obviously having taken to heart the advice given the lowest-ranking members of any military that to be safe one should salute anything on two legs. He trotted back around the bridge to his original post.

Richard stepped to the nearest general information vidscreen and found that the next supply ship, carrying ammunition, food, and medical and communications equipment would launch in half an hour. That gave him just enough time to rush back to his cabin, pull out the bag he had packed the day before in the hope he'd go down to the surface, use the bathroom (it seemed a prudent precaution), and take the lift to the central core. Holy Warriors from the ship's crew stood by at each of the three intraship transporters, platforms that slid along slots placed at equidistant intervals around the cylindrical core. Richard carefully transitioned from the spinning habitat ring to the nonspinning section, and a crewman shoved his bag into a box on the platform and strapped it in place. Richard seized one of the many handholds on the transporter, and they zipped the length of the ship in two minutes. "Thanks," Richard said. The crewman shrugged, handed him his box, and zipped away again.

Richard took a moment to take a couple of deep breaths—the relatively rapid transit of the core had unsettled his stomach a hair—then pulled himself along the soft silvery webbing that covered every wall of the zero-G part of the ship, tugging his luggage behind him. He entered an access tunnel, emerged a moment later in the shuttle launch bay, and flinched: the shuttles were all locked down, of course, but two of them, including the one he wanted, hung overhead from his perspective, fat cargo-carrying cylinders with a much smaller crew compartment at the bow like an olive attached to the tip of a sausage.

Richard knew better than to try to simply jump across the intervening distance: the zero-G training he'd had on board *Sanctification* had brightly and painfully illuminated the difference between mass and weight, and the unforgiving nature of inertia, and he knew he could very easily misjudge the amount of force with which he'd hit the far wall and break an ankle—or his neck. Instead, he continued around the brightly-lit space using the webbing, and finally reached his shuttle with five minutes to spare. The pilot, a man who looked solid enough to have been hewn out of a single—and very large—block of granite, took one look at his passenger, grunted, and pointed him to . . .

"What's that?" Richard said. It looked a bit like a medieval torture device, all black metal, straps, and buckles. There were six in the crew cabin, three on each side of the smallish, white-painted space.

"Is called a rack," the pilot said, apparently confirming Richard's impression. He had a thick Russian accent to go with his bearlike appearance. "I show. Go there." He didn't give Richard an opportunity to do otherwise, manhandling him into position with casual strength. "Straps go here, here—" he pointed to Richard's shoulders, waist, and crotch. "Pull in handles, so—" He demonstrated. U-shaped, padded handles swung away from the wall on hinges and locked in front of Richard's chest. "Helmet . . ." The pilot opened a locker on the other side of the small compartment and took out a dark blue crash helmet with an alarmingly battered look. It had a short bungee cord attached to the back. The pilot jammed the helmet onto Richard's head, almost taking his ears off in the process, clipped the bungee cord onto a metal loop on the wall, and fastened the chinstrap. Then he tapped something on the side of the helmet, and built-in headphones came to life. "You hear?" the pilot said.

Richard nodded.

"You hold on," the pilot said. "Ride rough."

Richard nodded again.

"Ride rough" hardly covered it.

The shuttle's launch cradle first dropped into the launch lock beneath it, then rotated so the top of the shuttle pointed toward the hull. A few moments while the lock cycled—no need to waste air in a nonemergency—three seconds of very gentle acceleration, and they had separated from the ship.

So far, so smooth. But within minutes, they plunged into the atmosphere, which announced its presence with a thin whine that soon grew to an all-encompassing roar. The supply craft bucked, pitched, yawed, did everything but flip end over end, and a couple of times Richard thought it might have done that. Richard's stomach fought to crawl up his throat and hurl itself and its contents into the crew cabin which, in addition to vibrating to the point of blurriness, had reached a temperature that seemed more suited to slow roasting a turkey than keeping its occupants comfortable. "Why . . . so . . . rough . . . ?" Richard called out when the turbulence slacked off just enough he thought he could get out the words without biting his tongue off.

"Some bad design," the pilot said. From his voice, he seemed unaffected by the turbulence, although of course that might have had something to do with the fact he enjoyed the embrace of a padded motion-dampening seat while Richard hung on the wall like a side of beef. "Some bad weather. Some evasive maneuvers."

"But . . . no . . . weapons . . ."

"Seems so," the pilot said. "Don't know for certain. Rather be all shook up and alive than calm and dead. Hold on tighter. Worst about to start."

Richard clenched his jaw, swallowed hard, and prayed he wouldn't embarrass himself by throwing up before they reached the ground.

Alas, as the Avatar liked to say, "All prayers are answered, but sometimes, the answer is 'no.' "

When they were safely on the ground, in a sports field commandeered to serve as a secondary landing site away from the town square for the cargo shuttles, the pilot summoned a cleanerbot to slurp up the widely redistributed remnants of Richard's morning toast, simbacon and near-coffee. He also provided Richard with a clean standard-issue (but insignia-free) light blue Holy Warrior one-piece to wear. Richard retrieved his bag from its locker and rather shamefacedly made his retreat out the tiny personnel hatch and down the five-step ladder to the blessedly solid ground. Bots were already unloading the contents of the fat cargo cylinder.

A fully armed and armored Holy Warrior waited at the bottom of the ladder. "Grand Deacon Ellers is expecting you," he growled. "This way."

As they walked through the streets of the town the Selkies had named after his grandfather, Richard looked around eagerly, finally able to experience it without the mediation of a video camera.

"Primitive" was his first impression. The building styles—lots of brick, with accents of shiny metal and glass and solar panels—reminded him of the seedier parts of the City of God, the ones that predated the Day of Salvation—which made sense, he supposed, since that style had been current when Grandpa Hansen had fled. The buildings didn't look new, though; they looked decades old.

He'd seen newer buildings in the vidfeeds, but they were all down by the water—or partially or completely under it. Or had been, before the Holy Warriors so quickly and efficiently blew them up.

He couldn't see any bomb damage here. He couldn't see any people, either, though the vidfeeds had shown a lot on the streets an hour ago. All hiding somewhere now, he supposed, or in flight, out of Hansen's Harbor. Not that they had anywhere to flee to. The interior was bleak and unappealing and the other towns much smaller. The assault craft had already attacked several of them, to drive home the message that the Holy Warriors controlled the planet. The refugees would probably meet other refugees coming the other way.

He felt sorry for the normal humans, though if they were smart, accepted the Body Purified, and didn't cause trouble, they'd suffer no further harm. But the Selkies . . .

He wanted—*needed*—to see the Selkies. With all the strange, near-treasonous thoughts and feelings that had come into his head in the last few weeks, he needed to know he had done the right thing in pointing the Holy Warriors at this planet.

First, though, he had to find out what the Grand Deacon wanted.

Richard and his escort emerged from a narrow alley into a broad courtyard surrounded by what probably passed for impressive architecture on Marseguro. Nothing stood taller than about four stories, but several of the buildings boasted columns, pediments, and the kind of glittering stucco that had been all the rage in public buildings on Earth at the time of Salvation. (Oddly, though Richard had long laughed at the style when he'd come across it in the City of God, he now thought it looked rather attractive. Context, he supposed.) An assault craft dominated the center of the square—the reason they'd had to land in the sports field—and multiple takeoffs and landings had cracked and blackened the once-white cobblestones. A bronze statue lay on its side in a now-dry fountain in the rubble of its broken pedestal. "Just a second," Richard told his escort. The pedestal still held a bronze plaque, scorched but readable. Richard leaned close. *Dr. Victor Hansen,* he read. *In memory and appreciation of the visionary geneticist who created the Selkie race and preserved it from extermination by the tyrants of Old Earth. Dedicated February 34, Year 34, on the fifth anniversary of Dr. Hansen's death.*

So you lived almost thirty local years after the landing, Richard thought. *Long enough to think you'd really pulled it off, that the Body would never find you.*

Too bad you didn't live a little longer so you could have met your grandson. We would have had a lot to talk about.

Although increasingly he felt as if he *had* met his grandfather. Which was why he kept talking to him directly in his mind. Which was absurd, and possibly slightly deranged.

Several times in the last few weeks he had thought about talking to a Body psychologist, but if he had—especially since his father had flagrantly demonstrated that mental instability ran in Richard's family—he suspected he would never have been allowed to come on this mission . . . and he couldn't have borne that.

It's just stress, he thought. *That's all.*

"Sir!" said his escort. "The Grand Deacon is *waiting.*" His tone made it clear he did not intend to leave the Grand Deacon in that unaccustomed state merely to satisfy Richard's sightseeing impulses.

"Coming, coming." Richard followed the Holy Warrior into the grandest of the semigrand buildings around the Square, the one with the biggest pillars and the glitteriest stucco, and the words GOVERNMENT HOUSE laser-cut into the Neo-Greek Revival pediment.

Probably as a potent symbol of occupation and defeat rather than for any practical purpose, the big wooden doors at the top of the broad flight of stairs leading up from the courtyard had been blasted into charred flinders. Beyond the wreckage, the lobby looked more like a government building than a palace, with a polished floor—a kind of

light-green stone flecked with silvery metallic flakes, in this
case—and a long counter on the left-hand side full of
wickets-for-standing-in-line-at. Sunlight streamed through
multiple skylights in the high ceiling of polished red wood
beams, providing plenty of natural illumination for the
Holy Warriors now running cables and setting up stands of
vidscreen-studded equipment that Richard recognized as
belonging to a mobile communications and headquarters
module. The Holy Warriors moved with purpose but without unnecessary haste, and mostly without talking, so that
Richard could clearly hear the one person who *was* talking,
at the top of his lungs, though he couldn't immediately see
whomever it was.

The voice was that of a young man, but it had the kind
of near-whining, making-excuses tone that Richard associated with a certain kind of much-younger child. "I don't
understand! Why won't you let me out? I'm trying to help!
I'm on your side! I'm part of the Body. My parents were
Believers. I've listened to *The Wisdom of the Avatar.* I can
quote—"

"Please don't," said another voice, which Richard recognized as that of Grand Deacon Ellers. "The one thing you
could do right now that would really help is to shut up."

"But—"

"That wasn't a request."

"But I—"

"Quiet, or I'll have you gagged!" Richard and his escort
rounded one of the vidscreen stands just as the Grand Deacon snapped that, giving Richard his first look at the source
of Ellers' annoyance.

It proved to be a short and skinny young man, maybe
twenty Earth years old, with light brown hair, a rather
scraggly beard and mustache, and blue, childlike eyes that
had widened with shock and hurt at the Grand Deacon's
sharp tone. Nevertheless, the youth did shut up, pressing his
lips together in a scowl that made him look about five, an
impression heightened by the temporary holding cell that
looked like a playpen imprisoning him.

"Grand Deacon, Mr. Hansen is here," the Holy Warrior
escorting Richard said, and snapped a salute.

Ellers sketched a salute in reply. "Dismissed," he said,

and turned his attention to Richard as the Holy Warrior turned smartly and lumbered off. Behind the Grand Deacon, Richard saw the prisoner's eyes widen further, then narrow and focus intently on him. "Mr. Hansen, thank you for joining me," the Grand Deacon said.

"My pleasure," Richard said. His eyes on the prisoner, he went on, "I was hoping I'd have the opportunity to see the Purification of Grandfather Victor's vile experiment firsthand."

The prisoner's eyes went wide again. "You're — you're — "

"I thought I told you to be quiet," Grand Deacon Ellers roared, turning on the young man, who wilted under the glare and sat down heavily on the floor of his cell. He pulled his knees up to his chest and wrapped his arms around them, then glared out at the Grand Deacon and Richard, who stepped up beside Ellers.

"Is this who you wanted me to see?" Richard asked.

The Grand Deacon grunted. "He claims he's the one who called us here. Says he activated a distress beacon. Even gave us a beacon ID number." He tapped on his forearm, then held it up, palm toward Richard. "Here it is." he said. Richard saw a string of digits on Ellers' nanodisplay, red beneath his skin like a bloody tattoo. "Look familiar?"

Richard recognized them at once. "Yes. That's definitely the ID of the beacon that led us here."

"So he's telling the truth?"

"I don't know how else he'd know that number."

"Hmmm." Ellers went over to the cell. "Stand up," he said.

The youth got to his feet.

"Tell me your name again."

"Chris Keating." The young man's gaze slid past the Grand Deacon to Richard. "Are you really Victor Hansen's grandson?"

"You're talking to *me*," Ellers snapped. "Why did you betray your planet?"

"My planet is Earth," Chris Keating said, so quickly Richard thought he must either really believe it or had overrehearsed saying it. "I don't belong here. None of us does. We belong inside the Body."

"Even the Selkies?" Ellers growled.

"They're abominations," Keating said, again instantly. "I don't care what happens to them. They're not real humans. Not like the landlings."

"Landlings?"

"Non-Selkies. Nonmods. Us." Chris waved his hand, indicating himself and them. "Normals."

"Do all the . . . landlings . . . feel like you do?"

Chris shook his head. "No. Most of them love the Selkies. But not me! And I'm sure there are others who hate them, too."

"These landlings who love the Selkies. Will they fight us?"

Chris laughed. "With what?" He leaned forward, laughter suddenly swallowed by a look of utter . . . *need,* Richard thought. "Will you take me back to Earth? *I have to go to Earth.*"

"We'll see," Ellers said. "If you cooperate . . ."

"Of course I will! I *called* you here!"

"So you said." Ellers glanced at Richard. "What do you think? Can we let him out?"

Richard blinked, startled at being asked. *What's Ellers playing at?* "Um . . . I think so," he said. "He seems harmless."

"Very well. Slowinsky!" A nearby Holy Warrior put down a spool of cable and saluted.

"Sir?"

"Release the prisoner."

"Yes, sir!"

While Slowinsky busied himself with the jail door, Ellers walked a few steps away and motioned Richard to come with him. "I don't have time to deal with him right now," Ellers said in a low voice. "I'm going to let you take care of him. Grill him for any information you can get—I'm sure Archdeacon Cheveldeoff will want to know everything you can learn. But most importantly, find out if he's telling us the truth. Test him. If you think we can trust him, bring him back to me. We've got our hands full right now, but in a day or so, we're going to be in a position to start hunting down any Selkies that have escaped our initial sweep. We could do with a reliable source of information."

Richard nodded. "I can do that," he said.

"Good." Ellers turned. "Mr. Keating," he said. The youth almost dashed over to him, like a puppy called to play fetch.

"Yes, sir?"

Ellers indicated Richard. "Mr. Hansen, here, is the one who detected the distress call. He is also a direct representative of the Archdeacon of Body Security, and therefore in charge of mission intelligence." Richard smiled inwardly. Only half of that sentence was true. But if Chris thought Richard was the intelligence chief, maybe he'd be more likely to talk. "I want you to take Mr. Hansen around the city. Show him the sights. Tell him whatever you think is important. Answer any questions he may have. Later— perhaps—we'll talk again."

Ellers summoned Slowinsky and another Holy Warrior whose name Richard didn't catch, assigned them to escort Richard and Chris, then turned to Richard. "Mr. Hansen, if you would care to join me for dinner at 1800 local time— your datapad will have been programmed to display that by now; it's in about six hours—you can report back then. I'll leave it to your discretion whether or not Mr. Keating should join us." He turned away. "Dismissed."

Neatly done, Richard thought as Ellers turned his attention back to setting up his headquarters. *He's got this Keating kid and me out of his hair. Any useful information he gets out of either of us is just bonus.*

"Well," said Richard to Chris Keating. "Why don't you give me the grand tour?"

Chapter 7

BEING THROWN IN JAIL had shocked Chris; he couldn't believe they would do that to the hero who had handed them Victor Hansen's bolt-hole. But when the tall, sandy-haired man in a plain blue jumpsuit had shown up—Victor Hansen's grandson, no less!—and been introduced as the one in charge of intelligence gathering, Chris had understood. Ellers simply hadn't had the authority to do anything other than throw him in jail. He was a military man; Hansen, the civilian, the representative of the Archdeacon of Body Security himself, must be the real power here. The Avatar himself might have sent him! And so Chris was more than happy to show him around Hansen's Harbor—especially with the reassuring presence of the two Holy Warriors to ensure that nobody who objected to the Purification of Marseguro put two and two together and decided to mete out a little vigilante justice to someone they might quite likely, Chris admitted, see as a traitor.

"Why did you do it?" Hansen suddenly asked as they walked down a rubble-strewn street. "Why did you betray your planet?"

The question echoed his own thoughts so closely it made him uneasy—and defensive. "I didn't betray anyone," he said, more hotly than he intended to speak to the man who might, after all, be the personal representative of the Avatar.

"The Holy Warriors have laid waste to half your city and must have already killed several hundred Selkies," Hansen said. "Your fellow Marseguroites—Marseguroians?—might disagree."

"You can't betray the Selkies," Chris said. "They're not

human. Can you betray an animal?" He kicked half a broken brick out of his way. "And we say Marseguroites."

Hansen shrugged. "If I locked my dog out of my house and refused to feed him, or kicked him every time I saw him, I think most people would think I had betrayed him. Selkies may not be strictly human, but they're more intelligent than dogs. From where I sit, it looks like you betrayed them—although of course I'm glad you did."

"If there were any betrayal, they betrayed us first," Chris snapped. His eyes narrowed as a thought struck him. *This is Victor Hansen's* grandson. *Why would they trust him? What if the Grand Deacon really* is *the one in charge, and he's put me with someone* he *doesn't trust to see if* I *can be trusted?*

Wheels within wheels. That kind of thinking made his head hurt.

"How did they betray you?" Hansen pressed.

He's in charge of gathering intelligence. He's supposed to ask questions, Chris thought. *He's not trying to annoy me.*

But he was.

"Selkies and landlings are supposed to be absolutely equal," Chris said. "But the Selkies breed like bugglefish and a lot of the landlings are sterile—something to do with radiation levels on the *Rivers of Babylon.* The Selkies' water tanks protected them, supposedly, but I've always wondered if maybe the Selkies are slipping something into the water supply.

"Anyway, there just aren't enough of us, and there are fewer all the time. And there are more and more of the Selkies. They've taken over the schools, taken all the best jobs, taken over the hospitals . . ." *Mom,* he thought, and his heart clenched like a fist in his chest. He wished she could have been alive to see the Selkie city in rubble. *She'd be proud,* he thought. *And so would Dad.*

"But that's not all." Chris fought the urge to lower his voice. *I'll never have to lower my voice again to say what I think about the Selkies.* "They've taken over the government, too. Or maybe they've always secretly run it. Supposedly, the elected Council, half Selkie, half landling, runs everything, but we . . . my parents and I . . . know that there's another Council, a secret cabal, that's really in charge. And it's all Selkie."

Hansen gave him a skeptical glance, eyebrows raised.

"It's true," Chris said. "Everything is set up to make the Selkies happy, and screw the landlings. And anyone who threatens Selkie control, threatens to stir up trouble among the landlings, is snuffed out. Like my father."

"They killed him?"

"The Council—acting on orders from the cabal, of course—ordered him to take a job at sea. The boat sank. The Selkies survived. They managed to save all the landlings, too . . . all but him." Chris' jaw clenched; he had to force himself to relax it. "They murdered him. That's what Mom said, and I believe her. They may have murdered her, too. Probably did. And they almost drowned me, tried to warn me to stay in my place." He grinned, a savage grimace he couldn't have prevented if he'd wanted to. "I guess I showed them."

"I guess you did." Hansen stopped. "I don't think we can carry on this way."

A tangle of steel, masonry, and glass blocked the road. "You're right," Chris said with satisfaction.

Hansen frowned at him. "Then why on Earth—sorry, on Marseguro—did you bring me this way?"

Chris nodded at the wreckage. "This is where I worked," he said. "A genesculpting lab. Most recently, we've been trying to modify native algae to provide more efficient feedstock for the bioreactors that provide air and fresh water to the Selkies' underwater habitats. We've been relying on Earth-native algae we brought with us, but some of the local species are much better producers of oxygen. Dr. Stanless thought—" He cut himself off. "Well, it doesn't matter. The Holy Warriors hit it this morning." He kicked at a lump of masonry. "Good riddance," he snarled. His vehemence surprised him. He hadn't realized how much he had come to hate the mind-numbing work Stanless had put him to. Day after day, he'd observed and noted and cleaned and refilled, punched buttons and turned dials, and none of it had been of the slightest benefit to landlings like him who never intended to or wanted to visit an underwater habitat. "Working here was my real betrayal," he said to Hansen. "Every day I worked in this lab I betrayed my fellow normal humans. I should have blown the place up myself."

"Is your version of giving me a tour of the city going to consist entirely of you taking me to places central to your personal life?" Hansen said. "Or may I request to see certain specific sights?"

Chris felt himself blush, and hated himself for it. Hansen, and the Grand Deacon before him, made him feel like a stupid little kid. *Maybe I am,* he thought. *Maybe I'm like the kid who tattles to the grown-ups when the other kids do something wrong.*

But you know what? Sometimes tattling is the right thing to do.

He frowned. He wasn't very happy with the simile he'd just come up with, because he'd been *exactly* that sort of kid. It hadn't helped his popularity with the other kids, landling or Selkie.

Out loud, he said, "Of course, Mr. Hansen. I'll show you whatever you want."

Hansen's answer surprised him, not so much for what he wanted to see as the strange vehemence with which he announced it. "Selkies," Hansen said. "Show me the Selkies."

"This way," Chris said, and led Hansen around the ruined laboratory to the road leading down to the pier.

Richard had surprised himself with his intense interest in Chris Keating's reasons for betraying his planet, and as he looked at the ruins of the laboratory where Keating had worked, it crossed his mind that maybe he wanted to understand Keating's betrayal to understand his own. Maybe Keating hadn't betrayed his planet, but hadn't Richard betrayed his grandfather?

Bull, he thought. He spoke directly to Victor Hansen again, as if he had asked the question. *You betrayed me and Dad and every normal human on the planet when you created your pet monsters.*

For the first time, it seemed like Victor Hansen answered, as an inner voice argued with him. *How could I have betrayed you when you weren't even born yet?* And then, *In a way, I am you, and you are me. How could I betray myself?*

I am you? *You* are me? *What the hell does that mean?*

And why am I arguing with myself?

His emotions, like his thoughts, were confused, guilt and anger all mixed up inside him, fighting like oil and water.

The kid led him down another street—almost choked in

places by rubble from collapsed and still-smoldering buildings—and for the first time, Richard got a good look at what the Marseguroites had dubbed New Botany Bay.

It was a mess. The Holy Warriors had concentrated their fire on the waterfront and the amphibian buildings that both rose above and descended below the water. Once-proud towers had been reduced to fanglike teeth of broken masonry and claws of twisted steel. In those buildings still more-or-less intact, the gaping black holes left behind by blown-out windows reminded Richard of a skull's empty eye sockets. Floating debris carpeted the surface of the water—bits of wood, bits of insulation, furniture, clothing . . .

. . . bodies.

Until he saw those dark but unmistakably human—human*oid,* he reminded himself as strongly as he could—forms floating in the turgid, oil-slicked water, he had known intellectually but not viscerally that the Holy Warriors' missiles were destroying more than just buildings. He'd told himself he was okay with that. He'd known from the moment he reported reception of the distress signal that this would be the result.

Hadn't he?

Guilt swelled up in him again, guilt he couldn't understand. *The Selkies are abominations! This planet must be Purified! I'm doing the will of God!* His mind raised its dikes against the welling tide of guilt, but it threatened to overtop them . . . and he couldn't figure out where it came from. It almost seemed separate and apart from him, pouring from some hidden portion of his brain, one that housed a different personality entirely than the one he thought of as himself.

The portion of his brain he'd been addressing, and arguing with, as though it were Victor Hansen.

Am I going mad? he thought. *Like my father?*

Maybe it's a good thing all the buildings are so short . . .

They rounded a corner, only to find the road, which led down to the broken-backed pier that stretched out into the fouled water of the bay like a long brown tongue, completely blocked by smoking, flame-licked wreckage.

Keating looked left, then right. "This way," he said. "This pile of junk must have been the Amphibian Club. Looks like it toppled across the road, so maybe the alley behind it is clearer."

He took a narrow path, just wide enough for one person at a time, between two buildings that seemed to have escaped with nothing worse than broken windows. Richard followed, his so-far-silent pair of bodyguards dogging his heels. He trailed one hand along the rough brickwork to his right. It looked a couple of centuries old, which was impossible, of course. Either the local climate played hell with building materials, or the settlers had wanted to create a false feeling of antiquity to help them forget they were on a brand-new—

He emerged into the alley, and something jumped on his back.

The weight smashed him down onto sharp-edged cobblestones. Strong arms wrapped around his neck. He couldn't breathe. *He's going to break my neck,* he had time to think, the gruesome image flashing into his mind—then he smelled burning meat and whatever had him gave a horrible, gurgling scream and rolled away.

Richard lurched up to his hands and knees, gulped some air, then scrambled to his feet. One of the Holy Warriors—Slowinsky, Richard remembered—stood over a body, laser pistol in hand. The other Holy Warrior had Chris Keating shoved up against the wall of one of the buildings they had just passed between, an armored forearm across his neck. Keating's eyes, wide and frightened, stared at Richard. "What happened?" Richard gasped.

"This *thing* was lurking on the fire-escape balcony," Slowinsky said, indicating the body. "Jumped you when you came into the alley."

"But didn't jump this guy," the other Holy Warrior rumbled. "I think he set you up."

Richard looked up at the fire-escape ladder that zigzagged up the brick side of the four-story building, then down at the "thing."

"A Selkie?" he said.

Slowinsky grunted. "See for yourself."

Richard walked over and knelt down. Oversized green eyes, like something from a cartoon figure, gazed sightlessly back at him, already clouding over. The flat, almost nonexistent nose, the nubs of ears . . . and the gills, triple slits on each side of the neck, relaxed open in death—all just as he had seen in his grandfather's notes, but seeing photos was different from seeing something in the flesh. Photos could have been manipulated, or computer-generated from scratch. But this thing, slumped inelegantly in an alley, shaved skull tattooed with a multi-colored spiral of stars, stinking of burned meat and evacuated bowels, blood leaking from mouth and nose and gill slits, pooling and congealing on the cobblestones, was indisputably real—and moments before had been alive.

From the same wellspring as the guilt, Richard felt pity and anger rise in equal measure. But he also felt his gorge rising and stood up hastily. He'd thrown up enough for one day. He rubbed his aching neck with his right hand, then went over to the Holy Warrior holding Keating. "Did you set us up?" he demanded.

Keating shook his head and tried to speak, but only managed a squeak. "Let him talk," Richard told the Holy Warrior, who gave Keating a little extra shove with his forearm, then released him. Richard didn't have to look behind him to know that Slowinsky had Keating well covered with the laser pistol.

As Richard had just done, Keating massaged his neck. "No," he said. "Why would I? I activated the beacon to bring you here! Why would I bring you here to kill Selkies and then try to help *them* kill *you?*"

Richard, hurting and knowing how close he had come to death, didn't want to give the boy the benefit of the doubt—but the facts were on his side. Keating had known the beacon ID number, so he must have activated it. *Unless the authorities found it and gave the serial number to this guy so they could get someone into our good graces to . . .*

No, that's crazy. Because that would mean the Marseguroite authorities had known the attack was coming. And if they had, those bodies wouldn't be floating in the bay. They would have evacuated the cities and dispersed the population, and by all the signs, they'd done nothing of the kind.

"He's telling the truth," Richard said. "Let him go." He turned around to look at the dead Selkie again. "But I'd still like to know why he didn't attack *you.*"

Chris went over and knelt down beside the dead Selkie for a moment, then lurched up and turned away and did what Richard had managed to avoid, vomiting up the contents of his stomach into the shadows on the far side of the alley. Richard looked up at the sky and swallowed hard.

After a moment, Keating emerged from the shadows, wiping his mouth and making a wide detour around the Selkie. "That's Peter," he said shakily. "Peter Stamos. He worked in the lab, same shift. He knew me, that's why he didn't jump me. He . . . he probably thought he was rescuing me. From you."

"A friend of yours?" growled Slowinsky, who had never reholstered his weapon.

"No!" The denial came as quickly as . . . well, as quickly as the denial would have come on Earth from someone asked if they harbored doubts about the Avatar's direct connection to God, Richard thought. *Fast learner. He should do well in the Body Purified.* "Just an acquaintance. I don't have any Selkie *friends.*"

"Looks like he didn't know that," Slowinsky said.

"Let's get to the water," Richard said. "When I said I wanted to see Selkies, getting jumped from behind by one wasn't exactly what I had in mind."

Keating nodded eagerly and led the way on down the alley. Richard and the Holy Warriors followed, but this time, he noted, the Holy Warriors followed with weapons drawn. *They screwed up,* he thought. *They forgot that just because there aren't any weapons, that doesn't mean there aren't any threats.* Considering they were supposed to be protecting him, he was glad they'd learned a lesson.

There were no more incidents between the ruined laboratory and the dock; in fact, they didn't see anyone living at all.

They did see several more bodies. Chris Keating, Richard noted, didn't look very closely. *Probably scared he'll see somebody else he knows,* he thought. *He's afraid to face all the consequences of his "heroism."*

The fact he *also* chose to avoid looking at the dead bodies was just . . . sensitivity.

Yeah, that's it.

Finally, as they walked out onto the ruined pier, they saw their first living people.

Half a dozen Holy Warriors stood on the pier, which was made of some unfamiliar material that looked a bit like wood and a bit like plastic. Richard wrinkled his nose. Whatever the stuff was, it stank like rotting seaweed.

Unlike his bodyguards, the Holy Warriors on the pier carried automatic rifles. They guarded a floating cage packed with Selkies.

Richard's knees suddenly felt weak and his heart fluttered as he looked at the massed moddies, males, females and . . .

. . . *children,* one part of his mind supplied.

Offspring, he insisted instead.

It was one thing to see one dead Selkie, it was another to see two dozen living ones. *Beautiful,* a part of his brain breathed, with a sense of pride. *Horrible,* said another. Richard clung to the latter reaction like the . . . offspring . . . in the cage clung to their parents, who petted their heads and hugged them for all the world like humans did. A little female maybe five standard years old looked up as Richard walked to the edge of the pier and looked down into the cage. "Look, Mommy," he heard her say. "He doesn't have a gun. Is he going to let us out?"

The mother turned her green, oversized eyes toward Richard. "Maybe, sweetie," she said, but not as if she really believed it. "Maybe."

Despite himself, Richard felt tears start in his eye. *Damn you, Grandfather!* he thought, turning away. *Damn you for creating these travesties of human flesh.*

They're not travesties. They're beautiful, the strangely traitorous part of his mind replied.

"How goes it?" he said to the nearest Holy Warrior, whom he thought he recognized from the ship. "Sexsmith, isn't it?"

The Holy Warrior nodded. "That's right, sir." He gestured at the cage. "Frankly, not so well. This is all we've managed to round up. All of the others—well, the ones that weren't killed outright, of course—seem to have fled into deeper water."

"They'll have to surface sometime," Richard said. "They can't eat underwater. Grandfather didn't engineer them that way."

He'd been concentrating so hard on convincing himself the Selkies weren't human that he'd forgotten they could hear and understand him. The Holy Warriors all knew his ancestry; their victims hadn't, until that moment.

"Your *grandfather?*" a voice growled from the water. Richard froze for an instant, then slowly turned and looked down into the cage at an older Selkie male, his close-cropped hair pure silver. "Victor Hansen was your grandfather?"

"I'm not telling you anything," Richard said.

"Your voice and face tell me enough," the Selkie male said. "Listen, everyone," he called. "This new landling is the grandson of Victor Hansen."

After a moment's stunned silence, the Selkies erupted into shouting. "It can't be!" "Then why doesn't he let us go?" "I don't believe it!" "The Creator's grandson would never—"

"Quiet!" shouted Sexsmith. He fired a burst from his automatic rifle over the top of the cage and the hubbub subsided. Sexsmith gave Richard an amused glance. "Looks like your cat's out of the bag, sir."

Maybe this is an opportunity, Richard thought. *An opportunity to show my devotion to the cause.* "That's right," he shouted to the Selkies. "My grandfather was Victor Hansen. But Victor Hansen was a monster, and the father of monsters. I'm here to right the great wrong he did, and make sure abominations like you don't pollute God's creation any further. I serve the Avatar and God Itself, not my twice-damned grandfather!"

Out of the corner of his eye, he saw the little female who had spoken when he first appeared turn and bury her head in her mother's shoulder. Angry at the involuntary pang in his heart, he plunged on recklessly. "Not only that, I'm the one who led the Holy Warriors here . . . with the help of your own Chris Keating, who activated the *Rivers of Babylon* emergency beacon."

That brought a collective gasp, and out of the corner of his eye, Richard saw Keating cringe. *Actions have consequences, boy,* Richard thought coldly. *Credit where credit is due.*

"Chris! Is he telling the truth?" The call came from a young male Selkie about Keating's age, at the very back of the cage. His bald head featured a red-and-blue spiral tattoo, and the formfitting wetsuit type of garment he wore glittered as though covered with silver scales.

Richard looked at Keating. The young man visibly stiffened his spine and lifted his chin. "Yes, it's true, John Duval," he shouted. "And you of all people should know why I did it."

The young Selkie looked genuinely shocked. "Not . . . not because of that silly game on the pier?"

"Not just because of it . . . but not *not* because of it, either. That was the rock that broke the keel, John."

John Duval's face reddened, making him look even more monstrous. "You betrayed the entire planet . . . led these monsters here . . . helped them kill who knows how many people . . . because you got *wet?*"

"Because you Selkies have lorded it over normal human beings long enough!" Keating yelled. "Because you're a bunch of subhuman monsters who—"

"Damn you!" John screamed.

The open-roofed "cage" extended two meters above the surface of the water. Richard would have bet that no Selkie could possibly make such a leap.

He would have lost.

From the back of the cage, John Duval plunged beneath the water and arrowed toward the front of the cage. The water boiled in his wake, and then he exploded out of it, up and over the front of the cage, landing on the pier in a cascade of salt water. He grabbed the rifle of the nearest Holy Warrior and smashed the butt of the weapon across its owner's face. As the Warrior screamed and fell back in a spray of blood, the Selkie whipped the rifle into firing position, aimed it at Keating, who stood frozen in shock, and pulled the trigger.

Nothing happened.

With a shriek of rage, Duval threw the rifle at Keating, turned, and dove into the bay, clear of the cage.

As he leaped, a single rifle shot rang out, shockingly loud, from just to Richard's left. Then the young Selkie was gone . . . but he left behind a faint red stain in the water.

"Got him," Sexsmith said. "Don't think I killed him, but he's wounded. He can't get far." He turned and shouted down the pier. "Khan! Veldron! Fire up the tracker boat!" As two Holy Warriors ran to comply, lowering themselves over the side of the pier and disappearing from sight, Sexsmith walked over to the Holy Warrior Duval had rifle-whipped. He sat clutching his nose, blood welling between his fingers and dripping on his chest plate. "Why didn't your weapon fire, Murphy?"

"Safety was on, sir," the wounded Holy Warrior said, rather indistinctly.

"Weapons are to be ready to fire at all times, Murphy. One demerit. It would have been two, but I'm too glad to be alive. The medics have taken over the town hospital. Get yourself up there and get your nose patched up. Report back when you can."

"Yes, sir. Thank you sir." Murphy got to his feet and headed up the pier, leaving a splotchy trail of red.

Veldron reappeared over the edge of the pier. "Boat ready, sir!"

"You heard about the DNA trackers?" Sexsmith asked Richard, who nodded. "This is our first chance to try the technology in the wild. We've married it up with a semi-autonomous underwater bot—we call it a 'hunterbot.' Our boy may already be floating belly-up out in the bay somewhere, but if he's only lightly wounded and thinks he can escape, the hunterbot will soon disabuse him of the notion."

Richard looked at Keating, who had found it suddenly expedient to sit down on the pier and put his head between his knees. *I've seen enough on land,* he thought. *And if I go back to the Grand Deacon, he's liable just to send me back up to* Sanctification.

He made up his mind. "I'd like to go out in the boat, see it in action," he said. As Sexsmith's expression turned skeptical, he played his trump card. "I'm sure the Archdeacon will want a complete report on the . . . um, hunterbot. If it works here, I'm sure Body Security will have good use for it on Earth and elsewhere."

Sexsmith hesitated, then shrugged. "All right," he said. "Suit yourself. Veldron!"

"Sir!"

"Mr. Hansen is coming along to observe. Is there a spare survival suit on board? Not that you should need it," Sexsmith said to Richard. "Regulations."

"Yes, sir," Veldron said.

"Good." To Richard, Sexsmith made a grand gesture in the direction of Veldron's head, the only part of him visible above the edge of the pier. "Have fun."

"Thanks." Richard went over to Slowinsky. "Tell the Grand Deacon where I've gone. And deliver Mr. Keating back to him with my compliments."

"The Grand Deacon is expecting you to join him for dinner at 1800," Slowinsky warned.

Richard waved a hand. "That's hours from now. I'm sure we'll be back. And if we aren't, the Grand Deacon will understand that I must fulfill my responsibilities to the Archdeacon first." *Sure* he will, Richard thought, but the worst the Grand Deacon could do would be to send him back to the ship, and Ellers probably intended to do that anyway.

"If you say so, sir," said Slowinsky, his tone implying that he didn't believe a word of it. "Come on, you." He reached down, hauled Chris Keating rather roughly to his feet, and led him away, back up the pier to the mainland, Richard's second erstwhile bodyguard bringing up the rear.

"Sir? We're waiting," Veldron shouted.

"Coming!" Richard jogged over to where Veldron and Khan had disappeared and discovered a metal ladder leading down to a floating dock. A tracker boat floated next to the dock, engine running, puffs of exhaust emerging from the oily water behind its transom as Khan, standing at the wheel in the upper half of the two-level, partially enclosed bridge, kept it in position. About the size of an ordinary Earth speedboat, painted dull gray and bristling with antennae and weapons launchers and dischargers, the boat had an open stern but a decked-over bow. In the center of that deck rode a gray torpedolike cylinder: the hunterbot, Richard presumed.

The boat rocked alarmingly even in the slight swell that made its way into the oil-fouled waters of New Botany Bay, and Richard climbed gingerly aboard it, wondering if he should mention he'd never been on a boat before . . .

. . . except, oddly, he felt as if he *had*.

The moment his feet hit the bottom boards, Khan shoved the throttle forward. The boat eased away from the dock, and Richard sat down hard and abruptly as he felt the boat sway beneath his feet.

They burbled along to the spot where John Duval had

hit the water, and Khan backed the propeller, bringing them to a bobbing halt. In the lower half of the bridge, Veldron busied himself at a curved console boasting three vidscreens and a surfeit of blinking lights. "Launching," he called, and pressed a button.

On the bow, something hissed, and a moment later, the hunterbot catapulted into the bay.

"Scanning for blood trace," Veldron said.

Richard wanted to get closer to the console, but the boat's motion made it risky. He elected to stay put and hold on. *If the boat is this unsteady when we're sitting still, what will it be like when we're moving?* he wondered uneasily.

"Got it," Veldron announced. "Hunterbot swimming clear. Homing signal activated . . . have you got it upstairs, Nassar?"

"Got it, J.B.," said Khan. "And . . . we're off!"

Richard braced himself for a surge of power, but the engine barely changed pitch, and as the bow turned toward the middle of the bay, they left the pier behind at something barely more than a walking pace. Richard unbraced himself. "That's it?" he said.

Veldron glanced back at him. "Whaddya want?" he said. "The hunterbot's fast, but the DNA scan takes a second or two every time it's activated, so that's the limiting factor. Don't worry, we'll still catch the fishy bastard. He might be able to outswim us for a while, but he'll have to rest eventually . . . and he's wounded, too. We'll probably have him in a few minutes."

Richard dared to ease his way forward, sliding along the bench that ran just under the gunwale until he could look over Veldron's shoulder. The main screen in the center of his console showed a green line stretching away before the icon representing their boat, spreading and fading the farther it got. "What's that?"

"Possible courses," Veldron said. "The tracker measures the currents to adjust for drift of the DNA it's detecting and extrapolates from that how it should adjust its course. Another reason it's slow." He grinned at Richard. "What, you thought we'd go galloping along like a speedboat and you came along for the thrill?"

"Something like that," Richard said, although actually, considering the way his stomach kept lurching, notgalloping suited him fine.

"Well, we'll pick up speed if we can get a reading from one of the surveillance satellites and don't have to rely on DNA tracking. But that will only work if he's close enough to the surface to produce an infrared trace, or leave a visible wake. I think he'll stay deep."

Richard watched the screen in silence for several minutes. "I can't believe it can pick up such tiny traces of DNA in all that water—and distinguish John Duval's DNA from all the other DNA."

"That's the genius of it," Veldron said. "Some smart guy in the Archdeaconate of Research and Development figured it out just last year. The scanning beam uses—what's wrong?"

Richard had grabbed for support as the boat lurched. It lurched again, and again . . . and kept on lurching.

Veldron laughed. "Oh, the motion. Yeah, we're leaving the bay, moving out into the open ocean. Looks like our boy's headed for deep water. Can't imagine where he thinks he's going. He's still bleeding, too, based on this." Veldron tapped the screen. "Really strong DNA traces. We could track him just from shed skin cells, but it would be slower." He shook his head. "I'm surprised he made it this far. Must not be a very serious wound. But we'll get him."

"In deep water? How?" Richard looked around. "Is there a minisub somewhere on the boat?" He couldn't imagine where.

"We don't even have to get our feet wet—"

As the boat lurched again, a big dollop of spray hurtled over the side and splashed into the bottom of the boat, where it quickly drained into the bilge. Somewhere, a pump started up. Veldron laughed again. "Well, okay, maybe we do. But we don't have to go underwater, doesn't matter how deep our escaped moddie goes. The hunterbot's armed. It'll take care of him for us . . . and any other Selkies it finds."

The boat lurched again, and more spray hurtled in, drenching Richard. "Gah," he said, and wiping salt water out of his eyes. As he did so, he looked up and saw swift-moving gray clouds scudding across the sky that had been mostly blue just moments before. He turned around to look back the way they had come, and his heart jumped in his chest when he discovered a wall of gray mist had swallowed the shore.

"Weather's turning," Khan called down, rather unnecessarily, Richard thought. "We may not be able to stay on station."

"Do the best you can!" Veldron called up. "The boffins want all the data we can provide before they turn the rest of these things loose."

"Turn 'em loose?" Richard said, tearing his eyes away from the waves that had begun to march past the boat, each bigger than the last. Spray splattered his face constantly now, coming both from the waves they ploughed into and over and from the rising wind, which blew the ridges of water into whitecaps and flung their peaks into the boat. It all seemed oddly familiar . . . from vids, maybe? . . . to his brain, but not to his stomach, which had begun to object . . . strenuously. He swallowed hard and tried to focus on Veldron, who seemed unconcerned.

"The hunterbots are designed to operate autonomously," he shouted above the rising wind. "You can use them to track a particular Selkie like this one," he tapped the screen, "or just let them loose to find any Selkies they can. In that mode, the default one, they just cast around like hound dogs, looking for Selkie DNA—based on that Selkie genome you provided."

Richard nodded.

"When a hunterbot detects some, it tries to track it. And when it finds a Selkie along the trail," Veldron grinned and made a slashing motion across his throat.

The wind howled, and Richard, now soaked to the skin, shivered in the cold blast. "Can't hold on station!" Khan shouted. "We're going to have to cut it loose!"

"Damn," said Veldron. "Okay!" he shouted back. He looked at Richard. "You look like you'll be glad to get back to dry land!"

"N-not at a-all," Richard lied between chattering teeth.

Veldron bent over and opened a locker under his console. He pulled out an orange package. "Put this on," he said. "Survival suit. Regulations say we should all have put one on before we left the pier, but Nassar and I both hate the things."

"W-why now? Are w-we sinking?" Richard said in alarm.

Veldron chuckled. "Takes more than a little squall to sink a boat like this. No, we're not sinking—but this will keep you warm—and dry."

Richard opened the package and began pulling on the one-piece garment inside. It seemed flimsy as paper, but the moment he had it on it stiffened to something more like soft rubber, and molded itself to his skin. "Might as well go whole hog," Veldron said, and handed him a helmet. Anxious to get the spray out of his face, Richard pulled it on. It sealed itself in place automatically. In seconds, he felt warm and dry and . . .

. . . seasick. He just managed to get his faceplate open and his head over the railing before retching up the mostly liquid contents of his stomach, still essentially empty—he hadn't eaten anything since he'd thrown up in the shuttle.

He hung there with his eyes closed for a moment. He had just opened them and was turning back into the boat when he heard Khan yell, "Shit!", a wordless shout from Veldron, and then the boat leaped up into the air like a dolphin, flinging him up and out. The world spun crazily around him, waves, mist, gray sky. He had a horrifying momentary glimpse of the boat, airborne and upside down, before he plunged into the ocean in an explosion of bubbles and spray.

Chapter 8

THE JOURNEY TO Dahlia's family's vacation habitat passed uneventfully for Emily and Dahlia, as most sub journeys did, since even the largest of Marseguro's nastiest deep-sea predators wasn't big enough to threaten a sub—despite the chilling tales of sea monsters the adventure vidders liked to spin—and even the most violent surface storm couldn't roil the water to the depth to which they were descending. Four hours after they left the bay, the radar profile of the shelter appeared centered, crisp, and clear, in their navigation screens. Half an hour after that, they could see its lights for themselves through the canopy; ten minutes after that, they had docked.

"Shall we take the air tunnel or swim it?" Dahlia asked. The sub had automatically increased its internal air pressure as they descended, so pressurization wasn't an issue, but when Emily saw the outside water temperature, she shivered.

"No, thanks," she said. "Not without a heated skinsuit. I'm a shallow-water girl. Let's take the air tunnel now and we'll go for a swim later."

"Okay." Dahlia flicked a switch on the control panel and the air hatch opened with a slight hiss. Lights came on, revealing a featureless white tube. "After you."

"So formal," Emily said with a grin. She hoisted her personal pack and stepped into the tunnel. It vibrated a little under her feet, which startled her until she remembered that somewhere out of sight bots were moving the supplies they'd brought out of the sub's hold and into the habitat.

The tunnel wasn't very long—five or six meters, maybe—and ended in another hatch, unlocked, of course: by long-standing Marseguro law, no deep-sea habitat *could* be locked, because someone might need it at any moment as an emergency shelter. This hatch led into an air lock— Selkies might be able to breathe underwater, but they still preferred not to have high-pressure water blasting into the air-filled part of their living quarters in the event of a seal failure. Since there was air on both sides of the lock at the moment, though, the inner hatch slid open instantly, revealing the interior.

As Emily had seen from outside—and as she knew anyway—the habitat was a sphere, the upper half full of air, the lower half full of water. Much like in her own home, the central feature of the air-filled section was a round pool. A splash ring about a meter wide surrounded it, and the main dryfloor was a short step up from that. About four meters wide, it was divided into four compartments: a kitchen, a living/dining/rec area (into which the tunnel opened) a sleeping area with four beds in it, and a bathroom, the only room that was fully enclosed.

Emily only had a moment to take in their surroundings before Dahlia shouldered her aside. "Well, don't just stand there," she said. "Let me show you around."

"I think I'm seeing most of it," Emily said wryly. "Not a lot of privacy. Good thing you didn't bring a boyfriend along."

"Oh, there are underwater rooms for *that,*" Dahlia said. "Up here is just for sleeping."

Emily laughed and followed her friend into the living room. Dahlia showed her the game and vidscreens and the audio system—all state of the art and very expensive; not for the first time, Emily wondered just how rich her friend's family really was. Despite both her parents having well-paying professional careers, she didn't believe for a second they could afford a private deep-sea getaway. But then, Dahlia's parents owned three of the microfactories that *made* most of this stuff. Maybe her dad got it at cost.

"There's enough food here for a year," Emily said as Dahlia showed her cupboard after well-stocked cupboard in the kitchen.

Dahlia shrugged. "Government regulations. Private habitats have to maintain the same rations as the government shelters. There are supposed to be enough of those to take in most of the population in the event of some kind of catastrophe, but just in case . . ."

"I've never known what kind of catastrophe they think the shelters would be any use in," Emily said. "An earthquake big enough to destroy the shore towns would probably damage the shelters, too. And an asteroid strike would probably just kill us off. You could die right away up top or die slowly down here."

"There's always the Body Purified," Dahlia said in a spectral voice. "They haven't found us in fifty years, but they could show up any day now and start wiping out all us depraved subhuman monsters." She wriggled her fingers at Emily. "Ooooooooooo . . ."

Emily laughed. "Depraved, I'll give you. Or at least perverted."

"My strength is as the strength of ten because my heart is pure," Dahlia said virtuously. "Even if the rest of me isn't." She moved on to the next door. "Now if you'll step this way, I'll show you our extra-fine toilet facilities."

After Dahlia finished showing Emily around, they returned to the kitchen, where they set the cookbot on "Gourmet" and gave it free rein. Dahlia even entered the nutrition override. "A little extra fat and salt won't hurt us just this once."

The resulting concoction, which went by an Old Earth French name that Emily didn't recognize and couldn't pronounce, but which tasted delicious, left them so sated they killed a couple of hours watching a vid. Some very good stuff had recently come out of the fertile minds and computers of Marseguro's small but burgeoning vid community, but tonight's, a tale of a star-crossed love affair between a Selkie and a landling set on a future Marseguro covered with floating habitats and underwater cities, left Emily cold, even though a couple of the actors were friends of hers. Still, it gave them time to digest. When it ended, they finally mustered enough energy to roll off the couches and into the pool (nicely heated, to Emily's relief).

Dahlia led her down into the underwater section of the habitat, which featured a wet-gym and not just one but two romantically lit "recreation chambers." Near the closed bottom hatch she opened a locker containing bright-yellow deep-sea skinsuits, more like the survival suits the landlings wore whenever they ventured out to sea than the usual minimalist Selkie garb. "Government regulations again," Dahlia chirped in Selkie as she pulled one on. Emily pulled on the other. The deep-sea skinsuits included, to her surprise, an oxygenator, full head cover and goggles, and even a small supply of emergency underwater rations in sealed tubes, the kind of thing you could squirt into your mouth and swallow without worrying about taking in too much salt water. "These are the only kind of skinsuits approved for deep-sea excursions," Dahlia went on. "Just in case landlings are in here. That's why they have oxygenators."

Emily nodded. "Do you ever just go for a swim without one of these?"

Dahlia chirped amusement. "Of course. You know how I love skinny-dipping! Especially if I have a boy to skinny-dip with." She laughed. "It's cold, but invigorating."

Emily cocked her head. "The swimming, or the . . ."

"Both! But even I can only stay out for a few minutes down here, and to really see the sights, we need more time."

She slapped a control on the wall, the hatch slid open beneath them, and they slipped out into the Deep.

Emily had to laugh at herself for her unconscious capitalization of the word. Deep? They were still on the continental shelf. The real Deep, the many-kilometers-deep abyss, lay several more kilometers out. Still, they were deeper than she'd ever been before, and as deep as most Selkies ever went, though she knew genesculptors were trying to find ways to further modify the Selkie genome to make them—or future generations, anyway—better able to utilize all of Marseguro: maybe even become true merpeople who would never need to surface at all.

Maybe the government's shelters do make sense, she thought. *We occupy such a small portion of the planet— we've still got all our eggs in one basket, as they used to say about Earth back in prespace days. It wouldn't take much to render Selkies extinct.*

It was the argument of the Expansionists, of course. The Consolidationists would argue that the odds of a species-ending event were so small they should concentrate on creating a society worth preserving before worrying about far-fetched threats.

That reminded her of the argument with her parents,

and she impatiently shoved such thoughts out of her mind.
I'm on vacation!

"This way," Dahlia said, and swam off into the gloom.
Light-piping on the skinsuit and her headlamp combined
to make her look like some ghostly figure composed entirely of photons. Emily followed.

The seafloor surrounding the habitat proved to be of
surpassing beauty, no doubt the reason Dahlia's family had
built there in the first place. A natural garden of black volcanic rock alternated with glittering fields of the glassy
structures built by the near-microscopic crustaceanlike
creatures dubbed "crablets." Many of the rocks sported red,
orange, and yellow anemonots. Fish swarmed among their
waving tentacles, including the largest pod of bugglefish
she'd ever seen, their black-and-white-striped snaky bodies
slithering over and over each other like an animated op-art
painting.

They returned to the shelter tired and finally hungry
again, climbed out of the pool, and shed the deep-sea skinsuits, leaving them by the edge of the water. "We'll need
them again tomorrow," Dahlia said, "and it's easier to get
into them up here. That's just a glorified storage cabinet
down below."

They had another delicious dinner, then turned in while
the soft strains of Mozart wafted from the audio system.

An indeterminate time later Emily's eyes flew open at
the sound of Dahlia's scream. A dark figure loomed over
her bed. "Emily," a voice croaked, and then the figure collapsed across her torso.

"Computer, lights!" Dahlia yelled, as Emily, too terrified
to make a sound, scrambled out from under the man's dead
weight, staggered to her feet, and pressed her naked back
against the wall, staring at the stranger.

Except, when the lights came up, she realized it wasn't a
stranger at all: it was John Duval. Her movement had sent
him tumbling back onto the floor, where he lay supine, eyes
closed, head lolling to one side. His silver-scaled skinsuit
had a hole in its left shoulder. Blood trickling from it had
already begun to pool on the bedroom's pale blue floor,
and a pink trail of mingled water and blood leading back to
the central pool gave mute evidence of John's struggle to
make it to Emily's bed.

In the middle of the pool floated a sputa, one of the one-person propulsion units used all over Marseguro whenever you needed to get somewhere faster than your own flippers could manage.

Emily dropped to her knees beside John. "John! John, can you hear me?"

"Computer, medical emergency!" Dahlia shouted, and a locker on the bedroom wall beeped and opened. What dropped out of it from vertical to horizontal looked like an old-fashioned four-poster bed—except Emily knew both the "posts" and the "canopy" were stuffed with automated medical scanning, diagnostic, and treatment equipment. "Let's get him into the docbot," said Dahlia. It wasn't easy—he was head-and-shoulders longer than Emily, and Emily was half a head longer than Dahlia—but adrenaline aided them. As they lugged John across the floor, Emily at his head, Dahlia at his feet, Emily worried about aggravating the still-unseen injury—but on the other hand, he had presumably survived a who-knew-how-long underwater trip with it, so it was probably as aggravated as it was likely to get.

They pulled him onto the bed and started stripping him of his skinsuit. Emily gasped as she got a clear view of his shoulder. "That's—that's got to be a gunshot wound."

Dahlia pulled John's skinsuit down around his ankles; Emily took a quick look at John's nude body, blushed, and then focused her attention on his shoulder until Dahlia—who certainly wasn't seeing anything *she* hadn't seen, and probably handled, often enough—pulled the docbot's body-temperature control sheet over him.

"Don't be silly," Dahlia said. "The only guns on the planet are kept locked up by the Council. What makes you think it's a gunshot wound?"

"It's round," Emily said. She stepped back as the docbot began its diagnostics, activating a full-body scan, extending a robotic arm to take blood, and Emily had only a vague idea what else. "And there's a small entry hole and a bigger, more ragged exit hole. That's the kind of thing they're always pointing out in historical adventure vids."

"You can't believe everything you see in a vid," Dahlia said, but she didn't sound as sure of herself as a moment before.

The room had begun to warm automatically as soon as the shelter realized people were up and moving around, but nevertheless Emily shivered and folded her arms over her breasts. Dahlia slipped away—Emily hardly noticed as she stared at John's face, waiting for the docbot's prognosis—and came back a minute later with a fuzzy pink dressing gown and—Emily did a double take—"Bunny slippers?"

Dahlia shrugged. "They're warm and comfortable—and comforting. It's hard to believe anything is seriously wrong with the world when you're wearing bunny slippers." She looked at John and bit her lip.

Emily pulled on the dressing gown, grateful for the warmth. But when she slipped her feet into the bunny slippers, they failed to work their promised magic: she was still very much aware, as she looked at John's unconscious form, that something had gone *seriously* wrong with their world. "What could have happened?"

"He probably just thought he'd surprise us," Dahlia said. "And had some sort of accident along the way."

"Surprise us?" Emily said. "Some surprise. He was starting a new job in the mapping corps, remember? He should be on a cat-sub heading out for a three-month voyage. Not bleeding to death down here in the middle of nowhere!" She realized she had raised her voice, and stopped.

"He's not bleeding to death," Dahlia said. "That fancy skinsuit of his has some built-in first aid functions, and it's self-sealing, to boot. It kept the wounds from leaking too much. And this is the latest model of docbot. It can handle a little thing like—"

"Gunshot wound to the left shoulder," the docbot suddenly announced.

"I told you!" Emily said, but she took no pride in being right.

"Blood loss. Shock. Hypothermia. Extreme fatigue. Minor muscle strain." The docbot stopped, and beeped. "Prognosis: good, with proper medical care."

Emily breathed a sigh of relief.

"Docbot, define 'proper medical care,'" Dahlia said.

"This unit will stabilize patient. Patient should then be transported to main hospital, with minimal transit time."

"Looks like our vacation is over," Emily said.

"Before it even really began," Dahlia said. "Well, it can't be helped." She sighed. "I liked being cut off from the world, but . . . guess I'd better send up a transmitter buoy so we can radio ahead and tell Hansen's Harbor we've got an emergency." She went to the edge of the pool, slipped out of her slippers, dropped her dressing gown, and plunged naked into the water.

"Docbot, how long until patient is stabilized?" Emily asked.

"Estimate three point five hours needed to restore body temperature and stabilize pulse and blood pressure," the docbot announced.

Emily looked at the unconscious John and chewed her lip. Finally she said, "Docbot, can patient be woken?"

"Ill-advised," the docbot said. "Necessary stimulant could interfere with stabilization of vital signs. Patient may wake on his own at any time, however. Brain activity is vigorous."

Emily knelt by the bed. She didn't touch John, but she spoke into his ear. "John, are you awake?" Nothing. "John?" she said a little louder, and this time was rewarded by a change in his breathing. Emboldened, she repeated, "John?" Then added, "It's Emily. John, wake up."

John's eyes fluttered, then opened. For a moment, they remained unfocused, gazing blankly up at the lens-studded underside of the docbot's scanner canopy, then suddenly he blinked four or five times in rapid succession and turned his head to look right at her. "Emily?" And then, to her shock, he began to cry, gasping for air between silent sobs, tears streaming from his huge green eyes. He turned his head away from her, obviously fighting to regain emotional control. She stood by helplessly for a moment, then tentatively reached out and touched his red-and-blue tattooed head, petting him as she might have soothed a restive baby. "Shhh," she said. "Shhh. John, it's all right, you're safe now."

"None of us are safe," John choked out. "None of us, Emily."

Dahlia returned at that moment, cinching her dressing gown around her waist. "Buoy's launched," she said. "It'll take a minute or two to reach the surface." She blinked at John. "You're awake!" She grinned. "Couldn't stay away from me, huh? But what did you do to your—"

"I was shot," John said. "By the Body!"

Emily frowned. "You mean *in* the body? No, in the shoulder—it's a nasty hole, but it's a flesh wound, it—"

"No!" John shouted. The docbot had restrained him at some point, so he could only move his head, but he flung it back and forth so violently Emily feared for his vertebrae. "I was shot by the Body. The Body Purified. It's here. It's invaded. And it's—they're—they're killing us like animals!"

Emily snatched back her hand and surged to her feet as though John had turned into a monster in front of her eyes.

"He's raving," Dahlia said. "I'll prove it." She raised her voice, although of course it really wasn't necessary. "Computer, status of transmission buoy."

"Buoy is on surface and active," the computer said.

"Computer, transmit following to—"

John's head jerked up. "Computer, cancel previous command!" he shouted.

"Command input canceled," said the computer.

"Now what?" Dahlia said.

"If you send a transmission, you'll tell the Body where we are," John cried, the words tumbling out like fish from a net. "They'll hunt us down and kill us, just like they killed . . . so many others . . ." He squeezed his eyes shut. Fresh tears tracked his face.

Dahlia glared at him. "This is going on too long," she said. "It's not funny."

"He's been shot, Dahlia," Emily snapped. "That's a rather extreme step to take for the sake of a practical joke."

"He wants us to stay cut off from civilization so it'll just be him and two girls trapped in this shelter for a couple of weeks," Dahlia said. "John has always wanted his own harem. And I'm not saying he wounded himself on purpose. I'm just saying he's not going to let a little thing like a hole in his arm keep him from fantasizing about threesomes."

Emily knew Dahlia and John had been lovers off and on for years. Presumably, Dahlia knew a lot of things about John that Emily didn't. But Emily had grown up with John, and while she didn't doubt he had a rich sexual life, both in reality and in fantasy, she didn't believe he would play a joke this cruel—or try to maintain it after he'd been injured.

And while she didn't doubt that her reputation for being unattainable would have made her an attractive sexual trophy for someone like John, she also didn't flatter herself to think that John wanted to thrash up some foam with her so much he'd completely change his personality to accomplish it.

"No," Emily said. "Dahlia, I believe him—or at least believe that *he* believes that the Body has invaded."

"You're as crazy as he is, then," Dahlia snapped.

"So you're locked in a shelter with two crazy people," Emily said impatiently. "Safest thing to do is humor us, isn't it? Don't send a transmission. Just listen. See what's being said on the communications channels."

Dahlia rolled her eyes. "All right," she said. "Computer. Scan communications channels and play strongest signal."

There was a long silence. "All communications channels scanned," the computer said. "Only encrypted signals found, at frequencies not normally used by Marseguroite traffic."

"What?" Dahlia glared at the ceiling, even though the AI was actually located somewhere in the wall on the opposite side of the shelter, if Emily remembered right. "Computer, play signal from Hansen's Harbor Public Broadcast Station."

"No signal present at designated frequency," the computer said.

"But . . . oh, stupid thing!" Dahlia looked at Emily. "It's probably just a glitch in our equipment," she said, but she made it sound like a question.

"No glitch," John said. He sounded calmer. Emily gave him a look, and he actually smiled at her. "Pain medication is a wonderful thing," he said. "Dahlia, the tower that housed the Public Broadcast Station is currently a pile of steaming rubble spread along a large chunk of what's left of Pier Two. The antennae cluster crushed two houseboats on its way down and narrowly missed taking out the harbormaster's building—not that it mattered, because the second sweep of the Body's assault craft blew the harbormaster and his building to bloody froth and flinders."

Dahlia stared at him, and suddenly sank down on the floor as though her knees had buckled. "You're serious."

"Serious as death," John said. "Literally."

Emily felt as if a great howling wind had started blowing

in the center of her head, a tornado that could suck in her sanity and control and rip it to shreds. "My parents?" she whispered. "Amy?"

"I don't know," John said. "I didn't see them. They weren't in the group of prisoners I ended up with." He took a shuddering breath. "I don't even know what happened to my own family. I was on my way to board the *Magellan* when the attack came. They seemed to be concentrating on the visible structures, so I hope the underwater habs were mostly spared. But when I escaped, they were working on launching a couple of subs. Good thing they didn't have those in the water when I made my run for it. I think they sent a surface boat after me, but a storm blew in. I'm pretty sure it lost me."

"But I don't understand," Dahlia said, sounding young and lost. "How did the Body find us after all these years?"

John looked grim. "You both know Chris Keating."

Emily remembered her unpleasant encounter with him in the Square, when she had tried to apologize. She made a face. "Yes, unfortunately."

Dahlia nodded.

"Apparently he hiked over to Landing Valley and activated one of the *Rivers of Babylon*'s distress beacons."

"What?" Emily couldn't believe it. "He couldn't—he wouldn't—I mean . . ." Her voice trailed off as she remembered some of the things he had said to her. "Oh, God."

"I'll kill him for it, if I get a chance," John said, and made it sound like a promise, not a threat. "I almost had a chance on the pier. They didn't know how far I could leap out of the water. I got clear of the cage and even got my hands on a rifle. But the damned thing wouldn't fire. That's when I escaped. I jumped into the bay."

"And that's when you got shot."

John nodded. "Somebody was awfully quick on the trigger. Nailed me in midair. But I could still swim, and there was a sputa stand just a few meters down. By the time they were searching the area right by the pier, I was already on my way out of the bay." He paused. "There's something else. I don't know if he was telling the truth, or not . . . I don't see how he could be . . . but someone else was on the pier. A civilian." He paused again. "He claimed to be Victor Hansen's grandson. And he said he was the one who picked up the signal from the distress beacon and told the Holy Warriors we were here."

"He's lying!" Dahlia said. "Trying to get under your skin. Victor Hansen's grandson would never betray us."

Emily heard the certainty in Dahlia's voice and really wanted to share it . . . except she remembered how equally certain Dahlia had been, just moments before, that *John* was lying. "It doesn't matter who he was. The question is, what do we do now?"

"John needs a hospital," Dahlia said.

"I doubt we still have one in Hansen's Harbor," John said. His voice seemed weaker than it had a moment before. "I think . . . I'm being . . . sedated . . ." he said, and then his eyes fluttered closed.

"Docbot, did you sedate the patient?" Emily demanded.

"Affirmative," said the machine. "Pulse and respiration showed signs of stress-induced irregularity outside the permissible parameters for proper stabilization of patient for transportation."

Emily turned to Dahlia. "Now what?" she said, trying to keep the despair lurking in the back of her mind from shouldering its way to the foreground. "This may be the safest place for him. It may be the safest place for *all* of us."

"I don't know," Dahlia said. "If we can't take him to shore . . ." She bit her lip. "Docbot," she said. "What is the patient's prognosis if the only medical care he receives is what is available in this habitat?"

"Nontrivial risk of death within twenty-four hours," the docbot said. "Tissue damage too great to be properly treated by this unit. Precise calculation of survival odds impossible."

"Docbot, provide *estimated* odds," Dahlia snapped.

"Best estimation, fifty percent chance of death within twenty-four hours. Risk rises thereafter. Best estimation, odds of long-term survival: no better than thirty percent. Best estimation, odds of survival without permanent disability: negligible."

"That's not good enough," Emily said. "We have to get him more help!" *But if we can't take him to Hansen's Harbor . . .*

Then it hit her. "Jumpoff Station," she breathed. "We'll take him to Jumpoff."

"The research station?" Dahlia said. "How is that any better than here?"

Emily hesitated. Most people thought of Jumpoff as only a small habitat, not much bigger than the one they were in, located on the very edge of the continental shelf, and used as base camp for expeditions into the abyss. But Emily knew better. She wasn't supposed to tell anyone, but she didn't suppose it mattered any more.

"It's a lot bigger than most people realize," she said at last. "It's almost a small town in its own right—the biggest underwater settlement on Marseguro. They do all kinds of research down there."

"Like what?" Dahlia demanded. "And how come I've never heard any of this?"

"It's secret stuff," Emily said. Emily's mother had put in more than a few stints at Jumpoff, and had told Emily about the station, though she'd never talked in detail about what she did there. Emily couldn't even imagine what kind of research needed so much secrecy, but she supposed the Council had its reasons. *Probably worried the Consolidationists would see whatever it is as a waste of money and try to close it down,* she thought. *Located there, it must have some sort of Expansionist agenda behind it.*

"Then how do *you* know about it?"

"My mother's worked there some. But never mind that. The important thing is that because so many people are living there at any given time, it has a full-blown hospital. They'll be able to give John the treatment he needs."

"It's six hours to Jumpoff from here by sub," Dahlia said. "It's only four hours to shore."

"Docbot," Emily said. "Effect of six hours' transit versus four hours' transit time on prognosis of patient, assuming he receives prompt medical attention at the conclusion of that transit."

"Negligible," said the docbot.

Emily looked at Dahlia and spread her hands.

Dahlia frowned, then nodded. "All right," she said. "Then let's get him on the sub. I'll pack some supplies if you'll go fire it up. We'll load the supplies, then take John over last."

"All right," Emily said. She gave the unconscious John a final glance, hesitated, then leaned down and kissed him lightly on the forehead. At the edge of the pool, she doffed the dressing gown and bunny slippers and pulled on one of the deep-sea skinsuits they'd left there the day before. "Computer, open air lock into sub access tunnel," she said. It slid open, and she headed down the air tunnel.

Once inside the dolphin sub, it took Emily only a few minutes to power up the controls and the engines. She flicked on the exterior lights, which showed the shiny length of tube leading to the sphere of the habitat, anchored to the seabed on three stout legs.

Something flashed in the beam of light between the sub and the habitat.

Fish, Emily thought at first, but something about the shape hadn't looked very fishlike. She activated sonar and the other sensors and got back a strong, sharp, and almost instantaneous return that the computer instantly analyzed as "Small submarine vessel, metal, self-powered by atomic battery."

Emily hit the comm button, hoping Dahlia had the habitat speakers turned up and the umbilical properly connected. "Dahlia, you there?"

No response.

"Dahlia, there's something out here I don't like the looks of. Respond, please."

Nothing.

And then Emily gasped and scrambled up out of the command chair as the strange metallic object stopped circling the habitat, dove straight to the bottom of the sphere . . . and disappeared

"Shit!" Emily hurled herself at the hatch, pounded her fist on it until it opened, and then dashed down the tunnel. The habitat door slid open as she approached and she burst in just in time to see Dahlia dive naked into the water from the other side of the pool. "Dahlia!" Emily screamed. "Dahlia!"

Her friend surfaced. "Don't worry, I'll be there in a second," she said. "I'm just going down to underwater storage to pick up some extra power packs for the—"

"Get out!" Emily screamed. "Get out of the water!"

"What?" Dahlia said. "Why?" And then she looked down, a puzzled expression on her face—and vanished, pulled underwater so fast a whirlpool swirled where she had been.

"Dahlia!" Emily started forward, but had only taken a step when water erupted from the center of the pool as though something had exploded in it—and the pool turned cloudy red.

Dahlia's head broke the surface again, and Emily felt a surge of relief that turned to horror as the head rolled over, revealing ripped flesh and shattered vertebrae. As other body parts bobbed to the surface, Emily screamed, a scream that turned to a choking cry as she vomited, falling to her hands and knees, emptying the green-and-yellow contents of her stomach across the pale blue floor. She hung there, breathing hard, then swallowed and scrambled up. Not looking at the pool and what floated within it, she hurried around the dryfloor to where John still lay in his drug-induced sleep, intending to drag him out of bed and somehow get him to the sub—but she'd just started to pull off his blanket when the lights went out.

For one heart-stopping moment of sheer terror, Emily stood in utter blackness. Then the pale green emergency lighting came on. "Power conduit failure," the computer announced. "Human intervention required to repair. Operating on backup batteries. Eight hours' power at current load."

Had the whatever-it-was that had killed Dahlia actually been smart enough to cut the main power conduit, or had that just been a side effect of its attack?

Either way, it didn't matter. Now she *really* had to get John out of here.

The habitat rang as if it had been struck by a giant mallet. "Computer, what's happening?" Emily screamed.

"Habitat was struck by a second high-pressure pulse."

A second . . . ? Oh. Emily suddenly knew what had torn Dahlia apart. No wonder the power conduit ruptured. *That thing has some kind of . . . of sonic depth charge.*

"Computer, report any damage!"

"Habitat is undamaged," the computer said in the same calm, unconcerned voice it always used—but what it said next filled Emily with horror. "Access tube to currently docked vehicle has failed, however."

"Computer, status of vehicle!" Emily yelped.

"Scanning." A paused. "Vehicle is no longer docked . . . Vehicle now on sea bottom."

Oh, no. "Computer, orientation of vehicle?"

"Inverted. Vehicle computer is no longer communicating . . . Vehicle appears to have lost integrity; numerous pieces of debris detected."

"Shit!" Emily seldom swore, but nothing else seemed to fit the situation. "Shit, shit, shit!"

The computer, not having been directly addressed, said nothing.

Emily looked at John, still unconscious and looking disconcertingly like a corpse in the pale green light. "Docbot," she said. "Patient status."

"Patient is stable and resting comfortably," the docbot responded promptly. "Prognosis has improved."

It has? For the first time, Emily felt a surge of hope. "Docbot, estimated odds of survival without further medical attention." She swallowed, then added, "Assuming power remains constant."

"Best estimate, seventy percent," the docbot said.

She closed her eyes. "Docbot, estimated odds of survival without medical attention once power fails?"

"Negligible," the docbot said. And it didn't put "best estimate" in front of that stark analysis, she noticed.

It'll have to do, Emily thought. *Oh, John.* But at least he had a chance. Unlike . . . Emily looked at the pool. Cleanerbots whirred within it, clearing it of . . . of . . .

Emily shook her head. She couldn't think about it. Not now.

But she knew damn well she'd wake screaming from dreams about it.

The sputa that had pulled John to the habitat still floated in the pool. "Computer," Emily said. "Location of small mobile vehicle that initiated pressure wave."

"Vehicle is again inside habitat," the computer said.

What? "Computer, close bottom sea doors, emergency speed!"

A vibration, an almost audible clang. "Doors closed."

"Computer, location of small mobile vehicle?"

"Unchanged."

Trapped you, you murderous piece of tin, Emily thought. Unless the thing was amphibious and could climb out into the air-filled part of the habitat . . .

If it could, it already would have, she reasoned.

She wanted to destroy it, wanted to destroy it more than anything she'd ever wanted to do before, but she didn't know how. At least she'd rendered it harmless for the time being . . . she hoped.

But she still had to get to Jumpoff Station, and that meant she needed the sputa.

I don't think I'll swim out and get it, Emily thought, as water suddenly surged and swirled for no apparent reason. Fortunately, she didn't have to; as the water bulged again, it pushed the sputa to one side . . . better yet, it pushed it to the same side as the door leading into the access tube air lock. Emily raced around the edge of the pool, being very careful not to slip and fall into the water, and hauled out the device, which looked like a winged torpedo. Nacelles on the ends of the wings held the propulsion jets; the fat part of the torpedo held the power source, a nearly inexhaustible atomic battery, and the pump that pulled water in and forced it out the jets. Two handles, steering planes, fins, and a rudimentary control and sensor panel made up the rest of the device.

Like every other Selkie, Emily had used sputas since the first time her parents had allowed her out of their hab on her own. She'd never handled one out of the water before, and she'd been worried about the weight, but she found she could lift it easily, and she shoved it into the air lock with little difficulty. She paused to issue final commands. "Computer," she said. "Turn off all power-using equipment except for the docbot and the emergency lights nearest to it. . . . and this air lock," she added hastily.

All around the pool indicator lights vanished as the refrigerator, entertainment units, and other electronics shut down.

"Should this unit shut itself down?" the computer inquired.

"No! Uh . . . no. Computer, record voice message."

"Recording."

Emily took a deep breath. "John, a lot has happened since the docbot sedated you. Some sort of bot seems to have followed you here. It's trapped in the pool. It killed . . ." She paused for a long moment before she could get her voice under control enough to continue. "It killed Dahlia and took out main power at the same time. Stay out of the pool, whatever you do, and stay put. I'm taking the sputa to Jumpoff Station to get help. I . . . someone . . . will be back. Computer, end recording."

"Recording ended."

"Computer, monitor docbot patient. If . . . when he regains consciousness, play him that recording."

"Understood."

Emily looked around. Had it just been yesterday she'd arrived here looking forward to a relaxing vacation before she went home and continued struggling with her parents over her choice of career? It seemed more like a lifetime ago.

For Dahlia, it had been the end of a lifetime . . . an all-too-short one.

"Computer, open inner air lock door." The door opened. She slipped into the cramped lock and dragged the sputa in after her. "Computer, close inner air lock door." It slid shut. "Flood air lock and open outer door." Water poured in. Despite the cold, Emily welcomed its clean embrace. Her nostrils snapped closed and her gills opened. She felt her heart change its rhythm, felt the muscles only Selkies had squeeze her lungs, forcing the air up and out of her mouth in an explosion of vomited bubbles, a tickling, pleasurable sensation. Her vision blurred for a moment until the third eyelid slipped over each eye. Then the outer door opened, and she pulled the now weightless sputa out, turned it around, and flicked on its headlight.

What had been just dim shadows against the gradually lightening water above snapped into sharp relief. The air tunnel lay, a twisted, crushed worm, on the ocean floor beneath the habitat, still attached to the largest piece left of the sub; probably its collapse had contributed to dragging the sub down, and the jagged spike of rock Dahlia had told Emily she privately called "Poseidon's Prick" had done the rest of the damage.

Behind her, the habitat rang. *Our little visitor must realize it's trapped,* she thought. *Time to get out of here.*

The habitat rang again . . . and again . . . and again.

At least, I hope it's trapped! Suddenly worried the habitat wasn't as secure a prison as she'd thought, Emily activated the sputa's rudimentary computer. "Computer, indicate course to Jumpoff Station," she chirp-clicked in Selkie. The system didn't have any speech capability of its own, but an indicator lit on the circular screen at the center of the control panel. Keep the indicator in the center of the screen, and she'd make it to Jumpoff in . . . six to eight hours, according to the computer.

The habitat rang again, and Emily thought she heard a sound like tearing metal. Saying a prayer for John's safety to whatever deity might be listening—Emily glanced at the priapic rock that had killed the sub; Poseidon, presumably, although he seemed to be thinking about something else— Emily squeezed the throttle on the right handgrip and accelerated away from the habitat into the unknown.

Chapter 9

YOU WOULD THINK, Chris Keating thought as he lay on his thinly padded bed, the only furnishing of note in his cell in the Hansen's Harbor Criminal Detention Center, *that almost having my head blown off on the pier by an enraged Selkie would be enough to convince the Grand Deacon I'm on his side.*

You would think that, but you'd be wrong.

In fact, after Chris had been returned to the Grand Deacon by the dour Holy Warriors who had formerly been Richard Hansen's bodyguards, the story they'd told of John's escape and Hansen's decision to board the boat pursuing him had seemed to increase rather than decrease the Grand Deacon's suspicion. Or maybe the Grand Deacon just didn't want to have to deal with whatever Chris represented, and decided to put him somewhere safe until he was ready.

Whichever, Chris wasn't given a chance to say a word in his defense before being hustled to the small-but-grandly-named Hansen's Harbor Criminal Detention Center. He wasn't the only prisoner; he'd glimpsed other landlings, some of whom he knew, as a Holy Warrior had hurried him down the single central corridor to his cell. He'd half-expected to see Dr. Stanless, but didn't—perhaps he was in the hospital. Or perhaps he was dead, but Chris didn't want to think that. He didn't really care about the Selkies, but despite that whole omelet-egg thing he regretted the landling deaths. He hoped the people he almost thought of as friends weren't among them, even if they were Selkie-lovers.

He'd already passed one night in jail, sleeping well despite everything. After all, he'd had a busy and stressful day, and had been woken early by the arrival of the landing craft.

But now, he found, time dragged, with nothing to read and no one to talk to. He amused himself by imagining what it would be like when Purification was complete and he was formally recognized for his part in its success, but you couldn't kill a whole day that way.

Well, the Grand Deacon would surely want to talk to him again soon.

Time passed. Meals arrived. He used the toilet, and the booth-sized shower stall in one corner. He stared at the ceiling. He stared at the floor. He stared at the walls. And as it started to grow dark again, Chris assured himself the Grand Deacon would surely want to talk to him the *next* day.

But as he settled in for another night on the thin mattress, a plaintive question followed him down to sleep.

But . . . what if he doesn't?

For twenty minutes, despite the noise of the sputa's water jets, Emily could hear/feel the almost constant ring/thump of the habitat as the killerbot tried to break out. At the very limit of her senses, it stopped—and something about the *way* it stopped, some ill-definable quality of the final vibration, made her shut off the sputa and drift, listening.

Nothing.

Maybe the machine killed itself, Emily thought. *All those blasts inside that enclosed space . . . or maybe it just gave up.*

Or maybe, she thought, and wished she hadn't, *it broke out.*

The thing had successfully tracked John for hours—and had been at least an hour behind him when he had arrived at the habitat. It didn't seem to have a problem with a cold trail, and Emily only had a twenty-minute head start.

If it had broken out.

Well, one way to find out for sure would be to float around until it showed up. Emily preferred to be kept guessing. She reactivated the water jets and roared away into the darkness again, still following the blip of light showing her the way to Jumpoff Station.

Her options were, to say the least, limited.

                              *   *   *

Richard woke to find himself floating facedown and underwater.

The survival suit had lived up to its name. Not only had
it automatically closed his faceplate as he hit the water, it
had adjusted his buoyancy to keep him well below the surface, far enough down that the storm above could only tug
at his limbs with phantom fingers.

Not that he figured all that out when he first woke. It
took him a few minutes of panicked flailing and heart-
pounding fear and disorientation before the parts of his
brain capable of rational thought managed to take over
from the parts of his brain convinced he was a) drowning
and b) falling. Apparently those more primitive brain parts
were unable to grasp the inherent contradiction between
those two states.

Once he had his body, pulse, and breathing under control, he turned on his back and looked up at the tossing
underside of the waves, not a sight he'd ever expected to
see.

The survival suit, a little self-contained submersible, had
its own AI and a heads-up display if he remembered right
from the training sessions he'd attended on *Sanctification*.
"Computer, activate display," he said.

To his delight, a collection of digital readouts appeared,
apparently floating in the water a few centimeters outside
his faceplate.

The survival suit reported that it was operating normally, that the water temperature was twelve degrees Cel-
sius, and that it was 1754, Hansen's Harbor time. He'd
apparently been unconscious for about half an hour. The
computer also informed him that he had incurred a long
but shallow gash in his left calf which it had biofoamed shut
and pain-deadened, and that it had successfully self-sealed
the matching gash in the survival suit's skin. "Blood loss
not trivial, but not life-threatening," Richard read. *Well,
that's a relief,* he thought. *But it's a good thing I'm not a
Selkie. That hunterbot would probably come after me with
that much blood in the water.*

Hmmm. I wonder . . .

"Computer, can you track the hunterbot the boat was
following?"

Apparently it could; it indicated a direction, but gave no distance.

Is the boat still on its trail? Why didn't Veldron and Khan come back for me?

"Computer," he said. "Locate boat."

The computer instantly indicated that, far from having followed the bot into the indeterminate distance, the boat was precisely 1,957 meters away . . . and, the computer noted helpfully, upside down.

Richard's stomach flipped in sympathy. "Urk," he said. "Computer, locate any other survival suits in vicinity."

The computer informed him there were three survival suits in the vicinity . . . 1,957 meters away, on the boat.

"Computer, any warm-blooded life in the water?"

Nothing.

This is not good, Richard thought. "Computer, any other boats or bots in the vicinity?"

"None detected," the computer said.

He was all alone.

The gray light filtering through the water had faded to almost nothing. Richard wasn't much of a swimmer, and swimming in the survival suit was problematic anyway. But if he remembered correctly . . .

"Computer, provide overview of features of this survival suit."

The computer obligingly listed them, sounding like a very boring salesperson, and confirmed what Richard had recalled: the backpack held the artificial gill, a filtering unit that created fresh water as needed—Richard took a sip—and a small propulsion unit; just a simple water jet, but it would move him through the water at something better than a walking pace.

"Computer, indicate boat direction and distance."

A blip lit up in his faceplate. "Computer, activate propulsion unit."

The backpack began to vibrate. He surged through the water . . . then rolled . . . corkscrewed . . . flailed . . . jack-knifed . . .

It took him several minutes to figure out how to control his direction using his arms and hands and flippered feet as control surfaces. By then night had fallen, and the blip representing the boat had moved to the bottom of Richard's display and started blinking red, which he took to mean the boat was behind him. He activated his helmet lamp, reversed direction, and was rewarded by the blip moving back to the top of his display and turning green.

Traveling the two kilometers to the boat took him more than a quarter of an hour. The oceanic microfauna glowed green and blue and orange in his headlight and flowed past his faceplate like multicolored snowflakes viewed through the windshield of a moving groundcar. They were mesmerizing, to the point that the computer beeped several warnings before he realized the distance to the boat as indicated in his display had shrunk to almost nothing and he must be on the verge of plowing head-on into it.

An instant later, he saw it in his headlamp, upside down, the red-painted keel disappearing out of the water above him, the gray-green superstructure pointing down into the depths.

"Computer, stop propulsion," Richard said. He floated, looking at the boat. *Now what?* He couldn't exactly swim up to it and flip it over.

Unless . . .

"Computer, can you link with the boat's computer? Is it still active?"

"Affirmative and affirmative," the computer said.

"Computer, link with boat's computer."

"Link established. Please refer to this unit as Suit Computer and the unit on the vessel as Boat Computer."

"Uh . . . right." Richard cleared his throat. "Boat Computer, can you hear me?"

"Affirmative." It had, of course, exactly the same dispassionate male voice as the suit computer. Every Body computer Richard had ever talked to used the same voice. You weren't allowed to change it . . . especially to a female voice. That would be enough to get you sentenced to at least a week of penitence.

"Boat Computer, status of boat."

"No significant damage. However, boat is upside down."

Well, I can see that, Richard thought. "Boat Computer, why did the boat capsize?"

"Collision with unknown object," the computer said. "Lack of damage to the hull and analysis of the impact suggests object was large indigenous life form."

What? Richard couldn't help looking around. Nothing swam in the shadowy waters at the very limit of his helmet light . . . but anything at all could be swimming in the black water beyond its reach. *You had to ask, didn't you?* "Boat Computer, do you have self-righting routines in the event of a capsizing?"

"Affirmative."

"Boat Computer, why haven't the self-righting routines been activated?"

"Boat is currently under manual control," the computer said. "Self-righting mechanism has not been activated."

"Boat Computer," Richard said, "deactivate manual control."

"Cannot comply," said the computer.

"Why not?"

No answer. He hadn't properly addressed it. "Boat Computer, why are you unable to deactivate manual control?"

"Primary control commands must be issued by a certified and rated ship's captain. Your voice pattern does not exist in my approved command identification database."

Great, Richard thought. "Boat Computer, can you tell me how to activate your self-righting mechanism manually?"

"Affirmative."

"Boat Computer, please tell me how to activate your self-righting mechanism."

The computer provided the instructions, which consisted of nothing more complicated than hitting a big red panic button on the main control panel. Presumably you were supposed to hit the button as the boat went over. Something had obviously prevented Veldron from doing so.

"Uh, Boat Computer," Richard said, "how does the self-righting mechanism work?"

"Water is pumped at high speed from starboard ballast tanks to port tanks," the boat said. "At the same time, high pressure water jets are expelled through openings in the starboard gunwale. If necessary, the jets pulse to set up a rocking motion. The self-righting mechanism is successful approximately sixty-nine percent of the time."

"Boat Computer, what happened to the boats in tests where the self-righting mechanism failed?"

"Twenty-two percent rolled over completely and remained inverted, usually with significantly more damage. Nine percent broke apart and sank."

Well, I guess I wouldn't be any worse off, Richard thought.

He looked at the side of the boat's hull, then down toward the submerged bridge. "Suit Computer, can you monitor my buoyancy and keep it neutral?"

"Affirmative," said the suit.

"Okay, let's do this, then."

Neither computer, sensibly, replied.

Richard swam down. When he cleared the gunwale and directed his headlamp into the cockpit, he found out why he'd seen no sign of the ship's crew. Veldron still hung in the straps of his command chair, eyes staring, head at an odd angle. Richard remembered the way the boat had leaped high in the air before it came down, and suspected the impact had broken Veldron's neck. He'd never had a chance to free himself.

Khan he discovered a minute later, as he swam even deeper to the upper bridge level. Either the impact or the flip-over had thrown him into the glass that surrounded the upper bridge on three sides. The glass had shattered, but the opening he had been hurled into had been a little too small for him to pass through completely.

He still hung in the window frame, skin and clothing floating in red strips like gruesome seaweed all around him, face shredded beyond recognition. The blood had long since cleared away, giving him the pale and shriveled look of a laboratory specimen pickled in formaldehyde.

Richard swallowed hard and willed himself not to throw up. It seemed like a really bad idea inside a survival suit.

Then he had to fight the battle all over again when he realized that the lower half of Khan's body blocked most of the control panel . . . including the part with the panic button he needed to reach.

He tried pulling Khan back through the window, but couldn't get enough leverage. He'd move a little the other way, though, and so Richard ended up bracing his feet against the post of the wheel and pushing Khan through the window, its jagged glass teeth shredding the corpse even more, though so little blood remained in it that only a small dark cloud accompanied the effort. By the time Richard had fed the rest of the beefy ex-Holy Warrior through the window frame, he'd forgotten what he was struggling with and was cursing the corpse under his breath like he would a bulky piece of furniture.

At last, Khan's hips were out of the wheelhouse. His legs followed easily after that, and finally Richard could access the necessary button.

He slapped it. It was almost the last thing he did.

The boat lurched sharply to the side as ballast shifted overhead in the tanks. The side of the wheelhouse that Khan hadn't gone sailing through smashed into Richard's side so hard it knocked the breath from his lungs. He grabbed hold of the wheel, the only thing he could, and struggled for air as water roared from the starboard gunwale in bubbling jets, twisting the boat even farther. It rolled sideways, the jets cut off, it rolled back slightly, and then the jets roared out again, rocking and pushing again and again until, finally, the boat gave a great groan and rolled over completely, dumping Richard hard onto the floor of the wheelhouse. Lights came on, illuminating the deckhouse, the foredeck, and the equipment room below. Khan's mangled body, lifted out of the water as the boat righted itself, slid across the wet bow planking and splashed into the sea. Veldron still sat in his seat below, his head now twisted completely around. Blood mingled with seawater dripped from his nose and mouth onto the deck.

Richard clawed at his faceplate, managed to unseal it, and lifted it up. He took deep, hard breaths of the damp night air. The storm had moved on, and strange stars were beginning to prick the sky between fast-moving galleons of cloud. "Boat Computer," he said. "Can I command you to secure the boat for the night?"

"Affirmative."

"Boat Computer, secure for night."

A red light came on on the port side of the boat, a green light to starboard, and a bright white light at the stern. Something splashed in the water aft: a sea anchor, Richard presumed, to keep the boat's bow facing into the waves.

Richard sat slumped a few minutes longer, then steeled himself and slid down the steps to the main deck. He unsnapped Veldron's body, then hesitated. His first thought had been to drag it down into the hold, but he didn't know how long he'd be out here and his food and other supplies were down there.

Khan had already had an inadvertent sea burial. Veldron might as well join his shipmate.

Not without difficulty, he dragged the corpse to the railing. "May God Itself, the Great Protector and Purifier, welcome you to the Perfect World Beyond, forever free from the fear of God's wrath," he intoned, and dumped the body into the water. Feeling a little giddy, he yelled out in the direction he'd last seen Khan's corpse, "That goes for you, too!"

And then he hauled his own weary-but-still-living body down into the dripping crew cabin—he could hear pumps and fans working hard to dry it—and flung himself on one of the two waterproof mattresses. Despite the survival suit—not that there was any way he was going to take *that* off—he fell asleep in seconds.

Emily wasn't kept guessing long: an hour after the pounding in the habitat ceased, she knew the killerbot had somehow managed to break through the doors and find her trail. The knowledge didn't come through some sixth sense or even through one of the standard five: instead, the minimal display on the sputa lit up as passive sonar (active sonar would have been the equivalent of standing in an empty field shouting "here I am!", so she'd made sure it was turned off) picked up the sound of a high-speed propeller in her wake, the sputa's onboard computer being perfectly capable of compensating for the noise of its own passage through the water.

It took her another thirty minutes of travel to confirm her worst fear: the killerbot swam faster. The closer it got, the better the sputa's computer could estimate its distance; and once it had a satisfactory solution, it began displaying it. Emily watched the digits slowly fall in ten-meter increments, matched that to the rate at which the distance to Jumpoff Station was decreasing, did some careful mental calculation, and swore silently.

The bot would catch her at least an hour before she reached the station.

She didn't know what other weapons it had besides the sonic depth charge, but she had no reason to think that it wouldn't make as quick work of her as it had of poor Dahlia. She needed to find some place to hide that it couldn't reach.

She needed to get out of the water.

"Computer, display chart. Fifty-kilometer radius." The screen display changed. She studied it for a moment. Yes, she'd remembered right. "Computer, display new course to chart coordinates A-36-D-12." The screen lit with an alternate course, one that angled away from her current vector at almost forty-five degrees. But the distance indicated was less than half of that to Jumpoff Station.

Emily hesitated a moment longer. John, if he was still alive, needed help. But he wouldn't get it if she were killed before she reached Jumpoff Station, and she would be if she kept on her present course. As long as she stayed alive, he still had a chance.

And anyway, never mind John's needs: she had her own strong need to stay alive.

She angled off on the new course.

For another hour she swept through the sea, her arms beginning to ache from holding on to the sputa, feeling a great fatigue working its way into her mind and limbs. She watched the readout of the distance to the following bot continue to decrease slightly faster than the readout of the distance to her destination.

It's going to be close, she thought—and then had a shock as a brand-new icon and distance readout suddenly blossomed on the screen.

A boat dead ahead had just started its engines.

Chapter 10

RICHARD GRINNED WITH relief as the engines started on the first try. He hadn't been sure the computer would allow him that much control, but apparently it would. It would also, it had told him when he asked, allow him to set its course. It would *not* allow him to fire weapons, but that didn't worry him—he hadn't even realized the boat *had* weapons.

He turned his attention to the navigation screens for the first time in a while, absentmindedly rubbing his aching calf. The painkiller provided by the survival suit must be wearing off. But the suit's biofoam dressing at least kept the gash sterile and sealed. Nothing to worry about, and they'd soon set it right back on shore.

Which is where he wanted to be, as soon as possible. *I never should have left it in the first place,* he thought. *The Grand Deacon was right to send baby-sitters with me.*

That thought gave him pause, as well as embarrassment. *If I go back without even being able to report where the Selkie fled to, I might as well have myself shuttled up to* Sanctification *and locked in my quarters—and save Ellers the trouble of ordering it done.*

On the other hand, if he managed to return with useful information . . .

He rubbed his calf again. He could put up with the discomfort a little longer. It couldn't hurt to check . . .

"Boat Computer," he said. "Run scan for hunterbot you were tracking before boat capsized." No doubt it was out of range, but . . .

An icon leaped to life on the screen: less than five kilometers away—and *closing*?

And then two things happened at once. Richard noticed another icon on the display, almost on top of the central blip representing the boat—and the water at the stern erupted, discharging something large and wet into the cockpit.

He yelped and spun, to find a female Selkie with short violet hair, wearing a bright-yellow skinsuit with glowing light-piping along the limbs, hauling into the boat something shaped like a torpedo with wings.

Richard's heart leaped into his throat. He had no weapons, not even a wrench he could turn into an improvised club. *Selkies are enormously strong,* he remembered telling the Grand Deacon. *And fast. Stronger and faster than we are, by far.*

The Selkie spoke, her words accented but understandable. "Who are you? Are you one of the killers from Earth?"

"I . . . I haven't killed anyone," Richard said. "I . . . there was an accident, we hit a . . . a whale, or something . . . and the crew . . . I'm just a passenger." *A passenger who led the killers from Earth right to this planet,* Richard thought, but didn't say.

The Selkie's huge green eyes flicked around the boat, and Richard felt a strange sense of admiration and pride as he took in her alien face.

Pride?

"There's no one else on board?"

"No. Not anymore."

"Then get down from there."

"I—"

So fast he didn't even see where it came from, she drew a knife. Its blade looked like glass, almost transparent in the misty morning light. "Now."

Richard slid down the ladder, and gave the Selkie a wide berth as she scurried up it in his place. She gave the controls a quick scan, and swore. "The damned thing's practically on top of us!"

The hunterbot, Richard realized. *It's after her. But what happened to John Duval?*

Then he had to hang on for dear life as the Selkie seized the manual controls, which Richard, confirmed landlubber, had hardly dared touch, and shoved the throttle to full. As the boat leaped ahead, the torpedo-shaped device she'd hauled into the boat slid across the deck. Before Richard could react, it smashed into his wounded calf. He yelped, but the Selkie ignored him.

"I hope we're out of—" she began, but never finished. A shock like a giant hammer blow from below struck the boat. The engines stuttered, but kept running, though they now had a vibration that made Richard's bones rattle and the pain in his leg even worse. At least the shock had moved the damned torpedo-thing off his foot. He bent down to check it. The blow had torn open the biofoam dressing and the survival suit's self-sealing skin. Blood trickled down his ankle to mingle with the water on the deck.

The Selkie came down the ladder. "We're lucky," she said. "It only got in one shot. But it feels like we've lost half a propeller, or warped a shaft, and there may be damage to the engine itself. I don't know how long we can keep running."

"How long *you* can keep running," Richard said. "It's not after *me.*"

The Selkie's mouth tightened. Her face, with its minimal nub of a nose and matching ears, already had a seal-like look. When she compressed her lips and narrowed her eyes like that, she looked totally alien. Richard couldn't look away, but again his emotions confused him. He should be horrified . . . but he found her strangely beautiful, and again he felt that strange surge of pride, almost as though the Selkies were *his* creation. . . .

Am I losing my mind? he wondered, not for the first time. She—*it's*—a monster.

A monster in the boat with him. A monster that held his life in her hands.

"Where are we going?" he demanded. Whatever the cause of his mishmash of emotions, they didn't seem to leave room for fear. "Back to Hansen's Harbor?" He indicated his calf. "I'm injured. I need a doctor."

"I've got a friend that needs one more than you do . . . if he's still alive." The Selkie lunged at Richard, so hard and fast that he gasped. With her face just centimeters from his, she snarled, "And I've got another friend who'll never need a doctor again, because that thing you put in the water blew her into bugglefish bait."

"I didn't—"

"Shut up." She pulled back. "We're not going back to Hansen's Harbor. We're going to a rock that has just one thing going for it: an underwater cave with two entrances. It's very dangerous, very unstable. We're going to lure that thing into the cave, and then we're going to see how it reacts to having a few tons of rock dropped on its back."

The boat shuddered, and the engine coughed. The Selkie glanced astern. A haze of blue smoke hung above their wake. "We'll be lucky if the boat gets us there. We may have to swim the last kilometer or two."

"Swim?" Richard said. "I told you, my leg—"

"The sputa can pull both of us."

"Why not just leave me on the boat? The hunterbot will follow you. I'll just slow you down."

"I may need your help doing what I want to do," the Selkie said. "And I don't trust you. Maybe this boat has weapons I don't know about, and the instant I'm in the water you'll blow me apart like that 'hunterbot' of yours blew apart Dahlia." She shook her head sharply. "No. I want you within reach."

Richard cast around for an argument that might convince her, but they all sounded weak even to him. If he really were a Holy Warrior, one of them would be dead by now, but a couple of week's training on *Sanctification* had hardly prepared him for hand-to-hand combat with . . . *that*. The Selkie might be female, and young, but she was faster and stronger—had been *designed* to be faster and stronger—than he could ever hope to be. And he was injured. He was at her mercy, and knew it.

I hope she shows some, he thought.

But a part of his mind, the same part that found her fierce and beautiful instead of frightening and hideous, wondered how much mercy he deserved from someone whose friends, family, and world he had helped destroy with his betrayal.

Betrayal? I did my duty!

The inner voice said nothing, but Richard's face heated with unaccustomed shame.

Finding the boat had been a stroke of luck, Emily thought. Finding it occupied only by a thoroughly cowed civilian landling instead of an armed Holy Warrior had been an-other. So it was probably too much to hope that the dam-aged boat would actually keep running all the way to Sawyer's Point, the cave-ridden, dangerously unstable bit of volcanic detritus she hoped would rid her of what the landling called a hunterbot (but she still thought of as a *killer*bot) once and for all.

Sure enough, they were still a good three kilometers from Sawyer's Point when the engine, which had been run-ning progressively rougher, suddenly sputtered, gave a loud bang, emitted a huge cloud of blue smoke, and died. Mo-ments later almost-invisible flames began licking around the boat's stern; apparently a piece of hot metal had found the alcohol tank. "Better seal your faceplate," Emily told the landling. "We just ran out of boat, and we're about to run out of time."

The landling looked at the growing conflagration—the flames were orange now that they'd found plastic to burn—and sealed his faceplate without comment. As his survival suit stiffened, she gave him a shove that toppled him over the gunwale and into the sea. *No point giving him time to get cold feet,* she thought, picked up the sputa, and leaped in after him.

Only to find him gone. *He couldn't have swum that fast!* Furious with herself, she activated the sputa's navigation screen, and saw the landling at once, heading away from the boat at a right angle to the course she intended to set for Sawyer's Point, and moving at a pace that could only mean one thing. She cursed herself for being an idiot. Why hadn't she noticed his survival suit had built-in propulsion?

Because our survival suits don't.

It wasn't much of an excuse.

Well, she couldn't do anything about it. He'd escaped, and he was right about one thing: the killerbot wouldn't be interested in him. It would come after her. She had to get to Sawyer's Point before it caught her . . . and then hope her scheme actually worked.

She put the landling out of her mind, aimed the sputa toward Sawyer's Point, and squeezed the throttle.

Richard felt proud of himself—terrified, but proud. He'd been hoping for a chance to escape, hoping that maybe the

Selkie didn't know about his suit's built-in propulsion, and then she'd handed him that chance on a silver platter by pushing him into the water. Probably she'd hoped to take him off guard and then jump in while he floundered, but he'd been readier than he'd looked, and the moment he'd hit the water he'd activated the water jet.

He'd also felt a twinge in his injured leg. *I must be leaving a blood trail. Good thing I'm not a Selkie or the hunterbot would be after me.*

But now the bot would leave him alone and concentrate on its proper target. *Can she really trap it, even kill it?* He supposed she could; no matter how terrifying the things might be, they weren't indestructible. A few tons of rock dropped on its back ought to squash it flatter than . . .

. . . than Dad when he jumped off the Meeting Hall. The metaphor came to him unbidden and unwanted, as thoughts of his father usually did.

He dealt with the family shame his way, and I've dealt with it mine, Richard thought. *He chose to kill himself, and I . . .*

. . . I chose to kill.

He'd denied that to the Selkie, but he couldn't deny it to himself, especially not the newly intrusive part of his mind that seemed intent on upending all his cherished rationalizations. He had pointed the Holy Warriors to Marseguro, and the Holy Warriors had already killed many of the planet's inhabitants, both normals and Selkies. Any Selkies they didn't kill they would confine, and later sterilize. To placate God Itself, to ensure It did not repent of Its sparing of Earth, the Selkies' whole inhuman race must end. Marseguro had to be Purified. He believed that.

Didn't he?

The Selkie are monsters. That alien face . . . those eyes . . .

Beautiful, that strange new voice in his head insisted. *Designed to be beautiful. A masterwork of the genesculpting art . . .*

Which made Purification a hideous mixture of murder and vandalism.

He shook his head. *She'd have killed you in an instant if she'd seen any reason to . . . if she'd known your role in the Purification of her planet.*

Maybe. But in his increasingly confused heart, he couldn't wish her dead.

God forgive me, but I hope she escapes.

He checked the navigation display. It had synchronized with the boat computer while he was on board, and showed him his distance from Sawyer's Point, now receding, his distance from the burning boat, also receding, his distance from the Selkie, receding as she raced toward Sawyer's Point, and his distance from the hunterbot, which had reached the boat's location sometime in the last few minutes. He blinked. Something looked odd. "Computer," he said. "Display hunterbot's course for the last fifteen minutes as a solid line."

The blip representing the bot elongated into a line, straight as an arrow from the edge of the display to the blip of the boat . . . and then, abruptly, curving away from the straight path to Sawyer's Point . . .

. . . curving to follow him instead.

"That's impossible!" Richard said out loud. "Computer, extrapolate your current course and bot's course."

His blip elongated, became a straight line leading off the edge of the display. After five extrapolated minutes, the bot's course matched his precisely, the two lines disappearing into one another.

"Computer, how long until the bot catches me?"

"One hour, two minutes," the computer said.

"Computer, how far to land at current speed, if course is altered as necessary to minimize time?"

"Four hours, thirteen minutes."

Richard swore, but the numbers were implacable. If the bot, impossibly, were following him, then he must also assume that the bot, impossibly, thought he was a Selkie—and would blow him into chum in one hour's time.

He'd started on the boat as a hunter. Now he was in the water as the hunted.

But he wasn't the only possible prey.

"Computer," he snapped. "Display least-time route to Sawyer's Point."

A new line formed, and a blip appeared for him to steer toward. He stuck out his left arm and leg and swung sharply around. With the blip centered, he began racing toward Sawyer's Point, and the blip that was the Selkie girl, almost at the Point already.

"Computer, ETA, Sawyer's Point."

"Fifty-nine minutes."

In his faceplate, the bot's marker altered course again. Its extrapolated course, still displayed, still matched up with his. "Computer, now how long until bot catches me?"

"One hour, four minutes."

He'd arrive at that piece of rock with five minutes to spare.

He hoped the Selkie would welcome his company.

Halfway to Sawyer's Point, Emily realized the killerbot had peeled off to follow the landling. The irony made her bare her teeth in a savage grin. For a moment, she considered abandoning her plan and heading for Jumpoff Station again, but she quickly rejected the idea. If the bot finished off the landling, it would almost certainly come after her again, and if she headed for open water now, she'd be worse off than ever when it caught her.

The wisdom of her decision was brought home shortly thereafter, when she saw that the fleeing landling had reconsidered his actions and was now heading toward her as fast as he had previously been heading away from her.

Moments after that, she surfaced to reconnoiter and saw Sawyer's Point dead ahead.

It rose precipitously from the sea, its base splashed white by the waves pounding themselves to spray against its black volcanic rocks. There could be no landing or climbing on its steep sides, made of rock as sharp-edged and splintery as glass. Even if you could find someplace to ascend, you'd slice off a hand or foot and bleed to death before you'd climbed ten meters.

Both above and beneath the water, Sawyer's Point was riddled with tunnels and caves, some volcanic tubes through which magma had once pulsed, some formed by erosion, some dissolved by seawater from below and rain from above, many formed by the action of the strange rock-eating microbes that some researchers thought were one reason Marseguro had so little dry ground.

Beautiful and dangerous, Sawyer's Point was strictly off-limits to teenaged Selkies and thus much frequented by them. Three young Selkies had died there just a year ago, and ever since then, sensors seeded around the rock had signaled Peaceforce headquarters in Hansen's Harbor whenever anyone ventured too close. Since Peaceforce headquarters was probably now a pile of rubble, Emily doubted anyone was paying any attention to those sensors now.

She'd been one of those teens who had ignored the restrictions, and she knew Sawyer's Point like the back of her hand—or, at least, she had, five years ago. How many of the tunnels and caverns she remembered remained unchanged she couldn't judge. If the one she was counting on was no longer there, or no longer open, then Sawyer's Point might well prove fatal to her, too.

Of course, it might anyway.

She plunged beneath the waves again, and directed the sputa down, down . . .

There! Thirty meters below the surface, the sputa's headlight picked out a gaping hole, about as wide as she was tall. She could only see it in the wall of black rock because unlike the rock, it reflected nothing. In front of it, the ubiquitous Marseguroite plankton twinkled in her light like stars.

Emily killed the sputa's jets. Then, floating just outside the cave mouth, she pulled her lightband from one of the almost-invisible pockets of her skinsuit and fastened it around her head. The forward half of the circlet lit up automatically. "Computer," she told the sputa, "surface and hold position until retrieved." She released it. Its headlight went out and it rose out of sight to wait for her to reclaim it.

If she ever did.

She reached up and pressed the back of the lightband to deactivate it. She'd need it later, but for now, she would wait in the dark for the landling's approach. With her light out, she'd be able to see his more easily.

Once he arrived, the killerbot wouldn't be far behind.

Richard watched the number indicating the distance to Sawyer's Point and the now-stationary blip of the Selkie count down, and the number indicating the distance between him and the hunterbot count down just slightly more slowly.

The Selkie's blip was almost, but not quite, on top of the blip representing Sawyer's Point. Since his suit could only track the sputa, not her, for all he knew she had left it outside and already entered the rock.

The thought alarmed him. If she had, how would he find the way in? Sawyer's Point rose sheer from the bottom, 200 meters down. The entrance she had taken could be anywhere. He couldn't search a hundredth of that mass of rock in the scant minutes he would have before the bot arrived.

Would the hunterbot's sonic depth charge blow him apart or squash him against the rock like a bug? he wondered sickly.

And then, too soon, he arrived at Sawyer's Point . . . and before he could panic, his display suddenly added a new blip: a warm-blooded life-form at a depth of thirty meters.

He hadn't been that deep before in the survival suit, but he could only assume it was good for it. He angled his hands and arms and aimed down into the darkness, feeling the suit stiffen around him to counteract the increasing pressure.

And suddenly, it wasn't dark. A light shone down there, barely visible at first but growing brighter as he descended . . . and then his own headlight picked up the shadowy form of the Selkie, who wore the light as a band around her head.

He hadn't seen a Selkie underwater before. Her nostrils were clamped so tightly closed he couldn't even see them anymore, making her look almost noseless. Her eyes had a clear membrane across them, and they didn't blink. And her gills . . . they were open, pink and pulsing, the thin membrane of their edges rippling constantly. They looked like horrific, killing wounds, slashes in the side of her neck, but, of course, they weren't killing her at all, they were keeping her alive, helmetless, thirty meters underwater.

Monstrous, he thought automatically, but at the same time . . . *magnificent.* No one but his grandfather had ever succeeded in creating a form of human with so many modifications, one that bred true, one that really *worked,* that didn't suffer from crippling health problems—breathing difficulties, fragile bones, horrific cancers, mental retardation. Victor Hansen's contemporaries had held him in awe, limited as they were to mere cosmetic manipulation—humans with tails, humans with cat's eyes. Victor Hansen had done what they considered impossible.

Not surprisingly, some had doubted his claims at the time, and in the years since Salvation, some Body theologians had argued that Hansen's achievements must have been overstated, that the Selkie race he claimed to have created must be little more than crippled, deformed freaks, that God Itself would not allow the Holy Human Genome to be tampered with to so great a degree.

But the Selkie girl in his headlight didn't look crippled or deformed. She looked . . . at home. Alive. Vibrant. Healthy. Bizarre, yes, monstrous, even, but . . . strangely beautiful.

God forbid, he thought fervently. *Attracted to a Selkie? The Avatar would put me in an execution sputnik and have my ashes scattered across three continents.*

No doubt the Selkies had some way to communicate underwater, but he didn't share it. He expected her to lead him into the cave behind her, but she didn't move, and he couldn't interpret the look she gave him. Then her gaze slid past him to the void beyond.

Of course, he realized. *She's waiting for the hunterbot. She wants to be sure it follows us.*

Or follows me. He still found it hard to believe he had become the bot's target, but without a doubt, here it came, the numbers showing its distance dropping rapidly now he'd stopped. Five hundred meters . . . four-fifty . . . four hundred . . . what was the range of its weapon, anyway? . . . three-fifty . . . three hundred . . . *Why isn't she moving?* . . . two-fifty . . . *She doesn't have a display! She can't be expecting that thing to show a light!* . . . two hundred . . . one-fifty . . .

Finally, she tapped his arm, pointed to the mouth of the cave, and plunged inside. He started to activate his propulsion system, thought about the sharp rock lurking inside the tunnel, thought better of it, and swam after her, his calf hurting and still, he suspected, leaking blood into the water.

The blood the hunterbot is following, even though I'm not a Selkie!

Feeling as betrayed by his own body as he had recently begun to feel betrayed by his mind, he entered the tunnel.

Emily swam through the tunnel as fast as she could, hoping she hadn't misjudged the killerbot's distance and the range of its weapon . . . and also hoping its AI wasn't smart enough to realize just how rotten the rock was in Sawyer's Point, because she knew full well one sonic depth charge would bring the tunnel crashing down.

Of course, that was precisely what she was counting on, but not just yet.

She knew the landling had followed her—what else could he do?—but she couldn't spare him a thought. If he kept following her and did exactly what she did, he just might get out of this alive . . . if either of them did.

She wasn't sure why she cared about that, considering what his fellow Earthlings were reportedly doing to her planet, but she'd never killed anyone before, and she didn't want to start.

The passage narrowed. She arrowed through an opening just big enough to let her pass and emerged into a giant cavern, a bubble blown in the magma long before. The upper third contained air, and so she swam up five meters and burst into the open. As she emerged, rainbows erupted from the bubble's lining of volcanic glass, made iridescent by the action of the rock-eating bacteria, which left a thin light-refracting slime on every surface. Spectacularly beautiful and much photographed after it had been discovered by one of the first-generation Selkies, Hendrix Cavern had also been the first part of Sawyer's Point declared off-limits. Geologists had warned that the slightest earth tremor or settling of the rock could shatter its fragile equilibrium and bring tons of rock crashing down into it, destroying its beauty forever: a terrible shame in the present and a crime against posterity—and Emily couldn't wait to make it happen.

She swam the cavern's thirty-meter diameter and climbed out onto a ledge. A moment later, the landling emerged. He didn't swim across the cavern: instead he activated his propulsion system and shot across the pool so fast he had to turn sharply at the last minute to avoid smashing headfirst into the rock, and even so banged into it so hard Emily couldn't help but wince in sympathy. He clambered out and unsealed his faceplate. "What is this place?" he said, staring around.

"Hendrix Cavern." She barely glanced at him, keeping her attention on the pool. She pointed behind her, where another tunnel began. "Go through there. It will drop you into water in another five meters. Keep following the tunnel and keep bearing left, and you'll emerge into the open ocean. Don't take any openings to the right or you'll never get out of the rock."

"What are you—?"

"Go!" Emily snapped, and to his credit, the landling didn't ask any more questions, but closed his faceplate and plunged into the tunnel.

Just in time. With a grinding noise, the killerbot burst into Hendrix Cavern.

Emily had hoped the action of the bot breaking through the rock constricting the opening into the pool might be enough to bring the cavern's roof crashing down all by itself, but no such luck. Instead, she saw her pursuer clearly for the first time through the crystal-clear water.

It resembled the pictures she had seen of Earth's giant squid, with a cylindrical body, an arrow-shaped "head" with diving planes on it, and four . . . no, six tentacles writhing and lashing around its stern like snakes tasting the water.

Which, if Emily had figured out how the thing tracked, was exactly what they were doing.

It was what she was counting on . . . although she was also counting on the bot being designed merely to attack things in the water. If it also had the ability to attack things out of the water, she was about to die.

She drew her glassknife from her skinsuit and, with only a moment's hesitation, drew its ultra-sharp blade across the ball of her thumb. Blood followed pain, and she plunged her hand into the pool.

The bot must have instantly picked up the warmth of her hand. She snatched her fingers out of the water just ahead of the tentacle that lashed at her with astonishing speed, barely slower in the water than it would have been in air. Even though she pulled her hand from the water, turned and leaped into the exit tunnel in one motion, she was still half in Hendrix Cavern when the killerbot discharged its sonic weapon.

The water in the cavern leaped up *en masse,* creating a tsunami that hurled her down the tunnel she'd barely entered. She screamed, the sound cut off as the water engulfed her, as her back slammed into the sharp rock and she felt her skinsuit and some portion of her skin tear away. At the same time, she felt a deep, rumbling, grinding vibration all around her, as Sawyer's Point groaned. The water shot her along the tube, and she frantically fended off razor-sharp rock and kicked and pushed as hard as she could to avoid being swept into one of the side tunnels she had warned the landling about. And then, suddenly, she exploded out into the open sea, skinsuit shredded in a dozen places and skin in a half-dozen, bleeding and bruised but, amazingly, still alive.

And the killerbot?

She hovered, gills working extra hard, and looked back at the wall of rock from which she had emerged. No way to be certain it was trapped, no way to be certain it had been destroyed, but she would know soon enough. If it made it out, it would follow her again. If it hadn't emerged by the time she got around to where she had left the sputa, it probably never would.

But how many more of those things are there? she wondered.

The landling would know, but he'd disappeared. She wondered if he'd made it out. If he hadn't, if he'd gone down one of the tunnels that curved, split, and narrowed, and especially if he had been in one of those when that surge of water came, then he was almost certainly entombed in Sawyer's Point, just like the bot.

She flexed her limbs. The lacerations seemed minor and the bleeding already less. She wouldn't bleed to death before she could get to Jumpoff Station, at least. It hurt to swim, but she headed around Sawyer's Point to retrieve the waiting sputa.

She put the landling out of her mind as an unimportant civilian. What she needed now was to get to Jumpoff Station, find out what was going on, and get help for John Duval (*if he's still alive*, she thought grimly). And then . . .

Then we figure out how to drive off these murdering Earth bastards.

She refused to believe that might be impossible.

Somebody will know what to do. Somebody will have a plan.

Somebody has to.

Chapter 11

RICHARD SPED TOWARD Hansen's Harbor, heart pounding, and watched his heads-up display. He had felt Sawyer's Point shrug as he emerged from the tunnel, and had seen a huge boulder race past him toward the bottom, trailing bubbles. But he hadn't hesitated, any more than he had when the Selkie had first thrown him into the ocean. He'd activated the survival suit's propulsion system and set course for Hansen's Harbor again, trusting that the Selkie had taken care of the bot, and that she wouldn't come after him when and if she emerged herself.

Trust, but verify, he thought, the old diplomatic phrase surfacing from somewhere in his subconscious, and kept watching the display.

He didn't see anything for fifteen minutes. The limited sensor capabilities of the survival suit didn't permit him to detect a Selkie in the water on her own from this distance. He wouldn't see her until and unless she hooked up with the sputa again and started it up . . .

. . . and there she is.

A blip separated from the blob that marked Sawyer's Point. He watched it. Would she come after him? The sputa was faster; she could catch him if she tried . . . but she didn't try. She headed off in an entirely different direction, and shortly thereafter faded from the display altogether.

He concentrated on keeping the blip pointing the way to Hansen's Harbor centered, and trying to reconvince himself of the sanctity of their mission. Nothing had changed. The Selkies were still subhuman abominations, not great works of art, no matter what some traitorous part of his mind might think, and the Body Purified's mission remained clear: such abominations could not be permitted to continue to pollute the Holy Human Genome, for just such pollution had drawn the wrath of God in the form of the giant asteroid fifty years ago, and only the Avatar's unflinching efforts to root out such pollution had earned God's pardon. Failing to destroy the Selkies would be tantamount to taunting God and daring It to destroy the human race after all, and Richard had no doubt that God could do that any time It wished, and quite likely would.

At least, he *thought* he had no doubt.

Didn't he?

That subhuman abomination saved your life, Richard thought. He'd had no way of dealing with the rogue hunterbot. If not for her knowledge of the local geography and her quick thinking, they'd both be feeding plankton by now. And she'd let him go, when she didn't have to, and before that, on the boat, let him live.

An animal wouldn't have hesitated to kill someone so demonstrably a threat. Neither would a subhuman monster. But she had. She'd acted, in fact, like a civilized human being, one who considered killing a last resort . . .

. . . unlike, say, the Holy Warriors.

That was an uncomfortable line of thought. Richard decided to think about something else.

Like, for example, why the hunterbot had altered course to come after *him* when it had sensed his blood in the water, and would other hunterbots do the same—because if there was one thing he was reasonably certain of, it was that there would be more hunterbots in the water at Hansen's Harbor.

All I can do is keep alert, he thought. *I'll be close to land by then. If I head for shore as soon as I detect one . . .*

It wasn't much of a plan. *Most of the hunterbots will be in New Botany Bay itself,* he reassured—or tried to reassure—himself. *I'll come ashore before I enter the bay proper and walk the rest of the way.*

Holding on to that thought, he sped along for another hour through pale-green water stabbed by shafts of ever-shifting sunlight from above. And then, suddenly, all his planning—such as it was—became moot: his display showed him another boat, straight ahead.

And as he watched, a smaller blip separated and raced toward him, the boat following in its wake.

Hunterbot!

He had nowhere to hide, no way to outrun the thing or its follower, no rocks to climb, and no Selkie to lure it to destruction. The best he could do was head for the surface and hope the Holy Warriors on the boat recognized his survival suit and called off the hunterbot before it blew him out of the sea.

He shot up through the water, the suit's water jet giving him enough momentum that he emerged three quarters of the way into the air before falling back with a huge splash like a broaching whale. The waves were modest by ocean standards, but still high enough that, low in the water as he was, heaving green hills cut off all sight of the boat. He couldn't see any sign of the hunterbot, either, but his display showed it getting nearer. His heart pounded as its blip met his blip and he gave an involuntary yelp as he felt a surge in the water beneath his feet . . . and froze as the hunterbot surfaced, wet gleaming metal emerging from the water just two meters away. The bot's tentacles remained tucked tightly to its side, though. It did nothing threatening at all . . . though he still had the feeling he was being watched.

He floated there, staring at it, until the boat suddenly appeared, almost on top of him. It slowed and turned broadside. A moment later, the two men aboard it threw a rope ladder over the side and helped him climb into the cockpit.

He opened his helmet. "Boy, am I glad to see you guys."

"We picked up the distress signal from your suit," the larger of the two Holy Warriors said. "Switched the hunterbot to homing mode instead of Selkie-tracking mode to pinpoint your location for us. But who *are* you?"

"Richard Hansen," Richard said.

The two exchanged glances. "You're Hansen?"

Richard nodded.

"Better call back the bot, Muhammad," the smaller man said. "We're heading back in." The bigger man nodded and went into the control cabin. The smaller man said, "The Grand Deacon has issued standing orders that whoever finds you is to bring you to him at once. I don't think he's very happy with you."

Richard said nothing.

In the boat, with the hunterbot once more aboard, the trip to Hansen's Harbor only took an hour. Richard really wanted to take off the survival suit, but considering he would have been dead if he hadn't been wearing it the last time he was in a boat, decided he could put up with it a bit longer. Once they docked at the pier at Hansen's Harbor, though, he stripped it off with great relish and climbed up the ladder to the pier (not without difficulty; his leg still hurt) once again wearing the unmarked Holy Warrior jumpsuit he'd been given by the cargo shuttle pilot . . . had that only been yesterday?

Unbelievable.

Two armed, armored, and grim-faced Holy Warriors met him and escorted him, limping, back through the town to Government House. Little had changed since yesterday, although the cage that had been full of Selkies floated empty, one side standing wide open. Richard wondered, with an unease that surprised him, what had happened to them. *Surely they weren't executed in cold blood,* he thought. *That was never the plan. They're to be allowed to live, just sterilized and put to work rebuilding the city in preparation for the arrival of pure human colonists. . . .*

Oh, is that all? And that's better, is it?

Again, Richard tried to put such thoughts out of his head. Ideas like that were dangerous, especially when he was about to talk to the Grand Deacon . . . who, in turn, would certainly be reporting to Cheveldeoff. Of course, Richard would be reporting to Cheveldeoff himself, but he had little doubt which report would carry more weight. He might be along as Cheveldeoff's personal observer, but he was also on probation, and he knew it.

Things hadn't changed much since his last visit with the Grand Deacon. Perhaps the sense of barely controlled chaos as people came and went had lessened slightly. Ellers, however, looked much unhappier than he had the day before, and from the way he looked at Richard, Richard suspected a large portion of that unhappiness was directed at him.

Ellers confirmed it. "What the hell did you think you were doing?" he snapped. "You didn't have permission to go out with a tracker boat. You're here to observe, not to take part in operations!"

"I thought it was important to observe the operation of the tracker boats and hunterbots," Richard said, keeping his voice level. "I didn't see how I could do that while remaining on shore."

"You should have requested permission," Ellers said.

"I'm not under your command," Richard snapped back, and instantly regretted it. *What's wrong with you? Are you trying to get yourself confined to the ship?*

Maybe he was. Then he wouldn't have to continue to observe the bloody results of his brilliant interstellar detective work.

Ellers' eyes had narrowed. "No," he said. "You're not. But the men you were with were. I've already issued orders to all Holy Warriors that they are not to allow you to accompany them on any operations without my express permission. Have you got a problem with that?"

Richard took a deep breath. "No. And . . ." He found it surprisingly hard to say. "I apologize, Grand Deacon. I had not thought through the possible consequences of my actions." *On Earth, or here.*

The Grand Deacon said nothing for a moment, his eyes searching Richard's face. "Apology accepted," he said abruptly. "We'll say no more about it."

"Thank you."

"But now tell me: what happened out there?"

Richard explained, as best he could, how he had come to be in the water without a boat and minus two Holy Warriors. When he finished, the Grand Deacon shook his head. "We know there are a lot of underwater habitats out there," he said. "We've found a few in relatively shallow water, but the deep-water ones . . . well, a few hundred meters of salt water makes a very effective sensor shield. It's too bad that Selkie bitch got away. I'd bet a sizable sum she was heading to one."

"I was hardly in a position to follow her," Richard pointed out, while inwardly seething at Ellers' use of the word "bitch" to describe the young woman . . . the *Selkie* . . . who had saved his life . . . *what's wrong with me?* He wondered again. *Why should I care what he calls her?*

Ellers waved a dismissive hand. "I'm not blaming you," he said. "In any event, we're analyzing the computer logs from your survival suit. Maybe there'll be enough data there to at least give us a direction; we can send out a couple of hunterbots along the possible vectors, and maybe we'll get lucky." He frowned. "Although I am also concerned by the rather astonishing fact that a hunterbot, hot on the trail of a well-identified and confirmed Selkie, abandoned that trail to follow you, instead. And you think it was because you were bleeding?"

"I think it must have been," Richard said. The Holy Warriors who had pulled him aboard their boat had resealed and bound the wound, but talking about it made him aware again of that particular, sharper pain mingled with the general aches of his much-abused body.

"I don't like it," Ellers said. "If the hunterbots start turning on our divers, their usefulness is questionable." He thought for a minute. "I want you to go to the hospital," he said finally. "I'll radio ahead and explain the situation. I want the medics to run whatever tests they can think of, comparing your blood and that of the Selkies. We need to know why that thing attacked you. And you should get that leg checked out anyway." Ellers gave him a hard look. "After that, you can continue your observations for Archdeacon Cheveldeoff. But you *will* get permission before doing anything like this again, do I make myself clear?"

Richard resisted the urge to say "Yes, sir." He wasn't in the military and while he might be at Ellers' mercy, he certainly wasn't—as he'd pointed out moments before—at his command. "Crystal clear, Grand Deacon."

"All right, get going. You two," he said to the Holy Warriors who had stood at attention throughout the exchange, "escort Mr. Hansen to the hospital. Dismissed."

The hospital was only a couple of blocks from Government House. The central part of the city seemed well-secured; maybe that was why the Holy Warrior on Richard's right, whose name tag read KAVANAGH, felt relaxed enough to chat. "Are you really Victor Hansen's grandson?" he said as they walked—or in Richard's case, limped—down the street, feet crunching on broken glass. Richard could count the number of unbroken windows he'd seen in Hansen's Harbor on the fingers of one hand.

"I really am," Richard said.

"So . . . look, I know you're not him, and you can't pick your relatives, but . . . well, why'd he do it?"

"Do what?"

Kavanagh gestured in the direction of New Botany Bay. "This. Create those monsters." He shook his head. "They give me the creeps. I feel kind of Unpurified just looking at them. Like I need a shower and a day's penitence. How could any normal human being create monsters like that?"

Leave it, Richard warned himself, but the newly rebellious part of his mind seized control, and he heard himself say, "They're not monsters."

He became aware of the suddenly more focused attention of the other Holy Warrior, whose name tag read DUNCAN. *Careful,* he thought, and again, *What's wrong with me?*

"How can you say that?" Kavanagh demanded. "Geez, have you seen them? Well, of course you have, I heard you were in the water with one. No nose to speak of, no ears, and those gills . . ." He shook his head. "And they're shameless. Those skinsuits they wear. They might as well go naked. I hear some of the ones they dragged out of the bay *were* naked."

"If they're not human, why do you care whether they're naked or not?" Richard said. *Shut up!* a part of him said frantically.

Kavanagh gave him a puzzled look. "Huh?"

"Never mind."

"So why'd he do it? Your grandfather? Was he, you know . . ." he made a circling gesture around his right ear. ". . . crazy?" He frowned. "Hey, I'd almost forgotten. Your dad was *definitely* crazy, wasn't he? I remember now . . . jumped off a building."

Duncan still watched him like a hawk. Richard's fist clenched. He wanted nothing more than to punch Kavanagh in the nose, but he knew whatever he did or said would be promptly reported back to the Grand Deacon. "No," he said carefully, wresting control away from the strange . . . well, the Body did not believe in demons or demon possession, but "demon" was still the word that came to mind . . . that seemed to have claimed half his brain. "I don't think my grandfather was crazy, even if my dad was. But remember, Victor Hansen created the Selkies before the Avatar's message had been widely disseminated. Humans had gotten away with doing whatever they wanted for decades without giving a thought to the will of God—the true will of God, as proclaimed by the Avatar. Grandfather was . . . misguided. He did not believe that creating a new race of . . ." Richard bit off the next word. He'd been about to say *humans*. ". . . subhumans was evil. He probably didn't think about the ethics and morality of it at all. It was an immoral age."

"But when the first one was born . . ." Kavanagh shook his head. "When he saw what it looked like, why didn't he just strangle it at birth and burn his research?"

What kind of monstrous father would strangle his child at birth, no matter what it looked like? Richard thought, but managed not to say. "I can't speak for my grandfather," he said instead. "It's not my place to defend him."

But for the first time in his life, he'd found that he wanted to, and that troubled him as they walked through the sliding doors into the reception area of the hospital.

Grand Deacon Ellers had clearly been true to his word. A Holy Warrior medic awaited them just inside. "You can go," he told the Holy Warriors, who nodded and left, Duncan giving Richard one last suspicious look before exiting.

The medic jerked his head toward the hallway that led off the deserted reception area. Richard followed him. "Pretty primitive conditions here," the medic said conversationally as they walked. "They don't seem to have advanced much since pre-Salvation days."

Richard looked around. He couldn't tell; to him it looked a lot like any other hospital he'd ever been in: the same white-and-blue corridors, the same beds, the same cryptic signs. But the beds were empty and the rooms they passed, offices and labs and patients' rooms alike, had a disordered look as though people had fled them in a hurry. "Where are the patients and doctors?"

"Still here," the medic said. "We just moved them all into a single wing, so we could secure it better. They're all normal humans, so it's no problem."

"There aren't any Selkies here?"

"No, they had their own hospital down in the harbor," the medic said indifferently. "One of those half-submerged buildings. Three times the size of this dinky place. Took a couple of direct hits. We don't have to worry about it." Two Holy Warriors stood guard at a fire door up ahead; the medic nodded to them and they let him and Richard pass without challenge.

Beyond the fire door, the hospital seemed more normal. People in blue, green, and white coats moved from room to room and an orderly pushed someone on a stretcher through swinging doors, but Richard didn't get a good look at any of them: the medic gestured to a door immediately to their right. "In here."

Richard followed him in, but in his mind, he couldn't help picturing that other hospital, the one in New Botany Bay. Early morning, nurses doing their rounds, patients sleeping . . . Selkie patients, but still . . .

And then . . . explosions, fire, screaming, smoke, crushing darkness, pain, death. Death. And more death. And those who survived . . .

. . . no rescue. No relief. A slow death instead of a quick death, in a place that should have been a place of shelter, a place of succor and relief from pain.

They were just Selkies, he thought fiercely. *They're not human!*

But again, he thought of the Selkie woman who had let him go and saved his life.

Dogs aren't human, either, he argued with himself. *But I wouldn't bomb a veterinary hospital.*

It's war. Things like that happen in war.

If this is war, why is only one side shooting?

The medic first took a look at Richard's leg. "Looks like the guys on the boat did a good job," he said. "It should heal fine. Come back in a couple of days and we'll check it again."

Then he stabbed a needle into the crook of Richard's elbow to draw blood. "It will take a few minutes to run the various tests. I could use this stuff," the tech gestured at the racks of diagnostic equipment that lined the walls, "but it's all museum pieces. I'll just run down to our own portable lab. You can wait here, if you like."

"Can I look around the hospital instead?" Richard said.

The tech looked startled. "Sure, if you want to. Both floors in this wing are guarded, and anyway, the staff and patients haven't given us any trouble." He shook his head. "I don't understand them, though. Here we've liberated them from the rule of mutants and they look at us like we're the bad guys. Stockholm syndrome gets pretty bad after a few decades, I guess. Well, I'll meet you back here in fifteen minutes." He went out.

For a moment, Richard stayed put. He wasn't sure why he'd asked to see the rest of the hospital. The strange confusion that seemed to have gripped him was unlikely to be eased by whatever he might see. *I'm an observer, damn it*, he told himself. *It's my* job *to look around. I don't have to make any policy decisions, anyway, thank God. I just have to tell Cheveldeoff what I've seen.*

He got down off the examining table and headed out the door.

Again, he was struck by how little difference there was between this hospital and those he'd visited on Earth. It even smelled the same, of strong disinfectant, mostly, occasionally mingled with the less pleasant smells associated with the very old and the very sick. He passed doctors and nurses who looked pale and worried and gave him a wide berth—the locals, he guessed. The patients watched him from their beds with eyes variously wide with curiosity, narrowed with anger, or clouded with pain or drugs. No one spoke to him except for the Holy Warriors guarding each floor. "Quiet place," one said. "Guess they haven't warmed up to us yet."

"Have you talked to anyone?" Richard asked.

"Most of them won't talk," the Warrior said. "Not to us. Except for one." He pointed down the hall. "Second door on the right. He's had a few things to say." He laughed. "Crusty old coot. Haven't heard language like that since basic training."

"Thanks." Richard headed down the hall toward the indicated door.

"He'll blister your ears!" the Holy Warrior called after him, and laughed again.

The "old coot" certainly looked old. He lay with his eyes closed, so painfully thin that he barely raised a bump in the blue blanket covering him, except for the twin hills formed by his feet. His skin had the white, papery appearance of someone who hadn't left his bed for a very long time, and was unlikely to leave it ever again. A handful of silver hairs stuck up at apparently random intervals from his brown-mottled pate. An IV fed something into his scrawny left arm, lying exposed on top of the blanket, and a metabolic monitor beeped, clicked, and flashed. Several of the indicators showed yellow warning lights.

Richard hesitated in the doorway, not wanting to wake the old man, but just as he'd made up his mind to leave, the man's eyes opened. They were a startling bright blue. "What do you want?" he growled. "Bastard."

Richard stepped closer. "No need to call me names," he said.

"Can't pull a gun and shoot you. What have I got but names?" The old man's face contorted. "I'd spit in your face if I had enough spit," he growled. "But my throat's too dry."

A carafe of water and two glasses stood on a table by the bed. Richard filled one of the glasses and held it to the man's lips. He hesitated, then accepted the drink. But he took only two swallows before a fit of coughing seized him. Richard pulled back the glass. "Damn it," the old man wheezed when he'd managed to gain control of his breathing again, "that actor lied."

"What actor?"

"The one that said dying is easy, comedy is hard. Dying is damn hard, too." The old man squinted at Richard. "You're not a doctor. And you're not one of those motherless Holy Warriors, either, unless you're out of uniform. So who the hell are you, and why are you bothering an old man on his deathbed? Haven't you got some nice Selkie babies to kill?"

"My name is Richard Hansen," Richard said quietly. "No, I'm not a doctor or a Holy Warrior. I'm just an observer."

"Hansen? Well, that's a kick." The old man wheezed a laugh. "A Hansen in Hansen's Harbor who's not related to Victor Hansen. Never thought I'd see the day." He snorted. "Wish I hadn't, considering it's the end of the world."

"Actually, I am related to Victor Hansen," Hansen said. He hesitated. *Is this really a good idea?* he wondered, then, *Well, what harm can it do. He's hardly going to climb out of bed and attack me. He already would have, if he could.* "I'm his grandson."

"His—" The old man squinted. "Damn these old eyes," he said. "I can't . . . come closer."

Stepping a little closer, but not too close, Richard leaned

down toward the old man, who turned his head to get a better view. His eyes widened.

"Shit," he said. "It's true. You look just like him, like a younger him. Like he looked when I first saw him."

Richard gasped as though someone had thrown ice water in his face. "You . . . you knew my grandfather?"

"Hell, yeah. I mean, I was just a kid . . . but of course I knew him. There weren't that many of us basics—that's what we called ourselves then—on the ship. We all knew each other, kids and grown-ups alike." That had obviously been a long speech for him. He had to stop and catch his breath, and for a moment he lay with his eyes closed, chest heaving. Richard wanted to shake him, but all he could do was wait. Finally, the old man opened his eyes again. "I'm the last one," he said. "Last one of the First Landers. Landlings live longer than Selkies, so there's none of *them* left. And even the kids that were littler than me when we landed are gone now. I've outlived 'em all. Wish I hadn't." He took a few more labored breaths. "Saw the beginning of Marseguro. Never thought I'd see the end." His voice roughened with emotion, emotion that also seemed to give him a burst of energy. "And never thought the grandson of Victor Hansen would be part of ending it."

"What . . . what can you tell me about him?" Richard said. "What happened on the ship? What was he like? How . . . how did he find this place? What—"

The old man laughed, a harsh, pain-filled sound. "Why should I answer your questions, you fucking traitorous genocidal asshole? You want to know about your grandfather? Here's all you need to know: he was a better man than you or that cocksucker you call an Avatar will ever be, and if he were here, he'd tell you the same thing I'm telling you: go to hell. I'll be along to join you soon enough, and then I'll kick your ass for all eternity . . ." He began coughing again, and this time he didn't stop. Several of the metabolic monitor's readings slipped into the red and an alarm began whooping. As doctors and nurses ran in, Richard backed out. "What have you done?" one of the doctors snarled at him as he went past. "You've finished killing the Selkies, now it's our turn?"

"I didn't . . ." Richard began, but no one was listening to him.

He watched the doctors and nurses work for a moment, then turn and walked away, deliberately taking a route that didn't lead him past the Holy Warrior who had pointed him to the old man. Avoiding everyone, he made his way back to the lab where the medtech had taken his blood. Shaken, he'd barely sat down on the examining table when the door opened. The medtech entered carrying a datapad. He gave Richard an odd look. "Are you all right?"

"Sure," Richard said. "I'm fine." But he wasn't, and he knew it. From the moment he'd landed on this planet, the foundation he'd built his life on had been slowly eroding. He felt like his very soul stood on shifting sands instead of solid rock.

And then the medtech gave his tottering belief system a good, solid shove.

"Well, I know why the hunterbot came after you," he said. "It's the strangest thing, and I can't explain it. I mean, it's obviously nonsense, but . . ."

"Just tell me," Richard said.

The medtech held out the datapad. Richard took it and glanced at it, but the strings of numbers and letters it displayed meant nothing to him. "Selkies have a great many difference in their genome from normal humans, but just to make it simple, we picked one particular extended sequence of DNA that every Selkie has. It doesn't seem to code for anything—it's what we call 'junk DNA'—but we've never seen it in normal humans. Until now." He came to Richard's side and pointed at something on the datapad. It still didn't mean anything to Richard. "You've got that same sequence, Mr. Hansen. Based on your blood, you're a Selkie."

If Richard hadn't been sitting, he almost certainly would have fallen. Because suddenly, a great many things made sense—and the sense they made hit him with the force of a whole world turning upside down.

Chapter 12

THE REST OF EMILY'S journey to Jumpoff Station passed uneventfully, compared to the first part: no boats, no strange landlings, no multitentacled killerbots tracking her down to blow her into pink froth . . .

She shook her head. *Dahlia. Maybe John, too . . .*

My parents . . .

How many are dead?

They'll know at Jumpoff.

Wishing she could somehow make the sputa go faster, she pressed on.

The station first appeared on her navigation screen, but just a few minutes later, she also saw its lights, and felt relieved. Until that moment, she hadn't wanted to admit her greatest fear: that the attackers had already destroyed the station and everyone in it.

She was even more relieved to detect two other sputas heading out from the station to intercept her. Their headlights blinded her to everything else as they approached, but when one swung in front of her, she glimpsed the helmetless operator. *Selkie,* she thought. *The station* must *still be intact, and still in our hands.*

But the greatest relief of all came when she swam up into one of the entry pools—Jumpoff Station consisted of a dozen habitats the size of Dahlia's family's, all linked together and surrounding a truly enormous sphere bigger than anything in New Botany Bay—and saw who was waiting for her. "Mother! Amy!" And then, without any warning at all, she burst into tears.

An hour later, with a sub already on its way to the habitat where she had left poor John, she sat on a bed in the hospital habitat, sipping blueblad tea and wrapped in a warming cloak. Amy sat beside her, her arm around her back, which would have been uncomfortable except that her multiple scrapes and cuts had just been cleaned, desensitized, and spray-sealed by the doctor who had just left the room. As it was, she welcomed the addition of Amy's body heat to that of her cloak. Selkies rarely suffered from hypothermia, but she'd almost managed it. She suspected it had more to do with shock than the temperature of the water.

Her mother had just delivered a different kind of shock, telling her in short, bald sentences what the Body Purified had done to Marseguro and its people—so far.

Casualties had been horrendous, she had said. Nobody knew how horrendous, because they didn't dare radio for fear of giving away their location. But they had heard the other towns talking before they, too, fell silent. "We think a lot of Selkies have made it to the emergency deep-sea habitats, or are en route to them," Emily's mother said.

Dr. Christianson-Wood looked tired, and somehow older than Emily had ever seen her look, even though Selkie faces didn't wrinkle as landlings' did when they aged. "We don't expect to see very many of them here, though, because we're so far offshore and most Selkies think this is just a tiny research hab."

"Dad . . . ?" Emily said in a small voice, dreading the answer. Amy squeezed her hand.

Her mother shook her head. "I just don't know. I . . ." Her voice broke, and she blinked and looked away before continuing. "It's only luck that I'm here . . . and even luckier that Amy is."

Emily looked at her sister. "What *are* you doing here?"

"I felt bad about . . . that argument we had," Amy said. "I knew Mom was planning to come out here, and I thought, maybe if I went with her, we could talk, I could make her see . . . it was just a spur-of-the-moment decision."

"We left in the middle of the night," her mother said.

"But you didn't tell me!" Emily said. "I thought you were still asleep."

"I didn't tell you because . . . we weren't really talking. I didn't even tell you we were going. I was . . . still upset with you. I left your father sleeping. I didn't even wake him." Her voice broke. She pressed her lips together and took a deep breath before adding, in a voice as cold and bleak as the bottom of the Deep, "I didn't even say good-bye to him." She fell silent, looking down at her hands. She fingered the ring on her finger. "I'll hope for the best until hope is gone."

"I didn't really make up my mind to go with her until just before I went to bed," Amy said. "I surprised her by getting up when she did. We found out about the attack when we reached Jumpoff." She squeezed Emily's hand again. "I didn't say good-bye to Dad, either. I haven't even really talked to him since . . ."

"Me, either," Emily said. "Oh, Amy." She hugged her sister close to her, and a moment later, their mother joined them, her arms around them as they had been so many times while they were growing up, but this time, Emily sensed, as much to take comfort from them as to give it.

They clung together for an indeterminate time, until at last Dr. Christianson-Wood pulled away, wiping her eyes. Emily wiped her own. She'd been focused on survival, then on getting help for John. Now, for the first time, she could think about the larger picture, and it terrified her. "What are we going to do, Mama?" she almost whispered. "They've destroyed our cities and towns . . . they've killed . . . God, they may have killed hundreds of us. Thousands. We have no weapons, no way to fight back. What are we going to do? Are we going to . . ." She paused, almost afraid to finish her question. "Are we going to surrender?"

Her mother had looked small and defeated as she stepped back from her daughters, but now she looked up, eyes flashing in the cold medical light, and her back stiffened. "We will not," she said. "And we *do* have weapons. We can—and *will*—fight back."

Emily blinked all three eyelids. "We do? We will?"

Amy seemed as startled as she felt. "What are you talking about, Mama?"

Dr. Christianson-Wood looked at her daughters as though taking their measure. "Have you ever wondered why this station exists, girls?" she said softly. "Or what we do here?"

"Research," Emily said. "Deep-sea research."

"It's on the edge of the abyss," Amy said.

"It is," her mother agreed. "In more ways than one." She

hesitated. "Emily, Amy, what I'm about to tell you has always been secret. Even most of the people who work here don't know about it.

"Yes, most of the research conducted here is what you'd expect: we launch probe-subs into the Deep, we map the ocean bottom, we experiment with technology that might allow Selkies, even landlings, to someday colonize every part of this planet. But there's a habitat, the only one not directly linked to the main complex, that is off-limits to everyone except a small group of people, mostly geneticists, a few medical doctors."

She started pacing. "Victor Hansen never believed Marseguro would remain hidden from Earth forever. He hoped that by the time the rest of humanity found us, the Body Purified would be just a historical curiosity, a brief fling with unreason in a time of threatened destruction. But he didn't rely only on hope. He launched a research program designed to protect Marseguro.

"For the last ten years, I've been the head of the program. And a little over a year ago, my research into Marseguroite viruses allowed us to bring the program to a successful conclusion." She stopped pacing and faced Emily and Amy squarely. "As Victor Hansen wanted, we've created a biological weapon, a weapon that strikes fast, and hard, and is almost impossible to defend against. A year ago, we deployed it. And now we're ready to use it . . . against the Holy Warriors."

Emily stared at her. She couldn't have heard right. "But . . . biological weapons were banned long before the asteroid threatened Earth. Victor Hansen himself helped negotiate the worldwide treaty! After the War . . ."

Beside her, Amy nodded vigorously. "They even scrubbed all the information about bioweapons research out of the computer networks. We learned about it in school."

"Yes, they were banned and rooted out on Earth, where there were multiple nations, nongovernmental organizations, and shadowy terrorist groups, any of which could have launched a plague that would have devastated the Earth as surely as the asteroid eventually threatened to do," her mother said. "But our situation is somewhat different, don't you agree? We have always had only one possible, well-defined enemy, the one that already tried to destroy us: the Body Purified. We would never use the weapon against anyone from Marseguro. It is a weapon with only one target. And now that target has presented itself, and beyond any doubt has given us *casus belli.*"

"But . . . one reason biological weapons were banned is because they affect *everyone,*" Emily said. "You can't limit their effect."

"On *Earth,* they couldn't limit their effects, because all humans are the same," her mother said. "*On Earth.* But not here. Here there are two kinds of humans. Selkies, and . . . and the others."

Emily felt cold again despite the warming cloak she wore. "You've made a biological weapon that only affects *landlings*?" she whispered.

"But . . . you can't . . . you'll kill all the non-Selkie Marseguroites!" Amy protested.

"No!" Her mother made a violent chopping gesture. "No," she said more softly. "If we did that, we truly would be the subhuman monsters the Avatar calls us. No, Emily, Amy, we won't do that. Before we made the decision to deploy the weapon, we created a vaccine—a hypervaccine, really, one that provides immunity within minutes of its injection, thanks to some cleverly designed nanobots. Those who receive it will live. Those who do not will die. Horribly."

"But how will you get the vaccine to our landlings?" Emily said. "Without warning the Holy Warriors?"

"Selkies have volunteered to go into every community and secretly vaccinate as many landlings as they can find—and give them their own doses of vaccine so they can then vaccinate everyone *they* can find."

"But . . ." Emily shook her head. She couldn't believe what she was hearing. "You can't possibly get them all. What happens to the landlings that are missed?"

Dr. Christianson-Wood turned even paler, but her voice remained steady. "They will die," she said. "And we will grieve for them. But civilian casualties are an inevitable result of war. If you are unwilling to risk them, you cannot win: and if we do not win this war, Marseguro will cease to exist, and so will the Selkies." She suddenly turned toward a vidscreen on the wall of the examining room. "I wasn't going to show either of you this—I wanted to protect you—but I must. I *can't* protect you from what we are about to do—and therefore I should not protect you from what has been done to us. So watch, and then judge." She raised her voice. "Computer, display vidrecord Alpha Three Nine Gamma, vidscreen nearest my present location. Start playback in ten seconds." She turned back to Emily as the screen behind her lit. "This is video from one of the assault craft that conducted the initial attack on Hansen's Harbor. We intercepted it before we decided the risk was too great and pulled down our floating arrays."

The playback began, and Emily watched in horror as the Body Purified destroyed her world.

Buildings she had known all her life vanished in orange blossoms of flame, then collapsed into smoking or steaming rubble. She heard Amy gasp as the above-water tower of the school where she had planned to study dance and Amy to study opera split like a gutted fish at the impact of a missile, half of it sliding into the water, the other half left shattered, twisted, and burning. And though few people were about at that time of the morning, she caught glimpses of bodies flung through the air to lie crumpled and still . . . and bodies floating in the now black-and-greasy water of New Botany Bay.

But not all were floating. Selkies began appearing on the surface, swimming up to see what was happening, some naked from their beds . . . and as she watched, the image tilted and turned. Lines of white fire traced the paths of bullets as they ripped into the bay and the Selkies swimming there, tearing apart flesh and bone, adding spreading washes of red to the already fouled water. Amy cried out and covered her eyes.

Emily closed her own eyes. "Shut it off," she begged her mother. "Shut it off."

"Computer, end vid playback," Dr. Christianson-Wood said, but Emily kept her eyes closed.

"We must strike back, Emily," her mother said softly into her personal darkness. "We must strike back, or be utterly destroyed."

Emily could still see the terrible images. She suspected she always would. She opened her eyes and looked at her mother's drawn face. "Yes," she said. "Yes. I understand."

And as she said it, something woke inside her, something hot and wild and angry. *I had one in my hands,* she thought. *I had one of those Earth bastards in my hands, and I let him get away. I* helped *him get away.*

I won't make that mistake again.

"And I want to help." She kept her eyes locked on her mother's. "I want to be one of the ones to help distribute the vaccine."

"Emily . . ." Amy said beside her, sounding horrified.

Her mother opened her mouth, almost certainly to say, "No," but something in Emily's expression must have stopped her. Slowly, she nodded.

"Fair enough."

"Mom!" Amy said. Her arm tightened around Emily's shoulders.

Emily shrugged it off and turned on her, though she knew the anger rising in her didn't really have anything to do with Amy's protectiveness. "We can't just sit here, Amy! You saw what they did. We have to help."

"There are other ways," Amy said. "They need people here, too. We're expecting refugees. There may be wounded. I've volunteered to—"

"And that's fine," Emily said. "For you. But not for me." Her throat tightened. "My God, Amy, they've probably killed Dad. They certainly killed Dahlia. They may have killed John. Who knows how many more of our friends are dead?" She looked at her mom. "Have we heard anything from Uncle Dwight in Firstdip?" Dwight was Dr. Christianson-Wood's brother. Emily's mother shook her head. "Or Uncle Phillip?" Phillip was Emily's father's brother. "He was out at sea somewhere, wasn't he?"

"Nothing," Dr. Christianson-Wood said.

Emily looked at Amy's tear-streaked face. "They may have killed our whole family. We may be all that's left. Doesn't that make you want to strike back?"

"Yes, but . . ." Amy held out her hands to Emily. "I don't want to lose you, too."

Emily took the proffered hands, hands that she remembered lifting her up when she was little, helping her to her feet after she'd taken a tumble, pulling her out of the water after they'd swum home together from school, hugging her on her birthday. Amy had always looked out for her, protected her little sister as best she could. "I'm not a little girl anymore, Amy," she said. "And neither are you. You can't protect me anymore."

"You may not be a little girl, but you're still my little sister," Amy said. "Emily, if you have to do this . . . please, please be careful." She squeezed Emily's hands; Emily squeezed back, hard.

"I will." But she knew it was a promise she couldn't really keep.

Dr. Christianson-Wood took a deep, ragged breath. "I'm proud of both of you," she said. "Emily, you know I don't want you to go, either. But if you must . . . I won't stop you. It's not a time for any of us to worry about our own safety." She touched a control; the door slid open. "You'd better come with me. We don't have much time."

They left Amy still sitting on the bed in the examining room, head bowed, holding Emily's warming cloak in her lap.

Emily's mother led her through air tunnels to her main lab in one of the smaller and more nondescript habitats, talking as they went.

Nobody knew when Victor Hansen had conceived of the last-ditch defense of Marseguro, she said. During his lifetime, he had done nothing to implement it. The very real threat of everyone starving to death in those early years had overshadowed the much more remote threat of being found by Earth's Holy Warriors, especially since Hansen had known Earth had its own recovery to look after in the aftermath of the Day of Salvation and the brief but violent Moon War. (Before they were destroyed by the same fleet the *Rivers of Babylon* had barely eluded, Luna's mass-drivers had landed a couple of wallops on Earth as hard or harder than those delivered by the pieces of asteroid that had not been deflected.)

But before he died at an improbably (as he himself said at his ninetieth Earth-year birthday celebration) ripe old age, Victor Hansen had left detailed instructions for the Council. Not all were followed—despite the reverence the Selkies held for Dr. Hansen, they knew well enough that while he might be their Creator, he certainly wasn't God— but his suggestion that they secretly research a doomsday weapon to counter some possible future attack from Earth had been.

"In every town, there are hidden germbombs." They'd reached the lab, and Emily's mother had called up a display of Hansen's Harbor on her biggest vidscreen. She pointed to the Square. "In Hansen's Harbor, there are several small ones, and one really big one—right here, under the pavement, not far from where the statue of Victor Hansen stood. Remember all that work on the fountain last year? That was the cover for installing the biggest bomb." She smiled grimly. "It seemed appropriate.

"When we send the signal, those bombs will explode. They're powerful enough to kill anyone nearby and destroy any vehicles that might be above them—but the explosion is only a way to make sure that the real destructive contents, our nasty little bugs, are spread far and wide.

"The thing multiplies unbelievably fast. It's highly infectious. It can be passed from one human to another with the most casual of contact: a touch, a sneeze, sharing an item of clothing. Not only that, it has a symbiotic rather than destructive relationship with many widespread Marseguro bacteria: that is, it can use their genetic machinery to reproduce itself without necessarily killing the host. That means that on Marseguro—or on the Holy Warrior ship, which I suspect has been thoroughly colonized by those otherwise harmless bacteria, whether the Holy Warriors realize it or not—it doesn't need to pass from human to human. It can reproduce on its own—not as fast, but fast enough. So simply quarantining those who are sick isn't enough to stop the spread of infection. It will colonize and contaminate air, water, and soil. And it will kill any nonmodified human it infects within a day."

"How?" Emily said. *Horribly, I hope.*

She needn't have worried. "It's a fast-acting hemorrhagic fever," her mother said. "A kind of super-Ebola. The first symptoms—if our computer simulations are correct, since we obviously haven't tested it in an actual human being—will appear within minutes of infection. A tickle in the throat, maybe a bit of soreness. A nosebleed. Within hours, a debilitating headache, followed by extreme lethargy, internal hemorrhaging . . . death."

"Is there a treatment?"

"None we've been able to devise," her mother said. "Except for the hypervaccine, and it has to be taken either before exposure or within six hours of exposure to be effective. It should be completely effective if taken before exposure, and about sixty-five to seventy percent effective after exposure, with its effectiveness dropping off as the time from exposure increases . . . as you'd expect."

"So the volunteers' task is to get the vaccine to as many of 'our' landlings as possible before the bombs are detonated."

"Yes. Without being killed, preferably." Emily's mother tried to smile, but couldn't quite make it convincing. "Please, without getting killed, Emily. Your father . . . your uncles . . . may be . . . I don't . . ." Her lower lip trembled and she pressed her mouth tight.

"I don't intend to get killed," Emily said. "They've already tried once, remember. If their super-duper underwater killerbot couldn't kill me, I don't see an ordinary stupid landling managing it."

As if the one has anything to do with the other, Emily thought, but she'd watched enough adventure vids to know how the dialogue was supposed to go in these situations. *You say what you have to in order to keep going. Otherwise, you might as well curl up and die.*

Her mother's left eyebrow raised; she knew all the clichés, too. "All right, then. Have you thought about where you want to go?"

Emily nodded. "There's only one place, isn't there? One place I know better than anywhere else." She pointed at the screen. "Hansen's Harbor."

Grand Deacon Ellers stared at the report from the medtech while Richard, once more back at Government House, stood silently by. "What does this mean?" Ellers growled.

"It doesn't mean anything," Richard lied. "It's just some fluke. You know I'm not Selkie."

Ellers gave him a look that matched his growl. "I can see that. But I don't understand how this could happen."

The medtech hadn't come back to Government House himself; instead, he'd called in an expert. The expedition included a geneticist of the Body-approved variety, a Dr. Jan Aylmer. A tiny woman with steel-gray hair, she had arrived just moments before and now peered nearsightedly at her datapad. Getting no satisfaction from Richard, the Grand Deacon turned to her. "Well?"

"I see two possibilities," Dr. Aylmer said. Her voice, so deep it could almost be called sultry, belied her tiny size. "One, this is merely coincidence. The number of base pairs involved, however, makes that extremely unlikely.

"Two, and I think this more likely: Victor Hansen used his own genetic material to create the Selkies."

Richard, who had come to the same conclusion the moment he heard the news, felt a chill that had nothing to do with the air temperature.

Ellers looked skeptical. "If he had, surely that stretch of DNA would not have survived in every Selkie, through — what, three generations now?"

"Not unless he *designed* it to survive. It's 'junk' DNA — DNA that does not, so far as we know, code for any proteins." She tapped the screen. "I think it's Dr. Victor Hansen's . . . well, call it a signature . . . and I think it originated in his own DNA."

"Then why does *he* have it?" Ellers indicated Richard. "If Victor Hansen had to carefully design the Selkies to ensure that that piece of DNA remained untouched from generation to generation, how did it end up in *him*? He may be Hansen's grandson, but that still means only a quarter of his genes are Hansen's."

"Perhaps the answer lies in Hansen's own genome," Dr. Aylmer said. "We do have a copy of it on record up on *Sanctification,* since he lived at the time when everyone's genome was sequenced and stored, by law, for medical and evidentiary purposes." She touched the screen of her datapad. "I think they've got the airnet up and . . . yes, here we go. Computer, ID me."

"Dr. Jan Aylmer, chief geneticist, Blessed Avatar Hospital, currently assigned to Extraterrestrial Purification Force, Holy Warriors."

"Computer, access and upload to this unit the genome on record for Dr. Victor Edmund Hansen."

A pause. "Done," said the computer.

"Computer, switch voice control to local access node."

"Done," said the computer, but this time the voice came from the display showing Richard's genome.

"Computer," Dr. Aylmer said, "compare genomes of Victor Edmund Hansen and Richard Arthur Hansen."

Another pause.

"Genomes are identical," the computer said.

"*What?*" the explosive syllable came from the Grand Deacon. Richard couldn't speak; the chill he'd felt had become cryogenic, freezing him solid.

"Computer, recheck and confirm," Dr. Aylmer snapped.

"Genomes are identical," the computer repeated.

Dr. Aylmer turned and stared at Richard as though he'd turned into a poisonous snake in front of her eyes. "Clone," she said. "He's a clone." She pointed a finger at him. "Anathema!"

Richard still couldn't speak. He'd guessed, when the medtech told him what he'd discovered, that the Selkies were his kin, almost literally cousins, children of the children of his grandfather. That had been troubling enough, but this?

This couldn't be happening. A clone? How? Why? It didn't make any sense.

But genomes don't lie, he thought. The results were right there for him to see. And they spelled the end of any hope he had of rising in the Body, of shaking off the taint of carrying Victor Hansen's genes. They spelled the end of everything.

He wasn't just related to Victor Hansen; in some ways, he *was* Victor Hansen, the most vilified man in the short history of the Body Purified.

No, it's worse than that. To the Body, a clone is no better than a moddie. To the Body, I'm not even human . . . I'm no more human than the Selkies. Maybe less.

He didn't realize he'd been backing up until he bumped into the wall. Grand Deacon Ellers' shocked stare transformed into a glare of fury. "Arrest this . . . thing," he said to the two Holy Warriors who stood at attention at the door.

"Grand Deacon—" Richard began to protest.

"Silence, or be silenced," the Grand Deacon said. The faces of the Holy Warriors headed his way might have been cast in steel; Richard had no doubt they would be glad to do the silencing. "Two good Holy Warriors are dead because of you, *clone*," the Grand Deacon snarled. "Trained, seasoned men, and yet they're dead and you, somehow, are alive. No wonder the Selkie bitch let you go—you're one of their inhuman kind. Hell, you're a clone of their God. You bear the mark of the beast in your very DNA."

But I led you here, Richard wanted to cry out. *You'd never have known this planet existed if I hadn't been searching for any clue.*

Except somehow he'd known where to look. And somehow he'd known other things since then. And thought other things. Things that made no sense, things that didn't come from *his* experiences, from the things *he'd* learned.

Clones are just identical twins. They don't contain the memories and personalities of the original person!

But that same strange part of his brain that had been bubbling up odd thoughts and emotions for weeks seemed . . . unsurprised.

God! Richard thought, as sudden realization almost choked him with panic. *Grandfather Hansen is inside my head!*

The Holy Warriors seized his arms and held him tight. The Grand Deacon suddenly strode over to him, and Richard flinched, fully expecting a blow. "So why did you really lead us here?" Ellers demanded. "Did you know we were about to find this planet anyway, and you thought this way you'd at least have a chance to warn them? What did you tell that Selkie bitch? She was your contact, wasn't she?"

Richard could only shake his head.

"Speak!" Ellers ordered.

"I didn't know I was a . . ." Richard swallowed; he could barely say it himself. ". . . a clone until this moment, I swear, Grand Deacon. Everything I have done I have done in good faith. Everything has happened just the way I said!"

. . . except for the little matter of tips coming from the ghost of my grandfather . . .

He'd thought he might be going mad. Now he was almost certain of it.

And if *he* were a clone . . .

Father, Richard thought. *Father must have been a clone, too. I'm not really his son at all. And he* did *go mad . . . did he hear these voices, feel these feelings? Is that what—literally—drove him over the edge?*

"Lies," the Grand Deacon said. "You're a clone of Victor Hansen. How can you possibly expect me to believe anything you say?" He gestured to the Holy Warriors. "Take him to the prison. The Interrogation Team can have him when they return from Firstdip."

Once again Richard found himself escorted by two Holy Warriors; but this time they weren't there to protect him but to guard him, and this time they didn't walk in front and behind, but half-dragged him, each holding an arm in a painful, iron-hard grip.

Despite their roughness, his legs felt so wobbly he was almost grateful for their support.

The Hansen's Harbor Criminal Detention Center, untouched by the Holy Warriors' aerial attack, stood in an empty cobblestoned courtyard several blocks from Government House, on the inland edge of Hansen's Harbor. A long, low building, it contained just a dozen cells and had a single entrance at one end, where two very bored-looking Holy Warriors stood watch in a guardroom. Inside, the cells opened, six on each side, off a central corridor. Whoever had laid out the cells must have gotten his ideas of jails from old vids, because the cells were made of concrete blocks and their doors were open steel bars. Harsh halogen lights lit the hall and the contents of each cell: a fold-down bed/bench, a toilet, a sink, and a shower stall.

Only two cells contained inmates, Richard saw as his guards dragged him down the hall to the cell farthest from the guardroom. In one a fat, balding man slept, or at least lay, with his back to the corridor. The other inmate, though, leaped to his feet and watched with wide eyes as Richard passed.

It was Chris Keating.

The door clanged shut and the Holy Warriors clomped out. Richard heard the door into the guardroom slam shut.

"Richard Hansen?" he heard Keating's voice. "Can you hear me?"

Richard ignored him. He sat on the barely-padded bed/bench beneath the tiny window, and put his head in his hands.

"Damn you, Victor Hansen," he whispered. "I've spent my whole life trying to escape you and what you did, and now I find out I *am* you."

Why had Victor done it? Why leave clones of himself

behind on a planet taken over by a religion that considered them monsters?

And from that strange repository of memory and emotion Victor Hansen had apparently *also* managed to leave behind in his clones, Richard dredged up an answer. It didn't feel like a guess, or something he had reasoned out: he just *knew,* the same way he knew his name or . . . former . . . address.

Grandfather didn't believe the Body would remain in power long, Richard thought. *And he didn't want the Selkies to be cut off from the rest of humanity forever. He left his clones in someone else's care* . . . Richard half-remembered a name, had it on the tip of his tongue . . . but he couldn't bring it forward, and lost it again.

Something must have gone wrong, and only one thing *could* have gone wrong. The Body. Somehow, the Body had learned of the clones' existence. The Body must have had them . . . decanted. At least in Richard's case, and probably in his father's.

Richard's father had told him his mother died in childbirth. He'd rarely said much else about her, except that he had loved her very much, and it had seemed like a miracle when they met, that such a beautiful woman would take such an intense interest in an ordinary Body functionary like him.

I'll bet it was a miracle, Richard thought. *A miracle of the Avatar. The Body arranged that marriage. The Body implanted me in her. And the Body made sure she died in childbirth, so the secret would remain safe.*

The Body raised me, and probably Father, for one reason: so that we could help lead them to Victor Hansen's Selkies. They must have known not only that we were clones, but that somehow . . . how, Richard could only dimly imagine . . . *Victor managed to implant a portion of his memories and personality in us, as well.*

Hansen's little experiment killed my father, Richard thought. *Except he wasn't really my father at all, was he? He was my* . . . *elder twin brother.*

From the point of view of the Body, Richard's father had been a failed experiment. Richard, though . . .

Richard thought of the Selkie bodies floating in the harbor, the greasy black smoke pouring up from the shattered buildings, the little Selkie girl in the arms of her mother, in a cage . . .

I've been a tremendous success.

For the first time in his life, Richard wished *he* had a building to throw himself off of.

The Grand Deacon is right, he thought blackly. *I am a subhuman monster . . . but not because I'm a clone.*

Because of what I've done.

"Richard Hansen! Richard Hansen!" Chris Keating kept calling from the other cell, but Richard, sunk in shame and bitter regret, berated by both his own conscience and the lurking ghost of his grandfather, barely heard him.

For ten minutes Chris Keating called Richard Hansen's name, but finally gave up and sat back down on his bed. *Why is* he *a prisoner? What's going on?*

The last time Chris had seen him, Hansen had been getting on the boat with the two Holy Warriors, about to set off in pursuit of John Duval. Now Hansen was here, and obviously no longer in the good graces of the Grand Deacon. *Did something happen on the boat? Or is he simply being disciplined for getting in the boat without permission?*

But he's an observer for Archdeacon Cheveldeoff. And the Grand Deacon said he's in charge of intelligence gathering. Why should he have *to ask permission?*

Too many questions, no answers, and none likely to be forthcoming. Chris didn't even understand why *he* remained in prison. Most of the other landlings he had seen in the cells had been kept and questioned for a few hours, then released. But not him, even after all he had done to bring about the Purification of Marseguro.

In a way it comforted him to see someone else imprisoned for no reason he could imagine. *The Grand Deacon is just being firm,* he thought. *This is an ungodly planet. Its Purification must not be impeded. He's not certain of me and has no time to make certain of me, so he's just put me here for the time being, for safekeeping. Maybe even for my own protection. Hansen told those Selkies what I did. If word got around . . .*

He shivered. Maybe prison wasn't such a bad place to be after all. *When things have settled down, Ellers will send for*

*me, and then I can show him just how helpful I can be . . .
and earn a ticket to Old Earth.*

Once he had the ear of the Grand Deacon, he could find
out what Hansen had done.

For now, he could only do what he'd been doing for two
days.

He waited.

Chapter 13

THE PROPHYLACTIC PATROL, as someone had dubbed them, set out from Jumpoff Station over the space of two hours as darkness fell far above on the second day of the invasion. There were thirty-six Selkies in all, twenty men and sixteen women, all wearing special black landsuits, the Selkie equivalent of the survival suit worn by the landling Emily now so much regretted allowing to escape.

The landsuits kept them both wet and cool. Wearing them, they could stay on land indefinitely. Better yet, the landsuits would also make it harder for infrared-based sensors or night-vision equipment to distinguish them from the background as they moved through the landling towns.

Each landsuit had also been equipped with two forearm dart-guns, loaded with four compressed-air-powered darts apiece. The guns were normally used to ward off hungry ocean predators. No one knew how effective the weapons would be on land, but they were the closest things to firearms available.

"We have one thing going for us: the invasion force is small," Emily's mother had told the assembled group as they suited up, Amy and other friends and family members of the volunteers looking on. Amy looked pale and worried, Emily thought. She suspected she did, too.

Her mother continued. "Survivors report no more than a dozen Holy Warriors in each small town, with maybe ten times that many in Hansen's Harbor, plus at least that many more supporting personnel.

"The Warriors are heavily armed, of course, and armored. Attacking them with improvised weapons or trying to overpower them would be suicide: the kill rate would be two or three hundred to one in their favor—or worse. Nevertheless, they are very few and even a small fishing port is a big place. If you keep your wits about you and keep your eyes open, you've got a good chance of going undetected."

"What if the landlings refuse the vaccinations?" a young man about Emily's age asked.

Emily shook her head. She already knew the answer.

"Then they will die," Emily's mother said. "That is their choice. Any other questions?"

"When will the detonation occur?"

Emily's mother looked at a man who stood behind her, one of the few bearded Selkies Emily had ever seen: Anton Scale, vice-chair of the Council. He nodded to her, assenting to whatever she was about to say.

Dr. Christianson-Wood turned back to the assembled Selkies. "The signal has already been sent," she said.

A shocked murmur ran through the group. She raised her hand. "I don't mean the germbombs have already detonated. I mean we've started a countdown." She glanced at a chronometer above the door of the main recreation hall where they were gathered, their somber black landsuits a sharp contrast to the brightly lit vidgames and vurtbooths lining the walls and the lights cycling through rainbow colors in the central pool that led to the underwater rec hall directly beneath. The design reminded Emily of the habitat belonging to Dahlia's family, and her heart clenched with sorrow and anger at the thought.

She still hadn't heard any news about John Duval.

"Detonation is at 0800 tomorrow," Dr. Christianson-Wood said. "Dawn, to ensure as much confusion as possible. You should all reach your targets by 2200 tonight. You'll have about twelve hours to vaccinate as many landlings as possible."

"What if there's a problem?" an older woman, probably in her mid-thirties, said from the middle of the front row. "What if we can't reach very many landlings? Will you delay the detonation?"

Emily's mother opened her mouth to reply, but Anton Scale stepped forward and held up a hand to forestall her. "This is a doomsday weapon," he said. "It always has been. 'Fire and forget.' Nothing *can* stop the detonation now. If this station is attacked and destroyed, if they run more bombing runs and level every town on the planet, they will still all be dead two days from now . . . and the Selkies that remain will begin to rebuild. They may intend to kill or enslave us all, but they can't do it in the time remaining to them."

There were no more questions. Emily glanced around the room. One or two Selkies met her eyes, than looked away. Many others stared at the floor, absorbing what they'd been told, or possibly praying, though from what Emily had seen, Hansen's Harbor's sacred buildings, Selkie and landling alike, had suffered the same fate as the secular ones. *They were probably specially targeted,* she thought. *No religion but the Body Purified can be permitted. They've driven Christians, Jews, Buddhists, Muslims, Animists, Wiccans, and every other flavor of unsanctioned belief to extinction or underground on Earth. They'd hardly spare them here.*

She looked up at Scale, who was talking in a low voice to Emily's mother. *He understands,* she thought. *There can be no negotiating with the Body. They don't want anything from us but our deaths. We're not human. We're a work of evil, and we must be eliminated.*

Which means we have to eliminate them first. Whatever the cost.

Finally, Emily looked at Amy. Their eyes met for a long moment; then Amy raised a hand in silent farewell, lowered her gaze, and slipped out of the room.

A moment later, the black-suited Selkies began slipping into the water.

They would travel in pairs, one pair each to the smallest communities of Parawing, Roger's Harbor, Rock Bottom and Good Beaching, two pairs each to the slightly larger towns of Beachcliff and Outtamyway, three pairs to Firstdip, and the remaining seven pairs to Hansen's Harbor.

Fred Notting, an engineer who had done occasional work with Emily's father, commanded the Hansen's Harbor group. He'd been working on a new habitat at Jumpoff Station at the time of the attack. He'd paired Emily with Domini Asolo, a young man in his late twenties whom she knew vaguely—he had been one of her mother's graduate students when she was still a little girl. As they waited for their call to set off—the Hansen's Harbor group would depart second to last—Emily's mother swam over. "Come talk," she chirped. "Domini, if you'll excuse us?"

He nodded, and Emily swam off a little way with her mother. The lights from Jumpoff Station provided plenty of illumination this close to the giant spheres, but not far away the darkness waited.

"The rescue team returned from the Schaefer habitat," her mother said.

"John?"

"Alive."

Emily felt a huge rush of relief. She hadn't realized how guilty she'd felt about leaving him in the failing habitat. "Oh, that's good news!" *About time we had some!*

"It could be better," Emily's mother said. "He's still unconscious, and they're worried about permanent disability."

Emily nodded, but she still felt relieved. John's chances were certainly much better at Jumpoff Station with proper medical attention than they had been in the clutches of a power-starved docbot.

"Your turn," Emily's mother said, gesturing at the Hansen's Harbor group. "Take care. I love you. And if you see your father . . ."

Emily nodded, gave her mother a quick embrace, and swam back to Domini.

The sputa journey to Hansen's Harbor was long, dark, and utterly uneventful. They detected no craft of any kind, sub or surface, and none of the murderous bots. In discussions beforehand they had decided that the killerbots would almost certainly be roaming New Botany Bay itself, so they had decided to land along an uninhabited section of the coastline south of the city, at a place where Marseguro's single road, which strung the towns and villages together like pearls, lay well inland and out of sight within thick brush.

Once on shore they programmed their sputas to return to deep water and sink themselves until called for. Then, at ten-minute intervals, they slipped off in pairs toward the town.

Emily and Domini were third in the lineup. "Good luck," Fred Notting said when the time came. They nodded and set off, staying close to the water, the previous pair having gone inland.

High clouds obscured the stars, so that the only light came from the faint glow of Hansen's Harbor itself, still a good six or seven kilometers away and on the other side of the outthrust ridge of land that formed one of the jaws of the mouth of New Botany Bay, whose circular shape suggested it had been formed by either an asteroid impact or a volcanic explosion. But Selkie vision needed no more light: they made good time, and within an hour had climbed the ridge to look down into the town.

The normal grid of street and building lights had gaping black holes, in some of which still glowed the duller, redder light of fire. Smoke blurred those lights that remained. The brightest light came from the Square. Emily could see a cargo shuttle there, and distant figures in shining blue-black armor moving around.

In their planning, they had divided the landling part of town into seven areas of roughly equal size. Each pair of Selkies would scour one of those sections street by street, vaccinating any landlings they found and giving those who could use them their own supply of one-dose hypos.

Emily and Domini's assigned area encompassed some of the oldest buildings in the city, recently turned into apartments, some craft shops and warehouses where they didn't expect to find anyone, and a few old government buildings, including the Hansen's Harbor Criminal Detention Center. The prison had been empty at the time of the attack, as it usually was on low-crime Marseguro, but they'd agreed they needed to check it in case the Holy Warriors had decided to use it as a holding pen for recalcitrant landlings.

They reached the first of the apartment buildings, coming up on its dark bulk from the inland side. Domini slipped down the gap between it and the next building, checked out the street, then motioned Emily to follow him.

Locked doors were a rarity on Marseguro for the same reason the prison normally stood empty. They slipped silently through the building's front door into its pitch-black lobby. "We'll start at the top and work our way down," Domini said. Emily nodded and followed him up the stairs.

Despite their luck with the building's front door, the first apartment they tried *was* locked. They had tools for that, though, and within seconds Domini had the door open. Inside, a vidscreen on standby glowed faintly green in the corner, providing just enough light to make out a couch and a couple of chairs, pictures on the wall, an opening into the kitchen, and another opening that appeared to lead into a hallway. They slipped through that. A door to their right opened into the bathroom, a door to their left into a bedroom. They crept in, and found two landlings asleep in a double bed.

They carried two kinds of hyposprays: one just the vaccine, the other a vaccine and a hypnotic. "Let sleeping landlings lie," was the motto, and so they each took out the hypospray charged with both vaccine and hypnotic, placed them against the necks of the man and woman in the bed, and fired.

The sharp hiss and inevitable sting made the landlings stir, but then the hypnotic tucked them back into sleep. Domini and Emily slipped out and moved on to the next apartment.

They found no one awake in that first apartment building. Three of the apartments showed signs of occupation, but were empty. But in the fifth apartment they entered, a wide-awake man waited for them, armed with a baseball bat (Emily didn't see the appeal, but landlings had recently taken to the old sport in a big way). When he saw they were Selkies, he relaxed. "I thought you were Holy Warriors!" he said. When they'd explained what they were up to, he took the vaccine, accepted a supply of his own, and slipped out to see what he could do to help the cause.

As they worked their way through apartment building after apartment building, Emily saw several names she recognized on annunciator panels, but one in particular stood out, in one of the smallest and most run-down buildings: Chris Keating.

I wish I'd drowned him when I had the chance, Emily thought. *The bastard called them here.*

Well, if she ran across him, he'd sure as hell receive no vaccination from her, though she couldn't prevent someone else from doing the honors, someone who didn't know who he was or what he'd done.

Get this over with, and then we'll deal with Keating, if he's still alive.

The night wore on. They saw no Holy Warriors in the

streets. At first, Emily wondered why they were so complacent, but then she thought of the ease with which they'd
taken the planet and the complete lack of armed resistance.
*Why shouldn't they be complacent? They think we're de-
fenseless.*

They'll know better soon enough.

They began to encounter landlings who had already
been vaccinated by other landlings. One, who gave his
name as Drew Harper, offered to accompany them. With
his help, they moved even faster, and as the sky began to
gray toward dawn, they completed their sweep of their part
of the city. All they had left was the prison. If it held any
prisoners, there would surely be Holy Warriors guarding
them, and so they had left it for last.

"I see two," Domini whispered to Emily as they crouched
in an alley from which they could look across the paved
courtyard surrounding the prison, a long, thick-walled
building with small windows. Guards meant prisoners. Any
Selkie locked up on land since the invasion would have
died a horrible death from dehydration by now . . . Emily
hoped to God *that* hadn't happened . . . so whoever was in
there needed vaccinating.

Domini lowered the heatscanner through which he'd
been observing the prison. Designed for use in the deep
ocean and looking like a pair of odd, lensless binoculars, it
could easily detect the thermal emissions of people through
the prison's cold walls. "Three prisoners. We have to get in
there."

Emily nodded. They had a plan, of course: a simple plan,
because they'd had no time to practice a complex one and
also because simple plans were usually the best—at least,
so she'd always heard, and she fervently hoped it was true.

"Drew, you stay here," Domini said. "Keep watch. You
see anyone coming, let out a shout and run like hell."

Drew nodded.

"Let's go," Domini said to Emily. They both stood, then
stepped out of the shadows and strode toward the prison as
though they belonged there. No one stopped them. Apparently, neither of the Holy Warriors in the guardroom had
yet glanced out the window.

That might be good or bad. It depended on what happened next.

They walked around to the imposing front door, made of native stonewood (an incredibly dense plant material that came by its name honestly), and positioned themselves side by side. Emily swallowed hard and hoped she'd be able to do what she was supposed to do next. She bent her right arm so that her right hand pointed toward the door. Beside her, Domini did the same.

And then Domini knocked.

At first, everything went perfectly. At least one of the Holy Warriors inside must have felt secure, because he pulled the door wide open. "What—" he began.

Emily heard a sharp "pfft" from her right as Domini fired the dart-gun strapped to his right forearm. A high-speed dart, designed to carry a scale-piercing punch through thirty meters of water, caught the helmetless guard in the throat and carried on through his spine and into and through the base of his skull. Blood, bone, and brains exploded from the back of the Holy Warrior's head, painting the low white ceiling of the guardroom a grisly, glistening red.

The corpse dropped. As it fell, Emily saw the second Holy Warrior, her target, farther inside the room. She fired, but the second Holy Warrior had had one second longer to react than his unfortunate companion—and had been alert enough to grab his weapon at the unexpected sound of a knock. He wasn't wearing his body armor, though, and Emily's dart tore through his chest, shattering his breastbone, piercing his heart, and slamming into the wall behind him. But he fired at the same instant, and the slug from his anti-personnel handgun ripped through Domini's belly and out his back, pulverizing his internal organs and smashing his spine.

Both men were dead before their bodies hit the ground, leaving Emily standing untouched, unharmed—and almost undone.

Her legs gave way and she fell to her knees on the pavement, then leaned over and retched, vomiting up the cold-pressed sea rations they had eaten when they first came ashore. She stayed there, bent over, her weight on the palms of her hands, her eyes closed, heaving until nothing remained in her guts to throw up, and then she stayed there longer, trying to catch her breath. Only the realization that daylight was breaking and more Holy Warriors could arrive at any moment drove her to her feet.

Domini's backpack, sticky with blood and bits of flesh, contained the remainder of their stock of vaccine. Emily pulled it off his body, taking a moment to close his wide eyes, glazing over now but still bearing a look of surprise, then staggered to her feet. She looked across the courtyard to where Drew still knelt, his eyes wide and white in the twilight, and waved to him. He hesitated—she couldn't blame him—but then got to his feet and dashed across the cobblestones. He didn't look at Domini's body. "We need to move fast," she told him. "There are cells down both sides of the interior hallway. You take the ones on the right; I'll take the ones on the left."

He nodded.

They went into the guardroom. Drew took one look and emptied his stomach as she had earlier. While he retched, she searched for a way to open the inner door, and found the keycard for it in plain sight on the blood-spattered desk the second Holy Warrior had been standing in front of when she shot him. The card, too, had blood on it, but the key slot accepted it, and the inner door, made of stonewood like the outer, swung open.

A second key slot caught her eye. She read the label on it, grinned, and shoved the key in.

Bright lights came on in the hallway and every cell door clanged loudly as it unlocked. Emily started down her side of the hall and found the occupant of the first cell, a fat man she didn't recognize, standing by his bed. "What's going on?" he demanded.

Emily swung open the door and entered the cell, digging in Domini's backpack for a fresh hypospray, fully charged and good for a dozen doses. "Call it a prison break," Emily said. "You're free to go, but you have to get this shot first."

The man started as she came in and he got a good look at her. "You're a Selkie! I thought they'd killed you all." He gestured at the cell. "That's why I'm in here," he snarled. "I tried to save my business partner and his family—Selkies. The motherless bastards that attacked us had locked them and a dozen more Selkies in a cage—like animals!—but they left it unguarded for a few minutes and I managed to get the gate open. All the Selkies escaped into the bay. I don't know what happened to them after that. I hope they made it somewhere safe. But the Holy Warriors saw me and threw me in here to rot."

"There isn't anywhere safe for Selkies right now," Emily said. "But soon there won't be anywhere safe for the Earthlings. We've got a nasty surprise for them. I can't tell you what it is—" *not with Holy Warriors likely to capture you before you've gotten across the courtyard,* "—but to be safe, you need this." She indicated the hypospray.

"Whatever you do to them, serves them right," he said, and held out his arm.

Emily vaccinated him.

"Many thanks," he said, and ran—surprisingly quickly, for a fat man—out through the guardroom.

While she had been dealing with him, Drew had gone past her and entered the third cell on the right. She heard voices in there but raced past without looking in, concentrating on the cells on her side of the hall. Empty . . . empty . . . empty . . .

And then, in the last cell, sitting on his bed with his head in his hands, she found the landling whose life she had saved at Sawyer's Point . . . before she knew what his kind had done to hers.

She reached out, took hold of his cell door, and slammed it closed. It locked with a satisfying crash.

The landling looked up at her, and she saw the shock of recognition on his face, too. He got to his feet.

"Did you hear what I told the first prisoner?" Emily said.

The Earthling shook his head.

Emily grinned—or rather, showed her teeth. Her heart raced, and she felt light-headed with rage. "Every non-Selkie human on this planet will die a horrible death tomorrow . . . every non-Selkie human who doesn't receive a dose of this, that is." She held up the hypospray. "We don't have guns on Marseguro, but we're not helpless primitives. You've slaughtered hundreds of us. Maybe thousands. But you're all going to pay."

"And we deserve it," the landling said dully. He sat down again. "Or at least *I* do. Do your worst."

His fatalism enraged her. She wanted him to beg for the vaccine, to plead, to cry, to experience just a little of the terror he and his kind had inflicted on her friends and family. "Don't you understand?" she yelled at him. "You're going to die. All of you! And I could save you—" Again she held up the hypospray. "But this time, I won't!" She thought of Dahlia, of the horrifying vid she had seen of the attack on Hansen's Harbor, of poor Domini's eviscerated body lying in a pool of blood on the pavement stones just outside the prison door. "Damn you, this time you're going to die, the way you should have died last time!"

The man in the cell lay down on his bunk and turned his back on her.

"Rot in hell!" she screamed at him, then turned and dashed out of the prison, through pools of blood beginning to turn sticky, weeping with rage and a grief she'd suppressed until then. Glistening red footprints marked her passage across the cobblestoned courtyard, as she ran to join her fellow Selkies and await the purifying plague.

A gunshot, the sound of locks unlocking, and bright lights switching on in the corridor brought Chris Keating out of a sound sleep. Heart pounding, he had just swung his legs over the edge when a landling he didn't know burst into his cell.

"I'm here to let you out," the stranger said. "But you have to have this first." He held up the hypospray.

"What?" Keating stared at it, brain still muzzy with sleep. "What's in it?"

"I don't know. Nobody's told me. I just know we all need it, all the landlings."

"You've had it?" The stranger nodded. "Who gave it to you?"

Someone raced down the hallway outside; Chris saw only a flash of black. "The Selkies. They're giving it to everyone."

Chris hesitated, but the open door beckoned and he finally held out his arm. The hypospray hissed, and the landling leaped up. "Nothing personal," he said, "but I'm getting out of here before any more Holy Warriors show up." He ran out without a second glance.

"Good plan," Chris muttered. He headed to the door, glanced right—

—and saw a Selkie in a black landsuit, a woman by the

curves of her body, though the landsuit's hood hid her face, talking to Richard Hansen through the bars of his cell.

He's dead meat, Chris thought. *And I am, too, if she sees me.* He dodged back into his cell, and pressed his spine against the wall until, a moment later, he heard the Selkie run past. Then he looked out again. He hesitated, torn between his desire to run and his desire to know what the *hell* was going on. The latter finally won and he ran down the hallway to Hansen's still-locked door.

Hansen lay on his bunk, his back to the corridor. "Richard Hansen?" Chris said. "Are you—" *Dead,* he intended to say, but Hansen answered that question by rolling over and staring at him.

"Got your shot?" Hansen said.

"Yes," Chris said. "What's it for?"

Hansen didn't answer. "Better run, then," he said. "Holy Warriors can't be far off."

"I'll let you out . . ." Chris said, but then realized he had no way to do so.

"Don't bother," Hansen said. "This is where I belong." He suddenly looked so angry that Chris took a step back, even with the bars between them. "So do you," he snarled. "Get out of my sight."

Chris stared at him for a long moment. "You're crazy," he said. "Just like your grandfather." And then he dashed for the guardroom.

What he saw there brought him up short. He edged around the walls, trying to avoid the blood that covered, it seemed, everything, and trying not to look at the ruined bodies of the Holy Warriors who had been guarding him. Outside the prison, he found a Selkie almost cut in two. He ran past the bloody corpse, dashed between two buildings that hid him from the prison, then kept running, zigzagging at random through back streets and alleys until at last he stopped and leaned his back against a cold concrete wall, breathing hard, confident no one was following him.

The Selkies are up to something, he thought. *If I warn Ellers . . . maybe he'll finally trust me. And take me back to Earth.*

He rubbed his sore arm. *But* what *are they up to?* The shot had to be some kind of preventive medicine . . . or maybe a way to distinguish Marseguroites from Earthlings.

A biological weapon? He shook his head. Not the sort of thing you whip up overnight, complete with vaccination. He knew enough genetics to know that. It must be something else . . . something else you need an antidote for.

It came to him. *A chemical attack! It's the only thing they could have pulled together this quickly. They're giving an antidote to as many of the Marseguroite landlings as they can—then they'll try to poison as many Holy Warriors as possible.*

Well, we'll see about that. There had to be some time left before the attack. Once Ellers knew something was planned, he could order his men into pressure suits. And then, Chris thought savagely, the Selkies would discover that what had happened to them so far was nothing compared to the terrible price the Holy Warriors would exact for such defiance.

He turned the corner of the building to head to the Square—and stepped right in front of two Holy Warriors. Their guns swung up. "Halt!" one snapped.

Chris skidded to a stop on the dew-wet pavement. "I'm going to see—"

The second Holy Warrior suddenly swung his rifle to his shoulder. The guide laser flashed red across Chris' eyes, momentarily dazzling him, and he flung up a hand. "I know him!" the Holy Warrior cried. "I escorted him to prison two days ago. He's escaped!"

"Shoot him if he moves," the first Warrior ordered. He strode forward and seized Chris' arms, pinning them behind him. "How'd you get out?" he shouted, his mouth inches from Chris' left ear. Chris winced. "Who helped you?"

"Selkies," Chris gasped out, then grunted with pain as the Holy Warrior twisted his arm upward.

"Liar," the Warrior snarled. "The prison is two kilometers from the water."

"Selkies . . . can manage just fine . . . on land," Chris said. "Ow!"

"Sam," the Warrior said, "get the prison guardroom on the horn."

Sam shifted his gun to his right hand but didn't lower it entirely. He lifted his left arm and talked to the wrist. "Computer, comm route," he said. "Prison guardroom."

"Signal sent," a tinny voice answered. A pause. "No acknowledgment."

"They're dead," Chris said. "Both guards, and a Selkie. Send someone—"

"Better check it out," the first Holy Warrior said. "He's secure."

Sam nodded and trotted off.

"You've got to take me to the Grand Deacon!" Chris said. "The Selkies have a plan . . . they're going to attack!"

"Let them try," the Holy Warrior said. "Don't worry, kid, the Grand Deacon is exactly who I'm taking you to. If you're telling the truth, he'll want to know. And if you aren't—" the Warrior barked a laugh. "He'll want to know that, too."

There's plenty of time, Chris told himself. *Plenty of time before they launch any attack. They only reached the prison twenty or thirty minutes ago. They wouldn't have cut it that close.*

But five minutes later, as the Holy Warrior frog-marched Chris into the Square, the ground beneath the toppled statue of Victor Hansen erupted.

The force of the blast knocked Chris and the Holy Warrior backward. Cobblestones smashed basketball-sized holes in the wall of the building behind them, and pebbles and dirt rained down. Chris found himself lying on top of the Holy Warrior, wriggling helplessly like an overturned turtle. Then the Holy Warrior pushed him hard in the back, hurling him into the air to crash down hard on his left side. For a moment, he couldn't think of anything but trying to recapture his knocked-out breath, but he could still see, and what he saw chilled him.

The Holy Warrior stood with his back to Chris, staring at a roaring geyser of white vapor shooting out of the crater in the Square left by the explosion. Overhead, a white cloud was already spreading and dispersing. This close to the source, Chris could feel the aerosol on his face as little pinpricks of ice, and when at last he managed to take a full breath, the stuff tickled his throat.

They did it, he thought. *The fishy bastards actually did it.*

He watched the Holy Warrior, expecting him to double over or collapse or at least start coughing, but instead the Warrior spun and yanked him to his feet so hard he thought his arm would come out of its socket. He yelped.

"I don't know what the *hell* that is," the Holy Warrior snarled in his face, "but I'll bet you do, and you're going to tell the Grand Deacon. Now!"

He half-dragged Chris across the Square to Government House, where a dozen more Holy Warriors stood looking at the thinning geyser of mist. As the Grand Deacon himself emerged, still pulling on his uniform jacket, the geyser's roar became a hiss and then stopped. The sudden silence seemed sinister.

"This one," Chris' escort growled, "showed up just before *that* happened." He pushed Chris forward, then unslung his rifle and kept it pointed at Chris' back as Chris stumbled to a halt directly in front of the Grand Deacon.

"You," the Grand Deacon said. His eyes narrowed. "You claimed you were the one who called us here. So why are Selkies breaking you out of prison?" He glanced over Chris' shoulder to the other Holy Warrior. "Your partner just called in. Calvert and Romanow are dead. So is a Selkie, wearing some kind of water-filled pressure suit. Hansen is still locked up. One prisoner unaccounted for."

"Jimmy Calvert was a friend of mine," the Holy Warrior behind Chris grated.

The Grand Deacon's gaze shifted back to Chris. "Calvert and Romanow were friends of a lot of these men," he said softly. "So you'd better give me a good reason why I shouldn't just turn you over to them."

"It's the Selkies!" Chris said. "They came into the prison, gave me a shot of some kind, told me to run. I came straight here. They're up to something."

The Grand Deacon looked at the geyser of white mist. "Tell me something I don't know."

"I think it's a chemical attack."

The Grand Deacon looked at him, and his eyes narrowed. "Chemical . . . or biological?"

"It *can't* be biological," Chris said. "Victor Hansen *hated* biological weapons, called them a 'subversion of the genesculpting art.'" The phrase came easily to Chris from long-ago history classes. As if making monstrous fishlike humans wasn't itself a subversion, a subversion of everything decent and good. "And they couldn't possibly have put together a biological weapon from scratch in the time you've been here. It's got to be chemical."

":'If it is, since we're still breathing, it's not a very effective one," the Grand Deacon said. He pursed his lips. "Unless there's a time component." He looked around at the assembled Warriors. "Anyone feeling anything?"

"Bit of a scratchy throat, Grand Deacon," said a nearby man wearing only a towel around his middle.

"Me, too," said another Warrior, this one fully armored. "I think it's just an irritant, sir."

The Grand Deacon cleared his own throat. "Now that you mention it . . ." He turned to his aide. "Everyone's on high alert already, but I want you to double patrols. This stuff may not be killing us, but it might not be intended to: it could just be meant to make us feel ill, make it harder for us to counter some more conventional follow-up attack. Order everyone to either take a shower or—" He looked at the half-naked man in the ranks, "—finish the one they were in the middle of." Everyone laughed. "Followed by full chemical decon procedures, level one—eye irrigation, nasal irrigation, the works. And then everyone into full pressure suits until further notice." The laughs turned to groans. The Grand Deacon coughed. "Dismissed." The assembled men hurried back inside.

Ellers turned back to Chris and coughed again. "Damn irritating stuff, whatever it is," he growled. "I'll get the medtechs working on it, but if you're carrying the antidote in your blood, we'll need more lab power than we've got down here." The Grand Deacon's voice had a noticeable croak to it. He spoke to his wrist. "Computer, comm route. *BPS Sanctification.*"

"*Sanctification* here," a tinny voice responded.

"I'm sending up a patient. A Marseguroite male, approximately twenty years old, standard. He was dosed with some kind of preventive drug. I want you to analyze his blood and tell me what it is—and make me some of it, if you can. We think it's designed to protect him from an aerosol chemical irritant." He paused. "But just in case . . . full biological quarantine procedures to be followed when the shuttle docks. Clear?"

"Roger."

The Grand Deacon nodded to the man who had escorted Chris to the Square. "You go up with him." He coughed again, and rubbed his nose with the back of his hand. Chris noticed a streak of red on it as he drew it away. So did the Grand Deacon. "*Damn* irritating," he grunted. He gestured at Chris. "If he causes any trouble, throw him out the air lock." He jabbed a finger at Chris. "Just remember, we can probably retrieve the antidote just fine from frozen bubbly blood." He went back into Government House.

"Just give me a reason," the guard warned. He grabbed Chris' arm and half-threw him across the Square toward the waiting cargo shuttle.

I'm going into space! Chris thought.

The pilot, a huge man, said, "Hello, Dodson," as he opened the crew hatch for them. He had a thick accent.

"Velikovsky," Dodson said. "Strap this one in good. I don't want him getting himself free."

"Will do," Velikovsky said. He grabbed Chris' arms and pulled him into the shuttle like a child lifting a marionette, shoved him into a contraption of metal straps and buckles attached to the wall, jammed a helmet on his head, and strapped the helmet down, too.

"What is this thing that has erupted in front of my shuttle and scratched my hull?" Velikovsky said as he took his own place in the pilot's seat and fastened his own straps. Dodson fastened himself into the rack opposite Chris. He had to shake off a fit of coughing before he could answer.

"Selkie chemical bomb," he said.

"Chemical?" Velikovsky squinted at him. "Not biological? Filthy genesculptors here."

"They don't have biological weapons," Chris dared to say again. "They don't have any weapons."

"Shut up," Dodson said, but then, "Kid's right. If they had any interest in self-defense, they'd have had guns. My guess is they scraped together some industrial chemicals, sneaked some explosives in under the Square in a tunnel we didn't know about to disperse them. Doesn't seem to amount to much. About what you'd expect from subhumans with fish brains. But the Old Man has told the ship to take precautions, just the same. Full biological quarantine when we arrive." He grimaced. "Guess I won't get that comfy shipboard bed I'd been hoping for."

"Well, better safe than sorry, no?" Velikovsky said. He pulled on a flight helmet. "Ready to lift, Ground Control," he said.

Chris couldn't hear Ground Control's answer, but Velikovsky laughed. "You sound terrible, Ground Control. Plenty of sleep, plenty of vodka. Old Russian remedy. We're away."

The engines rumbled to life, and Chris suddenly felt much heavier than usual. *Good-bye Marseguro, and good riddance,* he exulted.

Whatever happened next, he knew he would never be back.

Richard Hansen had had little to say to the Selkie when she gleefully proclaimed his imminent death. He had little more to say to the Holy Warrior who arrived a half hour after she left and demanded to know what had happened. "You tell me," Richard said, not bothering to get up from the bed where he lay with his hands behind his head, staring at the ceiling. "I was locked in here the whole time."

"Who did it?" the Holy Warrior snapped.

"The only person I saw was a Selkie woman," Richard said. "I gathered she objected to the slaughter of her friends and family. I also gathered she'd freed the other prisoners."

"And why didn't she free you, clone?"

"It seems," Richard said in a flat voice, "that I am *persona non grata* to both sides of this conflict. An inhuman monster to both the religious fanatics I led here and the people whose genocide I facilitated. And so, here I rot." He said nothing about the woman's mention of a horrible death coming for all the Earthlings. It could have been hyperbole or an empty threat meant to terrorize him, but even if it were the truth, he wouldn't lift a finger to save the Holy Warriors whose barbarity he had been prepared to celebrate just two days earlier.

Nor would he lift a finger to save himself.

"We are all in God's hand, and that hand may close into a fist at any moment," Richard thought, remembering a quote from the Avatar's book. "Ain't it the truth," he muttered.

"What was that?" said the Holy Warrior.

"Nothing." Richard rolled over and sat up. "Are you going to let me out or shoot me? Doesn't really matter to me."

"Neither," the Holy Warrior growled. "The Grand Deacon put you here; he can let you out if he wants. There'll be new guards to relieve me soon enough. In the meantime, you can just sit there and think about whether there's anything else you should tell us. I've got to check in."

He went down the hall.

A few minutes later, the thundercrack of an explosion rattled the city. Despite his professed disinterest, Richard leaped to his feet. He waited to see what would happen next. When nothing did, he sat back down and waited some more.

Emily climbed to the rendezvous point on the ridge surrounding Hansen's Harbor. The other dozen Selkies who had gone into the city were all there, almost invisible in their black landsuits in the dark shadows beneath the overlapping canopies of giant bumbershoot trees. They stared at her as she stumbled into the glade. "Where's Domini?" said a young woman whose name Emily didn't know.

"Dead," Emily said, and then, to her embarrassment, she began to cry, great racking sobs that shook her whole body. She fell to her knees and then onto her side, where she curled into a near-fetal position and wept and wept . . . and wept.

No one moved to comfort her; no one had any comfort to give, and others who had known Domini better sat quietly sobbing also.

But Emily's tears weren't only for Domini. She cried for Dahlia, brutally slain by the killerbot; for the terrified families screaming and dying beneath the guns of the landing craft; for her father, missing and most likely dead, with whom her last conversation had been an argument; for John Duval, wounded and harried across the ocean and now possibly dead or crippled; and for her old life and old dreams of dance and music, now as crumpled, shattered, and charred as the buildings of Hansen's Harbor.

The sound of multiple explosions ended her tears. She raised her streaked face, then got to her feet and went to the edge of the grove. There the hillside fell away steeply, offering an unobstructed view of the entire town and the bay beyond.

From the center of Hansen's Harbor and half a dozen other places around the edge of it, geysers of white mist rose and spread.

"It's done," a woman said behind Emily. "God, I can't believe it."

"Those poor bastards," said someone else. "They don't know what's coming."

"Neither did we," Emily said, surprising herself with how harsh her voice sounded. "Let them die. To hell with them."

Her tears were over. She might cry again for her people, but she would not shed a tear for the Earthling butchers.

"Now what?" said the woman who had spoken first.

"Now we wait," said Fred Notting. "And watch."

For the rest of the day they did just that. Shortly after the germbombs detonated, a cargo shuttle lifted from the Square and rode the white flame of its rockets into the sky. "Going back to their ship," Notting said with quiet satisfaction. "And taking the plague with them."

That had been their biggest worry, that the ship would remain uninfected and might have powerful weapons with which to extract vengeance from orbit. But the shuttle had launched well after the germbomb detonation and had been sitting practically on top of it. It had to be thoroughly contaminated, outside and in, as were any Holy Warriors inside it. And the Marseguroite virus that formed the plague's backbone was smaller and tougher than any Earth virus. Emily's mother thought it would survive any ordinary decontamination procedures, and once on the ship, even if any human carriers of it were quarantined, would quickly spread through its symbiotic relationship to the Marseguroite bacteria that, being harmless, the Holy Warriors would have had no reason to quarantine against and which were likely, therefore, widespread throughout the vessel.

"If they take anything aboard the ship from the planet, no matter how thoroughly they think they've decontaminated it, they'll be infected," she'd said. "Unless they blow all the air out of the ship and suit up in pressure suits, it will find them."

Whatever they think *they're carrying to the ship,* Emily thought, *they're really carrying death.*

The idea of a ship full of dead Holy Warriors circling Marseguro forever almost made her smile.

Their landsuits kept their skins moist and provided

them with water to drink, and the sea rations they'd brought with them, if uninspiring, were nourishing enough. They waited, and watched.

After the initial explosions, there was a flurry of activity for five or six hours. Ground transports rushed here and there, boats crisscrossed the bay, a few armored Holy Warriors dashed through open spaces in the city, and once an attack craft roared overhead, making them duck farther into the shadows of the bumbershoot trees.

As the sun passed the zenith and started easing toward the mountains, though, the amount of movement noticeably lessened, and by late afternoon, all vehicle traffic ceased. Emily studied the pier through binoculars. The Holy Warriors there had vanished. So had those who had been guarding the Square. She spotted a few foot patrols slinking through the shadowed streets, but they soon disappeared as well.

For the last couple of hours of daylight, nothing moved at all. The complete absence of Marseguroite landlings worried Emily. What if the vaccine hadn't worked?

"The Holy Warriors probably ordered everyone off the street," Notting said when she mentioned her concern. "They're just lying low."

Emily hoped he was right, because as the sun set behind the inland mountains, its final rays turning the sky, most appropriately, the color of blood, Hansen's Harbor looked like a ghost town.

"What's that?" a woman whispered, the desolation and silence having obviously affected her, too.

"What?" Notting said in a normal voice. He might as well have shouted, the word sounded so loud in the still evening air, and he repeated, "What?" in something closer to the whisper the woman had used.

"In the Square."

Emily raised her binoculars.

A single Holy Warrior had come into view. He staggered as he walked, like someone drunk. The setting sun had painted the scene orange, but the front of his armor seemed redder than it should have. *Blood,* Emily realized. *It's covered with blood.*

The Holy Warrior took one step, then another, then stopped. For a long moment he just stood there, wavering, then suddenly he doubled over. Dark red fluid spewed from his mouth, splattering the cobblestones with the force of a fire hose. He fell to his knees, mouth and eyes stretched impossibly wide, then tumbled forward to lie, facedown and unmoving, in the spreading scarlet pool.

Someone else who had binoculars stumbled away and threw up in the bushes surrounding the glade. Others closed their eyes; but Emily kept her glasses focused on the Holy Warrior, dead and prostrate in his own vomited blood, long after the others had turned away. *Payback,* she thought. *Payback at last.*

"We'll camp here overnight," Notting said. "At first light we'll survey the situation. If it's all clear . . ." He gave them a wan smile. "Then we have our planet back, ladies and gentlemen."

They cheered, then, and Emily cheered the loudest.

The flight into orbit was short and surprisingly rough, but Chris had a tough stomach—he'd never been in a boat, but he'd never thought he'd be seasick if he were—and when they arrived at *Sanctification,* just twenty minutes after launch, his heart pounded with excitement. *Once you're off a planet you're halfway to anywhere,* Chris remembered a teacher saying. *Well, that means I'm halfway to Earth.*

Dodson unhooked himself from his rack, then floated over to free Chris. He looked pale, and sweat beaded his forehead. "When I find the Selkie who cooked up this stuff, I will personally pull his guts out through his gills," Dodson said. "I feel like shit." With Chris half-freed, Dodson suddenly coughed and kept on coughing, so hard he ended up holding on to a metal handle on the bulkhead for support, his rifle clamped between his knees, covering his mouth with his left hand. Tiny crimson globules escaped from between his fingers and floated in the air between him and Chris, and when the spasm passed and he moved his hand to grip his rifle again, blood stained his lips and palm.

"You should see a doctor," Chris said.

"Shut up." Dodson straightened and finished unstrapping him.

The shuttle had been directed to a small zero-G landing bay, just big enough for one vehicle. Its outside doors remained open, leaving the bay in vacuum. Dodson pulled a pressure suit from a locker and shoved it at Chris. "Get in," he croaked.

Chris silently complied, though he found it awkward without gravity, and bounced off the walls a couple of times and once off of Dodson, who angrily shoved him away. When he was finally in, Dodson sealed the suit, then climbed into one himself, in half a dozen efficient motions, while Velikovsky held the rifle and watched Chris. Then Dodson took the rifle again and nodded to Velikovsky, who opened the inner hatch of the air lock. Dodson shoved Chris in, then slung his rifle over his shoulder and followed. Velikovsky sealed the two of them into the coffinlike space. The sound of air pumps quickly died away as they emptied the lock of atmosphere. At last, the outside door opened in eerie silence.

Dodson took hold of Chris' arm, bent his legs, and pushed off against the floor of the air lock. The two of them sailed across three meters of space, then collided with the padded walls, covered with silvery webbing. Dodson pulled them hand-over-hand toward an open hatch, Chris bobbing behind like a child's balloon.

The hatch proved to be an open air lock. Dodson clambered in, pulled Chris in behind him, then slapped a control. The outer door closed. The silence quickly gave way to the sound of hissing air, and at the same time, Chris felt his weight increasing: the "air lock" had to be an elevator, too, transitioning them from the microgravity of the ship's core to the spinning outer hull of the habitat ring.

A moment's heaviness, then they stopped. Dodson still gripped his arm. Their chamber suddenly flooded with a pearly white mist. "Decon," Dodson said, his voice crackling with startling volume in Chris' ear. "If your fishy friends did come up with a nasty little bug of some kind, this'll do for it."

"They're not my friends," Chris said.

"Shut up."

The mist cleared away. A brilliant purple light followed; Chris' pressure suit automatically darkened his visor almost instantly, but he still felt like his eyeballs had been scalded. And then, finally, the side of the chamber swung open, revealing a white, featureless corridor. At the far end, another door stood open. "Go down there, go into that room," Dodson said.

Chris hesitated. "What about you?"

"We get to go back to the planet so we don't contaminate anything," Dodson snarled. "Get going!" He gave Chris a sharp shove.

The last thing Chris heard from him over the suit radio was a long bout of hacking, gurgling coughs; then the elevator and he were gone.

A new voice spoke in his ear. "You can remove your suit helmet, Mr. Keating," it said. "Then please proceed to the quarantine chamber, where we will commence our tests."

Having nowhere else to go, Chris complied.

Chapter 14

FOR RICHARD HANSEN, the hours following the explosions in the Square and elsewhere passed not much differently from the rest of the time he had spent in the cell, with one exception: no meals.

He expected new guards to arrive and check in on their prisoner, and probably bring additional prisoners as the Holy Warriors rounded up people who were either involved in setting off the bombs or just unlucky enough to be in the wrong place at the wrong time. But after the Holy Warrior left, he saw no one. No guards, no Selkie women bent on rescue or revenge, no prisoners, Earthling or Marseguroite. No one at all.

They've left me here to rot, he thought. *Or starve to death.* At least he had water: the sink and shower continued to work.

The missed breakfast didn't matter much. By lunchtime, though, hunger clawed at his stomach, and by suppertime, those claws were long and sharp indeed. Something more had happened than just a few bombs being set off by Selkie resistance fighters.

He recalled the Selkie's parting words. *"You're going to die. All of you! And I could save you—but this time, I won't! Damn you, this time you're going to die, the way you should have died last time!"*

She'd held up something, he hadn't known what—at the time he'd thought it must be a weapon. But now, belatedly, it came to him: she'd been holding a hypospray.

An antidote? For a chemical weapon?
Or a vaccine?
Germ warfare?

If that were the case, the only thing keeping him alive might be his isolation in this prison cell, and a rescue might also be a death sentence.

Let me see if I have this straight, he told himself. *The clone of the creator of the Selkies sets a butchering army on them, is rescued by one of his original's creations, is condemned by the army's leader as being no better than one of those creations himself, is further condemned by the same Selkie who rescued him once, is saved from a plague by the prison meant to be his tomb, and will likely either die in that very prison anyway, or be released from it and* then *die.*

It might have made an interesting adventure vid. But to Richard it sounded more like just a screwed-up finish to a screwed-up life, and the piece of Victor Hansen squirming away in his brain didn't argue with that view.

All that remained now was to see which of the two possible endings occurred, and how painful it would be.

He went to bed hungry, and sleep took a long time to arrive; but "the body satisfies its own needs without regard to the spirit," as the Avatar had written, and eventually he fell into a restless sleep punctuated by vivid, ugly dreams.

He woke to hunger and silence.

No one had come, and as the day wore on and his hunger increased, he became convinced no one ever would.

The Selkies descended into the streets of Hansen's Harbor at first light and cautiously approached the nearest Holy Warrior outpost, a guard station on the main road from Hansen's Harbor inland. Fred Notting peered inside. He stared for a moment, then reeled out, retching, the sound loud in the otherwise utter stillness of the predawn light.

The others exchanged glances. No one moved except for Emily. *I need to see for myself what we've done,* she thought. *And it can't be any worse than what I saw at the prison.*

She was wrong.

She smelled the room before she entered it, a vile, nose-assaulting stench of mingled blood and urine and feces and incipient rot. The Holy Warriors manning the outpost had collapsed and died where they lay. Puddles of blood and piss, mingled with strange black flecks that looked like rice, surrounded the bodies. Faces stared at her, blood-filled eyes wide, mouths stretched so wide Emily thought the doomed men must have dislocated their jaws with the force of the final retching that had ripped apart their internal organs.

She swallowed, but she forced herself to look and to breathe the foul air. *This is what we did,* she thought. *They wanted us to die. But instead, we lived, and they died. It's the way of the sea. The way of all life.*

And very much, she thought with sudden viciousness, *the* human *way.*

She turned away at last. No one looked at her as she emerged. No one else went inside.

"Burn it," Notting grated.

As flames roared into the sky and black smoke poured up, the Selkies moved deeper into the town.

Everywhere the Holy Warriors had been, they had died, in scenes of mind-numbing horror. By the end of that long day, as the bodies burned, no one bothered to turn away anymore, and no one retched. As they found each body, they first stripped it of armor, armament, ammunition or communications equipment, which they set aside for later use: if the Holy Warriors reappeared, either from some unsuspected refuge on the planet or from orbit, they wouldn't have nearly as easy a time of it. Then they piled the bodies like bloody cordwood wherever they could find an open space, poured on alcohol and set them ablaze.

At first, only the Selkies who had been part of the Prophylactic Patrol carried out the grisly task, but soon the landlings they had vaccinated emerged from hiding to help as well. Together they cleansed and reclaimed the town.

A few landlings had not received the lifesaving shots. Those bodies were bathed and set aside for a proper burial at sea. *There will be recriminations and consequences,* Emily thought as she gazed at the line of sheet-wrapped figures. *How did we miss so many?*

And what had happened in the other towns? They still had no word.

The largest number of Holy Warrior corpses they found in Government House. As they moved from one blood-drenched room to another, Emily thought that the whole place might have to be demolished.

In what had once been the Chief Administrator's office, surrounded by vidscreens glowing the pale green of loss of signal, they found the man who must have been the commander, dead in his chair, head thrown back, red eyes staring at the ceiling, the front of his uniform stiff with dried blood.

A nameplate on his left breast pocket read ELLERS.

"Take him out and burn him with the others," Notting said.

Emily stayed behind as the others hauled out the corpse. "Have we heard anything from Jumpoff Station?" she said. "Do they know how things went?"

Notting nodded. "I talked to them this morning. The subs should be here in a couple of hours and individuals coming by sputa by nightfall."

"Do they know . . ." Emily's voice faltered. "Do they know about . . . Domini?"

Notting nodded again. He put a hand on her arm. "Don't blame yourself. It could just as easily have been you—or both of you."

"I don't blame myself." Emily looked down the hallway, where "Ellers" was just being loaded onto the elevator. "I blame them." A thought occurred to her. "Have we checked the prison yet?"

Notting shook his head. "It didn't seem very—"

"Domini is probably still lying there," Emily said harshly. "And the two dead guards. And there's another body in one of the cells . . . some Earthling the Holy Warriors had thrown in prison for some reason." *Some Earthling I rescued when I should have executed him*, she thought. "I'll go."

Notting opened his mouth as if to protest, seemed to think better of it, and instead said only, "Take Farley with you."

Emily nodded and left, passing a cluster of landlings heading for the Chief Administrator's office . . . the Administrator himself among them, she saw. They were all deep in conversation, and didn't even acknowledge her as they went past.

Most of the landlings survived, she thought, moving aside to let them pass. *The Holy Warriors weren't out to kill* them. *But how many Selkies died?*

The thought held surprising bitterness, and she frowned, troubled. There had always been some tension between

Selkies and landlings. But if the feelings she detected in herself had become more widespread, if the Selkies started thinking that the landlings had somehow escaped the brunt of the attack, or if the landlings were seen to be taking advantage of their new demographic strength, taking advantage, in other words, of the deaths of all those Selkies . . .

. . . and then, if the landlings who had lost friends and relatives in the germbomb attack blamed the Selkies . . .

She shook her head and moved on down the corridor to the elevator.

Recovery, for Marseguro, would involve a lot more than just fixing ruined buildings and burying the dead.

Her own internal recovery might be even more difficult, Emily acknowledged to herself as she and Farley, a much shorter and stouter Selkie woman a good ten years older, walked toward the prison. The person she had been just three days ago would not have been hoping to find the corpse of a man she'd once rescued—or any man—locked in the prison cell from which she could have freed him, slain by a horrible illness she could have prevented . . . but that was *exactly* what she hoped to find.

First, though . . . first, she would have to pass through that charnel house of a guardroom again.

She recognized the corner where she and Domini had paused before approaching the prison, and steeled herself. Farley must have heard her intake of breath, because she glanced up at her and said, "You can wait here if you want. I can deal with whatever's in there."

Emily shook her head. "I've already seen it once," she said. "And Domini was my partner. I want . . . I *have* to do this."

Farley nodded. "I understand."

Everything was as Emily had left it, but with the addition of a new body, that of another Holy Warrior, who had obviously died from the disease. Everything was also almost two days old. They couldn't do anything about the dried blood that seemed to be everywhere, or the smell, but they pulled the stiffened corpses from where they lay, put them together in the shade of the prison wall, and covered them with sheets taken from the cell closest to the guardroom, the one from which Emily had freed the fat man. They placed Domini's body separate from the others. The

Holy Warriors would be burned; Domini would be returned to the sea.

Finally, Emily and Farley went down the long corridor to the furthermost cell.

By now, Emily knew what to expect: the stiffened body, the terror-stricken eyes, the gaping mouth, the stench of blood and vomit and shit. Even though the Earthling she'd inadvertently rescued hadn't been one of those who had killed Domini, he had been in the boat that had launched the killerbot that had slaughtered Dahlia. She wanted to see that he had suffered.

Bloodthirsty? She knew it, and didn't care.

She didn't get her wish. When they reached the door of the cell, the man inside it, alive and well, stood to greet them.

Richard Hansen heard the doors opening and closing at the far end of the corridor and knew someone had come at last. Despite his growing hunger, he didn't cry out. Instead, he listened, trying to determine who was in the prison. If they were Holy Warriors, they'd be looking for him soon. If they were Selkies . . . they'd probably kill him.

But the soft murmur of voices told him nothing. As those voices approached, he stood, holding onto the wall with one hand for support, his two-day fast having left him shaky.

The last person he expected to see was the same Selkie girl who had rescued him once, then on their second meeting refused to rescue him and promised him he was going to die.

Her mouth fell open when she saw him. For a moment, they stared at each other. Behind the girl, an older Selkie craned her neck, trying to see him over the much taller girl's shoulders.

He finally broke the silence. "You again," he croaked. "Come back to finish the job?"

"Why aren't you dead?" the girl said.

"Not the friendliest of greetings." Richard felt light-headed, and suspected he had nothing to lose by saying whatever he wanted. "If you want me dead that badly, you'll have to do it yourself."

The girl raised her arm as if to point at him, but the older woman pulled it down. "You can't shoot him in cold blood!"

"Why not?" The cold flatness of the girl's voice made Richard shiver. *Nobody that young should sound like that,* he thought. *There's something else I've accomplished. Good work, Hansen.*

"He could be useful. And if you're telling the truth about not vaccinating him . . ."

"I am," the girl said.

". . . then we need to study him. Find out why he's immune. If even a few Holy Warriors survived and are hiding somewhere with their weapons . . ."

The girl took a deep breath. "All right." She lowered her arm. "Come on, you," she said. "My mother should be here in an hour or so. I'm sure she'll be happy to dissect you."

The way she said it, Richard wasn't at all sure it was a metaphor.

With the bloodthirsty girl leading the way and the older woman keeping his arm pinned behind his back, Richard stumbled down the long hallway and through the guardroom. It looked like an abattoir, spattered with blood and . . . bits. More blood stained the cobblestones outside, and four corpses lay in the shadow of the prison, wrapped in sheets, one set apart from the others. Whether they were Holy Warriors, Selkie, or local nonmods, Richard couldn't tell, and he wasn't given an opportunity to look.

They left the prison courtyard behind and made their way through the streets of Hansen's Harbor. Richard saw no Holy Warriors, living or dead . . . until they reached the Square.

Richard gasped, and tried to stop walking; but the stocky woman wouldn't let him, forcing him to stumble forward.

In the center of Square, near the toppled statue of his "grandfather" and a huge crater where the fountain used to be, lay row upon row of bodies. Plastic or blankets wrapped them, but here and there an arm protruded, or a leg, almost always spattered with blood, and almost always wearing the telltale blue jumpsuit of the Holy Warriors. "How . . . ?" Richard gasped.

"Shut up." The woman behind him twisted his arm to emphasize her command.

Several people, Selkies and nonmods, stood around the entrance to Government House. As Richard and his escorts approached, two nonmods came out, dragging two more plastic-wrapped bodies. A third nonmod appeared. "Those are the last ones, Mr. Notting," he said to a Selkie wearing a black pressure suit garment like those worn by the two women with Richard.

"I wish we still had one of them," growled a nonmod next to Notting.

"Maybe we do," said the Selkie girl, and the woman holding Richard's arm released him and pushed him forward so hard he stumbled.

Notting frowned. "Emily? Who's this landling?"

Emily. So that's her name.

"He's not a landling, Fred. He's a Holy Warrior."

Notting's frown deepened. "He can't be."

"The first time I saw him he was on a Holy Warrior boat that had been tracking the killerbot that killed Dahlia Schaefer," Emily said.

"But he's alive," blurted out the man who had just said he wished he still had a Holy Warrior in precisely that condition. "If he's alive . . . there could be others."

"I doubt it," Richard said. They all stared at him, as if he were a dog that had suddenly stood up on its hind legs and started spouting Shakespeare.

Notting came closer. The stocky woman grabbed Richard's arm again and held it tight. "Why do you say that?" Notting growled. "Do you deny you're a Holy Warrior?"

"I'm a civilian," Richard said. "And the Holy Warriors would be the first to deny I could ever be one of them. They've decided I'm subhuman, like you."

"You're no Selkie," said the man behind Notting.

"No," Richard said. "I'm a clone." He hesitated. *Oh, to hell with it.* "A clone of Victor Hansen."

Astonished, dead silence for a long moment, then Notting barked a laugh. "You're joking."

"I'm not," Richard said. "I didn't know it myself until two days ago, but it's true."

"You expect us to believe that?" said Emily, behind him. He couldn't turn to look at her, not with the stocky woman's grasp having just tightened to something beyond merely viselike.

"Not really," Richard said. "But it's the truth. And as you've so astutely observed, I'm alive. Maybe that's why."

Notting's eyes narrowed. He looked closely at Richard.

"There's certainly a resemblance," he said. "But why would a clone of Victor Hansen accompany the Holy Warriors sent to destroy Hansen's Selkies?"

Richard's arm and shoulder hurt, and when he glanced from Notting to the face of the man who had expressed a desire to have a live Holy Warrior in his hands and beyond to the glares of the other Selkies and nonmods, who had gathered since he'd arrived, he decided he'd been forthcoming enough. Twice in the past two days, he'd thought he was as good as dead. At one point he'd thought he'd even welcome his impending demise . . . but now he found he didn't particularly relish the idea of being torn to pieces by an enraged mob. *The body satisfies its own needs without regard to the spirit,* he thought again. *And staying alive is a pretty basic need.*

"I think I'd better tell my story to the authorities," he said. "If they still exist."

"Oh, they exist," Notting said.

"The Chief Administrator is in his office," offered the man behind Notting.

"This isn't a matter for the Administrator," Notting said. "I think Mr. Hansen . . . is that your name?"

Richard nodded. "Richard Hansen," he said.

"I think Mr. Hansen had better talk to the Council. I believe a quorum survives." He looked over Richard's shoulder. "Emily, will you and Farley escort him down to the pier?"

"Sure," Emily said. She stepped forward, back into Richard's sight. "But I think we should hand him over to my mother first, to figure out if he's telling the truth or not."

Notting nodded. "Good idea. All right, I'll leave him in your hands." He looked around at everyone else. "Let's get back to work."

The crowd broke apart. Emily set off in the direction of the pier, and Farley forced Richard after her.

"Who's your mother?" Richard said to Emily's stiff back. "How will she be able to prove I'm a clone?"

"My mother is Dr. Carla Christianson-Wood," Emily said without looking back. "She's the best geneticist on Marseguro. She knows the Selkie genome backward and forward . . . and she has full access to the Hansen archives." She glanced back at him for the first time, a fierce look on her face. "She's also the one who created the plague that just 'Purified' your precious Holy Warriors right off the face of the planet." She turned away. "She'll prove it . . . or disprove it."

Richard didn't reply, but he did wonder, as he stumbled through the rubble-strewn streets, whether he would be any better off in the hands of Emily's mother than he would have been in the hands of an enraged mob.

If she could unleash a weapon as terrible as the plague that had killed the Holy Warriors, he doubted he could throw himself on her mercy.

He doubted she had any.

The subs from Jumpoff Station hadn't yet arrived when Emily, Farley, and their unexpectedly living prisoner reached the shattered pier. Richard Hansen—if he really was who he said he was—found an undamaged bench to sit on and planted himself. Farley stoically took up a position behind him. But Emily couldn't stand still. She prowled the pier, glaring at the gaping holes in the bioplast planks, still reeking of burned seaweed. She'd stuck with the mission, helping locate the dead, going to the prison, escorting Hansen . . . but now she wanted—*needed*—to search for her father. She assumed he was dead, but she didn't *know*.

Like who knows how many other survivors? she thought. *We're all in the same hab. Nobody knows who's alive and who's dead, in Hansen's Harbor or anywhere else.*

Something caught her eye: a bulletin board where announcements concerning community activities had once been posted, near where the pier ran onto the shore. It had originally stood on two stout bioplast poles, and she'd passed it a hundred times. The poles were still there, but snapped off at the base. Someone, however, had propped the bulletin board back up again against a nearby bollard, and it appeared to have new notices on it. Emily strode over to it.

A gallery of faces stared up at her, each accompanied by a desperate note. "Has anyone seen . . . ?" "Any information regarding . . ." "Last seen wearing . . ." "Sweetheart, if you see this . . ."

Emily stared at the faces. Her eyes burned with tears, but the fury in her heart burned even hotter. She looked away, out over the greasy water of the bay. The bodies she'd seen floating in it in the vid her mother had shown her had been gathered up. If they hadn't been, she would have cheerfully added Richard Hansen to their number.

She resumed her pacing, but avoided the bulletin board.

As evening shadows crept across the bay and the sky once more turned the color of blood, the three big subs that had been moored at Jumpoff Station finally appeared, fully surfaced, Selkie crew members standing on their decks. The subs picked their painfully slow way through the flotsam and jetsam floating in the ship channel. Among other things, the blunt bows batted aside several quiescent killer-bots, some smart landling having found the master deactivation code for the mechanical monsters and broadcast it from the Holy Warriors' own communications equipment at Government House.

Somewhere in the wakes of the big subs, Emily knew, another couple of dozen Selkies rode sputas or drove dolphin subs like the one she and Dahlia had taken to the Schaefer family habitat.

Aboard the subs, besides her mother, were three members of the nine-person Council. Two other members had been located, one in Firstdip and one in Outtamyway, and would be in Hansen's Harbor soon, if they weren't already. No one had heard from the remaining four Council members, all Selkies. Since all four were in Hansen's Harbor at the time of the assault, all four were presumed dead.

Like Father, Emily thought. *Well, just a few more minutes, and I can hand this murdering landling over to my mother and go look for him.*

Going to let the grown-ups take over? an inner voice snarled.

Yes, she answered herself. *But I'm going to make damn sure they hear what I think about whatever plans they make from here on out. I think I've earned that right.*

The subs maneuvered gingerly up to the undamaged portion of the pier, and crew members jumped onto the pier with lines. Several more minutes passed before the sub was snugly moored. Eggshells wouldn't have broken if they'd been used as fenders, but that kind of care took time, and even though Emily could see the skill of the sub skipper, she would have appreciated more haste and less grace.

Finally, the hatch opened.

Dr. Christianson-Wood appeared first, and to her astonishment and embarrassment, Emily burst into tears and ran for her mother's embrace.

"There, there," her mother whispered, stroking her back. "It's all right, Emily. It's all right."

"Daddy," Emily sobbed. "I haven't found Daddy."

Her mother nodded. Her own eyes were wet, Emily saw, and suddenly everything flipped and instead of wanting her mother's comfort, she wanted to comfort her mother. "But I'm not giving up," she said. "I'm going to swim down to the hab. It might be intact. He might still be hiding down there. Or somewhere else . . ." Her voice trailed off.

"Maybe, Emily," her mother said. "I hope so." Something in her voice made Emily step back and take a good look at her. Her eyes glistened, but her face didn't look like that of someone who was about to emotionally crumble. It looked hard, set in stone—and even older than Emily remembered it from just a few days ago. "But if he *was* killed, I think you can safely say I've had my revenge." And then she looked past Emily at Richard Hansen, and her face became even harder. "Who's that?" she said in a flat voice. "He's an Earthling, isn't he? Why isn't he dead?"

"That's why I've brought him here—so you can find out." Emily took a deep breath. "He says his name is Richard Hansen." At the last name, Dr. Christianson-Wood's eyes shifted sharply to her daughter. "And he's not just claiming to be a relative of Dr. Hansen. He says he's his clone."

"A clone of Victor Hansen!" Her mother's eyes widened. She strode over to the Earthling. "Stand up!"

Hansen stood.

"What makes you think you're a clone?"

"Believe me, it was as much of a shock to me as to you," Hansen said. "But that's what the Holy Warriors' geneticist told me. She also said that I had a genetic sequence in my junk DNA peculiar to the . . . Selkies. You." He looked at Emily. "That's why the hunterbot came after me. It detected my blood in the water and thought I was a Selkie."

"I should have let it have you," Emily said.

"I'm glad you didn't," Dr. Christianson-Wood said. Her face had lost some of its new harshness and taken on a little of the light Emily had sometimes seen in the past when her mother was engrossed in a scientific problem. "Let's get him to my lab and I'll . . ." her voice fell. She turned and looked out across the ruins of New Botany Bay. "I forgot," she said. "My lab is gone." She turned on Hansen so suddenly he flinched. "I'll have to make do with what's on the sub." She looked at Farley. "Take him aboard. Tell the skipper I want him locked up until I can get to him."

Farley nodded, and propelled Hansen toward the gangway.

Emily's mother turned back toward her. "You look terrible. When did you last sleep? Or eat?"

Emily shook her head irritably. "I don't remember. But I can sleep or eat later." She looked back at the bay. "I have . . . I need to go see the hab."

Dr. Christianson-Wood pressed her lips together, then nodded. "You're right. Go. Look. Tell me what you find. But then come back here. You can use my quarters—just ask; someone will point the way. Get out of that landsuit and take a good long swim—in clean water," she added, glancing at the bay, whose water looked absolutely black now that the sun had vanished behind the mountains. "The sub's ballast decks are filtered and open for Selkie use. Try those." She looked over her shoulder at the sub. "A Hansen clone . . ." she said, almost to herself. "If it's true . . ."

"How could it be?"

Her mother looked at her for a long moment. "I can't tell you," she said at last. "Not yet. Not until I've confirmed it." She sighed. "And I can't do that right now, because the Council is meeting up at Government House in an hour."

"Couldn't they do without . . . without you?" Emily said, yawning. *My mother suggests I must be exhausted and suddenly I feel exhausted,* she thought. *We should harness that mysterious Mom-power as a weapon. If we're ever attacked again, she could just tell the Holy Warriors to play nice, and they would.*

Dr. Christianson-Wood looked oddly uncomfortable. "Ah. Well, um . . . the truth is, Emily, I'm an, ah, ex-officio member of the Council. Have been for years."

Emily's yawn turned into a gape. "Huh?"

"Big secret, just like the work out at Jumpoff Station," her mother said. "You know the constitution allows the

elected Councillors to appoint additional members to the
Council as circumstances require."

"Uh . . ." Emily cast her mind back through dim remem-
brances of civics classes. Mostly she remembered the boy
who had sat in front of her, whose looks and body had
turned all the girls' heads, but who had also, alas, turned out
to be gay. "If you say so."

"Trust me," her mother said. "It's in there. And I have
been so appointed. So I really had better get uptown.
You . . . do what you have to. If you find Daddy . . ."

"I'll come tell you," Emily said quietly. "Council meeting or no Council meeting."

Dr. Christianson-Wood nodded. "But if you don't, come
back here, get on the sub. Rest. Swim. When you wake up,
eat. And by then I'll be back and ready to tackle that . . .
little problem you brought me."

Emily nodded. She started toward the edge of the pier,
then stopped and turned back. "If you're a Councillor, Mom,
then tell me. What happens next? After all this . . ." Emily's
gesture took in the destruction surrounding them, and by extension all of the dead, Selkies and landlings and Holy Warriors alike. ". . . what happens? Where do we go from here?"

Her mother's face settled back into its new, harsher look.
"Emily," she said, "I have no idea. None of us do." And with
that, she turned her back on her daughter and strode inland.

Emily watched her go, left with that most unsettling of
childhood feelings: the grown-ups were in charge . . .

. . . but they didn't know what to do.

Then she shook herself, mentally and physically. "Why
am I still standing here?" she asked out loud. With relish,
she stripped out of the landsuit, leaving it in a crumpled
pile on the pier. Underneath, she had on a barely-there
two-piece skinsuit of the kind Dahlia had always favored,
the best choice for wearing under a landsuit. She bent down
to the discarded landsuit and from one of its pockets took
out the lightband she'd last used when she'd lured the killerbot into Sawyer's Point, and strapped it around her head.
Then she jumped into the bay.

The water closed around her, but she held her breath
instead of opening her gills, until she'd sunk far enough into
the bay that she hoped she'd left the worst of the oil and

other pollution fouling its surface above her. Even so, as
the water streamed through her gills, it tasted . . . wrong.
Metallic, and oily, and . . . foul.

I hope I'm not poisoning myself, she thought, then dove
deeper.

Lights still glowed along the bottom, the self-powered
globes that lighted the swimways. With their guidance, she
got her bearings, and swam past habitat after habitat. Some
of them looked undamaged, though cold and without
power, which gave her hope; but then she passed more that
had crumpled to the floor of the bay, or split from above
like a rotten fruit, and she despaired.

When she turned down the swimway that led to their
habitat, her hopes soared again: the first few habs looked
undamaged. But then the far end of the swimway came into
sight, and she backwatered sharply, horror stabbing her
heart like a fish-gutting knife.

The end of their swimway had led to the below-water
entrance of the largest of the amphibian towers, a tower
her father had designed, and which had housed his offices.

The Holy Warriors' missiles had caused the tower to
topple. Every habitat at the end of their swimway, their
own included, lay buried under tons of twisted steel and
shattered masonry. If Emily hadn't known exactly where to
look, she wouldn't even have been able to say where the
hab she had grown up in had been located.

"I left your father sleeping. I didn't even wake him," she
remembered her mother saying. *"I didn't even say goodbye
to him. . . ."*

There's still hope, she told herself frantically. *He might
have woken up before the attack, swum out . . .*

. . . and swum to his office, in the tower now lying in ruins
across their hab.

The fish-gutting knife ripped through her heart and her
hope. Vision blurred by the tears flooding the space beneath her third eyelid, Emily jackknifed and drove hard for
the surface, away from the worst horror of all the horrors
the past three days had visited on her.

Chapter 15

FROM ONE PRISON TO another, Richard thought, surveying the bare and barely-big-enough-to-stretch-out-in cabin into which he'd been locked on board the Selkie sub. But at least he still lived, unlike any of the Holy Warriors on the surface.

Aboard *Sanctification,* though . . . that was an open question. Had anyone infected made it up to the ship? If they had, then presumably it was a ghost ship now, or soon would be. If they hadn't, then the Holy Warriors in orbit would be perfectly well aware of what had transpired down on the planet, and would even now be planning their revenge. *And next time,* Richard thought, *the Purification will be total.*

And a sub sitting in the open moored to the Hansen's Harbor pier would be a primary target, which meant any minute now his approximately coffin-sized new digs might be completely appropriate.

As the minutes and then hours dragged by without any attack from orbit, though, the alternative scenario—that everyone on board *Sanctification* had died of the plague— became more likely. He slept, and would have dearly loved to eat, but nobody provided him with any food. He did have water, fortunately—the tiny cabin contained a palm-sized sink—but his stomach, unfilled for days, was cramping by the time the door abruptly opened to reveal Emily's mother, Dr. Christianson-Wood.

Accompanying her was the largest Selkie man he'd yet seen, his shaved head and naked upper body covered with intricate tattoos that slowly moved and changed color beneath his skin in a way that made Richard queasy. He tore his gaze away from the apparition and focused on Dr. Christianson-Wood, whom he strongly suspected held his life in her hands.

"I've come to test your claims," she said without preamble. "Follow me."

He stepped out into the narrow corridor, which the broad shoulders of the tattooed guard filled wall to wall. He followed Dr. Christianson-Wood and the guard followed him, along the corridor, down a companionway, then along another corridor to a door that opened into a relatively spacious chamber, a good four times the size of the one he'd just left. So much scientific equipment packed it, though, that it had very little free space. He just hoped the sharp shiny objects in the rack in the corner were surgical and not torture devices, although he'd always had a hard time telling the difference.

Dr. Christianson-Wood entered and motioned him to an examining table. "Sit down. Roll up your sleeve."

Richard complied. "If your blood tests require fasting, I'm more than prepared. In fact, if it requires fainting, I can probably manage that, too. Any chance of getting something to eat? Even a condemned man usually gets a last meal."

Dr. Christianson-Wood took a syringe from a drawer. "You haven't been condemned." But she opened another drawer and handed him a foil-wrapped bar.

Richard glanced at the tattooed giant in the hall as he tore it open. "But I've been convicted." He wolfed down the bar, which looked and tasted like he'd always imagined dried seaweed would look and taste.

He'd never tasted anything more wonderful.

Dr. Christianson-Wood held up the syringe. "You came with the Holy Warriors. You're an accessory, at least."

Richard finished the bar but said nothing more as she swabbed and stuck. He watched his blood, so dark red it verged on violet, bubble up into the syringe. She gave him a wad of fibrous material to hold in the crook of his elbow, then turned and busied herself with placing the syringe into a compartment of one of the more complicated-looking bits of equipment along the wall. "Will that device prove I'm telling the truth?"

"It will tell me if you're a clone of Victor Hansen," Dr.

Christianson-Wood said. "And if you share the section of DNA that deactivates the plague virus."

"And if I don't?"

Dr. Christianson-Wood closed the compartment door. It sealed with a hiss, and a vidscreen lit up. Dr. Christianson-Wood pulled a keyboard from a slot on the front of the machine and typed for a few seconds. The machine beeped and began to hum quietly.

"How long?" Richard asked, when it became apparent Dr. Christianson-Wood wasn't going to answer his previous question.

"Five minutes," she said. "Be quiet."

Richard complied. The five minutes passed at a glacial pace. At last, the machine beeped again. Dr. Christianson-Wood examined the screen; the readouts on it made no sense to Richard. *What if I'm* not *a clone?* he wondered suddenly. *What if the Holy Warrior geneticist lied? What if the voices in my head are just my own conscience? Would it change anything?*

He shook his head. *No, it wouldn't.* He owed these people. Every death on this planet was in some way his responsibility. He had to try, however hopeless it might be, to somehow make amends.

What if the only way I can do that is to let them execute me?

Then that's what I'll do. He snorted softly. *Not that I'll exactly have a choice.*

Dr. Christianson-Wood turned to look at him, her expression unreadable. She stared for a long moment, then glanced into the corridor. "You can go, Peter."

"Are you sure?" the giant in the hallway rumbled.

"I'm sure. He's not going to do anything."

"If you say so, Dr. Christianson-Wood." Peter sounded doubtful, but Richard heard his footsteps moving away.

Then he heard the door close. He looked up. "Now what?"

"You're more than just a clone of Victor Hansen," Dr. Christianson-Wood said. "As I suspect you know. He also gave you . . . literally . . . a piece of his mind."

Richard's blood ran cold. "How do you—"

"I'm the leading geneticist on Marseguro. I'm an appointed member of the Planetary Council. I am also the current caretaker of the Victor Hansen archives, and one of

the few people allowed to access any part of them I choose."
She leaned back against the equipment cabinet, and folded
her arms. "Dr. Hansen kept thorough notes. Among those
he kept secured until his death—and the Council has kept
secured since—are ones detailing his scheme to 'have his
cake and eat it, too', as he put it.

"Before he left Earth, Victor Hansen made five clones of
himself. He left the frozen embryos in the care of someone
he considered trustworthy . . . his wife, Dianne. His ex-wife,
really; she loved him, but nothing could convince her to
leave Earth. She did agree to keep the clones, though, and to
raise the first of them to adulthood, if she and they survived.
The remaining clones would then be put into the hands of
the first clone." Dr. Christianson-Wood leaned forward. "But
these weren't ordinary clones. Dr. Hansen believed he had
discovered a way of passing on, not just his genetic material,
but also at least a portion of his memories and possibly even
his personality. He believed he knew how to encode that information into a living brain. He built into his clones what he
called a gene-bomb: a genetic package activated at a certain
stage of development—he estimated it would 'go off' when
the clone was around thirty—which would begin rewiring a
portion of the clone's brain, encoding some of his memories
and beliefs and . . . well, he didn't really know, because he did
all this based on theory, without any experimental trials at all
beyond mice and computer models." She paused, and looked
away, at nothing in particular. "Dr. Hansen," she said after a
moment, "did not lack for ego." Then she blinked and turned
her attention back to Richard.

"Hansen did not believe the Body Purified would remain in power. He believed it would fade away. By which
time, he believed, his clone would be grown, and would
find, tucked away inside his head, the information he
needed to find Marseguro, and the wisdom to decide
whether or not it was time for Selkies and Earthlings to
join together once more."

She stepped even closer. "And now here you are," she
said. "The living image of a young Victor Hansen." And
then, without warning, her hand lashed out, cracking across
Richard's cheek like a whip, twisting his head half-around
and making his ears ring. "Damn you! Damn you to hell!
How could the clone of our creator help destroy us?"

Richard, hand on his burning cheek, turned his eyes back to her. He thought of all the reasons he'd had. He'd been doing God's will . . . well, God's will as proclaimed by the Avatar. He'd wanted to clear his family name. He'd wanted to advance his career. He'd . . .

All those reasons depended on thinking of the Selkies, as subhuman, evil, twisted creatures that God wanted destroyed.

But as a clone, the Body considered him just as subhuman, evil, and twisted as the Selkies.

And Emily had saved his life.

And . . .

He shook his head. "I don't have any reasons you'd understand or accept," he said. "I don't accept them myself anymore." He moved his hand from his stinging cheek to the back of his neck and rubbed hard. "And I don't even know if that's because of my own experiences or because Victor Hansen's ghost keeps whispering in my ear."

"Is that 'ghost' how you found us?" Dr. Christianson-Wood demanded.

Richard nodded. "Not directly. But I had a . . . what I thought was an intuition."

"Too bad it didn't take you over completely," the Selkie said bitterly. "But of course, it couldn't. Hansen himself figured it out, years later, when things had settled enough here on Marseguro for him to continue his research. His gene-bomb couldn't work: not the way he intended it. He suspected at best, his clones would have strange dreams, unexplained impulses, flashes of memory—which seems to be what happened to you. At worst, he suspected they would go stark, raving mad."

Richard nodded. "Father," he said.

"What?"

"My father—the man I thought was my father—he must have been a clone, too. He worked for the Body, until one day he went crazy. He killed himself." For the first time, though, Richard wondered if his father had actually intended to kill the Avatar, too, with that mad leap. He'd hit the pavement just a few meters in front of the motorcade. If he'd hit the Avatar's groundcar . . .

"The gene-bomb," Dr. Christianson-Wood said.

"Probably. I was thirteen. When I got older, the Body

made sure I ended up working for Body Security. They gave me the job of finding out where my 'grandfather' had fled with his . . . creations."

"Which means they knew about the gene-bomb, too," Dr. Christianson-Wood said. "They used you. They've probably decanted the other clones, too. They've just been waiting for one of you to point the way to Marseguro." She shook her head. "Damn Hansen. Always so sure of himself. He was an idiot to leave those clones behind. In a way he betrayed us himself." She snorted. "Since you're his clone, in more than one way."

Richard nodded. "Looks like it." He met her eyes. "And being a clone . . . that's why I'm immune to the plague?"

"Yes, you murderous bastard," Dr. Christianson-Wood snarled. "All Selkies contain that same stretch of DNA because all of us are descended from Victor Hansen. He sculpted our race from his own genetic material—just like he sculpted you." She lunged forward, flaring her gills and eyes at the same instant, so that she became instantly, monstrously alien. He flinched; he couldn't help it. "Genetically, I'm your daughter. We're *all* your sons and daughters. And you helped to murder us! Hundreds of us!" Her voice dropped to a deadly, poisonous whisper. *"Including my husband!"*

"I know," he said. "I know. And . . . I'm sorry. So sorry." The inadequacy of the words choked him; he couldn't say anything more. Instead, he hung his head, unable to look at the face of his . . .

. . . daughter?

Two days ago, I didn't have any relatives. Now I have a whole planet full of them.

Not as full as it used to be, jabbed his conscience, or the ghost of Victor Hansen—he couldn't tell them apart, any more.

Dr. Christianson-Wood straightened, and finally broke the lengthening silence. "Well," she said. "We have one other thing in common besides our genetic heritage."

Richard looked up, puzzled. "What's that?"

"You're a mass murderer. And so am I."

"I didn't . . ." . . . *kill anyone,* he wanted to say, but the lie died on his lips. "I led the Holy Warriors here. You designed the plague that killed them. But you were just defending your world."

"And you were defending yours . . . or so you thought. Defending it from God's ongoing threat of vengeance if abominations like the Selkies were permitted to live." She made an impatient gesture. "There are always justifications. Some are better than others. I think mine is better than yours. But it doesn't change our guilt. We're killers, many times over.

"But here's the bottom line, Richard Hansen . . . and whatever of Victor Hansen is in there." She came close to him again, uncomfortably close. *Underwater adaptation,* he thought distantly. *You have to get closer to communicate effectively.* To a nonmod—a landling—it seemed like an invasion of personal space, a threat.

Her strange oversized eyes almost filled his vision. He wanted to look away, but wouldn't.

"What can we do to ensure neither of us has to kill again?"

The moment was deadly serious, the stakes couldn't have been higher, and they were, after all, discussing mass murder, but Richard couldn't resist.

"Take me to your leader?"

Richard had a hard time reading Selkie faces, but he was almost sure he saw a flicker of amusement cross Dr. Christianson-Wood's at that moment . . . and maybe, just maybe, her tone was slightly warmer when she said, "I think that can be arranged."

When Emily reached the pier, she went straight to the sub and demanded the captain put her in touch with her mother. He took one look at her face and didn't argue.

The link was audio-only. Emily could only imagine the expression on her mother's face as she told her what she had found in the bay. When Emily finished, there was a long silence.

"I . . . suspected as much," her mother said. "We'll . . . we'll keep looking, Emily. It's all we can do." Her voice strengthened. "Get some rest, sweetie. We'll talk soon."

The connection went dead. Emily turned to the tech at the communications console. "I need to make another call," she said. "To Jumpoff Station . . ."

This time, the link had video. Emily looked at Amy, who had stayed behind to help in the hospital, where wounded Selkies rescued from other deep-sea habitats were still being brought. "Emily!" Amy said. "Are you all right? Have you found Daddy?"

"I'm fine," Emily said. "And . . . no." She told Amy what she had told her mother. Amy's face crumpled, but she didn't cry . . . quite.

"Oh, Emily," she whispered. "What are we going to do?"

Suddenly I'm *the strong one?* Emily thought. *I'm the one putting out my hand to steady* her? *When did that happen?*

"What we have to, I guess," she said. "There's a lot for everyone to do right now." She hesitated. "How's John?"

Amy's face lit up again. "He's doing great!" she said. "He's awake, and the doctors think he'll make a full recovery—probably regain full mobility of his arms and upper body with enough therapy. We've been spending a lot of time together, talking, when I'm not on duty."

You've been . . . ? John Duval and my sister . . . ? She shook her head. The world really had turned upside down if Amy were interested in one of her "kid friends."

"I've got to get some sleep," Emily said. "If we find out anything more about Daddy . . ." her voice trailed off. "We'll talk again soon."

Amy nodded. "Good-bye, little sister. Take care of yourself."

"Good-bye, big sister." And although she could never remember having said it before, Emily added, "I love you," before breaking the connection.

The captain, a middle-aged Selkie with the unusual-for-Selkies affectation of a mustache, dyed red to match his hair, had been standing discreetly by during her conversation. Now he cleared his throat. "We've got quarters set aside for you . . ."

"I need to do one more thing first," Emily said.

Five minutes later, she walked the length of the pier again to the bulletin board. Kneeling, she thumb-tacked to it the photograph of her father the captain had retrieved for her from the sub's computers, which contained a backup copy of the planetary database, downloaded from the Jumpoff Station computers before the sub began its journey. The photo had been taken above-water, on the top floor of the building that had crushed their home as it fell. His huge green eyes sparkled in the sunlight, and behind him, Hansen's Harbor, undamaged, spread to the rim of the encircling ridge. He looked young, and confident, and . . . immortal.

On the white space below the image, she had written, "Has anyone seen this man, Peterson Wood? Please contact Dr. Carla Christianson-Wood or Emily Wood at Government House."

She stared at the photo for several minutes, her mind a jumble of memories and fears, longing and loss, all tinged with dark fury, then finally made her way back to the sub, her borrowed quarters, and, a long time later, sleep.

When she woke, she found her mother had come and gone while she slept . . . and taken Richard Hansen with her. Considering her unsettling feeling the night before that the "grown-ups" didn't know what they were doing, that should have reassured her—obviously, wheels were turning and plans were in motion—but now it just annoyed her. "Where did she go?" she demanded of the sub captain. "And why didn't she wake me?"

The skipper looked taken aback. "She went ashore, Miss Wood, that's all I know. And why would she tell *me* why she didn't wake you?"

Emily wanted to snap something at him about how captains were supposed know *everything* that happened on their vessels, but instead she turned on her heel and stormed off the sub. She didn't expect to be out of the water long enough this time to need a landsuit; instead she wore a plain white skinsuit left for her in her quarters, one that showed less skin than the one she'd been wearing the night before.

The devastation didn't look any better in the morning than it had at dusk, although most of the fires seemed to have finally burned themselves out and thus the air had cleared a little. Efforts at cleanup had begun here and there. The workers she could see, mostly landlings, with just a smattering of Selkies, seemed to be focusing on infrastructure basics like power and communications broadcast towers and water and gas lines. Others, wearing face masks, gloves and rubber overalls, were undertaking the grimmer task of searching the wreckage for bodies.

A big Selkie with morphing tattoos she remembered from Jumpoff Station . . . Peter, that was his name . . . stopped her at the shattered doorway to Government House. "Council is meeting, Miss Wood," he rumbled. "No one allowed in."

The rage that now seemed to be Emily's constant companion boiled up. "Try to stop me," she snarled, standing on tiptoe to deliver the message wide-eyes-to-wide-eyes, gill slits flaring, tingling as they dried in the morning air. "You'll have to knock me down and sit on me. And then you'll have to explain it to my mother. And when you let me up, I'll make damn sure you never father a child. Now get out of my way!"

Peter blanched, but held his ground. "I can't, Miss Wood," he said. "But," he added hastily as she opened her mouth again, "I'll escort you in. Then it will be up to the Council."

Emily closed her mouth and her gills and took a deep breath. "So escort!"

Peter turned to one side, and for the first time she saw the second guard, a landling, previously hidden by Peter's bulk. His wide grin vanished as Peter rounded on him. "Let anyone else in and I'll swim you to the bottom of the bay and leave you there!" Peter barked. Then he strode inside, Emily in his wake.

Most but not all of the blood had been cleaned from the walls of the broad hall that led from the entrance to the Council Chamber—really, despite its grand name, little more than a glorified conference room. No Holy Warriors had died in it, so at least its deep green carpet and round stonewood table were unstained. A cube of blank green vidscreens served as the table's centerpiece, and around it the surviving members of the Council, Emily's mother among them, sat in green fishleather chairs. Three chairs remained empty.

In one of the four blue-upholstered chairs normally set aside for those having business with the Council sat Richard Hansen.

When Peter opened the door he paused as though about to announce her, but Emily brushed past him. "Why are you listening to this murdering bastard?" she said in a loud voice. "Why haven't you fed him to the nearsharks?"

Heads all around the table jerked to look at her. Only Richard Hansen and her mother seemed unsurprised and unperturbed. "Hello, dear," Dr. Christianson-Wood said. "I hope you slept well."

"Answer the question," Emily said. She pointed at Hansen. "Why is he here?"

A landling to the right of her mother rose to his feet. Thin to the point of emaciation, with a bald head and deep-set eyes, Ellison Jeter, Chair of the Council, had always looked rather like a walking skeleton. After the events of the past few days, he could have passed for the Grim Reaper himself. He pointed a bony finger at Emily. "Who let you in here?" he growled. "Peter . . . ?"

Emily heard the door closing behind her. Peter had obviously decided it would be prudent to return to his post.

"I let myself in," Emily said. "I saved this mudworm's life and I've regretted it ever since. I left him to rot in the prison where the Holy Warriors had put him. I found him alive and brought him here, and escorted him to my mother. I think I've earned a right to understand what you're doing with him. Why is he here? And why isn't he dead like all the rest of his murdering ilk?"

She stopped and waited. *I don't think I've ever used "ilk" in a sentence before,* a small part of her brain commented wryly.

Her mother's slightly amused expression hardened. "Don't be so quick to condemn people to death, Emily. Too many have died already."

Emily said nothing, unwilling to argue with her mother. God knew how she felt about the plague she had shepherded through her laboratory and finally unleashed against the Holy Warriors. It must have gone against everything she'd always professed to believe in. *It had to be done, Mom,* Emily thought. *It had to be.*

But then Richard Hansen had the gall to say, "I agree."

Emily's rage roared red-hot again. "*You* agree?" She rounded the table at a run. Anton Scale stood up just in time to grab her, or she would have flung herself at the Earthling. She pulled against his iron grip. "You bastard! After everything you . . . Dahlia and Domini and . . . Daddy . . ." To her horror, she found herself weeping. Scale released her arms and instead pulled her to him, hugging her, comforting her like a little girl. *His beard tickles,* she thought inanely. Then, *I wish I were still a little girl. I want my daddy!* She wept harder.

"We've all lost friends and family, Emily," Scale said quietly. "But we can't bring them back by killing one more man. Especially *this* man."

Emily sniffed and swallowed and managed to bring her lower lip under control. She pulled away from Scale and looked up into his shadowed eyes. "It sounds like you believe—"

"He *is* a clone of Victor Hansen, Emily," her mother said from the other side of Scale, who glanced over his shoulder at her, then released Emily and stepped to one side. "He carries the DNA sequence that protected us from the plague. That's why he's alive. He also carries a small part of Victor Hansen's memories and personality. And all of that means . . ." She spread her hands. "He's family."

Hot tears flooded Emily's eyes. "He's not . . ."

"You saved my life once, Emily," Richard Hansen said. She refused to look at him, but he kept talking. "I can't bring back the people the Holy Warriors killed, and I wish I'd never . . ." His voice trailed off. "Well, I wish a lot of things. But I can help you now. That's why I'm here.

"The Holy Warriors on the planet are dead. All of them, we think. But there's a ship in orbit. We don't know how many Holy Warriors are still alive up there." He nodded toward Dr. Christianson-Wood. "Your mother thinks her virus will have infected the ship even if they used standard antibiological decontamination procedures on any shuttle that went up there, and quarantined anyone arriving from the planet's surface. Maybe she's right, maybe not. But even if *they're* all dead, sooner or later there will be another ship . . . and *that* ship will carry many more Holy Warriors, and deadlier weapons, and your plague won't stop it, because they'll never set foot on the planet or breathe its air until every Selkie above and below the water is dead . . . and likely all the landlings, too.

"One way or another, this planet *will* be Purified."

Emily didn't want to believe him, or listen, but his words made too much sense and echoed her own fears. And from the somber faces of the Council and her mother, it was obvious *they* believed him.

"So what can *you* do?" she demanded. "How are *you* going to stop your all-powerful Holy Warriors?"

"I may be able to talk them out of attacking," Hansen said.

Emily stared at him. "Talk? That's all you have to offer?"

"It's all I have right now." Hansen looked around the table. "I have a . . . connection with the Archdeacon of Body Security. Although I'm sure he knows I'm a clone, it must be a closely guarded secret. Everyone else thinks I'm . . . one of his favorites. I may be able to convince any arriving force that everyone is dead from the plague, Selkies and landlings alike, and I'm the only survivor . . ." He paused, and sighed. "It's weak, I know. But it's the best I can offer."

"We'll have to deliberate on this," Jeter said.

"I don't think we have a choice," Emily's mother said.

Emily wanted to protest, to say, "Of course there's a choice!" but the words rang hollow in her own mind. Hansen's scheme offered faint hope, but faint hope might be the only hope they had.

"So we just wait for this new ship to arrive and attack?" said another Councillor, a Selkie woman with electric-blue hair and blue star tattoos around her eyes. For the life of her, Emily couldn't remember her name. *I never had to pay much attention to government before. It never seemed important who was in charge.*

Suddenly, it did.

"The first thing is to find out if *Sanctification* . . . the ship in orbit . . . has any surviving crew," said Hansen. "I need access to the Warriors' communications equipment."

"Don't trust him," Emily said. The words burst out of her. She believed in the threat, even believed Hansen might be their only hope, but giving him access to communications . . . "What if he orders them to attack?"

"We need to deliberate," Jeter said again.

"Do we have time?" said the blue-haired woman.

"We need to know *now,*" Emily's mother said.

The other Councillors chimed in and the room erupted in pandemonium as they argued with each other. Emily's thought about the grown-ups not knowing what to do came back full force. The trouble was, she didn't know what to do, either.

Then all their arguing became moot. The door suddenly banged open, and the noise died as everyone turned to look at the newcomer, a young landling with a black eye and bandaged head. "We're getting a signal from orbit," he said breathlessly. "Somebody's alive up there."

Everyone turned to look at Richard Hansen, even Emily—though she promptly despised herself for the reflex.

"I guess I'd better talk to them," he said into the sudden silence.

The quarantine chamber Chris had been ordered into aboard *BPS Sanctification* had very little to recommend it over his former cell in the Hansen's Harbor Criminal Detention Center. Like his previous lodging, it contained a bed, a toilet, and a shower stall. It *did* boast the added luxury of a table and chair. A twenty-five-centimeter cube of pale green plastic centered on the table puzzled Chris until it suddenly dissolved into the 3-D image of a man in a white coat. "Mr. Keating," the man said. "Please sit on your bed."

"What . . . ?"

"Please cooperate, Mr. Keating."

Don't these people know I'm here to help them? Chris grumbled to himself, but he did as he was told.

Once he was seated, a door hissed open and a bot trundled in on six small black wheels. Cylindrical, it had eight spindly metal arms, all of which ended in something either sharp or pointed.

"Hold out your right arm, Mr. Keating," said the man in the holocube.

Chris did so. The bot extended one of its own needle-tipped arms and plunged the point of the needle into the crook of his elbow. He winced. It held the needle in place for ten seconds, then pulled it out. A second arm whipped around and neatly applied a small round bandage. Then the bot rolled out again.

"Rest, Mr. Keating," said the man in the holocube. "Once we are certain you are not carrying any unknown pathogens, we'll release you."

The cube turned opaque again.

After that, Chris heard nothing for several hours, although food and drink appeared shortly after the bot left.

A previously invisible hatch above the table opened and two metal arms extended, holding a covered tray. They neatly deposited the tray on the table then withdrew again, the hatch closing, sealing, and vanishing behind them. Chris ate.

Shortly after that, a larger hatch opened, revealing a plain blue jumpsuit on a hanger, and a bag containing neatly folded underwear and socks, also blue. Chris took the hint, and took a shower.

Sometime after that, the lights dimmed, and he slept.

And sometime after that, Chris woke and sat up on the bed as the door that had previously allowed the bot to enter slid open.

The lights brightened, and the doctor he had seen in the holocube staggered in. Blood dripped from his nose, spattering on the front of his already red-soaked white coat. He carried a hypodermic, and lunged at Chris with it. "You're . . . immune . . . your blood . . . serum . . ."

Chris leaped up on the bed. The needle plunged into the mattress. The doctor fell to his knees, his elbows on the bed. For a moment he looked up at Chris as though intending to offer a prayer to him; then his eyes widened, his mouth gaped open, and he vomited up black-flecked blood that exploded across the snow-white sheets and blanket, splattering the wall and covering Chris' feet.

The doctor, eyes wide but no longer seeing, slid sideways to the floor. The hypodermic remained upright in the mattress, quivering.

Chris looked from the corpse to the open door, then jumped from the bed and ran, leaving bloody footprints behind.

Many hours later, Chris sat in the main recreation room of *BPS Sanctification,* staring at the blue-white sphere of Marseguro on the wall-sized vidscreen. He liked the room not only for the view (piped in from a camera somewhere aft in the zero-G section because the three-rpm rotation of the crew cylinder would have made a live view both dizzying and annoying) but because no one had died there. Everywhere else in *Sanctification,* corpses floated or sprawled or sat at their posts in some horrible zombified mockery of life.

The cleanerbots had taken care of most of the spilled

bodily fluids, except for the unfortunate few who had sealed themselves in pressure suits in a vain attempt to escape whatever was killing their fellows. The cleanerbots couldn't get inside the sealed suits, and Chris wasn't about to open them. The thought made him shudder.

Currently, the cleanerbots were working on taking away the corpses themselves, both suited and unsuited, to be dumped in the nanorecyclers, but they still had a long way to go.

Chris didn't understand it. The chemical bombs the Selkies had detonated below might have affected Dodson and Velikovsky, but how had they delivered the poison to the ship? The shuttle had been kept quarantined in vacuum.

It looked more like some kind of germ attack. But it *couldn't* be. Never mind the Victor Hansen-instilled horror of biological weapons. Never mind the fact the Selkies had had no time to concoct such a weapon. The Holy Warriors on *Sanctification* had taken all the necessary precautions against such an attack, and had *still* died.

Maybe it was a punishment from God. Not for attacking the Selkies—that was God's work if anything was, he had no doubt about it; if such abominations had been eliminated a century ago, God Itself would never have threatened to destroy the world—but for something else. Something they had done that had displeased God.

And then he had it. Like a light going on in his head.

Richard Hansen, he thought. *Grandson of Victor Hansen. They brought him aboard* Sanctification—*and with him, they brought sin.*

Chris' eyes narrowed as he remembered Hansen heading out on the boat. What had he done out there? Had he helped the Selkies? And what had he done before he even got to the planet?

He could have poisoned them, Chris thought. *Poisoned the food and water on the ship. Something that acts slowly, or something that could be triggered to act by something on the—*

Oh . . . my . . . God.

He had it. He had it all figured out.

Richard Hansen had poisoned the whole shipload of Holy Warriors . . . but he'd been clever about it. He'd used a two-stage poison, one that built up harmlessly in the body until it was triggered by contact with the second part of the poison.

And then he'd sneaked away to the Selkies on the pretense of chasing John Duval, and told them how to cook up the second half. They'd planted it in aerosol bombs near the Holy Warrior positions on Marseguro. They'd dosed their own landlings—Chris rubbed the spot on his arm where he had been hyposprayed—to ensure they weren't affected, then set off their bombs.

Sometime during the trip here, Hansen must have also planted the second half of the poison in *Sanctification,* either timed to be released a certain interval after the ship arrived at Marseguro, or controlled by a signal he'd managed to send up from the surface. *Something like a rat poison,* Chris thought. *They bled to death in their own skins. Poor bastards.*

They weren't punished by God. They were murdered. Murdered by Richard Hansen and the Selkies.

He felt familiar, renewed fury at the monsters that infested his world and had ruined his life . . . and were *still* ruining it, even after he'd finally managed to get off the planet into space. Now he was stuck here, until . . .

He smiled as the thought completed itself.

Until the next shipload of Holy Warriors arrives.

When they do, they'll need information, he thought. *They'll need to know everything they can find out about what's happening on the planet.*

They'll need me.

But that meant he needed fresh information.

If his suspicions were correct—and he didn't doubt they were—Richard Hansen remained alive and well on the planet's surface, probably scheming to sabotage the follow-up attack that would surely come, maybe even scheming to make himself appear a hero of some sort who could return to Earth to fame and adulation . . . and poison the Body Purified as he had the Holy Warriors, spreading the toxin of his grandfather's abominable ideas about modifying God's Holy Human Genome.

Well, Chris could put a stop to that. And ensure that the next shipload of Holy Warriors did a *proper* job of Purifying Marseguro.

He headed for the rec room door. After his thorough

exploration of *Sanctification*'s corridors during the last day, he knew exactly where to go.

Two minutes later, after tugging the pressure-suited body of the Holy Warrior who had been manning the post out of the way, Chris Keating activated the ship-to-planet communications system, and said into the microphone, "*BPS Sanctification* to Marseguro. Is anyone there?"

Chapter 16

THE COUNCIL ADJOURNED (at something approaching a run) to the lobby of Government House, where the Holy Warriors' communications station, the very place where Richard had first met Ellers and Chris Keating when he'd shuttled down to the surface, remained intact. Richard stood in front of one of the communications vidscreens and nodded to the tech, who did something at the main control panel.

The screen lit, and Richard found himself face-to-face with . . . Chris Keating.

They stared at each other.

"You bastard," Keating said. "I knew it."

"Everyone's been calling me a bastard recently," Richard said. *Technically, I suppose that's exactly what I am,* he thought, but didn't say out loud; Chris presumably didn't know he was a clone, and he wasn't about to tell him. "Is anyone else left alive up there?" He thought he already knew the answer: the Holy Warriors would hardly be allowing Chris Keating to access communications if any of them were alive to stop him.

Keating hesitated. "There have been some deaths," he said. "I'm not sure how many. Enough so I was able to escape and get to the communications station."

Escape? "You were a prisoner?"

"Of course!"

Off to the side, out of Keating's field of view, Emily shook her head. Richard didn't need her warning.

"There's no 'of course' about it. The last time I saw you, you were bragging about having activated the beacon that led the Holy Warriors here."

Keating's face smoothed. "I've changed," he said. "People do change." He smiled. "Isn't that what you've told your new 'friends' down below? Do they know that you were the one who heard the beacon and guided the Holy Warriors to Marseguro? Do they know the only reason you told them how to complete your poisoning of the Holy Warriors was so that you can return to Earth a hero when the reinforcements arrive?" Chris' smile grew wider. "Are you planning to poison the Selkies now, and claim the credit when the next ship arrives?"

Richard managed—just barely—to keep his face expressionless. *I poisoned . . . ?* He wondered what kind of bizarre theory Chris had assembled to explain events. Well, he wasn't about to set him straight.

"I don't think I'd call the people down here my 'friends,' " he said instead. "Though I hope I might be able to some day. As for the rest . . . they know the truth."

"I'll bet," Chris said. "So are you in charge now? The Great Savior from Earth?"

Richard looked at Jeter, whose skull-like face bore an expression as dark and threatening as a thundercloud. "No, I'm not," he said carefully. "I'm still a prisoner. Unlike you, I haven't managed a miraculous escape."

Jeter came to stand beside Richard. "Council Chair Jeter here, Mr. Keating. The Marseguroite Governing Council is in session and fully in control, though we've lost four of our members. Mr. Hansen replied to your communication on the assumption only a Holy Warrior would be talking to us from their orbiting vessel." Jeter's tone became icy. "Mr. Keating, if you are the one who activated the beacon at the Landing Site, you are directly responsible for the deaths of, at current count, two hundred and seventy-six nonmods and one thousand, four hundred and ninety-five Selkies. We expect those numbers to increase.

"I cannot speak for the Council, but I can speak for myself. I do not deny the possibility of someone changing. But it's going to take more than your say-so to convince us you deserve anything other than a traitor's execution."

"But . . . but Hansen led the Holy Warriors here!" Keating suddenly sounded like a petulant little boy. "You trust *him*? I'm one of you! *He's* from the Body Purified!"

"Who said we trust him?" Jeter said. "He has a long way

to go to earn that, Mr. Keating. But that's neither here nor there. How can you prove you were taken to that ship as a prisoner and not a willing accomplice to genocide?"

Keating licked his lips. "I . . ." His voice trailed off and he bowed his head. For a moment he looked like he was praying, but when he raised his head again, fury twisted his mouth. "I can't," he snarled. "I can't, and I don't want to." He leaned into the camera so that his face filled the screen. "I was glad to see the Holy Warriors attack," he said, his voice fierce and hard. "I was glad to see the towers of Hansen's Stinking Harbor in flames. Selkies in cages? What a laugh. And when Emily set me free from the prison, you know where I went? Straight to the Grand Deacon. I tried to warn him. I told him something bad was coming. I didn't know about Hansen's poison, or they would have all been in pressure suits when you set off the trigger dose and you'd all be fish food.

"But I'll tell you this. When the next ship arrives from Earth, I'll be here to warn them. They won't listen to a word you say, Hansen. They'll listen to *me*. And they'll Purify that worthless pissball you call a planet like nothing has ever been Purified before. They'll Purify it to hell and gone. And then I'll go to Earth and my just reward and you, all of you, fishfaces and stinking fish-loving landlings, and especially you, Richard Hansen, can literally rot in hell . . . because hell is what Marseguro is going to become. Chris Keating out."

The screen went blank.

Hansen looked at Jeter. "So much for me talking the next Holy Warrior ship into leaving us alone," he said. "We need a Plan B."

None of the Councillors spoke, but Emily did. "I've got one." Everyone looked at her. "We've got the Holy Warriors' weapons," she said. "We fight."

None of the Councillors looked happy, Dr. Christianson-Wood least of all. But one by one, they nodded.

"It won't work," Richard said flatly. "Not if they know what to expect. If Chris Keating tells them what happened, they'll bombard the planet from orbit, not just send down an armed party. *Sanctification* could have done it. The only reason Ellers didn't order it was to avoid killing nonmods—the Body prefers to give them the chance to 'repent'—and because planets with breathable atmospheres are few and far between, and even one mostly covered with water might be worth colonizing. Next time, that won't be a consideration. They'll gladly write off the planet to kill everyone on it, modded or nonmodded."

"So what do *you* suggest, clone?" Emily snapped.

"Several things," Richard snapped back, her unwavering hostility finally getting to him. "We have to stop Chris Keating from talking . . . and then, when the next ship arrives, we have to keep the Holy Warriors guessing."

"How?" said Jeter.

"Stop surface reconstruction," Richard said. "Leave the wreckage where it is, and move everybody you possibly can into your emergency deep-water habitats. When the Holy Warriors' reinforcements arrive, we want them to see a planet all but devoid of human life—not just Holy Warriors, but nonmods and Selkies, too. Leave them wondering what happened. Then, when they land, either the virus will get them . . . or we will."

"That doesn't do any good if Chris Keating manages to warn them," Emily said.

"I have a solution to that, too," Richard said. "But I'll need unfettered access to this equipment." He indicated the Holy Warriors' communications station.

Jeter studied him for a moment, then nodded. "Done."

"I'm staying with him," Emily said instantly.

Jeter smiled. "I was about to ask you to," he said. "I'm making you Mr. Hansen's personal guard. I'm sure Mr. Hansen won't object, if he is indeed on our side now."

"I have no objection," Richard said. He eyed Emily. "Um . . . she doesn't have permission to shoot me, does she?"

"Only in the direst of circumstances," Jeter said. "Emily?"

Emily's face looked like a threatening sky about to be ripped apart by lightning and wind, but she pressed her lips together and held back the storm. "All right," she said. "I'll do it. At least it's something. But if the Holy Warriors come back, I want a weapon."

"You'll have one," Jeter said. "Councillors, I believe we still have things to discuss . . . ?"

The Councillors moved back down the hallway toward

their meeting room. Dr. Christianson-Wood trailed the others, and gave a final, troubled look over her shoulder at her daughter and Richard before she disappeared from sight.

Emily folded her arms and glared at Richard. "Well?" she snarled. "Get to work."

Richard nodded. *I hope I know what I'm doing,* he thought, and turned his attention to the console.

After disconnecting, Chris sat in shuddering fury for a few seconds, then exploded out of the communications room, took the nearest elevator to the central shaft, and launched himself into zero-G. He needed to work off his rage before he could think straight, and half a dozen flying trips up and down the central shaft did the trick. By the time he had soared and grabbed and spun and leaped a few dozen times, sweat flew from him in glistening silver globules, and he could think again.

He transitioned back into gravity through one of the elevators. Once again in the rec room, he looked at the stabilized image of Marseguro in the giant vidwall, and indulged in a moment's vivid daydream of what the filthy planet would look like once the Holy Warriors sent reinforcements: dotted with mushroom clouds and glowing red craters where Hansen's Harbor and Firstdip and Outtamyway and all the other pustules that passed for towns now stood.

Richard Hansen would pay, just like the Selkies, just like the fish-lovers. When reinforcements arrived, it would be Chris Keating who finally got his due—and those who had taunted him, belittled him, stood in his way, killed his father and let his mother die, would get their just desserts.

He only had to wait.

He was sure it wouldn't be long.

He lay back in the relaxation chair and closed his eyes.

Not long at all.

In his office in the basement of Body Security headquarters on Earth, Archdeacon Samuel Cheveldeoff frowned at a vidscreen. "Still nothing?"

"No, sir." The face of the communications tech visible on the screen gleamed with sweat, and he blinked a lot. Cheveldeoff liked the fact that his underlings feared him, except when it led them to alter their reports to say what they thought he wanted to hear rather than give him the facts. Cheveldeoff liked facts, even unpleasant ones. What he really hated was falsehoods.

"Could something catastrophic have happened to the ship?"

"Unlikely, sir," the tech said. "The null-brane carrier wave is intact, which means *Sanctification*'s communications system and Cornwall drive are also intact and operational. But she is not responding to our attempts to contact her and there has been no message from her now for four days."

Cheveldeoff grunted. The last message, brief and cryptic as an old-fashioned telegram due to the energy costs of transmitting information through branespace, had said merely, "NO RESISTANCE. PURIFICATION PROCEEDING." He'd already met with the Right Hand to plan their public announcement, how best to coordinate it with the announcement of the Avatar's death, and how best to use both to leverage more Council votes for his ascension.

But four days . . . standard operating procedure required a daily check-in. Energy costs or no energy costs, four days was too long. The ship might still be there, but something must have happened to the crew.

Cheveldeoff hadn't become Archdeacon of Body Security through indecisiveness. "Thank you," he told the tech, who looked visibly relieved. "Continue monitoring."

"Yes, si—"

He cut off the channel. "Computer," he said to his office system, "List Holy Warrior warships currently in orbit."

"BPS Jihad," said the computer promptly. *"BPS Retribution. BPS Armageddon. BPS Angel of Death."* The list stopped. Cheveldeoff drummed his fingers on the table. It wasn't much of a list; most ships were still committed to the blockade of New Mars and the pacification of Tuin. Of those just listed, *Jihad* and *Armageddon* were both in space dock and out of commission for at least six weeks. *Angel of Death* was a tiny scout craft, barely even armed. That left *Retribution*. She was no *Sanctification*—she lacked both an Orbital Bombardment System and the docking and launching facilities needed to carry *Sanctification*-style assault craft—but she could actually carry *more* Holy Warriors, al-

beit relatively lightly armed, and her four dedicated troop-insertion shuttles could deliver those Warriors in greater force to the ground than *Sanctification*'s could.

That should do, Cheveldeoff thought. *Ellers said there was no resistance, so it's unlikely they've been wiped out in a military attack of any kind. Something else must have happened to them.*

The timing couldn't be worse, though. Cheveldeoff took a deep breath, then put through an encrypted call to the Right Hand.

He appeared at once. "Rasmusson here."

Cheveldeoff filled him in. The Right Hand scowled. "This is serious, Sam. Nothing has changed on the Council. In fact, you may be another vote down. And I think we have a month, tops, before we have to announce the Avatar's death and convene the Council. If you can't deliver Hansen's Selkies . . ."

"I'll deliver them," Cheveldeoff said. "*BPS Retribution* is in orbit."

"You'll go yourself." It was a statement, not a question.

Cheveldeoff smiled grimly. "I might as well. If the mission fails, there's not much point in coming back, is there?"

Rasmusson didn't argue otherwise. "Then you've got another problem."

Cheveldeoff nodded. "Braun."

"You have to involve him. He's next in the chain of command."

"I know." He was also, like Ellers but even more so, Shridhar's man.

"Make sure the crew includes a complement of men loyal to yourself," Rasmusson said. "You have agents among Braun's staff and top-level commanders." Again, it wasn't a question.

Cheveldeoff nodded. "Of course. But you don't really think Braun would sabotage the mission, do you? Ellers didn't."

"I hope not," Rasmusson said. "But that doesn't mean he won't try to sabotage *you*. If he could complete the mission, but make it appear the success was in *spite* of your interference, rather than *due* to your involvement . . ."

Cheveldeoff snorted. "I'm an old hand at those kinds of games," he said. "Don't worry."

Rasmusson smiled, very slightly. "I'm not," he said pleasantly. "Whatever happens on Marseguro, Sam, I will still be Right Hand. I would prefer that you become the next Avatar . . . but I can work with Shridhar, if it comes to that."

Not if the secret recordings I've kept of our interactions find their way into Shridhar's hands, which they will if you somehow betray me, Cheveldeoff thought . . . but very carefully did not say. Making that move would not only end the game, it would overturn the board. All he said aloud was, "I understand."

"Good. Good luck." Rasmusson reached out, and the screen blanked.

Cheveldeoff turned to a different screen. "Computer, comm link to Grand Deacon Braun."

A man's lean, mustached face abruptly appeared in the vidscreen. "Yes, Archdeacon?"

"Prepare *BPS Retribution* for departure," Cheveldeoff ordered. "Full complement of Holy Warriors, weapons and ammo. You to command."

Grand Deacon Braun nodded. "We're checking up on *Sanctification,* I take it?"

"Yes. I'll provide operation details when I join you in orbit."

Braun's eyebrows lifted. "You're coming . . . sir?"

Cheveldeoff let his eyes narrow. "Do you have a problem with that, Grand Deacon?" He had the satisfaction of seeing the normally self-assured Holy Warrior blanch. *Shridhar's not Avatar yet,* he thought. *He can't protect you until he is.*

"No, sir."

"I'll be there within two hours. Cheveldeoff out."

He cut the connection, sat back in his chair and stared off into space in the general direction of the virtual copy of Rembrandt's *Night Watch,* currently hanging on the north wall of his office, which today appeared to be paneled in dark wood. *Something's wrong out there, I can feel it.* He smiled. *And I'll deal with it.*

Cheveldeoff had a supreme confidence in his ability to deal with anything that came his way. He hadn't failed yet. *Nor will I this time.*

He leaned forward and started making additional calls. Rasmusson was right: he needed as many people loyal to him as possible aboard *Retribution*. Braun might fear him here, but he might lose some of that fear once they were light-years beyond the supposed reach of Body Security.

If necessary, Cheveldeoff wanted to be able to make it clear to Braun that he would *never* be beyond reach of Body Security—no matter how far they went.

In the lobby of Government House, Emily watched Richard Hansen's fingers fly over the multiple keyboards of the Holy Warriors' communications control console. "We're in luck," he said after a few minutes. "Ellers never got around to canceling my security codes."

"Yeah, lucky," Emily said. "So why didn't he?"

"Why should he?" Hansen countered. "He had me tucked away in prison, and he had a planet to Purify. It probably never crossed his mind. And then he was dead." He punched a few final keys. "There."

"What have you done?"

"Listen." Hansen sat back. "Computer, confirm that all communications control functions have been transferred to this station and are under my voice command."

"Confirmed," the computer said.

"Computer, confirm my identity and security clearance."

"Richard Hansen, Adviser to Archdeacon Cheveldeoff, security clearance Alpha Three."

"Computer, lock control functions to my voice command."

"Controls locked to your voice command," the computer said. "Note that override is still possible by Alpha Two, Alpha One and Alpha Prime security ranks."

"Understood," Hansen said. "Computer, shut down all communications systems until further notice."

"Are you sure you want to shut down all communications systems?" the computer said.

Hansen grimaced. "I wish these things would just take your word for it," he said. "Computer, yes, I'm sure. And please provide detailed confirmation as you do so."

"Commencing shutdown," the computer said. "Satellite Alpha, switching to standby mode. Satellite Beta, switching to standby mode. Geosynchronous branespace booster, powering down . . . ." The computer continued listing systems as it switched them off or put them on standby. When it said, "*BPS Sanctification* ship-to-ship communications functions disabled," Hansen gave Emily a thumbs-up and turned down the computer's audio volume, so that its continuing litany of disabled systems carried on at a whisper. "That's it," Hansen said. "Without security clearances Chris Keating doesn't have and can't get—since everyone with clearance higher than mine is dead—he won't be able to say boo to anyone."

"How did you know how to do that?" Emily said.

"It's my job . . . or was," Hansen said. "I analyzed communications, so my training included learning how to operate communications systems of all sorts."

"A communications analyst. And so you just happened to be the one who heard the *Rivers of Babylon* emergency beacon Keating activated."

Hansen shook his head. "I was actively looking for it. Cheveldeoff—the head of Body Security—had made that my primary mission. But I was looking in the wrong place. I wouldn't even have noticed the beacon if not for . . ." He tapped his head. "The gene-bomb my grandfath . . . grandclone . . . put in my head."

"I still can't believe I saved your life," Emily said bitterly.

"I'm glad you did," Hansen said. He pushed his chair away from the communications console and turned it to face her. "Not just because I'd rather be alive than dead—there were a few hours there when I'm not sure that was true—but so that I can help make amends."

Emily looked down at him. He looked back, his face deadly serious. She felt her fists clench. "Why should I believe you?" she said through a throat gripped so strongly by emotion she could barely squeeze out the words. "Chris Keating could be right. You could be orchestrating all of this so that when the next batch of Holy Warriors comes our way, you can betray us and be a hero back on Earth."

"Chris Keating also thinks I *poisoned* the Holy Warriors . . . and somehow got you to help me," Hansen said. "He's slipping into paranoia."

"Slipping? I'd say he plunged headlong into it some time ago."

"He had help." Hansen looked down. "The Body Purified is a powerful . . . organization. Its propaganda is extremely effective. I'd say Chris Keating was vulnerable to it and somehow got hold of it."

"Here on Marseguro?" Emily said incredulously. "How?"

"*The Wisdom of the Avatar of God* was readily available on Earth when your ancestors—and my clone—fled," Hansen said. "And not all of the normals . . . um, nonmods . . . on board the *Rivers of Babylon* were there by choice. Some of them were simply in the wrong place at the wrong time. It would have been astonishing, at that time in history, if some of them *hadn't* been part of—or at least sympathetic to—the Body Purified."

"Wouldn't we have known?" Emily said. "Or our ancestors?"

"Your ancestors were mostly children living in the water-filled holds of *Rivers of Babylon*," Hansen said. "And any followers of the Avatar would have had to have been suicidal to let anyone know what they believed. My guess is they went underground. Maybe they even changed their minds. But not all of them. Not Keating's family, I'm guessing. And if they remained Believers, they would have kept their books . . . books which have swayed older and less vulnerable minds than that of Chris Keating."

"Yours, for instance?" Emily stepped closer to Hansen, so he had to tilt his head back to look up at her. "Why did *you* believe it? You thought you were Victor Hansen's grandson, for God's sake. Why did *you* fall for the Avatar's gospel of hate?"

"Because I wasn't suicidal, either," Hansen said. He kept his eyes on hers, even though it must have been uncomfortable. "My father . . . my predecessor clone . . ." his voice took on a bitter tone, "was marginalized all his life because he was perceived to be the son of Victor Hansen. He killed himself. I swore I would restore the family honor . . . and on Earth, the only route to success and respect is through the Body Purified. Those who do not accept the Avatar's 'gospel of hate,' as you put it, are beyond the pale: impoverished at the least, often imprisoned, sometimes executed.

"So I convinced myself I believed. I convinced myself that modded humans were the ultimate evil, the usurpation of God's creative powers that led the Creator to the brink of destroying the world. I had to convince myself I believed that, because otherwise my quest was entirely about my own selfishness, and I didn't want to believe I was that shallow a person."

He took a deep breath. "But here, when I finally saw the Selkies I thought I hated . . . I just saw people. Funny-looking people, by my standards, but people. A terrified little girl clinging to her mother for comfort in a cage . . . a young woman who saved my life after I had done everything I could to destroy her kind . . . Just . . . people. And then the ultimate blow to my professed belief, when I found out I was a clone myself, and hence in the eyes of the Avatar and the Body Purified as much a nonhuman abomination as the Selkies . . . worse, that in a very real sense I *am* Victor Hansen, the man I thought I hated . . .

"That's when I found out I didn't really believe anything I'd claimed I did. That's when I found out that everything I had done really *had* been based on nothing but my own selfishness and ambition." He blinked hard three times in quick succession. "Maybe it's my conscience. Maybe it's really Victor Hansen's conscience. I can't tell anymore, and it doesn't really matter. It's all me, now. However I've become what I've become, I'm not your enemy anymore. I'm your ally."

Emily looked into his narrow landling eyes, bright with unshed tears, and something inside her, some tight knot of rage, loosened just a little.

She hadn't forgiven him. She didn't know if she could.

But maybe . . . just maybe . . . she could trust him.

A little. For now.

"Okay," was all she said. "Where to next?"

"That's up to the Council." Hansen turned back to the console and boosted the computer's volume again. At some point it had quit talking. "But there's one more thing I want to do here." He cleared his throat. "Computer, repower Emergency Beacon Alpha-Two aboard *BPS Sanctification*."

"Beacon repowered," the computer said.

"Computer, activate Emergency Beacon Alpha-Two, Code Black Three."

"Activated."

"What have you done?" Emily said, suspicion rushing back.

Hansen pushed back his chair and stood up. "When the next ship arrives, the only signal it will receive will be coming from that beacon. And that particular code means 'All dead here. Plague ship. Stay away.' " He shrugged. "And that's all I can do. Originally I thought maybe I could talk to any reinforcements myself, try to convince them to turn back, but I'd have to go through *Sanctification*'s systems, and there'd be no way to prevent Chris Keating from listening in — and maybe horning in — on the conversation."

"Will the beacon be enough to scare away another ship?"

"I doubt it. But it ought to keep their eyes off of *Sanctification* and on Marseguro, where we want it." He showed his teeth. "And Chris Keating can rot in orbit. He won't even have a clue what's going on." The bloodthirsty grin faded. "That's it. That's all the special expertise I can offer. Now . . . I'll do whatever is needed. I just want to help."

Emily's answering grin would have looked at home on a shark. "Then follow me." She headed toward the main entrance.

"Where are we going?" Hansen said, catching up.

"We're going to find some Holy Warrior weapons. And then you're going to teach me how to shoot them."

Chapter 17

THREE HOURS AFTER *BPS Retribution* entered the system *Sanctification* had been sent to Purify, Samuel Cheveldeoff stood on the bridge listening to the repeating voice loop that was the only communication signal they had so far detected. "This is *BPS Sanctification.* Code Black Three. This is *BPS Sanctification.* Code Black Three. This is *BPS Sanctification.* Code Black Three—"

Cheveldeoff motioned for the sound to be cut off, and the dispassionate male voice ended abruptly, replaced by the normal quiet hum of systems and murmur of voices from the crew manning the half-dozen bridge stations.

"Code Black Three?" he demanded of Grand Deacon Braun.

"It's a plague warning," Braun said. "Code Black means the crew is dead. Black Three means they're dead of an infectious disease."

Cheveldeoff nodded slowly. "And you're not picking up anything else?"

"Nothing," the Grand Deacon said. "*Sanctification*'s entire communications system—on board the ship, on the planet, the repeater satellites, even the branespace booster—they're all off-line or powered down. They could have been destroyed or deactivated through enemy activity, shut down deliberately by the crew—or they may have simply gone into standby because the computer didn't receive any human input for seventy-two hours. That would be consistent with a fast-acting plague."

Cheveldeoff stared at the holographic main tactical display, a spherical three-dimensional representation of the system from which the various bridge stations radiated out like spokes on a wheel. There wasn't much to look at: an icon representing the planet, an icon representing *Retribution,* an icon representing *Sanctification.* A green dotted line showed their projected course into orbit. A solid red line showed their route through the space they had already traversed.

"Aside from the emergency beacon, what do we know about *Sanctification*'s condition?"

"Long-range visuals show her intact," Braun said. "Spectrographic analysis reveals no atmosphere cloud around her, so we don't think she's been holed."

Cheveldeoff shook his head. "The beacon is telling the truth," he said. "They're all dead. I can feel it."

"You can't be certain, sir —" Braun began, but fell silent when Cheveldeoff turned his coldest stare on him.

"I'm certain. Forget the ship for now. If it's infected, it will take careful planning for us to visit it, and if it's empty, there's no point anyway, except to retrieve whatever records might be there. That's important, but not as important as finding out what's going on down on the surface. So get us into orbit, and let's get a good look. Prepare an armed reconnaissance party. Full pressure suits, and full decon procedures when they return to the ship. But don't launch them until I say so."

"Yes, sir," Braun said, and hurried off to give his orders. *So far, at least, he still defers to me,* Cheveldeoff thought. He'd been alert to any sign of betrayal since boarding *Retribution.* There'd been nothing. Some of the loyal operatives he'd managed to ensure were part of the ship's complement of ground troops reported grumbling about the mission among the rank and file, but Cheveldeoff would have been suspicious if there hadn't been grumbling at that level. Besides, the grumbling seemed evenly directed at him and Braun. However, he didn't have eyes or ears among Braun's most senior command staff, though some of the lower-ranking officers were his, and that worried him. He'd made it clear he expected to be part of every meeting of the senior staff, and he thought he would have known if they were meeting without him, but clandestine discussions over the ship's secure internal communications were almost certainly taking place.

Well. All he could do was stay alert. He smiled. *Good practice for when I'm Avatar.*

He looked at the decreasing distance to the planet detailed in the tactical display, and wondered what they would find on the surface. Ellers' initial reports had made it clear there was no armed resistance. Everything had been on track, and then communications had simply stopped. If there had been a plague, had it been something the Selkies were immune to? Or had it taken moddies and nonmods alike? And where had it come from? If the planet hosted a native plague that killed humans, how had Victor Hansen ever settled it in the first place?

He frowned. Could the Selkies have unleashed a biological weapon? Victor Hansen, in the years before Salvation Day, had campaigned tirelessly against biological weapons, helping to craft a strong international treaty banning them and personally setting up the inspection agency that enforced that treaty. It seemed unlikely he would have allowed research into biological weapons to continue on the planet he took his pet moddies to, a planet where he presumably intended to set up some sort of perfect society.

But still . . . he dared not discount the possibility entirely.

He needed more information. He stared at the tactical display and silently urged the ship to go faster. But the laws of physics were, unlike humans, unaffected by even the coldest Cheveldeoff stare, and the ship continued its agonizingly slow approach.

"*BPS Sanctification* to approaching vessel," Chris Keating said hoarsely. He wore an earbud transceiver, and he'd been saying the same thing over and over for hours, ever since the ship's computer had announced that another Holy Warrior vessel had entered the system. So far, he'd heard nothing in reply but static.

Richard Hansen, he thought. *Somehow, the bastard has jammed me.*

He'd had it all planned out, how he'd warn the Holy Warriors, tell them to attack the planet from orbit, tell them how Richard Hansen had betrayed them all. He'd visualized it in detail: they'd rescue him, take him back to Earth, fête him as a hero. . . .

But none of that could happen until he managed to speak to someone on the approaching ship.

Maybe when they're closer.

And so he continued to repeat, "*BPS Sanctification* to incoming vessel. Can you hear me? Please respond. *BPS Sanctification* to incoming vessel . . ."

For three weeks after his meeting with the Council, Richard threw himself into helping the surviving Selkies and landlings prepare for the inevitable follow-up attack. Emily became his almost-constant companion, leaving him each night only after locking him into the quarters he'd been given in one of the apartment buildings facing onto the Square. Sparsely furnished with a table and two chairs in the kitchen/dining area, a bed in the bedroom, and nothing else, the apartment beat a cell, he supposed, but not by much. It didn't even offer a view, since all its windows had been blown out, either by the explosion of the germbomb or the takeoffs and landings of the Holy Warrior shuttles. Rather than replace them, the work crews had simply boarded them over—acting on his own recommendations, he had to admit, since the only real repair work being done was to things out of sight, like sewers and water lines: everything else, as he had suggested, had been left in ruins to present to orbiting eyes as convincing a picture as possible of a dead or dying world.

He had found one other use for his expertise besides passing on his meager knowledge, mostly picked up during his two weeks on board *Sanctification,* of the care and operation of Holy Warrior weapons: the repair and upgrading of planetary communications. He had even managed to construct, from equipment left behind by the Holy Warriors, a secure, untappable and undetectable network for the Marseguroites to use when the attack finally came. Other than that, he'd simply made himself available for any and all tasks. He'd donned the uncomfortable and remarkably smelly local equivalent of a rubber suit, made from the sap of the bumbershoot trees that grew on the hills around Hansen's Harbor, and dragged the rotting remains of Holy Warriors out of the holes they'd died in . . . and he'd helped grieving relatives pull the bodies of loved ones from the rubble of buildings the Holy Warriors had leveled.

He couldn't work in the water, so he and Emily had been ashore when workers found the body of her father in the ruins of her home. That had been the only time she had left him during the day, turning him over to the scowling oversight of Farley. He'd watched her walk slowly away with her mother, the two of them holding on to each other so closely he couldn't tell who was supporting whom, and his guilt, never far from the surface, rose up and squeezed his throat so tight it hurt.

When Emily came back the next day, she said nothing beyond the necessary minimum to him all morning, and he knew better than to say anything to her. They spent the morning on the firing range, where Emily had become a crack shot with a standard-issue Holy Warrior automatic rifle, and adequately accurate with both slug-throwing and laser sidearms.

An ammunition microfactory had been delivered to the planet's surface at some point, and its associated bots had filled an old concrete warehouse to the rafters with ammunition before running out of raw materials. Supplied with new feedstock by the Marseguroites, the factory had no difficulty keeping the warehouse full, so there were no restrictions on ammo use during training—a good thing, considering the impressive rate at which Emily went through it that morning. Richard wondered just what faces she saw on the man-shaped targets she had chosen. He wouldn't have been surprised if one was his.

He didn't ask.

Three weeks after his first meeting with the Council, he met with its members again. The interior of Government House had been thoroughly cleaned and repaired by then, only a few discolored spots resisting the workers' scrubbing. Like everything else, though, it still looked completely ruined from the outside. The germbomb's explosion had sent half the facade sliding down onto the cobblestones in a pile of undifferentiated bricks, exposing the mundane gray cinder block underneath. Richard looked at the pile of rock with approval, then followed Emily into the still-wide-open main entrance—nodding to Peter as they passed—and down the long corridor to the Council Chamber.

Though it was only early afternoon, the Council had already been in session for hours, dealing with the thousand and one details of the contradictory tasks of both making the planet's cities and towns livable for landlings and Selkies and keeping them looking deserted. Many Selkies had moved out to the deep-sea habitats, Richard knew, but they were mostly children and the elderly and those needed to care for them and maintain the habitats. Able-bodied Selkies remained in Hansen's Harbor or the other towns, working hard on underwater repairs.

One isolated habitat far to the north of any others had been set aside for what they'd taken to calling the LDDF, for "Last Ditch Defense Force." If things went badly on land, the LDDF would attempt to mount a guerilla campaign. Richard privately thought that was a fool's hope—even the remotest habitats wouldn't remain secret for long once the Holy Warriors began seriously scouring the seas for them—but he supposed it was necessary for morale.

". . . last of the free-ranging hunterbots, we think," Councillor Petrie, the red-haired woman he hadn't had a name for the first time he'd been in this room, was saying as they entered. "A sputa patrol nailed it near Sawyer's Point. It may have been trying to rescue the one Emily trapped there; we've been picking up weak signals from it ourselves every now and then."

She sat down, and Jeter stood up. "Thank you, Linda," he said. "And perfect timing, Mr. Hansen."

I wish someone would call me by my first name, Richard thought. Out loud, he said, "I'm at your service."

Jeter nodded. "And have been for the past three weeks," he said. "We appreciate it. In fact, we've taken a vote . . ." he looked around the table, ". . . and we have decided unanimously that we will remove the restrictions we have placed on your freedom. You will no longer be locked in at night, and we will no longer require Miss Wood to guard you at all times."

Richard blinked, his own reaction surprising him: he felt both pleased and . . . sad. "Thank you," he said. "I promise I won't do anything to make you regret it." *Well, that sounded lame.*

He glanced at Emily, half-expecting her to object, but she didn't react. *She must have known. I wonder how she feels about it?*

He suddenly realized why he'd felt that tinge of sadness: Emily Wood was the closest thing he had to a friend on Marseguro.

Come to think of it, the Selkie girl who at one point

would gladly have let him bleed out in a jail cell was probably the closest thing to a friend he had *ever* had.

Now that *was* sad.

"We believe we have completed the most crucial preparations you helped us identify," Jeter said. "Now, of course, we're wondering . . . just how long do we have to wait?"

"I wish I knew," Richard said. "Grand Deacon Ellers didn't tell me his check-in schedule. I suspect, however, that it was daily. If that's the case, then they've known for three weeks on Earth that something has gone wrong. They will have sent messages of their own, which have gone unanswered. It will take time for them to decide on a course of action, and of course the transit time from Earth to here is about two weeks." He spread his hands. "I think the earliest they could arrive is next week. More likely the week after that. It all depends on—"

With a feeling of *déjà vu,* he saw the Council Chamber door thrown open, and the same tech who had burst into the room last time he'd been there burst in again. "We're receiving a signal!" he almost shouted.

"From *Sanctification*?" Jeter said.

"From the Holy Warrior sensor satellite Richard linked us to," the tech said, and hearing his first name, Richard thought, *Thank you.*

"And?" Jeter prompted.

"A second ship is approaching."

Richard's heart skipped a beat. "Or," he said carefully, "they could arrive today."

"Sound the alarm," Jeter told the tech.

Richard glanced at where Emily had stood a moment before, but she'd disappeared. He looked back at Jeter. "What do you want me to do?"

Jeter returned his gaze steadily. "I gave you your freedom, Mr. Hansen," he said. "That's up to you."

Richard stood very still for a moment. His original plan had been to try to talk the Holy Warriors out of attacking, but Chris Keating had fouled that up. He could flee to the underground shelters they'd constructed and wait out the coming events.

Or he could prove once and for all whose side he was on . . . and what he really believed.

He followed Emily.

* * *

Aboard *Retribution,* Cheveldeoff and Braun surveyed a vidwall in the main briefing room just off the bridge, watching the flow of data from the surveillance satellites they'd launched when they'd finally entered orbit. "Evidence of Purification is clear in all of the towns we've identified," Braun said. "The *Sanctification* contingent appears to have done an admirably thorough job of destroying major structures in and close to the water, while minimizing damage to land-based structures, in an effort to avoid unnecessary casualties among the normals.

"We've identified a few Holy Warrior-built control points and weapons emplacements," Braun went on, pointing them out with a laser pointer. The red dot flicked here and there too fast for Cheveldeoff to even register the structures indicated, but he didn't say anything. He didn't need the details, just the gist. "This indicates that Grand Deacon Ellers had taken over governance and was imposing order. Presumably that included a curfew, martial law, summary corporal and capital punishment—the usual measures."

"I'm familiar with the *modus operandi* of the Holy Warriors," Cheveldeoff said. "I wrote most of the manual. The question is, Grand Deacon Braun, are there any Holy Warriors on the planet now?"

Braun turned off his laser pointer with a click that fell just short, Cheveldeoff thought, of insubordination. "Not that we can detect, sir. Nor have we seen incontrovertible evidence of any other survivors. Certainly there is no evidence that any kind of large-scale human—or subhuman," he added hastily as Cheveldeoff cocked an eyebrow, "civilization continues to operate. There are some signs that rebuilding began, but then halted."

"Your conclusions?" Cheveldeoff said, although he'd already come to his own.

"A plague," Braun said. "As indicated by the Black Three code. A fast-acting plague that incapacitated and killed both Holy Warriors and planet-dwellers so quickly they could take no effective countermeasures."

"And where did this plague come from?"

"There's no way to be certain, sir," Braun said, "but—" he clicked on his pointer again and aimed it at a bombed-out building that looked no different to Cheveldeoff than any of the others, "—close analysis of this structure reveals it to be a biological laboratory. From the photographs, we've identified equipment identical to that used by the pre-Salvation genesculptors. Other equipment appears to be related to culturing microorganisms. Remembering that Victor Hansen created this society, it seems likely the Selkies and their normal collaborators were conducting gene modification experiments on local life-forms. Conceivably, they accidentally created something deadly that the bombing of the laboratory released into the environment."

Cheveldeoff nodded thoughtfully. Braun's theory made sense, and the ruined lab, if not definitive, certainly bolstered its probability. The biological warfare scenario seemed less likely if the plague had killed most or all of the planet dwellers as well as the Holy Warriors.

Time to seek further evidence. "Very well, Grand Deacon," he said. "Send down your armed reconnaissance party."

Inside Government House, Emily stood by the Holy Warriors communications station with Richard Hansen, her mother, and the Council, watching the tactical display Hansen had somehow conjured on one of the vidscreens. The new ship had entered orbit more than three hours ago, and so far had utterly ignored its silently orbiting sister ship, *BPS Sanctification.* "Looks like they bought the Black Three warning," Hansen said. "But look." He pointed to half a dozen icons circling the planet in different orbits. "They're surveying. By now, every square centimeter of Hansen's Harbor and the other towns has been scanned, photographed, and analyzed a hundred different ways."

"They want to know if anyone is alive down here," Emily's mother said. "But can they tell that from orbit? Can they spot us in here?"

"Not from what I know of the technology," Hansen said. "And the habitats are deep enough they should be safe from orbital scans. Let them get down here in shuttles, though, and they'll soon track us down."

"They wouldn't live long enough," Emily said. "The plague . . ."

"Won't affect men in pressure suits," Hansen said.

"Which they will almost certainly be wearing, if they believed the Black Three code."

"What do you think they'll do?" Dr. Christianson-Wood said.

"Probably send down an armed reconnaissance force," Hansen said. "I've worked with Cheveldeoff a long time. He wants firsthand accounts. He never believes intelligence that comes into his office until he's sent an agent to verify it personally. If he's true to form, there'll be a shuttle full of Holy Warriors heading our way very soon."

"We'll be ready for them," Jeter rumbled.

"As ready as we can be," Hansen said. He frowned. "I wonder . . . Computer, access *Sanctification* tactical computer."

Emily stiffened, hands gripping the automatic rifle she'd been practicing with for weeks, the rifle that no longer felt awkward in her hands but more like an extension of her own arms. "What are you doing?"

Hansen shot her a look. "Still don't trust me?" he said. "I'm not doing anything the new ship can detect. And if we're lucky . . . Yes!" He pointed. The icon representing the new ship in their own tactical display had suddenly sprouted a string of new numbers—and a name. Emily leaned in closer.

"*BPS Retribution,*" she read.

Hansen whooped. "*Retribution*! That's a piece of luck."

"Why?" said Jeter, and Emily gladly let someone else play straight man for a while.

"*Retribution* is an old troop carrier," Hansen explained. "Lots of Holy Warriors on board—more than *Sanctification* had—but it's what it doesn't have that's important. It doesn't have assault craft—and it doesn't have an Orbital Bombardment System."

Emily felt a smile spread across her own face. The possibility more assault craft would swoop down on them again or, worse, the new ship would simply lob mass-slugs at them from space had worried all of them. If Hansen were right, then all they had to worry about was—

He stiffened. "Here they come."

Emily looked into the tactical display again. A small glowing speck had detached from *Retribution*'s icon. As she watched, the separation increased. It sprouted its own numbers and name: *BPS Fist of God*.

"When will we know where they're going to land?" Jeter asked.

"We won't," Hansen said. "They could change their destination right up until the last moment. But I think it's a safe bet they'll land in one of the towns. And knowing Cheveldeoff, I'd be willing to bet they'll land right here in Hansen's Harbor. In fact—" he pointed toward the door. "I'll be surprised if they land anywhere else but the Square. In about twenty minutes."

Emily hefted the rifle and checked the clip and chamber with smooth, practiced motions. Then she held the rifle at arm's length so she could inspect the dart-guns once again strapped to both wrists. Finally, she propped the rifle butt on her hip. "Well, we'd better prepare the welcome party, hadn't we?"

Cheveldeoff sat in the main briefing room of *Retribution* with Grand Deacon Braun, watching the video feeds streaming back from the descending shuttle. The twenty-four Holy Warriors on board *BPS Fist of God* could be accessed individually, but for now Braun had the feed coming from the shuttle's exterior cameras. The craft had just broken through a low bank of clouds hanging over Hansen's Harbor, giving them their first clear view of the town.

"Ellers clobbered it good," Braun said. "It looks worse up close than it did from orbit."

It did. Although there were signs some rubble had been cleared away, most of the debris lay untouched. Bricks and twisted steel and overturned, burned-out ground vehicles clogged the streets. Nothing moved except for stray bits of hardcopy skittering through the wreckage, pushed by a strong sea breeze.

Fist of God made one low pass over the town, then settled into the main square, where something had blasted a huge crater in the once-white cobblestones, near a toppled and scorched bronze sculpture. Cheveldeoff leaned forward as the cameras made a slow pan around the courtyard. All the buildings looked damaged: windows broken, roofs holed, facades fallen, pillars snapped off at the base. More paper swirled by as a dust devil howled across the square and disappeared into an alley. Otherwise, they might have been looking at a still photograph.

"Holy Warriors, check suit seals and sound off!" a voice crackled. Braun touched a control, and a new picture popped up in a separate window inside the main image. "Ground Commander Speitzl," read white letters across the bottom of the window, which showed the length of the troop hold inside the shuttle, full of Holy Warriors in full pressure suits, strapped into the two facing rows of seats, their weapons secured on the rack between them. "Ashcroft, tight!" "Umstattd, tight!" "Hughes, tight!" and so on through twenty-four names.

"Unship weapons," Speitzl said. Almost in unison, the two-dozen warriors reached out and pulled their rifles free of the rack. At the same instant, the straps holding them in their seats unsnapped and retracted.

"On your feet."

They stood. The seats disappeared, moving up into the ceiling.

"About face."

They turned sharply to face the now-bare outside walls.

"Go, go, go!"

The outer walls fell away, forming ramps down which the Holy Warriors charged, except for the four who stayed in the shuttle to provide covering fire from the raised turrets fore and aft.

Not that any was needed. The exterior view remained empty of life.

Cheveldeoff nodded. *As I expected.* "Tell Speitzl to secure the shuttle, then send out patrols to the Holy Warrior positions we identified. Starting with that big building facing the Square. They seem to have set up communications there." He stood up and turned toward the door. "I'll be in my quarters if anyone—"

Someone screamed. Cheveldeoff whirled back to face the vidscreen.

Down on the planet, all hell had broken loose.

From the darkness of the windowless, burned-out shell of a building that had once been the Office of Land Dweller Affairs, Richard watched the shuttle settle in the Square, its shrieking landing jets threatening his eardrums. Hot air drove a wall of dust and grit over the long-suffering fallen statue of Victor Hansen. Then the jets cut off, and the massive hydraulically cushioned landing struts groaned as the shuttle's full weight came to bear on them.

In the sudden silence, Richard could hear his ears ringing.

Sanctification hadn't carried this kind of shuttle, but he'd seen them in action often enough in various squelch-the-heresy and stamp-out-rebellion operations over the years. He'd told the others what to expect. For a few minutes, the shuttle just sat there, its name, *Fist of God,* gleaming on its flank in golden script. Then, with no warning at all, the sides dropped and twenty Holy Warriors swarmed out, ten to a side.

They hit the ground at a run, then dropped prone, weapons pointed out in a circle of potential death. Inside the shuttle, which Richard could now see right through, four additional Warriors crouched in turrets behind heavy machine guns that could deliver withering suppressing fire if required.

But just as Richard had suspected—or at least hoped—the Warriors weren't wearing their normal body armor. Instead, they were in pressure suits. They obviously feared the plague more than any potential ambush. The pressure suits would keep out the killer virus Dr. Christianson-Wood had developed, but they wouldn't do a thing to stop bullets or lasers.

Emily crouched beside Richard. They didn't speak. They both knew what was supposed to happen next.

Richard would have waited a few minutes longer, in hope some of the Warriors would get to their feet and thus make better targets, but Fred Notting, who had been given overall command of the "welcoming committee," didn't have the same degree of patience.

"Go," said a voice in Richard's ear, in the Holy Warrior earbud transceiver he wore, tuned to the secure communication system he'd helped set up. And from all around the Square, the ambushers opened fire.

Richard had known exactly how many people the incoming shuttle held, and how many would come out of each side. They'd positioned their forces accordingly. In the few moments since the Holy Warriors had emerged, each one of the Marseguroite defenders had identified his or her target.

The most crucial were the four heavy gunners. They could only be hit from above, and so four snipers had been sent to four roofs around the Square, crouching out of sight in doorways as the shuttle descended.

When the command came, Richard was peering through his sight at the helmeted head of a man looking almost directly at his position. The reflective pressure suit faceplate kept him from seeing the man's face. He could almost pretend it wasn't a man at all . . . almost. Without giving himself time to think about it, he squeezed the trigger, firing a triplet of high-velocity armored bullets.

The smooth glass bubble didn't shatter. Three round holes appeared in front, a red-and-gray mist spurted from the back, and the pressure-suited figure slumped.

Richard swung to his secondary target—Emily's primary—but she'd taken care of it . . . *of him,* he corrected himself, unwilling to whitewash what they were doing. He'd never killed someone directly before, though he knew he had killed thousands indirectly. It had to be done. He believed that. But he would not lie to himself any longer about the consequences of his decisions and actions.

He lifted his head to survey the overall situation.

On his side of the shuttle, every Holy Warrior sprawled or slumped on the ground, dead or incapacitated, including the commander, crumpled against the side of the shuttle, a red smear marking where he had stood just seconds before. It looked like all the Holy Warriors on the far side of the shuttle were also *hors de combat* . . . but the snipers had gotten only three of the four machine gunners. Vengeful or panicked, it didn't really matter which, the surviving machine gunner was spraying the buildings on the far side of the Square, including Government House, with a murderous hail of bullets. As Richard watched, one of the surviving pillars holding up the Government House pediment split under the stream of fire and collapsed. A moment later the pediment crashed down on top of it, blocking the building's main entrance with rubble . . . and bringing down a large section of roof, along with the sniper who had been on it.

"We have to get him from this side!" Richard yelled, and scrambled up. Emily had already decided the same thing and led him by two steps as they burst into the open. Others from their side of the ambush followed, but Richard and Emily were the closest. They were halfway to *Fist of God* when its sides started to rise. A dead Holy Warrior, half on and half off the ramp, tumbled out like a rag doll. "The shuttle's lifting!" Richard shouted. "You take the gunner, I'll take the pilot." With the bulkhead almost a meter off the ground, he had no time for anything more. He jumped, cleared it, fell, rolled. He glanced left and saw Emily tumbling down the slope of the lifting bulkhead and the gunner in the turret turning toward her, but he had no time to watch what happened. He turned right and crashed through the door into the shuttle cockpit. Behind him, he heard a burst of rifle fire.

The pressure-suited pilot barely had time to turn toward the door before Richard's rifle butt smashed his right shoulder. He yelled, the sound muffled by his helmet, and dropped the laser pistol he had in that hand. Richard kicked it away and the pilot lunged after it with his remaining hand. Richard's rifle butt came down on his outstretched left arm, and it snapped with an audible crack. The pilot collapsed, cradling his arm and moaning.

"Doors closed. Commencing automated takeoff in ten seconds," said the shuttle's computer. "Nine. Eight. Seven."

Richard's shipboard Holy-Warrior training had not included anything about flying a shuttle, but he knew how to read. A large red button clearly marked MAIN POWER EMERGENCY CUTOFF nicely put a stop to the countdown.

The pilot moaned again. With two useless arms, though, he didn't seem much of a threat. Richard ignored him and turned back toward the main compartment, remembering the shots he had heard. *Emily!*

"The shuttle's lifting!" Hansen shouted. "You take the gunner, I'll take the pilot."

Why not the other way around? Emily thought, but had no time to argue, not with the side bulkheads of *Fist of God* rising and the machine gunner demolishing everything on the far side of the Square and possibly slaughtering their compatriots at the same time. She angled left, and leaped.

She didn't quite make it. Her left foot caught the lip of the bulkhead. She fell headlong, and her rifle flew from her hand and skittered down the rapidly increasing slope. She slid down after it and ended in a crumpled heap at the bottom.

The bulkhead closed behind her and sealed. The machine gunner, his field of fire cut off, boiled out of his turret like a mad animal, unshipping his rifle and screaming something about God and vengeance. Emily twisted onto her back and lifted herself up as his barrel swung toward her—and shot him in the stomach with all four steel-tipped darts in her dart-guns.

The miniature harpoons ripped through his pressure suit as if it weren't there, tore apart his guts, and burst out the back, splattering bloody chunks of flesh across the ceiling. His rifle fired once, the bullets burying themselves in the bulkheads. His shout about God's vengeance turned into a high-pitched scream, then a gurgle fading to silence. With a final cough, the Holy Warrior pitched forward, his helmeted head slamming into the floor just inches from Emily's outstretched feet.

She heard the door to the cockpit opening behind her and lunged for her rifle. She grabbed it, twisted around again—

—and found Richard Hansen looking down at her, breathing hard. "Good work," he said.

She took a deep breath of her own. "The pilot?"

"Alive but incapacitated." Hansen held out a hand to her, and after a moment's hesitation, she took it and let him pull her to her feet. "We may need him."

"What, your limitless knowledge of things Holy Warriorish doesn't extend to flying shuttles?" she said, and to her own surprise, found herself grinning. *I'm teasing him,* she thought. *And* smiling *at him.* She felt sure she'd never done the former before and hadn't done the latter more than twice. *Well, I can't be suspicious forever. And after that . . .*

She remembered the barrel of the machine gunner's rifle swinging toward her, but she didn't glance back at his body. She'd thought she'd never tire of taking revenge on the Holy Warriors, but she'd seen—and shed—enough of their blood now to begin to realize her thirst for vengeance wasn't unquenchable after all.

I guess I'm not cut out to be a brutal killing machine.

Hansen—hell, she might as well go all the way and think of him as Richard—looked surprised at her smile, but then he matched her grin with one of his own. "I'm afraid not," he said. Then he grimaced and rubbed his knee. "I barely cleared that damn bulkhead. The Holy Warriors didn't teach me levitation, either, worse luck."

"It's probably in the advanced course," Emily said. "Along with walking on water and raising the dead."

Richard laughed. "Probably." Their eyes met, and Emily looked away, suddenly feeling oddly self-conscious. "So," she said, studying the blank bulkheads and the weapons rack down the center of the compartment, "how do we get out of here?"

"This way . . ." Richard hesitated. "I think." He led her tentatively toward the bow.

He's a landling, he is . . . or was . . . an enemy . . . and he's the clone of someone I could quite accurately describe as my Creator, Emily thought. *I can't start thinking about him in those terms.*

But remembering how good it had felt to laugh and smile with him, she wondered if she really had a choice.

"*Damn* them!" Cheveldeoff roared. He paced the briefing room, turning his head to keep his glare on the feeds from *Fist of God,* which showed the Selkies and their human accomplices dragging the bodies of the entire reconnaissance party away into the surrounding buildings. "And especially damn *him!*" He stopped and jabbed a finger at a figure that had just passed the camera, a much shorter Selkie female in black by his side. "Richard Hansen. A murderous traitor like his devil-spawned grandfather." Braun didn't know Hansen was a clone, and even in his rage, Cheveldeoff wouldn't give *that* bit of information away freely. "And I trusted him. Blood will tell, Braun. Blood will tell."

"Your orders, Archdeacon?" Braun said, his own face expressionless.

He's sensing an opportunity, Cheveldeoff thought, suddenly cautious. *A weakness. I ordered the shuttle down. He's not on my side. He wants me to fail, so he can step in and save the day.*

"I can send down another shuttle," Braun suggested.

"Two shuttles. We'd know what to expect this time. We could establish a beachhead."

"No." Cheveldeoff made a chopping motion with his hand. "You establish a beachhead when you want to invade and occupy. I don't want to invade and occupy. I want to destroy."

"We don't have any orbit-to-ground weapons," Braun said.

Cheveldeoff stopped his pacing, spun and snarled at the Grand Deacon, who paled even if he didn't—quite—flinch. "Don't tell me what I already know! I'm fully aware we don't have any orbit-to-ground weapons on *this* ship—but this isn't the only ship we have."

"What about the plague?" Braun said, and added, "sir," just in time to not sound insolent. "We'll have to manually bypass the security protocols to take over command of *Sanctification* from the computer. You can't do that work in space gloves. Someone will have to unsuit."

In those moments when duty required him to choose between two difficult possibilities, Cheveldeoff often felt an icy calm descend on him, a coldness that allowed him to make his choice on a completely rational basis, without regard for the moral niceties and ethical quibbles lesser authorities allowed to cloud their judgment. *That's why I'm Archdeacon,* he thought, relishing the feeling that gripped him now, as though he had plunged into a pool of cold, crystal-clear water. *That's why I'm going to be Avatar.*

"There may not *be* a plague, Grand Deacon," he said. "It may be as illusory as the utter desertion of the town below. But even if it exists, those who must unsuit must unsuit." His gaze bored into Braun's pale blue eyes. "But you will *not* permit anyone who unsuits to return to *Retribution* until we know for *certain* if this plague exists. Do I make myself clear?"

Braun's mouth tightened and his nostrils flared, but all he said—wisely—was, "Yes, sir."

"Board *Sanctification.* Activate the Orbital Bombardment System. And give *me* targeting and fire control. Do it."

Braun saluted and left the briefing room. Cheveldeoff looked back at the vidwall. Sometime in the past few minutes it had gone blank. Probably someone on the ground had suddenly realized that *Fist of God* had eyes and ears.

I don't have to see you to know you're there, you God-damned travesties of human beings, he thought. Then, out loud, he quoted the words of the first Avatar, "Vengeance belongs to God—and I am God's instrument."

He turned his back on the vidwall and strode out of the briefing room. *This planet* will *be Purified, O Wrathful One,* he vowed in silent prayer. *I swear it.*

Chapter 18

RICHARD SHOT A SIDEWAYS glance at Emily as they made their way past the shattered front of Government House, where medical personnel were carefully putting the badly injured-but-still-living sniper on a stretcher. With the front entrance blocked, they'd have to go in through the freight entrance at the back. Their route between Government House and Town Hall took them out of sight of everyone for a few seconds. Richard opened his mouth to say something, then closed it again.

She smiled, he thought. *She called me Richard instead of Hansen. She even joked with me.*

He felt like a young teenager. *Does she like me or doesn't she?*

She's a Selkie, he thought. *She lives most of her life underwater. Selkies even have sex underwater. I could drown!*

And besides that, she's more than 10 years younger. It'll never work out.

He intended the thought as a private joke—surely he didn't feel *that* way about her—but to his surprise, he realized he really did feel *that* way about her.

She attracted him . . . she attracted him a lot. And had for a long time. He just hadn't admitted it to himself.

She may like me, he thought. *It doesn't mean she wants to bear my children. She* can't *bear my children. Grandclone Victor made sure of that.*

Oy. Just drop it, Richard. This isn't the place, and it certainly isn't the time. Be happy that at least she's unlikely to shoot you on the spot, and leave it at that.

But later, maybe, if they survived . . .

They emerged from darkness into light, literally if not, in

Richard's case at least, metaphorically, jumped up onto the concrete loading dock, and made their way in through the storerooms and kitchens to the Council Chamber.

They found something of a celebration in progress, excited talk and laughter echoing down the hall so that they heard it before they saw it. *Time to be a wet blanket . . . or maybe, for the Selkies, a dry one,* Richard thought, as he and Emily entered to shouts of, "They're here!", applause, and claps on the back.

He put up his hands for quiet. Jeter saw him and helped him out by pounding his gavel. The room fell silent. Everyone looked at him.

Emily included.

He liked that.

He cleared his throat. "Sorry to be the bearer of bad news," he said, "but we haven't won yet."

"Let them come back," one of the Councillors called. "We'll be ready for them."

Richard shook his head. "They won't come back. Not the same way." *Not unless Cheveldeoff has turned into an idiot since I used to play chess with him.* "They're going to want to destroy us, and there's only one way they can do that." He pointed up. "From orbit."

"But you said they don't have any orbit-to-ground weapons on the . . . um, *Retribution,*" Jeter said.

"They don't," Richard said. "But they know *Sanctification* does. And now that they know they need them, our plague beacon isn't going to stop them from boarding her."

Faces fell around the room. But Jeter kept looking at him steadily. "So you're going ahead with the second part of your plan?"

Richard nodded. "The job's only half-done."

Jeter shook his head. "You're going to get killed."

"Well . . . some would call that just desserts," Richard said. He very carefully did not look at Emily, but out of the corner of his eye he saw her drop her gaze, and it warmed him. *At least* she *doesn't feel that way anymore.*

Apparently Jeter didn't either. He frowned. "I'm tired of hearing that, Richard," he said, using his first name for the first time. "You've proven yourself over and over, especially just now, out on the Square. You don't have to die. We may be subhuman abominations, but we don't practice human sacrifice."

First name and *a joke,* Richard thought in wonder. *I might be accepted here some day after all.*

If I live long enough. Jeter was right: if he attempted what he had in mind, he probably wouldn't.

But there really wasn't any choice. If a shuttle hadn't already left *Retribution* for *Sanctification,* it would soon enough, and if Cheveldeoff got control of *Sanctification*'s Orbital Bombardment System, *none* of them would live much longer.

"I have to try," he said.

Emily's head suddenly came up. "Then I'm coming with you!"

He shook his head. "No. It's not an attack. Numbers don't matter. It will either work, or it won't."

"If numbers don't matter, then two are as good as one," she shot back. "And just maybe two is better. You'll need someone to watch your back."

"You've never been in zero-G," Richard said, and then stopped, surprised, as everyone in the room burst out laughing. "What?"

Emily flared her gill slits at him. For some reason it made him blush. "Selkie, remember?" she said. "I grew up in zero-G." She grinned. "Wanna bet I get around in it better than you?"

"Uh . . ." Knowing he'd already lost the argument, Richard gave in. "All right," he said. "You can come . . . um, I mean, I welcome the company."

She bowed her head a little. "Thank you so much," she said sardonically.

Jeter's own smile faded. "When?"

"I need to talk to the pilot." Richard hesitated. "He might need a little . . . persuasion . . . to tell me the truth."

"I can help there," Dr. Christianson-Wood said. Emily gave her a look halfway between startled and dismayed, and Dr. Christianson-Wood laughed. "I'm not talking about torture, Emily. Simple brain stimulation. He'll answer truthfully, and it won't hurt him at all."

"What about the plague?" Richard said.

"I'll give him the vaccine," Dr. Christianson-Wood said.

"I'm not a monster." She blinked suddenly, and looked away. "Not entirely, at least."

Emily looked away, too, and Richard wondered if she were remembering that *she* had been perfectly willing to let *him* die in a cell without giving *him* the vaccine. *Well,* he thought, *if she's coming with me, I'd just as soon she was a little ruthless.* He looked at Emily's mother, who had engineered the disease that had brutally killed a shipload of Holy Warriors and not a few of her own fellow Marseguroites, and thought, *No worries there, if like mother, like daughter.*

He thought of what he'd done himself, on both sides of the conflict. *No worries here, either, I guess.*

He cleared his throat. "No time like the present," he said. "In fact, maybe no time at all."

"Let's go, then," Dr. Christianson-Wood said, and led the way.

The first that Chris Keating knew of the arrival of *Retribution*'s Holy Warriors aboard *BPS Sanctification* was the shrilling of an alarm that woke him from a deep sleep.

He sat upright on the couch in the rec room and stared around, trying to figure out the source of the high-pitched squeal. The ship's computer clarified things for him. "Unauthorized docking. Unauthorized docking. Unidentified shuttle craft in Bay One. Repeat, unidentified shuttle craft in Bay One."

Docking? Chris stumbled to his feet and half-ran, half-staggered to the vidscreen he had managed to slave to the main tactical display. He couldn't change the view from the last one the dying crew had used, however, since the computer only allowed him the absolute minimum control over any ship's systems—little more than "Lights on, lights off"—and all he could see was a blip representing the other Holy Warrior ship.

He rubbed his face vigorously with his right hand, trying to wake up. He'd spent hours, until he was hoarse, calling that ship. Eventually he'd crawled back here for a nap. How long ago had that been?

He didn't know. He'd long since lost track of time.

Had they heard him and finally decided to rescue him?

Maybe they'd been replying all along, and for some reason he hadn't been able to hear them?

Or did they even know he was on board?

"I've got to get up there," he said aloud, then grimaced. *Talking to myself,* he thought. *That's a bad sign.*

Chris was good at zero-G maneuvering now, after weeks in orbit. Once he was out of the rotating habitat ring, he zipped down the central shaft and to the docking bay access tunnels in minutes. But he grabbed the maneuvering webbing and pulled up short of the hatch leading into the docking bay. *They've got to be nervous. And they may not know I'm here. No point in getting shot.*

All the way to the bay, he'd been accompanied by the computer's monotonous periodic warning of: "Unauthorized docking in Bay One. Unauthorized docking in Bay One." But suddenly it changed. "Security Alert. Security Alert. Unauthorized computer access. Unauthorized computer access. Unauthor—"

And then, silence.

Chris gripped the webbing even tighter, and waited.

Abruptly, the hatch slid open. A pressure-suited Holy Warrior popped out and convulsively grabbed the webbing himself as he caught sight of the young Marseguroite.

Chris tentatively raised one hand. "Uh, hi," he said. "I'm Chris Keating. Welcome to *BPS Sanctification.*" Then he couldn't help but break into a huge grin. "Boy, am I glad to see you!"

In *Retribution's* briefing room, Cheveldeoff and Braun watched the feed from the *Sanctification* boarding party. Docking had proceeded without difficulty, although *Sanctification's* main computer continued to squawk about it. They'd been worried about the ship's anti-boarding armament, but apparently the crew of *Sanctification* had had no concern about being attacked in space by the Selkies and had not armed it. The computer complained, but it didn't attack.

Watching through the shuttle's exterior cameras, Cheveldeoff saw the salvage crew emerge. Their first task would be to get out of the docking bay, which required manually severing the computer's control of the dock's hatches. As he watched, a Holy Warrior removed a plate from the floor and inserted something into the opening. *Sanctification*'s computer squawked something different, then fell silent.

"Got it," Cheveldeoff heard over the suit-to-suit channel. "The hatch is opening. I'll just go through and . . . Holy Wrath of God!"

"Computer, switch to helmet camera of man just transmitting," Cheveldeoff snapped.

The image flickered, and changed.

Cheveldeoff found himself looking at a young man—little more than a boy—with shaggy brown hair and a few wisps of chin hair that hardly qualified as a beard. Barefooted and bare-chested, he wore nothing but rumpled blue pajama bottoms, far too big for him, kept on only by a tight knot in the strings. "Uh, hi," he said, raising a hand. "I'm Chris Keating. Welcome to *BPS Sanctification*." He grinned, which made him look even younger. "Boy, am I glad to see you!"

"Who the hell is *he*?" Cheveldeoff demanded of Braun.

"I have no idea," Braun said. "He's obviously not a Holy Warrior. And the only civilian on board *Sanctification* was Richard Hansen. He must be from the planet. But how he got there . . ."

"He's not a Selkie," Cheveldeoff said. "He's human." He frowned. "And he's obviously been unaffected by the plague . . . if there is one." He turned to Braun. "I want to question him. Get him into the shuttle."

Braun nodded, and gave the orders.

Chris wasn't exactly sure what he was expecting, but being grabbed like a piece of cargo and hauled across the docking bay and into the waiting shuttle certainly wasn't it. Nobody had said anything to him, although that might have been because they all insisted on keeping their pressure suits on and their helmets sealed. He could have told them they had nothing to worry about—that the *Sanctification* crew had been *poisoned* by Richard Hansen, not killed by anything infectious—but he hadn't had a chance yet.

Two Holy Warriors manhandled him into position in front of a comm terminal. A blank green vidscreen lit, revealing a square-jawed, bullet-headed man with a nose like a squashed grape and brown eyes that glittered like polished stone. "Who are you?" the man demanded without preamble, his voice a *basso profundo* rumble.

"I'm Chris Keating," Chris said. "Um . . . who are you?"

"Samuel Cheveldeoff," the man growled. "Archdeacon of Body Security. And that's the last question you get to ask until I'm done asking mine. What are you doing aboard *Sanctification*? What happened to the crew? And what happened on the planet?"

At last, Chris thought, and told Cheveldeoff everything he knew or guessed—how his family had remained faithful to the Body all these decades, how he had set off the emergency beacon in the hope it would finally bring richly deserved Purification to Marseguro, how thrilled he had been when the Warriors from *Sanctification* attacked, how he had met Richard Hansen . . . and how Richard Hansen had betrayed the Holy Warriors, half-poisoning them on the ship, then finishing them off with the chemical bombs he had told the Selkies how to build. "He planned to present himself as a hero when you showed up," Chris said. "I'm surprised you haven't—"

"A chemical weapon killed them? Not a plague?" Cheveldeoff interrupted him.

Chris nodded. "It couldn't have been a plague. If there were any diseases like that on Marseguro all of us normal humans would have died a long time ago, wouldn't we?

"The Selkies could have created it. A biological weapon."

"No!" Again, Chris shook his head. "Victor Hansen hated biological weapons. The Selkies wouldn't dare go against their Creator. And anyway, they didn't have time. I should know, I'm . . . I'm a geneticist." *Okay, I'm a laboratory technician*, he thought. *But they don't need to know that.* "It's impossible to create such a selective pathogen in two days. Absolutely impossible."

Cheveldeoff grunted, and looked over to his right, as though someone had said something. "What?" he said, not to Chris. "Damn. All right. I'm done here anyway." He turned back to Chris. "You'll forgive me if I don't take any chances. Stay on *Sanctification*. Help the crew there with anything you can. Once we're sure there's no infection, then . . . we'll see. If you're telling the truth, I'll personally make certain the Avatar knows you are a hero of . . . what did you call this planet?"

"Marseguro," Chris said. He felt himself grinning like an idiot, but he couldn't help it. "It means 'safe sea,' apparently."

"Marseguro." Cheveldeoff looked away again. "All right, I'm coming." The vidscreen blanked.

Still grinning, Chris turned to the Holy Warrior who had escorted him there. "You heard him," he said. "What can I do to help?"

The Warrior snorted. "Stay out of our way," he said, his voice issuing from an external speaker on his helmet. He grabbed Chris and hauled him out of the communications room with no more respect than he'd shown shoving him into it.

"Hey!" Chris protested, but the Warrior ignored him. So did the others, shoving him out of the way like a stray bit of floating debris when he tried to talk to them. Eventually, he settled for sulking in the background, following them as they moved through the ship, disabling and rerouting systems. They seemed in a hurry, and upset about something.

He wondered what it was.

Eventually the crew, now in the habitat ring, stood outside a hatch Chris had never been able to open, labeled ORBITAL BOMBARDMENT MAIN CONTROL. They had pulled up a large section of deck planking and were standing looking down into the cables snaking through the hole. To Chris' astonishment, one of them reached up and removed his helmet. As he did so, exterior speakers on the other's suits came to life. "Smell any germs, O'Sullivan?" someone cracked.

"It smells fine," O'Sullivan said. He sniffed. "Although I think the kid there needs a shower." He began undoing zippers and snaps on his now-deflated pressure suit and shimmied out of it. Underneath, he wore a blue jumpsuit with his name stitched across the left breast. Rank insignia Chris had no idea how to read marked both sleeves.

Chris ignored the gibe. "All of you could unsuit, you know," he said. "There's nothing to worry about. I mean, look at me. I've been living here for weeks, and I'm fine."

O'Sullivan glanced at him. "Gee, thanks, I feel much better now," he said. "Now shut up." In his sock-covered feet, he turned and descended into the opening in the floor. "All right," he said, looking up at his still-suited compatriots, "here goes nothing."

*   *   *

"Message from *Sanctification*," Braun said quietly to Cheveldeoff as they stood side by side on the bridge of *BPS Retribution*. "They're working on the final switch-over. You should have control of *Sanctification*'s Orbital Bombardment System within a couple of hours."

Cheveldeoff glanced at the Grand Deacon. *He's still waiting,* he thought. *Waiting for me to screw up. Well, he'll have a long wait.* He turned his attention back to the main tactical display. In the middle of his interrogation of Chris Keating, he'd been informed that *Fist of God,* whose complement of Holy Warriors they had seen slaughtered, had just launched. Some time ago, it had vanished behind the planet. It should be coming up behind them, rising over the horizon as it ascended and accelerated to rendezvous with *Retribution.*

But who was on board?

There. "*BPS Fist of God* reacquired," said the computer. "Rendezvous in twenty-two minutes."

"Computer, open communication link to *Fist of God.*"

"Ready," said the computer.

"Occupants of *BPS Fist of God*, this is *BPS Retribution.* Identify yourselves." No response. He hadn't really expected one, but it never hurt to ask. "Occupants of shuttle *Fist of God,* respond." Still nothing. "Computer, end transmission." He turned to Braun. "We asked them," he said. "They didn't answer. The shuttle is on automatic approach, which means we get control of it for final docking." He smiled. "It might be contaminated, Grand Deacon. When we gain control, order it to open itself to space."

The Grand Deacon's smile was as predatory as Cheveldeoff's. His loyalty to the Archdeacon might be questionable, but not his desire for revenge on those who had killed his troops. "I can't think of a better way to rid a spacecraft of . . . contamination, sir. It will be my pleasure."

"See to it." Cheveldeoff turned back to the tactical display to watch.

Less than fifteen minutes later, *Fist of God* moved through the handoff point. Control passed from its computer to that of *Retribution.*

Two minutes after that, the shuttle fired retro rockets that brought it to a halt, relative to the ship.

And one minute after that, the sides opened.

Air exploded out, its moisture forming an expanding cloud of ice that swirled and glittered in the sunlight. Odds and ends of equipment spun and flashed in the cloud . . . but no bodies, pressure suited or otherwise.

Damn! "Braun?"

"Scanning," Braun said. "Stand by." A minute crawled past. "Empty," Braun said abruptly. "No one aboard. No one in the seats, no one in the cockpit, no one in the holds."

Cheveldeoff felt his fists clench and consciously relaxed them. "Then where the hell are they?"

Chapter 19

THROUGH THE FACEPLATE of his borrowed Holy Warrior pressure suit, *BPS Sanctification* loomed in front of Richard like a . . . *well, like an orbiting starship,* he thought, simile failing him.

They had bailed out of *Fist of God* while it was in Earth shadow from *Retribution,* carrying the POTs—Personal Orbital Transportation devices, the space equivalent of the Selkies' sputa. The wounded pilot had told them all about the POTs when properly brain-stimulated by Dr. Christianson-Wood. He'd also told them exactly how to program the automated return of the shuttle, what would likely happen to the shuttle when it reached *Retribution* ("They'll either open it to vacuum or blow it out of space"), how to use the *Fist of God*'s computer to calculate their best intercept course for *Sanctification,* what he'd had for dinner the night before, how he felt about his ex-wife, his deep longing to someday be a professional singer, and the nasty thing he'd done to his sister when he was twelve (and very nasty it had been, too).

Richard suspected he was still talking.

They'd left sometime during his account of getting beaten up in kindergarten and returned to *Fist of God.* They'd found the POTs right where the pilot had said they were, and the computer had been extremely helpful once presented with the security codes the pilot had handed over. It had programmed the POTs for them, told them when to enter the air lock, and expelled them at the proper time with careful bursts of gas. They'd watched the shuttle dwindle into a moving star while they coasted on their new trajectory.

Once both *Fist of God* and *Retribution* were below the horizon, the POTs came to life, driving them into a new orbit that now, two hours later, had brought them to a gentle rendezvous with *Sanctification.*

Emily, as she had smugly expected, had indeed had no difficulty at all getting used to zero-G. Richard's stomach felt unsettled, but not as badly as when he had first gone into space. Those weeks on *Sanctification* had eased his tendency to space sickness, it seemed.

If Richard turned his head, he could see Emily four meters to his left and slightly behind him. They hadn't spoken since they'd left the shuttle, not daring to break radio silence in case either *Retribution* or *Sanctification* — or both — were listening.

He looked back at *Sanctification* as a beep sounded in his helmet. "Programmed maneuvers completed," said a tinny version of the shuttle's computer voice. "Manual controls engaged."

The computer had done its part. Now it was up to them to make a safe landing.

Richard knew what to look for: four service air locks spaced equidistantly midway between the spinning habitat ring at the bow and the shuttle docking bays at the stern. But he couldn't spot them in the glare of the sun, and the ship was growing bigger with alarming speed.

Time to end radio silence.

"Computer," he said. "Activate suit-to-suit communication."

"Activated."

"Emily, are you there?"

"I'm here," the response came immediately. "What's next, Rocket Richard?"

Richard grimaced. Ever since she'd decided to use his first name instead of calling him Mr. Hansen, and in general become friendlier, she'd been experimenting with nicknames. "Richard is fine," he'd told her. "Just Richard."

Apparently, she'd decided to ignore his suggestion.

Oddly enough, despite his protests, he wasn't at all sure he really minded.

"We need to slow our approach. Two-second forward burst on my mark, count of three. Ready?"

"Roger."

"One . . . two . . . three . . . mark."

Two puffs of gas from each of the chairlike POTs, and the approach of the ship slowed markedly. But Richard still couldn't see any hatches.

"Computer," he said hopefully, "Magnify and enhance."

"The Mark 6 Space-Capable Pressure Suit does not have the inherent ability to modify visual input," the computer replied. "Please install a Mark 9 Enhanced Vision Helmet or a Neo-Zeiss Mark 67 Visual Enhancement Overlay Device."

Richard sighed. "Never mind."

"Are you looking for a hatch?" Emily said. "Because I can see two of them."

"You can?" Richard squinted. He still couldn't make out any details in the sun-drenched white surface.

"Nictitating membranes," Emily said. "Polarized, even, thanks to Dr. Hansen. They act like sunglasses. Reduce glare, enhance contrast. You should get some."

"Very funny. All right, you'd better take the lead, then." He nudged himself sideways, and eased slowly up on Emily's right side. "Computer, match our trajectories and velocities."

"Vector matching complete," the computer said after a brief puff of gas from Richard's POT.

"Computer, slave POT controls to Suit Two."

"Controls slaved."

"Okay, Emily, you've got the helm."

"Affirmative. Hold on."

To what? he wondered.

He needn't have worried. Emily maneuvered them in with as much finesse as a veteran spacedock worker, until they floated stationary relative to the ship, close enough to reach out and grab the stanchions that surrounded all four sides of the two-meter-by-two-meter hatch.

"Now comes the fun part," Richard said. "We find out if my computer codes still work."

"They worked when you shut down communications," Emily said.

"Yes, but by now there must be Holy Warriors on board. And they're undoubtedly mucking around in the computer. There are no guarantees."

"*Now* you tell me," Emily muttered.

"Better late than never!" Richard poked a gloved finger at a glowing red button beside the hatch; a panel slid open, revealing an oversized keyboard. With one finger, he entered the twelve-character alphanumeric code he'd memorized back when he still thought the will of God—and his own career and ego—could be best served by sending a shipload of bloodthirsty killers to ravage a peaceful planet.

He had changed, but the code hadn't: the hatch opened.

They clearly couldn't both fit in the lock with their POTs. Richard only hesitated a second. "Dump the POTs," he said. "We probably won't need them again, and if we do, the ship must have some."

It made perfect sense, but Richard still felt a brief surge of worry as he unbuckled from his POT and gave it a gentle shove. It drifted slowly away, out of reach within seconds. *No going back now,* Richard thought, and then had to laugh at his groundlubber brain, which insisted on thinking he could simply retrace his steps to the shuttle. The shuttle was either destroyed or on board *Retribution* by now. There hadn't been any going back since the moment they'd squirted into space. There was no "back" to go back *to*.

He turned to Emily, who had likewise dispatched her POT, and swept his arm toward the air lock. "After you, miss."

Emily made as much of a bow as she could in a pressure suit, and pulled herself into the lock.

Sanctification swept through the terminator. The air lock's interior changed in an instant from a forbidding black hole in a glaring wall of metal to a welcoming, well-lit cubbyhole in a forbidding sea of blackness.

Taking that as an omen, Richard followed Emily inside.

As she waited with Richard for the air lock to cycle and let them through into *Sanctification,* Emily slipped her laser pistol from its holder. The thing could only manage a few shots before it needed recharging, but as Richard had had to remind her—underwater wasn't *quite* the same as zero-G, and shooting guns underwater just didn't come up on Marseguro—mass-throwing projectile weapons and microgravity didn't go together well, thanks to Newton's Third Law.

Richard pulled out his own laser pistol. Together they

watched the light over the inside door. At last it turned green. The door opened, and . . .

. . . nothing. Just an empty spherical chamber maybe six meters in diameter, with hatches across from the air lock and above, below, and to either side. Silvery webbing covered the bulkheads, as though a giant Earth spider had been hard at work.

Richard holstered his pistol, reached up, and took off his helmet. Emily did the same.

"They're not waiting for us," he said. "That's something. And if they're working on the Orbital Bombardment System, they're clear up in the habitat ring. On the down side, that's where we have to go, too."

"Well, if we have to fight, I'm not doing it wearing this," Emily said. She began undoing the straps and zippers that held the pressure suit in place. "I can barely move."

Richard hesitated. "We might need them," he began, then stopped and laughed. "And if we do, there are plenty on board. You're right." He began struggling out of his own suit. ·

Underneath the pressure suit, Emily wore her black, water-filled landsuit . . . in a way, just a different kind of pressure suit, something to protect her from a not-entirely-friendly environment. She flexed her neck, encased in a watery collar. Her gills were cramping from being cooped up for so long. The collar kept them moist, but the suit's water supply held little oxygen, so she couldn't really use them. What she wouldn't give for half an hour in the open sea. . . .

Richard, now wearing a blue jumpsuit and soft white leathery slippers—"standard Holy Warrior microgravity ship wear," he'd explained when he'd taken it from the shuttle's storage locker and put it on, down on Marseguro—pulled his laser pistol from the floating, crumpled form of the pressure suit. Emily grabbed hers, too, but she also took a moment to check her wrist dart-guns. They'd saved her life twice now. She'd become attached to them.

"Ready?" Richard said.

She nodded.

"This way." He pushed off from the wall and sailed across, landing on the webbing on the far side of the chamber and grabbing on. Emily followed him. Using the webbing, they worked their way to the hatch opposite the air lock. It opened at the touch of a button on a panel beside it, and they slipped through.

A square cross-section corridor ran away from the hatch, more hatches opening periodically from each of its four sides. "Straight ahead," Richard said. "The far end of this corridor should open into the central access shaft, the zero-G highway that runs fore to aft. That'll take us to the habitat ring, where the bridge is."

"Wouldn't it make more sense to have the bridge on the nose of the ship?" Emily said. "So you could just look out and see where you're going?"

"You can't fly something the size of *Sanctification* by the seat of your pants," Richard said. "You don't need to see where you're going. So you might as well put the bridge in gravity and make it easier for the crew to function. Besides, one reason for the central shaft is to allow shuttles or life-craft to fly through the ship to get out if the docking bays are damaged. The nose of the ship is just one big hatch. Come on."

She expected him to launch himself down the corridor like a missile, but instead he grabbed hold of the webbing and began pulling himself along it. Emily followed.

All the hatches were closed. Emily wondered what had happened to the dead Warriors she knew must inhabit the ship. *It's like those old Earth stories about ghost ships.* She'd never been superstitious, but she still had to repress a shiver.

She spotted the opening at the end of the corridor that presumably led into the central shaft. "The end is in sight!"

"Not to me," Richard grumbled. "But it's about time. My arms are wearing out."

"Why not just push off?" Emily said. "From here you could probably shoot through the opening without touching anything—"

"And zip right across the central shaft, smash into the far wall and break my neck," Richard said. "I prefer slow and steady." The opening, dim and blue, loomed ahead. "The ship's still running day/night cycles for the crew, looks like," Richard said as he pulled himself the last couple of meters. "Just our luck to hit a night cycle . . . oof!"

As he emerged from the corridor, something traveling fast toward the stern collided with him, and he disappeared. It happened so quickly Emily didn't have a clue what the fast-moving object had been. She gripped her laser pistol and launched herself through the opening.

Too fast! She lost her grip on the webbing and fell into the central shaft, drifting across its thirty-meter diameter unable to do anything but wriggle. But by jackknifing, she at least managed to turn herself around to see what had happened to Richard.

He drifted in the shaft, struggling with another figure, a half-naked barefoot landling youth—

Chris Keating.

As she watched, Richard shoved hard, and Chris sailed into the shaft wall with an audible thud and grunt. Richard accelerated in the opposite direction, more or less toward Emily.

Chris grabbed the webbing and clung like a wallcrawler, staring up at them. Emily raised her pistol, ready to fire—

—and Chris scuttled away, still heading toward the stern. He'd never said a word.

"Where's he going?" Emily said. He'd already gotten too far away to waste a precious laser shot on. As she watched, he swung through an opening and disappeared.

"Could be anywhere," Richard said. Something in his voice made her look more closely at him. He had drifted within a couple of meters of her but would soon pass her— tossing Chris away from him had given him a lot more impetus than her leap into the shaft had given her. He held his left arm cradled against his body, and his laser pistol had disappeared. "I think my arm is broken," he gasped. "Keating hit me like a ton of bricks."

Emily looked around. "We're almost across the shaft. Will you be able to grab the webbing?"

"I'll have to, won't . . . unnh." He'd hit the wall. He groaned, but grabbed a silvery rope with his right hand and held on.

Emily reached the wall herself a minute later. She spidered her way down to him. "Let me see your arm."

"It's all right," he said. "I'll . . ."

"It's *not* all right, Dicky," Emily snapped, knowing the nickname would annoy him and hoping it would also refocus his mind.

"Don't call me—" He stopped and said, "You're right. But what can you do with a broken arm?"

"I can't set it, but I can wrap it up." She looked around. "If I can find something to wrap it with."

"There's nothing in the shaft."

"I can look in some of the compartments—"

Richard shook his head. "No. There's no time. I don't know where Keating is headed, but we have to figure he'll tell the Holy Warriors we're here. And we can't fight them all. Our only hope is to carry out our original plan. We have to get to the bridge."

"But your arm . . ."

"It's not going to kill me. It just hurts. I'll live. Let's go." And he started to crawl forward, one-armed. He moved at about the same pace as a squeegeefish scraping muck off the bottom of a rock pool, and Emily only followed for a few seconds before saying, "Stop."

"We can't—"

"I said stop, all right?" She made her way in front and stuck her bare foot in his face. She wriggled her webbed toes at him. "Grab hold."

He didn't argue, for once, just grabbed hold of her ankle.

"No tickling," she said. "Especially not the webbing. Or I'm likely to kick your teeth in. Purely by accident, of course."

Richard managed a wan smile. "No tickling. I promise."

She tucked the laser into a pocket of the landsuit, took hold of the maneuvering webbing, and began pulling them hand over hand toward the bow, the habitat ring—and the bridge.

Chris hurried toward the docking bays, a sharp pain in his side from the collision with . . . Richard Hansen. He couldn't believe it. Hansen himself, the Machiavellian mass-murdering monster, returning to the scene of his crime . . . with Emily Wood, the sea-bitch herself.

He needed to warn the Holy Warriors . . . but he couldn't get back to the habitat ring without going through the central shaft, and Hansen and Wood were there, and armed— he'd seen a laser pistol in Wood's hand.

And besides, if he went back, he'd lose his only chance to do what he had to do if he wanted to be sure of getting off this hulk.

The Warriors are soldiers, he thought. *They can handle one normal and one moddie. There's no way Hansen and*

Wood can do anything to stop them before they have the Orbital Bombardment System up and running. And when they do—boom. No more Hansen's Harbor, or Firstdip, or any other settlements. No more Selkies. No more Marseguro.

No more landlings, but he could live with that. *Toadying fishfuckers, the lot of them.*

He rubbed his aching right side. A cracked rib, almost certainly. But he must have hurt Hansen, too. Something had snapped when they'd collided.

The Holy Warriors can take care of themselves. It's about time I took care of me.

He kept heading aft.

"Status," Cheveldeoff snapped, for the fifth time that hour.

"Nothing has changed." Braun didn't quite manage to keep the impatience out of his voice. "*Sanctification*'s central computer is a higher order AI than *Retribution*'s. There are difficulties in convincing it to allow us to hand over control to what it sees as a less-capable system, even though we have hardwired a shunt past the—"

"I don't want the technical details, Grand Deacon," Cheveldeoff said, with more than a hint of dry ice in his tone. "I want an estimated time of completion."

"Half an hour, minimum. Sir."

Cheveldeoff glared at the tactical display. "And how long until the next opportunity for maximum-velocity, maximum-mass bombardment of Hansen's Harbor?"

"Forty-seven minutes. After that, there are lesser-velocity launch windows, of course, but the maximum-damage launch window won't open again for one full orbit—a little under two hours."

Cheveldeoff turned the full power of his coldest stare on Braun. "I can wait if I have to, Grand Deacon. But I don't want to."

The Grand Deacon's lips thinned. "Understood."

"Good." Cheveldeoff stared at the tactical display again. He'd been waiting for the other shoe from *Fist of God* to drop. So far they hadn't picked up anything . . . but *Retribution*'s sensor suite wasn't even close to state of the art. The ship hadn't been left in Earth orbit during major operations on New Mars just because the Archdeacon of Naval Operations didn't like its name, after all.

Still, they couldn't have missed a second shuttle launch. Cheveldeoff had begun to allow himself to believe Braun's comforting theory that the shuttle had been preprogrammed to return to the ship automatically by an overcautious—and now presumably thoroughly dead—pilot, and its launch had taken the Marseguroites as much by surprise as it had the Holy Warriors.

He'd left *Fist of God* drifting outside the ship. Nothing from the ground would be allowed aboard *Retribution* until he was certain they weren't dealing with either a natural or Selkie-made plague.

He resisted the urge to ask Braun for the status of the salvage party again. He would wait. But if he didn't have orbital bombardment control within forty-seven . . . make that forty-five . . . minutes . . .

Well, Cheveldeoff's spies informed him that Braun's loyalty to Shridhar wasn't as solid as all that. When the mission succeeded, Cheveldeoff suspected Braun, recognizing Shridhar's bid for the Avatarship was doomed, would start sucking up to the Archdeacon in earnest. Cheveldeoff also suspected Braun was smart enough to realize that if he did anything to obstruct Cheveldeoff's efforts, and the mission succeeded anyway, he'd soon find himself running anti-Islamic revival operations in Saudi Arabia.

Cheveldeoff had long worked by the theory that the best way to ensure obedience was to punish someone. Anyone. The Marseguroites' punishment was sure. The Grand Deacon's still hung in the balance.

As for Richard Hansen . . . Cheveldeoff only regretted that if Richard Hansen were in Hansen's Harbor when the mass hurled from orbit arrived, he'd never see it coming.

Chapter 20

RICHARD CRADLED HIS left arm and held on to Emily's webbed foot. Keeping his arm motionless kept the pain bearable enough that he only gasped once. But any movement caused bone ends to rub against each other and agony to skewer his arm like a red-hot poker. The second time it happened, he squeezed his eyes closed. *How in hell am I going to do what I need to do with one good arm?*

Emily slowed. "Now what?" she said.

Richard opened his eyes and blinked away tears. On the other side of a webbing-free, meter-wide strip of bare silvery metal, the central shaft continued—except the webbing on the other side of the strip rolled past at about the speed a man could run, as the entire shaft rotated at three revolutions per minute.

Eight small cubical elevator heads protruded from the rotating shaft, four equidistant around the shaft about twenty meters from where they waited, and four more forty meters beyond that. Brightly lit, they were all Richard could see in the dim blue light . . . but they were the last thing he wanted to use. Anyone monitoring ship's systems would immediately detect an elevator being put into operation, and either shut it down or have a welcoming committee waiting for it when it reached the outer deck.

Somewhere out there, though, there were also hatches, each of which opened onto a shaft called, for reasons lost to history, a Jefferies tube. The tubes provided access to various systems for repair and maintenance. Each had a ladder in it that allowed the person doing that repair and maintenance to climb from the outer deck to the central shaft and back again. And one—the one Richard wanted—led to the corridor just outside the bridge.

"We're looking for hatches," he said. "They're painted yellow . . . no webbing on them. But I can't see them in this light. Can you?"

Silence for a moment as Emily set her oversized eyes to the task. "I think so," she said finally. "Half a dozen of them, at least. Which one do we want?"

"Farthest. Closest to the bow." Richard closed his eyes as a wave of pain and nausea swept over him. He swallowed hard four or five times. He would *not* throw up. He would *not* . . .

As seemed to happen every time he issued that command to himself, he promptly disobeyed it.

At least the air circulation system took the globules of liquid and floating undigested bits of the military rations he'd eaten back on the shuttle toward the stern. *Maybe they'll hit Chris Keating,* Richard thought.

Emily waited stoically until he'd quit heaving and coughing. He spat a couple of times, and wished he had water to rinse his mouth. "Let's go," he said, taking hold of Emily's foot again. "The usual method is to . . . unnh."

Not bothering to wait to hear what the usual method was, Emily had simply launched herself . . . and him . . . onto the rotating webbing. She grabbed hold. The jerk as they were swept "up" made him gasp.

"Sorry, Ricky," she said.

"Just get us to the hatch."

Even this close to the center the spin imparted weight, enough so that instead of bobbing along like a cork behind Emily, Richard found himself being dragged across the webbing like a balloon without quite enough helium in it. He turned onto his right side to save his broken arm as best he could. As a result, he had a perfect view of the lone pressure-suited Holy Warrior emerging from one of the elevators.

The Holy Warrior's half-silvered helmet hid his face, but Richard didn't have to wonder long if he'd been seen: the Warrior instantly launched himself toward them.

"Look out!" Richard yelled at Emily.

The shout was too late to do her any good, but she must have seen something out of the corner of her eye, and Victor Hansen had given the Selkies unbelievable reflexes by nonmoddie standards. So fast he hardly saw the motion, she turned, drew, and fired.

He couldn't see the beam in the clear air, but sparks, bright as stars in the dim light, burst from the neck of the Warrior's pressure suit. For a moment, Richard thought the suit had stopped the laser, but then the oncoming body separated into two parts. The still-helmeted head drifted up and away from them, while the now-headless body continued forward in a slow, stately, end-over-end spin, spewing shimmering scarlet globules.

The body bounced off the webbing and over Richard's head. He ducked. Blood spattered the webbing around him. One crimson globe hit him on the cheek, clinging and half-blinding him; he frantically wiped at his face with his good hand.

Selkie faces were always pale, but Emily's looked paler than usual. "Too close! Did he call for help?"

"No way of knowing. Let's get to that hatch." He grabbed Emily's heel again, and she resumed the scramble.

By the time they reached the hatch, the Warrior's body and head and most of his blood were drifting back down the shaft in the air circulation currents. Richard was surprised he could still see them; then he realized what must be happening.

The night cycle had ended. "Dawn" was breaking.

The hatch opened readily to Richard's security codes, and bright light strips came on in the Jefferies tube. He couldn't see the bottom—not surprising since he calculated the tube was roughly the height of a twenty-story building.

Emily looked down, then at Richard. "Are you sure you can do this?"

"I don't have much choice, do I?"

"We could take the elevator."

He shook his head. "Too dangerous."

"They may not even know we're here," Emily argued.

The webbing to their right suddenly came apart in a puff of acrid smoke, its severed ends glowing red for a moment. Richard dove headfirst into the shaft, grabbed hold of the ladder with his right hand, and swung around, crashing into it so hard his ears rang. Emily jumped in behind him and clung to the ladder just below the raised hatch.

A glowing red line streaked across the inside of the hatch and vanished, leaving behind a long black mark. Emily slapped at the controls. The hatch slammed shut and sealed with a hiss.

Through the red roaring haze in his head, Richard heard a faraway voice say, "They know."

It took him a minute to realize the voice had been his own.

"Intruders in *BPS Sanctification,*" Braun suddenly announced to Cheveldeoff on the bridge of *Retribution,* just five minutes away from the end of the estimated half hour until handover of the Orbital Bombardment System.

"Intruders? *How?*"

"They must have used POTs," Braun said. "Probably launched themselves from *Fist of God* out of our sensor range, then just coasted to a rendezvous with *Sanctification.*"

"And why didn't we see them?"

"Our sensor suite is old and overextended."

Is it? Cheveldeoff thought. *Or are you being very careful to only do what I specifically order you to, and since I didn't tell you to look for coasting pressure suits, you didn't instruct your men to look for them, either . . . so that if these "intruders" succeed in screwing up the mission, the fault will be entirely mine?*

Deal with the immediate problem first. "How many?"

"We have visual confirmation of two, a normal male and a female Selkie. There could be others we haven't seen."

I'll bet I know who the male is. Cheveldeoff's mind flashed back to the sight of Hansen and a Selkie girl walking away from the shuttle after the ambush of the reconnaissance party. "Where are they?"

"They're in a Jefferies tube . . . not sure where it goes yet. We're checking ship schematics . . . got it." A pause. "It leads to just outside the bridge."

"Then I suggest you get some of your people to just outside the bridge, Grand Deacon."

Braun's brows knit. "That order has already been given, Archdeacon."

"Good to know you aren't entirely incompetent," Cheveldeoff snarled. "Here are *my* orders: kill them, and get me control of the Orbital Bombardment System within the next twenty minutes."

The Grand Deacon didn't move. "Those orders," he said carefully, "have *also* already been given. Sir."

Oh-ho, thought Cheveldeoff. *Time to show some teeth.* "A word in private, Grand Deacon?"

Braun nodded. Cheveldeoff led him into the briefing room. The door closed automatically behind them, and Cheveldeoff whirled and put his face just inches from Braun's. "Grand Deacon," he said, soft as a breeze but with the focused intensity of a blowtorch, "let's be perfectly clear. I know, and you know I know, that you favor Shridhar in the upcoming vote to select the next Avatar. I don't know your reasons; I don't care. What I do care about is this mission. You may think, Grand Deacon, that by sabotaging this mission you are only sabotaging me, and ensuring that your favored candidate wins the post of Avatar. Perhaps he has offered you my job if you succeed in causing this mission to fail.

"But know this, Grand Deacon. No matter who eventually becomes Avatar, when we return to Earth, I will still be head of Body Security for several weeks or months to come. And during that time, I will have little compunction about using all of the considerable powers I will still enjoy making your life, and the lives of all those dear to you, hell. Of course I cannot, in my official capacity, order anyone's death or torture, but I cannot vouch for some of my more overenthusiastic followers, who might take it upon themselves to punish those who have openly declared their enmity toward me . . . something I am beginning to suspect you may be on the verge of doing yourself."

Cheveldeoff moved even closer to Braun, who kept his eyes rigidly focused on the wall behind Cheveldeoff's head. He dropped his voice to the barest whisper. "Do I make myself clear, Grand Deacon?"

Braun pulled his gaze down as though from a great height, and looked into Cheveldeoff's eyes, his face pale but utterly stoic. "Perfectly, sir," he said. "Now if you'll excuse me . . ." He turned and went back out through the briefing room door onto the bridge.

And Cheveldeoff felt an unaccustomed pang of uncertainty. In his experience, no one remained as calm as Braun just had in the face of such threats from the Archdeacon of Body Security.

What's he up to? he wondered. *And why haven't my spies found it out?*

Unsettled, he returned to the bridge.

Emily didn't like the way Richard looked. Of course, the over-bright, over-blue lighting of the Jefferies tube didn't do his complexion any favors, but she didn't think his paleness was entirely a result of the lighting, and it certainly hadn't caused the sheen of sweat on his face. "Can you move?" she said.

"I'll have to, won't I?"

"I could carry you—"

He shook his head. "No. You need your gun hand free."

She couldn't argue with that.

"Let me by," he said, and she squeezed to one side so that he could heave himself up the ladder to just under the hatch and punch buttons on its keypad. "I've keyed in a manual combination. I doubt they have complete control of the computer, so they shouldn't be able to bypass it easily. They won't come after us this way."

"But they'll be waiting for us down below?"

"If they can get there fast enough. But unless they're already there, they've got to follow a roundabout route—that part of the habitat ring is practically a maze, and the layout of the rooms and corridors is somewhat mutable; it's a security feature. We, on the other hand, are taking a straight line. So let's move."

Emily took the hint and began to descend.

Their weight increased as they went down deck by deck, and with it, the number of moans and grunts coming from Richard. But he didn't complain or ask for help, and as they came closer to the bottom of the shaft, Emily focused her attention downward, straining her eyes for any glimpse of movement, afraid the first—and last—she would know of the arrival of the Holy Warriors below her would be the flash of a laser.

But there was the bottom hatch, still closed. Emily stopped. "It should open automatically," Richard panted above her. "They're locked against entry to keep unauthorized people out of the tubes, but there's no default need to lock them against people inside them."

Emily nodded. "If they're waiting on the other side, we won't have much of a chance, will we?"

"If we don't try this, Marseguro doesn't have any chance at all," Richard said. "A half-ton rod of ceramic-tungsten alloy impacting at eleven kilometers per second makes a hell of a hole."

Emily felt a flash of her old anger at him. *None of this would be happening if not for you!*

But that wasn't really fair . . . not anymore. Chris Keating was the real culprit . . . and above all, the Avatar of the Body Purified, whose bloody-handed predecessor had driven them to Marseguro in the first place and whose so-called "wisdom" had turned Keating against his own people.

Hell, maybe *she* was even partly to blame for having jumped Chris on the pier that day with John Duval and her Selkie friends.

Lots of blame to go around. Lots of actions by lots of people, leading to lots of consequences, good and bad. Her anger at Richard faded. *At least he's tried to make up for what he did. Whether it's because of Victor Hansen's gene-bomb or his own conscience, he's changed.*

She grinned. *So have I,* she thought, and jumped off the ladder.

The hatch opened underneath her and she dropped heavily into the corridor below, crouched, laser out, ready to cut in half anything that moved.

But nothing did.

"All clear," she shouted up to Richard.

He dropped down a moment later, hit the deck with a groan and fell to his knees. He remained there for a moment, leaning on his one good arm, then sighed and straightened. She held out her free hand and helped him to his feet.

"Thanks," he said. He looked around. "We can't have very long. This way." He led the way down the corridor to the right.

After a few meters, he stopped in front of a heavy black pressure door with the crossed-sword-and-starship emblem of the Holy Warriors embossed on it in red. "Computer," Richard said, facing it. "Biometric scan, please."

"Scan complete," the computer said. "Greetings, Richard Hansen."

"Computer, open bridge door."

The door didn't budge. "Input verbal security codes."

Richard reeled off a string of numbers and letters. Emily held her breath.

"Codes accepted," the computer said. "Standing down bridge security. Laser turrets deactivated. Sonic stunners deactivated. Please wait for pressurization."

"Laser turrets? Sonic stunners? Pressurization?" Emily said.

"Security features," Richard said. "If the bridge is abandoned by the crew, the computer takes steps to ensure that no one without authorization can gain control of the ship."

"How long will it take to pressurize?"

"Just a minute or two—"

From down the hall came the clatter of footsteps.

Emily spun and dropped to one knee. The first Holy Warrior to round the corner screamed and fell back out of sight as her beam slashed across his leg.

"I don't know if we have a minute or two," Emily said.

"They can't come around that corner without you nailing them," Richard said.

"Is there any way for them to circle around and hit us from two directions at once?"

Richard hesitated. "Yes. But it will take them—"

"—a minute or two," Emily said. "Great."

She caught a hint of movement and fired. The beam harmlessly scored the wall . . . and an indicator on top of the pistol flashed yellow. *Charge warning,* Emily thought. *This just gets better and better. You'd think the Holy Warriors would make sure their laser pistols were fully charged before hanging them in a shuttle for anyone to use . . .*

. . . and just how many shots do you get after the charge warning appears, anyway?

She found out two shots later, when she pressed the trigger and nothing happened. Since both shots had missed, the odds remained unchanged . . . as did the bridge door, still stubbornly closed.

"Computer," shouted Richard, "How much long—look out!"

Emily had glanced at him just for a second. Now she jerked her head around again to face the corner. Only her Selkie reflexes saved her life. She saw the emerging Holy Warrior as if he were moving in slow motion, saw his laser pistol coming up, and threw herself forward, firing her right-hand dart gun as she fell. The darts slammed the Holy Warrior back against the wall. He slid down, leaving a trail of blood, and slumped to the ground.

Some sixth sense—or more likely Selkie hearing—warned her to twist around the other way. A Holy Warrior had just started to come around the corner in that direction; he leaped back as she turned, and the darts fired from her left wrist shattered harmlessly against the wall.

Out of darts, out of time, she thought . . .

The bridge door opened.

. . . but not out of luck.

Richard darted in. Emily followed. A searing pain lashed through her right calf as she jumped, and she screamed and crumpled to the ground just inside the bridge.

"Computer! Secure bridge!" Richard shouted, and the door slammed shut behind them.

Emily felt a surge of fear. "It will blow the atmosphere!"

"Not with authorized people in the room. Different procedure." Richard knelt beside her. "Are you all right?"

"My leg . . ." Emily stretched it out in front of her. The pain made her gasp.

A laser had sliced a six-centimeter gash in her calf muscle, passing right through. Since the laser had cauterized the wound at the same instant it made it, she hadn't bled much, but nothing she'd ever felt had hurt worse. A puddle of water had formed under her calf from the hole in the landsuit, but its self-sealing skin stopped the leak before more than a couple of hundred milliliters escaped.

"I'll live," Emily said weakly. "Can't fight, though. No ammo." She felt light-headed; shock. "Might pass out . . ."

"End game," Richard said. "Either I can make this tub do what I want it to, and we win, or I can't, and we lose."

"Warning," said the computer suddenly. "Unauthorized access of Orbital Bombardment System. Unauthorized access of Orbital Bombardment System. Unauthorized remote control initiated. Unauthorized remote control initiated." A pause, then, "Launch detected. Five-hundred-kilogram mass."

Richard swore. Emily felt her heart skip a beat, then another, then settle into a strange, syncopated rhythm. The room whirled.

"Too . . . late . . ." she whispered, and fell into darkness.

*   *   *

"Who authorized that mass launch?" shouted Cheveldeoff on the bridge of *Retribution*. "Because I sure as hell didn't!" He clenched his fists. *Is Braun slipping into outright mutiny?* He looked around the bridge. The Holy Warrior manning the communications console returned his gaze steadily. *One of mine,* Cheveldeoff thought. *But he's the only one in here who is.*

Braun said nothing, listening to a voice in his ear. "A glitch," he said after a moment. "During the switch-over."

"Show me where it hit!"

The tactical display changed to a three-dimensional image of Marseguro. A spot of light blossomed in the middle of the ocean, ten thousand kilometers from the continent, almost halfway around the planet.

"Wasted!" Cheveldeoff snarled. "And the angle was all wrong. It burned off most of its speed and a good chunk of its mass in the atmosphere. It won't even raise a ripple in Hansen's Harbor."

Braun spoke quietly to his earbud transceiver; listened, then said, "Roger that," and looked at Cheveldeoff. "Fifteen minutes to reload. You'll still get your shot this pass."

No mutiny yet, then. "I'd better. What about Hansen and that moddie bitch? Dead?"

Braun shook his head. "Not yet. They killed two Holy Warriors and made it onto the bridge. They're both wounded, though. They may not be able to—"

"They're on the bridge!" Cheveldeoff roared. "Damn you, Braun—"

"They can't do anything there," Braun said. "Hansen is an intelligence analyst, not a spaceship pilot."

"*Sanctification* is moving, sir," a Holy Warrior shouted—not Cheveldeoff's man.

"They can't do anything, can they?" Cheveldeoff spun to face the crewman. "Moving where?"

"Unknown, sir." A pause. "She's slowing." Another pause. "I think she's changing orbits, sir."

"Restore tactical display!"

The globe vanished, replaced with the display he'd been watching for hours.

"Detailed view!"

Numbers and projected trajectories flashed into view.

Cheveldeoff took one look. "She's not *changing* orbits, you idiot, she's *de-orbiting*. He's scuttling her." He looked at the numbers again, and his lips pulled back from his teeth in what might have been mistaken for a grin. "But he can't scuttle her fast enough. Computer! Confirm control of *Sanctification* Orbital Bombardment System has passed to this vessel."

"Confirmed," said the computer.

"Computer, program *Sanctification* Orbital Bombardment System as follows: target, Hansen's Harbor. Mass: largest available. Velocity: maximum possible." He leaned forward. "Put it in the middle of that precious Square of theirs."

"System programmed," the computer said. "Please confirm auto-launch."

"Computer, confirm auto-launch."

"Auto-launch in six minutes . . . mark."

Cheveldeoff straightened and took a deep breath. "Grand Deacon," he said, without looking around.

"Yes, sir," said Braun.

"Call your people back." He paused. "Except for the one that took off his suit. He stays."

Braun sucked in a sharp breath. "You're leaving him to die?"

"He could be infected. If he returns to the ship, we may all die."

"That Keating kid said . . ."

"Grand Deacon," said Cheveldeoff. With the hammer about to fall on Hansen's Harbor, he no longer felt any uncertainty at all, and he turned and gave Braun the hardest of his extensive repertoire of hard stares. "*Don't* argue with me."

Braun's mouth worked, but all he said was, "Yes, sir." He moved away, talking into his transceiver, and left the bridge.

Cheveldeoff watched the tactical display. "Checkmate, Mr. Hansen," he said softly. "Checkmate."

Chapter 21

IT TOOK RICHARD ONLY two minutes to discover that his plan to disable the Orbital Bombardment System from the bridge would not work.

He'd suspected as much when he'd told Emily that the Holy Warriors had hardwired a shunt around *Sanctification*'s security systems. He'd worried they had cut the ship's computer out of the control loop entirely . . . and the ship's computer had just confirmed he'd been right to worry.

Their best hope had been to get to *Sanctification* before the Holy Warriors even boarded it. Failing that, they'd had to get to the bridge before the Warriors gained control of the OBS. Having failed *that,* he seemed to be out of options.

He glanced at Emily. She lay unconscious, face pale, on the steel plates of the bridge floor, a pink pool of mingled blood and water beneath her wounded leg. He wanted to go to her, do something for her, but there was no time.

How little time was brought home an instant later. The ship jerked, just a little, and the computer said, "Unauthorized launch from Orbital Bombardment System."

Richard felt cold. "Computer, show me where it hits."

Screens lit. He watched the slug slash a claw mark of white fire through the atmosphere. It impacted in a snowball of vaporized water in the deep ocean a long, long way from Hansen's Harbor, and he relaxed . . . a little. *What was that?* he wondered. *Warning shot?*

Nonsense. Cheveldeoff didn't give warnings. It must have been a glitch. When Cheveldeoff acted, he wouldn't miss.

"Computer," Richard said, "how long until ship is in position for a maximum-velocity, maximum-damage mass launch aimed at Hansen's Harbor?"

"Thirteen minutes, forty-six seconds," the computer said.

That's it, Richard thought. *That's how much time I've got.*

He stood on the bridge, his broken arm cradled against his side, each beat of his pounding heart driving another hot steel spike of pain into it. *So it comes down to this. My whole life, leading to this moment.*

He had dreamed, once, of rising high in the hierarchy of the Body Purified, of making the name Hansen respected instead of vilified. Less than half a year ago? It seemed an eternity.

He had learned a lot since then, about himself, and about other things.

He had learned he would never rise in the Body Purified. By the teachings he had accepted all his life, or at least given lip service to, he wasn't even fully human: he was a clone, an abomination, a subhuman monster with no right and no place in the assembly of God.

Chris Keating thought Richard had engineered everything that had happened to gain prestige and power back on Earth. But even if he had carried out the bizarre scheme Chris had concocted in his Avatar-addled brain, even if he had carried out such a scheme and it had *worked,* he could never have prestige and power because of who—what—he was.

He glanced at Emily. But he had learned something else. He'd learned that the abominations and subhuman monsters he had come to help destroy were, like himself, neither: they were just people, maybe people who looked different and even thought different, but people. Good people, bad people, indifferent people.

Monsters and abominations acted according to their character, like wild animals. The Avatar had proclaimed that moddies must be destroyed because their very existence offended God Itself: they were imperfect copies of God's perfect creation, corruptions of God's Holy Human Genome.

But unlike animals, people—even different-looking people—could *choose* their course of action. They could choose to do evil . . . or choose to do good. They could kill, or heal. Hinder, or help. Stand by and do nothing . . . or take a chance, and act.

Richard had chosen a course of action on Earth. He had chosen to fight back against what he saw as the unjust treatment of his father and himself, to take a chance and attempt to prove his worth to the Body Purified with a great deed, like a prince in some old fairy tale. He had chosen to set the Holy Warriors on the path to Marseguro.

But discovering the monsters of Marseguro were no more monstrous than himself, that they were simply a different kind of people, had left him with another choice: to help them, or let the Holy Warriors keep hurting them.

Thinking back, he thought he might have made his choice without realizing it when he saw the little Selkie girl in the cage with her mother at the Hansen's Harbor pier. Or maybe he had made it when Emily had helped him escape the hunterbot. Or perhaps he had made it when he suddenly found himself on the other side of the equation, when Grand Deacon Ellers had ordered him locked up, not because he had done anything against the Holy Warriors, but simply because he was a clone.

Maybe it had taken all of those things together to turn him around.

Or maybe none of them had turned him around; maybe the part of his brain rewired by Victor Hansen had turned him around, in which case, maybe his decision hadn't been his decision at all, but an echo of the decision his "grandfather" had made half a century ago when he decided to create a new race of humans.

No, he thought. *I don't buy that. So what if he rewired a portion of my brain? We rewire our brains all the time, through what we think and feel and experience. I am what I am. My mind is my mind. However I reached my decision, it is* my *decision.*

That it had been the right decision, he had no doubt, and though it had led irrevocably to this point, he wouldn't have changed it even if he could.

He looked at Emily again. She had made her own irrevocable decision when she chose to accompany him into space. If she had chosen otherwise, he had to admit, he would already have been dead several times over. She'd helped him get this far. Now it was up to him to make good use of what she had won for him.

His feeling toward her remained tender . . . but confused. He suspected—hoped—she had similar feelings toward him.

He hoped they would still get the chance to discover where those feelings might lead.

He suspected they would not.

He spoke at last, surprising himself with the steadiness of his voice. "Computer. Confirm I am the only surviving member of the registered crew of *BPS Sanctification*."

"Confirmed," said the computer. "All other crew members are deceased."

"Computer, transfer full command of this vessel to me, as ranking member of the crew."

"Security clearance required."

Again Richard reeled off the string of numbers and letters he had memorized during the trip to Marseguro.

"Clearance sufficient," the computer said. "Mr. Hansen, the ship is yours." The traditional phrase sounded odd coming from a talking machine.

"Computer," said Richard, "Course change. De-orbit ship for impact in the ocean, minimum distance from land two hundred kilometers." That should be far enough away to prevent radioactive or chemical contamination, and near enough that the Marseguroites could salvage valuable resources from the wreck.

"Cannot comply," said the computer.

Richard felt cold. *No!* He couldn't have come this far, made the final decision, only to be forced to ride out the destruction of the entire population of Marseguro while watching helplessly from the bridge of the very ship carrying out that destruction. "Computer, explain!"

"Stated course is tantamount to self-destruction," the computer said calmly. "Self-destruct commands can only be issued by officers of Grand Deacon rank or higher."

Damn! Richard thought quickly. "Computer," he said. "Program quickest and most effective course to halt use of Orbital Bombardment System."

"Done," said the computer.

"Computer, execute new course."

"Course executed," said the computer.

Richard didn't bother asking what the new course *was*. It didn't matter. "Computer, will new course prevent operation of Orbital Bombardment System before ship reaches coordinates for maximum-damage launch against Hansen's Harbor?"

"Negative."

Richard closed his eyes. "Computer," he said. "Is there a weapons locker on the bridge?"

"Affirmative."

"Computer, open bridge weapons locker."

A panel slid open in the wall beside the bridge door. Richard darted to the newly opened compartment and peered inside. Laser pistols, laser rifles, slug throwers, automatic rifles, a sniper rifle—an impressive arsenal, but not what Richard . . . there! A rack of grenades.

"Computer, explain operation of grenades found in bridge weapons locker."

"Press red button to arm. Press green button before throwing. Use LED panel and associated buttons to set delay between pressing of green button and detonation, range zero to six hundred seconds."

He didn't have time for that. "Computer, what is the default delay on these grenades?"

"Three seconds."

Good enough. The grenades hung on an equipment belt, but he couldn't possibly strap it on with only one good arm. Instead, he slung it over his neck and chest like a bandolier.

Then his eye caught on something else: a pouch with a red circle on it, the Body's symbol for a first-aid kit. With his good hand, he opened it and found what he'd hoped: a hypospray full of general-purpose analgesic. Without hesitation he pressed it against the side of his neck. It felt like he'd sprayed needles of ice into his skin, but almost instantly the agony in his arm lessened. He unzipped the top of his jumpsuit and stuck his broken arm inside it, Napoleon-like. *Best I can do. Now . . .*

"Computer, locate Holy Warriors."

"All surviving Holy Warriors except one are returning to their shuttle."

"Computer, where is the one Holy Warrior who is not returning to the shuttle?"

"Outside Orbital Bombardment System control room," the computer said.

Might have guessed. "Computer, open bridge door."

The door opened. Richard gave Emily one last regretful glance, then darted out into the hallway and ran toward the OBS control room.

Emily's eyes fluttered open. Her heart had steadied, but she gasped as the pain in her leg registered. She didn't pass out again, though. She lifted herself on her elbows.

Richard had vanished. The bridge door stood open. Next to it, so did the door of a locker full of weapons. Inside the locker she could see an empty rack.

"Computer," Emily shouted, not even sure the ship would acknowledge her, "Where is Richard Hansen?"

It must have been programmed to answer nonsensitive requests for information from anyone, because it promptly responded, "Richard Hansen is approaching the Orbital Bombardment System control room."

"Computer, show me a map."

The main screen lit with a schematic of the habitat ring. A green line traced a path from the bridge through a half-dozen hatches and corridors to a room labeled "OBS Control." A red dot labeled "Acting Captain Richard Hansen" (*Acting Captain?*) was approaching the room.

Another red dot, labeled "Unknown Holy Warrior" waited for him.

Emily struggled to her feet, yelping involuntarily as she put weight on her leg. She limped to the weapons cabinet, grabbed a laser pistol to shoot and an automatic rifle to use for a crutch, then set off at a reasonably rapid hobble after Richard Hansen.

Saving his life has gotten to be a habit. I don't see any reason to break it now.

As he approached the OBS control room, Richard slowed, even though his internal clock screamed at him to hurry. With one corner to go, he got down awkwardly on his knees, then his belly, and wormed his way to where he could peer around it.

A Holy Warrior crouched in an opening in the deck

plates just in front of the OBS control room door, his rifle resting on the deck, his head barely showing—which put him at eye-level with Richard. Their eyes met. For an instant they stared at each other, then Richard realized what was about to happen and scooted backward.

Bullets spattered against the far side of the corridor and ricocheted off the floor right where his head had been a second before.

In the echoing silence after the burst of rifle fire, Richard heard the Holy Warrior cough.

He's not wearing his pressure suit. The plague's got him.

Maybe that would make it easier to do what he had to do. Richard reached for one of the grenades he'd brought with him . . .

"Let's try something else first," said a voice.

Richard's heart thumped hard. "Good thing I didn't already have one in my hand," he said, turning his head to look at Emily. She leaned against the wall, a rifle in her left hand serving as an impromptu crutch, a laser pistol in her right. "Are you trying to scare me to death?"

"Sorry," Emily said. "You're just lucky I'm not a Holy Warrior."

"Unfortunately, he *is.*" Richard nodded toward the corner. "The last one left on board, or will be soon. And he's settled in right where we need to get to if we're going to keep Cheveldeoff from turning Hansen's Harbor into a glowing crater sometime in the next five or six minutes. If that isn't a time for grenades, I don't know what is. One to take care of the Holy Warrior, another one in that hole he's standing in to break the shunt they must have hardwired in to take *Sanctification*'s computer out of the control loop."

"That's your plan? Throw a grenade into the hole and hope for the best?"

"It's all the plan I've got time for," Richard said. "And it's *your* bloody city I'm trying to save."

"We need an expert to return control to *Sanctification,*" Emily said. "He's our expert. He must be the one who wired it. Why else would he be out of his pressure suit?"

"Why should he help us?"

"He's *out of his pressure suit,*" Emily repeated. "He's infected."

"All the more reason for him to fight to the death. I say

we take him up on it. We'll just be putting him out of his misery." Richard stopped. He couldn't believe he was talking about murdering a human being in such cold terms, but the ethical calculus seemed clear, though brutal.

"Give me two minutes," Emily said. "If I can't persuade him to help us, then it's bombs away."

We may not have two minutes, Richard thought, but Emily had a point—a strong point. Just throwing a grenade into the works might or might not break the shunt. And if it didn't, there would be no second chance.

And there was one other thing, a small thing, maybe, but it tipped the balance.

He was sick of killing.

"Go ahead," he said. "Two minutes."

Emily had come down to the OBS control room expecting to help Richard kill the Holy Warrior and retake control of the weapons threatening Hansen's Harbor . . . and, after that, she was certain, every other town and identifiable habitat on the planet until her people and the landlings who had helped them were wiped from the face of the universe.

She understood the stakes. But when she realized only one unsuited-and-therefore-infected Holy Warrior held down the fort, she also realized there might be a better way than brute force to solve the problem.

Now that Richard had agreed, she had to deliver.

She limped to the corner. "Holy Warrior," she shouted. "Can you hear me?"

A long silence, then, "I can hear you." The man's voice sounded ragged and hoarse, and he coughed again after speaking.

"What's your name?"

"O'Sullivan. What's it to you?"

"My name is Emily." No answer. "How are you feeling?"

A ragged laugh. "Like hell. Looks like this really is a plague ship, after all. You'll be sick soon enough."

"No, I won't. I'm immune." Emily paused. "And I have a vaccine."

Another long silence, but even across several meters, Emily could hear the Holy Warrior's strained breathing, the struggle to draw air through swollen bronchial tubes into lungs already beginning to fill with fluid. "You're lying," he said finally. "There isn't any vaccine. If you're immune, it's because you're a moddie."

Emily glanced at Richard, who nodded.

"She's not lying," he shouted. "Holy Warrior, this is Richard Hansen speaking. You know who I am."

"You're a bloody traitor," the Holy Warrior snarled. "I know that much."

"But I'm not a moddie. I'm a normal—" he shot a look at Emily, as though to apologize, "—human being, like you. And I'm not sick, even though I've been breathing the infected air of this ship as long as you have. That's because I've had the vaccine."

Which isn't strictly true, of course, Emily thought, *but . . .*

"Doesn't change the fact you're a traitor," the Holy Warrior mumbled.

"Did you *plan* to stay behind here, O'Sullivan?" Emily shouted. "When they told you to take off your suit, did they tell you you'd be stuck here?"

"Just until quarantine was over," O'Sullivan said. "Unless I got sick." He coughed again. "And I got sick." He frowned. "After the others left. They don't know. I've got to tell—"

"Cheveldeoff gave orders to leave you here to die," Richard shouted. "You could have been quarantined in the shuttle. You could have been put into isolation and treated. But this way Cheveldeoff could use you, use you to ensure we didn't manage to disconnect the command shunt you've installed. I know Cheveldeoff. I worked with him. He's good at using people, O'Sullivan."

"So I die," O'Sullivan said. "At least I die with honor, serving the Body Purified."

"You die a mass murderer, O'Sullivan," Richard said. His eyes blazed, and he seemed to have forgotten talking to the Holy Warrior was Emily's idea. Emily gladly let him take over. Richard understood the Holy Warriors and the Body Purified in a way she doubted she ever could. "Cheveldeoff is going to hit Hansen's Harbor with a maximum-impact OBS strike in the next couple of minutes if we don't stop it. Thousands will die."

"Moddies and their sympathizers," O'Sullivan said.

"Women and children. Young men. Girls. Old men.

Grandmothers. Babies. Toddlers. Schoolchildren," Richard said. "Struck down from heaven, just like Earth would have been if not for the Miracle. But that was God's judgment. This is man's. This is Cheveldeoff's—and yours, because you can put a stop to it.

"It's God's right to destroy us like an artist erasing a mistake. But It doesn't need men for that. It doesn't need fallible men like you, or evil men like Cheveldeoff, or . . . whatever kind of man I am. The God who sent Its Hammer against the World, and chose at the last minute to push it aside, does not need human hands to carry out Its punishments.

"So if you choose to let those people on Marseguro live, O'Sullivan—and if you choose to live yourself—you aren't acting against God. You're just acting against Cheveldeoff.

"You know the stories about him, what he's capable of. Is acting against him really such a bad thing? Especially when it means you get to live yourself?"

Silence. Emily gripped her rifle, and saw Richard's hand close over the grenade again. *No time,* she thought. "On my mark," Richard whispered. "Five . . . four . . . three . . ."

An inarticulate cry came from around the corner, then a hammering sound, tearing sounds, and finally a flash of light. Emily exchanged a look with Richard, then both of them peered around the corner.

White smoke hung under the ceiling, hazing the blue-white lights. O'Sullivan, coughing, blood dripping from his nose, tossed his rifle across the floor at them and crawled out onto the decking. "Cheveldeoff can go to hell, if the Devil will have him," he said. "And if God wants to kill you all, let It do it Itself." He wiped his nose with his sleeve, looked at the blood on it and said, "What was that about a vaccine?"

They'd decided back on Marseguro that Emily should bring several doses of vaccine just in case they found non-mods still alive on *Sanctification.* Emily unzipped a pocket on her landsuit and pulled out a hypospray. "Right here, O'Sullivan," she said. "Right here."

"Good for you, O'Sullivan," Richard said. He'd managed to leverage himself off the floor with his one good arm and stood leaning against the bulkhead, face pale.

O'Sullivan looked at him, then spat blood on the floor at his feet. "You're still a bloody traitor."

"I can live with that," Richard said. A deep, throbbing gong sound suddenly reverberated through the ship. Richard's eyes widened. "Uh-oh," he said. "I think I'd better get back to the bridge."

He turned and disappeared back down the corridor toward the bridge, leaving his belt of grenades behind.

"Now what?" Emily called after him, but got no answer.

O'Sullivan rubbed the place on his arm where she had sprayed him with the vaccine. "Atmosphere warning," he said. "We're falling out of orbit." He snorted. "Looks like your vaccine may have been wasted, moddie."

"The name's Emily," she snapped.

O'Sullivan opened his mouth to say something else, then closed it and looked down at the deck plates. "Emily," he said. "Um . . . thank you. I've seen how the *Sanctification* crew died. I . . . wouldn't want to go like that. I'd rather die burning up in the atmosphere."

"I'd rather not die at all," Emily said. She put out an arm. "Let's get to the bridge. Maybe we can help."

O'Sullivan hesitated, then took her arm. "All right," he said. "Guess I've made my bed. Might as well lie in it."

"That's the spirit," Emily said dryly. "Come on."

Calm and certain, Cheveldeoff watched the tactical display as the minutes ticked down to the moment when *Retribution*'s computer would issue the order that would send half a ton of ceramic-tungsten alloy slamming into the heart of Hansen's Harbor at forty thousand kilometers an hour. The shuttle carrying the salvage party had cleared *Sanctification* and would be docking with *Retribution*—in an unpressurized hold, with the crew destined for indefinite quarantine—within an hour. *Sanctification* continued to lose altitude, but *Retribution*'s computer assured him that the course change would be insufficient to prevent a devastating attack. With Hansen's Harbor and its stock of weapons and ammunition taken from *Sanctification*'s dead Holy Warriors vaporized, Cheveldeoff's remaining troops could quickly reduce the smaller population centers and underwater habitats, even if *Sanctification* burned up in the atmosphere and prevented any further use of the OBS.

The time to launch slipped to under a minute . . . under thirty seconds . . . twenty . . . ten . . . five, four, three, two, one . . .

Nothing happened.

Cheveldeoff felt as though a trapdoor had opened under his feet.

Nothing happened!

"Launch command issued," the computer said without prompting. "No response from *Sanctification.* Orbital Bombardment System not under this computer's control. Probable cause: hardware failure of shunt mechanism."

"Computer, reissue command!"

"Command reissued." A pause. "No response. Analysis unchanged."

Cheveldeoff's hands clenched into fists. "Grand Deacon!" Braun stood on the opposite side of the tactical display from him, consciously or unconsciously keeping the maximum distance between them. "I heard," he said.

"Well, *do* something about it!"

Braun hadn't let a readable expression cross his face in his conversations with Cheveldeoff since their confrontation in the briefing room, but Cheveldeoff could well imagine the glee boiling merrily beneath that bland exterior. *The bastard loves to see me fail. Well, he won't be laughing soon.* Cheveldeoff scratched the right side of his nose. The Holy Warrior at the communications console casually got to his feet and moved one console over, bending over it. He pulled out a keyboard and began to type.

"I'm open to suggestions . . . sir," Braun said.

"Are you?" Cheveldeoff resisted the urge to "suggest" that Braun do something anatomically improbable with a laser pistol. "What I *suggest,* Grand Deacon, is that you prepare to execute our main invasion plan."

Braun's eyes narrowed. "Sir?"

"You heard me. Their only weapons are in Hansen's Harbor. We'll land inland, and take the smaller centers first. Then we'll strangle Hansen's Harbor at our leisure."

"Fighting in pressure suits, sir? The plague . . ."

"You will fight naked if I order you to, Grand Deacon," Cheveldeoff snarled. "This planet *will* be Purified. You *will* make that happen. Do I make myself clear?"

A long moment of silence as the Grand Deacon stared at him, his face unreadable. Then, "Yes, sir," Braun said. "I will call a briefing of the subcommanders for one hour from now."

"Good idea," Cheveldeoff said icily. "Just do your job, Grand Deacon. That's all I ask." *Because it sure as hell won't be your job for long.*

The Grand Deacon inclined his head slightly, then spun on his heel and left the bridge.

Cheveldeoff turned back to the tactical display. He glanced at his agent, who had returned to his usual post. Cheveldeoff smiled. He had his own briefing to conduct before the subcommanders met: every man on the ship he knew to be loyal to him had been warned to expect orders within the next hour.

But vital as those orders were, giving them could wait. "Computer, visual of *Sanctification.*" The ship appeared, wrapped in an orange borealis as she encountered the outermost wisps of atmosphere. "Still there, Mr. Hansen?" Cheveldeoff growled under his breath. "At least I'll have the pleasure of watching you burn."

He crossed his arms and waited for the end.

Chapter 22

RICHARD KNEW IT MUST be his imagination, but he couldn't help feeling the temperature inside *Sanctification* had already gone up a couple of degrees by the time he reached the bridge. "Computer," he shouted as he entered, "situation report."

"*Sanctification* has entered atmosphere," the computer said. Its usual lack of inflection, no doubt meant to reassure, infuriated in these circumstances.

"Why?"

No answer.

I didn't say "Mother, may I," Richard thought. *Calm down and concentrate.* "Computer, why has *Sanctification* entered atmosphere?"

"*Sanctification* is following the orders of Acting Captain Richard Hansen."

Following orders . . . ? I didn't . . .

Or did I?

"Computer, restate last order."

"Execute quickest and most effective course to halt use of Orbital Bombardment System."

"Computer, does this course take us into the atmosphere?"

"Affirmative."

But . . .

"Computer, you previously indicated you could not self-destruct on my order!" Behind him, Emily entered the bridge, leaning on the arm of the still-very-sick-looking Holy Warrior, although his nosebleed seemed to have stopped.

"Affirmative."

"Then why . . ." *That won't work.* "Computer, explain why you are driving *Sanctification* into the atmosphere if you cannot self-destruct."

"Non sequitur," the computer said. "Prohibition against self-destruction does not prevent entry into atmosphere."

I'm wasting time. "Computer, change course. Lift out of atmosphere."

"Unable to comply."

"Computer . . . !"

Clarity came from an unexpected source.

"It's the emergency landing protocol," croaked the Holy Warrior.

Richard stared at him. "The what?"

"Emergency landing protocol. These ships have an automated landing system. They're too expensive to just throw away—that's why they won't self-destruct. But as a last resort a captain can order them to land themselves."

"Without a spaceport?" Richard said. "Without a landing cradle?"

"I told you, it's a last resort," the Holy Warrior said. "The landing site has to be carefully chosen. If it's not within a very few degrees of perfectly level, or if it's too rough, the struts will collapse and the ship will roll. And possibly blow up," he added helpfully.

"Computer!" Richard called. "Are you executing the emergency landing protocol?"

"Affirmative."

"Computer, can you abort it?"

"Negative," said the computer. "Once initiated, emergency landing protocol passes out of control of the computer."

"That's in case the central computer has been 'killed' along with most of the crew," said the Holy Warrior, who was beginning to get on Richard's nerves.

"You seem to know a lot about it," Richard growled at him. "Got any sage advice for the Acting Captain?"

"Sure." O'Sullivan coughed, then grinned. "Hold on. The emergency landing protocol doesn't really take into account the possibility that there might be anyone aboard left alive. Things could get a little rough."

"Hold on," O'Sullivan had said, and Emily did her best, strapping herself into one of the empty crew chairs that ringed the cylindrical "tank" of the tactical display. "Things could get a little rough," he'd added.

That proved to be a miracle of understatement. They'd barely strapped themselves in before they found that out. "Rotation ending . . . now," the computer announced.

Emily's body pressed painfully into the straps that held her into the crew chair as the rotating section of the hull—moving at about 100 kilometers per hour where they were—braked hard into motionlessness relative to the rest of the hull. Richard groaned as the straps cut into his broken arm, and O'Sullivan started coughing again.

But the rough part had just begun.

The ship shuddered and bucked, throwing them up and sideways, crushing them under multiple Gs, hanging them upside down in their straps as the floor suddenly became the ceiling. The temperature climbed and kept on climbing, overwhelming the cooling mechanisms of Emily's landsuit, strained by the loss of water when the laser cut her leg, until she felt she might be boiled alive like a crustacean in a pot. She risked a broken neck by shooting a look at her companions. Both had their eyes closed. Fresh blood streaked O'Sullivan's face—his nosebleed had started up again. Richard's head rolled loosely from side to side. Sweat glistened on his white face and plastered his hair to his forehead.

The buffeting went on and on, accompanied by a deafening roar, like the wind of the worst storm Emily had ever experienced multiplied a hundredfold.

A particularly hard jolt broke loose an equipment cabinet. It careened across the floor, smashing into other cabinets. A sudden drop hurled it into the air; it crashed down with killing force just centimeters from Richard's head.

Richard didn't flinch.

Emily closed her eyes and wished she were unconscious, too.

The roaring changed pitch, lessened . . . then redoubled with a new bass note she hadn't heard before . . . and then . . .

. . . stopped.

So did the buffeting.

The ship creaked and groaned. The floor began to slant. The wayward cabinet slid another meter and fetched up against the base of the tactical display. Emily waited for the ship to roll, as O'Sullivan had warned it might . . .

. . . but the slanting stopped, the creaking and groaning diminished to just an occasional pop—and then the floor moved again, leveling out.

"Emergency Landing Protocol completed," said the computer. "Ship condition: good. Relaunch capability: intact. Minor interior damage. Bridge and other gimbaled rooms reoriented to local gravity. Detailed report available upon request. Awaiting further orders."

Emily felt like an enthusiastic sadist had beaten every square centimeter of her body with a grappling hook, but she forced herself to unbuckle and swing her legs over the side. To her left, O'Sullivan groaned, but she ignored him, instead pulling herself upright and then lurching, almost falling, against Richard's chair. "Richard," she croaked, then summoned up more breath and more energy and said, "Richard!"

His eyes fluttered, opened, closed . . . then opened again, and this time focused. "Emily?" He blinked. "Wait. We're . . . we made it?"

"Down in one piece," she said. "I don't know where . . . but if it's solid ground, we can't be too far from Hansen's Harbor."

"Help me . . . help me sit up." Emily unbuckled him and pulled him to a sitting position. He slumped for a moment, eyes closed, then opened them and said, "Computer. How far are we from Hansen's Harbor?"

"Sixty-nine kilometers," said the computer.

"Computer, external cameras."

The tactical display tank flickered, then displayed a view of the surrounding area. Richard blinked. "What's that cylinder thing . . . ?"

Emily looked and laughed. "I should have guessed," she said. "Sixty-nine kilometers . . . we're in Landing Valley." She pointed. "That's all that's left of the *Rivers of Babylon*. And that low building next to it is the Landing Valley Museum."

"We've set down by the *Rivers of Babylon*?" Richard laughed. The laugh turned into a wincing cough, then he managed to compose himself. "The best landing site then and now." He frowned. "But sixty-nine kilometers? Computer! Activate radio communications." He looked around. "Activate manual controls at bridge communications station."

"Ready," said the computer.

Richard, broken arm still slung inside his jumpsuit, hobbled over to one of the bridge stations and began awkwardly typing with his remaining hand. "I'm connecting to the secure comm network I set up for the Council," he explained as he did so. "At least, I hope I am . . . yes!" He cleared his throat, then pressed a button. "This is Richard Hansen aboard *BPS Sanctification*," he said clearly. "Emily is here, too, and . . ." he glanced at O'Sullivan, who had managed to get himself into a sitting position, ". . . a guest. Chris Keating may be on board somewhere, too."

Chris! Emily had forgotten about him. *If he didn't strap himself in when the atmosphere warning started to sound, he's probably just a pulp at the back of the central shaft.* She couldn't work up much sympathy at the thought.

Richard was still talking. ". . . need armed reinforcements here ASAP. Also any qualified air pilots you can scrape together. I doubt Cheveldeoff expected us to make it down in one piece, but it won't take him long to come after us now we're here. And if he gets here first . . ."

Emily glanced at the still-open weapons cabinet by the door. *The whole ship is crammed with weapons,* she realized. *If Cheveldeoff gets them—especially those assault craft, if they're still intact—it's game over, despite everything.*

But if our people get here first . . .

She grinned. Then the Holy Warriors would be marching into the teeth of people armed, armored, and unencumbered by pressure suits—and with a lot of incentive to win.

She thought of Cheveldeoff targeting Hansen's Harbor, of the havoc wrought there by *Sanctification*'s own Holy Warriors, and her grin turned into something much fiercer and much less amused.

A *lot* of incentive.

"No, sir, I don't know how a desk clerk like Richard Hansen managed to activate *Sanctification*'s Emergency Landing Protocol," Grand Deacon Braun said. "Perhaps he had help from the Holy Warrior you insisted I exile there."

Cheveldeoff, Braun, and the subcommanders of the

Holy Warriors aboard *Retribution* stood around the oval table in the main briefing room. There were chairs, but Cheveldeoff had not asked anyone to sit down. The vidwall showed a still satellite photo of *Sanctification,* in one piece, on the ground in an inland valley near what appeared to be a single hull section from an antique starship—presumably *Rivers of Babylon.*

"Are you telling me the loyalty of your men is in question?" he said softly. "Because that loyalty is your ultimate responsibility, Grand Deacon. If you cannot vouch for it—"

"Loyalty is a two-way street, sir," Braun said. "I betrayed my loyalty to my men when I ordered that Corporal O'Sullivan be left behind with no evidence he was, in fact, infected with anything at all. I can hardly fault him for doing whatever he had to to survive."

Cheveldeoff stood very still. He had never heard the Grand Deacon skate so close to outright insubordination—hell, outright *mutiny* . . . and he had no illusions about his own hold over the subcommanders gathered in the room with them. He had given his orders to his loyalists throughout the ship. They were in position to seize all the key stations . . . but they would only do so on his order, and he had to get out of this room alive and able to communicate to give that order.

"I don't suppose we'll ever know the truth," Cheveldeoff said finally. "And whether you believe it or not, Grand Deacon, I regret the necessity of leaving Corporal O'Sullivan on board *Sanctification* as much as you.

"Let us set aside *how* Richard Hansen did it, and move on to what *we* are going to do to complete our mission. I take it your plans have changed with the successful landing of *Sanctification.*"

Braun stood very still himself for a moment. Cheveldeoff could almost see him weighing the pros and cons of continuing down the path of mutiny against those of drawing in his horns and concentrating on the Purification of Marseguro. Success, after all, would wipe away all other concerns once they got home . . . or so he must have decided, because in the end he simply nodded and said, "They have. If the locals gain control of the armament on *Sanctification* before we do, especially the airpower shuttles, our position will become . . ."

The door slid open, and a Holy Warrior came in, dragging—

Cheveldeoff stared. The Holy Warrior was dragging a boy wearing tattered pajama bottoms and nothing else, a boy with a few wispy whiskers on his chin and a mat of tangled brown hair.

"Chris Keating?" Cheveldeoff said.

The Holy Warrior looked startled and relaxed his grip. "We found him in the hallway outside," he said. "I don't know where—"

Keating pulled himself free and straightened up. "Mr. Cheveldeoff," he said, and strode forward, holding out his hand.

Cheveldeoff was so bemused he took it for a moment before snatching it back. "How the hell did you get on board?" he bellowed.

"Stowed away," said Chris. "Spare pressure suit, empty equipment locker. Good thing, too. I hear *Sanctification* made it down intact." He grinned. "Which is more than I would have if they had gotten me down there with it. But you're in luck. Here I am, and I can tell you what's what and who's who down there. To properly Purify that cesspool of a planet, Mr. Cheveldeoff, sir, you need me." His grin faded. "I don't think you've fully appreciated that. I don't think anyone has."

"Lock him up," Cheveldeoff growled. "Full quarantine." He looked around the room. "Proceed with your plans, Grand Deacon."

"The plague, sir?" Braun said.

Cheveldeoff wanted desperately to wash his hand, but he very carefully folded it behind his back with its mate instead. "What plague, Grand Deacon? Chris Keating himself told us it was a chemical attack that killed *Sanctification*'s crew, not anything biological. If that were not true, he would hardly have risked us all by coming here, would he?" Considering the little creep had just shaken his hand, he dearly hoped his logic held water.

"No, sir," said Braun.

"Carry on, then," said Cheveldeoff. "I'll be in my quarters. Report when you're ready to launch." He went out. *Braun backed down again. Maybe I'm overly concerned.*

Well, he'd keep his loyalists in position, just in case.

As he walked toward his quarters, Cheveldeoff cleared his throat, trying to get rid of an annoying tickle that had just started.

Too much talking, he thought. *I'd better rest my voice for a while.*

One small part of his brain, however, gathered a seed of panic to itself, planted it, and waited for it to grow.

The reinforcements from Hansen's Harbor arrived two hours after the message went out from the grounded *Sanctification.* By that time, Richard had a pretty good idea of the extent of damage to the ship, thanks partly to the computer but especially thanks to O'Sullivan, whose knowledge of the Holy Warrior vessel seemed encyclopedic, far exceeding what Richard had picked up in the few days he had spent on board. O'Sullivan obviously felt much better since receiving the vaccination. In fact, he'd become positively garrulous, showing them around the ship as if he owned it.

Parts of it, of course, they couldn't even get to. The bridge and other vital control rooms maintained proper orientation when the ship landed, but less important rooms were supposed to be secured for landing. With the crew dead, they hadn't been. The violent descent and just the fact half the rooms were sideways and a quarter completely upside down had played havoc with everything not nailed down.

Weapons and ammunition, however, were all properly stored and readily accessible. And the all-important air-attack shuttles had ridden out the descent in fine style, their gimbaled landing pads keeping them upright and ready for launch at a moment's notice. Richard suspected that just such a launch would be called for the minute they had pilots who could fly them . . . if anyone could. Until someone more qualified got a look at their controls, that was anybody's guess.

One room they found contained a docbot that made quick work of setting his arm and cleaning and sealing Emily's leg wound and pumping them both full of fast-heal—although it would also have pumped her full of drugs she didn't need that might have killed her if they hadn't been monitoring it closely: apparently her perfectly normal Selkie vital signs indicated to the docbot deathly illness.

Throughout the two hours, Richard wouldn't have been surprised to see shuttles from *Retribution* dropping out of the sky. He didn't relax after the reinforcements from Hansen's Harbor showed up; they remained vulnerable until the weapons from *Sanctification* had been dispersed and the assault craft were either under Marseguroite control or disabled.

Eventually, he had to sleep, first giving strict orders (not that he had any particular right to issue orders, but somehow people kept doing what he said) to wake him if the Holy Warriors showed up or if they received any communication.

He slept well and long . . . too long. He checked and double-checked the time, then hurried into his clothes and out of the captain's cabin he had appropriated for his nap, out the nearest access hatch and down the ladder extruding from it to the ground.

"Why didn't you wake me?" he demanded of Council Chair Jeter, who had shown up with the first batch of reinforcements and stood watching crates being loaded onto a groundcar in the early morning light.

Jeter raised an eyebrow. "You said to wake you if something happened. Nothing happened."

That brought him up short. "Nothing?"

"Nothing untoward. It took all night, but we've dispersed almost all the weapons and ammunition. The pilots are still puzzling over some of the controls for the assault craft, but they're confident they can get them in the air if they have to, even if they can't use the weapons systems. But so far, we haven't heard or seen anything of the Holy Warriors." Jeter pointed to the First Landing storage cave in the steep red hillside a hundred meters away, where they'd set up headquarters. "Emily is in there with her mother. Dr. Christianson-Wood said she'd like to talk to you when you woke up."

"Uh . . . okay." Bemused, Richard trudged across the blackened near-grass covering the valley floor.

No sign of the Holy Warriors after more than twelve hours? Cheveldeoff couldn't have been fool enough to let a plague-infested shuttle on board his ship . . . could he?

The storage cave had been the colonists' first shelter. The Selkies had relied on the water tanks on the ship for their comfort and survival, while the landlings had lived in the cave. Very little natural rock remained exposed. Corridors and rooms had been carved out and lined with fast-setting-but-damn-ugly gray concrete. It felt exactly like what it was, a bunker providing shelter from a possibly hostile world.

Richard found Emily and her mother in the only room in the complex with a window, a small round portal camouflaged from the outside by an overhanging rock. Through a screen of near-grass stems, it provided an adequate if slightly obscured view of *Sanctification* and the people bustling around it.

Dr. Christianson-Wood, wearing a plain white landsuit, stood looking out that window as he entered. The rooms had long ago been stripped of their original furnishings, but someone had moved in a folding table and chairs, and judging by the empty food and drink containers piled in an old cargo crate in one corner, people had been taking their breaks here. Emily sat at the table, wearing an electric-blue landsuit with green lightning bolts slashing down the sides. He'd gotten so used to seeing her in black that the bright colors startled him.

"You wanted to see me, Dr. Christianson-Wood?" Richard said. "Hi, Emily. Get some sleep?"

"Not as much as you," she said. "But some." She nodded at her mother. "We've been talking, mostly."

Dr. Christianson-Wood turned from the window and faced him. "We've been talking about what we should do next," she said quietly. "Because we can't stay here."

Richard opened his mouth; closed it again. He'd been so focused on the here and now that he hadn't looked any further down the road. But of course she was right. Even if the Holy Warriors aboard *Retribution* decided not to attack—and now that the Marseguroites had the weapons and assault craft from *Sanctification,* it would be suicide—they'd only bought a temporary reprieve. Cheveldeoff would head back to Earth, and return with however many ships he needed to purify Marseguro—purify it right down to bare and glowing bedrock.

He won't bother with Holy Warriors next time. It will be orbital bombardment from the beginning, and likely with nuclear weapons. "You're thinking of evacuating on *Sanctification*?" he said quietly.

"That's what I'm thinking." Dr. Christianson-Wood

shook her head. "But it won't carry the entire population. Not even close. And anyone who is left behind . . ."

"Hidden habitats," Richard said. "New ones, stealthed so they can't be detected from orbit. Move the population into the deep oceans. Send out *Sanctification* for help."

"Who will help us?" Dr. Christianson-Wood said. Her gill slits flared, pink, gaping mouths on her neck, and her oversized eyes opened wide. "Who will help us against the Body Purified? Against Earth?" She glared at him, then relaxed. "No one, that's who. Fifty Earth years ago, at least, even the colonies that opposed the Body Purified barely tolerated moddies. Has that changed?"

Richard had to shake his head. "No."

"Then all we can do is hide." She sighed. "I did the best I could, with my nasty little plague. But in the end . . ." Her shoulders slumped. "I killed all those people . . . became a mass murderer . . . for nothing."

"*Not* for nothing," Emily snapped. "We've been over this. For *survival.*"

"But we still may not survive," Dr. Christianson-Wood said. "Certainly many of us won't."

"But many will," Richard said. He understood Dr. Christianson-Wood's pain because it matched his own, the pain locked down deep where he'd also tried to bury the unassuageable guilt of the agony he had brought to this planet and its people. "Many will survive on *Sanctification.* The ship recognizes me as Acting Captain, and O'Sullivan has the technical know-how we need. She came down in good shape. We can get her back into space. And she can carry hundreds, even if she can't carry everyone. The Selkies will survive. I'll see to it. They're . . ." His voice trailed off. He'd just realized that he was echoing, almost word for word, what Victor Hansen had said before the *Rivers of Babylon* headed into space from Luna fifty Earth and forty Marseguro years before, ultimately ending up in the broad, flat valley bottom right outside the window. *Well, why not? I am Victor Hansen, or at least part of me is.*

"We'll have to decide who gets to go, and who stays," Dr. Christianson-Wood said. "It won't be easy."

"No, it won't," Richard said.

"It may be easier than you think," Emily said. She stood up. "I won't go, for example."

Both Richard and Dr. Christianson-Wood jerked their heads toward her. "Yes, you will," said Dr. Christianson-Wood.

You tell her! Richard thought.

"No, I won't." Emily came over to her mother. "You asked me, back before this all started, what I was going to do with my life. You didn't want me wasting it on something frivolous when so much work remained building Marseguro, expanding our presence here. Well, in the past few weeks I've learned you . . . and Daddy . . . were right. I've fought . . . I've *killed* . . . so Marseguro will survive, Mother. I'm not going to run out on her now."

"But if you're on *Sanctification,* we can find a new planet. A new world to build," Richard said. "For the Selkies . . ." *And I don't want to leave you behind!* But he couldn't say that.

Not yet.

Especially not with her mother standing right there.

"This planet is my home," Emily said. "I won't let it be destroyed without a fight. We have the shuttles. We have the know-how to make planet-to-orbit missiles, smart bullets, dumb dust, even missile interceptors."

"But you may not have time to—"

"But we may," Emily said. "You didn't think we even had time to take the weapons off of *Sanctification.* But where are the Holy Warriors?"

As if on cue, a young man burst into the room. "Transmission coming in," he gasped. "For you, Mr. Hansen."

Richard glanced from Dr. Christianson-Wood to Emily. "I guess we're about to find out." He turned to the young man. "I'm right behind you," he said, and followed him out of the cave.

Chapter 23

*L*OCKED UP AGAIN, Chris Keating thought gloomily, sitting in the brig of *Retribution*. On the plus side, at least they'd given him proper clothes—a blue Holy Warrior jumpsuit and shoes. Until they had, he'd begun to think he'd never be warm again. The pressure suit he'd donned in the shuttle locker must have had heaters on it, but he hadn't known how to raise them from what must have been a minimal default setting, and he'd felt like a walking iceberg by the time the shuttle had docked with *Retribution*.

He'd almost hidden in the locker without the suit. If he had, he would have been dead the instant they'd left *Sanctification,* because shortly after launch they'd blown out the atmosphere. He'd expected them to repressurize at some point, but they never did. And when he finally dared to exit the locker and peer out of the shuttle after they reached *Retribution,* he'd found it locked down in an unpressurized bay, Marseguro swimming in space outside the open hatch.

What had happened to the crew, he had no idea. He'd found an air lock, cycled through, and stripped off his pressure suit without seeing anyone.

Retribution felt much smaller than *Sanctification,* but had a similar layout. Chris had avoided the open central shaft and made his way toward the bow through secondary passageways. He'd been nabbed, not trying to get into the briefing room as the guard seemed to think, but trying to get to the bridge. It didn't matter; his real goal was Cheveldeoff, and lo and behold, he'd finally met the Archdeacon face-to-face, shaken his hand, offered his help . . .

. . . and had been cooling his heels in here ever since.

A sound brought him upright, an unmistakable sound with no place on a spaceship:

Gunfire.

More shots, and the distant thump of an explosion. Running footsteps outside the door, passing without slowing. Vibrations. More noises. A hint of shouting voices . . .

What's going on?

A particularly loud bang rang his cell like a gong. The normal lighting flickered, went out, and gave way to the sickly green glow of emergency lights . . . and his door unlocked itself and slid open.

Chris peered out. The brig cells all opened into a central area with a circular desk at which the guard on duty passed his time. But no one sat there now. All the other cells stood open and empty.

Another rattle of rifle fire.

Feeling more naked than he had when he'd been running around in nothing but pajama bottoms, Chris crept out into the open and headed for the sound of fighting.

The first burst of gunfire brought Cheveldeoff to his feet behind the desk in his quarters, laser pistol in his hand. He held his breath, and listened.

More shots. A few shouts.

"Computer, status report," he said.

"You are not authorized to issue commands to this unit," said the computer.

What?

He slapped at the comm button on his desk. "Bridge, this is Cheveldeoff. What's going on?"

No answer.

Cheveldeoff coughed. The damn tickle had turned into a scratch and now a raging sore throat. He felt something trickle from one nostril, and brushed at his nose with the back of his free hand.

It came away red.

What the hell . . . ?

The part of his mind nurturing the seed of panic let it bloom. *Plague! Keating lied. He's a carrier!*

I have to get to the sick bay . . .

Gripping the pistol, he opened the door to his quarters . . .

. . . to find the Holy Warrior he'd last seen manning the communications console on the bridge—Greist, that was his name—just reaching out to open the door from the other side.

Two other Holy Warriors Cheveldeoff recognized as part of the loyal contingent that he'd managed to get assigned to the mission stood behind Greist. "Braun twigged," Greist said without preamble. "There are running battles all over the ship for all the key positions we'd lined up. We're holding engineering and the shuttle bays, but Braun still has the bridge. We've been working on the crew since we launched, but Braun still has the edge in manpower." He coughed. "What's left of it. People are getting sick, sir, all over the ship."

"Damn," Cheveldeoff said. His throat felt like sandpaper, and he wheezed when he drew a breath. "Keating brought it on board. Whatever killed *Sanctification*'s crew and the Warriors on the ground. We've got to get to sick bay. There must be something they can do."

Greist shook his head. A tiny ruby drop flew from one of his nostrils and landed on Cheveldeoff's cheek; he wiped it away. "Braun's men hold sick bay."

"Then I've got to talk to Braun," Cheveldeoff said. "We need a comm channel to the bridge. He's killed my computer privileges, but he has to be getting reports from key stations."

"The brig is closest," one of the Holy Warriors said. "There should be a comm station there with manual controls."

Cheveldeoff nodded, his throat so raw the motion felt like he'd swallowed glass. He wiped more blood from his nose. "Let's go," he said. "I don't think any of us have much time."

The brig stood open. All the cells were empty. "Didn't we put Keating down here?" Cheveldeoff said.

"Looks like something blew the security circuits," Greist said. "Keating must have run for it." He sat down at the desk. "Comm channels work." He looked up. "I can put you through to the bridge."

"Do it." Cheveldeoff cleared his throat, but it didn't really help; it still felt like ground glass and sandpaper.

"Bridge," a voice said tersely—Braun's voice.

"Braun, it's Cheveldeoff."

Silence for a moment. "Your plan has failed, Cheveldeoff. I knew you intended to take the ship. I moved first. You've only got a couple of key stations. You can't get any more. Tell your men to stand down."

I don't have time for this, Cheveldeoff thought. The panic had bloomed and spread and now threatened to choke off all reason. "How many of your men are sick?" he snapped.

Another pause. "I don't know what you mean."

"Braun, Keating lied. There's no poison. It's a plague, and he brought it on board this ship when he stowed away on the shuttle. It's the same plague that killed *Sanctification*'s men. It will kill all of us if we don't . . ."

"If this is some kind of ploy . . ."

"How many of your men are sick?" Cheveldeoff demanded again.

A very long pause, this time. "A lot," Braun said finally.

"You."

Pause. "Yes."

"Braun, I surrender," Cheveldeoff said, ignoring the sudden, startled stares from Greist and his men. "Give me computer control, and I'll put an end to the fighting. If any of us are going to survive, we need access to—"

"Shit!" Greist swore.

Gunfire. Cheveldeoff ducked behind the desk, but not before a spray of blood and bits of bone and meat spattered his upper body. Which of his men it had come from, he had no idea.

All three, he discovered when he raised his head. Greist and both of the others lay dead, slumped against the console. The back side of it had been as shattered by gunfire as their bodies. Wires sparked and smoked. An alarm suddenly shrilled.

"Braun?" Cheveldeoff said. He coughed. "Braun!"

No answer.

"Braun, we have to—"

The door into the corridor slammed shut. The doors into each of the cells followed an instant later.

"Security breach detected," said the computer. "Brig is locked down."

"Computer!" Cheveldeoff yelled. "Open brig doors."

"You are not authorized to control this system."

"Dammit, computer—" a fit of coughing choked off his voice. He covered his mouth with his right hand.

"You are not authorized to control this system."

Cheveldeoff pulled his hand away, The blood staining it hadn't come from his slaughtered men.

He couldn't stop coughing. His chest felt on fire. He couldn't catch his breath. And every cough sprayed scarlet across the floor.

His gut twisted, then burned, then spasmed with a pain so sharp he might have been stabbed. He doubled over, retching now mingling with the coughing. So much blood . . . he didn't even know he *had* that much blood.

Then: pain. Pain such as he'd never known, pain such as he'd never imagined, though he'd imagined a lot of pain in his life, mostly inflicted on others.

He screamed, then, or tried to, but he had little voice left, and the scream died in the final twisting, retching spasm that tore through his guts. His insides seemed to be trying to hurl themselves from his mouth. He had no choice but to stretch his jaw, as wide as he could . . .

As black-flecked blood spewed across the cold metal floor of the brig, Cheveldeoff's last dim thought was how ugly it looked, and how glad he was someone was dimming the lights.

By the time Chris Keating found the first body, he hadn't heard any shooting for at least ten minutes.

He stared down at the dead Holy Warrior, who stared back. A laser beam had taken off the top of his head. His unmarked face bore a mildly surprised look.

Why are they fighting amongst themselves? Chris wondered. He felt angry. *Why aren't they busy Purifying Marseguro? What's* wrong *with them?*

"It's not fair," he muttered. Everything he did went wrong. He'd called in the Holy Warriors, only to be locked up. He'd gone to warn them about the Selkies' plans to poison them, but he'd been too late. He'd made it to *Sanctification* only to watch everyone die. He'd failed to warn Cheveldeoff in time when he entered the system . . . and when he did talk to Cheveldeoff, the Archdeacon had ordered him kept on board *Sanctification*. He'd managed to get to *Retribution* and, most generously, he thought, consid-

ering how he'd been treated, had once more offered his
help—only to be locked up *again*. And now the Holy Warriors, the soldiers of the Avatar, were killing each other instead of slaughtering Selkies.

It's a test, he told himself. *The Avatar spoke of God testing us, but not to destruction . . . unless we* fail *the tests.* Then
comes destruction.

He didn't feel he had failed any of the tests he'd faced,
but maybe Cheveldeoff was failing *his*. Maybe the Holy
Warriors were failing *theirs*.

He turned his back on the dead Warrior and pushed farther into the ship.

"Halt!" shouted a hoarse voice from behind him before
he'd gone another hundred meters. He put up his hands
and turned slowly to face the Holy Warrior who, armed
with a slug thrower, stood behind him. "State your loyalty,"
the Warrior croaked.

"I'm loyal to the Avatar," Chris said, wondering if that
answer would get his head blown off. But the Warrior just
grunted.

"Aren't we all," he said. "Don't be smart. You know what
I mean."

"No, I don't."

The Warrior came cautiously nearer. He looked pale,
and sweat beaded his forehead, glittering as he passed
under one of the cold green emergency light strips in the
ceiling. "You're not a Holy Warrior! You're that kid that
came over from *Sanctification*. You're supposed to be in the
brig."

"The power went out. The cells opened," Chris said.
"You couldn't expect me to just sit there."

"I suppose not." The Holy Warrior cleared his throat,
swallowed, and grimaced as though he'd tasted something
bad. "You'd better come see Grand Deacon Braun. *Cheveldeoff* ordered you locked up. His orders aren't operative
anymore. The Grand Deacon may have other plans."

Chris cautiously lowered his hands. The Warrior didn't
object, just motioned down the corridor with the slug
thrower. Chris walked in the direction he'd already been
headed. "Where *is* Cheveldeoff?"

"Locked up in his quarters, last I heard. Sick." The Warrior coughed. "We're all sick."

Oh, no, Chris thought. *No, Hansen couldn't have . . .*

But Hansen had been on *Sanctification.* They'd literally run into each other. And he'd been coming from the direction of the shuttle.

He put something on the shuttle, and they brought it aboard with them. He's poisoned them. Just like the others. Damn him!

He didn't say anything to the Holy Warrior. But he'd tell the Grand Deacon. If they knew it was poison, not an illness, they might be able to find an antidote.

"When are you planning to attack?" he asked the Warrior.

The Warrior laughed, coughed, laughed again. "Attack?" He hawked and spat, the sputum glistening bright red where it landed on the floor by Chris' advancing foot. "We're not attacking."

Chris' feet stuttered. "You're not?"

"Keep moving," the Warrior said, and gave him a shove that sent him into a staggering run for a couple of meters. "No, we're not. We've already broken orbit, course loaded and locked.

"We're heading to Earth, boy. And then we'll come back with a proper fleet and Purify that worthless ball of water back there till there aren't three microbes left alive.

"Here we are."

The Warrior ushered Chris into a briefing room, the same one where he'd shaken hands with Cheveldeoff.

Braun sat behind the table. He looked worse than the Holy Warrior who had escorted Chris. Wads of tissue at his right hand were stained red, and his eyes were devilish, black pupils floating in a sea of red. "Get out," he told the Warrior when he saw Chris. The Warrior sketched a salute and left.

"Hansen got the poison on board, didn't he?" Chris said. "You've got to get me to sick bay. I was given an antidote. Maybe they can . . ."

"It's not poison, you miserable little shit," Braun said, almost conversationally. "It's a plague, bioengineered by Hansen's God-damned Selkies, and, yes, you will get yourself to sick bay, because if any of us are going to live, we're going to need whatever antibodies you have swimming in your skinny little veins."

He struggled to his feet . . . then his bloodshot eyes rolled up into his head, he made a gagging sound, and he dropped like a felled tree. Chris heard his body thrashing around on the ground behind the table, heard horrible gurgling and retching sounds, and slowly backed away until he'd pressed himself tight into a corner. "Not again," he whimpered. "Not again not again not again . . . please, God . . ."

But for whatever reason, God Itself did not seem to be answering the prayers of Chris Keating, or any of the other frantic but increasingly fewer prayers issued from *BPS Retribution* that day.

And so, a few hours later, once more alone on a ship full of bloody corpses, Chris Keating made his way to the communications room.

"I think it's recorded," the tech who had come to fetch Richard from the cave said breathlessly as they climbed up the ladder into the strangely canted corridors of *Sanctification*. The communications room was gimbaled, but it was also currently on top of the ring, and getting to it required something approaching mountain-climbing skills. Richard looked at what he had once thought were decorative niches in the walls and now realized were handholds, looked at his arm, still in a sling—just climbing up the ladder had been hard enough—and said dryly, "Surely there's an easier way."

Emily, who had limped her way to the ship, said through gritted teeth, "I'm sure there must be."

The tech looked from one to the other, and comprehension dawned on his face. "Oh! Um . . ."

"I'm sure it can't be too difficult to route it to the portable comm station you set up outside, can it?" Dr. Christianson-Wood said.

The tech's face cleared. "Oh, of course. I should have thought of that. I'll have it in a minute."

He scrambled like a monkey up the handholds to the communications room. Dr. Christianson-Wood sighed and shook her head, and led the one-armed Richard and her limping daughter back down the ladder and over to one of the tents the Hansen's Harbor contingent had put up. A small console of black metal had been set on a folding bioplast table. A moment later the tech reappeared and touched a control, and an all-too-familiar voice filled the tent.

". . . Chris Keating calling Richard Hansen and anyone else listening in the Marseguro system," the voice said. "Congratulations, Hansen, your poison has done its work. They're all dead. How does it feel to be a mass murderer?"

Richard exchanged glances with Emily and Dr. Christianson-Wood, and saw in Dr. Christianson-Wood's eyes a dawning horror that puzzled him until he heard Chris confirm what she must have already guessed.

"But don't get too cocky, you son of a bitch. *Retribution* is already en route to Earth, course locked in, computer in command. I'm just along for the ride, but once we reach Earth and I tell my story, there's going to be a whole fucking Holy Warrior battle fleet heading your way to scrub that slimepit of a diseased planet down to magma.

"Enjoy your last few weeks, you and your Selkie whore and all the rest of the monsters and monsterfuckers on that God-forsaken ball of mud. The Avatar is coming, and God's vengeance will not be denied a third time."

A click.

"This is Chris Keating calling Richard Hansen and anyone else listening in the Marseguro system . . ."

"Kill it," Richard said, and the tech touched the controls again, silencing Keating in mid-rant.

"How did he get on board *Retribution*?" Dr. Christianson-Wood whispered, face stricken. "*How could they have let him on board?* They must have known what happened to *Sanctification*."

"I think he sneaked on board," Richard said. "He was heading toward the shuttle bay when we . . ." he flexed his arm, ". . . met."

"He's a carrier," Dr. Christianson-Wood said. "God Almighty, he's a carrier of the plague I made. The plague that killed every Holy Warrior. He's a carrier . . . and he's going to Earth."

"They'll quarantine him . . . ?" Emily said, but she said it as a question.

"Will they?" Dr. Christianson-Wood sank into a chair and covered her face with her hands. "*Will they?* And even if they do, can they stop it? *Sanctification* must have quarantined the shuttle that took Chris up in the first place, and every last one of them died.

"God, what have we done? What have *I* done?"

Her daughter put her hands on her shoulders, but had no comfort to give.

Half a Marseguroite year later, Richard Hansen stood once again on the bridge of what had once been called the *BPS Sanctification,* and now bore the name *MSS Victor Hansen.* A miniature statue of his . . . original . . . graced the alcove that had been a weapons locker, and a full complement of both Selkies and nonmods—the term "landling" no longer being acceptable in polite company—crewed the consoles surrounding the tactical display.

A screen by his currently unoccupied captain's chair lit with Emily Wood's face, the central pool of an underwater habitat in the background. "Getting close to launch," she said.

"Very," said Richard. "How's the new deep-water Selkie village coming?"

"On schedule, for a wonder," Emily said. She glanced behind her. "I guess we learned some things building the first two. If the Holy Warriors show up, we've at least got a chance of surviving whatever they can throw at us. And if they don't show up . . . well, it's about time we settled more of this planet, anyway." She grinned. "Funny thing, there don't seem to be any Consolidationists left anymore."

Richard just nodded. After half a year—more than half a year, in Earth terms—he didn't believe the Holy Warriors were still a threat. Even with Cheveldeoff dead—*especially* with Cheveldeoff dead—vengeance would have been the primary aim of the Avatar once he found out what had happened on Marseguro. The fact that a Holy Warrior fleet had not yet appeared in the system had to mean that things on Earth were bad . . . very bad.

"How's your mother?" Richard asked. "I haven't spoken to her for . . ."

"The same." Emily shook her head. "Half the time she thinks Dad's still alive and the attack never happened, some of the time she's almost catatonic, and sometimes . . . sometimes she just sits and rocks and weeps. Amy has been wonderful about looking after Mom. And John has been wonderful about looking after Amy." Her face hardened. "The Body Purified took my family and my friends and tried to take my world, Richard. Don't ask me to approve of what you're trying to do."

"I won't," Richard said. "But the Council agreed with me."

"I know." Emily blinked and managed a small smile. "Look, I didn't call to argue all that out again. Just . . . don't let the Body get you, too."

Richard smiled back. "I won't."

Something splashed into the water behind Emily, raising a small tsunami. She looked over her shoulder. "What the—no, no, no, that should go into the main—" She glanced back. "Got to go. Be safe. Come back. Love you."

The screen blanked.

Richard found himself grinning, and couldn't stop. But then, he didn't want to.

He raised his head, checked the time. "Computer, status report."

"All systems operating within normal parameters," the computer said. "Ready to launch on command."

Richard looked around at the crew, who looked back with blue eyes and brown eyes and green eyes, small and large, with and without nictitating membranes. Some had gills, some didn't, but they were all human.

And so were the people of Earth.

The holds were filled with water for the Selkies—and the microfactories necessary to create the hypervaccine for Dr. Christianson-Wood's plague. The course was laid in and locked.

They weren't fleeing Marseguro, and they weren't heading out to find a new home. They were going back to their old one, to see if they could save its people—some of them, at least—from a threat as deadly as the incoming asteroid that had led to the rise of the Body Purified. That one might have been sent by God, but this one had definitely been sent by man. And even if it had been, in some way, justified, it had never been intended to slaughter the innocent.

The Body believed God had miraculously rescued Earth from Its own threatened vengeance last time. This time, the very people hounded and murdered by the Body to appease God would provide the rescue.

Richard suspected the Avatar, if he still lived, would soon face a serious theological crisis.

He glanced at the statue of the original owner of his personal genome, and wondered what he would have thought of it all. Then he snorted.

Richard Hansen knew exactly what Victor Hansen would have thought of it all . . . and had already thought it.

He turned, surveyed the crew, and nodded to them. "Computer, launch," he said.

On a mission of mercy, *MSS Victor Hansen* headed for Earth.

TERRA INSEGURA

This one is for my best friend in high school, John "Scraw-ney" Smith. All those after-school writing sessions together finally paid off!

Acknowledgements

My sincere thanks to my perspicacious and patient editor, Sheila Gilbert, whose insight makes every book better; to my hardworking agent, Ethan Ellenberg; and to Stephan Martiniere, whose gorgeous cover art delighted me the moment I saw it.

My heartfelt gratitude to my long-suffering (not to mention radiantly beautiful) wife, Margaret Anne, and my practically-perfect-in-every-way daughter, Alice, for sharing me with my computer.

A grateful tip of the hat to Dr. Robert Runte, who read this before anyone else did and offered sagacious advice.

And finally, effusive thanks to all those who read and enjoyed *Marseguro*. May you enjoy this one even more!

Chapter 1

*B*UMP.

Emily Wood jerked awake in the pilot's chair of the tiny sub, heart pounding. Her eyes flicked over the control panel, searching for red lights that would indicate they'd hit something.

But nothing had changed. All the indicators still glowed green. The sub continued to purr along on autopilot, and the Marseguroite ocean outside the transparent canopy remained as black and impenetrable as always, with dawn still hours away on the surface, a hundred meters above.

Emily glanced at the woman in the chair beside her, but her mother still slept, her graying hair an unruly halo around her head, the gill slits on the side of her neck showing the slightest trace of pink.

It was a sign that her sleep had been helped along by drugs: relaxed like that, gills dried out faster, so normally a Selkie's gills remained as tightly closed in air when the Selkie slept as when she was awake.

But it was also a sign Dr. Carla Christianson-Wood, formerly the foremost genetic engineer of Marseguro and a member of the Planetary Council, really was asleep, not just keeping her eyes closed because she couldn't be bothered to take an interest in anything around her.

These days, that was just as likely.

Not even the news of the impending marriage of Emily's sister Amy to her old school friend John Duval had stirred much response. But least she had boarded the sub under her own power, even if she hadn't said a word since they'd left Newhome Station five hours ago.

Emily sighed and settled back against the soft black

pseudoleather. *Something in my dream,* she thought, though the dream remained clear in her mind and nothing had happened within it that should have jolted her out of it.

Richard had been in it, of course. He often showed up in her dreams now, more than a week after he had left Marseguro aboard *MSS Victor Hansen,* bound for Earth. She both missed him and worried about him. No one knew what the *Victor Hansen* would find on the home planet. If the Body Purified remained in power . . .

She didn't like to think about that possibility. If the Body Purified remained in power, Richard faced imprisonment or death.

But the other possibility was maybe even more horrific: that the crew of the *Victor Hansen* would find Earth devastated by the plague the Marseguroites had created to kill the Holy Warriors who had attacked and occupied their world six months ago.

The *Victor Hansen* carried vaccine, and the knowledge of how to make more . . . but would there be anyone left alive on Earth to save?

The crew, in other words, faced a mission fraught with uncertainty and danger . . .

. . . rather like her relationship with Richard.

With a finger, she traced the stitching of the pseudoleather covering the arm of the chair. She and Richard had fought together. They'd become friends . . . more than friends. She'd thought—fantasized—about their becoming lovers . . . but it hadn't happened. Not yet.

Once, she'd thought . . . but the moment had passed. She hadn't been ready. She'd told him so. He'd taken it well . . . but another moment hadn't come.

His fault, or hers? She wasn't sure. They'd been working apart for much of the past few months, Richard focused on bringing the former *BPS Sanctification* back to life as *MSS Victor Hansen,* while she'd had her mother to worry about, and her sister Amy, and the job she'd taken on coordinating construction of the new deep-sea habitats the Planetary Council had started to build as insurance against further attacks or natural disasters. They'd hardly had a moment together since they'd ridden the crippled *Sanctification* down from orbit.

And now he was gone. Maybe for good.

She shook her head. *No*, she thought fiercely. *He'll be back. He promised.*

As if *that* guaranteed anything.

She checked the board one more time, then settled back in the chair and closed her eyes, hoping to recapture the dream. She and Richard had been walking along the shore of . . .

Bump. Bump.

She jerked upright again. No denying it this time!

She scanned her controls. Nothing, but the little sub didn't have the greatest suite of sensors, and those it had were all focused in front of it, to guard against collisions with other vessels or one of Marseguro's sea predators.

Could it be a daggertooth? Emily had never heard of one of the killer whale-sized creatures trying to attack a sub, but . . .

Of course, it could be something entirely new. Except for one island continent, the whole world was ocean, almost completely unexplored. Emily felt a surge of excitement. *Here there be monsters? If I could get a photo of a new species . . .*

She still wasn't worried. A predator might check out the sub, but since it obviously wasn't edible, the creature would lose interest in a moment. Maybe as it swam away, she could . . .

And then Emily was thrown forward hard, only the pilot's harness she kept fastened by habit keeping her from smashing her nose into the control panel.

Her mother opened her eyes at last. "Emily? What's happening?" She almost sounded scared, which perversely pleased Emily. Any real emotion from her mother was so rare these days she leaped at it like a drowning landling lunging at a twig, hoping it was a harbinger of recovery.

"I don't know," Emily said. "Something has grabbed us, I think. We're at a dead stop." She peered uselessly through the canopy. The sub's headlights showed only plankton, swirling in twin cylinders of light that faded away into darkness within a dozen meters. And still nothing showed on the sensors. "It's under us, whatever it is. It must be a predator, something bigger than we've ever . . ."

She stopped. Her mother's eyes had closed again, the drugs pushing her back into sleep. Emily was talking to herself.

The floor canted. They were descending. Emily glanced at the depth gauge. Pressurized, the sub was good to three hundred meters. She had no idea how deep the ocean was at this point, but she'd bet it was deeper than that. If this thing pulled them far enough down . . .

She could flood the sub. Flooded, it might survive all the way to the bottom. But she and her mother would not, not unless they put on deep-water suits. Even before the pressure crushed them, they'd asphyxiate, their gills, though far more efficient than any fish's, unable to draw enough oxygen.

Getting her mother into a deep-water suit would have been a nightmare under ideal conditions. Now . . . she looked at the older Selkie woman, once more asleep, gills once more over-relaxed. *How many pills did she take?*

A strange vibration rolled through the sub. It felt mechanical, not biological, and it was followed by a series of clanks that were most definitely mechanical: metal against metal. Then came a high-pitched whine that set Emily's teeth on edge. *Drilling,* she thought. *It must be another sub. We've been grabbed by another sub, and someone is trying to get in.*

But that made no sense. If someone needed them, they could wait until their next radio check-in, due in an hour. No one would send a sub to grab them in the middle of the ocean. No one would have any reason to.

Unless . . .

Emily's already oversized eyes widened even further. "Shit!" She scrabbled at the buckles of her harness, got free, then scrambled out of her chair and plunged through the cockpit's after hatch into the hold.

Like the rest of the sub, the hold was full of air on this trip, because they were carrying all the food for the upcoming wedding reception, including a magnificent wedding cake, five tiers high, with Amy and John re-created in colored sugar atop the highest layer. The cake resided in a large box placed safely on the floor. As Emily burst into the hold, she saw the box rise on one side, then tip over. It crashed to the floor, breaking open and spilling pink icing and yellow cake across the decking. The spun-sugar Amy and John skittered across the floor but somehow remained intact.

A metal tube protruded into the hold from where the box had been, shiny silver shavings of metal scattered around it and clinging to its tip.

Something hissed. White mist spewed from the tube. Emily took one abortive step toward the deep-water suits racked at the back of the hold before the floor somehow rose up and smacked her on the cheek. She found herself staring at the sugar figures of Amy and John, lying in a welter of crumbs. They seemed to whirl around Emily in a bizarre wedding dance, and then everything went black.

"Impressive, isn't it?"

Richard Hansen just barely managed not to jump as the voice sounded in his left ear. It wouldn't do for the captain of the *Marseguro Star Ship Victor Hansen* to appear anything less than perfectly calm at all times. It particularly wouldn't do to flinch violently in zero gravity, which could send him on an unintended journey down the cylindrical corridor, bouncing off the padded walls as he went . . . and given his stomach's usual reaction to violent maneuvers in zero-G, possibly throwing up as well. And it *particularly*, particularly wouldn't do for Richard to give the owner of the voice the satisfaction of knowing he'd been startled.

"Isn't it," Richard said mildly, without looking around. "Hello, Andy."

An amused snort, and Andy King drifted across the corridor to cling to the webbing next to Richard, and look out with him into the main equipment hold of the *Victor Hansen*. Assault vehicles, cargo shuttles, boats, submarines, ground vehicles—some armed and armored, some not—small airplanes (ditto), racks of personal weapons and body armor: there was enough matériel in the hold to equip a small army: a lot more of an army than they had, for sure, since their entire ship's company numbered seventy-eight souls, fifty-two Selkies and twenty-six nonmods. But then, if it came to fighting—if, against all their best estimates, the Body Purified still held sway over Earth and refused to even talk to them—they didn't stand the proverbial snowball's chance in hell.

Or, as they used to say on Marseguro, a landling's chance
in deep water, though the term "landling" was no longer
considered polite when talking about a nongenetically
modified human. ("Normal" was even worse, since it implied Selkies *weren't.*)

Richard realized Andy was looking at *him*, not at the
equipment ranged around the hold, and turned to face his
first officer.

"You're thinking again," Andy said, as though accusing
him of a misdemeanor, if not a capital crime. He was a bald-
headed, round-faced, brown-skinned, short-but-muscular
Selkie. He wore a black landsuit: one hold of the *Victor
Hansen* had been flooded, lit and equipped with oxygenators to provide the Selkies with a swimming area, but most
Selkies still wore landsuits while on duty to enable them to
remain at their stations as long as necessary in the event of
an emergency.

Like the rest of the crew, Andy King had no space experience. But he had captained the largest ocean-going vessels, surface and sub, that Marseguro boasted, and he knew
how to gain a crew's respect and keep it disciplined. He'd
also become, in the few months that Richard had known
him, a good friend.

"Does it show?" Richard said wryly.

Andy made a circular gesture near his vestigial ears.
"Smoke," he said. "Burning smells."

Richard laughed. "Well, I promise not to do it again."

Andy's smile faded. "I didn't just come to insult you—
respectfully, of course," he said. "I've got news. Planetary
Communications forwarded it just before we entered
branespace."

"Nothing good, I take it."

Andy shook his head. "No. O'Sullivan's been murdered."

"*What?*" O'Sullivan, the former Holy Warrior who had
thrown in his lot with Richard and Emily aboard this very
ship and done more than anyone else to help her return to
space under her new name, had sent good wishes to the
crew just two days before, as they broke orbit. Richard
couldn't believe he'd been killed. And murder? Crimes of
any sort were rare on Marseguro; murder almost unknown.
Richard didn't even know when the last had been committed.

Unless you counted all the people killed by Holy Warriors in the attack he had facilitated on the planet.

He shoved that thought away, as he did a dozen times a day. "Do they have a suspect?"

"They have the killer himself," Andy said. "A Selkie. I didn't recognize the name. He shot O'Sullivan dead in the street, then slung his body over his shoulders, walked to Peaceforcer headquarters, dumped the body on the doorstep, and turned himself in. Said he was avenging his daughter. No Holy Warrior could be allowed to breathe the air of Marseguro after what they'd done, that kind of thing." Andy shook his head. "There's a lot of anger, a lot of tension between land . . . nonmods and Selkies. O'Sullivan was a hero to a lot of nonmods. I'd say the tension just got worse."

"Which is why this mission is so important," Richard said. "We're Selkies and nonmods—Marseguroites, all—working together for the good of people we haven't met, in the name of our common humanity." He couldn't help smiling a little. "It's a team-building exercise."

Andy winced. "I've always hated those."

Richard changed the subject. "Well, you claim you didn't come down here just to insult me, and as it happens, I didn't come down here just to be insulted. I'm looking for Smith. He's supposed to be in there," he indicated the hold, "somewhere, but I don't . . ."

"Here I am, Captain."

This time Richard did jump. So did Andy. Neither let go of the webbing, though, and so were at least spared the embarrassment of floating away.

Smith, the *Victor Hansen*'s quartermaster, was a stolid nonmod with a uniform air of grayness about him: short gray hair, short gray beard, gray eyes. His skin had a grayish tint. Even his pale-green standard-issue jumpsuit looked a little gray around the edges, Richard thought.

His first name, of course, was John.

"You wanted to see me?" Richard said—a little too quickly, to cover his startlement.

"Yes, Captain," Smith said. "I found something you should see . . ."

Ten minutes later Richard, Andy, and Smith floated inside the quartermaster's cube-shaped zero-G office. Most of the senior staff operated in the ship's rotating habitat ring, where something approaching normal gravity existed. The quartermaster needed to be close to his stores though, like the rest of them, his sleeping quarters were in gravity.

The room's walls were, naturally, gray. (Richard had sometimes wondered—though not enough to actually ask the computer—if the *Sanctification*'s quartermaster had also been named Smith; he couldn't remember a thing about the man, though he must have met him sometime during the two-week-long flight from Earth.) Glowstrips broke up the plain metal walls at meter intervals, and almost-invisible seams marked the various panels that could be opened to access storage compartments—and a vidscreen, which Smith now activated.

"As you know, Captain—"

Richard sighed. "Please don't start your explanation like that, Smith. It makes me feel like I'm trapped in a bad adventure novel."

Smith blinked, which was as close as he ever came to looking flustered. "Very well, Captain. Well ... um ... as you ... um ... that is, we've been having difficulty penetrating the quartermaster's personal security to access his records, which for some reason are segregated from the main ship's data store. As a result, we've been uncertain how much of the ship's original supplies remain aboard. Thanks to our own manual inventory we know what we have, but we haven't known what we're missing." Smith's thin lips curled up in a tight smile. "Until now. Computer, display file Smith 23A."

The vidscreen lit up with a series of text entries, accompanied by small pictures of various items. "I've gained access," Smith said, entirely unnecessarily.

Andy whooped. Richard didn't go that far, but he gave the quartermaster a huge grin. "Fabulous! How'd you do it?"

Smith snorted. "The quartermaster's software encryption was unbreakable. However ..." He reached into the right breast pocket of his jumpsuit and drew out a small rod that glittered like a jewel in the light from the glowstrips. "I found this taped to the underside of his bed. It's a data crystal, and it unlocks the files."

Hanging on to the webbing with one hand, Richard shook Smith's hand with the other. "Great work, John."

Smith shook his head. "I should have looked for something like that sooner. But thank you, Captain."

"So what have you found out?" Andy said. He gestured at the display, still flicking automatically through page after page of records. "This kind of thing makes my eyes glaze over."

"As near as I can tell, we're primarily missing only what you would expect—some small arms, ammo, personal armor, that sort of thing. However, there are two major items which remain unaccounted for." Smith turned back to the vidscreen. "Computer, display items UWV108 and ASV03."

The screen blanked, then showed two images side by side. Andy and Richard leaned in. "A sub," Richard said.

"Pretty big one, by the look of it," Andy agreed.

"And a shuttle?" Richard looked closer. "It doesn't look like any of the others, though . . . it's huge!"

"The sub is a Jonah-class attack submarine," Smith said. "Crew of eight. Designed to sneak up on other subs and either sink them or board them. A nice toy, if we're ever able to retrieve it. The shuttle, though . . ." Smith paused. The thin smile broadened; for a moment Richard thought the quartermaster was actually going to show his teeth in a grin. "It's something special. It's a GDPSS." He looked at them expectantly.

Richard glanced at Andy. Andy shrugged. They both looked back at Smith, who sighed.

"A Grand Deacon Personal Star Shuttle. It's twice the size of any other shuttle aboard, and that's not all: it has Cornwall engines."

"It's a mini-starship?" Richard took another look. "A second ship for our navy?"

"If we can find it," Smith said. "According to these records, it was off-loaded the day after the attack. Presumably, it was intended to take Grand Deacon Ellers back to Earth once Marseguro was pacified, so he could move on to other things while *Sanctification* remained on station."

"But we've seen no sign of it," Andy said. "Wouldn't we have noticed . . . ?"

"Computer," Richard said.

"Yes, Captain," the computer replied instantly.

"Computer, whereabouts of shuttle ..." he looked at Smith.

"*Divine Will*," Smith supplied.

"... *Divine Will*."

"*Divine Will* is not on board," the computer said.

"I know that, you ..." Richard stopped himself. He was pretty sure arguing with the computer was not a captainly thing to do. He tried again. "Computer. State the last known whereabouts of the shuttle *Divine Will*."

"*Divine Will* is on Marseguro."

Richard sighed. "Computer, *where* on Marseguro is the shuttle *Divine Will*?"

"Precise coordinates unknown."

"Why?" No answer. It's just a machine, Richard reminded himself for the umpteenth time that day. "Computer, *why* are precise coordinates of shuttle *Divine Will* unknown?"

"Shuttle *Divine Will* launched without proper authorization on Day 22 of current mission. Shuttle descended erratically. Shuttle disappeared from ship's sensors beneath ocean surface at coordinates ..." It reeled off a string of letters and numbers.

They meant nothing to Richard. "Computer, display those coordinates on a map of Marseguro."

The screen obligingly shifted to a map. Richard recognized the northern tip of the island continent at the bottom of the screen. A red spot glowed in the waters offshore. Andy pointed at it. "It went down a good fifteen kilometers offshore. And way north of any settlements or habitats. No wonder we had no idea."

"Day 22," Richard said thoughtfully. "That's when the plague hit the ship. Whoever took the shuttle must have realized what was happening and tried to escape. Probably collapsed or died during the descent, and the ship hit the water and sank. Computer," he said, raising his voice, "was impact of shuttle *Divine Will* sufficient to destroy it?"

"Negative," the computer said.

"Computer, what is the maximum depth of water shuttle can withstand?"

"Two thousand meters," the computer replied.

Richard whooped. "Another starship, waiting for us!"

"If we get back," Andy said.

Randy waved him off. "We'll send a null-brane pulse as soon as we emerge from branespace." He turned to Smith. "Great work, John," he said. "Congratulations. If this were a proper military, I'd promote you."

"Thank you, Captain," Smith said. His face actually colored a little.

Richard and Andy took their leave, pulling themselves along the webbing toward one of the transport platforms that would whisk them along the ship's giant central shaft to the habitat ring. "So tell me, Captain," Andy said as they went, "which are you looking forward to more when we emerge from branespace in two weeks: letting Marseguro know where to look for a second starship, or talking to a certain Selkie girl?"

Richard resisted the temptation to kick him. "I doubt I'll get to talk to Emily," he said. "I'm sure she's busy. Amy's wedding."

"Uh-huh." Andy was quiet for a moment. "I envy you," he said at last. "I don't have anybody waiting for me on Marseguro."

Richard said nothing. Most of the crew didn't: it had been planned that way. It was one reason he'd kept his distance from Emily over the past few months. There had been that one night, after the victory celebration, they'd kissed, and they'd almost . . .

. . . but she'd pulled away, said she wasn't ready. And afterward he had kicked himself for even letting things progress that far, knowing he would soon be off on this dangerous adventure. If anything happened to him . . . well, she was young. She was Selkie. He didn't want her pining after him instead of getting on with her life.

If he made it back, then maybe . . .

"Emily is her own woman," Richard said. "She may not be waiting at all."

Now why did I say that? he wondered. The possibility stung.

Well, whether she's waiting for me or not, I'm glad she's safe back there on Marseguro. "Hurry up, Number One,"

Richard said over his shoulder. "We're going to be late for the staff meeting."

"Race you to the platform," Andy said, and after that, they were working too hard to talk.

For the moment, that suited Richard just fine.

Chapter 2

EMILY WOKE IN THE DARK to confusion and a pounding headache, wrists bound behind her back so tightly her hands felt numb. Where was she? What had happened to the sub's cockpit?

Where's Mom?

She blinked. It wasn't completely dark. Maybe it would have been to a nonmod, but her Selkie eyes saw a faint, indirect glow, and as her vision cleared and the headache receded slightly, she could see enough to get a sense of the space she lay in. Small, but . . . living quarters of some kind? Certainly she lay on a bed, not on a bare floor. And that looked like a tiny sink and counter over there. *Submarine quarters,* she thought. *But not our sub. And not any sub I've ever been in on Marseguro.*

That really left only one other possibility, and so when the door suddenly opened and flooded the tiny space with light so bright it made her wince and turn her head away, she wasn't surprised to glimpse a man in the powder-blue uniform of the Holy Warriors.

She'd hoped to never see that uniform again. She'd seen enough of them, generally splattered with blood, during the battle to free Marseguro from the Body Purified's occupation, and the long cleanup afterward.

Why was this Holy Warrior still alive, when the plague had taken all of his comrades?

"She's awake," the man said. Emily turned her head back to see a different Holy Warrior take the first one's place. Both men were bearded, something she'd never seen in the original force. *Makes sense if they've been hiding in a sub all this time . . . but they're doomed now. Mom and I are*

*carriers of the plague. Everyone on Marseguro carries it. It's
only a matter of . . .*

"Bring her out," the second man said. "I want to talk to
her." He stepped out again, and the first man bulled into
the room, grabbed her by the arms, and hauled her to her
feet. She tried to kick him, but he spun her around and propelled her headfirst into the narrow corridor outside the
door. Then he marched her down it to what was probably
one of the largest spaces in the sub, since its curved walls
suggested it extended the full width of the hull. Some sort
of wardroom, furnished with four unpainted metal tables
bolted to the walls, two on each side, each with four attached, red-painted chairs.

Three more Holy Warriors stood at the far end of the
wardroom. Her mother sat in one of the chairs, arms tied
like hers, face cheek-down on the metal table, eyes closed.

"Mom!" Emily tried to pull free. The second man she'd
seen said, "Let her go," and a moment later she fell to her
knees at her mother's side.

Dr. Christianson-Wood's eyes were open just a slit, but
only the whites showed, glittering in the light. Her skin
looked waxy. But she was breathing. Emily gulped a sigh of
relief. For a moment she'd thought . . .

"What's wrong with her?" said the Holy Warrior who
seemed to be in charge.

Emily struggled to her feet and turned to face him.
"Who are you?" she demanded.

"Don't tell me you don't recognize the uniform," the
man growled.

"I know you're Holy Warriors. I want to know your
name. I want to know who I'm talking to."

The man cocked his head. "Fair enough. After all, I
know who you are, Emily Wood. I'm Alister Stone, commander of the Body Purified submarine *Promise of God*."

"What do you want, Commander Stone?"

"We've got what we want, Emily Wood," Stone said.
"We've got your mother."

"And me?"

He shrugged. "You're incidental. Bit of a nuisance, really. Unless you can help us talk to your mother, I might
decide to just put you out the air lock. At depth."

Emily ignored the threat. "Why do you want my mother? Why do you need to talk to her?"

Stone's lip curled. "Because she designed the filthy plague that murdered every other Holy Warrior on this planet."

Emily felt as if he'd slapped her. "How—"

"How do I know? Because we've been down here since it started, listening. We know what happened to all of our comrades. We know what happened to *BPS Retribution*. We know about the vaccine—and we stole some for ourselves, so don't start listening for a cough."

"You've been hiding out—underwater—for six months?"

"Lots of rations on board these subs, Miss Wood. Enough to keep us going this long."

"But . . . why? What do you hope to accomplish?" Emily looked down at her unconscious mother. "What do you want with my mother?"

"Retribution," the Holy Warrior said. "Like the name of our former ship."

"But that won't get you anything in the long run," Emily said. "When we don't show up at our destination, there'll be a search. Subs, surface ships . . . they'll find you. And then you'll have to deal with a whole planet full of people who'll know what you've done. How long do you think you'll last then?"

"Oh, there'll be a search," Stone said. "And they'll find exactly what we left them to find: debris—wedding presents, that sort of thing—" he showed his teeth in a wolfish grin," —floating on the surface, and in the deep-sea trench you were crossing when we grabbed you, the flattened remnants of your sub, five hundred meters below its crush depth."

John . . . Amy . . . Emily imagined them getting the news, their grief, the wedding postponed . . . "You can't hide forever," she snarled. "Your rations will run out. Your recycling equipment will foul. You'll have to surface . . ."

Stone's grin widened. "Will we?"

"No sub remains underwater forever," Emily said.

"We're not going to be remaining on the sub." Stone moved closer, uncomfortably so, until his face was only centimeters from hers. "Listen to me, Emily Wood, and listen well. We are going to board the shuttle *Divine Will*, lying sunken but intact in relatively shallow water just fifty kilometers from our current position. We are going to take that shuttle, and your mother, back to Earth. And then we will hand her over to the Body Purified for trial and punishment, and accept our reward from the Avatar with all due humility."

"But the plague—" Emily said. "You must know—"

"That it returned to Earth with *Retribution*?" Stone shook his head. "Ridiculous. Do you really think something your mother cooked up in a lab on this water-soaked rock could overwhelm the Body Purified on Earth itself? It may have sickened a few people, but it won't have swept the planet as you naively hope. The Body Purified still rules Earth, Miss Wood. Count on it." He leaned in even closer, until she could smell his slightly sour breath and feel its heat on her face, and lowered his voice to an intense, vicious whisper. She forced herself not to flinch away. "You'd *better* count on it. Because if we get to Earth and find no authorities for us to answer to, we will use you two Selkie bitches as God Itself intended men to use women, and discard the broken bloody remains without a moment's regret. Because never forget, Miss Wood . . . you . . . are . . . not . . . human!"

Emily felt an old familiar rage building inside her, the rage that had driven her during the battle for Marseguro, when she had watched men die horribly—at her own hand, from the plague, and at the hands of others—without pity or regret. "You try," she snarled, "and I'll snap your spine like a twig. Because I'm stronger than you, Alister Stone. Stronger, and faster, and smarter. Not human? Maybe not in your eyes. But if I'm not human, it's because I'm better, not worse." She showed her teeth. "New and improved. Humanity 2.0."

Stone's lips tightened and his eyes narrowed. "Blasphemy!" he spat—literally; she felt the spittle hit her cheek, but she forced herself to ignore it. For a moment she was sure he would slap her, but instead he stepped back. His mouth curved in a cold smile. "You may indeed be stronger than me," he said. "But your mother . . ." He glanced at Dr. Christianson-Wood. ". . . is not. Would you prefer we start with her?"

Emily stiffened. "Don't touch her."

"We won't . . . for now." He gestured to the first Holy Warrior Emily had seen. "Release her hands, Abban." He looked back at Emily. "Look after your mother. I want her awake and talking when we present her to the Avatar. But cause any trouble, and I'll reconsider the advantages of presenting her to the Avatar catatonic . . . or dead."

Emily fought the fury inside her, tried to turn it cold instead of hot. *While there's life, there's hope*, she thought. It wouldn't do either of them any good if she got herself killed. Her mother needed her. "I'll behave," she said finally.

"I know you will," said Stone. He looked at Abban again. "We're only a couple of hours from the *Divine Will*. She can stay in here with her mother. Keep a close eye on her."

"Aye, aye, sir." Abban saluted.

Stone turned to the others. "Pass the word," he said. "I want everything ready to transfer to *Divine Will* the instant we arrive."

A chorus of aye-ayes followed, and the men dispersed fore and aft. Stone gave Emily one more long, hard look, then went forward.

Emily sat beside her mother. "Mom," she said. She glanced at Abban, who stood by the forward hatch. He watched her, his hand resting on the black grip of the sidearm in his belt holster. She looked back at her mother. "Mom, can you hear me?"

Slowly, as though emerging from a fog, her mother's face somehow . . . came into focus. She raised her head from the table, blinked at Emily, and managed a small smile. "Emily," she said. The cheek that had been pressed against the table was bright pink. "Have I been sleeping?"

"Yes, Mom," Emily said carefully. "Don't you remember what happened?"

"We were . . . going somewhere?" Her mother frowned, and looked around the Spartan wardroom. "Have we arrived? Where are we?" Then her eyes drifted over to the Holy Warrior in his distinctive blue uniform. She stared for a moment, her eyes growing wider and wider—and then she screamed, the sound bright and piercing as a laser. Abban whipped the gun from his holster and pointed it at them, holding it in both hands, finger on the trigger.

Running footsteps sounded, and a moment later Stone and four crewmen, whether the same ones as before or others Emily couldn't tell, burst into the room. "What have you done?" Stone shouted above her mother's unending screams. He shoved Abban's gun down; the Holy Warrior lowered it but didn't holster it.

"Shhh, shhh," Emily said, kneeling by her mother, putting her arm around her, but her mother would only look at the Holy Warriors, eyes jumping from one to the next. Emily stood and confronted Stone. "Get them out!" she shouted. "Get them all out!"

Stone hesitated, then nodded. "Everyone out," he said. "Close and bolt the doors. Abban, you stand guard outside the forward hatch. Biccum, stand guard aft. Move."

The Holy Warriors exited, all of them this time, Abban the last to go, looking back over his shoulder at them as he finally holstered his gun.

The hatches closed, leaving Emily alone with her mother. Dr. Christianson-Wood's screams tapered off, but her eyes still darted around the room as though she expected the Holy Warriors to reappear from thin air.

Maybe she does, Emily thought. "It's okay, Mom, they're gone." She knelt and put her arm around her mother once more.

Her mother turned wide, stricken eyes to her. "Ghosts!" she whispered. "Ghosts, Emily. Didn't you see them? They're all dead . . . all the Holy Warriors . . . I killed them . . . I killed them all . . . but they were here! They were here a minute ago!" She grabbed Emily's hand. "They were here!" But then her face softened and her eyelids drooped. She blinked. "Weren't they?"

"They were here, Mom," Emily said. She squeezed her mother's shoulder. "But they're not ghosts. They're survivors. They were in this sub when the plague hit. They figured out what was going on, and they got hold of some hypervaccine somewhere. They're immune." She took a deep breath. "And they don't think Earth is dead, Mom. In fact . . ." She swallowed. "In fact, they're planning to take us there."

But her mother's eyes were almost closed, and Emily didn't know how much she'd really heard and understood. "Don't be silly . . ." Dr. Christianson-Wood murmured. "We don't have a spaceship. Richard took it." And then she was asleep again, head dropping heavily onto Emily's shoulder.

Emily held her as once her mother had held her. She didn't cry. She wished she could.

In the sudden silence, all she could hear was the steady thrumming of the sub's propellers, the hiss of ventilation . . . and her own thoughts, which were not very comfortable companions.

Her future had suddenly narrowed to only two possibilities. The best: imprisonment on Earth, a life of slave labor. The worst: horrible death or gang rape. Oh, she'd meant what she'd said to Stone, but of course they could tie her down or drug her or in some other way keep her from fighting back. She would struggle, but they'd have her in the end.

So forget about her. Her focus had to be on her mother. She turned her head, studied her mother's slack, waxy face. Dr. Christianson-Wood had always been so vital, so in charge of herself and whatever situation she found herself in. But something had broken inside her when she'd heard that Chris Keating had taken her plague to Earth.

On Marseguro, it had been one hundred percent fatal among nonmodded, unvaccinated humans. Dr. Christianson-Wood's colleagues believed—hoped—it would not be quite as deadly on Earth, because a portion of its effectiveness depended on interaction with Marseguro-native viruses. But only a portion: it seemed likely it would be at least as deadly as Ebola-Zaire, which, before effective treatments and vaccines were developed in the early twenty-first century, had sometimes killed as many as nine out of ten.

And, unlike Ebola, it was easily spread. It could pass from person to person with a breath or a cough or a handshake, or linger in the very air of a building. Worse, most small mammals—rats, mice, cats, dogs—could carry it without themselves being infected. So, probably, could birds.

Dr. Christianson-Wood herself had been unable to provide any input: in her mental breakdown, she seemed to have rejected all the knowledge and experience that had enabled her to make the plague in the first place. She could not or would not draw on it: she wouldn't even make the effort.

Her mental breakdown had been followed by a physical one. She had always been strong, athletic. Now she looked weak and underfed, and her hair, still mostly blonde just months ago, was now almost entirely gray.

In a strange reversal, Emily had become the strong one, the grown-up, the one who had to have all the answers and make everything all right when the world seemed broken.

She took a deep breath. She *would* be strong, whatever the future held. For her mother. For herself.

And one thread of bright hope wove its way through her personal tapestry of darkness, a thread she held in her mental grip like a lifeline: they were going to Earth . . . and so was Richard.

When they reached the home world, *MSS Victor Hansen* would already be there. And if things on Earth were as bleak as the Marseguroites thought, she might be the only ship in orbit, the only ship to greet the shuttle when it arrived.

By Emily's count, Richard still owed her several rescues. She hoped he'd get a chance to even the score.

Chris Keating crouched in an empty garbage bin and listened to wild dogs howling in the streets of the City of God.

More dogs than people inhabited the city these days. Chris hadn't seen a human being now in a month, unless you counted the flotilla of aircraft that had roared low over the burned-out shell and toppled spire of the House of the Body two weeks ago. Chris had stood in the rubble-strewn street outside the Body's central place of worship, torched at some point during the days of violence that followed the outbreak of the plague, and shouted himself hoarse, jumping, waving, begging the Avatar and his surviving followers to take him with them, but of course they hadn't heard him. Even if they had, they probably would have left him behind.

God Itself has some other role in mind for me, Chris had comforted himself. *God wouldn't have gone to such extraordinary lengths to ensure I would be on Earth at this time if I weren't part of Its plan.*

He still wondered how Richard Hansen had done it. For a long time he'd been convinced that the deaths on Marseguro, on board *Sanctification* and, later, *Retribution*, had

been a sophisticated chemical attack planned by Hansen.
But he'd had to change his mind shortly after he'd reached
Earth.

He'd tried to radio Earth Control when *Retribution* arrived in orbit, but though he'd been able to send a final
message to Marseguro as the ship had left that system, he
no longer had communications control by the time he
reached Earth: the computer kept telling him that attempts
had been made to compromise its programming and it had
therefore initiated Security Protocol something-or-other.
He would have told them what had happened on the ship,
and they would have taken precautions, even though at
that point he still hadn't believed the plague was a plague.

Why should he? He'd worked in a genetics lab. It was
impossible — absolutely impossible — for the Marseguroites
to have created a plague, specifically targeting normal humans, in the few days that had passed between the Holy
Warriors' initial attack and the day the Holy Warriors
started dying. Therefore, it *couldn't* be a plague. It had to be
something else, most likely a chemical agent of some kind
that Richard Hansen had somehow smuggled aboard.

The Holy Warriors who had boarded the ship, and taken
him off of it, and brought him to the City of God, had been
looking for armed intruders or mutinous crew, not viruses
or poisons. And shortly after they detained him and took
him to the Holy Compound in the City of God, they began
to die.

"Damn Hansen," Chris muttered, as he did several times
a day. He'd obviously been wrong about the deaths being
caused by a poison. But he was obviously right about the
Selkies having been incapable of creating such a finely
tuned plague. The only thing he could figure was that Victor
Hansen, creator of the Selkies, had himself designed the
disease organism before he died, and that Victor's grandson, Richard, had brought that knowledge to the Selkies as
part of his own twisted plan to gain power.

Because if there was one thing Chris was absolutely certain about, it was that every disaster that had befallen
him — and the Body Purified, of course, but especially
him — could be laid squarely at the feet of Richard Hansen.

By the time the Body Purified had realized what was
happening, the plague was out of control. Incredibly infec-

tious, incredibly deadly, carried by animals—there had been no controlling it. It had swept the world like a tsunami.

The hospitals filled with the infected, then overflowed with the dead. Few bodies ever made it to the morgues. Mass graves were dug and bodies bulldozed into them by the dozens, but soon enough there was no one to drive the bulldozers. The Holy City's infrastructure continued functioning on automatic. Lights stayed on, water flowed, Body hymns wafted from loudspeakers five times a day. Bots emptied the already-empty garbage bins, like the one he crouched in now, and roamed the streets searching for debris, finding little but the occasional leaf or animal corpse: the human bodies had all been cleared away long since, delivered to the back doors of morgues, where they piled up in rotting, reeking heaps. Chris had gotten downwind of one a few days ago and had retched till he'd thought his stomach would come out his nose.

The howling had faded. Chris poked his head up, then climbed out and brushed dirt from his stylish black pants and tight-fitting red shirt. No point dressing in rags when the city was full of unused clothes, he'd decided. Fresh meat and produce had become impossible to find, but the city contained enough frozen, canned, and irradiated food to last him the rest of his life.

For his lodgings, he'd selected the penthouse of Paradise on Earth, the tallest and swankiest hotel in the city. The smell of decay wasn't so bad fifty floors up: down here on the streets, it hung over everything, fainter than it had been, but not gone.

Not by a long shot.

He'd come out today to pick up some warmer clothes from Splendid Raiment, his favorite clothing store. The leaves were starting to turn, and the nights were cooler than they had been. The City of God, built on the ruins of what had once been known as Kansas City, was a long way from the Arctic, but it was also a long way from the moderating effects of the ocean that had kept the climate of Marseguro's single land mass temperate all year 'round.

He'd been halfway to Splendid Raiment, located about two kilometers from his hotel, when he'd heard the dogs howling. He didn't think they were on his scent, but at the

same time he knew that the plentiful supply of food . . .
something else that didn't bear thinking about . . . the dogs
had enjoyed for days must be approaching inedibility even
for them, and that they were increasingly going to be looking for fresh meat. Probably they were hunting the deer
that had begun wandering through the deserted streets, but
Chris saw no reason to offer them an easier alternative.

Now he emerged from the alley onto the street, and
looked both ways.

It was the main boulevard of the city, the one that ran
past the ruins of the House of the Body straight to the Holy
Compound, the city-within-a-city where the Avatar and all
the highest members of the Body hierarchy had dwelt in
happier times. Paved in spotless blue ceramic tile, it glittered in the sun. The white stone sidewalks and white stone
buildings that lined it were almost too bright for him to
look at, and he'd foolishly left his sunglasses back in the
hotel.

Well, he'd pick up another pair at the store.

Nothing moved along the boulevard. Directly across
from Chris lay Mercy Park, immaculate lawns and mani-
cured flower beds surrounding a cheerfully plashing fountain, whose central, pyramidal spire of golden metal
spouted water in glistening streams into bowls held in the
outstretched hands of dozens of nude men, women, and
children. Chris had wandered over once to read the inscrip-
tion: apparently it represented God Itself pouring out Its
mercy onto the grateful people of Earth.

With no one to tread on the grass, trample the flowers or
spread their litter, the park had never looked better. As he
watched, a tiny gardenbot trundled into view, carrying a
single wilted flower in its manipulator claw.

Chris crossed to the park side of the boulevard and
headed away from the Holy Compound toward the commercial district, still four blocks away. The sun shone warm
on his shoulders, and birds chirped in the trees. He couldn't
help grinning, and tilted his face to the sun to enjoy the
warmth even more. Despite everything, he was happy to be
on Earth, happy to be far away from Marseguro and its genetically modified monstrosities. The Body had long since
cleansed Earth of such things.

Then why has God visited this punishment on Earth? a

rebellious voice whispered inside him. *Why did It save the Earth all those years ago, if It intended to destroy it now?*

Chris shook his head. He would not question God's Will. He dared not: only the mercy of God had enabled him to survive this long.

The mercy of God, and the mercy of the Selkies, who had given him their vaccine before the plague was unleashed against the Holy Warriors.

No! He shook his head again. Their mercy had been unintentional. They would certainly have let the plague take him if they had realized it was he who had brought the Holy Warriors down on their blasphemous planet in the first place. No, God's mercy, not that of the Selkies, had been at work in that moment. God wanted Chris Keating alive, and It wanted him where he was right now.

Why else allow him to escape Marseguro to *Sanctification*, escape *Sanctification* for *Retribution*, and come at last safely to Earth? Why else ensure that he was released from detention when it became clear everyone else was dying?

He'd been terrified of being trapped in his cell. He'd banged on the door and screamed until his hands were bloody and his voice gone, and then, when he'd almost given up hope, the door had been opened by a Holy Warrior whose face was mottled and splattered with blood that ran in trickles from his nose and eyes.

"You seem to have escaped it," the Warrior had wheezed. "I won't leave you to starve in there."

Chris had thanked him and run, run as fast as he could, out of that charnel house . . . and into the greater charnel house of the City of God.

He had dreamed of coming to Earth, to the City of God, since he'd first listened to the contraband recordings of the Body's holy book, *The Wisdom of the Avatar of God*, that his grandparents had smuggled to Marseguro decades ago. He'd dreamed of seeing for himself the new order the Body had imposed on the scarred but Purified Earth.

He'd arrived just in time to see that order unravel.

Lost in his thoughts, he'd been watching his feet instead of his path; he looked up to discover he was already across the street from Splendid Raiment. He crossed and climbed in through the shattered front window. One reason he favored it was that it had been locked up before the riots began, and no one had died in it. Finding a space free of the reek of corruption and the buzzing of flies was rare enough to make it his favorite store even without the fact that he thought the clothes in it made him look damn good.

It was too bad no one else seemed to be alive to appreciate it. Not that he hadn't imagined what it would be like to find another survivor: a beautiful young girl, of course, lost and alone and desperate for human company . . . for male company . . .

He shook his head. The hotel had a rich collection of vids he'd begun to explore, with much, if unavoidably lonely, pleasure. He'd have a romantic date with himself that evening. For now . . .

He spent a few minutes browsing through the coat racks, finally settling on a long black overcoat that looked warm and also had enormous pockets he could fill with anything he came across that might be useful. On his way out, he grabbed some multi-shades, dialed them to their second-darkest setting, and stepped out into the sunlight.

A block from the safety of his hotel, he realized he was being stalked.

When he first glimpsed movement out of the corner of his eye, he thought it was the dogs . . . but it had looked too big to be a dog. A human?

Chris' pulse quickened. Unlikely though he knew it to be, his fantasy of the beautiful young girl resurfaced. Certainly he had no reason to think another human survivor would be a threat. With a whole city to loot, what could he possibly have that another survivor would want?

Unless they knew I was on board the Retribution *when it brought the plague back to Earth,* he thought uneasily. *Which they just might, if they're from the Holy Compound.*

Well, it couldn't hurt to pick up the pace just a little —

And then, from the alley on his right, from behind the trees in the park, and from the lobby of his hotel itself, dark figures emerged.

Chris stopped. *What the hell . . . ?*

They weren't human. Not fully. No more so than the Selkies. Maybe less. They wore no clothes except for straps and belts that held tools and weapons, but they weren't naked. Instead, they were covered in thick fur, not like a gorilla's but more like a cat's. Ears larger than a normal human's, pointed and tufted, sat high on their heads and twitched and swiveled like a cat's. Their faces were catlike, too, nose and jaws extended to make a kind of muzzle, though without the harelip of a cat or dog. Just like the Selkies, they had human-looking mouths, the full lips looking incongruous on the animallike faces—but unlike the Selkies, when those lips were drawn back into a grin . . . or a snarl . . . they revealed sharp fangs. One female, staring at him without blinking, ran her tongue over the tips of those fangs.

After one shocked, frozen moment, Chris dropped the coat he was carrying, turned, and ran the only way open to him, into the park.

They followed instantly, in unnerving silence. And they were fast—incredibly fast. As he dashed headlong toward the fountain, two of the creatures ran past him as if he were strolling, leaped up onto the fountain's lip, and turned to face him.

Chris stopped. He had no choice. He turned slowly, encircled, taking in more details of the creatures as he did so, particularly their hands, shaped the same as his but covered with fur on the backs and black pads of naked skin on the palms. As they came nearer, needle-sharp white claws sprang from the tips of each finger and toe. "What . . . what do you want?" Chris finally managed to squeak out. "Who are you?"

"We are the Kemonomimi," said the biggest, a huge male whose fur did nothing to hide just how male he was. He made Chris feel small in more ways than one, and his voice rumbled like thunder. "You will come with us."

Chris could smell them now, a musty scent, not unpleasant, but . . . feral. Disturbing. They stopped just out of reach, but close enough he had no doubt they could rip him to pieces with their formidable natural armament before he took two steps.

"But . . . where? Why?"

"You will come with us," the male repeated, then nodded. Chris felt his arms suddenly seized from behind. He tried to struggle, but they were strong, so strong . . . stronger than anyone he'd ever met, except for Selkies.

They're moddies, he thought, horrified. *But . . . Earth was Purified. There are no moddies on Earth. This is impossible!*

The Kemonomimi didn't seem to realize that they

couldn't exist. He felt his hands being tied together, then someone jerked a black hood down over his head. A moment later he felt himself being lifted; then he was thrown over a furry shoulder like a . . .

. . . well, the image that came to mind was of an animal trussed for butchering.

He remembered his earlier thoughts about the dogs searching for fresh meat in a city where even the plentiful carrion was becoming too gamy, and hoped fervently that he hadn't just become the main course for that evening's Kemonomimi feast.

No, he thought, as the creature carrying him broke into a loping run that caused his head to bounce hard against its back with every step. *No. God Itself has spared me for a purpose. That purpose cannot be to feed moddie monstrosities. It can't.*

But he couldn't help remembering something the Avatar had always emphasized: God's ways are mysterious. To think you understand them is to verge on blasphemy. And those who blaspheme deserve death.

It's not fair! Chris thought.

But fair or not, it seemed, once more his fate lay in the hands of moddies.

Chapter 3

"EMERGING FROM BRANESPACE in five ... four ... three ... two ..."

The blank screens showing the view outside the ship suddenly filled with light: the light of Sol itself. "Computer," Richard snapped. "Tactical situation: *Sanctification* status, other ships in system. Specify sizes and types."

"*Sanctification* has been recognized and approved for Earth approach by System Defense," the computer said. "System Control has provided data for insertion into assigned orbit; executing maneuvers now. Other ships in system: twelve. In orbit around Earth: One commercial freighter. Two forty-person ground-to-orbit shuttles. One hotel ship. One Holy Warrior vessel."

Richard and Andy exchanged glances as the computer continued. "In orbit around Luna: One Earth-Luna transport. In orbit around Mars: Two commercial freighters. Docked at Europa Station: One passenger liner. One government freighter. In solar orbits: One commercial freighter. One vessel of unknown type." A pause. "Correction. Vessel of unknown type has just leaped to branespace. In solar orbit: One commercial freighter."

"Somebody running away from us, or just from Earth in general?" Andy wondered.

"Computer," Richard said. "Why are you unable to identify the type of vessel that just jumped to branespace?"

"Unknown vessel was not within *Sanctification*'s sensor range and was not transmitting standard identification codes to System Central," came the reply.

"I don't like that one bit," said Andy.

"Me neither," Richard said. "But whoever they were,

they're gone now. Let's worry about who's left." He cleared his throat. "Computer, size, armament, and current status of military vessel in Earth orbit."

"Vessel is *BPS Vision of Truth*," the computer replied. "Calcutta-class Earth-to-Luna troop transport. Unarmed. Status unknown."

"Computer, establish communications link with *BPS Vision of Truth*," Richard ordered.

A pause. "Unable to comply. *BPS Vision of Truth* does not respond."

"Crew dead? Or lying low?" Andy murmured.

Richard shook his head. "No way to tell. But let's see if anyone else is talking." He raised his voice again, though there was really no need; the computer would hear a whisper as easily as a shout. "Computer. Scan all in-system voice communication channels for conversations related to *Sanctification*'s appearance in the system."

Another pause, then, "No in-system voice communication detected," the computer said.

Richard felt relief, followed immediately by a chill of horror—was no one left alive in the entire system? "Computer, send out general broadcast to all ships in system, null-brane and light speed. Message follows: '*MSS Victor Hansen*, formerly *BPS Sanctification*, to all ships. What is the status of Earth system? Please respond.' End message. Send."

"Message broadcast," the computer said.

"Computer, inform me the moment any response is received."

"Confirmed."

Richard turned to Andy. "So which of our scenarios do you think we've jumped into?"

They'd talked about all the possibilities they could think of long before they'd set out from Marseguro, of course; talked about them, brainstormed them, and drilled the crew in procedures to deal with them. Finding everybody in the system dead had been one of those possibilities, but Richard had never considered it very likely: there was no reason a ship in orbit should be infected if its crew realized in time what was happening on Earth.

Of course, that had brought up the disturbing possibility that they would jump into the system and into the teeth of a fully operational and very angry Body Purified fleet. They seemed to have avoided that one, since no one was either shouting or shooting at them.

That didn't mean there weren't Holy Warriors lurking on *BPS Vision of Truth*, or on the Moon, or on one of the half-dozen stations orbiting the Earth and Mars, staying silent, awaiting their chance to attack the *Victor Hansen*. That possibility seemed so strong that they'd drilled that scenario the most.

As Richard had learned when he'd first come aboard the ship, prior to the Body Purified's attack on Marseguro, she'd been designed with mutable spaces in the habitat ring: walls that could move, folding, unfolding, rotating or withdrawing altogether, blocking off the routes invaders might otherwise follow to the bridge or other crucial locations and at the same time herding them into places where they could be imprisoned or killed. With some careful modification and programming—thanks largely to the late O'Sullivan (Richard felt a pang of mingled grief and anger when he thought of the former Holy Warrior's murder)— they had created hidden spaces that even the computer no longer remembered existed: important, because as far as the computer was concerned, this was still a Body Purified ship, and how it would behave once they were in orbit around Earth had been the greatest uncertainty of their mission.

In the event of an attack, the entire crew could go underground—although, given the aquatic nature of most of the crew, the actual code word was "Submerge"—and make plans to counterattack. During the last drill, they'd gotten everyone under cover in eight minutes and fifty-three seconds.

Five minutes would have been better, Richard thought, but he'd take what he could get.

"Everyone in the system could be dead," Andy answered Richard's query, echoing his own worst fear. "But then again, they could simply be playing it safe. If central authority has broken down, ships and stations are going to be hurting for supplies pretty soon. Piracy might start looking pretty good."

Richard nodded thoughtfully. "And we're the biggest ship in the system, and a warship to boot. Pirates won't want to tangle with us, and everybody else will think we just might *be* pirates, trying to get them to reveal themselves."

"Makes some sort of sense," Andy said.

"Reply received," the computer said. "Null-brane."

"Computer, identify source."

"Heavy Freighter *Bearer of Burdens*."

"Computer, plot location of *Bearer of Burdens* on main tactical display, scaled as needed."

A cylindrical, three-dimensional diagram of the system appeared in midair at the center of the bridge. A spot of light marked their location, with a solid red line marking their path into the system and a dotted green line their projected path, barring course changes. Another spot of light, blinking blue, indicated the source of the transmission.

"The other solar-orbiting ship," Andy said. "Not really orbiting at all. She's outbound clear across the system from us. Figures she has nothing to worry about."

"Computer, play message," Richard ordered.

The voice that came over the bridge speakers was female, and as clear as if the woman speaking were standing there with them: null-brane transmissions weren't afflicted by static. Nor did they suffer from speed-of-light lag. They either made it through instantaneously without change, or were reduced to unintelligible gibberish.

"*MSS Victor Hansen*, this is Captain Leora McFadden of the heavy freighter *Bearer of Burdens*, outbound for Stableford. You'll forgive me if I'm suspicious you're who you say you are: your ship IDs as *BPS Sanctification*. The few of us left alive in Earth space have been wondering when a Body warship would come back. I don't think you'll find anyone very interested in a rendezvous.

"But whoever you really are, there's no reason you shouldn't know the situation in Earth system before you do something foolish like taking someone aboard.

"Earth system is dead. A plague has killed the vast majority of the planet's population. Not all, apparently: someone calling himself the Avatar still broadcasts orders occasionally, but I haven't heard anybody responding to them. There have been a few bursts of communication that indicate groups of survivors are hanging on in various remote locations, but for the most part . . . Earth is one giant ball of corpses.

"Luna Station was infected early on. I think a couple of habitats managed to cut themselves off from the rest of the station and ride out the initial die-off, but they fell silent a week or so ago; I suspect they weren't self-sufficient and eventually had to open up again, and the plague took them.

"Europa Station seemed to be fine for a while, but I haven't heard a peep out of it recently. Don't know if it was the plague or in-system pirates: ships without Cornwall drives had nowhere to go, and Europa didn't want to let them in. They may have tried to take the station, and if something went wrong . . . well, decompression will kill you just as messily as the plague.

"The orbital stations around Earth went silent at the same time as Luna. Somehow the plague got to Mars, too.

"We waited long enough to make sure we weren't infected, and now we're getting the hell out of here. Stableford hasn't welcomed any Body ships for a long time, so it should be clear.

"So whoever you really are, *MSS Victor Hansen*, you've pretty much got the system to yourselves . . . and you're welcome to it. Just don't drink the water and don't breathe the air.

"McFadden out."

"Computer, send following message to *Bearer of Burdens* —" Richard began, but the computer interrupted him.

"*Bearer of Burdens* has entered branespace," it said. "No message can be sent."

In the tactical display, the blue icon winked out. Richard sighed. "Computer, tactical display off."

The system diagram disappeared. Richard walked over to the captain's chair and dropped onto its plush black upholstery. "It's as bad as we thought," he said. "Maybe worse. Earth . . . all those millions of people . . ."

"Most of whom who would have killed everyone on Marseguro if they'd had the chance," Andy said. His eyes weren't really focused on Richard; he seemed to be looking at something Richard couldn't see.

Richard got to his feet. "Let's take a walk, First Officer," he said. "Second Officer Raum, you have the bridge."

Cordelia Raum, a pink-haired Selkie with a scar across her face caused by shrapnel on the day of the Body's attack on Marseguro, nodded and came up to the captain's chair.

Andy looked from her to Richard. He raised his eyebrows but followed Richard out through the massive bridge security door, currently locked open. Just outside the door stood a statue of Victor Hansen, a copy of the one that had once stood in the courtyard at the center of Hansen's Harbor. It had been placed there, welded onto a steel pillar, during the ship's renaming ceremonies three months ago. Richard tried not to look at the thing. It was unnerving to see an older version of your own face on a statue.

Richard turned to the right and led the way around the next corner to the briefing room where he typically met with the senior staff. He led Andy inside, turned and closed the door.

Normally, when they were alone, neither stood on formality, but Andy must have sensed something of his mood: he stood at what a Holy Warrior would have called parade rest, and looked straight ahead as Richard sat on the edge of the glass-topped table and folded his arms.

"I was disturbed by your comments on the bridge, Number One," Richard said. "You seemed to be implying that the people of Earth deserved whatever the plague has done to them."

"They attacked Marseguro," Andy said.

"No," Richard said. "They didn't. The Body Purified did. The Holy Warriors did. But not the people of Earth. Most of them are as innocent as Marseguroites killed in the attack by the Body. Y—" Richard stopped. He'd been about to say "your," and that sounded like an accusation he didn't want to make. "*Our* plague was only intended to defend Marseguro. We never wanted this. At least, I hope we didn't. But if you *did*—I need to know."

Andy's gaze flicked to Richard, and his eyes, green like those of every other Selkie, narrowed. "No," he said. "My apologies, Captain. I misspoke. Of course I didn't want the innocent to suffer. But don't ask me to mourn the Holy Warriors or the Body Purified."

"I won't," Richard said. "But we must all remember that this is a mission of mercy. Not one of revenge. Especially now, Andy, because very soon we're going to have to decide how to distribute the vaccine."

"We don't know enough yet," Andy said.

"Not yet," Richard agreed. "But our list of scenarios is

narrowing. We know the system has been devastated by the plague. We know, thanks to Captain McFadden, that there are survivors—maybe just in isolated pockets, but survivors nonetheless." He turned his head to look directly at Andy. "And we know something else. The Avatar is still alive—and broadcasting."

"McFadden didn't say anything about anyone responding," Andy said.

"She wouldn't necessarily hear them, would she?" Richard shook his head. "If the Avatar is still alive, then the Body is still alive. Maybe in retreat, but not destroyed. Remember, the Body is *designed* to survive apocalyptic conditions. Whether through luck or divine revelation, the first Avatar built underground shelters all over the planet long before the Fist of God—the killer asteroid—approached. They kept the faithful mostly unharmed during the meteor bombardment that followed the Day of Salvation. Those shelters, hardened, self-sufficient, still exist: it's a holy duty to the Body to keep them operational. Some of the faithful will have fled to those before the plague reached their regions. There are other Body bases and compounds, isolated, secure. And the Body is ruthless enough to do whatever is necessary to prevent the spread of the plague to areas it wants protected."

"If it had time, maybe," Andy said. "You know how fast the plague moves. And all it would have taken was one infected person—hell, one infected *mouse*—to wipe out everyone in even the most secure location."

"Nevertheless, the Avatar probably survives," Richard said. "And the Avatar has access to the planetary computers that control all the resources of the planet. Microfactories, transportation, distribution nodes, surveillance systems. Exactly what we need to find survivors and distribute vaccine to them."

"Shit." Andy glared at Richard, who didn't move. "You're still considering negotiating with the Body! You know how *I* feel about that."

"Yes." They'd argued through this scenario several times already. Even if they hadn't, Andy's comments on the bridge moments before would have made his position clear. "But in the end, the decision will be mine." Richard stood up and stepped close to his First Officer so he could look him squarely in the eye. "So I need to know now, before that moment of decision arrives: will you support me?"

"It may not come to that."

"But it may."

Andy drew himself to full attention. "If it does," he said stiffly, "I will obey any orders you give me . . . to the best of my ability. Captain."

What does that mean . . . exactly? Richard wondered. He started to ask; then stopped himself. After all, this might all be moot. Until they arrived in orbit themselves, they couldn't be certain what the situation was on Earth. "That's . . . enough," he said. He tried a grin, but he didn't get one back.

"Permission to speak, Captain?" Andy said.

"Of course, Andy."

Andy relaxed from attention. "You're worried I'll be blinded by the thirst for revenge," he said. "And maybe you're right to worry. But here's the thing, Richard: you could be just as blinded by your thirst for redemption."

Richard blinked. "I don't—"

"You blame yourself for the attack on Marseguro. And so you blame yourself for the plague being unleashed, and for it making its way back to Earth. You're desperate to make up for all of that. But the fault for what has happened to Earth doesn't lie with you: it lies with the bloody Body Purified. The Body didn't have to attack Marseguro just because you told them where it was. But they did. Their fault, not yours. The plague followed from their aggression. Like it says in the Christian Bible, they sowed the wind and reaped the whirlwind."

Richard's mouth quirked. "I didn't know you were religious."

"I'm not. But Tahirih . . ." Andy's voice broke off and Richard mentally cursed himself for asking the question. Tahirih, Andy's wife, had died in the Body's initial attack on Marseguro. Andy cleared his throat and continued. "The point is, Richard, the Body got what was coming to it. It needs to die, for the good of Earth, for the good of all of humanity, nonmods and moddies alike. Don't let your desire to make up for your perceived sins blind you to that. Use the Body if you have to, but don't trust it."

"Not much chance of that," Richard said. "But I'll take

your comments under advisement." He turned away from Andy and raised his voice. "Computer. ETA until Earth orbit."

"Fifty-two hours, thirty-six minutes," the computer replied.

"Computer, general address to the ship."

"Ready," said the computer.

"Attention," Richard said to the ship at large. "Senior officers report to the briefing room in one hour." He paused. "Ladies and gentlemen, it appears the situation on Earth is every bit as grim as we feared. But there are survivors. This is a mission of mercy, ladies and gentlemen, and I expect all of you to do whatever is necessary to ensure that we save as many of our fellow humans on Earth as possible. Captain Hansen, out. Computer, end general address." He glanced at Andy. "You have the bridge. I'll see you back here in an hour."

"Aye, aye, sir," Andy said, once more at attention. Richard nodded once, and went out.

As he walked toward his quarters, Richard replayed the conversation in his head. He hoped like hell he wouldn't end up negotiating with the Body. But he'd made up his mind a long time ago to do whatever was necessary to save the largest number of people. If that meant giving the Body a new lease on life, well, how much of a lease could it be on a plague-ravaged world?

He hoped it wouldn't come to that. He hoped they could find a way to not involve the Body. But if they couldn't . . .

There had already been so much death and destruction, and so much of it could be laid squarely at his feet. He knew that. Decisions made for the wrong reason, decisions made for the right reason that had gone wrong, failing to make a decision when he should have . . . the ways he had failed were myriad. In the end, Marseguro had been saved, and he had contributed to that, he guessed. But he never forgot—could never forget—that Marseguro had only been in jeopardy to begin with because he had helped the Body find it.

Now the tables were turned. Now Earth was in peril. And though he hadn't created the plague devastating the planet, and no one had intended for it to infect Earth, the fact remained that this, too, was the direct result of his determination . . . less than a year ago, though it seemed two lifetimes ago . . . to clear his family name and rise as high as possible within the Body hierarchy. One thing had followed another. Thousands . . . probably millions, by now . . . of people had died, domino falling on domino, all set in motion, at least in part, by his actions.

Yet what could he do but make more decisions, the best decisions he could with the information he had at hand? If he could not stop the dominoes from falling, at least he might be able to divert them into a different direction, one that minimized the suffering and death. And if that meant negotiating with the Body, then he would negotiate with the Body, up to and including the Avatar himself.

And hope that his crew would all, like Andy, obey his orders . . .

"To the best of my ability," Andy added. The phrase niggled at him. It sounded like . . . an out. As if his desire for revenge wouldn't let him commit fully.

And what about your own desire for redemption? he thought. *Is it blinding you to the dangers of the Body, like Andy said?*

He shook his head. No. Far from being blind, he was seeing more clearly than ever the cost of the conflict he had helped instigate. It had to stop.

Andy had quoted the Christian Bible. Richard remembered another part of it, which talked about "A time to kill, and a time to heal."

Surely the time to kill was past. Surely it was time to heal at last.

His cabin door slid open at his approach as the computer recognized him, and he stepped into his spacious-but-Spartan captain's cabin. He'd brought few personal items to Marseguro from Earth, and he hadn't acquired many more in the months since—and he'd stripped the cabin of everything that had belonged to its previous occupant.

The only bit of decoration was a holopic of Emily Wood, standing on the shore in her yellow-and black zebra skinsuit, the Marseguroite ocean stretching out green and glittering to the horizon behind her. Glistening drops beaded her suit and skin, and she smiled at him, the holopic making it seem she turned to watch him cross the cabin floor and sit on the bed.

"*You'll* understand if I have to negotiate with the Body, won't you?" he said to her.

She said nothing, of course. And the uncomfortable thing was, he didn't know what she'd say even if she were there with him. Despite all they had been through ... he didn't really know.

He hoped she'd have supported him, at least for the sake of her mother, undone by the horror of what she had unleashed on Earth. But she also had her own reasons to hate the Body, which had killed her father and several of her friends.

He couldn't be certain what she'd say, if worse came to worst and he had to treat with their enemies. And that troubled him most of all.

He lay back on his bed and threw an arm over his eyes. "Computer, wake me in thirty minutes," he said.

"Affirmative," the computer said.

But though he did his best, sleep wouldn't come.

Andy King sat in the command chair on the bridge and stared at the tactical hologram without seeing the vector lines and ship ID numbers it displayed. Instead, the images that filled his mind were those from six months before, when the Holy Warrior assault craft had swept down over Hansen's Harbor and shattered his world.

He'd been on deck aboard the *Bel Canto* that morning, preparing for a cargo run up to Firstdip. The sun had just edged over the horizon when he'd heard the scream of jet engines, a sound he'd never heard before except in vids. Marseguro had only a handful of aircraft, and they were all low-speed fanprops.

He'd looked up, puzzled but not yet alarmed, to see the three enormous black delta-winged craft, each almost as big as the *Bel Canto* herself, sweep low over the city. Missiles riding on tails of flame speared the city, blossoming into ugly flowers of orange and black. Fire rippled along the leading edges of the strange crafts' wings, and explosive slugs ripped up streets and shattered walls and windows.

He'd gaped, stunned, horrified, unable to speak or move: then the trio of craft had banked and turned back toward the city ... and he'd suddenly realized their second pass would take them right over the harbor.

"Get off!" he'd screamed at his crew, four Selkies, two landlings, all on deck, all staring up at the sky like he was. He'd shoved the nearest man into the water, then leaped in himself. His gills opened as he plunged under and he dove deep—but not deep enough that he didn't feel the awful impact of the explosions above, as missiles tore through the *Bel Canto*'s hull. Chunks of metal ripped through the water all around him, trailing bubbles. One sliced through both skinsuit and skin, laying open his right calf so that he trailed blood as he dove still deeper.

Here in the harbor anchorage there were no underground structures, nowhere to go, so he sat on the muddy bottom of New Botany Bay until the thump of explosions had ceased to make the water shudder. Only then did he resurface, cautiously, barely poking his head into the air.

Beneath a filthy, smoke-streaked sky, Hansen's Harbor lay in ruins, its towers shattered and burning. Some had fallen completely, and he instantly knew that half the underwater city must have been buried in rubble. "Tahirih!" he'd screamed, and dove again, swimming as fast as he could through water that reeked in his gills of oil and explosives and . . .

. . . blood.

He'd reached the floating lights that marked the swimways, had followed them as he had followed them so many times when he'd come back from a voyage, turned at the first intersection, swam toward the shore . . .

. . . and found his way blocked by the ruins of one of the towers, tons of steel and stone and glass forming an impenetrable thicket of wreckage.

Somewhere beneath that, he had left his wife sleeping.

"No!" he had click-screamed in Selkie. He'd pulled at the wreckage, but even as he bloodied his hands on twisted steel and shattered stone, he knew it was hopeless. It would take heavy equipment days just to dig down to the habitats that had lined this street. If anyone still lived down there, could they survive that long? The Selkies could breathe underwater, but the water had to circulate, had to be reoxygenated . . .

He needed help. They all needed help.

Then he had swum to the surface and discovered that no help would be coming.

Rounded up with the other Selkies, locked up first in a cage in the harbor then, after John Duval escaped, in one of the larger surviving underwater habitats, he had waited, helpless, for the Holy Warriors to decide his fate. Cut off from everyone else, none of the prisoners had known what was happening in Hansen's Harbor ... until one day, their guards fell ill, then disappeared. And the next day, two Selkies had swum into the habitat to free them ... and tell them the Holy Warriors were all dead.

Then, at last, equipment had been brought in to dig down to the buried habitats, though on shore the ruins were left largely intact to confuse the follow-up force of Holy Warriors everyone knew would be coming.

No survivors were found. Few of the bodies discovered were even whole. Andy had identified Tahirih only by the delicate pattern of winding vines tattooed on her shaven head; her face was ... gone.

He'd lost other people that were important to him that day: friends, distant relatives. The Selkies who had been aboard the *Bel Canto* all survived. The nonmods, unable to swim deep enough or stay down long enough, had all been killed.

When the Holy Warriors returned, he'd been one of those in the Square with Richard and Emily. He'd felt a fierce joy as he'd pulled the trigger and seen a Warrior collapse with a bullet in his brain ... but revenge couldn't bring back Tahirih.

He'd volunteered to join the crew of the *MSS Victor Hansen*, because, he'd told himself and everyone else, he didn't want the innocent people of Earth to suffer like he'd suffered. And he didn't: he would gladly vaccinate any survivors they found ...

... any survivors, that was, who didn't wear the uniform of the Holy Warriors and hadn't served within the Body Purified, the fascist death-cult that considered him and all those like him abominations in the sight of the bloodthirsty God it served.

But now Richard Hansen—the man he had sworn to obey as captain of this vessel and commander of this mission—was hinting he wouldn't hesitate to do exactly that, if he thought it the best way to get the vaccine to the maximum number of people quickly. And if the Body got the vaccine, Andy knew what it would mean, because he and Richard had discussed it over and over as they'd mapped out various scenarios for their arrival: around the world, surviving Holy Warriors would receive the vaccination first. Only then would they spread out to vaccinate the other survivors, and at the same time retighten the Body Purified's slipping grip on the planet.

And if that happened, then instead of destroying the Body, destroying the Holy Warriors, destroying the evil that had slaughtered Selkies without mercy on Marseguro, then the crew of the *Victor Hansen* would be helping it, healing it, ensuring it remained alive, like a zombie from some horror vid.

So they can come back to Marseguro and Purify it "properly" next time.

He was First Officer of the *MSS Victor Hansen*. He had sworn to serve the ship and obey the captain's orders.

And so he would. *To the best of my ability*.

But Andy King knew one thing: it was *beyond* his ability to obey any orders that would let the Body rise from the well-deserved grave the Marseguroite plague had shoved it into.

He might be worrying about nothing. The situation might never arise.

But if it did . . . he knew he could find others with like minds among the crew.

He glanced at the chronometer. Time for the staff meeting.

"You have the bridge," he told Second Officer Raum.

"Aye-aye, sir," Raum replied. She reminded him of his dead wife . . . except for the scar on her face. He watched her slender fingers slip fluidly over her control panel for a moment longer than was really necessary, then headed for the briefing room.

Chapter 4

KARL THE FIRST, Third Avatar of the Body Purified, did not claim to talk to God directly. His predecessor, Harold the Second, had made such a claim, but back then Karl Rasmusson had been Right Hand, not Avatar, and as such knew enough of Harold's myriad weaknesses of both personality and intellect to discount out of hand the claim that he had frequent intimate conversations with the Creator and Destroyer.

On the other hand, Karl had no doubt whatsoever that the First Avatar, Harold the First, had indeed had such a hotline to the Wrathful One. The existence of human beings on Earth was proof enough of that. Harold the First had foretold the miracle that had seen a previously undetected asteroid shunt aside the approaching planet-killing asteroid known as the Fist of God at practically the last possible moment. The odds of such a thing happening by chance were, well, astronomical. And the Avatar had positioned himself so perfectly to take over the planet in the wake of the initial panic, the devastating meteor storms, and the ensuing chaos, that he *must* have been telling the truth when he said God Itself had spoken to him and told him what to do.

Harold the First had talked to God. Harold the Second had not. And Karl the First . . . ?

Well, he was listening. He was listening *very hard,* because a little divine whisper in his ear would have been a welcome sign that God still cared about what happened on Earth. Because without such a sign, all the evidence seemed to point to God Itself turning Its back on the planet, its people, and the Body Purified.

Karl stood on the porch of his modest dwelling, which looked exactly like a log cabin even though not a speck of it had ever grown on a tree, and looked out through a carefully maintained clearing in the pine forest to the rocky shore of Paradise Island and the fog-shrouded water of the Pacific Ocean beyond. Somewhere behind him, the sun had risen, but it was still hidden by the mists it had not yet burned away. On a clear day, he would have been able to glimpse the low blue hump of another island, fifteen kilometers away over open water, but so far today his own island sailed alone through swirling clouds of gray.

It seemed appropriate, since that was what Karl felt he had been doing for some time now.

He'd never intended to be Avatar, never *wanted* to be Avatar. He'd liked being the Right Hand, the man who really ran things, no matter who the Council of the Faithful had selected as the current physical representative of God Itself. He'd hoped (and discreetly lobbied for) the ascension of Samuel Cheveldeoff, former Archdeacon of Body Security, when Harold the Second had suffered his unfortunate illness (a stroke brought on by a prodigious drinking binge). Cheveldeoff's success at purifying Marseguro was to have ensured that ascension.

Unfortunately, Cheveldeoff's ship had fallen silent, like *BPS Sanctification* before it. With the Marseguroite mission clearly a failure of monumental proportions, the Council of the Faithful had unanimously raised Ashok Shridhar to the position of Avatar when Harold the Second had finally (with a little judicial medical help) succumbed.

Karl had met with Ashok the First, established, with the help of certain information he had judiciously collected about Ashok's pre-Ascension activities, who *really* ran things, and had settled in for what he thought would be a few more years of very pleasant (for him, anyway) *status quo*.

And then *BPS Retribution* had returned.

Obviously under AI control, she had arrived silently, except for automated recognition signals. She had placed herself in a standard parking orbit around Earth. No one aboard responded to hails and the computer either didn't know or wouldn't say what had happened. The experts thought the AI had been tampered with in an attempt to subvert the command hierarchy, and had responded (as it was designed to) by becoming unresponsive to anyone. Essentially, it kept saying it would only speak to its captain, but it didn't know where its captain was, or even who he was.

The consensus was that there had been a mutiny. Nobody was thinking of disease. Why should they? Germ warfare had been abolished long before the Body took over, and with its distaste for genetic modification of any kind, even the thought of it was anathema.

So the Holy Warriors had taken no special precautions when they boarded *Retribution*, and no special precautions when they found the lone survivor, Chris Keating, who swore up and down that the dead had been murdered by Richard Hansen via mysterious chemical means.

Chris Keating, Karl thought. The name was burned in his mind. Immune to the plague, but a carrier. *Does he still live? Did he starve in prison? Or did someone figure out what he'd done and put a bullet in his head?*

In a way, Karl hoped he still lived, because then the possibility remained that someday Karl would have an opportunity to personally make him pay an appropriate price.

The Holy Warriors should never have taken Keating from the ship, of course. But they had. And they were the first to pay the penalty for their foolishness . . . but far from the last.

The doctors had never seen a disease like the one that gripped every man who had gone on board the *Retribution.* It started with a cough, proceeded to joint pain and fever and nosebleeds, and killed with alarming rapidity and efficiency, as victims bled to death internally or literally drowned in the blood that flooded their lungs. And "contagious" didn't begin to describe it. Just being in the same room with someone infected, or in a room connected by an air vent to a room containing someone infected, or using a bathroom used by someone infected, or . . .

They'd questioned Chris Keating. Why wasn't he infected? He'd told them he'd been given a shot by the Selkies, who had somehow protected the normal humans living on Marseguro from the disease. They'd taken his blood, tried to use its antibodies to formulate their own vaccine . . .

But it was too late. The doctors died before their work was half begun.

The Body authorities tried to stop the spread of the disease, but too many people had already been infected before they realized what they were dealing with.

A few—a very few—people seemed to be naturally immune, though no one knew why. Even fewer—maybe one in a hundred thousand—managed to fight off the disease and survive. Almost everyone else, everywhere on the planet, died.

The new Avatar, Ashok the First, briefed by men who had talked to Chris Keating in person before anyone knew about the plague, died in his office, vomiting blood across the diamond-topped desk hewn from one of the meteors that had slammed into the planet after the Day of Salvation. *Appropriate,* Karl thought blackly. The desk was a symbol of how God Itself could choose to destroy or to save. Once before It had chosen to save Earth. This time, It seemed to have chosen to destroy it . . .

And yet, a remnant clung to life. Almost too late, some members of the Body had realized that their only hope lay, not in isolating the victims, but in isolating the survivors.

The Body existed because the first Avatar had had the inspired foresight to build self-contained shelters beneath all of the Body's Meeting Halls. The largest complex of such shelters lay beneath the Holy Compound. The commander of Holy Warrior forces in the Holy Compound made it there first with a handful of his best men, all pressure-suited. They let in other survivors. Anyone could enter through one of the outer air lock doors into the shelter, which was essentially a buried spaceship. But no one came through the inner door until they had spent a full twenty-four hours inside the cramped air lock itself. In the end, one hundred and thirty-seven people had made it through. Another forty-six had fallen ill in the air lock and been expelled, alive or dead, their choice.

Among the other survivors: the forty-seven people, including the Right Hand, Karl Rasmusson, who waited in orbit aboard the Earth-Luna Shuttle *Reflected Glory* while plague felled humanity like a scythe through ripe wheat.

Not a single member of the Council of the Faithful, normally charged with selecting a new Avatar, survived. Fortunately, the inspired laws of the Body provided for that contingency: if the Avatar died without the Council being able to appoint a successor, the Right Hand ascended.

And so Karl Rasmusson, through no wish of his own, had become Avatar Karl the First.

He would have preferred to stay in orbit, but *Reflected Glory* was intended for short hauls only; food and water soon began to run low, and the air grew increasingly foul. And so he'd returned to the Holy Compound. Not everyone aboard the ship had agreed with that decision, but the half-dozen Holy Warriors who formed his personal bodyguard soon convinced them.

Reflected Glory carried enough pressure suits for thirty people. The new Avatar and those who had been part of his entourage each got one. That left eighteen suits to divide among thirty-five people. Six of those went to out-of-uniform Holy Warriors who had been on recreational leave. The remaining suits were handed out through a lottery. Only one of those who didn't get a suit had to be clubbed to death. The others decided to remain on board the landed shuttle, keep it sealed, and hope the plague burned itself out before they had to exit.

They watched as Karl and the rest of his tiny band of followers exited the shuttle and headed across the vast flat expanse of the spaceport toward the looming towers of the City of God, only dimly visible through the thick haze of acrid smoke that hung over everything.

The smoke came from buildings that burned, unattended, all along their route. They stepped over and around the bodies of men, women, and children, bloated and bloodstained. The corpses lay in the streets, huddled in vehicles, sprawled in parks and ornamental pools. Occasionally a large bot would trundle by, corpses stacked like cordwood in the bed of its trailer.

Not everyone was dead yet. A few survivors shrank back against walls when they saw the armed, pressure-suited Warriors coming, and clung there, coughing. A few of the bravest trailed along, begging for help, but the Warriors warned them off — with rifles, if necessary.

Window glass crunched under Karl's boots as they

passed another looted store, and he shook his head. The looters must have known they were as doomed as everyone else. What possible use could they have for a holovid or cookbot?

The two-story gates of gleaming copper at the main entrance into the Holy Compound were closed and sealed, but unguarded. Karl went into the gatehouse and ordered the Compound's AI to open the gates: it complied.

Like the city, the Holy Compound was occupied only by the dead or the dying. The Holy Warriors shot two men and a woman who came running toward them, coughing, faces streaked with blood, begging for help. As the woman fell, Karl recognized her as a former secretary of his. After that, the other walking dead kept their distance. Karl's party had no further trouble until it reached the entrance to the shelter. As he ordered the AI to let them in, some of the survivors rushed them. None of them got within ten feet, falling in a hail of automatic weapons fire, but a well-hurled missile smashed the faceplate of one of the Holy Warriors. His comrades shoved him away from them. As the door closed, he was putting his pistol in his mouth.

Stripped, irradiated, sprayed, washed, then irradiated, sprayed and washed again, they emerged four stories underground into an island of normality. One hundred and thirty-seven people were living in the shelter, swelling to one hundred and sixty-six with the Avatar's arrival.

It had been intended to house a hundred at most.

From the smell alone, it was obvious it wouldn't do for long-term residence. But at least it had a communications center that allowed him to contact other Body sanctuaries around the world.

No one had good news.

The plague had spread to every corner of the globe. Only the most remote outposts remained unaffected, and only by way of ruthlessly preventing the arrival, or even the approach, of anyone from the outside world. More: since the virus could be carried by small mammals, every cat and dog had to be slaughtered, every mouse and rat exterminated, and none could be allowed to enter the protected area. Birds, too, might be carrying the plague—though no one was certain—and so also had to be shot on sight.

Difficult measures to enforce: too difficult for some sanctuaries, which fell silent shortly after he contacted them.

He also managed to contact a few sanctuaries outside of the Body's hidden shelters: remote communities, mostly, high in the mountains or in the middle of deserts, where the plague hadn't reached. When he identified himself as the Avatar, they became guarded and unwilling to talk. Most refused further communication from him. It had infuriated him, but until he reestablished control—if he reestablished control—he could do nothing about their rebelliousness.

None of the places he contacted were in any position to take in the large number of survivors still in the Holy Compound shelter. Karl had then turned to the computer, searching the database for a place that could. It had to be remote, free of the plague, and able to maintain the necessary containment measures until . . . if . . . the disease somehow burned itself out.

He had found . . . this place. Paradise Island, formerly a resort for high-level members of the Body hierarchy. Avatars vacationed here. So had Karl, once. Fishing bots and extensive gardens provided some fresh food to complement the thousands of tons of stored supplies. The island boasted recreation facilities, communications facilities, and a full hospital, whose laboratory would enable the few scientists who had survived to continue studying the virus.

There was no need to remind them of what it would mean if their samples escaped containment: an error would carry its own death penalty. For all of them.

The island also boasted its own large population of survivors, including various relatively high-level Body officers who would form the core of his new staff, and a sizable contingent of Holy Warriors, since the island had always been an obviously tempting target for attack by anti-Body terrorists. That contingent had been further enhanced by escorts of some of the officials who had fled to the island even before Karl arrived, and the complete complement of the mainland garrison that watched over the island's ferry port. The total population of survivors on the island, in the end, numbered over 3,000, of which fully seven hundred were Holy Warriors, armed and armored: a small army.

It was a shame, Karl thought, that their enemy could not be defeated by guns.

Staring into the mist, he prayed, not for the first time, that God Itself would tell him what he must do, how he could turn Its wrath away from Earth and once more gain Its favor.

The sound of gunfire interrupted his murmured prayer, as the automated weapons that ringed the island's shore locked onto some unlucky bird and blasted it into bloody feathers. The sound reminded him of the propane "bird-banger" cannon that had frightened birds away from the vineyards surrounding his childhood home in the Niagara Peninsula.

He wondered how his father would have felt about his son becoming Avatar, then snorted. It wouldn't have mattered: Pietr Rasmusson thought only about his vineyard and his wine. It had broken his heart when his eldest had chosen to enter Body service instead of following in his footsteps. Karl's younger brother Gunther had taken over the vineyard instead. The last Karl had heard, Gunther's wines were carrying on the family tradition of winning awards.

Karl winced and closed his eyes. No more. His brother and his brother's wife, along with their four children, were almost surely dead. They and their grapes were probably rotting together in the fields, a feast for the birds at last.

As if on cue, the guns fired again.

As the echoes died, Ilias Atnikov, Karl's former chief of staff, and now the new Right Hand, stepped onto the porch. "Your Holiness," he said softly—Atnikov *always* spoke softly—"we've just received a transmission from AI at System Control. It reports a new starship has just entered the system."

Karl felt a surge of . . . hope or fear, he wasn't sure which. His prayer had barely died on his lips. Could this be an answer, so soon? "Can we identify it?"

"It has identified itself, sir," said Atnikov. "It's *BPS Sanctification*."

"*Sanctification!*"

"Yes, Your Holiness. However, it has broadcast a message to the whole system using a different name."

"What name?" Karl demanded.

Atnikov raised his voice. "Computer, play message broadcast from *BPS Sanctification* at 0635 local time."

"Message follows," said the computer. Its uninflected male voice, apparently coming from thin air, was immediately followed by the voice of a living man: "*MSS Victor Hansen*, formerly *BPS Sanctification*, to all ships. What is the status of Earth system? Please respond."

"*MSS Victor Hansen*?" Karl's heart quickened still more. "It's from Marseguro!".

"It seems a reasonable deduction," Atnikov said.

Karl looked back out at the misty ocean, taking a moment to compose himself. If the Marseguroites were aboard *Sanctification*—he'd be damned if he'd call the vessel by the name of the monster who had birthed the Selkies, the inhuman creatures who had created the plague—then the secret of the vaccine that had kept Chris Keating alive and could save all the survivors of Earth was there, too.

And one way or another, he, Karl the First, Avatar of the Body Purified, the chosen human vessel of God Itself, Creator and Destroyer, would have it.

It was the sign he had been praying for. God had heard his prayer, and It had, indeed, spoken to him . . . in, as always, Its own way.

Which meant It had a purpose for him, and the means by which salvation had been delivered told him what that purpose was.

Once he had the vaccine, then all the abominations of Victor Hansen would die as horribly as the millions they had murdered.

He looked up at the pearl-white sky. "I swear it, Creator and Destroyer of All Things," he whispered. "I will Purify this world and theirs with fire and the sword. Or I will die in the attempt."

He looked at the sky a moment longer, then turned to Atnikov. "Let's go," he said. "We have plans to make."

"Yes, Avatar," said his Right Hand, and led him inside.

Richard Hansen came onto the bridge of the *Victor Hansen* and, as he had for the past two days, looked first to Second Officer Raum, who had been the officer on duty during the night watch, the third since they had arrived in Earth's system. "Anything?"

"No, sir," she said, then had to cover a yawn with the back of her hand.

Richard had already known that, of course. If there had been any response from the planet below to their endlessly looping message, he would have been awakened immediately. But he still had to ask.

"Very well," he said. "You stand relieved."

"Thank you, sir." She got out of the captain's chair, sketched a salute, and then went out through the bridge door just as Andy King came through.

"I don't think we're going to hear anything, Andy," Richard said.

Andy said nothing. Richard wondered if he were secretly pleased. After all, the most likely people to hear from would be the Body.

"I think we're going to have to send a shuttle down," Richard went on. "Let's call a staff meeting to discuss possible—"

"Signal from Earth," said the computer, its voice as calm as always.

Richard and Andy exchanged a glance. "Computer, map and show location of signal's origin and play message."

The tactical display lit with a globe of Earth, zoomed in, and stopped, displaying the coast of British Columbia, north of Vancouver Island, where a multitude of islands of all sizes nestled off a mountainous shoreline cut with deep inlets. One island, in particular, was highlighted. Some of the other islands had names associated with them; that one did not.

"*MSS Victor Hansen . . .*" The voice that crackled into the bridge sounded strained and worn. "Receiving your transmission. Please respond. *MSS Victor Hansen . . .*"

"Computer, establish two-way link." Richard studied the tactical display. The message had been routed to them by one of the Body's communications satellites: they were currently on the other side of the planet from the source. But that didn't mean the speaker was a Holy Warrior or any other kind of Body official: their own broadcasts had been routed through those satellites, too. It was the only practical way to ensure anyone with an active receiver might hear them.

"Link established," the computer said.

"This is *MSS Victor Hansen*, Captain Richard Hansen speaking," Richard said. "Can you hear me?"

Crackle, then the sound of cheering. "Yes, *Victor Hansen*, we hear you! God, it's so good to know there are still people alive out there . . ."

"Good to hear voices from Earth, too," Richard said. "Who are you? And what's your situation?"

"My name is Jacob," the voice said. "There are a couple of hundred of us on this island . . . we were on vacation when we heard about the plague. We've been stuck here, afraid to go to the mainland. We've got lots of water, but food's running short. We've been patrolling the shore, shooting birds like crazy. So far no one has fallen sick. But we need help." The voice broke. "God, we need help so bad—"

Richard looked at Andy. "Are there any Body officials in your group?"

"A couple of Lesser Deacons who were on vacation," the voice said. "And four Holy Warriors on leave. They're the ones shooting the birds." The voice turned almost frantic. "What difference does that make? Won't you help us? Please!"

"Stand by, Jacob." Richard had moved over to the captain's chair while he talked; now he reached down and touched the manual control that muted his end of the signal. "What do you think, Andy?"

"It sounds legitimate," Andy said. "But that doesn't mean anything. It could be a Body trap."

"Or it could be just what we've been hoping for," Richard said. "A group of survivors without strong Body ties. A beachhead on the ground from which we can launch a planetwide effort to locate and vaccinate survivors."

Andy nodded slowly. "We haven't heard from anyone else," he said. "Things must be getting pretty desperate for all the survivors, wherever they are. I think we have to trust them."

"I think so, too," Richard said, and inwardly felt a huge weight lift from his spirit. He hadn't liked wondering if he could trust Andy to back his decisions. Now he wouldn't have to. He reactivated the bridge microphone. "Jacob, thanks for waiting. Yes, we'll help you." He glanced at Andy, who nodded. "More than you might expect. We have a vaccine."

Silence on the other end, then a new outbreak of relieved shouting and cheers. "We can't tell you . . . thank you! Thank you!" Jacob said. "How soon can you join us?"

"Within twelve hours, I would think," Richard said. "Our computer has your location. Is it possible to land a shuttle there?"

"Yes, it's . . . it was . . . a pretty nice resort. Big landing field. You shouldn't have any trouble."

"Excellent. I'll give you a precise ETA when I can." Richard deliberately didn't look at Andy as he added, "I'll talk to you soon in person. Richard Hansen out. Computer, end transmission."

Only then did he turn to face Andy again. His First Officer was glowering at him, pretty much as he expected.

"You'll talk to him in person? What crap is that . . . Captain?"

"I have to go myself, Andy," Richard said. "I know Earth. I know what the political situation was before I left. I have a pretty good idea of where we'll have to go to find the resources we'll need to gear up for planetwide distribution of the vaccine. I have to talk to these people."

"We can't afford to lose you," Andy said. "The ship recognizes you as its captain. Without you—"

"And the ship recognizes you as First Officer," Richard said. That had taken some careful programming by Simon Goodfellow, the computer genius they'd recruited early on in the process of turning *Sanctification* into *Victor Hansen*, but he'd managed to make it happen: the ship's computer, eternally loyal by design to an unbroken chain of command, now thought that Andy King—and all the other ship's officers—had enlisted in the Holy Warriors some six months ago and made the most remarkably quick climbs in rank in the history of military service: battlefield promotion after battlefield promotion, sometimes two or three on the same day. Andy King was now officially recognized by the ship as having the rank of Grand Deacon, Third Class—roughly equivalent to lieutenant commander in one of the old national Earth navies. "If something happens to me, the ship will accept you as the captain."

Andy couldn't argue with that. But he didn't look any happier. "There are other precautions we should take," he said. "An armed bodyguard—"

"Agreed," Richard said. "We'll discuss the makeup of the landing party together." He also readily agreed to take the other precautions they'd already planned to protect the vaccine from simply being seized and handed over to the Body. The doses he would take would be locked inside a high-security container that could only be opened by Richard without destroying its contents. "Okay?" he said at last, when all of Andy's objections—except the big one, against Richard going at all—had been dealt with.

"Okay," Andy said grudgingly.

"Good." Richard glanced at the chronometer. "I need to go talk to the scientists," he said. "Call a staff meeting for one hour from now. In the meantime, you have the bridge."

Andy watched Richard walk out and took a deep breath. He had a bad feeling about the whole situation, but he didn't know why. The voice from the surface had sounded convincing enough. Though it was odd the island this apparent luxury resort was on had no name on the map. "Computer," he said. "Display best satellite imagery available of island from which last transmission originated."

The tactical display blurred, then refocused to show a wooded and rocky island. The scale helpfully included in the image revealed it to be about ten kilometers long and maybe six wide at its widest point. The north end was rounded and mountainous, the southern end flatter and much narrower, petering out into a series of islets and rocks, splashed white with surf. In the middle of the island were several buildings, just nondescript roofs from his vantage point. Boats were tied up to a series of piers along the eastern shore, and not far inland from them there was, indeed, the long flat scar of an airstrip. Half a dozen aircraft were parked next to hangar buildings along the western edge of it.

"So far, so good," Andy muttered. But he still wished Richard weren't going himself. If it was a Body trap, Richard would be a huge prize . . . thought not as big as the vaccine he would be carrying with him.

Well, he thought viciously, *if the Body does capture or kill Richard, then I will be the new captain of* MSS Victor Hansen. And *in full command of its weaponry. Including the very same assault craft that killed Tahirih.*

Your bloody God Itself isn't the only one who can rain down destruction from on high.

He settled back in the chair. The dice were thrown. Now they just had to wait to see what numbers came up.

Karl Rasmusson leaned back in his chair as the transmission ended, and turned to Henry von Eschen, formerly chief of his security detail and now, as ranking officer of the surviving Holy Warriors, the new Archdeacon of Holy Destruction. "That went well," he said.

"I thought so, too... Your Holiness 'Jacob.'" Von Eschen grinned. "They fell for it."

"Seems that way." Karl glanced over his shoulder at the half-dozen Holy Warriors who had moments before been cheering the news that *MSS Victor Hansen* was carrying a vaccine against the plague. "Good work, all of you. You're dismissed."

The Holy Warriors filed out of his office. Karl waited until the last one was out and had closed the door behind him before turning back to von Eschen. "You're sure no one else has heard Hansen's messages?"

Von Eschen nodded. "As expected, *Sanctification*'s computer automatically routed its transmissions through Body satellites. It was a simple matter to ensure the only place those messages were relayed was here."

"And Hansen won't suspect?"

"No. At our instruction, the satellite falsely confirmed to *Sanctification* that the broadcast was going out over the whole planet."

Karl nodded. "Good." He pulled a datapad over to him and studied again the text message that had appeared on it while he was pretending to be the grateful civilian survivor Jacob. "And you're sure about this, too?"

"Computer confirms."

"And the shuttle?"

"It checks out."

Karl grinned. "Make sure Hansen gets down here safely first. Then do it."

"Yes, Your Holiness." Von Eschen saluted and went out.

God does *hear prayers*, Karl Rasmusson thought again. "I am the Avatar of the Body Purified, and God Itself is with me and in me," he murmured.

Those were the words of the Ascension Ceremony. When he had said them perfunctorily aboard the *Reflected Glory*, he'd given them little thought. When he had been Right Hand, he had even silently scoffed at them every time they were spoken by Harold the Second at the annual Ceremony of Reaffirmation.

But now . . .

"God Itself is with me and in me," he whispered again; and for the first time since he'd become Avatar, he truly believed it.

Chapter 5

CHRIS KEATING WOKE to find himself bound, blindfolded, and gagged, lying on his side on what felt like bare metal. He tried to roll over and couldn't. He listened, but all he could hear was a deep rushing and roaring. The cold surface beneath his left ear thrummed.

A vehicle? he thought. *Aircraft? Boat? Groundcar?*

He waited, but nothing else happened. He wiggled to attract the attention of whomever might be in the vicinity . . . and to get some blood flowing to his limbs . . . but nothing changed.

Where are they taking me? he wondered.

It appeared he'd have a long wait before he found out.

Emily Wood sat in the wardroom of the sub with her mother for the two hours it took them to travel to where the *Divine Will* lay on the bottom of the ocean. After an hour or so, Dr. Christianson-Wood stirred and opened her eyes, but she sat staring into space, occasionally muttering something to herself that Emily couldn't catch. She paid no attention to Emily or her surroundings at all.

At the end of the second hour, a subtle shift in the vibration of the sub told her the engines were slowing. A few moments later they stopped. She heard distant shouts and clanking sounds, and after a few minutes the forward door opened and Alister Stone came in, Abban right behind him, sidearm drawn.

"We've reached the *Divine Will,*" Stone said without preamble. "Time to get you aboard."

"We can swim," Emily said.

"We can't," Stone said shortly. "We've got a three-man

minisub aboard we're going to use to ferry people across. We've told the shuttle's computer to open the cargo hold and let it flood. We'll take the sub into the hold, pump it out, let people out, rinse, and repeat."

"What makes you think that shuttle is still good?" she said. "Salt water is highly corrosive. And it's been down here for months."

"The computer says it's fine," Stone said. "I guess we'll find out when we launch."

"Or when you get into orbit. Or when you jump into branespace. Or on landing. One failure, and—"

"—and we all die." Stone shrugged. "You included."

Emily got to her feet and took a step toward him. Abban lifted his weapon, and she stopped. "Why not give yourself up, Stone? Marseguro could use your expertise. We're not vindictive. The Planetary Council will offer amnesty if I recommend it. You could start a new life—"

"A new life?" Stone's lip twisted. "A new life with the monsters who murdered my friends? A new life with *things* like you? I'd rather die. And I'd rather die doing my duty than die a traitor when the Body comes back to rip this filthy sponge of a planet to shreds."

"How do your men feel about it?" Emily shifted her eyes to Abban.

His pistol didn't waver, but his eyes flicked from her to Stone. Stone glared at him. "The same," he said tightly.

Emily turned back to her mother. "Have it your way," she said. "But I think it's a mistake."

"Then we'll all live—or die—with the consequences," Stone said.

Emily touched her mother's shoulder protectively. "I should—"

"You should shut up and do what I tell you!" Stone snarled.

Emily blinked and very carefully didn't smile, but she couldn't help but think, *I got to you, didn't I?* And the only reason she could think of was that Stone wasn't as sure of his men as he pretended. Some of them might not be as fanatically committed as their commander.

She wasn't sure how that could help her. Maybe it couldn't. But maybe it was worth poking at, like a weak spot in a brick wall. She just might break through to someone. And if she could get any sort of ally among the Holy Warriors, it could make all the difference on the trip to Earth, and maybe even after.

But then her spirits dropped like a rock falling into the Deep. The trip to Earth. God, she couldn't believe it was really going to happen. But here they were, about to board the *Divine Will*. And once they were in space, there would be no chance of escape.

She looked at her mother. *There's no chance* now. If it had just been herself, she might have tried something once she got aboard the minisub. But she couldn't leave her mother to be dragged to Earth alone, as a war criminal at best, as a plaything for Stone and his crew at worst.

"Get her moving," Stone snapped. Without a word, Emily tugged her mother to her feet. She stood willingly enough, and walked when Emily applied a little pressure to her arm, but she still didn't seem to be registering anything around her.

Emily wondered how she'd react when they were separated for the trip to the shuttle, but she took no more notice of Rusk, who accompanied her on the first trip over, than she had of Emily.

Emily waited in the big sub's internal docking bay, guarded by Abban and another Holy Warrior whose breast-pocket name tag proclaimed him to be Biccum. Stone stood a little way off, talking in a low voice with another man whose name she didn't yet know.

Forty-five minutes after they'd watched the minisub submerge, it reemerged into the big sub's bay, water streaming from its transparent canopy. "Biccum and the Selkie," Stone commanded. "Then Abban and me."

"Shouldn't you stay and go down with your ship?" Emily said.

"I'm transferring my flag," Stone said. "Move."

Settled in the smaller sub, Emily couldn't help but think of her own little sub, now lying crushed on the ocean floor. Just a few hours ago she'd been packing it in anticipation of John and Amy's wedding, her happiness tempered only by her constant concern for her mother and the more distant worry for Richard.

Now it was happiness that was distant, so distant she couldn't see how she could ever find her way back to it again.

The journey from sub to shuttle took only a few minutes. Stuck in the windowless passenger compartment, she couldn't see a thing. She could only listen: thumps, clangs, the rhythmic swish of pumps. The sub suddenly listed to the left, then stopped at about a ten-degree angle. And then the hatch undogged and swung open.

Biccum crawled out first, then turned to offer her a hand as she followed. Surprised, she took it. Once on the wet deck plates of the cargo hold, she looked around for her mother, but of course she'd been taken somewhere farther inside the shuttle. Biccum pointed her to a hatch. It opened at his touch on the control plate. Inside was a ladder, leading down into a corridor that, at first glance, appeared to extend almost the entire length of the shuttle. Emily had expected something utilitarian, but the corridor was lit with subtle, hidden lights, and painted in muted tones of blue and green. The netting that covered the walls to provide easy hand- and footholds in zero gravity was cleverly designed to look like intertwining vines, complete with leaves and red, yellow, white, and blue flowers. The air was cool and dry ... and tainted, just faintly, with a hint of decomposing flesh.

The crew, Emily thought.

Rusk stood at the bottom of the ladder with her mother, whose glazed eyes made it clear she was not seeing the corridor at all. "We're supposed to confine them in one of the cabins," Biccum said as he climbed down after Emily. He glanced at her. "We'll be making a couple of final runs with the sub after everyone is aboard to bring over the cargo we're taking back ... including a landsuit for your mother."

Only one? Emily, who could already feel the tingle of dryness along the edges of her gills, felt a sudden chill. *Of course only one. They didn't plan for me.* "What am I supposed to do?" she said.

Biccum looked uncomfortable, but shrugged. "I don't know. You'll have to talk to Stone about that." He pointed toward the rear of the shuttle. "That way."

"How long is the trip to Earth?" Emily asked as she followed Rusk and her mother, Biccum bringing up the rear.

"Two weeks."

Two weeks? She swallowed, mouth—with horrible appropriateness—suddenly dry. "I won't make it."

"Talk to Stone," Biccum said again.

Emily changed the subject. "What kind of shuttle *is* this?" She reached out and ran her fingers through the zero-G webbing. It felt soft as velvet to the touch.

"Interstellar conveyance for Grand Deacons and the like," Biccum said. His tone was almost friendly, at least compared to any other Holy Warrior she'd ever spoken to. She gave him a closer look. About the same height as she was, he had a bald head and bushy black eyebrows, and either the thickest neck she'd ever seen or no neck at all. He smiled, startling her. "I've never been in one myself until now."

Rusk, thin and dark-skinned, shot him a sharp look over his shoulder, brown eyes glittering, but he said nothing. They moved slowly down the corridor at her mother's shuffling pace. "It's even bigger than the sub," Biccum went on. "We could have carried two more attack craft on *Sanctification* if we hadn't brought it, but Grand Deacon Ellers insisted. He figured we'd have Marseguro Purified in no time, but we'd have to stay on station here for a while to keep things quiet . . . and he didn't intend to hang around in person for that. There was supposed to be an Ascension fight shaping up back home and he wanted to be in the thick of it."

Emily didn't know what an Ascension fight was, or particularly care, but she was glad to have found, if not an ally, at least a possible source of information among the Holy Warriors. "Interesting," she said.

"Shut up, Biccum," Rusk snarled at last. "Stone didn't say nothin' about chattin' with the pris'ners." He had a different accent from Biccum's, though Emily didn't know enough about Earth to know what part of the planet he might have come from.

"He didn't say *not* to talk to them either," Biccum retorted, but he fell silent for the rest of the slow trip to their quarters. When the door opened, Emily gasped. Three rooms, tiny, but still; three entire rooms in a shuttle?

Not really a shuttle, she thought. *More like a mini-starship.*

One of the rooms was a dining/sitting room with a small table with low sofas on either side of it and a vidscreen/ entertainment unit in the bulkhead next to the door. From it, open sliding doors revealed a bedroom, taken up almost entirely with bed, and a bathroom with very odd-looking fixtures.

In fact, everything looked odd. It took a few seconds for Emily to realize that everything had two configurations: one for when they were in gravity, like now, and one for zero-gravity. That strange collapsed tube pressed up against the ceiling of the bathroom, then, must be a zero-G shower or bath. Emily eyed it doubtfully, all too aware it might be all that stood between her and an agonizing death.

"The Grand Deacon's own quarters," Biccum said. "Commander Stone said you'd need it, with two of you."

"I'm surprised he didn't keep it for himself," Emily said. "I expected something more dungeonlike."

"Naw, Stone doesn't go in for luxuries," Biccum said. "He's one of the men."

"Biccum . . ." Rusk snarled.

"Right. Well, here you are. I'll be outside the door." Biccum turned to Rusk. "Well, go on, Rusk, what are you waiting for? You're supposed to help shift cargo!"

Rusk gave him a blistering look, but turned and went out. Biccum went out, too, but as he closed the door behind him, he . . .

Emily blinked. Had that been a wink?

Holy Warriors are human, too, she thought as she guided her mother to the bed and helped her lie down on it. It had been easy to forget that during the war. It had been easy to celebrate every time she saw one die . . . or every time she killed one. After the first few, she'd felt no more empathy for them than she did for squigglefish.

Or so she had told herself.

But now . . .

Biccum seemed almost kind. She didn't think for a second he'd help her escape, but he wasn't a monster himself, just a man in service to a monstrous ideology. A man she might have been friends with, if he'd been born and raised on Marseguro instead of in the Body Purified.

She watched her mother, lying on one of the couches

beside the table, blinking sleepily up at the ceiling. After a moment she closed her eyes and began to breathe deeply.

Mom knew that from the start, she thought.

Her mother had known her plague would kill men who didn't deserve to die, men who served the Body only because they had no other choice, men who might harbor doubts but couldn't act on them, men trapped inside the system.

Richard had escaped that system, had realized . . . on his own, or with the help of the gene-bomb Victor Hansen had left inside his brain . . . that he had to turn against the Body. How many others among the Holy Warriors might have done the same, but were never given the chance? Her mother's plague was no respecter of persons: every non-mod, friend or foe, who didn't receive the vaccine in time, died.

Emily's mother had steeled herself to that knowledge, but when she'd learned the plague was on its way to Earth . . .

She'd retreated, unable to face what she'd done.

Emily went into the bedroom and lay down. Her mother hadn't said anything, but she must be starting to feel the effects of dehydration, as well. She hoped Stone would hurry up with the landsuit.

And after that . . .

She rolled over onto her side and stared at the zero-G bathtube again.

Stone didn't bring the landsuit himself: instead it was Rusk, who handed it over without a word and retreated again at once. Emily woke her mother and helped her pull on the heavy suit, its reservoir tank already filled. A slight frown had settled on Dr. Christianson-Wood's face, and she kept blinking around the cabin as though trying to work out where she was. *The drugs are wearing off,* Emily thought uneasily. *And we don't have any more.*

The drugs kept her mother calm, kept her from hurting herself or someone else when she lost herself in hysteria. Without them, Emily didn't know what would happen. Especially when her mother remembered, as she eventually would, that they were on a shuttle filled with Holy Warriors bound for Earth.

She'd better talk to Stone about it.

She went to the door and knocked. It swung open at once, out into the corridor, revealing Biccum's broad face. "Yes, miss?"

"I need to talk to Stone," she said.

"I'll let him know."

Stone showed up about half an hour later. "What is it?" he said without preamble, standing in the doorway without coming in.

She told him about her mother. "If you have any sedatives on board, I might be able to . . ."

"We don't," Stone said. "The crew of the shuttle used everything in the med station trying to save their lives when they became sick. In the end they killed themselves . . . using the supply of sedatives. We've been disposing of the corpses for the past thirty minutes."

"I don't know how my mother will react when she fully wakes up," Emily said. "She might—"

"I suggest you control her," Stone said. "See to it that she doesn't hurt herself. I want her undamaged when we hand her over for trial. And if anything happens to her . . . I don't need you."

Emily's mouth tightened. "I remember."

"Good. Now don't bother me again. We lift within an hour."

Twenty minutes later, Biccum knocked, then came inside. Rusk, she saw, remained outside on guard. "Beg pardon, ma'am," Biccum said, "but we need to rig your quarters for zero-G." He glanced into the bedroom at her mother, asleep once more. "We'll start in here."

Emily nodded and stood out of the way. With a few twists and clicks, Biccum turned the ordinary couches into acceleration couches, complete with harnesses for takeoff and landing and single lap belts to enable passengers to "sit" in them without gravity. He helped Emily prod her mother into one of them and strap her in, then went into the bedroom, where, in a few moments, he had transformed the ordinary-looking bed into two tubes like sleeping bags. In the bathroom, the bathtube descended and was sealed and the previously passive toilet came to rather sinister hissing life at the touch of a button, the water in it vanishing away, the seat replaced with an odd kind of flexible seal. It had a seat belt, too.

"All done, miss," Biccum said at last, crossing the sitting room to the door.

"Thank you," she said.

He smiled. "You're welcome." And out he went.

They must have been waiting for his signal on the bridge, because five minutes later an alarm whooped and Stone's voice came from speakers in the ceiling. "Prepare for launch. Five minutes . . . mark."

Emily strapped herself into the couch beside her sleeping mother. Dr. Christianson-Wood's head tossed restlessly, and her mouth formed unheard words, then she subsided, though she continued to frown slightly in her sleep.

"One minute," Stone said.

The seconds crawled by.

"Beginning ascent," he said abruptly.

The actual event was anticlimactic, which in a shuttle that had been submerged in salt water for six months was a very good thing. The shuttle swayed slightly, presumably rising through the water, then the slight vibration shaking the deck plates changed frequency and the ride smoothed out. Acceleration suddenly pressed Emily hard into her couch. It lasted only a few minutes, then eased off. She felt lighter and lighter and . . .

The straps on the couch creaked slightly as she turned her head and her motion lifted her off the seat. Zero-G. They were in space.

They were going to Earth.

Her mother's eyes fluttered open, and she blinked up blankly at the ceiling (if you could still call it that), then turned to look at Emily. "What's . . . sweetie, what's happening?" she said faintly. "I've had . . . nightmares."

"Go back to sleep, Mom," Emily said. "I'll tell you later."

Her mother blinked at her a few times, then her eyes, still dragged down by the drugs slowly fading from her system, closed once more.

And what will you tell her? Emily thought bleakly. *That the nightmare is real, and just beginning?*

Her gills had moved beyond tingling to burning and itching. She moved her head irritably, then sighed and unstrapped.

She'd better make the acquaintance of the zero-G bathtube.

                    *   *   *

Richard Hansen hung in the hold of one of the *Victor Hansen*'s cargo shuttles, checking the straps securing the precious security chest full of vaccine—and, even more importantly, the microfactory programming for creating more vaccine. Of course it was secure—it had been checked and double-checked already—but he needed something to occupy him while the minutes dragged by until they launched for the rendezvous with Jacob and the other survivors at the island resort.

Andy King floated in. "Not particularly good management technique, double-checking the crew's work," he said mildly.

"I know," Richard said. "But it's better than biting my fingernails in the cockpit."

He waited for Andy to tell him—again—that he shouldn't go himself, expecting to reply—again—that the decision had been made, but Andy surprised him. "I hope the mission goes well," he said. "Good luck, Captain."

Richard blinked. "Thank you, Andy." He turned back to the straps and gave one last unnecessary tug. "I think we're set."

"Launch in fifteen minutes, then?"

Richard nodded. "Launch in fifteen, as planned."

"Very good. I'll return to the bridge." Andy held out his hand. "Good luck, Richard."

Richard shook Andy's hand firmly. "Thank you, Andy. Take good care of the *Victor Hansen*. She's the only starship we've got, unless we manage to drag that missing shuttle off the bottom of the sea."

"Makes me acting admiral as well as acting captain, doesn't it?" Andy said with a grin. He turned and pulled himself out along the ratlines still joining the shuttle, now floating free in the central tunnel of the *Victor Hansen*, to the curving walls of the tunnel's interior.

Richard pulled himself up out of the cargo hold into the passenger compartment. The shuttle could easily have carried a dozen or more, but for this trip the crew, all volunteers, consisted of just six, counting himself, evenly divided between nonmods and Selkies. Looking through the open hatch forward, he could see a young Selkie woman with black-and-pink hair: Melody Ashman, his pilot. Next to her sat her copilot, Pierre Normand, a slender Selkie with a fuzz of electric-blue hair covering his pate and lightning-bolt tattoos on each cheek, both contrasting sharply with his unadorned matte-black landsuit.

Strapped into passenger seats were Jerry Krall, another Selkie, bigger than Pierre but with more sedate taste in hair and tattoos—the former plain brown, the latter lacking—and Ann Nolan, a nonmod woman, older than Melody, so petite she looked childlike next to Jerry. They were the technicians who would explain the making of the vaccine and program the first microfactories to produce it, assuming all went well.

Finally, all by himself at the back, Richard saw the remaining nonmod, Derryl Godard, tall, thin, wraithlike, dressed all in black, hair and eyes just as dark. He held a long black case across his knees, which Richard knew contained a Holy Warrior sniper rifle. His job: keep watch over Richard's first meeting with the supposed survivors and kill without mercy at the first sign of treachery—or the first sign of Holy Warriors. He also carried the control that would order the security chest to destroy its contents.

Hope for the best, plan for the worst, Richard thought. "Everyone set?" he said.

A chorus of "Yes, sirs," and "Aye, ayes," came back. Only Godard remained silent, though he gave a slight nod when Richard glanced back at him.

Richard strapped himself into the seat behind Melody, frowning. He only knew a little of Godard's story. Like everyone else, he had lost people he cared about in the Body's attack on Marseguro. Like many others, he had responded by training hard with the Holy Warrior weapons that had become available in the aftermath of the plague, and had been one of those who had helped ambush the follow-up landing by Holy Warriors from *BPS Retribution*, sent from Earth to discover what had gone wrong with the initial assault. But unlike most, he had continued to train, day after day, hour after hour, becoming without a doubt the best shot on Marseguro.

And then he'd volunteered for the *Victor Hansen*.

Yet Andy had assured Richard that although Godard would shoot without hesitation, he was not on some private mission of revenge.

Richard hoped Andy knew what he was talking about.

Jerry went back into the hold to sit across from Derryl, while Ann took the other cockpit seat. Richard leaned forward. "We're in your hands, Melody."

She nodded and said briskly, "Computer, establish link to bridge; keep open until otherwise ordered."

"Link established," said the computer's uninflected male voice.

"Bridge, this is shuttle *Sawyer's Point*. We are secured and ready for launch." They'd named the shuttle in honor of the volcanic spire that Emily Wood had brought crashing down on the killerbot that had been tracking her . . . and Richard. It had been his first inkling that he wasn't who he thought he was, that he was literally a blood relation of the Selkies he had brought the Holy Warriors to destroy.

"Roger, *Sawyer's Point*. Reeling in ratlines." Through the cockpit window, Richard watched two of the lines retracting into the walls of the hold.

"Isolating launch bay."

Massive bulkheads irised shut in front of the shuttle, blocking off the bulk of the central tunnel of the ship. They would exit through the stern.

"Evacuating launch bay."

A gale sprang into existence outside, and for a moment the bay filled with fog as the air pressure dropped precipitously. Just as quickly the fog vanished, the roar of the pumps attenuating with it into silence.

"Opening rear hatch."

Richard couldn't see that, but flashing yellow light reflecting off the bulkhead separating them from the rest of the ship told him it was happening.

"Launch."

The bulkhead receded, faster and faster; then they were out in space, the sun glaring from behind them, lighting up the long cylinder of the *Victor Hansen*, sleek and silver, thicker at the stern where the drives and shuttle docking bays were located, and banded at the front by the fatter cylinder of the habitat ring. It fell away above them, and then slid out of sight behind them as Melody took control and began their descent.

"Here we go," Richard said to no one in particular.

The first thin screams of tortured atmosphere rose from

outside the shuttle ten minutes later, and for the first time they touched the plague-infected atmosphere of Earth.

"They've entered the atmosphere," Grand Deacon von Eschen told Karl Rasmusson quietly.

"Good," the Avatar said. "Send the signal."

Chapter 6

ANDY KING SAT IN the captain's chair on the bridge of the *Victor Hansen* and watched the tactical display. The blip representing the shuttle entered Earth's atmosphere and began the descent to the resort island.

The display didn't show much else: just satellites and a few space stations. The satellites continued their automated functions, whatever they might be; the space stations were silent, floating tombs. The other ships orbiting Earth, the freighter, the two shuttles, the hotel ship, and most importantly, the Holy Warrior vessel *BPS Vision of Truth*, remained dead. They were alone in orbit.

About forty minutes after *Sawyer's Point* exited the ship, Pierre Normand's voice crackled onto the bridge. "*Victor Hansen*? *Sawyer's Point*. We're down in one piece. We'll update you shortly."

Andy touched the manual control that activated his end of the always-open communications link they'd established with the shuttle. "*Sawyer's Point*, *Victor Hansen*. Acknowledged."

Even as he spoke, a new blip appeared on the tactical display. It disappeared almost instantly: if he hadn't happened to have been looking at exactly the right part of the display, he never would have seen it.

He opened his mouth to say something, but his acting first officer, Cordelia Raum, beat him to it.

"Unknown vessel, bearing . . ." She stopped. "Um . . . it's gone, sir."

"I saw something, too, Cordie," Andy said. "Check it out."

Raum bent over her board. After a moment's silence,

she looked up. "It read as a shuttle, but just for an instant," she said. "Then it disappeared. Some sort of atmospheric echo, maybe? If it were real, the computer would have said something."

Andy's eyes narrowed. "Maybe," he said. "But let's play it safe. Sound General Quarters." As klaxons sounded, he activated the comm link again. "*Sawyer's Point, Victor Hansen.* Captain, we may have a situation up here. Please respond."

Nothing. Andy frowned at Raum, who frowned at her board, fingers flying over the controls. "The comm link to the shuttle is down, sir!"

"Computer," Andy said. "Reestablish comm link to shuttle *Sawyer's Point.*"

"Unable to comply," the computer said.

"Computer, why are you unable to comply?" Andy snapped.

"We are currently experiencing severe electromagnetic interference on all communications wavelengths," the computer replied.

We're being jammed, Andy realized. *And that blip was no atmospheric echo.*

He'd already sounded General Quarters. There was nothing else he could do but wait for the other shoe to drop.

Sawyer's Point burst out of low-hanging clouds and swept down the length of a broad valley, dark evergreen forest disappearing into the fog on either side. A few seconds later the forest ended in a cluster of buildings and four large piers, then they were roaring over gray-green tossing ocean. The island appeared out of the fog ahead of them, and the shuttle's braking rockets roared. Moments later, they settled onto a broad pad at one end of the landing strip, its concrete burned black by countless takeoffs and landings.

The shuttle creaked as it settled onto its landing struts. The engine noise died away, leaving only the faint hum of the ventilation fans and the ticking of cooling metal.

"We're down," Melody said unnecessarily.

"Let the *Victor Hansen* know," Richard said.

"Already done, sir," Pierre Normand said. Then he

cocked his head, listening to his earbud. "Ground Control has contacted us. It's Jacob. He welcomes us to Earth and wonders if they can approach the shuttle now."

"Any visual?"

"No, just voice, like before," Pierre said.

"Let me talk to him." Pierre touched a control, then nodded.

"Hello, Jacob," Richard said.

"Captain Hansen! I can't tell you how wonderful it is to see you. Can we come out or do you need to secure things first?"

"Let's not rush anything," Richard said. "You'll forgive me for being cautious, and nothing personal, but this could still be a Body trap. I'll tell you what: I'll meet you on the landing strip, alone. Then we'll talk about what to do next."

Jacob chuckled. "I don't blame you at all, Captain. Okay. You're about a hundred meters from the control tower where I am. Do you see it? You're pointing right at it."

Richard leaned out of his seat and looked out through the cockpit window. Directly ahead, dim in the fog, a tower loomed at the edge of the concrete pad. "I see it."

"I'll meet you halfway."

"I'm on my way." Richard unbuckled. *You don't have to do this yourself,* he could almost hear Andy say. Those on board the shuttle expressed *their* disapproval with silent frowns. He ignored them, just like he would have ignored Andy.

He did, however, turn to Godard. "Get your weapon," he said. "I want you outside the shuttle . . . just in case."

Godard nodded, and unbuckled.

Andy King watched the tactical display. It didn't change.

But he felt something odd, a faint . . . bump. Barely perceptible. "Computer," he said. "Status."

"All systems nominal," the computer said.

"Computer," Andy began again, but got no further.

"Bridge, we're being boarded!" a voice yelled over internal communications. "Holy Warriors! They're coming through the . . ."

The voice cut off.

"Computer, secure all access routes against boarders!" Andy snapped.

"Unable to comply," the computer said.

What? Andy felt a chill. "Computer, why are you unable to comply with last order?"

"Order has been countermanded by higher authority," the computer said.

"Damn!" Andy slapped the internal communications controls. "Crew, report!"

"They're in the main access tunnel," an unidentified voice came back. "We can't even get there. All of the hatches are locked."

"Casualties?"

"One. Teddy Simons," came another voice, ragged, breathing hard. "He was right there when they came in through Hatch 12. The bastards killed him on sight. But they haven't fired another shot. They haven't had to. We can't get at them!"

"Computer," Andy said. "Location of party that has just boarded the ship."

"Command party has just entered the habitat ring," the computer said.

Command party!

"Weapons?" Raum asked.

"No," Andy said. "Stand down." He stood up, looked around at the four men and two women currently on the bridge. "All of you," he said.

They knew what he intended. They'd drilled it often enough. As one, the bridge crew shut down their stations, stood up and moved away from them.

"This is First Officer Andy King," Andy said to the ship at large. "Submerge. Repeat, submerge."

He looked around at the bridge crew. "Let's go."

The statue of Victor Hansen outside the bridge doors watched impassively as they filed out.

Richard stood outside the shuttle, breathing the air of Earth for the first time since he had boarded the *Sanctification* for the attack on Marseguro, more than half a year ago. The fog had lifted a little, just enough that he could see the base of the control tower clearly, though mist still wreathed the top. And there, right on schedule, came Jacob . . . or someone he presumed was Jacob. Not surprisingly, the man walking toward him was wearing a pressure suit . . . civilian, though, not Holy Warrior issue. A good sign.

"No one else visible," Melody's voice said in his ear.

"I'm going to meet him," Richard said, and he did.

Jacob appeared to be a bit shorter and slimmer than Richard. The half-silvered bubble of his pressure suit made it impossible for Richard to see his face. He raised a hand as Richard approached, then touched a control on the suit's neck. "Welcome to Earth!" he said, his voice tinny over an external speaker.

"You're Jacob?" Richard said.

"In a manner of speaking," the man said cheerfully. "Though you might know me by another name." And he touched another control that turned his suit helmet completely transparent.

Richard blinked. He knew that face, but he couldn't . . .

And then it hit him, with the force of a fist to the stomach. "You're . . . Karl Rasmusson. You're the Right Hand of the Avatar!"

"Ready," said Godard in Richard's ear. Richard's jaw clenched. All he had to say was the code word "Firstdip" and Rasmusson would die . . .

Along with himself and everyone on the shuttle. There could be no doubt now that Holy Warriors were nearby. He held his tongue.

"Well, not anymore. Now, I am the Avatar: Karl the First, at your service. Not through any choice of my own," Rasmusson added with a bit of a smile. "I much preferred being Right Hand. But thanks to you, I have Ascended, and taken the oath before God Itself to serve It and keep the Body Purified."

"You are also in the sights of a sniper," Richard said softly. "At my signal—"

"Look down, Mr. Hansen," the Avatar said.

Richard's eyes narrowed, but he glanced down. There were three small red dots in the middle of his chest.

Sniper laser guides didn't have to be in visible wavelengths. These were a message.

Richard looked up again. "Killing me won't do you any good. The vaccine is in a secure chest. Only I can open it. If anyone else tries, or if I give a signal . . . the vaccine will be destroyed."

"All of it?" Rasmusson said. "Surely some of it is aboard *BPS Sanctification*."

"*MSS Victor Hansen*," Richard corrected sharply. "Flagship of the Marseguroite navy. And any vaccine there is out of your reach."

Rasmusson smiled. "Is it?"

Richard felt a chill that had nothing to do with the fog. "Pierre," he said.

"Monitoring," Pierre said tensely.

Richard kept eyes on the Avatar. "Any communication from *Victor Hansen*?"

"Negative."

"Call them," Richard said.

A moment's silence. When Pierre's voice came back, it sounded strained. "No response, sir. But, sir . . . we just received a message from the ship."

"Replay it."

A crackle, then a voice Richard had never heard before: "This is *BPS Sanctification*. Bridge secured."

Karl Rasmusson cocked his head. "Trouble?" he said.

Richard's fist clenched. He wanted to smash it through Rasmusson's faceplate, but that would accomplish nothing except getting himself killed.

"We have your ship, and your crew," the Avatar went on conversationally. "Aboard that ship we will no doubt find a great deal more vaccine, and the data which will allow us to mass produce it. You have one unarmed shuttle, five crewmembers, a secure chest filled with entirely *redundant* vaccine, and three bright red dots over your heart." The Avatar smiled. "I suggest you surrender."

"I can still kill *you*," Richard said.

"I'm sure that's true," the Avatar said. "But if we both die within the next few seconds, it changes nothing. The Body will still control *Sanctification* . . . as it always has, of course; your so-called captaincy was essentially a work of fiction. Your crew will still be captive. Your shuttle and your crew here will be destroyed. All of you will die, and to no purpose."

"You'll be dead, too. Right now that seems a fair exchange."

The Avatar sighed. "Mr. Hansen, you know as well as I that upon Ascension to this position my own personal safety became secondary to the needs of the Body. If I die, God Itself will welcome me into the afterlife as a martyr and a hero."

Richard stared at him. Ice-blue eyes stared back. Richard's heart sank. "You really believe that, don't you?"

"I do."

"I didn't expect . . ."

"True belief in someone who has spent his life pulling strings in the shadow of Avatar Harold the Second?" Rasmusson shook his head. "Then you didn't think things through. I preferred to be Right Hand, never sought to be considered for Ascension, because I thought that being Right Hand allowed me to better serve and protect the Body. I am not interested in power for its own sake. I serve the Body; the Body serves God. It is the only way to ensure that It does not destroy Earth once and for all."

Richard stood stock-still for a long moment. He could bring this conversation to a bloody end with a word, but he had no doubt the Avatar was telling the truth. Karl Rasmusson was as much a fanatic as the First Avatar had been. His orders would already be in place: if he were struck down, not only would Richard die, so would his entire crew.

If the Body truly held them captive. Because therein lay his only hope: that Andy King had ordered the crew to Submerge. If he had, then the crew might be trapped in orbit, but they weren't imprisoned. They were in hiding in the rooms and access routes that they had systematically blinded the computer to during the months of retrofitting.

Simon Goodfellow, his pet computer genius, had assured Richard they'd left no traces of that tampering: that to the Holy Warriors, it would seem that the crew had fled aboard the (in-reality empty) escape pods launched automatically as part of the plan.

Goodfellow had promised Richard something else, too, offering him an option so drastic that Richard had hoped it would never be necessary. But now it sounded like it might be.

It wouldn't be his decision to attempt it, though. It would be Andy King's. Because for the moment, and quite possibly permanently, he was out of the fight.

He couldn't—wouldn't—sacrifice the shuttle and its crew. And at least one good thing could still come out of all this: the vaccine would be distributed. Lives would be saved. Even if ultimately that led to a resurgent Body, it was better than allowing the plague to continue killing innocent people indiscriminately. He'd said as much to Andy, when he'd raised the possibility he might eventually have to negotiate with the Body.

His own life might not be among those saved, of course, but in the grand balance, perhaps that wasn't all that important to anyone except himself . . .

. . . and, he dared hope still, Emily.

Glad yet again she had remained safe, at least for the time being, on Marseguro, he took a deep breath, then said, "Very well, Avatar. We surrender."

"Captain . . . ?" Melody said tensely in his ear. "Are you sure about this? Derryl's got a clean shot. Give the word, and—"

"You heard me, Melody," Richard said. "Godard, stand down. Everyone, stand down. Open the hatch. Let the Holy Warriors aboard." He kept his eyes on the Avatar, who never looked away. "They won't hurt you."

"Your crew won't be harmed, provided they cooperate," the Avatar said. "I promise." He turned away and spoke in a low voice into his helmet microphone, then turned back to Richard. "Now, if you'll perform the introductions . . ." He indicated the shuttle.

With the sense of failure settling on him like a heavy black cloak, Richard led the Avatar of the Body Purified to *Sawyer's Point*, already swarming with pressure-suited Holy Warriors.

Aboard the erstwhile *Victor Hansen*, Andy King held on to the zero-G webbing lining the walls of the giant cylindrical chamber that had once been a fuel tank but now no longer even existed as far as the ship's computer was concerned, and surveyed his crew. They were all there, every nonmod and Selkie . . . all except for Able Crewman Teddy Simons, age twenty-four, promising splashball player and talented singer/songwriter, shot down by the Holy Warriors as they first entered the ship.

The Holy Warriors' method of precluding counter-attacks—ordering the computer to seal off all access to the route they took the bridge—had worked against them. It had given the crew time not only to respond to Andy's "Submerge" command and vanish into the hidden areas, but to take the entire existing stock of vaccine and the microfactory programming modules for creating more into hiding with them.

They had food and water enough for weeks stored in these secret spaces. But eventually they would run out. Before that happened, they had to retake the ship. And before they could retake the ship, they had to deal with the computer.

The nonmod hanging next to Andy in the webbing was thin and gray-skinned, with a sunken chest and sunken cheeks. Pale blond hair, almost white, stuck in wispy, sweaty strands to his mostly bald head. *He wouldn't last two minutes in a physical fight,* Andy thought. But right now Simon Goodfellow held the key to all their hopes.

"Can you do it?" Andy had asked the question a moment before, and it seemed to hang in the air between them. The rest of the crew, ostensibly out of earshot, somehow seemed to be holding its collective breath.

"It will take time," Simon responded at last. "I'll need uninterrupted access to a main data conduit for at least two hours. And a programming/diagnostic workstation, of course."

Andy frowned. "I thought you planted the databomb back on Marseguro. Why can't you just trigger it?"

"I did plant it," Simon said. "But these ship AIs are extremely—insanely—well-protected. Not trusting types, Body engineers. Getting the activation command to the databomb through all the defenses designed to prevent tampering with the ship's brain . . . we had weeks to get the thing in there. But if we'd made it too easy to access, it wouldn't have remained hidden. The AI itself would probably have found it and rooted it out before now. Two hours, minimum." He smiled a slightly superior smile. "I can explain in more detail . . . if you have a year or two to study AI mechanics."

Andy took a deep breath, held it for a moment with his eyes closed, then let it out explosively. He didn't have to like Simon Goodfellow, but he sure as hell needed him. "Fine," he growled. "So where can we find a main data conduit, and where can we find a programming/diagnostic workstation?"

"There's a PDW tucked away in here," Goodfellow said.

"That's a relief," Andy muttered.

"The best place to get at the main data conduit would be the corridor outside the bridge. There's an access panel there."

Andy stared at him. "Um, no," he said. "How about the second or third best? Preferably some place we can actually defend while you go about it."

Goodfellow grimaced. "Well . . . I suppose I could do it from the VR training room. But there's no access panel. We'll have to cut through the wall. It'll add more time."

"Beats standing around outside the bridge waiting to be shot," Andy said dryly.

Simon turned a shade paler. "Um. Yes, I see your point."

Andy thought hard. "I might have an idea," he said at last. "It'll take some planning. And we'll have to be patient. If everything worked the way we planned, they'll believe we all fled to the surface. But we've got to give them time to search the ship, wait until they're off their guard." Andy wanted nothing more than to act *now*, this minute, to take the *Victor Hansen* back and turn the tables on the Holy Warriors . . . but he couldn't.

For the moment, the only wise action was inaction.

He sighed and looked around at the assembled crew. "So," he said. "Anybody got a deck of cards?"

Karl Rasmusson glared at the pressure-suited Holy Warrior in the vidscreen. Slightly out of focus behind him, the Avatar could see the bridge of the *Sanctification*. "Are you certain, Grand Deacon Byrne?"

"Yes, Avatar." Karl couldn't tell for sure through a faceplate but he suspected Michael Byrne—who, after all, had only been a Grand Deacon for about a day, since the Avatar had contacted the erstwhile captain aboard his orbiting troop ship, *BPS Vision of Truth*—was sweating. As he should be. "No crew left aboard. The computer confirms it. Ten escape pods launched as we approached the bridge. If they only had a skeleton crew, that would be enough to ferry them all down to the surface."

"We saw them launch," Karl said. He leaned forward. "But something else launched, too, Grand Deacon. Besides escape pods. Something larger."

Byrne paled even further. "The assault craft," he said. "All three of them. Unmanned, as far as we can tell. They seem to have laid in an emergency program to deny their use to anyone else should the ship be taken."

"Not surprising, considering the history of this particular ship," Karl said. "Do you have other bad news for me, Grand Deacon?"

"Yes, sir." Byrne swallowed. "The Orbital Bombardment System has been scrapped, ripped right out. Even the alloy rods are gone."

"Foolish of them, when they were sailing into Earth orbit. I'm surprised they didn't try to use it to threaten us into submission. But never mind that." Karl leaned forward. "What about the vaccine?"

Byrne shook his head. "Your Holiness, I'm sorry, but . . . nothing. There's none here. And the computer says it knows nothing about it. As a result . . ." Byrne spread his hands. "We don't dare remove our pressure suits while we're on board, and we're keeping vacuum between *Sanctification* and our shuttle. We return to it in shifts to sleep and eat."

Karl drummed his fingers on his desk and stared at the wall for a few moments. Finally he looked back at Byrne, who didn't particularly seem to welcome the attention. He gave the man a small smile: completely terrified underlings were of little use, after all. "Very well, Grand Deacon. You've done well. A shame about the vaccine, though. Keep your eyes open . . . for it, and for a possible counterattack. There are plenty of flight-ready spacecraft scattered around the planet that they could conceivably get their hands on. If you see a ship you don't recognize it, warn it, then destroy it if it doesn't identify itself. No second warning."

"Yes, Avatar."

"Avatar out."

Karl killed the circuit. He sat back in his chair, and looked around his office. Half the size of his old one, maybe a quarter the size of the Avatar's office in the Holy City, it had a determinedly faux-rustic appearance to match the fake-log-cabin exterior. Undressed "logs" of bioformed plastic formed the walls. The carpet, artfully worn, featured dogs hunting stags and foxes. The fireplace snapped and crackled just as if it contained real wood instead of a hologram, and the antlers above the hearth looked as though they might once have really belonged to a deer, possibly the victim of the equally authentic-looking muzzle-loading musket hung on hooks just beneath them.

His desk, though of polished wood, was crammed with electronics, of course. And although normally he could look across it through a huge plate-glass window over a descending slope of fog-wreathed trees to the Pacific Ocean, right now a half-dozen large vidscreens hung in that space.

The one he'd just been using blanked and withdrew into the ceiling. He turned his attention to the next one over, which showed Richard Hansen sitting on a bed in a room that contained nothing else except the security chest containing the vaccine—assuming Hansen hadn't been lying to him all along, of course.

Two pressure-suited Holy Warriors, only visible to the camera as disembodied legs, stood behind Hansen to ensure he didn't attempt to destroy the vaccine.

I've been a little too clever, or else not clever enough, Karl thought. *I thought they'd fight for the ship. I didn't expect them to just abandon it and take the vaccine with them. I didn't think they'd have time.*

Now that chest contains all the vaccine in my control. And I need it.

So . . . how best to convince Richard Hansen to give it to him?

Karl Rasmusson had been playing power games for a very long time. He specialized in using his opponents' weaknesses against them. And he had Richard Hansen's weakness pegged:

Richard Hansen cared about people.

Karl did, too, in his own way, but he cared about them as a mass far more than as individuals. He needed people to carry out the work of the Body, to bring God's will to fruition. When, someday, humanity had been completely Purified, when all the far-flung colonies had been brought under the Body and the last abominations rooted out, then God would open the universe to humans and death and pain would become a thing of the past. Those far-future people would thank the Avatars who had worked tirelessly to achieve their utopia. But unfortunately, he couldn't allow concern for here-and-now people to block the path to that future paradise.

Nor truth, for that matter.

He would talk to Richard Hansen in a few minutes. Let him contemplate the vaccine chest for a few minutes longer.

He glanced at a third screen, where the other five members of Hansen's crew were crowded together in the compound's only other quarantine room, but then turned to the fourth screen, where a Lesser Deacon stood at attention, awaiting his attention. "Report," he said.

"We lost tracking on the escape pods and the assault shuttles when they hit atmosphere, Your Holiness," the Lesser Deacon said. "We think the crew disabled the tracking signals before launch, and without them . . ." his voice trailed off.

Karl said nothing. Once not a sparrow could have fallen on the planet without it being observed by one of the Body's surveillance systems, but without people riding herd on them, those systems degraded quickly. Now the surveillance net had so many gaping holes in it that an entire invasion fleet could have already landed in, say, Afghanistan, and they'd be none the wiser. They were barely able to keep an eye on *BPS Sanctification*. "Best guess?"

"The escape pods all landed in remote regions that are sparsely inhabited or completely uninhabited, Your Holiness."

The whole planet is sparsely inhabited now, Karl thought, but didn't say.

"The escape pods aren't big enough to carry vehicles," the Lesser Deacon continued. "They're stuck, or at best weeks from walking out. I suspect they'll be entirely focused on staying alive."

"What about the assault craft?"

The Lesser Deacon shook his head. "The same situation, I'm afraid."

Then I hope Byrne was right about them being unmanned, Karl thought. "Thank you, Lesser Deacon." Karl glanced at one of the smaller screens beneath the desk's polished surface. "Another matter, then. You've investigated these reports of aircraft being spotted near various Body compounds . . . ?"

"Yes, Your Holiness," the Lesser Deacon said. "And we have visual sightings that confirm your suspicion. The aircraft are manned . . . if that's the word . . . by Kemonomimi." And now the Lesser Deacon smiled for the first time. "And those we *have* been able to track: they're flying from the airport of a town called Newshore."

"I've never heard of it."

"It was built during the Third Wave of reconstruction following the Day of Salvation, Your Holiness." The Lesser Deacon's smile broadened, revealing teeth. "It's located on the coast of British Columbia. Less than three hundred kilometers north of Paradise island."

"Ah!" Karl returned the man's smile. "Thank you, Deacon."

"Lesser Deacon, Your Holiness," the man corrected.

"Not anymore."

The man grinned so broadly it looked like his face would split. "Thank you, Your Holiness!"

"Dismissed."

Karl flicked off the channel. That screen, too, rose into the ceiling. Now he could once again see down to the endlessly rolling waves splashing against the rocky shore. God Itself lived in that ocean, and in the air, and in the trees, and in space, and in the past few days, Karl had begun to feel Its presence more and more strongly.

First Richard Hansen had been delivered into his hand. And now ... the Kemonomimi. The catlike moddies that had first come to his attention as First Hand.

The Holy Warriors had never been able to find a community of them, if such a thing existed, but sightings, though sometimes years apart, were consistent. Harold the Second had personally called off the expensive, fruitless searches that Karl kept mounting, reasoning (inasmuch as Harold the Second reasoned anything) that they weren't causing any trouble, so why not let them be?

God had answered that argument with the plague.

"We accept your chastisement, O God," Karl said out loud, still watching the ocean. "We understand why you have visited this disaster upon us. We failed to Purify the Selkies of Marseguro, and here on Earth the Kemonomimi abominations have also been left Unpurified. But we will not fail again. We will purge the Earth of the Kemonomimi. We will purge Marseguro of the Selkies. And then we will offer ourselves unblemished before you that you may extend your protection once more. As Your Avatar, I swear it!"

The waves rolled on unchanged, but Karl Rasmusson, Third Avatar of the Body Purified, knew in his heart that God had heard . . . and approved.

He turned his attention back to the screen displaying Richard Hansen's cell, and activated the communications circuit.

Richard sat in the isolation chamber and wondered when he would hear from the Avatar . . . and what the Avatar would have to say.

If Andy had successfully carried out Submerge, the Holy Warriors would have found no trace of the vaccine on board the *Victor Hansen*. Which would suddenly make the vaccine—and microfactory programming—inside the locked security chest far more valuable to the Avatar than before: and Richard's cooperation far more necessary.

If the Submerge had failed, then Richard had lost all bargaining power . . . and the Avatar would be able to do whatever he wanted with him.

It didn't surprise him at all that when the blank vidscreen in the isolation chamber came to life, his heart skipped a beat, then kicked into a much higher rate.

The Avatar's face appeared. He smiled pleasantly. "I'd like you to open the security chest now, Mr. Hansen," he said. "I will begin vaccine distribution the moment you do so."

That did nothing to slow Richard's heart. *Did Andy pull it off . . . ?* "Have you harmed my crew?" he asked.

"No," the Avatar said.

"Will you?"

"I will not," the Avatar said. "*If* you open the chest. If you do not . . . well, in the absence of a vaccine, you are a threat to everyone on this island. You are all carriers. I will have no choice but to treat you as hazardous material."

"You've got the vaccine from the ship," Richard said, but he was almost certain, now, that the Avatar did not.

"Of course," the Avatar said. *Of course, nothing!* "But delivering it here where we already have a supply is a waste of time. From orbit, we can quickly distribute it to our other enclaves around the world."

He doesn't have it! Richard thought.

But then, unbidden, came another thought:

So what?

So what if Andy had successfully Submerged the crew and hidden the vaccine? It could be days, if ever, before they regained control of the ship. In the meantime, people all over Earth continued to die, or fought an almost hopeless battle to keep the plague at bay.

It was just as he'd told Andy on the ship. The Avatar had access to everything needed to distribute the vaccine as quickly and efficiently as possible. The Marseguroites had . . . nothing. It was his fault, of course; he'd thought he was being overly cautious and in fact he hadn't been cautious enough. He shouldn't have come down himself, shouldn't have brought vaccine. He should have sent a scouting party first to find out if "Jacob" was on the level. But he'd been so anxious to start helping people. . . .

The road to hell is paved with good intentions. Clichés became clichés because they contained truth, and he'd just proved the truth of that one in . . . to use another cliché . . . spades.

Mission of mercy. Not revenge. He'd made that point to Andy. Now he had to live up to his own high-minded rhetoric.

However good it would feel to destroy the vaccine in the chest . . . it would benefit no one. Not the dying people of Earth, not his crew, on Earth or aboard *Victor Hansen*, not even the people of Marseguro. It would be a stupid, futile gesture. It would simply get him and the shuttle crew killed . . . and ensure that unknown numbers of survivors died, even though help was at their planetary doorstep.

"All right," he said abruptly. "If you promise not to harm my crew."

"I promise," the Avatar said. "Before God Itself."

Richard took a deep breath. "Very well." He glanced at his pressure-suited guards. "May I . . . ?"

"Let him go to the chest," the Avatar commanded.

Richard stood and crossed to the chest, a gleaming silver crate of roughly the same proportions as a coffin. He knelt and put his hands on the palm readers, bent and let the light beam scan his retinas, felt the nip of the DNA sampler against his index finger.

Without fanfare, the chest opened.

Inside were five thousand prepared doses of the hyper-vaccine and two microfactory programming modules for making more. The doses, each in a cylinder of gleaming black metal, shone in their padded racks. The silvery hyposprays for administering them lay in rows like weapons, but weapons designed to save lives instead of take them. The programming modules, each the size of a deck of cards, gleamed gold. It looked like, and in many ways was, a chest of treasure.

"Thank you, Richard," said the Avatar, using Richard's first name for the first time. Richard wished he wouldn't. "Hildebrand, take Mr. Hansen to join his crew. Pufahl, stay put until the medical team gets there. They're suiting up now and should be along in a few minutes."

Richard followed Hildebrand out of the isolation cell and down a short corridor to the larger ward, where his crew waited. Hildebrand ushered him in, then closed and sealed the door. Richard looked around at them. "I gave them the vaccine," he said without preamble.

"What?" Pierre Normand's face darkened. "You gave the vaccine to the Body?"

"Otherwise they would have killed all of us," Richard said.

"They've already killed enough of us," Pierre snarled. "If a few more of us had to die in order to ensure the plague took every last Holy Warrior, it would have been a fair trade."

"They've already got the *Victor Hansen*," Richard said.

"But if Andy King—"

"I suggest you *submerge* your feelings," Richard snapped. "That's an order."

He saw the sudden recognition of the code word take hold in each of their faces . . . and with it, he hoped, the realization that everything they were saying must be being monitored. Pierre subsided, but he didn't look any happier.

"If the plague were only taking Holy Warriors, that would be one thing," Richard said. He didn't mind the Avatar overhearing *that*. "But it's also taking—has already taken—countless innocent lives. Vaccine distribution *must* begin as soon as possible. And . . . circumstances being what they are . . . only the Body can make that happen."

Silence. "What do we do, sir?" Melody Ashman finally asked.

Richard sat down on the floor and leaned his back against the wall.

"We wait." *And pray,* he added to himself but didn't say out loud.

The only God he'd ever worshiped didn't seem likely to be on his side.

Karl rubbed his arm where the vaccine had been administered, and stepped aside to watch as the long line of Holy Warriors and Body functionaries who had made it to Paradise Island stepped up one by one for their own shots. "Can we manufacture it?" he asked the tall, gaunt-faced woman who stood watching over the proceedings, her silver-gray hair drawn back in a tight bun.

Dr. Allison McNally looked around, then motioned the Avatar a few paces away, out of earshot of the assembled men and women. "There are difficulties," she said in a low voice. "The programming modules are for a very old kind of microfactory . . . and they're not even remotely compatible with any of the three on this island. We've tried to simply read the contents to burn new modules, but . . . there are also aspects of the programming we don't understand. The Marseguroites . . ."

"Are decades behind technologically," Karl said. "Are they not?" He kept his voice mild, but he could feel anger, like a corrosive acid, eating up at his control from below.

Dr. McNally must have detected something of his incipient rage, she paled. "In some ways," she said. "But not in others. Their technology has advanced over the past seven decades just as ours has, but in different directions. Their knowledge of genetic manipulation is superior to ours, as you'd expect, since research into such matters has been essentially stalled for—"

"—for very good reasons," Karl said. "To preserve us from the wrath of God."

Dr. McNally paled further. "I am not questioning the will of God," she said, very carefully. "I am merely explaining why the programming modules are not usable at this point in time. It will take work and study and experimentation to re-create this vaccine with our equipment, unless we can find a microfactory of the correct vintage, and frankly, I wouldn't even know where to begin looking for one."

"How long?"

Dr. McNally took a deep breath. "Days. Weeks. Months. I

can't say with certainty. Perhaps if the Marseguroites helped . . . ?" Her voice trailed away.

Karl looked at the lines of personnel getting their vaccines, the stock diminishing with each hiss of a hypospray. "I'll think about it," he said. "In the meantime, there will be no vaccine distribution beyond this island. How many personnel do we have to vaccinate?"

"Three thousand, one hundred and sixty-four," Dr. McNally said instantly.

"Leaving us with one thousand, eight hundred and thirty-six doses."

"Yes, sir."

"Carry on."

Karl walked away, seething. The solution seemed obvious: ask the imprisoned shuttle crew for help. But theologically . . .

Theologically, Karl thought, *I can't.*

To go to subhuman monstrosities like the Selkies, cap in hand, begging for help, would be blasphemous. It would imply that Selkies were, in some measurable fashion, superior to normal humans. And clearly they were not: one only had to look at them to see that.

No. If God Itself had so arranged things that they could not manufacture the vaccine, and had not been able to retrieve any more from *BPS Sanctification*, then God wanted them to complete the Purification of Earth with the resources It had made available to them: five thousand doses of vaccine, no more. Destroy the Kemonomimi, and *then* God would provide the means to save all the people of Earth . . . and Purify Marseguro as it should have been Purified to begin with.

So, then. Time to be about it.

He quickened his pace. "Computer," he said to the air, knowing the microphone in his collar would transmit his command, "please ask Grand Deacon von Eschen to meet me in my quarters as soon as possible."

"Confirmed," the computer said in his ear.

The one thing they lacked, the Avatar thought, was detailed information about the Kemonomimi physical capabilities. They looked catlike, they were strong and fast, but how strong? How fast? How smart?

Well, he thought, *we have the clone of their creator im-*

prisoned. He altered his direction of travel to take him to the quarters where Richard and the others were being held.

Purification had been delayed, but not derailed. Karl Rasmusson, Third Avatar of the Body, would complete it . . . and save the Earth once and for all from the ever-looming wrath of God.

Chapter 7

HALFWAY BETWEEN MARSEGURO and Earth, the *Divine Will*'s computer cut the water rations. The first Emily knew of it was when she tried to soak herself in the zero-G bath, as she had been doing for hours every day . . . only to discover she could no longer get water.

Floating naked in the empty bathtube, she stared through its transparent wall at the speaker in the ceiling. "Computer, repeat?"

"Water for baths is now restricted to every third day," the computer said. "This restriction will continue indefinitely."

Every third day? Starting from when?

"Computer, when will I next be able to take a bath?"

"In two days."

Emily felt a chill. She'd already delayed this soaking longer than she should have. Her gill slits already tingled, and her skin itched. Was this some nasty trick of Stone's?

"Computer, explain!"

"Recent prolonged submersion in salt water has damaged several systems," the computer said. "Corrosion has resulted in unintended venting of approximately one half of our water supply. Survival protocols dictate that water rations be cut to all crew."

Emily closed her eyes. She wanted to argue with the computer, but she knew that was futile. It could only follow its programming.

She'd have to talk to Stone.

Dry, she pulled herself out of the bathtube, tugged on a jumpsuit, and floated into the bedroom.

They'd been in space for a week now, and the drugs that

had kept her mother calm had long since worn off. But to Emily's surprise, there had been no rages, no hysterics. Dr. Christianson-Wood remained calm, if confused. Half the time she asked after her husband, Emily's father, killed in the Holy Warriors' attack on Hansen's Harbor. Sometimes she seemed to think she was still a child, and Emily was *her* mother. And sometimes she simply sat staring into the distance.

At the moment she slept, snug in her landsuit, tucked into her sleeping bag. That suited Emily. She went to the vidscreen in the living area. "Computer, contact Commander Stone."

After a moment, the screen lit with Stone's face. "What is it?"

"The computer has cut the water rations," Emily said. "I can't fill the tube. I need—"

"We're short of water," Stone said. "We all have to put up with it."

"I don't need it to drink," Emily said. "I need—"

"You need to remember that you are a prisoner, not a guest," Stone snapped.

"Leaving me to dry is torture," Emily said quietly.

Stone laughed. "You can only torture a human being," he said. "You aren't one." And the screen blanked.

Emily's gills burned.

Two days, she thought.

God help me.

Shortly after Richard had handed over the vaccine, the crew of *Sawyer's Point* were shepherded from their isolation wards to what looked like a guest cottage, with four bedrooms, a large living area, and even a well-stocked kitchen. With nothing much else to do, they'd started a never-ending card game. Richard was up six hundred points over Melody Ashman and dealing the sixty-seventh hand of Blind Man's Hearts when the front door of the cottage opened and a Holy Warrior—Hildebrand, if Richard remembered right—stuck his head in.

He wasn't wearing a pressure suit.

They've been vaccinated, Richard thought. *It's begun.*

"Hansen," Hildebrand said. "Out here."

"Play this hand without me," Richard told the others. "I'll be right back."

He followed Hildebrand out of the cottage and across a gravel path to an artificially rustic lodge that had once served as the central meeting place for this neighborhood of the island resort. Its main room was a thicket of upended chairs on round wooden tables, and it took a minute for Richard to spot the Avatar. Karl Rasmusson sat in a big deerhide-covered chair by the enormous fireplace, in which what looked like real logs (though Richard suspected they were holographic) blazed away.

"Join me," the Avatar said, indicating the matching chair on the other side of the hearth.

Richard sat. Hildebrand stood behind him.

"Everyone on the island has now been vaccinated," the Avatar advised. "It's a great relief, as I'm sure you appreciate." He smiled. "The local wildlife appreciate it, too, since we're no longer blasting everything living out of the sky and sea. We even let a couple of sea otters ashore this morning, and the gulls are all over the docks again."

Richard said nothing.

"No doubt you are concerned about your crew," the Avatar went on. "I assure you no one was injured in the retaking of *BPS Sanctification.*"

"I'd like to talk to them," Richard said.

"That won't be possible," the Avatar replied smoothly.

"Just my first officer," Richard said. "Priscilla Wylie?" I'm sure she identified herself when you—"

"Yes, I know the woman," the Avatar said. "But I'm afraid I can't allow you to talk to her, or anyone else."

That clinched it. Priscilla Wylie had been Richard's kindergarten teacher. Andy had slipped the Body's clutches: the Submerge had worked. Richard allowed himself a touch of elation.

"Although . . ." the Avatar looked thoughtful. "Perhaps something could be arranged. If you can help me with something in return."

I know something you think I don't know, Richard thought. "I've already given you the vaccine," he said out loud. "I have nothing else of any use."

"You have information," the Avatar said. "Or at least you may." He leaned forward. "You're Victor Hansen's clone. He planted a gene-bomb in you to implant you with elements of his memories and his personality. So tell me . . . what do you know about the Kemonomimi?"

Richard blinked. *The what?* "Nothing," he said honestly. "I've never heard the name before."

"Are you sure?" The Avatar leaned back in his chair again, and gestured. From somewhere in the thicket of up-ended chairs appeared a woman in a black dress, wearing a white apron: she placed a tray containing a steaming pot and two cups on the low table between the two chairs. "Coffee?"

Richard shrugged. "Sure."

The Avatar poured. "Cream and sugar?"

"Both, please."

The Avatar put in a generous amount of sugar and cream, stirred the coffee, then handed him the cup. "The Kemonomimi," he said as he did so, "were your . . . original's . . . first creation."

Richard stopped with his coffee cup halfway to his mouth. "What?"

"A decade before he created the first generation of Selkies, Victor Hansen created the Kemonomimi. We don't know much about them. They're feline in appearance, and in ferocity. As with the Selkies, he brought several dozen modified embryos to term, then raised the children in secret. But something went wrong. He designed them to reach physical maturity very rapidly, in just nine years. In their tenth year, as they entered puberty, they became rebellious. They escaped the compound in the Canadian Rockies where he was raising them, and killed several normal humans in the process. They fled into the wilderness.

"That was long before the Day of Salvation, of course. They were forgotten in the ensuing chaos. But within the past fifteen years or so, we've begun to sight them occasionally. We've even captured one or two. But we've never been able to find where they're hiding.

"I was the one who discovered they were yet another monstrous creation of Victor Hansen's." He sipped his coffee.

Richard remembered the strange moddie he'd seen in the House of the Body on the Salvation Day, the one that had attacked the Voice and been shot down by Holy Warriors. Had that been a Kemonomimi? "I know nothing about them."

The Avatar sighed. "Well, it was worth asking."

"The gene-bomb didn't really work, you know," Richard said, perversely feeling he needed to explain.

The Avatar smiled. "Of course, I know," he said. "I approved the gene therapy that partially defused it . . . and quite possibly kept you from going mad, like your father."

"He wasn't my father," Richard said. *Though I thought he was.* "He was my elder twin brother."

"Touché." The Avatar sipped more coffee. "In any event, if we hadn't modified the gene-bomb, you might have offed yourself even more messily than he did."

Richard remembered that time; he'd felt Victor Hansen inside his head like a second personality, trying to overwhelm him, blot him out, and he shuddered. "I can't believe I'm saying this," he said, "but thank you."

"You're welcome." The Avatar put down his cup. "Unfortunately, it appears that in the process we destroyed some of your memories. Or else Victor Hansen didn't include the memories of the Kemonomimi in your gene-bomb; that's quite possible. He was not a man to admit that he had made a mistake."

Then I'm definitely not like him in every way, Richard thought. *I know all too well how many mistakes I've made.*

"Well." The Avatar stood. "It was worth asking. Take your time with your coffee." He turned to Hildebrand. "When he's done, escort him back to his quarters."

Richard watched the Avatar pick his way out through the tables. Were the Kemonomimi, too, based on Hansen's DNA? Were they also Richard's cousins . . . brothers . . . sisters . . . children, even . . . like the Selkies?

Whether they are or not, they're in the Body's sights, Richard thought. *Marked for Purification. Another race of humans threatened with extinction at the Body's hands . . . and I've helped make it possible, by handing the vaccine over to the Avatar.*

Grandfather Hansen created races. I seem to be destined to help destroy them.

He put down his coffee cup and climbed to his feet. "Take me back to my prison," he told Hildebrand.

He didn't say it out loud, but inside he thought, *It's where I belong*.

Emily drifted in a sea of pain. She knew she was floating, naked, in a fetal position in the middle of her bedroom aboard *Divine Will*, but the knowledge was distant and unimportant. She couldn't focus her mind on anything except the agony in her gills, the fire consuming her skin. The tingling had progressed to burning, burning that intensified until it became an agony she had never imagined. At first she had attempted to wet her gills and skin with a washcloth, soaked in the little water the computer would allow, but it hadn't been enough, and as the pain had progressed, she had lost the ability to even do that much. Now she floated, and hurt, and hurt some more, and she doubted she could survive until the next allotted bath time . . . or even manage to get herself into the bathtube when that time came.

Except . . .

Someone was helping her. Someone was bathing her gills with water: not enough water, but enough to lessen the pain. Someone was sponging her drying skin. Someone . . .

She forced her swollen eyes open enough to see what was going on.

"There, there," her mother murmured, gently running the soaked washcloth over her parched gill slits. "I know it hurts, honey, but it will be better soon."

"Mom?" Emily croaked.

Dr. Christianson-Wood smiled at Emily, the first genuine smile Emily had seen from her mother in a very long time. "Take the cloth," she said, pushing it into Emily's hand. Emily gripped it and began sponging her own gill slits again. With both hands free, her mother began slipping out of the landsuit that, with its own constantly recycled, purified and oxygenated water supply, had kept her from suffering the same agony as Emily.

"Mom . . . no," Emily said.

"Nonsense," her mother said firmly. "I'll be fine for a few hours while you recover. Then we'll trade off again. Between that and the baths we're allowed, we'll manage the rest of the journey."

Her mother sounded so normal that Emily couldn't help it. She began to cry.

"Stop that," her mom said. "You can't spare the water."

That made Emily laugh, then cry even harder. She hadn't realized until that moment just how much she'd missed her mother.

But now, it seemed, at least for the time being, she had her back.

And, she thought as she wrapped herself in the blessed wet embrace of the landsuit, not a moment too soon.

Chris Keating had no way of knowing how many hours he had lain in the aircraft, dozing, awake, or somewhere in between, when suddenly the sound of the engines altered pitch. A few minutes later a solid bump banged his head painfully against the deck, then the engines roared so loud he feared for a moment that they would explode. Instead, they fell to silence, and he realized that his journey had ended.

Minutes passed and nothing happened; then he heard voices. A clunking sound, and fresh air swept across his face, damp and cool. He wriggled, so the owners of the voices would know he was awake, but they didn't seem to care: he was picked up unceremoniously, tossed carelessly and painfully over a bony, fur-covered shoulder, then carried down half a dozen steps into the open.

"Bring him over here," said a strangely familiar male voice. Chris was carried a few more steps. "He probably won't be able to stand after being tied up that long," the voice said. "Put him on that crate."

Chris was lowered off of the bony shoulder and manhandled into a sitting position on something hard, square . . . and wet. Cold water promptly soaked through his pants and chilled his buttocks.

"Untie him," the voice said.

The ropes binding his legs and hands were swiftly undone, and as blood rushed back into his extremities, Chris gasped and tears sprang to his still-blindfolded eyes. If he'd been standing, he would have fallen, and probably screamed on the way down.

"Now take off the gag," the voice said.

The cloth binding his mouth went the way of the ropes,

and Chris gulped a deep, damp, cool, and pine-scented breath. "Who are you?" he demanded, or tried to, but his voice came out in a barely audible croak.

The owner of the voice seemed to have understood him, though. "You'll see in a moment," he said. "Literally. Take off the blindfold."

Someone yanked away the blindfold, and Chris squeezed his eyes shut against the sudden, painful flood of daylight. Then he blinked away tears, looked up . . . and gasped.

He sat on a plastic crate in the middle of a long concrete runway. Beyond a stretch of open green ground rose a collection of modest one- and two-story buildings, interspersed with tall pines. And beyond those . . . unbroken forest, climbing up steep slopes until it disappeared into the fog.

At least a dozen of the catlike moddies . . . Kemono-mimi . . . surrounded him. And directly in front of him stood the last person he had expected . . . or wanted . . . to see.

"Richard Hansen!" he blurted out.

But the eyes in that hated face narrowed. "No."

"But you look—"

"I," said the man coldly, "am Dr. Victor Hansen."

The *Divine Will* took ten more days to reach Earth. They weren't comfortable days for Emily or her mother, but it appeared they would be survivable—thanks to the recovery, or at least partial recovery, of Dr. Christianson-Wood, and also thanks to help from an unexpected source.

Emily was so glad to have her mother back to something approaching normal that she didn't mind the constant switching back and forth of the landsuit or the hours spent in the bathtube until she couldn't stand the filthy, deoxygenated water any more.

She tried tentatively a time or two to talk to her mother about the nature of their trip, and their captors. But her mother brushed aside the efforts. "I don't want to think about that right now," she said. "I'm just . . . staying focused. On making sure we both make it okay."

Emily worried what would happen the first time a Holy Warrior made an appearance in their quarters. Four days after the computer announced water rationing, two days after Emily's last chance to use the bathtube and one day before she could use it again, she found out.

They had just exchanged the landsuit, so that Emily's mother was wearing it again and Emily momentarily wore nothing at all. The door swung open without warning. Emily looked up to see Biccum looking in. He took one look at her, turned bright red, and slammed the door shut again.

Emily couldn't help it; she laughed.

"Um, sorry, Miss Wood," came Biccum's voice through the annunciator panel. "I'm sorry. I should have knocked . . ."

"Don't worry about it," Emily said, pulling on her skinsuit with practiced ease. She glanced at her mother, but Dr. Christianson-Wood didn't seem perturbed by the fact a Holy Warrior had just walked in; she just looked amused. "I'm dressed now. You can come in." *We're your prisoners; you can do whatever you want*, she thought, but didn't say.

The door opened. Biccum peered cautiously in. He still looked flushed and he didn't meet her eyes. "I really am sorry. I—"

"It's all right," Emily said. "What is it?"

"Um . . ." Biccum finally got up the courage to look her in the face. "I heard . . . you need water. I've brought you this." He held out something oblong and shiny.

Emily took it. "It looks like a datachip," she said.

"It is. It's my water. Uh, some of it. I mean, let the computer scan it and it will route some of my water ration to your quarters. So you can get wet . . ." He paused, blushed again, and mumbled, ". . . I mean, take a bath. A little more often."

Emily stared at him, bemused. "Um . . . thank you," she said.

"Yes, thank you," said Dr. Christianson-Wood firmly. "That's very decent of you."

Biccum gave her a startled look. "You're welcome?" He made it sound like a question. Then he backed out through the door. "I should . . . um, I hope it helps. 'Bye."

The door closed.

"You've made a friend," Dr. Christianson-Wood said. "Even if you embarrassed him horribly."

"It's not my fault he didn't knock," Emily said. She looked at her mother. "Are you . . . all right?"

Emily's mother looked away. "I . . . I think I will be," she said softly. "I'm . . . reintegrating, I think I'd call it. I've been focused inward, drowning in my own depths. You . . . when you were in so much pain . . . it pulled me out. Pulled me to the surface." She looked up. "I know we're prisoners of the Holy Warriors," she said. "I know we're going to Earth. I know that they want to punish me for . . . for what I did. I know all of that. And I'm terrified, Emily. But . . . but I'm not lost anymore. I've found my way out. I've found myself."

Emily felt a huge rush of relief, a tsunami of relief that washed her own fear away, at least for the moment. "Thank God," she said. "I've been so worried about you, Mama." She hadn't called her mother that in ten years.

Dr. Christianson-Wood smiled, wide green eyes bright with unshed tears. "I know, Emmy," she said. "I'm so sorry to have put you through all that worry . . . so sorry that you're suffering now because of what I did. I can't even claim not to deserve it. But you—"

"You *don't* deserve it," Emily said. "Don't start talking like that. You did what you had to to save us all. If not for you—"

Her mother made a brushing-off gesture. "My reasons don't matter, Emily. I made the best decisions I could at the time. But whatever my motivation . . . the results have been horrible. I'll have to live with the consequences when we get to Earth. Whatever they may be." She held up a hand, forestalling Emily's next protest. "Let's not talk about it now. Your boyfriend just gave you a present. Wouldn't you like to make use of it?"

Emily looked at the datachip, and laughed. "It was rather sweet of him," she said. "Which is not something I ever thought I'd say about a Holy Warrior."

"They're just people, Emily," her mother said. "People like us. Even the worst of them." Her face closed down again. "Even the ones who attacked Marseguro. Even the ones I . . ." Her voice trailed off.

Emily held her breath, afraid her mother would . . . go away . . . again, but Dr. Christianson-Wood shook her head and carried on. "Go on," she said. "Get in the bath. You know you want to."

She did. Silently thanking Biccum, she went into the bathtube, smiling to herself as she slipped out of her skinsuit again and remembered how red he'd turned when he'd walked in on her. "Just people," she told herself. "Just people."

She climbed into the tube, sealed it, and let it fill with clean water. As it closed over her cramped gills, and she opened them wide, wider than the landsuit allowed, she remembered how, for a time, she had relished watching Holy Warriors die, had even relished killing them.

Somewhere along the way she had lost that bloodthirstiness. She wondered if she could get it back if she needed it.

She wondered if she wanted to.

Sharing the landsuit and making use of the extra water ration provided by Biccum, they passed the final few days of the journey to Earth comfortably enough. When they talked, they talked of shared memories, family stories, vids they'd watched and books they'd read.

The one thing they didn't talk about was the future.

The first they knew of their arrival at Earth was Stone's voice over the intercom. Emily was wearing the landsuit and Dr. Christianson-Wood the sedate navy-blue skinsuit she'd been wearing aboard the sub when they were taken. They were floating in the living room, playing a word game they'd found programmed in the entertainment unit. When the intercom came to life, Dr. Christianson-Wood's hand twitched, erasing her last move. Then she looked up, listening. So did Emily.

"All hands," he said. "We're entering Earth orbit. Our sensors and communications are barely functioning, so we're not sure what the situation is down below, though from what we can tell, things are . . . quiet. Too quiet." He paused, and Emily knew everyone in the crew must be thinking the same thing: the plague had hit Earth hard. "We're going to land and reconnoiter," Stone concluded abruptly. "All hands prepare for reentry."

Without a word, Emily shut down the entertainment unit. A moment later, someone knocked.

"Come in," Emily said.

The door opened, revealing Biccum. "I've come to make sure you're ready for reentry," he said. "You need to strap in to the acceleration couches. We've only got a few minutes."

"What was that about communications?" Emily said.

Biccum glanced over his shoulder, then lowered his voice as he started strapping her in. "We can receive, but we can't transmit," he said in a low voice. "*BPS Sanctification* is in orbit—"

Emily's heart skipped. *Sanctification*? Not *Victor Hansen*?

"—and it challenged us. Since we couldn't respond, it warned us off, said it would destroy us if we tried to come closer. We've been challenged from the ground, too, but only by an automated system. If we try to land anywhere there's a Holy Warrior base . . . we may get shot down."

"So where—"

"We've picked up . . . another signal. A commercial homing beacon of some kind. No threats of being shot down. We're going to ride it down." He shook his head. "Aside from that, everything is just . . . empty. Like the whole planet is deserted."

Emily glanced at her mother. Dr. Christianson-Wood closed her eyes as though in pain, but then opened them again and focused on Biccum.

"So we're going to land away from any major population centers, and see what we can see," he went on. "If it's the plague . . ." He looked grim for a moment. "If it's the plague, we'll set up one of the microfactories we brought from Marseguro and start manufacturing vaccine. If there's some other reason, well, we'll sort that out when we get there." He finished tightening their straps, and gave them both a determined, if slightly forced, grin. "See you on Earth!" He went out, and the door closed behind him.

"Mom . . . ?" Emily said.

"I'm all right," Dr. Christianson-Wood replied. "I'm ready to . . . find out what happened. What I did."

Emily opened her mouth to reply, but a sudden jolt snapped her teeth shut so hard she was lucky not to bite her tongue. A high-pitched whine began, deepening to a steady roar. *Atmosphere,* Emily thought. The buffeting grew worse, and worse, and worse still, until it was as bad as it had been when she'd ridden *Sanctification* down during its automatic deorbiting procedure. *Something's wrong,* she thought, her fingers gripping the arms of the chair so tight they hurt. *This can't be right.*

Then Stone confirmed it. ". . . don't have : . . plete control," he shouted over an intercom now so full of static only portions of his words could be understood. ". . . slow our desce . . . can't control where . . . come down . . . ooks like . . . shit!"

That last word came through loud and clear.

Ten seconds later an enormous impact flung Emily hard against the straps of her acceleration couch. She heard a shriek of tearing metal, distant thumps and what sounded like an explosion, all mixed together. The lights went out, but were almost immediately replaced by the cold blue glow of the chemical emergency lights, strips embedded in the ceiling that turned everything a color Emily associated with sunshine filtered through four or five meters of seawater. And then . . .

It felt like utter silence in comparison to what had come before, though in fact she could still hear distant thumps and hissing noises and shouting voices. "Are you all right, Mom?" Emily called.

"I'm fine . . . oh!" The floor of the shuttle, once more emphatically the floor now they were back in gravity, had suddenly tilted. More shouting from panicked voices. The shuttle began to sway, a motion Emily recognized instinctively.

"We're in the water," she said. "We're sinking."

The floor tilted further, until they were hanging in their acceleration straps. More crashes and thumps came from somewhere inside the shuttle: it sounded like equipment breaking free and falling against bulkheads. The shuttle continued to sway for a minute or two, and then suddenly, with a final, solid thump, the motion stopped. The floor tilted back toward the horizontal, and finally, all was still.

"I'm going to get out," Emily said. "Stay put."

"Be careful," her mother said.

Emily unstrapped herself and picked her way across the slanted floor to the door. She put her ear against it, but could hear nothing on the other side but a distant roaring sound . . .

. . . rushing water.

Then the door suddenly swung open, and water surged around her feet. Biccum stood ankle-deep in the corridor outside, blood streaming down his face from a gash on his forehead. His eyes were wide and panicked. "We're underwater!" he cried. "On the bottom! There's water coming in everywhere!"

"Pressure suits?" Emily said.

"We can't get to them. They're already underwater. We need—" He gave her a pleading look. "We need your help. If you can get to them, bring them back, please, there are only three of us in this section, we haven't heard anything from the rest of the shuttle, if you can just get us three pressure suits."

They're Holy Warriors, Emily thought, but then, *no. They're people.*

"I'll try," she said. She looked over her shoulder at her mother, who was also unstrapping. "Mom, you stay—"

"Not likely," her mother snapped. "I'm coming with you."

"But . . ."

"Quit treating me like I'm made of glass, Emily," her mother said. "It's about time I started saving lives again."

Emily couldn't very well argue with that. "All right," she said. "Show us, Biccum."

"Dave," he said. "Call me Dave. This way."

The water in the corridor behind was already visibly higher than it had been when Biccum had opened the door. As he led them down the slight slope, it grew deeper still, until finally Biccum had to stop and grab hold of one of the curving metal handles of an equipment rack set in the wall.

"At the end of the corridor," he said. "There's a hatch. It's open. The pressure suits are inside. There's an air lock beyond that that leads out of the ship." He looked like he would say something else, but he didn't.

He's just told us how we can escape and leave them to drown, Emily thought. *But he's not going to beg us not to do it.* She looked at her mother, and saw that she had realized the same thing. But all she said was, "Let's go. This tub is filling up fast."

Emily nodded. "I don't need this," she said, reaching up to unzip the landsuit. She glanced at Biccum. "Maybe you should close your eyes."

He blinked, then blushed, said, "Oh," and squeezed them firmly closed.

Emily slipped out of the landsuit, its weight oppressive now they were back in gravity. Salt water swirled around her thighs. It felt good. "Go back up the corridor as far as you can," she told Biccum, putting the landsuit into his hand. "You might want to open your eyes once you've turned around. It'll probably help." Biccum nodded, turned and began climbing back up the corridor, the heavy landsuit held under one arm. He didn't look back. Emily smiled a little, then went the other way with her mother.

When the water was chest-deep, they plunged beneath it and opened their gills. The momentary shock of transition gave way to the pure pleasure of once again breathing seawater, albeit seawater with an odd tang to it. "It tastes funny," Emily chirp-clicked to her mother, and using the Selkie underwater language again after so long was a joy in itself.

"Different ocean," her mother said. "And possibly pollutants from the crash."

Emily chirped disgust, then looked around. The shuttle's emergency lights were more than bright enough for Selkie eyes, and she spotted the hatch at once. Together she and her mother swam down into the room below the corridor. As promised, three suits hung there. They freed them, then paused for a moment.

Just beyond the racks of suits was a closed air lock door.

"We could leave now," Emily said. "Escape. We don't owe the Holy Warriors any favors."

"No," her mother said. "We've had our revenge for the attack on Marseguro. That slate is clean. Maybe we do owe them: maybe we owe them . . . some of them, anyway, the ones like Biccum . . . the chance to live and grow into better human beings."

Emily couldn't decide whether her mother was being profound or hopelessly naïve. But she did know she didn't want to swim off and let Biccum or anyone else drown. She turned and swam back into the main corridor.

As she passed through the door, the shuttle shuddered, jerked—and suddenly tilted. In an instant the corridor's relatively mild inclination switched to vertical. The water around them boiled and foamed. For a moment Emily floundered, disoriented, then her Selkie senses reasserted themselves and told her emphatically that *that* way was up: and an instant later, as if to prove the point, something big plunged into the water from above.

A man. One of the Holy Warriors. He flailed helplessly, striking out in all directions. His left foot caught Emily in the ribs, and she dropped the two pressure suits she was carrying and grabbed it. "Hold still!" she clicked, but of course the Holy Warrior couldn't understand, or even hear her clearly. Her mother grabbed one of the man's arms. Together they drove toward the surface, and a moment later the man's head burst into the air. He gulped a huge breath, coughed, and choked out, "I can't . . . can't . . ."

"Swim?" Emily said. "Somehow I guessed."

She looked around. The water continued to rise, taking them up the corridor, now a near-vertical shaft with water cascading down its sides over the blue emergency lights. Far up, still ten or fifteen meters above them, a door stood open. Two pale faces peered down. "Is he all right?" one shouted. It was Biccum.

"Yes," Emily called back. "But I've dropped the suits I was carrying."

"I've still got mine," her mother said.

"Stay still and you'll be all right," Emily said to the man. "Mom will keep you on the surface. I've got to go back down." She flipped and drove downward with her broad, webbed feet.

The suits had settled at the far end of the corridor, past the hatch they had brought them out of. Emily grabbed them and started back up the corridor. The water's surface was now just three or four meters below the room where Biccum and the other Holy Warrior waited. She emerged into air, closed her gill slits, took a lung-breath and said, "Got them."

She looked at the man who had fallen on top of them. His eyes, so wide with fright they were almost as large as her own, looked back at her. She thought she remembered his name from Marseguro.

"You're Koop, aren't you?" she said.

He nodded. "Evan," he said. "Evan Koop."

"Well, Evan, let's try to get you into this one down here, before the water lifts us to the others," she said. "Then we'll have one less to deal with. Hold still." She passed one of the pressure suits to her mother, then plunged under the water. She unsealed the suit. It would have water in it, but as long as the helmet remained clear of it, that wouldn't matter.

The suit was bulky, designed to go over clothes in an emergency, and she had no trouble slipping the man's legs into it and pulling it up. She guided his arms into it. The life-support pack was only a pad a few centimeters thick built into the back of the suit, and the "helmet" was a transparent inflatable hood. She pulled it over his head, sealed it, and touched the suit's activation button. The helmet expanded into a clear plastic globe, and the man grinned with relief. "It works!"

"Good."

They were within a meter of the room containing Biccum and the other Holy Warrior, whom Emily hadn't gotten a good look at yet; she was keeping her transparent nictitating eyelids over her eyes both to protect them and so she could see clearly underwater, but they tended to throw everything above water into soft focus. She tossed up the second suit she'd rescued; her mother tossed up the one she carried. "You two can dress yourselves," she said to Biccum and the other man. They grabbed the suits and disappeared.

Emily glanced at Koop. He wasn't looking up at all: his focus was entirely down into the water, and Emily suddenly realized that with his helmet in place he had a clear view of her nude body. She sighed. *Men,* she thought. *Nonmods or Selkies, they're all the same.*

The water reached the open doorway and suddenly poured into the room beyond. Emily stayed in the corridor, although any pretense at modesty seemed kind of silly at this point. "Are you two—" she began, then stopped. As he finished sealing his pressure suit, the man who had been with Biccum turned around, and at the same instant Emily finally recognized him as Abban—and realized he had a standard-issue Holy Warrior slug thrower in his hand, small, but more than powerful enough to blow her head off.

"You two climb in here," Abban said. "I figure we've got just enough time to tie you up before the water fills the room." It was already approaching his knees.

"We just saved your lives," Emily snarled, fury almost choking her.

"Thank you. Now get in here."

Naked and dripping, Emily complied. Biccum looked away. Abban didn't. His eyes, clearly visible through the transparent helmet, ran over her body from head to foot, then back again.

Emily's mother climbed out beside her daughter.

"Biccum, tie them up," Abban ordered.

"I don't—"

"Do it!" Abban ordered. "We've got to secure them before the water rises. Then we can get them to shore, turn them in to the Body—"

"The Body doesn't exist anymore," Emily said. "The plague reached Earth. Haven't you been paying attention?"

"God wouldn't let the Body be destroyed," Abban snarled. The water was up to his thighs. "Do it!" he snapped at Biccum.

Behind Emily, Koop said "Abban, don't you—"

"Shut up, Koop. I outrank you and Biccum both. Follow orders or I'll see you up on charges of insubordination."

"All right, all right," Biccum said. He looked Emily full in the face. "I'm sorry, miss," he said. He stepped forward, past Abban—then half-turned and slammed his arm down onto Abban's forearm. The gun splashed into the water and Emily pounced on it.

She raised it to see Abban and Biccum struggling in waist-deep water. She couldn't shoot without hitting Biccum. She didn't want to shoot at all. But if she had to—

She didn't. As the two men struggled, they fell with an enormous splash. There was a strange popping sound, and when the men rose to face each other again, Emily saw that Abban's inflatable helmet had been punctured by something. It hung loosely on his face. "Abban—" Biccum said, reaching for him.

"Get away!" Abban snarled. "I swear, Biccum, I'll see you shot for—" His eyes suddenly widened. He looked down at the water, rising faster than ever; it was up to his belly. "Oh, God," he said. He looked wildly at the others. "I need—you've got to find another pressure suit!"

"There were only three," Emily said. "Biccum—Dave—are there any others in this section?"

Biccum shook his head. "No," he said hoarsely. "The others are up there—" he pointed toward what should have been the bow but was now straight up. "We can't get though the bulkhead without computer access. And the computer is dead."

"You've got to cut through—" Abban said.

"With what?" Biccum said. "God, Abban, I'll do whatever I can—but we have nothing."

"But . . ." Abban looked down at the water. It had risen to his chest. "But . . ."

Emily thought furiously. Maybe they could rig a diving bell, something that would hold enough oxygen to get Abban out of . . .

Or maybe . . .

But her thoughts went nowhere. The water was up to Abban's neck now. He began screaming, praying, begging. They lifted him up, kept him above the water as long as they could, hoping an air bubble would form and stabilize, but the air seemed to have some unseen escape path, and the rising water never faltered.

In the end, they all floated in the flooded compartment and watched Abban drown. He flailed for a few minutes, eyes wide and bulging, then suddenly opened his mouth and sucked water into his lungs. He spasmed, jackknifed, mouth opening and closing, and then abruptly fell limp.

Emily turned away. "Let's get out of here," she chirp-clicked to her mother.

They motioned to Biccum and Koop and started down the corridor toward the air lock. As they approached it, Emily heard a noise . . . a mingling of tapping and scraping sounds.

"What's that?" her mother asked. "Rescuers?"

"I don't see how it could be."

They swam into the pressure-suit locker and over to the air lock. Biccum moved up beside Emily. "Let me," he said, his voice sounding odd but perfectly audible to her Selkie ears even through the filters of helmet and water. "There are manual controls in case of emergencies . . ." He opened a panel next to the air lock door, revealing what looked like a hexagonal bolt head and a hand crank clamped to the wall. He pulled the crank free, attached it to the bolt head, and started cranking.

The door began to open. No air bubbled out of the crack that appeared. "The outer door must be open," Biccum panted. He cranked more, then stopped. "What the . . ."

Light streamed through the centimeter-wide opening, white light, not the blue-green light of the emergency strips, light that dimmed and faded as though its source were moving around on the other side. "There's somebody out there," Emily chirp-clicked to her mother.

"Looks like we haven't escaped the Body after all," her mother replied.

"There's somebody out there," Biccum said, echoing Emily though he had no way of knowing it. He gave her a questioning look; she wondered when exactly she had taken command. *Me, commanding Holy Warriors,* she thought. *That's a switch.*

She mimed continuing cranking, and Biccum nodded and kept turning the handle.

The door opened further. The light dimmed, as though its source had moved away. Emily looked through the opening, but all she could see was that light, surrounded by indistinct shapes, beyond the outer door of the air lock, which indeed stood wide open.

Finally the door was open wide enough for her to slip through. Emily motioned Biccum to move back. She looked down at her naked body. Well, at least they won't see me as a threat, she thought wryly, and slipped into the outer air lock.

The light steadied on her form. She floated, keeping stationary with gentle motions of her arms and legs, gills rippling. The water still tasted odd, but fresher than that filling the wreck of the *Divine Will.*

One of the shapes behind the light moved forward, came in front of the light, and swam toward her, a silhouette. She squinted, trying to see. Her heart suddenly pounded. The shape didn't have a pressure suit on, or scuba gear; it looked . . .

The swimmer entered the air lock, illuminated by the blue-green emergency lights, and Emily gasped.

A Selkie woman in a plain white swimsuit looked back at her with eyes as wide and green as her own.

Chapter 8

KARL RASMUSSON LOOKED at the projection on the largest screen in his office and let Grand Deacon von Eschen tell him what he was seeing. "This satellite image is a few months old, of course—we don't currently have control of any of our reconnaissance satellites—but obviously the topography won't have changed. The Kemonomimi haven't been entirely careless: Newshore is barely accessible by land. When normal humans still lived there, they flew in or came in by boat. Not a single road leads to it."

"Could this have always been their hiding place?" the Avatar asked.

Von Eschen shook his head. "No, this was definitely a Body town. There's a small meeting house, a school, a geothermal power plant, all the usual accoutrements for one of these reconstruction villages. A lot of them were built in remote places. The Avatar felt that seeding people around the planet could help preserve the race in the event of . . ."

His voice trailed off.

"Another catastrophe," Karl finished for him. "Like the plague. And he was right. Most of the survivors who aren't in Body enclaves are probably in towns like that one." He looked at von Eschen. "Are there any normal humans there now?"

"We don't know," von Eschen said.

Karl turned back to the image. "Why did the Kemonomimi pick Newshore?" he said. "Why leave their hideout in the mountains, wherever it was? It's kept them safe for seventy years."

"We *assume*," von Eschen said with careful emphasis,

"that wherever they were they didn't have access to aircraft. We also assume that their hideaway was somewhere very close to this town, probably somewhere in this range of mountains that cuts Newshore off from the interior." A laser pointer highlighted jagged peaks just to the east of the small collection of buildings and the unmistakable lines of two intersecting runways that marked the town on the image.

"No roads," Karl said. "How do you propose to attack, then, Grand Deacon? By boat?"

Von Eschen shook his head. "We don't have enough boats. And they'd see us coming and melt away into the interior before we got there."

Karl frowned. "But you said—"

"Your Holiness," the Grand Deacon said quickly, as if suddenly realizing that making the Avatar feel foolish might not be a good career move, "*almost* inaccessible is not the same as *completely* inaccessible." The laser pointer moved again, and a winding path lit up, leading from a broad inland valley through the mountains down to the town. "There is a pass, along the river that eventually flows into the sea at Newshore. It's narrow, but no trouble for men on foot."

"What about an air assault?"

"We have no air weapons systems," von Eschen said. "And our transport aircraft wouldn't stand a chance from any concentrated weapons fire on approach to the Newshore airport. If we had recovered the assault craft from *Sanctification* . . ."

"Yes, well, and if the Selkies hadn't ripped out *Sanctification*'s Orbital Bombardment System this whole discussion would be moot, wouldn't it?" Karl shook his head. "God is testing us, Grand Deacon. It has given us just enough vaccine for everyone on this island. It has stripped our forces down to men on foot, lightly armed. It has denied us air power and sea power, blinded our technology, thrown us back on our own resources. God, Grand Deacon, wants us to prove our commitment to Its command. And when we win the victory, God will know that we are once more worthy of Its continuing aid and protection, and a new Body will arise from the grave of the old: a better, stronger, more perfect Body to do the will of God Itself!"

"Yes, Avatar," the Grand Deacon breathed. His eyes shone in the light from the screen.

Karl found that he was standing, though he didn't remember getting up. His heart pounded and his head felt light. This *is what it means to be Avatar!* he realized exultantly. *God Itself is with me. I can feel Its touch. I can feel Its presence. It speaks to me...*

God speaks to me.

And I speak for God.

Avatar!

"Arm everyone, Grand Deacon," Karl said. "Everyone who can walk, everyone who can fire a gun. Gather supplies. Do whatever you must to enable us to cross to the mainland and march on the Kemonomimi. The sooner, the better."

"Forty-eight hours, Your Holiness," the Grand Deacon said. "Forty-eight hours."

"Good. Dismissed."

The Grand Deacon left. The giant screen drew back into the ceiling beam from which it had descended. Karl looked down the slope to the ocean. For once the sky was clear, and the setting sun drew a line of fire across the glassy water, a path of light that led to the horizon, and beyond.

A path to God, Karl thought. *A blood-red path.*

Red with the blood of the Kemonomimi. Red with the blood of the abominations of Victor Hansen.

The ancient religions were heresy, of course, but those high in the hierarchy of the Body studied them to recognize them when they saw them. Karl Rasmusson knew that in many of the old, false religions, blood sacrifices served to purify worshipers and turn away the vengeance of God.

A hint of truth in the superstitions of the past, he thought. *God trying to speak, but humanity unwilling to listen—until the First Avatar was born.*

We're listening now, God, he said in silent prayer. *I'm listening now.*

You will have the blood you demand. I swear it.

The sun sank into the sea, and the path of light vanished as though it had never been ... but the sky still glowed red, the red of blood and fire.

"All set?" Andy King whispered into his mike. Pressure-suited, he hung in one of the shafts the computer no longer remembered existed, one that emptied up through a floor plate into the virtual-reality training room where Goodfellow's precious data conduit lurked behind the wall.

Below Andy, the shaft led down to one of their secret access routes, right up against the hull. Fifteen meters sternward from the bottom of the shaft, a shaped charge had been placed that, when detonated, would blow a hole in the hull. As the air rushed out, the computer would seal the two hatches into the VR room, isolating it from the rest of the ship.

Andy just hoped the makeshift air seals they had rigged in their own crawlspaces held, or everyone in his crew who wasn't pressure-suited—which was most of them; they only had access to a half-dozen suits—would be forced to flee into the areas of the ship the computer could still see, where they would be instantly detected.

Simon Goodfellow hung below him, his face pale and sweating through the transparent bubble of his helmet. He didn't speak, but nodded.

"Set," Cordelia Raum said in Andy's ear.

"Do it," Andy said.

Not all of the charge's force went out through the hull: he felt the explosion as a pressure wave that slammed past him, shoving him hard against the rungs of the ladder to which he clung. An instant later, air rushed the other way, howling out through the hole in the hull. A thick fog enveloped him momentarily, then was sucked away.

A few final phantom tugs of fleeing atmosphere, then the utter stillness and silence of vacuum. Andy looked down at Goodfellow. "All right, Simon?" he said.

"Yes," Goodfellow squeaked.

"Seals held," Raum reported.

"We're going in," Andy said.

He climbed up the last few rungs of the ladder and pushed aside the already loosened deck plate.

The VR training room contained the multipurpose simulators the Body used to train Holy Warriors in the operation of the ship's auxiliary vehicles. Everyone in the *Victor Hansen* crew had spent time in one of its four boxy simulators, learning to operate the shuttles, assault craft, boats, and submarines that filled the ship's equipment holds. The simulators, each about three meters tall, four meters wide and maybe five meters long, crouched down in tangled nests of hydraulics. Four curved white control desks for managing the simulations stood along the two longer walls of the room, two on each wall. The room was big enough that the curvature of the habitat ring's hull could be clearly seen, making it look as if the doors in the shorter walls were located slightly uphill from where Andy had made his unorthodox entrance.

Those doors, each about twice as wide as a normal door and taller, too, so that equipment could be easily moved in and out, were both closed: and above them, bright red lights flashed a steady warning rhythm. *Vacuum sealed for your protection,* Andy thought.

The rest of the room looked perfectly normal, except for frost glinting here and there on walls and floor.

Andy pulled himself up, then drew his laser pistol. "Get to work," he told Goodfellow. The tech climbed out clumsily, weighed down by a huge black backpack, and would have overbalanced backward and fallen back into the shaft if Andy hadn't grabbed his arm. He gave Andy a wan grin, looked around, then made a beeline for the wall between the two simulator control desks to his right. He set down his backpack, pulled out something that looked like an oversized handgun with a strange black shield surrounding the barrel, and pressed it to the wall. As he slowly moved it horizontally across the metal, a thin black line, edges glowing red, appeared behind it.

Andy turned his attention to the doors. The computer knew they were in there. The computer also couldn't do anything about it: the AI might be the ship's conscious brain, but the pressure seals were under the control of the ship's autonomic nervous system. The computer could no more open those doors than a man could command his heart to stop beating: not until the hull breach was sealed and the room repressurized. And since the hull breach had occurred in an area they had blinded the computer to back on Marseguro, it should be having fits trying to figure out exactly what had happened—and giving the Holy Warriors on the bridge fits in the process.

They'd figure it out eventually, of course. But with the computer out of the loop, the bots that would normally be sent out to fix a hull breach would be useless: they were all under central control. The Holy Warriors would have to go outside themselves, locate the breach visually, and then attempt to seal it. All that would take time.

Enough time?

Andy didn't know. But they'd thrown their dice. They'd either retake the ship, or die trying.

He sat down where he had a good view of both doors, and settled in to wait.

"Who are you?" Emily chirp-clicked. The woman cocked her head, obviously able to hear but not understand. She made noises in return, similar to the Marseguroite click-speech but unintelligible to Emily.

A second Selkie pushed into the air lock, a teenaged male, maybe sixteen, standard, wearing white trunks. He looked at Emily and his mouth fell open. The older woman elbowed him in the ribs, and he closed his mouth and dropped his eyes, but he didn't stop stealing looks.

Then Biccum stuck his helmeted head into the air lock and both Selkies backed up fast. The boy pulled a wicked-looking knife from the belt of his trunks.

Emily turned and shoved at Biccum. "Get him back inside!" she chirp-clicked to her mother. "And get me something to write on. I think the pressure suits have whiteslates."

Biccum's head jerked out of sight: Dr. Christianson-Wood had apparently pulled him back into the shuttle by his ankles. A moment later her hand extended a white rectangle with a silver stylus floating from it on a string.

Hoping the strange Selkies could read English, Emily grabbed the whiteslate and wrote, "Please help us."

She passed the slate to the woman, who took it cautiously. The boy's eyes were now locked on Emily's face—which showed great concentration on his part, she figured—and his knife remained ready.

"We don't help Holy Warriors," the woman wrote, the motion of her hand sharp and angry. Emily felt a surge of relief: they would be able to communicate.

She scribbled furiously. "Only two Holy Warriors alive," she wrote. "We were prisoners. These two saved us."

She passed the slate. The woman's eyes flicked over it.

He nodded, turned and swam back out into the open water, where the dark shapes of—presumably—other Selkies clustered, trying to see what was going on.

"Come with us," the woman wrote.

"The Holy Warriors?" Emily responded. She couldn't leave them to drown . . .

"Prisoners," the woman wrote. "Blindfolds."

Emily nodded, took the slate, and wrote on it for the benefit of Biccum and Koop, "They'll help us. But you have to go as prisoners. Blindfolds."

She passed the slate inside. Biccum looked at it, then looked at her. His mouth quirked. "Tables turned?" he said, his voice thin but loud enough for her Selkie ears to pick it up. "I can live with that. Since the other option would appear to be dying with it. But how do you blindfold a pressure suit?"

"I'm not . . ." Emily began, but then felt a touch on her foot. She turned back. The woman was holding out two opaque bags, probably used for gathering shellfish, easily large enough to go over the pressure suits' helmets. Emily smiled at her and passed them through.

Something else came out the other way: her mother must have swum back up to their quarters, and now held out Emily's zebra-striped yellow skinsuit.

With great relief, Emily pulled it on. Selkies weren't as body-shy as nonmods, as a rule, but she still felt she'd put on enough of a show for one day. *I'm not cut out to be an exhibitionist,* she thought.

She suspected the teenage boy with the knife would be disappointed.

With Biccum and Koop blinded by the bags, all four of them finally emerged from the *Divine Will.* The water outside was a deep blue-green: it had to be daylight up above. A dozen Selkies of both sexes, ranging from the teenage boy to middle-aged, floated outside, along with the same number of small transportation devices similar to the Marseguroite sputa: handheld, steerable torpedoes, essentially. Their headlights were the source of the illumination Emily had seen through the air lock door.

She felt the strange Selkies' eyes on her as she emerged, and was doubly glad to have her skinsuit.

Her mother swam up beside her. "I don't believe it," Dr.

Christianson-Wood chirp-clicked. "Selkies? On Earth? How have they survived? Why hasn't the Body hunted them down? And why are they here in the first place? I've read Victor Hansen's diaries. He didn't say anything about leaving any Selkies behind on Earth."

"Maybe they'll tell us, once we're in air." Emily turned to look at the shuttle. Its hull was crumpled and torn in a dozen places, and its bow was a tangled mass of metal and glass: it must have taken the brunt of the crash, and it looked like something up there had exploded, too. She'd wondered if other Holy Warriors might still be clinging to life in the shuttle. Now she wondered how any of them had survived.

The woman in white held out her hand for the whiteslate. Emily passed it to her, and she wrote, "Follow us."

Emily nodded, and the whole strange party of Selkies towing Holy Warriors swam away from the wreck of the *Divine Will*.

Chris Keating looked around at the assembled Kemono-mimi and debated the wisdom of telling "Victor Hansen" that he was full of crap. Assuming these cat-people were the original Hansen's creations, and in light of the fact that even those of them not armed *to* the teeth were armed *with* teeth—and claws—denying the identity of the person they apparently accepted as their creator didn't seem wise.

He opted for a cautious, "Really? I, uh, thought he was—uh, you were dead."

"As I wanted the world to think," Hansen said. His eyes raked Keating like lasers. "But as you can see, I'm very much alive. As, unaccountably, are you."

"Is that why you brought me here?"

"Why else?" Hansen gestured at the assembled cat-people. "My Kemonomimi were on an important . . . er-rand . . . for me in the Holy City when they spotted you: the only living human, so far as they could tell, in that entire metropolis. They radioed me for instructions and I ordered them to bring you back with them." He stepped closer. "Why haven't you succumbed to my clever little virus?"

"Your virus?" Chris blinked. "I thought . . . uh, heard . . . that it came from outer space. Marseguro."

Hansen's face darkened. "What you heard was a lie," he

snarled. "A lie created by those hideous freaks, those . . . fish-people."

"Selkies?" Chris said, and wished he hadn't.

"That's what they call themselves," Hansen said. "But to think such inferior creatures could have created anything as perfect as my virus . . . it's laughable." He didn't look like he was about to laugh. He looked like he wanted to kill someone. But he took a long, deep breath and some of the color faded from his face, that face that was so much like Richard Hansen's.

It's true, then, Chris thought. He'd been told, while still imprisoned, that Richard Hansen was not Victor Hansen's grandson at all, but a clone. Which meant *this* "Victor Hansen" must also be a clone.

How many copies of himself did Hansen make? Chris wondered. *The man was a raging egomaniac.*

Which meant, he suspected, that so was the man in front of him, who seemed convinced he was the original.

Hansen was still staring at Chris. The anger had faded from his face. "How . . . interesting . . . that you heard this virus came from Marseguro," he said. "Considering only those at the highest levels of the Body Purified were told that particular lie." He abruptly turned on his heel, snapped, "Alexander. Napoleon. Bring him," and strode off.

Two towering Kemonomimi males, one glossy black, the other tiger-striped, stepped out from the encircling pack. Strong furred hands, retractable claws just showing from the tips of the fingers, gripped Chris' arms. He didn't resist; either one of them could have broken him in two, and both looked like they'd as soon eat him as escort him.

They propelled him in Hansen's wake across the runway to a broad sidewalk, and along it to the low building, punctuated by a control tower barely three stories tall, that had obviously been what passed for an airport terminal in the tiny town. A blue patch of sky had been showing when they'd removed his blindfold, but gray fluffy clouds swallowed it as they walked, and heavy drops of cold rain began to fall just as they reached the glass doors at the back of the building, clearly marked EXIT ONLY. They went through them anyway, into a large room decorated in earth tones, with comfortable-looking dark-brown chairs lining olive-green walls. Large windows gave a view of the runway. The crowd of Kemonomimi had dispersed: Chris could see them walking in twos or threes away from the field toward ground vehicles and other buildings. Just before Hansen led him through a door marked AUTHORIZED PERSONNEL ONLY, Chris thought he glimpsed much smaller Kemonomimi—children?—running through the rain to greet one of the couples.

Hansen, Chris, and his guards continued down a gray-carpeted corridor, punctuated at regular intervals by doors of dark, reddish wood, to an open door at the far end. Chris' guards pushed him into the room beyond in Hansen's wake.

"Wait outside," Hansen told them. They exchanged silent looks, but stepped back into the corridor. Hansen closed the door firmly behind them.

The room had obviously been the office of whomever had overseen operation of the airport. Two chairs upholstered in charcoal-gray leather faced a curving desk of the same dark-red wood as the door. Vidscreens covered one wall; a few personal knickknacks decorated a shelf nestled among the blank, glassy surfaces. Chris' gaze wandered to a photograph: a smiling woman, sun shining on her blonde hair, a small girl, her smile and hair matching the woman's, held protectively in the woman's arms.

Chris felt an unaccustomed pang. *All dead,* he thought. *All dead because I came to Earth . . .*

No. He pushed the thought away. *Not because I came to Earth. Because Richard Hansen betrayed real humans and helped the Selkies. Because Victor Hansen created those monstrosities in the first place. Because the Body failed to carry out God's wishes.*

Proof: Seventy years after the Day of Salvation and the supposed Purification, two cat-people stood outside this room, and a clone of Victor Hansen stood within it.

Chris tore his eyes away from the photograph, and bit down hard, clenching his jaw against the rage he felt. He had to play it cool, or he'd join that smiling family in death.

Hansen indicated one of the chairs that faced the desk. Chris sat. Hansen rounded the desk to the larger chair behind it. "Now," he said, sitting down, "I want answers. But . . ." He leaned back. "I'm generous. I know you must be curious about me, so I'll tell you about myself first.

"Yes, I'm Victor Hansen. The *original* Victor Hansen. I

faked my death all those years ago and put out the ridiculous story that I fled Earth in the company of the worst mistakes of my career, the Selkies, to cover my true plan."

He spread his hands. "How old do I look to you?"

A trick question? "Um ... mid-thirties?" Chris said. "Maybe younger?"

Hansen laughed. Apparently he'd said the right thing. "Exactly," he said. "*Exactly*. And yet, seventy years ago when I supposedly hijacked a spaceship and fled Earth forever, I was already in my fifties." He leaned forward. "I have made many great discoveries in my life," he said, "and one terrible, terrible mistake.

"Of all my discoveries, three stand out." He held up one finger. "First, I discovered how to mold the human genome at will. And then, late in life, I made two more great discoveries." A second finger went up. "I discovered how to reverse aging." A third finger extended. "And finally, I discovered the secret of suspended animation."

Chris nodded. It seemed safe.

Hansen wasn't really looking at him, anyway. His eyes stared past him, off into the distance. He spoke as if he were talking to a large crowd, giving a long-prepared speech. In fact, the cadence of his voice as he told his story reminded Chris of the recordings of *The Wisdom of the Avatar* he had discovered among his parents' things, the recordings that had led him to activate the interstellar distress beacon that had brought the Body to Marseguro for its long-delayed Purification.

Not that that had exactly worked out the way he'd planned, but God Itself had a plan, of that he was certain. Just as he was certain that the plan involved him. Because why else would God have ensured he be brought to this strange place at this strange time?

Why else was he still alive?

To stay that way, though, he kept his mouth shut and listened to Victor Hansen's sermon.

"... and thus I reversed the aging process in myself, made myself decades younger," he was saying. "Then I entered a state of suspended animation. And when the time was right, I emerged from the darkness." A shadow crossed his face. "And a terrible darkness it was," he said softly. "There were ... unanticipated side effects. I dreamed terrible dreams in which I wasn't myself, dreams in which I wandered the world in the company of Holy Warriors and other functionaries of the cursed Body. But finally, one morning, I woke and found everything had become clear. I remembered who I was, and although I didn't remember what I had done to advance myself so far into the future, so young and strong, I soon reasoned it out." His voice softened. "A terrible loss, that particular memory. To know you have cheated death, and not to be able to remember exactly how you did it . . . well. At least I remembered the most important things: my greatest triumph, and my greatest mistake.

"I remember creating the Kemonomimi." Hansen's eyes were bright, but he was still looking off into the distance, though his actual line of sight only encompassed an open door at the side of the room that appeared to lead to a toilet. Chris glanced at it longingly. He could *really* use a toilet.

"The Kemonomimi are what humans should always have been," Hansen said. "Stronger, faster, tougher. Their senses are superior. They need no clothes because they're almost impervious to cold. They're . . . perfect. The perfection of humanity.

"I remember how proud I felt when the first youngsters, already sexually, physically, and mentally mature at age ten, escaped into the wild . . . though I regretted the deaths of some of my employees during the escape, of course." He blinked, then carried on. "My beautiful Kemonomimi fled into the mountains, built a society, and successfully hid from every attempt, first by the government of the day, and later, after the Day of Salvation, by the Body Purified, to hunt them down."

He smiled proudly, but the smile soured into a scowl. "But then . . . I also remember creating the fish-people. The Selkies. And they were my greatest mistake.

"Humans' distant ancestors crawled out of the sea. We were never meant to crawl back into it. Water creatures are inferior. The fish-people can barely function on land. Keep them out of the water too long and they die a horrible death. They were *wrong*. I should have destroyed the embryos long before I implanted them in the artificial wombs. But . . . I didn't." He shook his head. "Why, I have no idea. My memories from that time are lost, wiped out by age reversal and suspended animation. I remember nothing after creating the Selkies.

"But no matter. The Selkies escaped to this other planet, this . . . Marseguro. A great pity, and someday I will rectify that, but for now the important thing is that there are no fish-people on Earth. Earth belongs to the Kemonomimi, *my* Kemonomimi. My virus made sure of that."

Chris had considerable personal experience with theories extrapolated from too little evidence. Right up until everyone on Earth started dying, he'd been convinced the deaths of the Holy Warriors on Marseguro, *Sanctification*, and *Retribution* had been due to some kind of diabolical poison cooked up by Richard Hansen. Now, of course, he realized that his judgment had been clouded by his own hatred of Richard Hansen and his belief—one he apparently shared with this clone of their creator, oddly enough—that the Selkies were too inferior to have created something as clever as the plague.

He didn't think his judgment was being clouded now, though, as he concluded that this Victor Hansen clone was one seriously deluded individual.

"You . . . remember creating the virus?" Chris said cautiously.

"No," Hansen said instantly. He rubbed his temple with one hand. "No," he said again. "I've tried and tried, but . . . it's not there.

"But I *know* I did it, just as I know I extended my life and slept through decades unchanged. I must have created the virus, for it is cleverly designed to kill almost everyone except those carrying a specific genetic sequence—a sequence from my genome, a sequence I put into my created races as a kind of artist's signature. In other words, this plague was clearly designed to free the Earth of inferior 'normal' humanity, in order to make room for my perfected version: the Kemonomimi."

Okay, then, Chris thought. *I think I know where we stand. You're crazy, and I'm entirely at your mercy.*

I hope this is all part of Your plan, God, because it's just a little nerve-racking from where I sit.

"Now it's your turn," Hansen said. He sat behind the desk and turned those intense blue eyes that Chris remembered so well from Richard Hansen's hated face toward him. "Why are you alive? And who told you that lie about the virus coming from Marseguro?"

Chris thought furiously. Hansen obviously would never accept the truth: that he had come from Marseguro himself and been vaccinated against the virus by its true creators, the Selkies.

"I was . . . a prisoner of the Body," Chris said after a moment. "For political reasons. I . . . um, did some work as a medtech and made the mistake of wondering why we weren't allowed to use gene therapy on humans. When they confronted me, I . . . said some other things. They locked me up."

"That would not stop my virus from finding you," Hansen said.

"No," Chris said, really wishing Hansen would quit using a possessive pronoun when referring to the plague. "But it kept me alive long enough for the Body doctors to experiment on me. They . . . developed a vaccine. They gave it to me to see if it had any adverse effects. That's when I heard the story about the plague coming from Marseguro—the doctors talked about it. But then someone brought the plague into the prison, and within a day . . ." Chris let his voice trail off.

"A vaccine?" Hansen frowned, then said, reluctantly, "Possible, I suppose. But if what you say is true, how did you escape the prison?"

"A guard took pity on me, let me out," Chris said. It was always nice to be able to sprinkle a little truth in among your lies. "If he hadn't, I would have starved in that cell."

"Did anyone else receive this vaccine?" Hansen said.

"I have no idea," Chris said. "All I know is I didn't see anyone else alive in the City of God until the Kemonomimi showed up."

"What about the Avatar?" Hansen said. "Did you hear how *he* fared?"

"No," Chris said. "But I saw aircraft fleeing the Holy Compound after I'd been on the streets for a few days. They'd managed to keep the plague out that long, at least."

Hansen studied him. "Indeed they did," he said.

"What?" Chris blinked at him. "How did you—"

"The Avatar and as many surviving Holy Warriors and Body functionaries as he could muster have established themselves at Paradise Island, about three hundred kilometers south of here along the coast," Hansen said. "That's why we have decided to make this town our new home."

Chris waited for more explanation. Instead Hansen abruptly stood. "You must be tired and hungry," he said. "The Kemonomimi will look after you. I'll talk to you again before long."

Chris got hastily to his feet. "Thanks," he said. He squeezed his legs together. "Um . . . before I do anything else . . . may I use your toilet?"

Hansen blinked, then laughed. "Of course."

"Thanks." Chris dashed for the door.

Inside, he took care of business, then took a good look at himself in the mirror. He looked older than he expected, with chin stubble the same uninspired sandy brown as his ragged, shoulder-length hair, and dark circles under his eyes. His fine red shirt was torn and his tight-fitting black pants spotted with mud and covered in dust. "What have you gotten yourself into, Chris Keating?" he said out loud.

His reflection had no answer.

Chris sighed, washed his hands—*wouldn't want to spread disease*, he thought, wishing he could share the joke with someone—and stepped back into the office. "I'm all yours," he said: but though he spoke the words to Hansen, in his heart he directed them to God Itself.

Then Alexander and Napoleon came in and took him away.

Chapter 9

FORTY-FIVE MINUTES PASSED in the evacuated simulator room aboard the once—and future, Andy King hoped—*MSS Victor Hansen* with nothing much happening. Simon Goodfellow had cut a jaggedly rectangular section out of the wall, revealing neatly bundled cables of various colors. He'd hooked one of those cables to a strange black keyboard that he had unfolded like a fan and set up on its own thin-legged tripod of black metal, then donned a set of VR goggles. Mostly now he just sat, moving his head from time to time, and very occasionally dancing his fingers across the keyboard.

While he'd been setting up his equipment, Andy and the remaining four crewmembers who had volunteered to wear the pressure suits had been setting up a rough barricade of deck plates around him to shield him from any weapons fire that might make it through the doors if—more likely *when*—they opened.

That done, Andy placed two crewmembers at each end of the room, facing the doors. Two Selkies, Brenda Slade and Sam Hallett, crouched behind the control desks at one end and two nonmods, Arthur Schmidt and Hala Khoury, at the other. That some sort of counterattack would come, Andy was certain. How soon, and what form it would take, he had no idea.

And then he found out. His earphones crackled. "There's a repair team on the outer hull," Cordelia Raum reported. "They're probing the hole."

Andy nodded to himself. "All right," he said. "You know what to do. Execute when you think the moment is right."

"Roger that."

A repair team on the outer hull was the best they could have hoped for. It meant the Holy Warriors wanted to seal the hole and then repressurize the room so they could open the doors and attack.

It also meant several Holy Warriors were even now gathered on the hull in the vicinity of the hole. Which meant . . .

"Executing," Raum said.

With no air to carry the blast, Andy felt nothing but a slight jolt as the two additional shaped charges they'd installed blew out sections of hull adjacent to the initial damage.

A moment's silence; then, "Repair efforts have ceased," Raum said. "I think they lost at least three men. The rest are retreating."

"Good work. They won't try to pressurize again. Which means they'll try something else. Stay alert, everyone." He glanced at Goodfellow. "Status, Simon."

"Getting there," Simon said. "Not there yet. Leave me alone."

"I was hoping," Andy said mildly, "for some indication of how *much* longer you need."

"At least an hour," Simon said. "Longer if you keep bothering me."

Andy started to reply, then thought better of it. He looked away just in time to catch an amused glance from Hala Khoury, ensconced behind one of the two nearest control desks, and shrugged.

"You think they'll try Plan B?" Raum said in his ear.

"What else can they do?" Andy said. "I just wish I knew how many men they can muster."

Plan B would be tougher for the Holy Warriors to arrange, but certainly not impossible. The computer wouldn't open the sealed doors as long as the corridors outside them were still pressurized. The only way into a depressurized area was to treat the next pressurized area as a giant air lock: put people into it in pressure suits, then lock down the next available pressure seal and depressurize the area with the people in it. Once that was done, the computer could be instructed to open the doors into this room, and the Holy Warriors could mount an attack.

Which was why Andy had his meager forces arrayed the way they were, watching for the flashing red lights above those doors to go out.

"First Officer Andrew King?" a voice said in Andy's ear. He jerked and looked around, then remembered the vacuum and felt like an idiot. He checked his data panel: the voice was coming over an overriding emergency frequency built into the Body-designed suit. With a tap on his wrist controls, he switched to that frequency.

"King here," he said.

"We can end this without bloodshed," the voice said. "Surrender your crew and you won't be harmed."

Andy laughed. "You expect me to believe that?" he said. "The Body has already killed my friends and family on Marseguro. The Body will always kill my kind. I'm a Selkie, you know. A moddie. A . . . whaddyoucallit? . . . oh, yeah. 'Abomination.' "

"I know what you are," the voice said. "And I'm Grand Deacon Byrne, acting commander of *BPS Sanctification*. You killed everyone I ever knew with your filthy plague. You've killed millions. I'd love to see you dead, and I'm sure the feeling is mutual. But I still say we can end this without bloodshed. Enough have died on both sides. Why add to the number?"

Andy looked at Simon. As long as Byrne was talking, he wasn't attacking.

"Why should I surrender?" he said. "Looks to me like I'm in pretty good shape right here."

"You're fooling yourself," Byrne said. "We know what you're trying to do, and it won't work."

"It won't?" Andy felt a chill, but he kept his voice light, aiming for a tone of polite interest. "Really? Why not?"

"You can't regain command of the AI," the Grand Deacon said. "The security protocols are unbreakable. It will only recognize the ranking Body officer as its captain, and even though you've convinced it that you're a Body officer, your fictitious persona doesn't outrank me, or any of my men. You can't change that with a data terminal, no matter how clever your programmer thinks he is."

Inwardly, Andy smiled. *He doesn't know what we're trying to do at all,* he thought. Out loud, though, he allowed a small hint of concern to creep into his voice. "I don't know anything about AIs," he said truthfully. "But why should I believe you instead of my own expert?"

"Your 'expert' comes from a planet that's been out of the mainstream for seventy years," Byrne said. "He's deluded. And he's deluding you."

Andy pretended to think. "Suppose I don't surrender," he said at last. "What then?"

"I think you know," Byrne said.

"You've already tried to repressurize this section. How'd that go for you?"

"There are other ways," Byrne said. "I'm not going to discuss it further. Surrender, or we'll kill you all."

"Suppose I make you the same offer?" Andy said softly.

"Fine," the Grand Deacon snarled. "Have it your way, moddie. Truth be told, I prefer it."

With no air to carry the sound as it contacted the deck, Andy might have missed the roof panel falling altogether if he hadn't happened to glance that way at just the right moment. But the instant he saw it dropping, he realized what must be happening, and flung himself to his feet and dashed forward.

He reached the fallen ceiling plate just as something small, round and black dropped from the newly opened shaft.

Acting on instinct, he grabbed the object and threw it back up the shaft as hard as he could, then dove to one side.

Just in time. The laser grenade went off somewhere inside the shaft, pumping out high-energy beams in all directions. Half a dozen came down the shaft, scoring the floor with white-hot gashes that slowly faded, a cloud of vaporized metal settling around them like mist.

A moment later a body dropped out of the shaft, its pressure suit holed in a number of places. It lay still, smoking. Blood began to pool on the deck plate.

After a moment, more blood began to drip from the hole in the ceiling.

Andy switched back to the frequency the Marseguroites were using amongst themselves. "Close one," he said. "Stay ready—"

Even as he spoke, he saw the light go out on the door he was facing.

"Here they come!"

He ran back to his place behind the corner of one of the simulators.

The door rose slowly. The instant it cleared the floor, the blank white backsides of the control panels Arthur Schmidt and Hala Khoury crouched behind smoked and sparked as lasers swept the room at floor level. A black line scored the barricade protecting Simon, and hydraulic lines at the base of the simulators ruptured, spraying fluid that exploded into a fine brown mist in the vacuum.

Then the door's ascent suddenly went from slow to fast, and two Holy Warriors rolled into the room and came up firing. Hala Khoury's laser burned one down instantly; the other vanished out of Andy's sight. He would have run around the simulator to go after him, but just outside the door another Holy Warrior crouched behind a long black tube on a black metal tripod.

Andy shouted a warning, but the heavy beamer had already fired. The control desk Hala crouched behind flared like a torch and fell apart. Hala jerked up, then fell over sideways and lay still.

Most of her head was missing.

An instant later Andy's laser found the helmet of the heavy gunner's pressure suit and sliced off its top, taking a chunk of the gunner's skull with it.

Andy looked around. The control desk Brenda Slade had been hiding behind had suffered the same fate as Hala's, but she wasn't lying there. He could see a body down by the door, and another slumped over a beam weapon like the one at his end in the corridor, but nobody alive.

He pulled back and ran to the other side of the room.

Brenda and Sam Hallett were struggling hand-to-hand with a Holy Warrior behind Sam's control desk. Andy looked the other way, and saw that another Holy Warrior, having somehow lost his weapon, was sitting on Arthur Schmidt's back, trying to undo his helmet. Andy fired, and the Holy Warrior's suit split across the back. The Holy Warrior stiffened, tried to reach behind him, then fell sideways.

Breathing hard, Andy looked around. Brenda and Sam had dispatched the Holy Warrior they'd been struggling with. That made five Holy Warriors dead, maybe six if there were another one up the shaft, and he'd only lost . . .

One, he'd started to say, but then he realized Schmidt wasn't moving. He ran to him and rolled him over, only to find dead, bloodshot eyes staring up at him: the Holy Warrior had managed to rip out the suit's air hoses before Andy's laser had found him.

"Shit!" Andy gave the Holy Warrior a savage kick, then strode over to Simon. "Simon, status!" he snapped.

"I told you . . ."

"Damn it, you bloodless little robot, look around you!"

Simon sighed. "This isn't—" he flipped up the lenses on the VR goggles, and for the first time saw the bodies all around him. His face paled. "I didn't—what happened?"

"Arthur Schmidt and Hala Khoury just died so you can do your job, that's what happened," Andy snarled. "Now tell me: what is your status?"

Simon swallowed. "Five minutes," he said. "I swear. Five minutes . . ."

The doors suddenly slid shut again. "I hope you have them," Andy said. He looked around. Brenda and Sam were staring at Hala's body. Tom had his arm around Brenda, whose suited shoulders heaved. Andy went over to them. "They'll try again," he said. "If they get a chance."

"They can't have many more men," Sam said. "Can they?"

"They don't need many more," Andy said.

They waited. Andy could imagine all too well what was happening on the other side of those closed bulkheads. They'd be repressurizing. They'd be manning the heavy guns again. They knew there were only three of them, they knew they only had light weapons. They'd probably just stand back and sweep the room with the heavy beamers. If the *Victor Hansen* crewmembers were lucky, they might pick off one of the gunners, but . . . Andy looked at Simon. The deck plates protecting him wouldn't last ten seconds with a heavy beamer on them.

Simon's promised five minutes crawled into ten, then fifteen. Andy didn't say anything. He flicked his eyes from the shaft in the ceiling to the still-closed bulkheads, over and over.

"Last chance, Mr. King," Byrnes' voice said, so suddenly Andy jumped.

He keyed the Holy Warrior frequency. "You had our answer last time," he replied grimly.

"We both lost people," Byrne said. "But there are more of us than you. You'll be dead two minutes after those doors go up."

"So will some more of your precious Holy Warriors," Andy snarled. "And you all arrived on one shuttle. There can't be very many of you left either."

"Enough to do the job. Do you surrender, Mr. King?"

Andy looked at Simon, who had to be hearing the same broadcast over the same overriding emergency frequency . . . and just at that moment, Simon straightened, took a deep breath, turned around, and gave Andy a thumbs-up. Andy grinned, pointed at Simon, made his thumb and finger into a gun, and "fired" it at the tech.

Simon nodded, turned around, and touched a single key on his keyboard.

"I believe the better question, Grand Deacon Byrne, is . . . do *you* surrender?

"What the . . ." Andy could hear confused, shouting voices in the background. "*What have you done?*"

"I just killed this ship's AI," Andy said. "Dead as a doornail. You have no command over anything."

"Neither do you!" snarled Byrne.

"Maybe," Andy said. "But I don't really need it, do I? Not like you do, Grand Deacon. Because you're trapped. Without the AI, you can't leave the bridge: security protocols have sealed it tight. You're stuck in there until your suits run out of air. Then you'll have to open your faceplates. And then . . . well, you know what happens then. A tickle in the throat, a bit of a cough, a little nosebleed, and within a day you're puking your lungs out and dying in your own bloody vomit.

"So here's my ultimatum to you, Grand Deacon Byrne. We've routed manual control of the ship's systems to here. We can let you have safe passage to your shuttle . . . so you can fly back to your ship and tell your precious Avatar that *BPS Sanctification* is once more *MSS Victor Hansen*."

"You're still dead," Captain Byrne snarled. "The ship's air won't last forever. Without the AI, systems will start to crash. You can't run something the size of this ship manually with practically no crew. And you've launched all your shuttles and escape pods. You've accomplished *nothing*."

"My accomplishments," Andy said, "are none of your

concern. All you have to do is," and he savored the next four words like bites of the most delectable dessert he'd ever eaten, "get ... off ... my ... ship." He waited one long moment. "Well?"

Silence for five seconds. Ten. Then: "All right."

Andy nodded to Simon. "Let them out."

Simon's fingers tapdanced across the keyboard. "They've got a clear passage to their shuttle ... they're leaving the bridge."

"Keep watching them until we know they've launched," Andy said. He clapped Simon on the shoulder. "Good work. You've saved us all."

Simon grinned awkwardly. "It was nothing."

"Glad to hear it," Andy said. "Because now comes the hard part. Once they're gone, you've got to get this ship's AI up and running again."

Simon's smile faded, and he gave his console a speculative look.

Andy's own smile disappeared as though it had never been as he looked back at Hala and Arthur, still lying where they'd fallen. *I'm tired of losing people to the Holy Warriors*, he thought. *It's got to stop.*

It's got *to.*

"We're ready," Grand Deacon von Eschen said quietly.

The Avatar stood in his office with his hands behind his back, looking through the window and down the once-again fog-shrouded slope to the Pacific Ocean, which today belied its name, smashing against the rocks of the island's west coast as though trying to tear it apart.

"What's the weather forecast?" the Avatar asked.

"Not good," the Grand Deacon admitted. "Of course, we don't have full meteorological capability, but what we've been able to piece together from the sensors scattered out west of the island and a handful of satellite photos ... it looks like we're in for a couple of days of this." He gestured out the window. Rain splattered against it, and the trees bent and swayed as violently as the ocean waves.

"Could we cross in this?" the Avatar asked, but he already knew the answer.

"Yes," the Grand Deacon said. "But not safely. Our boats are small and our crews inexperienced. There are rocks along the coast and the wind would be blowing us right at them. If something went wrong . . ."

"God wants us to wait," the Avatar said. He looked up at the sky: though Body doctrine made it clear God imbued every part of the universe with Its life force, something in humans persisted in seeing the sky as more Godly than the Earth.

Well, he thought, *if God's everywhere, then there's more of It out there than there is down here on this puny speck of dust, isn't there?*

"Yes, Your Holiness," the Grand Deacon said.

The Avatar turned away from the stormy view. "Bring Richard Hansen to me," he said. "I want to talk to him."

"Yes, Your Holiness."

The Grand Deacon saluted and left. Karl wondered idly if he would bring Hansen back himself, or order someone else to do it. He'd noticed that people responded to the Avatar's wishes in unpredictable ways, and ways very different from how they had responded to the wishes of the Right Hand.

There's power, then there's absolute power, Karl thought. *And with absolute power comes absolute responsibility.*

Which was one reason he wanted to talk to Hansen.

He'd once suggested to Cheveldeoff that they sacrifice Hansen to the people, use him to cement Cheveldeoff's position as the next Avatar. But instead Hansen had led the Body to Marseguro . . . and now he had returned, hard on the heels of Marseguro's killing plague.

He's been at the center of all that has happened, Karl thought. *And that means he's an agent of God, whether he realizes it or not.*

Karl believed he knew exactly what God wanted him to do. But that didn't mean he shouldn't try to discern God's wishes as clearly as possible.

A discreet knock sounded at his door. "Enter," he said, and turned to face the clone of Victor Hansen, ushered in by . . . Karl smiled . . . the Grand Deacon himself.

"You can leave," he told the Grand Deacon. "But post a guard."

The Grand Deacon gave Hansen a suspicious look, but withdrew.

"Sit," Karl said.

Hansen looked around at the office. "Kind of small for the Avatar, isn't it?" he said.

"Circumstances being what they are," Karl said, "it suffices." He indicated one of the seats across the desk from him. "Please."

Hansen sat. He looked . . . tired, Karl thought. Defeated. He smiled. "I'd like to talk to you, Richard," he said. He sat behind the desk. "There's something I've been wondering about." He folded his arms on the desk and leaned forward. "Why?"

Richard didn't know what to expect when the Grand Deacon came to fetch him from the Marseguroites' prison cottage. As far as he knew, he had nothing else to tell the Avatar, nothing to offer him of any value. They'd established he knew nothing about the Kemonomimi. He'd already turned over their supply of vaccine. The Avatar was hardly in a position to threaten Marseguro—*Not yet*, Richard thought bitterly—so whatever knowledge he had of the Selkie planet was of no use.

He felt of little use to anyone. Bringing the vaccine to the island in person had been one more disastrous decision in a string of them that had begun with his determination to blot out his father's shame by helping to find the Selkies.

But the Grand Deacon took him to the Avatar's office, and the Avatar had him sit down, and then the Avatar asked him the one question he didn't expect: "Why?"

He understood the question instantly. But he pretended not to. "Why what?"

The Avatar leaned back in his chair and steepled his fingers. "You were raised in the Body. You were *loyal* to the Body. The gene-bomb Victor Hansen built into you was at least partially defused. You have been steeped since childhood in the teachings of *Wisdom of the Avatar of God*. You know that what the Body teaches is true: God Itself saved Earth from seemingly certain destruction. It was an obvious and unmistakable miracle. After it, no reasonable man could doubt that God exists, and has a plan for Earth that we thwart at our peril.

"Yet that is exactly what you did. You tossed aside God's plan. You tossed aside everything you had been taught, everything you believed. You threw in your lot with the kind of abominations that brought God's wrath down on Earth to begin with. You helped these abominations fight off the Body's Holy Warriors. And when they created a monstrously evil plague that only kills normal humans, not moddies . . . you still aided them.

"That plague has killed millions on Earth. Friends, enemies, everyone you ever met on this planet has most likely fallen to it. And yet you continue to be loyal to the monsters of Marseguro?"

The Avatar slammed his hands down on his desk so suddenly that Richard flinched. "Why?" he thundered. "How could you betray humanity?"

Richard could feel, deep in his heart, the pull of the belief in which he had been so thoroughly indoctrinated. *Repent,* it urged him. *Repent. This is the Avatar, God's chosen vessel on Earth. Confess to him that you have made a terrible mistake, that you will return to the fold, that you will serve God again . . .*

. . . but another part of him pushed back, hard. He'd made deeper and more lasting friends among the "monsters" and apostates of Marseguro than he had ever found on Earth, and it was on Marseguro, for the first time in his life, that he had learned to love.

He refused to see that love as monstrous or unnatural, or the object of that love as an abomination.

He looked straight into the Avatar's ice-blue eyes. "I do not deny that what happened on the Day of Salvation *seems* miraculous," he said. "But I deny your interpretation of it. I deny the Body's interpretation of it. I deny the existence of a God that commands us to kill in Its name. I deny the truth of a faith that labels fellow humans monsters or abominations simply because they look different or live differently. I deny a Creator of life that would restrict Its creations from creating new life in their turn. And as for the plague—" Richard's face twisted. "No one on Marseguro wanted the plague to reach Earth. We just wanted to be left alone. Chris Keating brought the plague here. Ask your God about *that.* If It's so happy with your precious Body Purified, why did It allow Chris Keating to bring back a virus that destroyed it?"

He sat back, but he didn't look away. The Avatar studied him for a long moment. "Fascinating," he said at last. "How fascinating to catch a glimpse of the machinations of God. That It can use even an apostate like yourself to Its ends . . . astonishing."

Richard couldn't help it. He laughed. "God has been using me?" he said. "Then God has a weird sense of humor."

"Of course God has been using you," the Avatar said. "As it has used Chris Keating: to send us a message."

"A *message?*" Richard felt a hot stab of anger in his heart. "Millions died so you could receive a *message?* God couldn't just slip a note under your door?"

"Not for this." The Avatar leaned forward again. "The message from God is: the Body has been lax. The Body has grown soft. It has come to rely on its own strength, instead of on God's. It has mistaken its purpose on Earth. It is not here to govern, it is here to Purify. It is not here to make sure the crops get harvested and iron gets mined and people have pleasant little lives in clean, safe cities. God is not interested in individuals. God is interested in the survival of Its chosen race, Its ultimate creation: humanity.

"Now God has pared humanity down to a remnant. God will use that remnant to complete the Purification of Earth. And then God will have at last a *pure* human race, a *warrior* race, to spread out among the stars, as God has always intended.

"That Purification starts with the Kemonomimi. God used you to provide us with the vaccine for the plague. Now that we can leave this island, we will destroy those abominations once and for all. And once they are destroyed, God will bless the Earth again. The Body will rebuild: stronger, harder, sharper, a razor-edged blade to slash away the evil branches that have sprung from the pure stock of humanity.

"Marseguro will fall. Then the other colonies. Humanity, true humanity, pure humanity, will spread among the stars: planet by planet, until God's chosen race is so widespread nothing can threaten its existence again . . . except God Itself."

The Avatar sat back and smiled a satisfied, mocking smile. "And you . . . with Chris Keating's help . . . made it all possible. I was once the Right Hand of the Avatar, but you, Richard Hansen, clone of the foulest violator of God's law the world has ever known—*you* have been made the Right Hand of God Itself."

Once more Richard felt the pull of his old life, the majesty and terror of God Itself, all around him, pushing, guiding, forcing, threatening . . . and, if you did Its will, protecting.

But whether because of the gene-bomb Victor Hansen had implanted in his clones or his own experience, Richard Hansen no longer believed in a God like that.

And he was no longer afraid of that God's Avatar.

"Your reasoning is circular," he said. "Everything that happens is God's will, you claim: therefore everything I do, or you do, or anyone else does, is God's will. Nothing can happen that is not God's will.

"Which means, Your Holiness, that Victor Hansen's creation of the Kemonomimi and the Selkies was God's will, and this God you claim to worship is ordering you to destroy something, to kill hundreds more on top of the millions who have already died, that It caused to be created in the first place.

"I reject that kind of God, a God that is nothing more than a bored child pushing toys around in a sandbox. My decisions are my own. As are yours. To a greater or lesser degree, depending on our circumstances, we all have free will. We choose to do good, or we choose to do evil.

"I've made evil choices. But recently I've been trying to make good ones. And that's the only reason I'm here. I came—we all came, nonmods and Selkies alike—to offer help to the survivors of the plague that Marseguro unwillingly and unwittingly unleashed on Earth.

"We chose to do good. And now you, Your Holiness, rebuilding your army, withholding vaccine from other survivors, focusing instead on your determination to kill the Kemonomimi and the Selkies and anyone else who does not believe as you do—you are choosing to do evil."

He stopped. The Avatar looked at him. Richard didn't know what he'd expected—anger, perhaps, an order that he be removed, even executed, but the Avatar only looked faintly amused.

"And what," asked the Avatar, "are good and evil if God Itself is but a myth?" He shook his head. "You tell me these things as if they have never been considered before in the history of the world, instead of hashed and rehashed for millennia. But those arguments were settled, once and for all, when the First Avatar heard God's voice, and acted on it.

"Here's what it comes down to, Richard." Karl Rasmusson leaned forward. "I am the Avatar. I have been chosen by God to be the Avatar. And unlike the Avatar before me, I have listened to what God told the First Avatar: a man we know heard God clearly, since the miracle of Salvation Day attests to his connection to the Creator and Destroyer of All Things.

"What is good and what is evil are determined by God. Human opinions mean nothing. Human choice means nothing, if it is not informed by God. Your 'choices' are made without reference to the will of God, and therefore are not choices at all. Only those who believe and have submitted themselves to God Itself in the Body Purified have true freedom of will."

"But if that is so," Richard asked softly, "why hasn't God simply caused all of us 'unbelievers' and 'apostates' to believe and repent?"

"The decision to serve God is always made freely," the Avatar responded. "Once it is made, you have the choice every day of continuing to serve God, or to return to your old ways. But once you step outside the Body, your free choices are forfeit. Until you return to the Body, you serve as God's pawn, as a cog in Its great plan for the universe."

"Then the only 'choice' God allows is to serve It," Richard said. "You're saying I can choose to return to the Body and do God's will every day . . . or I can choose to remain outside the Body, in which case God will use me to do Its will anyway."

"Exactly," said the Avatar.

"Then freedom is a myth."

The Avatar's blue eyes bore into Richard's. "Exactly," he said again. "Richard Hansen, you could serve the Body again. Even though you claim to have none of Victor Hansen's memories of the Kemonomimi, you are still his clone—Victor Hansen himself, in very many ways. You could help us when we reach the Kemonomimi, help talk them into surrendering rather than fighting. If they surrender, we need not kill them."

"Just sterilize and enslave them," Richard said. "Like you planned to do with the Selkies."

"They cannot be permitted to continue to breed and pollute God's Holy Human Genome," the Avatar admitted. "But it is better to be alive and unable to reproduce than to be dead."

"And then I suppose you'll want me to help you retake Marseguro?" Richard said.

"It would be helpful," the Avatar said, "but not necessary. I understand you may have emotional entanglements with the Selkies. I would not force you to return to that planet. You could serve here on Earth, helping to distribute the vaccine, helping to rebuild the planet.

"It is the only free choice left to you," the Avatar said, and his voice hardened. "You have served God unwillingly and unknowingly. Continue to serve It like a puppet, or choose to serve it as a free man. But you *will* serve God."

Richard felt anger rising in him then, welling out of the same deep source from which he had earlier felt the tug of loyalty to the Body. *I gave myself to God freely once before,* he thought. *And the result was death and destruction, death and destruction that continue. Marseguro would remain undetected and hundreds there would still be alive, Earth would be uninfected and millions still alive here, if I hadn't made that choice.*

I sure as hell *won't make it again.*

"God," Richard growled, looking down, hands clenched, "can try to make me Its puppet. But I'm going to be pulling on those strings for all I'm worth. I'd rather be an unwilling puppet than a willing slave. In other words," he lifted his head and looked the Avatar straight in the eyes, "God Itself can kiss my ass."

Was that a flicker of anger at last in the Avatar's face? If so, it didn't carry over into his voice. "Very well," he said mildly. He looked out the window at the waves exploding in spray on the island's shore. "I believe God wanted me to offer you this last chance to serve It freely. I believe that's why we have been delayed by weather." He turned back to Richard. "And now that I have made that offer—and you have made your answer—I believe the weather will clear. We will sail to the mainland tomorrow, and from there march on the Kemonomimi."

He walked past Richard and opened the door. "Return him to his quarters," he said to the guards. As they entered and none-too-gently hauled Richard to his feet, the Avatar added, "You and your crew will remain here under guard. When we have completed our mission, we will return, and then I will deal with you as God instructs." He stared hard into Richard's eyes one last time. "I am being merciful," he said softly. "All of you will have one last chance to submit freely to the Body, and live. If you do not, then I am quite confident it will be God's will to see you shot." He stepped out of the way, and the guards pushed Richard out.

Richard didn't look back. *If there is a God,* he thought, *It may well have other plans for* you, *Avatar*.

He looked up at the sodden gray sky. Somewhere beyond those clouds, Andy would be trying to retake *Victor Hansen*. If he succeeded, all of the Avatar's plans could yet be seriously upset.

Not that he should mind, Richard thought savagely. *After all, it's all God's will.*

One of the guards gave him a shove that almost tripped him up, and he concentrated on the gravel path.

When the door closed behind Hansen, Karl Rasmusson allowed himself the luxury of slamming his hands down on his desk. The effrontery of the man! Raised in the Body, steeped in the truth of the First Avatar's words, witness to the recordings of the undeniable miracles of God on the Day of Salvation, and he *still* dared to deny God's will?

"Why did you want me to talk to him?" he asked God out loud. He looked out at the storm. As he had expected, it seemed to be easing. "You must have known what he would say."

And even as he asked the question, he knew the answer: God had wanted him to talk to Richard Hansen not for Hansen's sake, but for his own. God needed him to face head-on the doubts that might otherwise eat away at his faith. God needed him to see how powerless and hopeless were those who turned their backs on It.

His spirits suddenly lifted. Richard Hansen had served his purpose. He lived only at God's—and the Avatar's—pleasure. Karl no longer needed to think about him.

When the weather lifted, he would sail with his vaccinated army to the mainland. They would march on the Kemonomimi, whose polluting presence on the Earth had brought the plague down upon them all. He would Purify the Earth and, like the First Avatar, turn away God's wrath. And, unlike the second Avatar, he would not falter afterward. He would follow God's will wherever it might lead, whatever it might require: across the Earth, across the solar system, across the galaxy.

The clouds broke apart. Shafts of sunlight stabbed down on the restless ocean, striking diamond-bright sparks of light from the tossing waves, and Karl Rasmusson, Third Avatar of the Body Purified, knew without a shadow of doubt that it was a sign of favor from God.

Chapter 10

THE STRANGE SELKIES DROVE Emily, her mother, and the two pressure-suited Holy Warriors through the funny-tasting blue-green water, doubled up on the transportation devices Emily decided to call sputa, since they were close enough to Marseguro's Self-Propelled Underwater Towing Apparatus. The Holy Warriors were kept in the center, each riding with one of the largest men in the group, the rest of the Selkies surrounding them. Emily and her mother were shown a little more trust: Emily was put with the woman she had seen first, holding on tightly to her waist. Her mother was put with the teenage boy. From the looks the teenager shot in her direction, she suspected he would have preferred that the arrangement be reversed.

After an hour her arms were aching, and she began to wonder just how far they had to go. Then, suddenly, she saw something in the turquoise distance. As they approached and she got her first good look at it, Emily would have gasped if she had been in air.

An enormous artificial island rode the waves above them, tethered to the ocean floor by cables twice as thick as Emily's body. She couldn't begin to guess at it size—the metal underbelly disappeared into darkness in all directions.

And in the deep shadow of that steel ceiling: a sphere, attached to the island's underside.

At first she thought the sphere must be about the same size as a large Marseguroite habitat, but her sense of scale, already thrown out of whack by the enormous mass of metal floating overhead, kept adjusting itself as they approached it until at last she realized it was far larger than anything on Marseguro, at least a hundred meters in diameter. Tubes a good three meters in diameter led off from it in three directions to smaller spheres, just visible in the murk, and shadows hinted at further spheres beyond that.

It's not just a habitat, it's a whole underwater city, Emily thought. And it's completely hidden from above by . . . that.

Whatever *that* was.

A Marseguroite habitat would have blazed with light and been surrounded by traffic, from skinsuited Selkies to sputa and subs, but this one was absolutely dark. If she hadn't known better, she would have thought it dead and deserted.

She glanced at her mother. She, too, was staring upward at the metal ceiling looming above them.

When they were within five meters of the habitat's massive curved wall a section of it split open, spilling light into the water. They drove in, then up. Seeing a surface above her, Emily let go of the strange Selkie's waist with relief and kicked up on her own. A moment later they all broke into the air in a large pool surrounded by four men and two women, all armed, all aiming their weapons—odd, streamlined things that looked as if they were made out of obsidian instead of metal, but definitely weapons—at the center of the pool.

Emily found herself looking down a shiny black barrel. "Is that really necessary?" she exclaimed in English.

The man with the gun started so violently she was probably lucky he didn't shoot her by accident. "You speak English?" he said, then clamped his mouth shut even before the woman in the white bathing suit, who had surfaced just beside Emily, said, "Shut up, Herb."

Then she looked at Emily. "I think we have a lot to talk about," she said. "But before we get out of this pool you're going to have to explain *them*." She gestured at Biccum and his companion, both floating in the pool, still blindfolded. "Why are you protecting Holy Warriors?"

"They . . . well, one of them, anyway . . . was kind to me," Emily said. "He may have saved my life. He certainly saved me a lot of agony. I owe him." She paused. "And . . . I've seen enough dead Holy Warriors in my life."

"I haven't," the woman said shortly. "Very well. We'll let them into the Republic. But they're going to be prisoners."

The Republic? Emily thought, but, "Of course," she said.

"And they'll have to stay in their suits," the woman went on, looking at Biccum and Koop. "The station is infected with the plague. We made sure of it."

"No, they won't," Emily said. "They've been vaccinated."

The woman's head snapped around as though she'd been slapped. "What?"

Emily sighed. "You said we had a lot to talk about. That's part of it. Wouldn't it be better to do so somewhere more comfortable . . . and more private?"

Emily's mother swam up beside them. "I agree," she said. "And I can't speak for my daughter, but I'm starving."

Emily smiled at her. "In this case, you *can* speak for your daughter."

The woman looked from Emily to her mother, and her expression softened slightly. "Agreed," she said. "Take the Holy Warriors to the brig," she said to the man she'd called Herb. "Kujawa, you go with him." Another man nodded. "I'm assured they can safely remove their pressure suits, so get them out of those down here. They won't be trying to escape with no way to breathe.

"I'll take these other two to my quarters for questioning. The rest of you . . . get back to work."

Emily swam to the nearest ladder and climbed up onto the edge of the pool. Someone handed her a towel, and as she wiped off the excess water, she glanced around. Gray steel walls, gray steel ceiling, harsh lighting: utterly utilitarian. Whatever the place had been, it certainly hadn't been a luxury hotel.

She sniffed the air: humid, saturated, warm, just the way Selkies liked it. She glanced at Biccum, struggling out of his pressure suit under the watchful eyes and ready guns of Kujawa and Herb. Sweat poured down his face and he looked miserable—but at least he was alive. She caught his eye and gave him a smile; he gave her back a wan one of his own, then was abruptly taken by the arm by Herb and hurried away, Koop in the grip of Kujawa behind him.

"This way," their hostess said. She led them out a different hatch than the one the Holy Warriors had been taken through, and along a corridor every bit as gray and utilitarian as the pool room had been, lined with submarine-style doors. They hadn't gone far, however, before the woman stopped, looked behind them, and said sharply, "Where do you think you're going, Shelby?"

Emily looked back. She hadn't noticed the teenage boy was following them. He'd pulled on a plain white T-shirt over his trunks. She'd thought his short-cropped hair was black when she'd seen it underwater, but now she saw it was actually died a deep cobalt blue. He looked down at the metal floor and pushed at it with one bare toe. "I thought . . . I'd come along. Mom."

Mom? Emily glanced back at the woman. The same sharp chin and prominent cheekbones . . . she could see the resemblance, now that she looked.

"This is Presidential business," the woman said. "I don't need you spreading rumors and exaggerations all over the Republic."

"I won't say a word unless you tell me I can," the boy—Shelby—said. Like every other Selkie, he had big green eyes, and as he raised his head shyly and looked up at his mother through his long eyelashes, he looked so puppylike that Emily laughed. Her mother chuckled, too.

The woman's face softened some more. "All right," she said. "But if you breathe one word to anyone before I've made an official announcement . . ."

"I won't," Shelby said, and he hurried forward to join the group. He looked sideways at Emily but didn't say anything.

Several intersections and three flights of narrow metal stairs later, they reached another submarine door that looked exactly like all the others they had passed. The woman placed her hand over a panel to one side, and with a clank the door unsealed and swung inward.

They stepped through into the first room Emily had seen that wasn't gray. Instead, the walls were a warm, sunny yellow. The furniture looked handmade, from some kind of driftwood stained a deep chocolate brown. Throw rugs softened the black vinyl floor, and pillows were everywhere, most embroidered with sea motifs: fish, whales, coral, and seabirds. Through another door, Emily glimpsed a short hall with more rooms leading off of it.

One corner of the main room was filled by what, despite differences in design from any Emily had ever seen, was recognizably a cookbot. Emily's mouth watered at the sight of it, and she looked at their hostess hopefully, but the woman simply gestured to the couch and chairs. "Have a seat," she said. She looked at Shelby. "You can sit in the corner."

Shelby promptly threw a pillow into the corner by the door, plopped down on it cross-legged, and watched with wide eyes as Emily and her mother seated themselves more sedately on the couch. The woman took one of the chairs.

"First, names," the woman said. "I'm Sarah McLean, and that, as you'll have gathered, is my son Shelby, age sixteen. I won't tell you my age." She smiled briefly, the first smile Emily had seen from her. "I'm the current president of the Free Selkie Republic, which is our rather grandiose name for this large habitat and . . ." She hesitated. "Um, a number of smaller ones." She paused expectantly.

"My name is Emily Wood," Emily said. "And this—"

"I can talk for myself," her mother said. "I'm Dr. Carla Christianson-Wood."

"Emily. Carla," President McLean said. "Then here's the big question." She leaned forward. "Where are you from, and how the hell did you end up in that Holy Warrior shuttle?"

Emily looked at her mother, who looked back silently. Emily sighed. "That," she said, "is a very long story."

President McLean leaned back. "Then I suggest you get started," she said. "Because until I'm convinced you're not a threat to the Free Republic, you're prisoners. And if you are a threat . . ." She left the sentence unfinished.

Emily cleared her throat. "Very well," she said. "First, where we're from." She looked into McLean's eyes, eyes identical to her own, eyes designed by Victor Hansen. "We're from Marseguro."

Shelby gasped. The president's eyes widened. "That's impossible!"

"Then you have heard of it."

"Of course I've heard of it. We were horrified when we heard that the Body had discovered it and sent an expedition to Purify it." She studied Emily and her mother. "I think some history is in order," she said. She looked at her son. "And since you're here, why don't you tell it? Assuming you've been paying attention in history class . . . ?"

Shelby straightened, bright-eyed. "Of course I have!" He cleared his throat. "When Victor Hansen fled the anticipated assault by the Body Purified against Luna aboard his stolen starship *Rivers of Babylon*, not all the Selkies he had created went with him. The initial Selkies gestated in artificial wombs, not in women's bodies, and were born within a few weeks of each other, and thus were all of the same age. But Hansen was only able to get one generation to Luna. The first generation—the original Selkies—were forced to fend for themselves on Earth. In the chaos of Purification, many were killed ... but not all. Some fled into the oceans, and over time, they came together to form the Free Selkie Republic, which has now remained hidden from the Body Purified for seventy years." He stopped his recitation. "How's that?" he asked his mother.

"Succinct," she said. "Thank you."

Emily blinked. "I've never heard any of this!"

"That's because Victor Hansen didn't intend for the Selkies on Marseguro to ever find out about it," her mother said unexpectedly. Emily gave her a startled look, then suddenly realized ...

"You had access to his secret diaries," she said. "You knew about the Earth Selkies!"

Her mother shook her head. "Not exactly. Hansen was convinced they had all been killed even before he left Luna. But he didn't want the Selkies of Marseguro to know they'd ever existed, because he was afraid it would drive the Marseguroites to attempt some sort of rescue, thus exposing themselves to the Body." She nodded at Shelby. "But everything he says ... is true."

"Of course it is!" Shelby said. "I always tell the truth."

His mother cocked an eyebrow at him.

"Well, almost always," he said, and settled back on his cushion.

"The Body never talked about Marseguro again after announcing it would be Purified," the President went on. "I had begun to think it had just been a ploy, part of somebody's political maneuvering in the run-up to the selection of the new Avatar."

"It's very real," Emily said. "It's our home. And, yes, the Body attempted to Purify it. But we defeated them."

"How?" the President said harshly. "I know what Holy Warriors can do—*have* done, to crush dissent all over this planet. How did *you* defeat them?"

Emily looked at her mother, who nodded. Emily turned back to the President. "The plague," she said simply.

"What?" McLean sat up straighter. "The Body said it was a virus that escaped from some old gene engineering lab. When it started, the Body kept talking—well, until there was nobody left to talk—about how it proved once again the dangers of modifying God's Holy Human Genome and how the Holy Warriors would redouble their efforts to bring all rogue genetic engineers and moddies to 'God's implacable attention.'"

"The plague did not originate on Earth," Dr. Christianson-Wood said. Emily looked at her with concern, but her voice, though it wavered a bit, remained strong. "It originated on Marseguro. And it is in no way natural. We created it." She closed her eyes, opened them; gave Emily a long look, then turned to President McLean. "*I* created it."

"No way," Shelby breathed. His mother shot him a look that made his shoulders hunch, then turned her laserlike gaze back to Dr. Christianson-Wood.

"A rather grandiose claim," she said. "You're saying you, personally, designed a virus that is almost one hundred percent fatal in unmodified humans?"

"Yes," Emily's mother said.

"And then you unleashed it on Earth?" McLean's voice gave no indication of how she felt about that, but Dr. Christianson-Wood reacted violently.

"No," she snapped, slamming her hand down on the low table in front of the couch. "I created it as a last-ditch *defense* of *Marseguro*. I created it because I knew—*all* of us knew—that if the Body Purified found us, they would sterilize us, enslave us, slaughter us. It was *only* intended to drive off nonmod invaders and ensure they could never invade again."

"You appear to have overachieved," McLean said levelly.

"But I never wanted this!" Emily's mother's voice broke for the first time. "When I heard . . . it almost drove me mad. I've barely started to climb out of the depression it plunged me into. I never wanted all these deaths on my conscience. All the millions—every one of them—dead because of something I cooked up in my lab, something I nurtured, something I tucked away at night in liquid nitrogen. That virus might as well be my own child."

Emily winced, but said nothing. McLean still sat straight and still, watching Dr. Christianson-Wood. "If you didn't send it deliberately," she said, "then how did it get here?"

"A traitor," Emily said. "A traitor to Marseguro. The same traitor who triggered the interstellar beacon that allowed the Body to find us in the first place. Chris Keating. He managed to get aboard a Body ship and rode it back to Earth. He'd been exposed. He carried it here."

"Why didn't he die?" Shelby asked, his eyes wide. His mother shot him a look, but didn't tell him to be quiet.

"Because he was vaccinated," Emily said.

"Like the Holy Warriors from the shuttle?"

Emily nodded.

"But why vaccinate him?" McLean demanded. "Why vaccinate *them,* if you created this virus to destroy them?"

Emily's temper snapped. "He got vaccinated because the person vaccinating him didn't know what he'd done. The Holy Warriors stole vaccine and vaccinated themselves. And I'm getting sick of this. We're Selkie. You're Selkie. Do you really think we're all part of some elaborate scheme to betray you to the Body?"

"Emily," her mother said, but Emily ignored her.

"The Holy Warriors on that shuttle kidnapped us. They dragged us into space against our will and flew us here with only one landsuit between us. They threatened to gang-rape us, for crying out loud. And they planned to put my mother on trial for genocide.

"Now it sounds like you're planning to do the same. Damn it, we're on your side!"

"How do you know what side that is?" McLean said, and now Emily could hear anger rising through the infuriating icy calm the President had maintained until then. "You—and you—*all of you*—you haven't been here. You've been enjoying your freedom on Marseguro all the years we've been struggling to avoid being found and slaughtered. Every year I've lost people, people who were glimpsed by fishermen or Holy Warriors on patrol, people who killed themselves rather than face interrogation that might have revealed the Free Republic. Two years ago, I had to order the scuttling of an entire outpost. We evacuated a hundred Selkies, but their homes, their belongings, everything they'd worked for their whole lives—gone.

"Every year, we grow fewer. There aren't enough young people, and there aren't enough women." She gestured at the walls around her. "There used to be more than two thousand of us living in this complex. Now most of the smaller habitats are deserted: we only visit them to tend the hydroponics and the vortex power generators and the microfactories. We're down to fewer than a thousand Selkies here, maybe half that many again in all the smaller outposts combined. We're aging and dying out. We've only survived this long because we've been smarter than the Body."

"We've been hiding from the Body, too," Emily pointed out. "We just had a larger hiding place. And when we were found, we fought back . . . just like you would. And we lost hundreds. Maybe thousands." She leaned forward. "We're not your enemies. The Body is."

McLean blinked and looked down. "Old habits of paranoia die hard," she said. She looked up again. "And to answer your question—no. We're not interested in putting you on trial for genocide, Dr. Christianson-Wood. Quite the contrary. If what you've said is the truth, we'd rather honor you as a hero. Because as far as we can tell . . . you've almost killed the Body Purified."

"I'm not a hero," Emily's mother said savagely. "Don't you *dare* call me that. I did what I had to do, but I never intended . . ." Her voice shook. "All those deaths—"

"Landlings," McLean said.

"People," Dr. Christianson-Wood snapped.

"People who would cheerfully kill you on sight."

"Not all of them."

"Enough of them."

"Women. Children."

"Breeders of Holy Warriors. Future Holy Warriors." The two women glared at each other, and Emily, her own anger fading somewhat . . . but only somewhat . . . stepped into the momentary silence.

"I have a question." She thought. "Two, actually."

McLean looked at her, face still tight with anger. "Go ahead."

"First. Earth isn't as much a water planet as Marseguro, but if I remember right, it's three-quarters of the way there. How did our shuttle happen to land almost on top of your 'Free Selkie Republic'?"

"If your shuttle hadn't fallen apart during descent, it *would* have landed on top of us," McLean said. She pointed up. "That artificial island up there is an old commercial spaceport. It's been abandoned since the Day of Salvation; just a dead hunk of metal tethered to the top of a sea mount in the middle of the Pacific Ocean. This," she gestured at the walls around her, "was where the workers lived, safe from typhoons and launch disasters. The first-generation Selkies found and moved into it.

"Because it was a spaceport, we've been able to use its old equipment to hack into System Control. There hasn't been much to see for the past few weeks . . . until just recently. A Holy Warrior starship showed up a few days ago . . . and then, your shuttle.

"When your shuttle got warned away by the starship and automated systems at the various Body outposts, we decided maybe we could use a shuttle . . . and so we activated an old landing beacon to bring you here. But you crashed instead, and . . ." she shrugged. "Here you are."

Emily nodded slowly. "I see," she said. "All right, I buy that."

"Good," said the President. She glanced at her son. "Because I always tell the truth." She looked back at Emily. "Your second question?"

"You said the plague had 'almost' killed the Body. What did you mean by that?"

McLean stood up abruptly. "That, I'll have to show you," she said. "Shelby, stay here."

"Aw . . ." the boy had stood up, but now he sat down again.

"You have homework to do," McLean said. As she led Emily and Dr. Christianson-Wood out, Emily glanced back to see the boy, crestfallen, dragging himself toward the bedrooms.

The President led them down this time, eventually swimming them through water-filled tubes lit by yellow glow-strips, then up into a wet porch. "Main control for the whole complex," she said as they climbed out into the air and toweled off. "We've made it as hard as possible for landlings to get to . . . just in case we're ever boarded."

Emily looked around. The room reminded her of the bridge of the *Victor Hansen*, but on a larger scale. Several Selkies sat at consoles, monitoring . . . what?

"Heating and cooling, fresh water extraction, protein synthesis, swimway oxygenation, the usual things," McLean said when Emily asked. "That's not what I brought you here to see." She paused in front of a particularly large console built into the curving wall. "This is central communications. Hello, Patrick."

The tech at the controls, a skinny young Selkie in a bright-orange landsuit, waved a hand. He had headphones clamped to his ears and was watching a screen that seemed to be displaying fuzzy surveillance video from . . . where? Emily could see pine trees, but it was either foggy where the camera was or it had serious technical difficulties.

"Any change?" the President asked.

Patrick pulled off the headphones. "No," he said, rubbing his nub of an ear. "They seem to have finished loading their boats hours ago. My guess now," he nodded at the screen, "is that they're waiting for the weather to improve."

"Who's they?" Emily asked.

"The Avatar," President McLean said. "And his army."

Emily jerked.

Dr. Christianson-Wood turned pale. "But you said—"

"I said 'almost killed,' " McLean said. "Almost isn't entirely. The Avatar—whoever he is; he could have been a janitor before the plague hit for all I know—has been holed up on an island with several hundred Holy Warriors and other Body survivors.

"We've known about Paradise Island for years. It's a luxury resort for the most important members of the Body hierarchy. We've got an outpost just fifty kilometers south of it, and we do our best to keep a watch on it, without getting close enough to get detected. That's how we knew the Avatar had fled there. But the only reason we've got that—" she pointed at the fuzzy vidscreen, "—is because Patrick here is a genius who managed to hack into a supposedly unhackable undersea data line. This video comes from a hidden camera that used to send video directly to Body Security in the City of God."

"I doubt even the Avatar knows it exists," Patrick said. "We think Cheveldeoff installed it as a way to gather material to blackmail Body officials with. This island saw some wild parties under the old Avatar."

"In any event," McLean said, "a few days ago, something happened. A shuttle came down from the Holy Warrior starship that had just arrived in orbit. It wasn't long before we saw *this*."

Another vidscreen flicked to life above the first. Emily looked up and gasped. Holy Warriors in long lines were moving past men in white coats, who methodically dosed each with a hypospray. "They're being vaccinated!"

"So it appears," McLean said. "Which is one reason I still have one or two doubts about your story." She looked at Emily, her face hard once more. "If they're being vaccinated . . . where did the vaccine come from?"

On the lower of the two vidscreens, Emily suddenly saw movement: a man being half-dragged by two Holy Warriors. Something about the man seemed familiar . . .

Ignoring McLean's question for a moment, Emily said to Patrick, "Can you zoom in on that prisoner?"

"Eh?" Patrick looked at the screen, then glanced at McLean. She frowned, but nodded. Patrick turned back to his controls. "Sure, just hold on a second . . ."

He pushed at a slider. The prisoner seemed to leap toward them, and Emily thought her heart would stop as an enormous surge of both fear and joy swept over her. "We didn't bring the vaccine," she said, her voice sounding distant, barely audible above the sudden roaring in her ears. "He did." She pointed.

"My God," her mother breathed beside her.

McLean looked at the man on the screen. "Who is he?"

"Richard Hansen."

Patrick spun in his chair to look at her; McLean froze for an instant, then turned more slowly. "Hansen? As in . . . ?"

Careful, Emily thought. *We don't want to . . .*

"As in Victor Hansen," her mother said. "Richard Hansen is a clone of our creator. And he brought the vaccine here to try to save as many people as possible."

"A clone of—?" Patrick said, but McLean had already jumped onto the latter half of Dr. Christianson-Wood's statement.

"As many Holy Warriors as possible, you mean."

"People," Dr. Christianson-Wood said sharply. "Just . . . people."

So much for not telling them everything we know, Emily thought. She watched Richard hungrily until he was pulled out of the frame by the guards.

Richard a prisoner. Vaccine going to the Body instead of the general population.

How did everything go so wrong?

"We've got to rescue him," she said.

"*We?*" President McLean gave her a cool look. "You mean *us*."

"Yes," Emily said.

"But you just said *he* brought the vaccine," McLean said. "He gave it to the Body. Now the Avatar and his Holy Warriors will be able to leave that island.

"We know there are other enclaves of survivors around the world. We've heard some of them talking to each other. They're free of the Body right now—that's the one good thing the plague has accomplished. But now that it has the vaccine, the Body will regain power. Survivors will have to submit to it again, or die. And we Selkies . . ." She stepped close to Emily, until their faces were just centimeters apart. "We could have inherited the Earth. Now we'll be forced to stay in hiding. Or else the Body will find us, and kill us." She thrust out one finger at the screen. "Why the hell should I rescue *him*?"

"Because," Emily said, but her throat closed down on whatever she had been about to say.

And what had that been exactly? *Because I love him?* She didn't think that would sway Sarah McLean.

"Because he's *not* one of the Body," Emily's mother said sharply. "He's their enemy. He fought them on Marseguro. He seized control of an entire Body starship, for God's sake. That starship? That's ours now. And he's its captain. He's on our side."

"He's got a funny way of showing it," McLean said. She started to say something; stopped, then finally shrugged.

"However. As it happens, a rescue mission is already underway."

Emily gaped at her. "But you said—"

"Not for him," Sarah said. "He didn't figure in our plans. But he's not alone there. Patrick, show them."

Patrick's fingers flicked across the controls. The top screen's image changed. Now it showed prisoners being hustled across the compound by Holy Warriors. Some were nonmods.

Some were Selkies.

"That's Melody Ashman," Emily said. "And Pierre Normand ... Jerry Krall ... they're all from Marseguro. They must have been aboard the shuttle with Richard."

"We couldn't figure out how there could be Selkie prisoners we didn't recognize," McLean said. "But we knew we had to find out. And we knew we couldn't leave Selkies in the hands of Holy Warriors.

"So we sent a sub from our outpost near the island. At around two AM—" she glanced at a time display on Patrick's console, "—that's about six hours from now—a rescue party will put ashore."

"But they're going after the Selkies," Emily said. "You're not planning to rescue any of the nonmods, are you?"

McLean said nothing.

"You have to—"

"I don't have to do anything," McLean snapped. Then her voice softened. "In any event, I can't. I have no way of communicating with them. They'll report back when they're well clear of the island. If all goes well, that will be early tomorrow morning our time."

She turned. "I'll show you to quarters."

The Marseguroites followed her silently, each lost in her own thoughts.

Chapter 11

IN THE MIDDLE OF the night, Richard woke to gunfire.
He had no idea how long he'd been asleep, but it didn't
feel like very long: he'd tossed and turned for hours after
he'd lain down, unable to brake the endlessly turning wheel
of self-recrimination and worry in his brain.

All of that had been ramped up by what they'd wit-
nessed out the windows of their cabin/prison at dusk: lines
of Holy Warriors marching down to the quay and boarding
the ships that waited there, leaving behind only a skeleton
staff to look after the buildings, and an unknown number of
guards to keep watch on them.

As the ships had sailed away in the gathering night,
Richard had glanced at the others. "They're going to attack
the Kemonomimi," he said.

"Poor bastards," Melody said. "I wish we could warn
them."

Richard said nothing and turned in early.

Now, head still fuzzy from too little sleep, interrupted
too soon, he sat up in bed and listened, wondering if he'd
dreamed—

No, there it was again. The unmistakable crack of Body-
issued firearms. He'd heard the sound too often on
Marseguro—sometimes with his own finger on the trigger—to mistake it for anything else.

But who—?

He got up and pulled on his green Marseguroite navy
uniform, then emerged into the hallway beyond to see the
rest of his crew already gathered there, in various states of
undress. The cabin had four rooms; he had one to himself,
as did Ann Nolan. Melody and Pierre, to his surprise,

though apparently no one else's, were sharing another one. *The captain is always the last to know,* he thought. By necessity, Jerry Krall and Derryl Godard were sharing the remaining room, though Richard didn't get the feeling either one of them much cared for the arrangement.

Melody, a sheet wrapped around her, said, "What's going on?"

"I wish I knew," Richard said. "Everyone get dressed, then come to the common room. Be quick."

They disappeared back into their rooms. He went down the dark hall, not daring to turn on a light, and knelt on the sofa to look out the window.

The hall across the road from the cottage, where he had had coffee with the Avatar, was ablaze, flames leaping high into black billowing smoke. He glimpsed dark figures in front of the fire. Two grappled; one fell, joining at least two other motionless forms he could see on the ground.

Abruptly, the door rattled. Richard leaped off the couch and turned to face it. A pause, then suddenly, with no warning at all, the lock exploded. Something stung Richard's cheek; he touched the spot, and his finger came away red.

The door smashed inward. A black figure stood silhouetted against the flame, a bright white light shining from the side of its head. Richard could see no details, but he could tell the figure held a handgun in one hand and a knife in the other. He held himself still as the light found his face.

The figure gasped, and lowered its weapons. "Creator?"

A woman's voice. "I . . . doubt it," Richard said. "Who are you?"

Her hand went out, fumbled on the wall—and as the lights switched on, it was Richard's turn to gasp.

A Selkie woman stood in the door. The light came from a headset that looked similar, though not identical, to the standard comm headsets of the Holy Warriors. She wore a black skinsuit not that different from those worn on Marseguro. But the thing that astonished him was that he'd never seen her before.

She wasn't from the *Victor Hansen*, and that meant she wasn't from Marseguro.

"Richard, what . . . ?" Melody Ashman led the rest of the group into the room. They were all fully dressed now, the Selkies in the black landsuits they wore during the day, the nonmods in pale-green Marseguroite uniforms like Richard's own. Melody froze so suddenly when she saw the strange Selkie that the others barreled into her from behind with classic slapstick timing. "Who—?"

The strange Selkie tore her eyes off Richard and looked at Melody. "I don't know who you are either," she said cheerfully, "and I sure as hell don't know how that's possible, but some of you are Selkies, and that's good enough for me." She holstered her gun and sheathed her knife with practiced ease, and grinned. "Hi. I'm Lia Wu, and I'll be your rescuer this evening."

"Rescue?" Richard said. "How—?"

"Well, we were planning to swim everyone down to our submarine just offshore, but I see that won't work for all of you. Fortunately, the Holy Warriors made things easy for us by leaving *en masse* earlier this evening, so I think we can safely use boats."

"The guards . . . ?"

"Are no longer a problem," Wu said. She turned her light back on Richard. "Does that concern you?" she said softly.

"No," Richard said. *Just a few more deaths to add to my account.*

"Good. As for the ordinary staff—they're not going to cause us any trouble either. They're all locked up. By the time they break out, we'll be long gone." She touched something on the belt of her landsuit, and spoke to, apparently, thin air. "Are you copying all this?"

She listened, then laughed. "Roger that." She jerked her head toward the door. "Grab anything else you have to take, and let's go."

Richard looked at the others. No one moved. "We're wearing everything that belongs to us," he said.

"Except for the deck of cards in the kitchen," Jerry said.

Richard groaned. "Leave it. I never want to play cards again."

Wu nodded. "Then follow me." She led the way into the smoke-filled air, past two Holy Warrior corpses on the gravel path, and then into the woods, down toward the rocky beach where the Pacific rolled in, the surf still heavier than usual after the recent storm. A nearly full moon gleamed through wisps of ragged, fast-moving clouds, alternately illuminating and casting into shadow the white-capped breakers. As they drew nearer, Richard saw a dark shape on the water: an inflatable boat, one man sitting in its stern, another waiting on shore. They had to get closer still before he could hear the soft thrum of its propulsion unit above the noise of the waves.

"All aboard," said Wu. "I hope none of you are subject to seasickness."

"Can Selkies get seasick?" Richard murmured to Melody, the closest Marseguroite to him.

"Oh, yes," she said. "Yes, they can."

He glanced at her. She gave him a wan smile, teeth and huge Selkie eyes gleaming in a momentary ray of moonlight, then vanishing into darkness again. "You?" he said in surprise.

"Selkies were designed to live underwater, not float around on top of it," she said defensively. "It's not natural!"

Then they were climbing aboard the boat, its rubber bottom heaving in time with the surf. Richard sat down much harder than he intended on one of the semirigid benches that spanned the boat's width.

With everyone aboard, the boat pulled away from the shore, and Richard held on for dear life. He'd mostly gotten over his tendency toward spacesickness, but he hadn't been on a surface boat since that day months ago when he'd joined the Holy Warriors tracking the hunterbot as it chased John Duval—that day that had ended with him floating in a survival suit and being chased by the hunterbot himself.

Of course, in hindsight it had been quite a special day, because it was the day he'd met Emily Wood.

Even if, later, she'd wished she'd let the hunterbot blow him apart.

Memories of Emily, wonderful as they were ... well, memories from the later, less potentially lethal, part of their relationship, anyway ... were apparently not an effective prophylactic against seasickness. Abruptly, he had to scramble for the starboard side of the boat, and threw up into the heaving water.

He heard Melody retching off the port side.

Nobody else seemed to be having any problem with the motion, and they studiously ignored him as he sat up and wiped his mouth and wished he had clean water to rinse it with. He looked back at the island. The flames from the burning hall flickered above the trees, and he wondered if the Avatar were still close enough to see it. If he did, would he bring the Holy Warriors back?

Probably not, Richard thought. *The Avatar would note that everything and everyone he'd left behind had just been burned to a cinder, and praise God for telling him so clearly that he is doing the right thing and mustn't turn back.*

His stomach, to his annoyance, heaved again. He didn't think he had anything left in it.

A moment later he was sure.

At last he spotted a low, dark shape in the water. A few minutes later they were clambering aboard a sub larger than anything on Marseguro. With the others, guided by Lia Wu, he descended a ladder through an open hatch near what he guessed was the bow, though he couldn't see enough detail to be sure, and a moment later stood shivering in the compartment at its base, surrounded by landsuits plugged into recharging hoses. The Marseguroites stood shoulder to shoulder in the cramped space.

"Next stop, the Free Selkie Republic . . . or rather, its nearest outpost," Wu said. "We'll be there in a couple of hours. I'd tell you to make yourselves comfortable, but this isn't a particularly comfortable conveyance. However, we've cleared out the forward cabin—" she indicated one of the two doors, currently dogged shut, that led out of the room, "—and put in two extra cots. As long as you don't mind close quarters . . ."

"As long as it's warm," Richard said. His teeth were chattering; he glanced at Ann, who looked just as miserable, and Derryl, who looked . . . exactly the same as always, stone-faced, unmoved. The Selkies, with their extra layer of subdermal fat, all looked comfortable enough—except Melody, whose pale skin had an unmistakable tinge of green about it.

"It's warm," Wu said. "Steve?"

"Follow me," said one of the men who had crewed the rubber boat. He led them through the forward hatch down a typical submarine corridor, narrow, with storage lockers of some kind on either side, then finally into a chamber that spanned the width of the sub—maybe four meters—crammed tight with six narrow cots, three abreast, two deep, with barely enough room to squeeze among them. No hatches exited the room forward, and the curve of that wall told Richard they were right in the bow.

He picked a bed and flopped down on it. The others quickly sorted themselves into the other bunks. The Selkies left their landsuits on.

Nobody spoke until Steve had left the room. Then they all started at once.

"Can you believe it?"

"More Selkies?"

"Here on Earth?"

"But I thought the Body killed them all."

"Obviously not. They must have been in hiding."

"For seventy years?"

"Just like us."

"Yeah, but we had a whole solar system . . ."

Richard let the conversation and speculation roll over him, but kept his eyes closed, one arm thrown over them. His stomach felt more settled. His brain did not. He had all the same questions as his crew, and no answers.

Wu had said she was taking them to an outpost of the "Free Selkie Republic," whatever that was. Presumably they'd get some answers when they got there.

At least they were out of the Avatar's hands.

But what was happening on board the *Victor Hansen*?

With us free, and the ship back in our hands . . . we might be able to do something to save the Kemonomimi.

Assuming that the Free Selkie Republic has any interest in doing anything of the sort.

What would they think when they found out the Marseguroites had come to Earth to offer a vaccine to the nonmods?

What would they think when they found out that he had handed that vaccine over to the Avatar—and that that decision had led to a plague-proof army of Holy Warriors?

What would they think when they found out that that army was on the march against another race of Victor Hansen-created moddies?

He didn't have any answers to any of those questions.

He suspected he might not like them when he did.

*   *   *

"Damn it!" Andy King glared at Simon Goodfellow. "You *promised* me you could do this."

"I said I *thought* I could." Goodfellow looked even paler than usual, and his hair hung across his balding head in greasy strings. He'd hardly left his console in the simulator room for days. *He certainly hasn't showered*, Andy thought, wrinkling his nose.

"You said," Andy said, "that you had successfully made a copy of the AI's kernel. You said, once you wiped the AI, you could reboot it, and then enter our names as the properly assigned crew. That's what you said."

"I said I *thought* I had successfully copied the AI's kernel. I said I *thought* I could reboot it. I never promised." Goodfellow blinked at Andy. "If I'd been *certain* I could do it, we would have done it on Marseguro and made sure the Body could never take control of the ship. But we didn't do it, because the risk was too great."

Andy clamped down on his temper. "So now you're saying you *can't* do it?"

"No," Goodfellow said. "I still think I can do it. But it may take longer than I'd thought. It's not just a matter of plugging in the datasphere and dumping its contents into the kernel. There are physical defenses that have to be dismantled, shunts to be installed, careful testing to be done before we even make the attempt."

"In case you haven't figured it out," Andy said, "we're in a hurry. We don't know what the Body will do next. If they can get control of another ship, or a ground-based space defense system . . ."

"And if I make the attempt and it fails," Goodfellow said, "we won't get another one. The computer will be permanently dead, incapable of being revived. The ship will need a whole new AI. And I don't happen to have one in my pocket. Do you?"

Andy took a deep breath and looked away. They were in the simulator room where they had fought off the Holy Warriors, but Goodfellow had a lot more equipment spread around the data conduit than he had before. "If I ever design a spaceship," Andy growled, "I'm going to make damn sure you can control everything on it manually if you need to."

"Fine," Goodfellow said. "But in the meantime, we're

stuck with *this* one. And the longer you harass me, the longer it will take me to get everything lined up for our one and only chance to take control of it again."

Andy closed his eyes. "Fine," he said in resignation. "Keep me posted."

"Of course," said Goodfellow, and turned back to his terminal, effectively dismissing the First Officer.

I thought I *was in command here?* Andy thought as he walked back to the shaft leading down into the now re-sealed and repressurized spaces where they had hidden during the Holy Warrior occupation.

He snorted. *Yeah, right.*

The motley fleet of vessels carrying the Avatar's remnant of Holy Warriors reached the mainland at first light. Karl Rasmusson stood on the bridge of what had once been the cruise ship *Ocean Breeze* and was now redesignated *Fist of God*, watching through binoculars as the first Holy Warriors began unloading materiel onto the pier of Blackstone, the deserted town that had once served primarily as the embarkation point for ferries to Paradise Island. The ships would have to take turns unloading, the pier wasn't big enough for more than two or three to dock at a time.

"Your Holiness," said a voice from close beside his elbow. He lowered the binoculars and turned to his Right Hand, Ilias Atnikov. "If you could come to the bridge . . . there's a message from the island."

"Not good news, I suspect from your tone of voice," the Avatar said. "Lead the way."

He refused to speculate on the message's content. Instead, as he climbed the narrow metal stairs to the bridge, he took a moment to appreciate the irony of a ship like the *Ocean Breeze*, intended only to transport Body functionaries and their families on pleasant sightseeing cruises along rocky, forested shores to see calving glaciers, suddenly transformed into *Fist of God*, the flagship of the Body navy, a task it was monumentally unqualified for.

He suspected more than a few of the surviving Body members saw him in similar terms. As Right Hand, he'd been almost invisible, apparently little more than a glorified secretary. The higher-placed members of the Body hierarchy, like the late Samuel Cheveldeoff, knew who *really*

controlled things as Harold the Second sank further and
further into hedonistic somnolence, but the rank and file
did not. For Karl Rasmusson, of all people, to emerge as the
Avatar after the catastrophe of the plague must have
shocked them—and brought home just how great the disaster that had befallen the world was.

Karl's own moments of doubt were now past. God Itself
had proved to his satisfaction that It had complete confidence in him, and that gave him complete confidence in
himself. He could only hope that his actions would assuage
the doubters. Failing that, he could only hope that their
own faith would see them clear to giving him unqualified
support.

Because failing *that,* he would have no choice but to follow the Purification of the Kemonomimi with a cleansing
of his own ranks, and they were thin enough he would prefer not to have to thin them further.

It's a test of faith for all of us, the Avatar thought. *God
rewards those who pass Its tests ... and terribly punishes
those who fail.*

"Here you are, Your Holiness," Atnikov said.

The Avatar looked at the only lit screen on the board,
and recognized the face of John Duncan, chief administrator of the former resort. "Your Holiness!" he blurted the
moment he saw the Avatar. "We've been attacked. All the
Holy Warriors are dead, and two of my staff. They burned
the mess hall. We were locked up, we just escaped—"

"Slow down," the Avatar said sharply. "When did this
happen?"

"This morning, early, maybe two AM," Duncan said. "We
were asleep, then we heard shots, and the next thing we
knew they were hauling us—"

"And who are *they*?" the Avatar said. There were plenty
of "revolutionary" groups that had promised over the years
to bring the Body to its knees, but any such group must
have suffered from the plague as much as the Body had.
That left—

Duncan confirmed his suspicion. "Selkies, Your Holiness."

Selkies! Crew from *MSS Victor Hansen.* They'd fled the
takeover of their ship ... at least some of them must have
managed to guide their escape pods somewhere close to

Paradise Island, so they could try to rescue Richard Hansen. "The prisoners?"

"All freed," Duncan said. He pressed his lips together nervously, then blurted, "Will you be returning, Your Holiness? We're defenseless now. We need—"

"They got what they wanted," the Avatar said. "They won't attack again. No, I won't be returning. Bury the dead and repair the damage. Report in if anything else happens . . . but I don't think it will." He paused, remembering something Duncan had said. "My condolences on the loss of your staff members. Did they have family?"

"Not since the plague," Duncan said. He blinked hard a couple of times. "None of us have family anymore."

"Things will get better," the Avatar said. "Tell your staff that. When we have finally finished the Purification of Earth, under God's renewed protection, things *will* get better."

"Yes, Your Holiness," John Duncan said, but he didn't meet the Avatar's eyes.

Don't you believe me? Karl wanted to snarl at him. *Don't you believe* God?

But it would have accomplished nothing. "Avatar out," he said instead, and touched the control to manually end the transmission.

He looked out the big glass windshield at the handful of buildings that made up Blackstone, only slightly dimmed by mist this morning. "Ready a boat for me," he told Atnikov.

"Yes, Your Holiness." Atnikov crossed the bridge to confer with the captain. Karl kept his gaze on the shore.

No looking back, he thought. *If Hansen is free, it's because God wanted it that way. Maybe he still has some part to play in God's plan that I can't see yet. All I can do is carry out* my *part.*

The Kemonomimi were ten days away on foot. In ten days, the Earth would at last be free of Victor Hansen's foul legacy, truly Purified at last, ready to receive God's blessing.

Ten days.

Karl Rasmusson smiled. *No time at all, really.*

Chapter 12

THE KEMONOMIMI treated Chris well enough, except perhaps for the tiny Kemonomimi woman who came in twice a day with a syringe and took a sample of his blood. She wouldn't tell him why.

In fact, nobody would tell him anything.

For days they held him in a small suite in what had been a small hotel. Meals appeared at regular intervals in the discreet room-service dumbwaiter, hidden behind a rather ugly red-and-brown abstract painting: the first time the elevator beeped to announce there was a tray inside it, it took him fifteen minutes to figure out where the noise—and the maddeningly delicious smells—came from.

The suite boasted an entertainment unit well-stocked with vids and feelies and games and texts, and Chris made good use of it, but after the first couple of days, he began to feel pangs of stir-craziness. After a week, he dreaded waking up to face another day in his comfortable prison . . . and found himself looking forward to the visits by the taciturn blood drawer.

At least the windows gave him a clear view of the airstrip. Aircraft continued to come and go. Kemonomimi moved hither and yon, often unloading bundles from aircraft and hustling them into one of the storage buildings alongside the runway.

And then, without any warning at all, Victor Hansen summoned him again.

The sun was actually shining that day, and Chris blinked in its bright light as Napoleon and Alexander, his guards from a few days before, led him along the sidewalk between landscaped flower beds, now gone to seed, to Hansen's appropriated office.

The first thing Chris noticed, after Napoleon and Alexander ushered him in and closed the door on him, was that the photograph of the previous owner's family had vanished. So had every other personal knickknack. Now the office was as impersonal as Chris' hotel room, although with better art.

The second thing he noticed was that Hansen wasn't alone. One of the chairs had been pulled into the corner, and sitting cross-legged on it was a Kemonomimi woman with fur as white as fresh-fallen snow over all of her body except her hands and feet, which were pitch-black. She looked like she was wearing gloves and boots, when in fact she wasn't wearing anything at all—and the fur didn't entirely cover what clothes would have. Chris tried not to stare at her. She had no such compunction about staring at him. Her eyes, amber yellow, narrowed as she looked at him.

Hansen stood with his back to Chris, hands folded behind him, looking out the window at the sunlit runway. An aircraft taxied along it, the sun glinting off its clean white flanks.

"Keating," Hansen said without preamble. "I have a question for you."

Chris looked at the clone's back warily, then glanced at the woman. Her eyes narrowed further, and he quickly looked away again. "I'll . . . answer it if I can," he said.

"Yes," Hansen said. "You will." He turned. "Do you serve God?"

Chris blinked, sensing a minefield. "I . . . guess," he said. "I've never thought about it very much."

Hansen snorted. "A prudent answer. A politician's answer. You're afraid if you say yes, I'll have you killed as someone too loyal to the Body to keep around.

"But you're wrong." Hansen spread his hands. "I, too, serve God. I always have. Though perhaps not the God you know.

"The Body Purified has done its best to stamp out not only all genetically modified life, but much of humanity's religious heritage. What do you know about Christianity, boy? Or Islam? Judaism? Buddhism?"

"Nothing," Chris said, which was almost true. There were Christians on Marseguro, a few Buddhists, a vanishingly small number of Jews, no Muslims that he was aware of, a smattering of other religions. Chris had never paid much attention to any of them. Having grown up in a family that secretly adhered to the Body, he knew that all other religions were both false and abhorrent, targets for God's wrath. The fact they existed among the nonmods who had accompanied the original Victor Hansen—unwillingly, in his parents' case—to Marseguro was only one more sign that the planet needed Purifying.

A few Selkies had taken up some of the nonmods' religions—Buddhism was particularly popular—but the closest most Selkies came to religion was venerating Victor Hansen. He very carefully didn't look at the woman. He suspected the Kemonomimi were the same, only their "god" still lived among them.

The real Victor Hansen, according to the history books, had tried very hard to stop his Selkies from treating him like a god. This Victor Hansen, Chris suspected, had no problem with it at all.

"I don't follow any religion," Hansen said abruptly. "Yet I serve God—at least, God as I conceive It—in my own way.

"Christianity and Judaism have in their holy book a mythological account of the creation of the world. In it, God creates various aspects of the world—day and night, sea and dry land, sun, moon and stars, green plants, etc.— over seven days. On the penultimate day, He—they saw God as a male—created the first man. On the seventh day, He rested. The book notes that God created man in 'His' image.

"To the ancients, that may have meant that God looked like a man. But I see it differently. As I see it, God created us in Its *spiritual* image, not its physical one, for, of course, It *has* no physical image. And at the core of God's spiritual nature is Its creativity. Why did it create the universe? Because It could. Because creating things gives It joy.

"If we are indeed created in God's image, than creativity must also be at the heart of our spiritual nature." Hansen walked over to the woman and sat on the arm of her chair, putting his arm around her shoulder. She bumped her head against his side and spread her lips in an alarmingly sharp-toothed grin. "And so, in obedience to God's will, I, too, create. And of all the humans that have lived on this Earth, I have come closer to God than any other, because I have created a new race of humans. This, by the way, is Cleopatra." He caressed the woman's furred cheek, and she took his hand and kissed it.

The sight sickened Chris. Maybe that was why he said, "*Two* races," then instantly wished he hadn't.

Hansen gave him a hard look. "Two races," he said. "But then, since I am *not* God, I sometimes make mistakes." He kissed Cleopatra on the forehead, then stood and came over to the desk to face Chris once more. "So," he said. "I serve God. Do you?"

"That's what I've tried to do," Chris said, still hedging.

"But you say you were imprisoned by the Body for daring to suggest that life, God-created life, could be improved upon."

Chris tried to remember the cover story he'd made up on the spur of the moment days earlier. "Um, yeah, that's right."

"Were you imprisoned justly?"

Think fast. "No. I don't think so. It's ... well, I've never thought of it quite the way you've put it, but I guess that's the way I feel. God made us creative and gave us the tools to modify life. Why shouldn't we use them?"

Because using them brought God's wrath down on us! he thought, but didn't say. God frowned on dishonesty, but It didn't actually forbid it—not in a good cause. Which keeping Chris Keating alive certainly was, at least as far as Chris was concerned. And since he was the only properly God-fearing loyal member of the Body Purified within the Kemonomimi camp, staying alive *had* to be a service to God.

"Good." Hansen sat down behind the desk. "The Avatar plans to attack us."

Chris' heart jumped. "How do you know?"

"Reconnaissance drones. The Avatar left Paradise Island with most of his remaining Holy Warriors last night. Today they are landing at Blackrock—"

"Stone," said Cleopatra. She had the same lisping accent as the other Kemonomimi he had heard speak.

Hansen looked at her, obviously irritated. "What?"

"Blackstone, not Blackrock." She smiled. "You made a mistake."

"I . . ." Hansen pressed his lips together. "Oh. Very funny." He turned briskly back to Chris. "They are landing, as I said, at Black*stone*, the nearest town on the coast."

"But . . . the plague . . ."

"Either they've decided it's burned itself out or they've been able to produce enough of the experimental vaccine that saved your life to inoculate their troops," Hansen said.

Which would have made perfect sense, except, of course, Chris had entirely fabricated said vaccine. "Where are they headed?"

"Here, of course," Hansen said. "To Purify us. You grew up in the Body. You know how the Avatar thinks. He sees the plague as a punishment from God for allowing moddies like the Kemonomimi to survive." He smiled. "It's funny, really. It has been my plan for a very long time to eventually mount an attack on Paradise Island. The old Avatar visited it regularly—so regularly that we could have been assured of killing him and most of the highest members of the hierarchy. When my plague hit, and I realized the Body still clung to Paradise Island like barnacles on a rotting boat, the attack made even more sense. And rather than hide out like pirates in a cold, wet camp somewhere along the shore, we were able to make use of this no-longer-occupied town . . . and its idle aircraft. With the ability to move freely at last, with no fear of Body detection, I sent a team to the Holy City to pick up a . . . vital component which I had arranged for but had not yet been able to smuggle out. They brought it back—and you along with it.

"But now we don't have to attack Paradise Island. The Avatar has left it and is coming straight to us."

"So . . . where will you run to?" Chris said.

Cleopatra laughed. It didn't sound entirely human to Chris; there was a hint of a feline yowl to it that made the hair stand up on the back of his neck.

Hansen chuckled, too. "Run? We're not running anywhere." He leaned back in his chair. "We're going to sit right here. And when the Avatar gets a bit closer, we're going to kill him and all the Holy Warriors with him . . . just like we planned from the beginning."

He pointed at Chris. "And you're going to help us."

* * *

The quarters President McLean showed Emily and her mother to were pleasant enough, though depressingly military in appearance: gray walls, gray floor. "Most of the Selkie quarters have their own air locks for slipping outside," McLean said. "I'm afraid these quarters do not. If you would like to swim, the deck below is flooded."

"Still don't trust us?" Emily said.

"I don't trust anyone." McLean left, closing the door behind her. It sealed with a hiss.

"Nice," Emily muttered.

"Don't be too hard on her." Emily's mother dropped onto the dark-blue couch. The rest of the furniture consisted of a small round table and two chairs in the corner, by a door Emily presumed led to the bedrooms . . . and, she hoped, a bathroom. "She's responsible for keeping her people safe. She does what she has to."

Emily sat beside her. "You sound tired."

Dr. Christianson-Wood laughed. "Really? I can't imagine why." She leaned her head back and closed her eyes.

"How are you . . . feeling . . . otherwise?" Emily said cautiously.

"You mean am I going to go catatonic on you again?" Dr. Christianson-Wood asked without opening her eyes.

"Well, um . . . yeah."

Now Emily's mother did open her eyes. "No," she said quietly. "I don't think so. Whatever that was, it's past. Though, in some ways, I wish I could go back there."

"Mom!"

"I didn't have to think," her mother said. "No thoughts, or very few. Just a blank grayness. I didn't have to . . . deal. With the consequences of my actions." She closed her eyes again—squeezed them tightly. "God, Emily. All the people who died here . . ."

"Not your fault. We've been through this."

"Intellectually, I know that's right," her mother said. "And someday that knowledge may help me feel better. But right now . . ." She shook her head. "What I think and what I feel are two different things."

"Richard's here," Emily said. "That means the vaccine is here, too. There'll be survivors. *Many* survivors. Without the amplifying effect of Marseguroite life-forms, they can ward it off with strict quarantine. Right? Just like any other infectious disease."

"But for how long?" Emily's mother said. "And if the Body has Richard, *they* must have the vaccine. They'll give it to Holy Warriors first. They'll use it to reestablish the Body's control. Marseguro may be safe for a generation, but eventually the Holy Warriors will come again." Her voice fell to a whisper. "I haven't even saved Marseguro. I've just delayed the inevitable."

"A generation is a long time," Emily said. "Things can change. Here, and on Marseguro. A new war isn't inevitable."

"I'm beginning to think war is always inevitable."

Emily took that disquieting thought to bed with her—the hallway did indeed lead to bedrooms, two of them, and a small but functional bathroom.

She lay in the darkness of the tiny bedroom, alleviated only by the glow of a clock on a table by the bed, and stared up at the ceiling.

Was her mother right? Was war inevitable? Was violence built into the human genome? *The "Holy Human Genome,"* she thought bitterly.

Once she wouldn't have thought so. She'd thought Marseguro was as close to utopia as humans had ever come. Nonmods, Selkies, different people, different opinions, different religions, even, all living together, arguing sometimes, sure, but never resorting to violence.

But then . . . Chris Keating had shattered it all and brought violence down upon them. And once Marseguro had been attacked, Emily and her mother had both discovered that they, too, could use violence in the service of a cause: self-defense, perhaps, but the people they killed were dead just the same.

Why didn't Victor Hansen remove our capacity for violence, while he was at it? she thought.

· But she answered her own question. *If he had, we'd all be dead or imprisoned now.* The Body would have seized Marseguro and slaughtered, enslaved, and sterilized the Selkies without resistance.

Humans, she thought bitterly. *We're just a thin layer of civilization painted onto the grinning skull of millions of years of bloody battles.*

She wasn't sure how the religionists explained it. If God had created everything, why did murder lurk in every human heart?

She supposed they'd blame sin, tell her that humans had once been perfect and peaceful, but had chosen to follow the path of death and violence.

And yet, they could not have followed that path if the capacity for it didn't lurk within them from the beginning; hadn't been placed there, in fact, by God.

If humans really were created in God's image, as she'd heard the Christians say, then maybe the God of the Body Purified *was* the true one: a God whose own capacity for capricious violence when disappointed by Its creations was perfectly mirrored in those creations' own ability to hurt and kill.

When she finally did drift off to sleep, Emily's dreams were full of blood.

She woke to knocking. It took her a few minutes to figure out where she was, and then she stumbled to her feet and pulled on the robe she had found in the closet of her room. She half-staggered through the darkened apartment, banging her shin painfully on the coffee table, and opened the door.

Shelby stood there, wearing only skimpy blue trunks. His skin glistened with water; he'd obviously made his way to them through one of the flooded decks. "We've heard from the sub," he said. "They rescued *all* of the prisoners — Selkies and nonmods alike."

Emily's heart skipped a beat.

"They'll be at the outpost near Paradise Island in a couple of hours," Shelby went on. "And Mom . . . um, President McLean . . . wants me to take you to main control as soon as you can get ready."

"What's going on?" her mother said from behind her. Emily turned and gave her a huge hug.

"They got them all," she said in a choked voice. "*All* of them. They're safe."

"Thank God," her mother said, hugging her back.

Emily said nothing, but her dark thoughts of the middle of the night came back to her.

God, she thought sourly, *had nothing to do with it.*

As far as she could tell, It didn't really believe in happy endings.

*   *   *

Lia Wu woke the *Sawyer's Point* crew with a cheery, "Good morning!"

Richard opened his eyes. *Where? . . . Oh!* Remembering, he sat up and turned to look at Wu, standing in the aft door. "Um, good morning."

"I hope you're all well-rested after your . . . oh, about two-hour . . . night," Wu said. "We're almost to the outpost. I'm afraid I can't offer you breakfast, but you'll be able to eat once we've disembarked. Which we need to prepare for. The Selkies can swim, but the rest of you will need water-breather gear, unless you can hold your breath for, say, fifteen minutes?" She looked at him expectantly.

"Um . . . no," Richard said. "I might manage three or four."

"Is that all?" Wu looked intrigued. "Interesting."

These Selkies don't interact with nonmods, Richard thought. *We're as exotic to them as . . . well, as Selkies were to me.*

"Well, the Free Republic has some old suits: original equipment, I think. We'll have them swum across. As far as we know, they still work."

As far as we know . . . ?

Wu crouched beside his bunk as the others begin to stir and stretch. "There's something else," she said in a low voice. "Apparently there are a couple of friends of yours at the main complex."

"Friends?" Richard blinked. "You mean others from the *Victor Hansen*?"

"I don't know," Wu said. "They just said to tell you that Emily and her mother are waiting to talk to you."

Richard felt like he'd been punched in the gut. He stared at Wu, stunned.

"I take it you're surprised," Wu said wryly.

Richard found his voice. "That's . . . impossible. Utterly impossible. We left them on Marseguro!"

Wu shrugged. "I'm just telling you what I was told." She stood up. "We'll be tethering in about half an hour. I'll see if I can round up some swimwear." She went out.

"I can't tell you how glad I'll be to get out of this landsuit and go for a proper swim," Melody said. She sat on the bunk across from Richard, looking at him. "Did she just say what I thought she said?"

Richard spread his hands helplessly. "I don't see how it's possible, but it must be true. How else would they know Emily's name?"

"But we have . . . had . . . Marseguro's only starship. They *can't* be here."

"I know."

No one could offer even a far-fetched explanation. If the Body had returned to Marseguro and somehow captured Emily, she certainly wouldn't now be in the company of the Earth Selkies the Body didn't even know existed. But the Earth Selkies couldn't possibly have gone and fetched her: they had no access to spacecraft and couldn't possibly know Marseguro's location anyway.

I guess I'll have to ask Emily in person, Richard thought, and felt almost giddy at the thought.

Wu returned with swimwear for everyone, and the sexes demurely turned their backs to each other while they stripped and put on the simple white suits. After a few minutes Wu came back and took away the nonmods' uniforms and the Selkies' landsuits. She held one up and looked at it closely. "Interesting design," she said. "Better than what we've come up with. It's hard to cobble together new technology when you're having to obtain all your supplies surreptitiously. We do have a couple of microfactories, but the feed stocks . . ."

Richard stiffened. "You have microfactories?"

"Yes," Wu said. "Three at the main complex, one in each outpost. Older models—pre-Day of Salvation, in fact—but the nanofabricator juice is still viable and of course they're self-repairing—"

Richard looked at Ann Nolan. "Older models," he said. "Like ours."

She grinned. "I'm way ahead of you. We'll have to download the software from *Victor Hansen*, but if we can program new modules . . ."

"What?" Wu said, looking from one to the other.

"Not now," Richard said. "But I think we may be able to make good use of those microfactories, if you'll let us."

"That'll be for the President and Council to decide," Wu said. "Way above *my* level of responsibility."

A bell clanged twice, then twice again. The vibration of the engines changed pitch, then died away altogether.

"We've stopped," Wu said unnecessarily. "Time to go."

She led them back to the landsuit-packed room through which they had first entered the sub, but carried on past it and down a flight of spiral stairs to a lower deck. From there they went aft, into a room where water lapped at the sides of an open floor hatch about a meter and a half in diameter. A couple of large Selkie men stood beside it, both with strangely rounded, shiny black riflelike weapons slung over their backs: something that could be used underwater, Richard guessed from the look of them. A third Selkie, likewise armed, stood back a little way. The Free Selkie Republic obviously wasn't taking any chances. "They'll escort the Selkies over first," Wu said. "Then they'll bring back the waterbreathers for you landlings." She nodded to the Earth Selkies. "Whenever you're ready."

"Aye, aye, ma'am," said one, and jumped into the pool. The other guided in the Selkies from Richard's crew: Jerry Krall, Pierre Normand, and finally Melody Ashman. Once they'd all entered the water, the second Earth Selkie jumped in, too.

Richard, Ann, and Derryl sat and waited in silence, while Wu spoke in a voice too low for them to hear with the remaining armed guard.

Maybe twenty minutes after they'd disappeared, the two Selkie men returned. They climbed out, then hauled up a huge mesh bag that they dumped on the deck at their feet.

Wu came over. "Let's see . . . anybody know how these things work?"

"Let me," said Ann. "They look a lot like what we used to use on Marseguro years ago." She started pulling things out of the bag. "Here we go. Slip into this backpack. Pull this hood up over your head . . ." She demonstrated as she talked. "Pull down the goggles, bite down on the mouthpiece . . . mmph mere moo mo!" She spat out the mouthpiece. "I mean, and there you go!" She looked at Wu. "What depth are we at?"

"Ten meters."

"Shouldn't have to worry about decompression, then," Ann said. She began handing out the waterbreathers.

The backpack had two straps that went across chest and stomach; the top strap had a small glowing readout on it. Ann twisted it up and took a look. "Not fully charged, but good for half an hour. We won't need it that long. The pack will expel or suck in water as necessary to ensure you keep neutral buoyancy."

"Great," Richard said. He pulled on his own rig, with a little help from Ann (Derryl, not surprisingly, needed no help), stuck in the mouthpiece, and took an experimental breath. The air tasted like sweaty socks, but it was breathable. He pulled on the goggles and gave Wu a thumbs-up.

"Off you go, then," she said.

As before, one Selkie jumped in ahead of them, the other guided them through the hatch. Richard jumped and sank through a welter of bubbles. For a moment he thought he would keep on sinking, but as promised, the backpack vibrated, jetting out ballast, and in a moment he stabilized.

He looked around. It had to be daylight up above, because a deep green light suffused everything, fading to blue in the distance. The sub was a long black cigar shape looming overhead. And the outpost of the Free Selkie Republic . . .

A cylindrical habitat, maybe fifty meters in length and half that in diameter. He couldn't see much detail, but as he followed the "come-along" gesture of their Selkie leader and swam toward the structure, writing on its side came into focus. "Commonwealth of American States Pacific Ocean Administration," it said.

The words gave him a shiver. The Commonwealth of American States had been the last secular government for this part of the world before the Day of Salvation and the rise of the Body. This thing must be almost a century old.

A time before the Body, he thought. *When will we see a time* after *the Body?*

They entered through a water lock, swimming up into a water porch. Richard climbed onto the deck, unbuckled the backpack, and pulled off the goggles. Within a few minutes Derryl, Ann and Wu joined him. Their Selkie guard took their waterbreathers, then Wu led them down the habitat's long central corridor to a control room at its centre and up a spiral stair. Vidscreens and blinking lights lined the walls of the circular room, the only other light coming through the clear dome overhead. Four Selkies were stationed around the room, watching consoles or listening on headphones.

But Richard hardly saw any of that. The moment his head rose above the surface of the control room floor, his eyes were drawn like magnets to the largest of the vidscreens, and the face of the young Selkie female who filled it. That face split into a delighted grin as he came within range of the video pickup, and Richard felt something hard and frozen deep inside him dissolve into warmth as he saw it.

"Emily!"

Chapter 13

IT TOOK THE HOLY WARRIORS most of the day to unload and divvy up equipment. They had six all-terrain cargobots, twenty-seven packhorses (part of the recreational complement of Paradise Island)—and lots of strong backs.

"We can't surprise them," Grand Deacon von Eschen had told him back on the island. "They have aircraft. Possibly reconnaissance drones. They'll almost certainly see us coming."

"Let them," the Avatar said.

"What if they flee inland?"

"Let them," the Avatar said again. "We'll track them down. They've come out into the open. They can't disappear again. And I don't think they'll even try."

The Grand Deacon frowned. "I don't follow."

"They believe the Body is finished," the Avatar explained. "Why else show themselves? And when they look at our forces, they won't see what *I* see—a dagger, small but deadly, hand-forged and honed by God Itself to Purify the Earth. They will see only a tiny, lightly-armed, ragtag army. They will believe they can defeat it."

"But they're outnumbered, even so. You can't be sure—"

"I'm sure," the Avatar had said. "God has made me sure."

The Grand Deacon, of course, had no answer to that.

And sure enough, as the day waned and the Holy Warriors made camp, preparatory to starting the march on the Kemonomimi the following day, Karl, standing outside his tent, heard, faintly but unmistakably, the droning buzz of an aircraft engine. He looked up and saw it, a tiny silver speck, still catching the rays of the sun that had just slipped behind the ocean horizon.

Grand Deacon von Eschen came to stand beside him. "The Kemonomimi know we've left the island," he said softly.

"And so God's plan continues to unfold," the Avatar responded. Von Eschen said nothing, but after staring up at the aircraft another long moment, he went back to his own tent.

Karl watched the aircraft until it was out of sight. He knew the Grand Deacon had his doubts that the Kemonomimi would do what the Avatar predicted, but Karl felt only calm certainty.

Once I had doubts, he thought. He could remember those days, those dark days when the Avatar had been a shambling, drunken, drugged-out wreck, concerned only with the next dissolute party, the next night's bed partners. Karl Rasmusson had kept the Body going, making decisions for the Avatar and in the Avatar's name, but as he'd watched the Avatar destroy himself, he'd begun to doubt God.

How could such an animal be the Avatar of God? How could he believe in a God that would set such a thing up as Its representative on Earth? How could God Itself actually *live* inside that . . . thing?

But now Karl understood. The previous Avatar had been part of God's plan to humble the Body, to humble Earth, to remind them both God was in charge.

More: the travesty that had been Harold the Second had helped to shape Karl Rasmusson into the perfect tool for God to seize when he needed a new Avatar, a strong Avatar, one who would understand what needed to be done . . . and be willing to do it.

And so he watched, with perfect equanimity, the Kemonomimi aircraft disappear into the gathering dusk. Whatever the Kemonomimi did or did not do, God would deliver them into Karl Rasmusson's hands.

He knew it, as surely as he had ever known anything.

Chris Keating sat very still after Victor Hansen's extraordinary announcement. *He's bought it,* he thought. *He thinks I'm on his side. This could be my chance . . . my chance to finally, finally prove to the Avatar himself that I am loyal to God and to the Body, to finally earn the rewards I've worked so hard for since I first activated the distress beacon on Marseguro.*

My big chance. As long as I don't blow it.

"I'll do whatever I can," he said carefully. "But I don't see what use I can be to you."

"Really? Take a good look at yourself."

Chris looked down. They'd found some clothes his size somewhere in the town, so he wore new black pants and a soft plaid shirt. Brown hiking boots. Otherwise, he was as thin as always, no taller than ever, completely unimpressive—and he knew it.

He looked up. "I don't get it."

Victor Hansen laughed. So did Cleopatra. "You're alive," she said. "You're immune to the plague. That makes you, if not unique, extremely rare."

Hansen glanced at her, and Chris thought he saw annoyance on his face. But his expression smoothed as he turned back to Chris. "Cleo is exactly right. Your obvious immunity will make you of great interest to the Avatar. If you approach his forces, he'll certainly have you brought to him for questioning."

"And what do I tell him?" Chris said.

"The truth. Well . . . up to a point. That you received the experimental vaccine, that a guard released you. But then you have to convince him that you saw the error of your ways and want to return to the fold, that once you were captured by those hideous abominations, the Kemono-mimi—"

Chris glanced up at Cleo. She raised her eyebrows and he looked away again.

"—you realized the wisdom of the Body's prohibition against genetic modification. Tell him you escaped and came to warn him.

"And then you tell him that you know our plans: that we are going to flee inland before he reaches the town, and that you know a place where he can take us by surprise." Hansen reached down and opened the middle drawer of the desk; he took out a map and slid it across the desk to Chris. "Here."

Chris looked at it. He wasn't very good at reading maps:

there'd been little need of them on Marseguro, where a plain blue sheet of paper would have been a perfectly accurate map of most of the planet's surface. "What's special about it?"

"It's a narrow valley, a pass through the coastal range from the inland valley they'll have to follow to get here. And it's where we'll have a surprise waiting for the Avatar."

"An ambush?"

"Not exactly," Hansen said. "A bomb. A very special bomb. A bomb that will destroy the Avatar and all his forces."

"Nuclear?"

"Close enough," Hansen said. "Matter-antimatter, actually."

Chris blinked. "Where did you get *that?*"

"The Holy City, of course," Hansen said. "It was supposed to be smuggled to us by a . . . friend. I'm afraid he fell to the plague before arrangements could be made. Fortunately, with the Body essentially out of the way, the team that also discovered you was able to retrieve it from its hiding place."

"A friend?"

Hansen sighed. "Mr. Keating, the Body has many enemies. The Body has also had firm control of all channels of communication, however, so the actions those enemies have taken have been little known among the general population . . . except locally, among those members of the general population injured or killed when bombs go off or water supplies are poisoned."

Chris had never dreamed . . . "Terrorists have attacked the Body?"

"Repeatedly, if not very effectively," Hansen said.

"The Kemonomimi?"

"No. The trouble with . . . I prefer the term 'direct action' to 'terrorism,' by the way . . . is that the Body is very good at rooting out and destroying groups that take that route. This has limited the number of attacks over the years, but certainly hasn't stopped them entirely. And it has made it clear to me that if one is going to strike, one must make that strike decisive. Hence our original plan: to decapitate the Body by destroying Paradise Island while the Avatar and many of his top officials were vacationing on it. To do that, we needed a special weapon. Which the Holy Warriors themselves were kind enough to invent for us."

"But how did this . . . friend . . . of yours get his hands on it?"

"He was one of the scientists who invented it," Hansen said. "He was also, fortunately, highly susceptible to bribery and blackmail." He shrugged. "And now he's dead. But we have the weapon . . . and the codes needed to arm and detonate it remotely."

"What if the Avatar takes me with him to this valley where you intend to blow him up? You're asking me to commit suicide!"

"Offer to fight," Hansen said. "Enlist in the Holy Warriors. You should be able to find an opportunity to slip away before the force enters the valley. Put a mountain between it and yourself, and you'll be fine. Don't worry. We'll be shadowing the force and will make sure you're clear before we do anything . . . irrevocable."

Chris wanted to laugh out loud. *He's handing me everything I wanted on a platter,* he thought. *I'll talk to the Avatar, all right. I'll tell him exactly what's going on. He'll never go near that valley. And I'll not only enlist in the Holy Warriors, I may damn well be in charge of them by the time this is all over!*

But he kept his expression troubled and modest. "If you really think I can pull it off," he said, "I'll do it. I want the Body ended as much as you do."

"I doubt it," said Hansen. He nodded to Cleo, who got up and gave Chris an exciting, if morally troubling, look at her long-tailed backside as she bent over and opened a cabinet door. From a hidden refrigerator, she pulled three bottles of beer. She put two on the desk, then took the third herself and returned to the corner chair. Hansen picked up the two on the deck, flicked them open with his thumbs, and handed one to Chris. "There's a huge stock of this stuff in the basement under the airport restaurant," he said. "Good thing, because I'm pretty sure the brewery's out of business." He raised his bottle. "To the end of the Body," he said.

Chris clinked bottles with him. *To the end of you and all your kind,* Chris thought, and took a swig of the bittersweet brew.

"Now let's talk about Marseguro," Hansen said. "Because once the Body is out of the way and the Kemono-mimi are finally free to follow their destiny, it will be time for me to set about rectifying my most serious mistake and ridding the universe of those water-breathing freaks." He took another swig of beer. "The Body made a tactical error. They tried to capture the planet, instead of simply killing everyone on it. I'll know better." He held the beer bottle up to the light, examining the play of light on its dewed surface. "Nor will I need an army . . . well, not an army of Kemonomimi, anyway. Not with the special weapon I've already prepared for the task." He smiled, as if to himself, then suddenly lowered his gaze back to Chris.

"But I need more information about my target," he said. "So . . . tell me about Marseguro."

He wants me to tell him about Marseguro so he can destroy it? Chris thought. *Now* that's *a conversation I can enter into without any reservations at all.* He settled back. "What would you like to know?" he said, and took another long pull on his beer.

Richard couldn't believe it. He drank in Emily's image on the vidscreen and could feel a grin as big as hers splitting his face. He couldn't have suppressed it if he'd wanted to.

Emily stepped back from the vid pickup and, for the first time, he saw who was standing beside her. He blinked. "Dr. Christianson-Wood?"

Emily's mother smiled. "Yes, I'm really here," she said. "All of me."

On the other side of Emily stood a Selkie woman he didn't know, in a white swimsuit that made a stark contrast to Emily's bright-yellow zebra-striped skinsuit. Emily indicated her. "Richard, this is Sarah McLean, President of the Free Selkie Republic."

"Pleased to meet you . . . Madame President." Richard said.

McLean seemed immune to all the smiling going on around her. "I'm not sure I can say the same about you," she said. She stepped forward, until she filled the screen, her image blocking out his view of Emily and her mother. "We need to talk. And not over this vidlink. In person."

"Of course," Richard said. "Um . . . where are you?"

"You don't need to know." The President glanced at something out of frame. "I'll come to you." She looked back at him again. "You and your crew make yourselves comfortable. I'll arrive within . . ." she glanced off screen again . . . "eight hours."

"Emily—"

"President McLean out."

The screen went blank.

Wu had come up the ladder behind Richard. He looked at her, and she shrugged. "I'll show you to your quarters."

The next few hours would have passed with agonizing slowness if Richard hadn't been so tired. Wu showed him to a tiny cabin with a cot and not much else in it except for a bubblelike porthole. Once he'd taken a good look at the view it offered of blue water and drifting plankton, there was nothing to do—and, for that matter, nothing he wanted to do—but sleep.

Which he did, waking to a knock on the cabin door. "The President will be boarding the habitat in five minutes," Wu said when he opened it.

Richard nodded. He found the head, two doors down, and looked at his unshaven face, framed by mussed, tangled hair, in the round, steel-rimmed mirror. He stuck out his tongue at his reflection, then headed toward the wet porch.

The President was climbing out onto the edge of the pool as he entered. Her gaze slid right over him, though, because she was too busy turning to glare at the teenaged Selkie boy climbing out of the water after her. "Shelby Alister McLean, I've a good mind to lock you in your room until you're eighteen. What the hell did you think you were doing, stowing away? You know weight tolerances are tight on the sub-planes. What if you'd overloaded it? You could have killed us all!"

The boy looked down at the deck plates, one bare foot sliding back and forth in a puddle. "I didn't . . ."

"You didn't think at all, did you?"

"I don't . . ."

"Oh, never mind. We'll settle this later. Now get out of the way."

The boy shuffled off to one side as another Selkie swam up to the air. Violet hair broke the surface, and Richard's heart skipped a beat. "Emily!"

She erupted out of the water almost like a dolphin, hit the deck with both feet, and an instant later barreled into him like a Richard-seeking missile, a large, muscular missile that wrapped its arms around him so tightly he could hardly breathe.

After what seemed both an eternity and all-too-brief an instant, Emily disentangled herself from Richard and stood back, grinning at him.

Over her shoulder he saw that the boy had raised his head and was looking straight at them. He looked . . . well, Richard still couldn't read Selkie faces as well as he could nonmods', but he could have sworn the boy looked . . . jealous.

Dr. Christianson-Wood was now hauling herself out of the water much more sedately than Emily had. Richard went to her and shook her hand. "Dr. Christianson-Wood," he said. "I can't tell you how happy I am to see you looking so . . . well."

"Thank you, Richard," Dr. Christianson-Wood said.

He turned to the President. "Madame President?" He held out his hand.

McLean didn't take it. Instead, she looked past his shoulder at Wu. "Where can we talk?"

"I've cleared the forward wardroom," Wu said.

"Take us there." McLean walked past Richard, who raised an eyebrow at Dr. Christianson-Wood. Emily's mother's mouth quirked in a half-smile, then he turned to follow the president. Emily fell in beside him, and the teenager brought up the rear. But not for long. "Shelby, get lost," McLean said without looking around as they reached a hatch at the end of the main corridor.

"But—"

"Go!"

The boy gave the President a dark look, gave Richard an even darker one . . . and then gave Emily a completely different sort of look, one Richard, who had once been a teenager himself, immediately recognized. As the boy walked back down the corridor, his bare back somehow radiating sulkiness, Richard whispered to Emily, "You've got an admirer."

Emily's mouth quirked. "Tell you why later," she whispered back.

The wardroom was probably the largest room in the habitat, since it spanned the full width of the cigar-shaped hull. Big curving overhead windows provided a view of the underside of the waves ten meters above. There were four rectangular tables and, in one corner, a miniature galley: microwave, sink, refrigerator, counter space.

President McLean planted herself at the head of one of the tables and gestured for the others to sit down. Richard sat to McLean's right, Emily at his side, while Dr. Christianson-Wood sat across from them.

"I've heard part of the story of how and why you came to Earth, Richard Hansen," McLean said without preamble. "But now I, as President of the Free Selkie Republic and representing the full Council, want to hear it all . . . and whatever reasons you can offer why we should not consider you a sworn enemy of our state for the aid you have provided the remnant of the Body Purified."

Richard looked up at the green light filtering down into the room. "Ah," he said. "It's a long story—"

"You've got nowhere to go," said President McLean. "And neither do I."

Emily's hand found Richard's under the table and squeezed it reassuringly. He squeezed back.

"For me," he said, "it all began when the man I thought was my father committed suicide . . ."

It took him well over an hour to relate all the events that had led him to Marseguro and everything that had transpired there and since. McLean frowned through much of his tale, and the frown deepened when he explained how he had been tricked into delivering the vaccine to the Avatar on Paradise Island.

But the biggest reaction came when he mentioned the Kemonomimi.

McLean had been looking down, hands folded quietly in front of her; suddenly, her head snapped up. "The Avatar asked you about the Kemonomimi?"

"Another race of moddies? Created by Victor Hansen? Here on Earth?" said Dr. Christianson-Wood.

Richard nodded. "So the Avatar said. I haven't seen them, but he was convinced enough that they existed that he left the island with all his forces to destroy them." He frowned. "Or maybe I *have* seen them," he said. "One of them, anyway. The Salvation Day service, just at the time I began to figure out where Marseguro must be ... during the Penitents' Parade, a moddie jumped the Lesser Deacon. She looked ... feline. The Holy Warriors shot her."

"Fascinating," Emily's mother said. "Victor Hansen's diaries ... there were strange references that hinted at some previous genetic experiment that had gone wrong. But he was never specific. And there were gaps ... huge gaps in his diaries, years' worth where he'd either recorded nothing or destroyed what he'd written." She nodded at the President. "He never mentioned Selkies left behind on Earth, for instance. And in his scientific papers he sometimes cross-referenced work we have no record of elsewhere."

"And I had no inkling of their existence from the shadows of memories that his gene-bomb imprinted on me," Richard said. "He obviously excised them from that, as well."

"He didn't want us know about them," Emily said. "But ... why?"

"Because they're savages," President McLean said.

The three Marseguroites looked at her. "You've heard of them?"

"Yes," she said. "About five years ago, we managed to steal some pretty sophisticated AIs, one of which we set up to monitor Body communications for mention of moddies, thinking it might give us warning if the Body discovered our existence. We got more than we bargained for. Within a week, the AI just about scared us to death when it overheard numerous mentions of expeditions trying to find some mysterious moddie camp.

"But they weren't searching for us. They were in the mountains. People had been slaughtered in their homes in remote areas of the Canadian Rockies. Transports had been ambushed, aircraft shot down. All by these other moddies.

"I've got no love for the Body or most nonmods," she looked straight at Richard, "but I don't condone murdering civilians."

"Nor do I," Dr. Christianson-Wood said sharply. "But I did. On my world, and on yours. Millions have died horribly simply because I did what I thought needed to be done to protect my kind. Your Kemonomimi may no more be savages than we are. They're simply trying to survive. Those 'murders' may have been necessary to prevent their eradication."

"Well, they won't be able to prevent it much longer," Richard said. "Not if the Avatar reaches them." He looked at President McLean. "You may not approve of what you've heard of their actions," he said. "But they're not your enemy. The Avatar is. You openly attacked Paradise Island. Unlike the Kemonomimi, you left people alive. He knows there are Selkies out here, now, or he soon will. And the plague is no longer a deterrent. Once he's dealt with the Kemonomimi, he'll come looking for you—and sooner or later, he'll find you."

"Which brings us back to your choice to give him the vaccine," President McLean said. "By your own account, you had the chance to destroy it, once you found out you'd been tricked . . . but you didn't. If the Body attacks, it will be because you enabled it to." Her eyes narrowed. "Just like you enabled it to attack Marseguro."

Emily squeezed his hand again, but Richard pulled it free almost angrily. "You aren't telling me anything I haven't already told myself. I did what I thought was best at the time. I didn't know about the Free Selkie Republic. I didn't know Emily was here. I didn't know about the Kemonomimi. All I knew was that people were—*are*—dying all over the planet, and it looked like the only hope to get the vaccine to them was to put it in the hands of the Avatar.

"None of us can change our past actions. All we can do is choose what we do next." He locked gazes with the President. "Warn the Kemonomimi. Join forces with them. Together, you can overcome the Avatar."

"Fight him?" President McLean laughed. "We can't take on an army of Holy Warriors—on land!"

"But I can," Richard said. "A small, lightly armed one, anyway, which is all the Avatar has left to him." He looked up through the blue-green water. "Up there, in orbit, I have a starship. And that starship has assault craft and holds full of weapons and ammunition."

"Your starship has been taken."

"I have every reason to believe she has been, or soon will be, taken back. Even if she hasn't, there's only a skeleton crew of Holy Warriors aboard, and my crew is in hiding, ready to strike back.

"Give me a shuttle, and I'll give you my ship." *I hope.* "And then *we'll* have the upper hand, and the Avatar will have no choice but to give up his dreams of Purifying Earth of all of us . . . abominations."

"What do you mean, 'us?' " McLean said. "You're not a moddie."

"No," Richard said quietly. "I'm a clone."

McLean sat very still for a long moment. Then, "I'll have to talk to the Council," she said abruptly. "I'll let you know what we decide."

She got up without another word and stalked out of the wardroom.

Dr. Christianson-Wood looked at Richard and Emily. "I'm going to . . . explore," she said, and followed the President.

"Why—" Richard began, but didn't get any further, because Emily was kissing him, almost devouring him, as though he were drink and she were dying of thirst.

An indeterminate time later they both surfaced for air. "I have a cabin," Richard said.

"I was hoping you might," Emily said.

Thinking about it afterward, it seemed to Richard they somehow teleported down the corridor to the tiny room he'd been given. And some time after that, as he spooned with her in the tiny bed, both of them naked, sweaty, and very, very happy, he said into her ear, "I take it you're ready for this, now."

She laughed. "I think so," she said. "But I may have to try it a few more times to be sure."

He tugged at her earlobe with his teeth, then murmured, "I'm not going anywhere."

For now, a voice whispered.

He ignored it.

Emily woke to the brightening that signaled morning, and for a moment wondered where she was; then she remembered, and smiled. She turned her head to look at Richard asleep beside her. For a while last night she'd thought they'd never sleep, and hadn't minded in the slightest. She knew they'd missed a meal, but somehow, no one had come knocking on their door, though it must have been obvious, in such a small habitat, where they'd disappeared to.

So much for being discreet, she thought.

Richard lay on his side facing her, and she studied his face, so much like the photographs of a young Victor Hansen in the museum back in Hansen's Harbor. She knew he was a clone of the creator of her race, and that they shared a not insignificant amount of DNA; but then, so did all the Selkies on Marseguro. That hadn't stopped them marrying and having children, and the tweaking Victor Hansen had done to the first generation of Selkies had ensured that the sometimes dire consequences of inbreeding hadn't befallen the population, though Emily couldn't remember exactly how he'd achieved that.

Her smile faded a little. She and Richard could never have children. Victor Hansen had seen to that, too. And yet, Victor Hansen had also given the Selkies a strong sex drive, to ensure they reproduced. Her attraction to Richard was part of that drive, but no matter how long they drove, or how hard and fast—and they'd driven long, hard and fast indeed last night—they could never reach that particular destination.

I don't care, she thought. *So we can't have children. We'll have each other.*

If we both survive the next few days, a part of her warned. She tried to ignore it.

The knock on the door that hadn't come the night before came now. "The President wants to see you both," said a voice Emily recognized as Wu's. "Half an hour."

"We'll be there," Emily called.

Richard stirred and opened his eyes. "What . . . ?"

"The President," she said. "Half an hour. She and the Council must have made a decision."

"I hope it doesn't involve shoving me out an air lock without a waterbreather," Richard said. He stretched and yawned.

Emily tried to speak, but her throat closed on her words. "I won't let that happen," she finally managed.

Richard blinked at her. "It was a joke."

"It wasn't funny."

"Um. No. Perhaps not." He grinned at her. "Breakfast?"

They found the rest of the crew of *Sawyer's Point* in the

wardroom, along with a couple of Selkies Emily didn't know—and who kept to themselves—and, inevitably, Shelby. The teenager had only half-finished his breakfast—a bowl of some unidentifiable glop that looked inedible to Emily— but when he saw the two of them come in together, he shoved away from the table in a hurry and strode out without looking back.

"Um," Richard said. "Well, can't say I blame him." Emily had told him the story of how she'd first met the Selkies of the Free Republic.

"I hope that's not going to cause any problems down the road," Emily said.

"It's not your fault he's a teenage boy," Richard said. "He'll grow out of it."

They spent a few minutes catching up with the others from *Sawyer's Point*, who kept exchanging grins when they didn't think Richard was watching. Everyone had had a long, long sleep and expressed their readiness for any-thing . . . everyone but Derryl who, as usual, said next to nothing beyond, "Captain Hansen. Emily."

Dr. Christianson-Wood was not in the wardroom, but she met them at the ladder leading up to the control room. She raised a hand in greeting as they approached. "You two look . . . relaxed," she said.

"Mom!" Emily said.

Her mother laughed.

"You can come up, now," said Wu. The three of them climbed into the rather cramped control room, President McLean turned to face them. On the screen behind her, Richard saw an indistinct image of half a dozen other Selk-ies gathered around a table.

"I and the Council of the Free Selkie Republic have dis-cussed matters," she said. "We agree that we must stop the Avatar now, while he is weak.

"Richard Hansen," she went on, looking at him directly. "Although the decision was not unanimous, we have de-cided to trust you.

"We'll get you a shuttle. You get your ship."

Chapter 14

ANDY KING SPRAWLED in his landsuit in the captain's chair on the still essentially useless bridge, legs hung over the armrest, watching the Earth spin in the tactical display, still showing the last view the Holy Warriors had chosen. Footsteps sounded behind him, and he turned around to see Simon Goodfellow.

"The reboot sequence is underway," Goodfellow said without preamble.

Andy's feet slammed to the deck plates. "You started it *without informing me?*"

Goodfellow blinked. "You've been going on and on about how important it is to get the computer working. I didn't think I needed to tell you I was about to do what you've been telling me to do."

Andy closed his eyes, took a deep breath, then opened his eyes again and let the matter drop. Simon seemed congenitally incapable of grasping the finer points of shipboard protocol—like the need to always check with one's commanding officer before beginning a technical procedure that could turn the ship into a useless lump of orbiting junk. "How long?"

"Two hours, twenty-nine minutes from start," Simon said. "Or . . ." He glanced at his watch. "Two hours, thirteen minutes from now."

"When will we know if it's working?"

"When it works," Simon said. "In two hours and thirteen . . . twelve . . . minutes from now, the computer will either wake up and ask for instructions, or it will remain silent forever."

"And the ship will shut down."

"And the ship will shut down," Simon said. "It's all or nothing. Either the reboot works, or else it wipes out everything. You might say that right now the AI is in a coma, but its brain stem is functioning. If the reboot fails, the brain stem dies, too."

"Life support, power, everything gone."

"Right," Simon said.

Andy nodded. "Very well," he said. He got to his feet. "I'll get down to the crew quarters and make sure everyone is ready for—" He stopped. Something had just happened: a sound, or maybe a vibration. Distant, but distinct, and definitely not part of the ship's normal, if currently rather subdued, function. "Did you feel that?"

"Feel what?"

Andy looked at the tactical display. Earth continued to swing below; they were just crossing the terminator, currently somewhere over North America. Nothing unusual there. He began moving from station to station, checking each in turn. All were frozen in whatever state they had been in when Simon had pulled the AI's plug, but some of their vidscreens showed exterior views.

There. Andy stared hard to be sure. The vidscreen was small and the lighting uncertain, but that bump on the hull . . . that shouldn't have been there. *A shuttle,* he thought. *The Holy Warriors. They didn't return to Earth. They just put themselves into a slightly different orbit. They knew we wouldn't be able to track them with the computer down, and now they've come back.*

We're being boarded!

"Simon," Andy said. "Go back to your data terminal. Stay there. Do whatever you can to make sure this reboot succeeds."

"There's nothing I can—"

"Then do nothing, but stay there!" Andy roared. "That's an order, damn it."

Simon blinked. "Um, okay. Uh, sir." He went out.

Andy pulled on one of the microcomm headsets they'd been using since they'd cut themselves off from ship systems. "Cordelia," he said.

"What is it, Andy?" Cordelia Raum's voice came back.

"The Holy Warriors are back," Andy said. "And we're in the middle of the reboot. The computer can't tell us where they are, but I'd say it's a safe bet they're heading to the bridge. We have to cut them off."

"I'll gather some people."

"Not some," Andy said. "All. Everyone who can hold a gun." He looked at the image of the shuttle. "They've come in through one of the external work air locks about three-quarters of the way to the stern. There's no way into the habitat ring from there. They'll have to come up the central shaft."

"Zero-G fighting," Raum said. "They're probably trained for it. We're not."

"We're Selkies," Andy said. "Well, some of us, anyway. We live in zero-G, remember?"

Raum laughed. "Affirmative," she said.

"Delegate four crew to guard the bridge," Andy said.

"Where will you be?"

"I've got a laser rifle. I'll be heading up to the shaft. See you there." He cut the connection before Cordelia could protest that the commanding officer shouldn't put himself in danger, that he should wait at the bridge in case the computer came back up . . .

Screw that, Andy thought. More than two hours? By then the Holy Warriors would either have the ship, be running away again . . . or be dead.

Andy preferred the latter option, and why should he let everyone else have all the fun of making it happen?

He found the nearest Jefferies tube and climbed up it toward the central shaft, weight dropping away as he progressed. As he neared the top, he slowed. The Holy Warriors had only just docked. They'd still be getting organized, slipping through the corridors toward the central shaft. Probably none of them had entered it yet.

Still, getting his head sliced off because he'd been too eager would be an embarrassing way to end his brief stint as acting commander of Marseguro's only starship.

He looked out carefully. The central shaft was pitch-black; its lights had gone out with the computer crash. A faint light shone up the Jefferies tube, though, and realizing it could silhouette him to anyone down the shaft, he cautiously pulled himself up and out. The spin here imparted just enough weight to keep him bobbing against the wall of the shaft like a balloon, but he could easily leap too high and be stranded in midair.

He closed the hatch, then pulled himself along webbing he couldn't see toward the elevator hut he knew was there somewhere.

He found it by the simple if somewhat painful expedient of bashing his head against it, and stood slowly upright, hooking his feet in the webbing, keeping his back to the elevator hut and the elevator hut between himself and the shaft. Then he unshipped the laser rifle and held it out at arm's length.

The rifle had an aiming vidscreen at the top that could be turned at right angles to the weapon, allowing him to shoot around corners.

It also let him see in the dark.

In the screen, the shaft glowed dimly green. Areas heated by machinery or with warm spaces beneath them glowed brighter than others.

And far down the shaft, one by one, small, bright dots were emerging into the shaft.

The Holy Warriors.

The shaft's atmosphere was too dense for him to make any effective shots at this distance, but he lined up one of the dots and activated the automatic tracking system. When the rifle's computer decided the range had lessened enough, it would automatically fire at that dot . . . and then the next . . . and then the next . . .

Which sounded like a surefire way to take out the whole troop, except, of course, the Holy Warriors had built the weapon . . . and had their own versions of it, and their own defenses against it.

He thought he might get one, if he were lucky. He doubted he would get two.

But one would be something.

He stood where he was, watching the screen and the approaching dots, wondering idly which man he had selected to die.

The screen flashed green. The laser fired. And then . . .

Holy shit!

The shaft exploded with light as the Holy Warriors opened up, not with lasers, but with automatic rifles. Tracers left blue-and-green streaks in the atmosphere.

Something smashed Andy's laser rifle from his hands, dislocating a finger in the process. He yelped in pain and pulled his hands in, then pressed his back against the elevator hut.

Suddenly, coming up here by himself seemed like a monumentally bad idea.

The gunfire ceased, leaving him in the dark, half-deafened, hand hurting. He debated crawling back to the Jefferies tube, but they were surely alert now and they'd have their own night-vision apparatus. If he showed even a sliver of warm body, they'd blow it off.

Which meant he'd just set up his own crew for ambush.

"Shit." He activated the microcomm headset. "Cordelia, come in. Come in!"

"We're almost there," Raum said. "We'll be popping up in—"

"No!" Andy said. "Don't. I did something stupid. I took a shot. It alerted them. They're bound to be using night vision. And they're using projectile weapons. Explosive bullets, I think. They don't have to nail you to nail you."

"Projectiles? In a spaceship?" Raum sounded shocked.

"Guess they figure they're unlikely to punch a hole in the hull from here," Andy said.

"But . . . that means you're stuck. Wherever you are."

"Yeah, well. As long as I keep my head down, no reason they should spot me."

Raum didn't say anything, but Andy could feel her disbelief and disapproval even over the comm link. "What do you want us to do?"

"With the elevators out, they'll have to come down a Jefferies tube themselves," Andy said. "I'll try to tell you which one they pick. You need to be waiting for them at the bottom."

"What if . . . you can't?"

"Then you'll just have to do the best you can," Andy said.

Silence for a moment. "Roger that," Raum said. "Good luck."

"You, too, Cordelia." Andy cut off the comm link.

We're all going to need it, he thought.

Once the President and Council of the Free Selkie Republic decided to trust Richard, things moved quickly. Now, just one day later, he and the crew of *Sawyer's Point* were once more aboard Lia Wu's sub, heading in the opposite direction from Paradise Island: south toward the Cape Scott spaceport at the northwestern tip of Vancouver Island, just a few hours' journey from the Republic's hidden habitat.

One difference: this time Emily was with them.

He'd urged her to stay behind. She'd refused. "You and I took *Sanctification* all by ourselves last time," she'd reminded him as they lay entwined in bed after another lengthy demonstration of moddie/nonmod unity.

"I don't want anything to happen to you," Richard said. His finger traced the lower curve of her left breast. "Not now."

"And what makes you think anything is more likely to happen to me than to you?" Emily said.

Richard sighed. "Can't I be chivalrous if I want to?"

"No." Emily had kissed the tip of his nose. "Chivalry is dead. I read that somewhere."

Richard looked at her now, standing at his left in the sub's control room, watching the crew at work, and hoped that no one would join chivalry in death once they got to the *Victor Hansen*.

If they did. They were betting on the spaceport having a ready-to-fly shuttle that could be piloted manually, and that sufficient information continued to flow through the orbital tracking systems of the Body that the shuttle's computer would be able to locate and rendezvous with the *Victor Hansen*.

Not impossibly large odds, at a spaceport the size of the Cape Scott one . . . especially since, Richard knew from his days at Body Security, Cape Scott had been developed in this remote location by the secretive Cheveldeoff as Body Security's private facility for launching missions into space. That implied to Richard that there would be a wide variety of spacecraft available. Still, it was hardly a sure thing. And they didn't know if Holy Warrior survivors still stood guard there or not.

The Earth Selkies understood they needed the *Victor Hansen*'s resources if they were going to have any hope of halting the Avatar's advance. But they didn't trust the Kemonomimi; as far as Richard could tell, the Council's view was that the Kemonomimi were a failed experiment, whereas the Selkies were a successful one.

Richard wondered what the Kemonomimi's view of the Selkies was ... if they even knew they existed.

The Selkies were willing to attempt to stop the Avatar, with the *Victor Hansen*'s resources. But they refused to warn the Kemonomimi first. If they stopped the Avatar, they'd consider talking to the other moddies. If they failed to stop the Avatar, then the Kemonomimi could face him alone. The Selkies would not expose themselves further to the possibly resurgent Body.

Richard thought they were wrong, but he had no way to persuade them, being essentially a beggar with his hand out.

"ARV launched," a crewwoman announced behind Richard.

"Let's see," Wu said. She went to look over the crew-woman's shoulder at a curving triptych of vidscreens. The images relayed from the dragonfly-sized aerial reconnaissance vehicle hovering just above the waves all showed variations of the same thing: gray water splashing on gray rocks and gray sky above. Only a few gray roofs showed inland. "Not very informative," Richard said.

"Or aesthetically pleasing," Emily put in.

"Another reason to hate the Body," said Wu. "Bad architecture. But the important thing is, nothing's moving. Radar and sonar are both clear, as well. And there's no radio chatter of any kind, open or encrypted."

"Because *everyone* there has been encrypted," Melody said.

Every turned to look at her.

She blushed. "Because ... they're dead? In crypts? Encrypted? Get it?"

"I won't even dignify that with a groan," Richard said, but he smiled as he said it.

"Push the ARV up to a hundred meters," Wu said. "Let's get a better look."

The images shifted, the water falling away and the view inland opening out. Dark-forested hills surrounded the spaceport, and waves splashed against rocky headlands in the distance. And in the spaceport itself ...

"Yikes," Melody said softly.

"My sentiment exactly," Richard said. It looked like something large had crashed on landing and skidded across the spaceport at a forty-five-degree angle to everything else, smashing trees into kindling, other ships into flinders, and finally buildings into rubble. The control tower, its windows blown out, stood at an angle more appropriate to an Italian postcard. The crashed vehicle itself, a battered and blackened cigar-shaped hulk, had fetched up just twenty or thirty meters from the sea. "A spaceship?"

"Orbital cargo vessel," Wu said. "Either the pilot or the ground controller probably had the plague and made a wrong decision—or dropped dead—at just the wrong moment." She pointed at something on the screen. "Zoom in." The shoreline seemed to leap toward them. "Made things easier for us, though. The fence is down." She tapped the screen.

It wasn't just down, it had been rolled up like baling wire and wrapped around a denuded tree.

"Let's surface," Wu told her crew. "Launch a boat."

Twenty minutes later the Marseguroites, accompanied by Wu and two of the sub's larger crew members, splashed ashore. One other sub crewman remained with the boat.

No one challenged them except for a crow that rose cawing from a dead, white-streaked tree jammed between two black rocks. They entered the spaceport through the hole in the fencing without difficulty, and headed to the flight line.

Richard saw a couple of bodies at a distance, but didn't suggest they investigate. He'd seen the bloody and bloated remains of plague victims often enough on Marseguro. He didn't need to see them on Earth . . . or any more evidence of the horror Chris Keating had unleashed.

Though there were surely many more bodies tucked away around the huge port, most people had probably died in their quarters, too sick to get out of bed. *A blessing, maybe . . .*

He snorted. A blessing? "With blessings like this, who needs curses?" He muttered the old Body saying under his breath, but Emily heard him, of course. Probably half the party did, with their damnable Selkie hearing.

"Are you all right?" she said, coming closer and taking his hand.

"Yeah," he said. "Just thinking." He gestured with his free hand. "All this destruction. All the deaths. I hope Chris Keating is proud of himself."

"I hope Chris Keating is dead and rotting," Emily snarled. "Or better yet, still locked away in solitary confinement somewhere wondering why nobody brings him food and water anymore."

"Maybe we should be grateful to him," Richard said. He squeezed her hand. "After all, he brought us together."

Emily didn't let go, but she turned to look at him. "I love you, Richard, but I would give you up in an instant if it meant I could roll things back to the way they were before Keating did what he did. If I could bring back my father . . . my friends . . ." Her voice choked off, and she looked away.

Richard didn't know what to say, because he couldn't tell her the truth: that he very well might make the opposite choice.

Of course, that attitude was incredibly selfish, and he felt bad about it, but ultimately the brain and body were primarily concerned with themselves. Altruism required work.

And, yes, of course those thoughts were incredibly egotistical, as well, but then, he came by that part honestly: as he sometimes forgot but his genome never could, he was the clone of Victor Hansen, the man who had created not just one, but two races of modified humans out of his own DNA.

Talk about thinking the world revolves around you . . .

Wu stopped suddenly. "There," she said, pointing off to the right. "I think we may have lucked out."

Richard looked. Tucked in between a couple of helicopters was a delta-winged craft that looked a bit like a miniature version of the assault craft carried by the *Victor Hansen*. "It's the right style to be set up for manual flight," she said. "And the fact it's on the flight line means it could be juiced up."

"Let's find out," Richard said.

Of course, it was really Melody Ashman and Pierre Normand, who'd be required to fly the thing, who gave the craft the once-over—and proclaimed it ready to go.

"What about navigation?" Richard said. He stood between and behind Ashman and Normand, who were tucked into the pilot and copilot seats. "No point going up there if we can't find the ship."

Melody tapped a screen. "It looks like we're getting automated tracking information from somewhere; probably an

AI under the tower that's still doing the best it can." She pulled out a keyboard and typed on it for a few seconds. "Good old manual controls," she said. "Gotta love 'em." More typing. "There." She banged a final key emphatically and let the keyboard retract. "Course laid in. Unfortunately, with where they are now, we're in for a bit of a chase to rendezvous. I'll know more once we're in orbit, but we're probably . . . six hours away from docking."

"Assuming they don't shoot us out of the sky."

"There is that," Melody admitted.

Richard turned and looked back into the tiny cabin. Pilot and copilot in the front, room for two passengers behind them. The reality hit him like a blow to the stomach. He turned to Emily, who stood close behind him. "Emily . . ." he said. He swallowed. "It's too small."

"What?"

"It's too small." He gestured. "We can't take . . . everyone."

Her face froze. "Richard—"

He shrugged helplessly and repeated, like a robot, "It's too small."

Emily looked down for a long moment. When she raised her head again, her eyes glistened. "Then I'll stay behind."

"Emily, I can't—"

"You can't do anything about it. I know." She put her hand on his chest. "But you *will* come back to me. Or else—"

"Or else?"

"Or else I'll kill you." She looked him in the eyes a long moment, then took a deep breath, turned, and went out.

Richard followed her. No one argued about who should go and who should stay: the choices were obvious. Richard had to go. Melody and Pierre, as pilot and copilot. And since they might have to fight when they got to the *Victor Hansen*, the logical fourth choice was Derryl, their silent warrior.

Jerry Krall and Ann Nolan would stay behind, because they would be needed if and when *Victor Hansen* was firmly in Marseguroite control once more, to download information from it that could be used to create vaccine-creation modules for the Earth Selkies' microfactories.

And Emily . . . Richard took her aside. "Keep working

on McLean and her Council," he said in a low voice. "Convince them to warn the Kemonomimi."

Emily's face suddenly lit up. "I'll volunteer to go myself," she said. "That way she's not putting any of her people at—"

"No!" The word exploded out of him. "You heard what she said. The Kemonomimi are dangerous. Let her—"

"—send someone else?" Emily snapped. "Possibly sacrifice a friend?"

Richard shook his head stubbornly. "It doesn't make sense for you to go. You don't know anything about Earth, or the Kemonomimi. You—"

"It sounds like nobody knows much about them," Emily said. She gathered his hands in hers. "Richard, I won't take foolish chances. I'll volunteer to go, but I'm not going to run up to the first Kemonomimi I see and yell ... what's that old expression? 'Take me to your leader!' But if I show how important we think it is by being willing to put myself in danger ... then maybe McLean will change her mind. And even if she doesn't ... well, the Kemonomimi still have to be warned." She squeezed his hands. "It's as simple as that."

"Damn it." Richard pulled her close and hugged her tight. "I hate it when you're right," he whispered into her ear. Then he pulled back a little ways and kissed her, long and lingeringly. Reluctantly, he stepped away at last and stared deep into her iridescent green eyes, the ocean-colored eyes he longed to drown in. "Be careful."

"Look who's talking," she said, her voice breaking a little. Another quick hug, then he forced himself to turn and walk toward the shuttle. Derryl Godard was the only one of the crew still waiting outside. He gave Richard an unreadable look, moved aside to let him enter, then followed him in through the tiny air lock, turning to close the double doors behind them.

Richard sat down in one of the blue-upholstered acceleration chairs and buckled up the five-point harness. Derryl sat beside him and did the same. Melody and Pierre were already in place.

"Let's go," Richard said.

"Aye, aye, sir," said Melody.

The ascent was only a little rough, and smoothed out as

they pierced the upper atmosphere and powered into orbit. Melody studied her controls as their acceleration ceased and Richard felt himself lift slightly from the chair, kept in place only by the harness. "Okay," she said. "I've got a better ETA." She leaned forward and peered at one of her screens. "Five hours, forty-nine minutes from . . . now."

The passenger section of the shuttle didn't even have any windows. Richard sighed and closed his eyes. Well, a nice long nap sounded like a good idea anyway.

Thanks to Emily, he hadn't been getting much sleep the last couple of nights.

He dozed off at once. He woke to a sound like someone striking a small silver gong in the distance. "What—?" It took him a moment to remember where he was. "What's going on?"

"I'm not sure," Melody said. "I don't know the system's audio cues." Her eyes flicked from screen to screen. "I'm trying to spot—Pierre, do you see—?"

"There," he said. He pointed at something. She peered at it.

"Ah," she said. The pilot's chair swiveled: she turned to look at Richard. "There's another Body shuttle already docked with the *Victor Hansen*. It's using the exterior lock I had programmed us to mate with."

Richard frowned. "It must be the shuttle the Holy Warriors used to board her. But . . . why wouldn't they have gone into the main boat bay? If they had computer control—"

"I don't think anybody has control of the ship right now," Pierre said. "*Sanctification—Victor Hansen* to us, but not to this shuttle's computer—is not responding to attempts to communicate." He tapped the console. "Our computer's getting frustrated. It keeps cycling through its communication options, faster and faster. But nothing. Can't even raise a proper identification code."

"Simon Goodfellow's databomb," Richard said. "Andy must have managed to activate it. They flatlined the AI."

"But that doesn't explain why that shuttle is where it is," Melody said.

"I can think of a good reason," Derryl said, startling Richard. They all turned to look at him; his dark eyes looked back from a face like stone. "The crew drove the

Holy Warriors off the ship, but only temporarily ... and with the AI out of commission, they had no way of knowing when the Warriors came back."

Richard blinked at him, astonished. He'd never heard Derryl say that many words in sequence before. Derryl frowned. "What? Why are you all looking at me like that?"

I guess he just hasn't had anything to say until now, Richard thought. "I think you're right," he said out loud. He turned to Melody. "Any way to tell how long that shuttle has been there?"

"It couldn't have been there when we made the boost to higher orbit," Melody said. "*Its* ID beacon is working just fine. If it had already been docked where it is now when I programmed in our course, our computer would have warned us sooner. I doubt it's been there more than an hour. Maybe less."

"Then they've just boarded," Richard said. "And we've got a chance to surprise them from the rear." He tried to lean forward, but of course his harness stopped him: weightless, he'd forgotten it was fastened. "Where else can you dock?"

"There's an emergency access hatch directly opposite," Melody said. "But we can't mate with it."

"Can we even open it?"

Melody nodded. "It's got manual controls."

"Get us as close as you can," Richard said. "We'll jump the rest of the way." He glanced at the sniper. "Derryl, get out the weapons."

"With pleasure," Derryl said. He unbuckled and floated to the back of the cabin. Richard followed.

They'd loaded the locker at the back before they'd left with standard-issue Body automatic rifles, "liberated" from some depot or other, laser pistols, Holy Warrior body armor, and visored helmets with built-in night vision and magnification capabilities. Those would have to wait until they were in the ship, though; they'd have to don pressure suits first to make the transition.

Neither the pressure suits nor the body armor appealed to Richard. "We're going to look just like Holy Warriors," he said to Derryl. "Any of our guys see us, they're liable to shoot us on sight. I'm sure they'd be really sorry about it afterward, but ..."

"Nothing to be done," Derryl said.

He was right, of course. Richard put that worry aside and focused on a different one. "I'm also not wild about the prospect of using projectile weapons inside a spaceship."

"Nothing here that could hole the hull from the central shaft," Derryl said. "The main reason lasers are commonly used shipboard is that a nonrecoiling weapon has some obvious advantages in a zero-G environment. But as long as you remember Newton's Third Law and brace yourself accordingly . . ."

"Mmmm," Richard said. No need to mention that he was about as clumsy in zero-G as . . . well, as a nonmod trying to swim stroke-for-stroke with a Selkie.

"Ready," Melody said. "Holding station."

"Then let's get suited up." Richard shoved his feet into the legs of a pressure suit. "I want our ship back."

"Aye, aye!" said Melody, and "Copy that," Pierre said. Derryl said nothing, but he picked up a rifle and sighted along it with practiced ease, then put it down again with a grim half-smile and started climbing into a suit.

They didn't bother with the air lock. Once they were all suited up and had secured their weapons and body armor in carry bags, they opened both doors at once and blew the shuttle's air out into space in one brief, violent hurricane of wind and fog.

They followed more sedately, gently launching themselves the three meters from shuttle to ship, grabbing the stanchions surrounding the emergency hatch as they hit. Richard went first, and as the others followed, tried his luck at opening the hatch using the external controls. Final proof that the computer was offline, if any was needed, came when he simply touched "Enter" on the keypad without entering his security code, and the hatch slid silently open.

The air lock was big enough for all of them, though barely. They crowded into it. Richard closed the outside door, cycled the lock, pulled a laser pistol from the bag of weapons, and opened the inside door.

There was nothing beyond but an empty spherical room, lit by the eerie blue-green of emergency lights. Webbing covered the walls, and ratlines crisscrossed the middle. There were openings above, to both sides, and directly ahead. Richard skinned out of the pressure suit, the others copying him, then strapped himself into body armor and grabbed a rifle. He jammed a helmet down over his ears. "Don't talk over the helmet radios," he said. "We just might be on the same frequency as the Holy Warriors."

"If we are," Derryl said dryly, "shouldn't we be listening to them?"

Richard blinked, then laughed. "Yes," he said. "And I'm an idiot." He flicked down his visor and the heads-up display kicked in immediately. "How did this thing work again?" he muttered to himself, trying to remember long-ago and cursory instruction in the helmets' use. "Look and blink . . . look at the menu you want, blink two times fast . . . aha." It worked: he found the communications menu, made sure his own microphone was muted, and then activated the helmet radio.

Nothing but static, but with maybe, just maybe, the tiniest *soupçon* of voices mixed in: unintelligible, but there.

Quickly he explained to the others how to work the helmet controls. "Experiment as we move," he said. "I don't know what's going on out there."

"Where do we go?" Pierre asked.

"Central shaft," Derryl replied, before Richard could. "Only way to the bridge."

The others looked at Richard. He nodded. "You heard him. Central shaft."

The corridors at least had some light, even if its green tinge made them all look like they'd been dead for a week (to Richard; he suspected to the Selkies it suggested sunlight through shallow water, or something else appropriately soggy). But the shaft . . .

The shaft was pitch-black. "Night vision," Richard whispered to the others. "Third menu from the left, fourth . . . no, fifth item." He double-blinked at the words apparently floating in space in front of him, and his vision shifted as the goggles began registering infrared and displaying it as visible light.

Now the shaft was a huge tube, mostly colored a very dark blue, although faint greenish and yellowish patches along its walls indicated warmer spots, probably where bits of the ship's power distribution network or hot pipes were close to the surface. At the far end, where the habitat ring rotated, the blue shaded to a deep emerald green: there was a lot more life support at work down there, warming up the multiple decks between the shaft and the hull.

And just approaching that habitat ring were half a dozen bright yellow dots, crawling along the side of the tube like some strange kind of glowing beetle: and now that they were in the shaft, Richard could hear over his helmet earphones what those distant Holy Warriors were saying.

". . . got the bastard?"

"Doubt it. Ducked behind the elevator head. But we'll get him soon enough. Nowhere to hide."

"The rest of them'll be on their way," the first man said.

"Then you'll just have to SHUT UP AND MOVE FASTER!" a new voice roared, obviously the commanding officer; after that, there was no more chatter.

"Derryl?" Richard whispered to the sniper.

He shook his head. "Not in this light, not at this distance, not with this weapon. If I still had my sniper rifle . . ."

"We'll have to get closer, then," Richard said. "Quietly. They've got no reason to look behind them. Let's keep it that way."

The quartet moved off, hauling themselves along the webbing that lined the shaft. Richard remembered the last time he'd made this journey, with a broken arm, Emily tugging him along like a balloon on a string.

"Transitioning," a low voice said in his ears, and it took him a second to realize it must be one of the Holy Warriors. Ahead, the Holy Warriors' glowing shapes suddenly swept up and around the curve of the shaft. They'd crossed into the rotating habitat ring, which here moved at about the speed a man could walk, though at the hull it whirled around at something close to 100 kilometers an hour. Which, of course, was why there was no way to dock directly with it.

"Nothing yet," the same voice whispered. "Todd, Barker, left side of that elevator head. Hough, you're with me. You others spread out. If anything moves, shoot it."

As far as Richard could tell, his group still hadn't been seen.

And then, with absolutely no warning, the lights came on.

Four glowstrips spaced equidistantly around the circumference of the shaft belied their name: they didn't glow, they blazed. His earphones erupted with startled shouts and Richard himself let out a shocked yelp. He couldn't possibly have reacted fast enough to save his eyes, but he didn't have to: his helmet visor instantly cut off the night vision and darkened, so swiftly he only felt a quick stab of pain. All the same, for a moment he was even more blind than he had been in the dark: the visor seemed to have gone completely opaque. *Designed to react to an explosives flash*, he thought. *It will come back in a—*

Ahead of him, weapons spoke. "Lie flat!" Richard shouted, hurling himself to the webbing. He looked at the heads-up display, calling up menus, trying to find the one that would adjust the visor's tint to let him see, and then suddenly he realized he *was* seeing. The visor had adjusted itself.

A firefight had broken out in the habitat ring. The only weapons he could hear were the rifles of the Holy Warriors: the defenders had to be armed with lasers. At least two bodies already floated in the middle of the shaft, tumbling over each other in a broken ballet, trailing blood, one in a Holy Warrior pressure suit, the other in a pale-green Marseguroite uniform. Richard felt sick, and wondered who it was.

Richard looked at Derryl. He nodded. "The spin won't make it easy, but I can do it."

"You split off, then. Pierre, Melody, follow me. We'll get as close as we can and jump 'em from the rear. Derryl, wait until we're . . ." Richard judged the distance. "Past the third segmentation ring. See it?"

"Aye, aye," said Derryl. He stuck his feet into the webbing and unslung his rifle.

"Let's move." Richard led the way, his heart pounding as he watched the battle ahead. The Holy Warriors seemed to have the defenders pinned down, and were slowly, bit of cover by bit of cover, moving closer. Richard guessed the defenders were using the Jefferies tubes as foxholes, but there were only four of those, and that meant only four people could be firing at any one time. There were a dozen of the Holy Warriors—*well, one less now,* he thought, as the bodies that had been in the habitat ring drifted by overhead.

The Marseguroite, a nonmod, didn't have a recognizable

face anymore, or much of a head. Richard still didn't know who he was.

He ground his teeth. The third segmentation ring, a broad band of shining metal, lay just ahead. He gripped his rifle tighter with one hand and pulled ahead. Once they opened fire, they'd have the Holy Warriors in a crossfire with the defenders—but they'd also be firing from a completely exposed position. The constant spinning of the habitat ring should make it difficult for the Holy Warriors to shoot back at them with any accuracy, but it made it just as hard for them to shoot at the Warriors.

Derryl said he could compensate. Richard hoped he was right.

They crossed the ring. "Fire at will," Richard said. He dug his feet and one arm into the webbing to hold himself in place, raised his rifle—

And heard the flat cracking sound of Derryl's.

The Holy Warrior just easing past the elevator head jerked and quit moving, falling in slow motion to the webbing. And with astonishing speed, the other Holy Warriors turned and discovered Richard and his crew behind them.

Richard pulled the trigger. The shots went wild, missing the Holy Warriors completely, ripping out chunks of the insulating padding that lined the ring like a giant quilt, as the Holy Warriors rotated over their heads. The Holy Warriors fired back, but nothing found its mark.

But Derryl's rifle spoke again, and the helmet of another Holy Warrior suddenly burst apart in a cloud of red and gray.

The ring kept coming. The Holy Warriors were getting closer. And Richard suddenly realized that staying put would get them killed. "Move!" he yelled.

He lurched upward as he said it and jumped, soaring across the shaft as the Holy Warriors opened fire again. Halfway across, something slammed into his chest so hard it knocked the breath out of him and he tumbled out of control, but the body armor saved him, and another Warrior died as Derryl fired again.

Spinning so fast he could hardly see, Richard slammed into the far side of the shaft, barely holding on to his rifle. Nauseated, he clung for a moment. Bullets tore into the padding just two meters from his legs, and almost without thinking he grabbed his rifle and fired back.

By pure luck, the Holy Warriors were at the closest point. His burst of automatic fire stitched a bloody line across the chest of one Warrior's pressure suit.

Behind that Warrior was another, though, and Richard saw the rifle swinging toward him that would surely finish him off—except the Warrior didn't fire. A puff of gray smoke erupted from his chest, and he stiffened, then just stopped moving, feet caught in the webbing, gun falling in slow motion.

The defenders had emerged from their foxholes.

Four Holy Warriors still lived. They threw down their weapons and held up their hands.

A moment later only three of them were alive as a final laser found its mark, but then the fighting stopped.

Richard tried to catch his breath. His chest hurt. Bodies floated in the shaft or bumped bonelessly against the habitat ring's inner padding, and a haze of blood and smoke swirled through the air.

Richard looked back at Derryl and gave him a wave. Then he looked around for Pierre and Melody . . .

. . . and saw them where he had left them, still tangled in the webbing, now soaked with blood, more blood floating in glistening scarlet globules all around them.

"God, no," Richard whispered. He jumped across the shaft, almost losing his breath again when he slammed into the far side, tossed his rifle and helmet away and pulled himself hand over hand to where his two crewmembers lay motionless.

They were dead, gaping holes torn in their bodies. From their postures, it looked like Melody had been tangled in the webbing and Pierre had tried to help free her . . . and then the Holy Warrior's bullets had found them.

My fault, Richard thought, a black roaring in his head, not wanting to look at their mangled bodies, but unable not to. *My fault. Pride. Hansen pride. I thought I knew what was best, just like Victor. I thought I could do whatever I want. I thought I could save the* Victor Hansen. *I thought I could save Earth. I thought . . .*

I thought wrong.

He was still sitting there, staring at their bodies, when Andy King found him.

Andy enjoyed adventure vids as much as the next person, but he usually only watched the latest Marseguroite efforts. Nevertheless, he'd once had occasion to visit the home of a friend whose hobby was ancient Earth "movies," and had been subjected to several risible and largely incomprehensible entertainment programs from the early twentieth century. When he'd expressed skepticism at the fortuitous timing of the arrival of military aid in one particular "western," his friend had laughed. "It's one of the clichés of the period," he said. "The cavalry always shows up in the nick of time."

Andy felt a new empathy for the rescued heroine of the western when, just as the Holy Warriors were threatening to overrun the *Victor Hansen* defenders, someone started shooting them from behind.

Not that he assumed they'd won yet, at that point: he'd already been disappointed that the sudden illumination of the central shaft (and God bless Simon Goodfellow for getting enough computer control back to make that happen, and his crew for rushing up the Jeffering tubes when it did.) hadn't blinded the Holy Warriors completely. His men had known it was coming and simply closed their eyes. The Holy Warriors must have been using night vision and hadn't had any warning, but their pressure suits seemed to have some sort of automatic mechanism for dimming the faceplate, because they'd resumed their attack faster than he'd thought possible.

It soon became apparent that there weren't enough Holy Warriors to fight a two-front battle, however, and within minutes the last of them surrendered, and if Andy was just a bit slow about realizing they had surrendered and shot one more of them anyway, who would ever blame him?

Only then did he see who their rescuers were.

Only then did he see Richard Hansen clutching the webbing, staring at two blood-spattered bodies, and realize that the cost of keeping *Victor Hansen* for Marseguro had been higher than he'd realized.

They gathered the dead, took them by elevator down to

the full gravity of the outermost deck, and laid them out in two rooms, the crew of *Victor Hansen* in one, the dead Holy Warriors in the other. Byrne, the commander, was among the dead; none of the remaining three outranked the others. Andy left them, under guard, to perform whatever rites they considered appropriate before the bodies were recycled, and went in search of Simon Goodfellow.

Of course, now that Richard was back on board, Andy was no longer the commanding officer of the *Victor Hansen*, but Richard seemed to be in no condition to take over. He'd barely spoken. Andy had last seen him sitting in the room with the bodies of Melody, Pierre, and Munish, the other Marseguroite casualty, head bowed, hands clenched in front of him.

Andy found Goodfellow in the simulator room. "Good work with the lights," he said. "I take it you've successfully rebooted the computer?"

"Sort of," Simon said. He sat at his data terminal, watching monitors and chewing on his lower lip. "There's . . . resistance."

"Resistance? To what?"

Simon pointed at a display on the screen that looked to Andy like a tangle of multicolored noodles. "The AI is . . . confused."

"Confused? It's a machine!"

"It's a very smart machine. Artificial 'intelligence,' remember?"

Andy sighed. "*Why* is it confused?"

"I couldn't wipe its memory completely and still have it be any use to us," Simon said. "It's finding gaps in its data. It knows something has happened to it and it's wasting processing cycles trying to reason it out. In human terms, it's suffered a massive concussion and partial amnesia."

"Uh-huh," Andy said. "So what are you doing to . . . deconfuse it?"

"Holding its hand," Simon said. He held up his own. "Figuratively. I'm watching it work its way through its memories. When it runs into a hole, I plug it with a reassuring subroutine that essentially tells it to move along, there's nothing to worry about there. It's worked to a certain extent. The lights came on when I asked for them, and I seem to have control of various other systems throughout the ship, but everything is still ... uncertain. Not every command is obeyed, or even acknowledged."

"So we still don't have complete control."

"No," Simon said. He frowned at Andy as if seeing him for the first time. "Didn't you go to see if the Holy Warriors were sneaking aboard again?"

"Yes," Andy said neutrally. "Some time ago."

"And ... ?"

"They were. We fought them off. They're mostly dead."

"Ah, good." Simon turned back to his console.

"Captain Hansen is back aboard," Andy said, mainly just to see if he could puncture Simon's geekish focus on the computer. To his surprise, Simon swung around at once, a huge grin on his face.

"Excellent! Just what we need!" He jerked a thumb at the console. "One reason the AI is struggling is that it is missing its captain. I've completely wiped any memory of the Holy Warriors taking command, so as far as it's concerned, Richard Hansen should be issuing its orders ... although it's confused enough that it's been letting me issue a few. When it shuts me out, though, it seems to be because it has suddenly realized I'm not the real captain. If Captain Hansen can come down here, we might be able to shock the system into some sort of stability."

Andy thought of Richard, sitting numbly in the make-shift morgue, and his jaw clenched. "The AI isn't the only system that needs to be shocked into stability," he growled. He'd been crouched down on his heels while he talked to Simon; now he snapped to his feet. "Captain Hansen will be down in a few minutes," he said, turned, and went to fetch him.

When Andy King returned, Richard tried to ignore him as he had before; but Andy wouldn't let him.

"Why the hell," Andy snarled, "are you still sitting there?" He grabbed Richard's arm and hauled him to his feet. "Captain. Sir. Technician Goodfellow requests that you assist him in the rebooting of the ship's AI."

"You go," Richard said. He tried to pull free. Andy didn't let go. In fact, he pulled Richard's arm behind his back and shoved his face up against the cold metal wall.

"I am not the captain," Andy said into his ear, his voice a burning whisper. "You are."

"You can't—" Richard tried to struggle, but Andy was a Selkie. He pushed Richard hard to the wall again.

"I can't make you act like a captain? No, I can't. But if you aren't the captain anymore, Richard, then I can damn well try to knock some sense back into you. You didn't answer my question. Why the hell are sitting in here with three dead bodies when you've got a ship to get back up and running?"

Cheek stinging, Richard felt a flicker of anger. "You don't understand, damn you," he grated, his words slightly distorted. "I got them killed. All three of them. If I'd made better decisions when we reached orbit . . . if I'd never gone down to meet 'Jacob' . . . hell, if I'd never insisted we come back to Earth in the first place . . ."

"Don't be so full of yourself! Everyone on the *Victor Hansen* is a volunteer. Everyone knew the risks. Some of us even knew the risks of having an inexperienced captain at the helm—lots of sailors on this ship, 'sir'—and yet we still decided to come. And as for you 'insisting' this ship come back to Earth with the vaccine, I seem to remember a certain Council of duly elected representatives having a little something to do with that decision. Or did you get yourself crowned king sometime while I wasn't paying attention?"

The flicker of anger fanned to a flame. "I'm still responsible," Richard snarled. "The Council agreed, but I pushed for it. They felt they owed—"

"Owed you what? Gratitude for saving them from Cheveldeoff? Who wouldn't have shown up at all if you'd never found Marseguro in the first place?" Andy said. "Hell, Richard, I don't see why you should be so cut up over the deaths of three Marseguroites, considering how many thousands you helped kill."

The flame roared into a bonfire of fury. Richard shoved back hard, threw Andy off him, and spun to face his First Officer, fists clenched. "You know how much I hate what I was, what I did. How dare you—"

"How dare you risk all the rest of our lives letting yourself sink into self-pity?" Andy snarled. "The mistakes you made when we entered this system are *nothing* compared to what you did before. But you managed to move on. You redeemed yourself. So move on again. Redeem yourself again. Snap out of this stupid funk and start acting like the captain again or, by God, maybe there'll be four corpses cooling in here."

"That's enough!" Richard roared. "You want a captain? Fine. I'm captain. And you're—"

Under arrest, he'd started to say, but he suddenly realized just how ridiculous that would sound. His anger evaporated like a puff of air in a vacuum.

"—absolutely right," he finished, almost under his breath.

"Sir?" said Andy. "I couldn't quite hear that last bit."

Richard snorted. "Yeah, right. Okay. You win. Take me to Simon. Let's get this ship up and running." He managed a wan smile. "And, uh ... confine yourself to quarters for insubordination. Not now. When it's convenient."

"Aye, aye, sir!" Andy snapped off a salute. Then he grinned. "Welcome back, Richard."

"Thanks," Richard said. He took one long final look at the bodies, each tucked neatly beneath a blue Holy Warrior blanket. If he'd gotten them killed, the least he could do was make sure their deaths weren't wasted. Down below, the Avatar was on the march. Another race of moddies was threatened with extinction. Around the planet, unknown thousands of survivors squatted in hiding in deathly fear of the plague.

Their mission wasn't over: far from it.

He turned away from the corpses of his crew. "Lead on." Then he followed Andy back into the corridors of the *Victor Hansen*.

Chapter 15

BACK AT THE FREE Selkie Republic outpost, Emily found Sarah McLean in the wardroom, eating a nondescript slab of something that might have been animal, vegetable, or mineral—it was hard to tell. With Captain Wu standing a diplomatic distance behind her and Shelby watching from the corner, bare feet pulled up onto the bottom of his chair, arms around his knees, Emily made her plea. The President chewed and swallowed automatically while she listened, but as Emily wound down, she lowered her fork and pushed her plate aside. "The Council decided not to warn them," she said. She sounded tired.

"Because of the risk to your people," Emily said. "But you wouldn't be risking any of *your* people. Just me."

"My people would be at risk escorting you . . ."

"I'm not asking for that," Emily said. "Just get me close. I'll walk in."

Silence. Emily glanced at Shelby: his wide green eyes were locked on her.

"It sounds foolishly dangerous," McLean said finally.

"It's important to me," Emily said. "I know you have decided that you do not want to risk any of your people contacting the Kemonomimi until the Avatar has either been dealt with, or . . . not. That's your decision. But as a Marseguroite, with fresh memories of what the Holy Warriors did to us, it's important to me to try to save the Kemonomimi from the same horror." *Seize the moral high ground!* she thought. "They're family, in a way: we all carry some of Victor Hansen's genes."

More silence. Emily hoped the President was feeling at least slightly ashamed. Maybe even enough to provide her with support after all. She didn't really relish the idea of walking into the Kemonomimi camp on her own.

But if she'd shamed the President at all, she hadn't shamed her that much.

"Very well," McLean's said suddenly. "Captain Wu."

"Yes, Madame President?" Wu said, coming up to stand beside Emily.

"Do not risk detection, but deliver Miss Wood as close to the Kemonomimi village as you safely can. Provide her with food and water and a landsuit. Give her a communicator. If you succeed, Miss Wood, or if the Kemonomimi allow you to leave, you may use the communicator to call the sub. You may also use it to call for assistance if you run into trouble *before* you reach the Kemonomimi. But if you call for assistance after you reach the Kemonomimi, you will not receive any. We will not attempt a rescue. Do you understand?"

"Yes," Emily said.

"Do you understand, Captain Wu? You are not to attempt to rescue Miss Wood, even if the Kemonomimi arrest her and threaten to kill her and you learn of it."

"I understand," Wu said.

"Miss Wood," McLean said. "We have no wish to see the Kemonomimi eradicated. But we do not trust them, and we will not expose ourselves to them. We have, however, chosen to trust you, and to trust that you will not do anything that would harm the Free Selkie Republic. Please do not betray that trust."

Of all the— "I won't," Emily grated.

"Then good luck." The President, stood, tossing the napkin that had been spread on her lap onto the table as she did so. "If you'll excuse me . . ." She glanced into the corner. "Shelby?"

"But, Mom—"

"Now."

With an exaggerated sigh, Shelby plopped his feet onto the floor and followed his mother out of the wardroom.

As the door closed behind them, Wu looked at Emily. "I won't disobey her," she said quietly. "If you get into trouble, we won't be there to rescue you."

"I know."

Wu sighed. "All right. If we leave in a couple of hours, we

can have you there by first light. It means traveling all night, but you can sleep on the sub, and we're divided into day and night watches here, anyway. The crew will be fresh. Will that suit you?"

Emily shrugged. "I don't suppose it matters."

"I'll go prepare the sub, then, and get your supplies loaded." Wu gave her a long, level look. "I hope you know what you're doing." She turned and went out.

"So do I," Emily muttered. "So do I!"

Two hours later she entered the sub through its wet porch, toweled herself off, and padded forward to the control room. Wu greeted her. "We mostly just have bunks in this sub," she said, "but you can have my cabin if you want. It's the first hatch on your left as you go forward."

"Thank you," Emily said. "What about you?"

Wu laughed. "Don't worry about me. I'm a night person."

"Wake me when we're close."

"I will." Wu made shooing motions. "Go on. Rest. You're going to need it."

Emily nodded and went through the forward hatch. She found Wu's tiny cabin at once, but then her stomach growled. She hadn't eaten anything since ... well, she couldn't remember. *Better fuel up,* she thought. There was a tiny galley in the bow of the sub; she headed that way along the narrow corridor, feeling the throbbing of the engines under her feet.

They were underway.

Three days into the Holy Warriors' ten-day march to the Kemonomimi, the Avatar sat on one of the two camp stools at the mouth of his tent and looked out at falling rain. It had started around noon, and by midafternoon had been coming down so hard he'd been forced to call a halt. Their tents could keep them dry, and they had enhanced-vision equipment that ensured they could see despite the sheets of falling water, but nothing could keep them from getting bogged down in the mud and slipping on rain-slicked vegetation and lichen-covered stones. They'd have to wait it out.

Which he was doing, with ill humor, wondering why God Itself couldn't make things just a little easier for Its servants, when Grand Deacon von Eschen, hooded and cloaked in rain gear, splashed across the ankle-deep stream running down the middle of the camp and trudged up the slope to Karl Rasmusson.

The Avatar gestured for von Eschen to sit on the second camp stool. "I hope you're here to tell me the scouts have spotted blue sky headed our way," he said.

"I'm afraid not, Your Holiness." Von Eschen shook his head. "But we've just had a message from *Sanctification*."

"They've found more vaccine?" the Avatar exclaimed, his spirits lifting.

"No," the Grand Deacon said. "The message was not from Michael Byrne. The message was from Richard Hansen."

The Avatar froze. "Impossible."

"So I would have thought," von Eschen said. "But there is no doubt about it."

"How did he . . . ?"

Von Eschen said nothing.

Damn it, God, why are you testing me like this? Karl snarled silently. "And the message?"

"I brought it with me." From underneath his dripping navy-blue rain vestments, he pulled a datapad, and thumbed it to life.

Richard Hansen's face appeared on the tiny screen, and his voice, tinny but recognizable, rang out in the tent. "Your Holiness," he said. "It is my pleasure to inform you that *MSS Victor Hansen* is once again in the hands of her Marseguroite crew, though I must sadly say that this was not accomplished without considerable loss of life, primarily among the Holy Warriors you sent to board her.

"The three surviving Warriors have been vaccinated and imprisoned. Please don't concern yourself about their safety.

"I'm contacting you now to urge you to reconsider your attack on the Kemonomimi. By now they must know you are coming, and will either fade away into the mountains, or will stand and fight. In either case, you will not find their Purification an easy task. It will be made less easy now that we control this starship.

"I propose that you return to Paradise Island while I talk to the Kemonomimi. There is no need to start the reconstruction of Earth with a war. Peaceful coexistence and cooperation would—"

"Kill it," the Avatar snarled.

Von Eschen turned off the display. "The message ends with a request for a response," he said. "If you do not agree to his terms, Hansen says, he will use the resources of the starship to stop our advance."

The Avatar snorted. "What resources? His crew scattered *Sanctification*'s assault craft to the four corners of the world when we took the ship. They can't retrieve them quickly, if they can retrieve them at all. He only has a handful of Selkies and nonmods to begin with, hardly enough to turn the tide against our army. And they themselves dismantled *Sanctification*'s Orbital Bombardment System." He shook his head. "We do not answer. We ignore his 'demands.' I don't know how he managed to retake the ship, but it's of no concern. Our concern is with the Kemono-mimi. We must Purify them to prove to God we are worthy of Its blessing and protection once more." He looked up; a patch of blue sky had just drifted over the mountain peak to the west, and the rain had definitely lessened. "Ah," he said. "Grand Deacon, I believe we may have just passed a test." He got to his feet. "We'll be able to continue our march in the morning. Make sure everyone is ready."

"Yes, Your Holiness," the Grand Deacon said. He stood, saluted, then splashed back across the camp.

The Avatar looked back up at the clearing sky. "Rot in orbit, 'Captain' Hansen," he said. "You gave us the vaccine. Your role in the work of God is done." He looked around the camp. "Mine remains unfinished."

Chris Keating stood with Victor Hansen and Cleopatra inside the waiting area of the air terminal building Hansen had made his headquarters, watching the rain sluice down the runway. "It won't last the day," Hansen said, looking to the west, where the sky was already noticeably brighter, although to the east the mountains were still completely lost in the clouds. The higher elevations were, no doubt, receiving a prodigious dump of that strange white stuff Chris had read about but had never encountered in person: snow.

Only the highest of the inaccessible peaks along the western shore of Marseguro's lone continent sported a crown of snow, and Chris had never been up there. No one on Marseguro had, as far as he knew. Certainly no Selkie would dare attempt to climb a mountain in a landsuit. They had enough trouble staying comfortable in warm, moist air. The cold, dry air of a mountain peak would be torture.

Wish I could haul Emily Wood up there, he thought.

"Tomorrow morning, then," Victor Hansen said. He put his arm around Cleopatra's waist and gave it a squeeze, then looked at Chris. "I'll have your pack prepared tonight. Warm coat, good boots, plenty of food and water. You'll have an escort, of course. They'll get you as close as is safe for them. You won't need to fear getting lost."

And you won't need to fear I'll simply take off, Chris thought. "I'm ready," he said out loud.

"Good." Victor returned his gaze to the rain-spattered windows. "We haven't been able to get a good read on the Avatar's position for a couple of days, but he can't be making good time in this weather. You should reach him in about four days. Five at the outside."

Chris nodded. "Does that give you enough time to get your bomb into position in the pass?"

Cleopatra nuzzled Hansen's neck. "The bomb will be where it needs to be," he said, rubbing his cheek against the top of her head. "I promise you that. You do your job, and we'll do ours. And then, once the Body Purified has been . . . well, Purified, in their own twisted sense of that word . . . then you and I can turn our attention to the Selkies of Marseguro."

"I wish you'd tell me more about this weapon of yours,' Chris said. "The one that will wipe out all the Selkies. I'm dying of curiosity."

"All in good time," Victor Hansen said. "All in good time."

A shaft of sunlight speared down on the runway.

Tap tap tap. Emily jerked awake in the pitch-darkness of her borrowed cabin. *What was . . . ?*

Tap tap tap. "Miss Wood?" said a voice muffled by the steel door. "Miss Wood? Captain Wu sends her compliments and asks you to join her in the control room."

Emily sat up and flicked on the lights, winced, squinted, and called, "Thank you. I'll be along shortly."

She used the head, brushed her teeth, put on her skin-suit, and within half an hour joined the captain in the control room, still yawning. Wu held two steaming cups of something; without a word she handed one to Emily, who sipped it cautiously. It was hot and not *too* unpleasant, if you concentrated really hard on the short list of all the worst things you had tasted in your life. "I can't send an escort with you," Wu said, "but nobody told me I can't help you with a little offshore reconnaissance."

Emily blinked at her. "I don't understand."

"We're about two kilometers out from Newshore and we've just launched a micro-ARV," Wu said. "Thought you might at least want to have a look at where you're going before you head there."

"I appreciate that," Emily said. "I hope you won't get in trouble."

"No reason I should," Wu said cheerfully. She drained her mug. "Finished with that?"

Emily nodded and handed her her own mug, still half full. Despite the liquid's foul taste, she had to admit she somehow felt more awake than she had just moments before. Wu handed both mugs off to a crewman, then led Emily to one of the stations along the walls. Large vidscreens curved around the seat there, occupied by a young Selkie woman who gave Emily a quick smile before turning her attention back to her controls. "All right, Malia, let's see what we can see."

"Aye, aye, ma'am," the crewwoman said, and pushed a tiny joystick forward with her right thumb while her left hand played over a keyboard. The screens lit up.

The ARV was currently just a few centimeters above the almost perfectly flat water. Emily could see the coastline, rock-strewn and dotted with trees, a cluster of buildings, a pier. Forested hills rose all around the town, climbing up in the distance to jagged mountains, silhouetted against pink eastern sky. A good-sized river emptied into the sea through the town, a curved wooden bridge spanning it not far from its mouth.

"A little more elevation, if you please, Malia," said Captain Wu. "And then zoom in on the town."

Malia nodded and pushed the joystick further forward, tapping again with her left hand. The buildings seemed to rush toward them at the same time as they dropped away below them, and now Emily could make some kind of sense out of them. An aircraft sat motionless on a runway. That low building with the single tower with the glass-walled room atop it must be the terminal. Houses were scattered among the trees, and just visible further inland slightly taller buildings rose, the largest maybe four stories—presumably Newshore's commercial district, if it had such a thing.

But then Emily forgot all about Newshore's buildings as she caught her first glimpse of its people.

Two figures strolled around the aircraft, apparently inspecting it, and although they were quite small on the screen, she could see them well enough to realize they looked . . . odd.

"Can we zoom in even more?"

"Of course," Wu said. "Malia."

Again the scene rushed toward her. The image danced and flickered, but now she could see the people more clearly.

They were heavily furred over every inch of their naked bodies. One had fur of almost pure white, with black stripes circling his torso and legs and . . . was that a tail?

It lashed as he turned to say something to his companion. Yes, definitely a tail.

His ears were large and pointed and tufted with black, and though located on the side of his head, not the top, seemed capable of independent movement, like a cat's. His eyes, too, looked catlike, with slit pupils instead of a normal human's—

She caught herself, shocked at her own turn of thought. Since when did a Selkie think of a nonmod as a "normal human"?

Since she came face-to-face with a version of humanity as different from her as she is from a nonmod, she thought. She glanced at Wu, who was staring at the screen with fascination and a hint of disgust on her face. *No wonder the Free Selkie Republic doesn't want to have anything to do with the Kemonomimi,* she thought. *They're not just different, they're* too *different. Too animallike.*

And what will they think of us? she wondered.

Well, I guess I'll find that out soon enough.

The second Kemonomimi, a female—a *woman,* Emily

consciously corrected herself—laughed at something the man had said. She was pitch-black from nose to tail, sleek and muscular and glistening and . . .

. . . *beautiful,* Emily thought. *She's beautiful.*

But oh, so strange.

"Pull out again," Wu said. "Let's see if we can find any more."

The image expanded. The two Kemonomimi disappeared around the back side of the aircraft. At the same time, though, a much larger group came out of the terminal building. "Zoom in on those," Wu said. Malia nodded and adjusted her controls. The image shifted, swelled—

—and Emily gasped out loud.

Wu turned on Emily, her face suddenly hard and unfriendly. "What is *he* doing there?" she snarled. "Have you been lying to us?"

Emily didn't answer. She couldn't.

On the screen, moving easily alongside half a dozen Kemonomimi wearing body armor and carrying rifles, she saw someone she'd never thought to see again: Chris Keating.

But even more impossibly, standing next to him was a man who looked exactly like Richard Hansen, holding hands with a sleek white Kemonomimi woman.

"Richard is in space," she said finally. "You saw . . . we all saw . . . him launch in the shuttle."

"We saw him launch. We don't know where he went after that," Wu said. "Maybe he flew here. And maybe your volunteering to warn the Kemonomimi was just your way of rejoining him. Maybe you're planning to betray us to the Kemonomimi."

"What?" Emily turned to stare at her, honestly bewildered. "To what possible end?"

"To . . ." Wu paused. "To . . ." She blinked, and then suddenly laughed. "I have no idea." Her laugh faded. "But whether it makes sense or not, that's what the President and Council would think if they were here."

"Good thing they're not, then," Emily said. She shook her head. "I don't know what's going on. That can't be Richard. But I do know who the other man is."

"Who?"

"Chris Keating." Emily said the name like it left a bad taste in her mouth, which wasn't too far from the truth.

"I take it you don't like him," Wu said dryly. She looked at the screen again. Keating and the man-who-looked-like-Richard were talking. One of the Kemonomimi handed Chris a large backpack and helped him struggle into it.

"I hate him," Emily spat. "He's from Marseguro. But he betrayed us. He activated the signal that brought the Holy Warriors down on our heads. And he's the one who brought the plague to Earth."

"Yeah?" Wu looked at Emily. "Maybe we should thank him."

Emily's mouth tightened, but she let that pass. "I don't know how he's survived. And I sure as hell don't know what he's doing with the Kemonomimi. He's a fanatic. He hates moddies, *all* moddies; lives and breathes the *Wisdom of The Avatar*. If he's helping them, or they're helping him, then either they're deluded or he is."

"Like your friend, there?"

"That's not Richard!"

Wu held up her hands. "Whatever you say. But you have to admit it looks—"

It suddenly sank in. "It's another clone," Emily said. "It must be."

Wu's eyes widened. "Another clone of Victor Hansen?" She stared at the man on the screen, who gave the Kemonomimi woman a lingering kiss on the lips, then took Keating by the arm and turned him inland, so their backs were to the sub. "But why is he here?"

"I don't know," Emily said. "But I think it's about time I went ashore and found out."

Wu stared at the screen for another long moment, then said. "I think you're right. Helm, take us south around the headland."

"Aye, aye, ma'am," said the Selkie at the sub's main controls.

Wu looked at Emily. "There's a good place to swim ashore there, and you'll be out of sight of Newshore. And if you change your mind, we can pick you up again there before you make contact."

Emily shook her head. "I won't change my mind." She pointed at the screen. "Especially not after seeing *him*."

Twenty minutes later they hovered in twenty-five meters of water at the mouth of the narrow cove just south of

Newshore's wider bay. Emily, wearing her black landsuit, with her waterproof pack of supplies strapped to her back, sat on the edge of the wet porch with her webbed feet in the cold water. "Last chance to reconsider," said Wu, the only other Selkie in the compartment; this close to Kemonomimi territory, Wu had doubled up everyone at the duty stations on the bridge, so twice as many eyes were watching the sonar, radar, and visual displays.

"Thank you for your help," Emily said. "Tell President McLean I'll be in touch."

"I'll tell her," Wu said. "Don't make me into a liar."

"I'll do my best." Emily gave a final wave, then slipped into the water.

She swam ashore uneventfully, never looking back at the sub. She clambered out onto wet rocks, turned to take a last look out to where she had left the sub . . . and jumped back so suddenly she tripped and fell painfully onto her rear end as a head rose out of the water directly in front of her.

Then, as the rest of the Selkie's body appeared, surprise gave way to dismay. "Shelby?"

He stood in water waist-deep, four or five meters offshore, holding his own dripping waterproof pack in his right hand. "My mother's wrong," he said. "She should have sent help with you."

"So you decided to come yourself?" Emily climbed to her feet and winced as she rubbed her bruised bottom. "Shelby, this is nuts! I can't let you do this."

"You can't stop me," he said. "I'm volunteering, just like you. I've thought long and hard about this. We need to warn these people. They're moddies, just like us. I don't know why my mother won't—"

"She's President," Emily said. "Her responsibility is to her people. *Your* people. The Free Republic has stayed hidden for decades. Warning the Kemonomimi could expose the Republic to the Body, if the Body prevails. She doesn't want to risk that. And she certainly doesn't want to risk her son. Nor do I." She shook her head violently. "No, Shelby, you can't come. You don't even have a landsuit, for God's sake!"

He held up his pack. "Want to bet?"

Emily ground her teeth. "Nevertheless, you can't come."

"You can't stop me."

"Oh, yeah?" Emily said. "There's a communicator in the backpack. I'm going to call Captain Wu and—"

Something in Shelby's expression stopped her. He wasn't even looking at her: he was looking beyond her, and his eyes had widened.

Already knowing what she would see, Emily turned around to face the armed Kemonomimi on the shore.

There were half a dozen of them, five men and one black-furred woman who held Emily's backpack in one hand and a pistol in the other. They wore helmets and body armor. Four of the men carried rifles, all of which were pointed in their general direction. The fifth man carried something else: a massive rocket launcher that Emily was sure a nonmod would have had to set up on a tripod. He had it aimed out to sea. It took her a moment to realize what that meant.

"No!" she yelled, but it was already too late: with an ear-splitting shriek, a missile blasted from the launcher and lanced across the water of the cove. Emily whirled, Shelby following suit, just in time to see the missile plunge beneath the surface of the water. A moment later, with a dull whump!, a column of water and steam erupted into the still morning air.

Then furred arms seized Emily from behind and she was dragged across the beach. Another Kemonomimi grabbed Shelby and pulled him after her.

Behind them, the suddenly troubled water of the cove splashed erratically against the rocks.

Chapter 16

THE LOADED BACKPACK Victor Hansen gave Chris was heavy, but not much heavier than he'd often carried when he hiked on Marseguro. Inside Hansen's office, with Cleopatra sitting on the edge of the desk most distractingly, Hansen had gone over its contents: ultralight tent and sleeping bag, collapsible heater/stove, dried food, a water purifier bottle, flashlight, rope ... the usual accoutrements of any hiking trip. The camouflage-patterned clothes he'd been given were warm, flexible, and tough. So were the boots. A self-adjusting warm/cool coat rounded out his equipment.

The one thing he *didn't* have was a weapon, unless you counted his belt knife. "They're more likely to shoot you on sight if you're armed," Hansen said. "And right up until you get there, you'll be escorted."

Chris didn't buy Hansen's excuse for a minute, but he was hardly in a position to argue.

"Any questions?" Hansen asked.

"No, I don't think so," Chris said. He adjusted the pack on his back. "I'm set."

"No more delay, then." Hansen held out his hand to Cleopatra; she took it, and they all went out onto the runway, where they were promptly joined by six waiting Kemonomimi, wearing helmets and body armor (but still no pants or boots), and carrying rifles, sidearms, swordlike blades and backpacks bigger than Chris'. Two more Kemonomimi, a man and a woman, were inspecting the aircraft Chris had arrived on. The sun hadn't cleared the mountains yet, but the cloudless sky was washed with pale pink, fading to deep blue out over the ocean.

Victor Hansen turned him away from the view and pointed inland. "You're heading toward that notch in the ridge where the river comes down. You should make it by nightfall. There's a good campsite near the top. We'll send up reconnaissance today to pin down the Avatar's location, but with any luck you'll get to him the day after tomorrow." He turned and kissed Cleo full on the lips, lingeringly; she rose on her toes and pushed her hips against him. Chris swallowed and looked away. A moment later Hansen took his arm and led him inland; Chris glanced back to see Cleo walking, hips and tail undulating in a most . . . interesting . . . fashion, back toward the terminal.

The six armed Kemonomimi fell in behind Hansen and Chris. Hansen led them to where the river ran along the airfield's border, stopping when the short-cropped bot-mowed airfield grass gave way to the longer, untidier flora of the wild. There Hansen held out his hand. Chris took it. "Good luck," Hansen said. "With your help, Earth will finally be free of the Body . . . and soon, Marseguro will be free of the Selkies." He released Chris' hand, then stepped back.

There didn't seem to be anything to say to that, so Chris took the hint and started up the trail that ran alongside the river, shadowed by his taciturn escort. Hansen hadn't introduced him to any of them—the *only* Kemonomimi Hansen had introduced him to so far had been Cleopatra—and looking at their grim, fur-covered faces, Chris guessed they weren't particularly interested in his introducing himself. *It's going to be a quiet trip,* he thought.

Well, that suited him. Making small talk with the abominations that had caused God to turn Its hand against Earth didn't exactly appeal to him anyway.

He had work to do . . . if not *quite* the work Victor Hansen thought.

"No reply," Cordelia Raum told Richard.

It had been twenty-four hours since he'd issued his ultimatum to the Avatar. The Avatar, it appeared, had no intention of responding.

"Did you really expect one?" Andy said.

Richard shook his head. "Not really. But I didn't see the harm in offering him a way out."

Andy snorted. "A way out. As if his fate is sealed if he

refuses to surrender to us. Do you know something you haven't told me?"

Richard rubbed his forehead. "I wish," he said. "But you know as well as I do what resources we have to draw on." He stared gloomily at the blue curve of the Earth on the main bridge display. "I think we were too smart when we set up the Submerge routine."

"If we'd left the assault craft on board, the Body would probably have them now," Andy pointed out. "And if they did, the Kemonomimi would already be dead."

Richard sighed. "I know, I know. So. What *have* we got that we can use against the Avatar?"

"Some pretty heavy weapons," Andy said. "Some ground vehicles, but I don't think they'll do us any good in that terrain. Light aircraft, unarmed. Cargo shuttles, too unmaneuverable to be of any use. And, currently, two personnel shuttles: the four-person flyer you came up in and the one the Holy Warriors . . . won't be needing anymore."

"Can we command that one?"

"Simon Goodfellow says yes," Andy said. "The reboot is proceeding smoothly, and that shuttle has been slaved to our AI. It will recognize the same chain of command."

"And it will hold . . . ?"

"Maybe twenty people at most, lightly armed," Andy said. "Fewer if they take some of the heavier equipment."

"Not enough, in other words."

"No."

"And no chance of getting one of the assault craft back."

Andy hesitated. "Define 'chance.' "

Richard straightened in the captain's chair. "You've pinpointed their locations?"

"Define 'pinpoint.' " Andy held up a hand. "I'm not being funny. We know within, say, a hundred kilometers, where each one went down. Presumably, if we took one of our surviving shuttles down, we could, eventually and with luck, locate them all."

Richard sighed. "I hear a 'but' coming."

"Good ears. Are you sure you're not Selkie?" Andy nodded. "But . . . although we know approximately where they are, we have no idea whether they're intact. They were never meant to fly themselves out of orbit. Simon programmed them as best he could, but he won't guarantee—"

"Simon won't guarantee that the sun will come up tomorrow," Richard said. "But it always has so far."

Andy made a noncommittal sound.

Richard rubbed his forehead again. "Let's start with the basics. Where are they?"

"One is somewhere in the Himalayas," Andy said. "Quite possibly in a crumpled heap in a glacial crevasse. One came down near the southern tip of Africa. Fairly flat there, it might be okay. And one is actually remarkably close to the Kemonomimi and the Free Selkie Republic . . . but since it's about two hundred kilometers offshore, I suspect it's too deep for any Selkie to reach."

"Even with a sub?"

Andy shrugged. "Unknown."

Richard nodded slowly. "All right. We have two shuttles. We send one to Africa with a recovery team. As for the other, perhaps if I ask nicely, President McLean will—"

"Transmission from the surface for Captain Hansen," the computer said suddenly.

"Computer, identify source," Richard said.

"Source self-identifies as President Sarah McLean of the Free Selkie Republic."

Richard shot a look at Andy. "Maybe Earth Selkies are telepathic." He raised his voice. "Computer, put it through."

The main display screen suddenly showed Sarah McLean, and Richard knew instantly something was wrong. For the first time since he'd met her, she looked flustered. Selkies' eyes always looked a bit watery to him, since they were so much larger, but hers looked so watery he could only think she'd been crying. And her gray-streaked black hair, longer than that of any Marseguroite Selkie he'd ever seen, but usually kept tightly under control in a bun or pony tail, hung loose around her face.

"President McLean?" Richard said. "What—"

"The Kemonomimi captured Emily as soon as she landed," the President said, her voice tight. "They must have spotted the sub. One of the Kemonomimi had a rocket launcher loaded with some kind of antisubmarine depth charge. Lia Wu's sub was severely damaged, but she managed to slip away before a ship rounded the headland from Newshore. She may still have to abandon ship before she gets back to this outpost."

Richard found he was gripping the arms of his chair so tightly his fingers hurt. He forced himself to relax them. "She's made contact, then," he said, keeping his voice steady. "That's what she wanted."

"She wasn't the only one the Kemonomimi took," McLean said. "They've got my . . ." A hard swallow. "They've got Shelby. My son. He apparently stowed away on the sub. I thought he was just sulking in his room here on the habitat. I never thought . . ." She swallowed again. "He swam ashore behind Emily. The Kemonomimi have him, too."

"Emily will look after Shelby," Richard said. "She won't let them hurt him."

"How will she stop them?" The President's eyes suddenly blazed. "Two of Wu's crew were injured in that attack, Captain Hansen. One of them may not make it . . . absolutely won't, if the crew has to abandon ship. And now my son is being held by those . . . savages? I want him back, Captain Hansen." She leaned forward, so her face almost filled the screen. "I gave you your ship back. Now I want you to forget the Avatar for the time being. I want my son back!

"I can't attempt a rescue myself," she went on. "The whole Free Selkie Republic only has half a dozen subs, the nearest is three days away, and Wu's is the largest. But *you* can be down there within hours."

Richard sat silent for a long moment. "If we attempt a rescue, we may get them both killed," he said.

"If we don't, they may kill them anyway," the President said. Her face hardened. "This is not a negotiable request, Captain Hansen. If you want the cooperation of the Free Selkie Republic in distributing your vaccine—distributing it to nonmods who some of our people might well think we'd be better off leaving to die—you will attempt to rescue my son. Do I make myself clear?"

Richard felt his temper rising, but pushed it down. "Perfectly," he said in as even a tone as he could manage. "But I hope you know what you're doing." Richard glanced at Andy. "Change of plan. Forget the assault craft in Africa. We need to get whatever forces we can on the ground near Newshore as soon as possible."

"Aye, aye, sir," Andy said. He turned on his heel, went to

his station, pulled on a headset and began talking in a low voice.

Richard turned back to McLean. "I have very limited resources," he said. "Far fewer than I'd hoped. But we'll bring down as many people as we can. We should be able to land within a few hours' walk of Newshore without the Kemonomimi seeing us. We'll reconnoiter on foot and then decide on a course of action."

"The Free Selkie Republic thanks you," McLean said formally. Then her voice softened. "And I thank you. I won't forget this, Captain."

"I'll keep you posted," Richard said. "Captain Hansen out. Computer, discontinue link."

The screen blanked, and Richard, keeping a tight hold on his own emotions, went to talk to Andy.

The Kemonomimi tied Emily's and Shelby's hands behind their backs, gagged them, then propelled them up a muddy track to a badly deteriorated paved road that ran along the shore until it plunged through the woods above the headland. The black-furred female led the way, with Emily walking between two of the males right behind her and Shelby, accompanied by his own pair of guards, behind her. The big Kemonomimi with the rocket launcher brought up the rear.

She became aware that the Kemonomimi on her left was staring at her. She stared back just as boldly.

His red-furred face had a hint of a stripe pattern, darker fur forming a kind of W shape over his eyes radiating out from his mouth and nose. Unlike a true cat, he didn't have long vibrissae, and his mouth and nose were close to human: no harelip. Thicker, darker hair, rather like a mane, swelled out from under the back of his helmet and flowed partway down the back of his armored vest.

"Can you talk?" he said suddenly.

The words shocked Emily. She realized she'd been thinking of him as an animal, not a human. *Just as the Holy Warriors think of us,* she thought.

"Do you understand me?" he said.

In fact she had a little trouble in that regard. His canines were sharper and longer than a nonmod's and they gave him a kind of lisping accent, with barely-there plosives. He made up for it with harsh gutturals, though.

The gag kept her from speaking, of course, but she nodded at him. His eyes widened, she felt a moment's satisfaction to think he had probably been thinking of her as something as inhuman as she'd been thinking of him . . . and then she felt shame. She'd claimed she wanted to talk to the Kemonomimi. It looked like she'd get her chance. And all she could think about was how weird they were.

I didn't want to talk to them this *way,* she thought. *Not trussed up like a feastfish on Landing Day. Not a prisoner taken by force.*

What had happened to the sub?

How could she offer hope for a peaceful alliance after that unprovoked attack?

"Quiet," snarled the black-furred female, turning her head so that Emily could see her gleaming teeth. "It is for the Creator to talk to these creatures, not you."

"I am sorry, Ubasti," said the male, and after that he kept his eyes resolutely forward.

So she's in command, Emily thought. *Interesting.* And then . . .

They're taking me to meet their Creator?

A few minutes later they came out of the patch of pine trees and left the road, striding across close-cropped green grass toward the landing strip Emily had seen from the sub, and the cluster of buildings alongside it. Looking to her left, she saw the water of Newshore Bay, houses close to the shore, small boats tied up to little piers, and the arched bridge she knew took the road they had been on over the river that emptied into the bay.

The nonmod who looked like Richard Hansen stood waiting for them by the terminal building, his arm around the white-furred female Kemonomimi she had seen from the sub, his own all-black attire—black pants, black boots, a black T-shirt, a black leather jacket—making a striking contrast to her, which Emily was quite sure was intentional. The stranger had a pistol holstered on one hip and a long knife or short sword sheathed on the other.

"Good work, Ubasti," the man said as they approached.

"Thank you, Creator," Ubasti said. She walked up to

Emily and pulled the gag off her face with sudden, brutal force. Emily jerked her head and glared at her, but the black-furred Kemonomimi had already stepped past her to do the same to Shelby.

"What's your name?" the man said, his voice very much like Richard's, but full of an arrogance she'd never heard from her lover.

"Emily Wood," she said. "What's yours?"

The man cocked his head to one side, a gesture so much like one she had seen Richard do a thousand times that it made her heart ache; but his next words shocked her. "I'm Victor Hansen," he said. "And I'm your creator."

"That's impossible," Shelby said in the kind of sneering, contemptuous voice that only a teenager could manage. "Victor Hansen left Earth seventy years ago. He never came back."

"A lie," said the man who called himself Victor Hansen. "A lie told by the Body . . . and apparently by the Selkies, too."

"Prove it," Shelby said. Emily wanted to tell him to be quiet, but "Victor Hansen" just laughed.

"My dear fishboy," he said, "I don't have to prove anything to you. Now be quiet."

Shelby drew in his breath as though about to speak, but Ubasti's hand, still holding the pistol, lashed out. The butt of the gun clubbed the boy behind the ear, and he cried out and dropped to his knees, gasping, blood dripping onto the concrete.

Emily jerked at her bonds, but Ubasti's flat eyes turned toward her and she subsided. "There was no need for that!" she cried. "You could have killed him!"

"He won't interrupt again," Ubasti said.

"Now, now, Ubasti," Victor Hansen said. "I appreciate your devotion, but that was perhaps a little extreme. Please don't damage either of them further unless I tell you to."

Ubasti inclined her head in his direction. "Of course, Creator." She stepped back, but she didn't holster her gun and she resumed her watch on Emily.

Victor . . . Emily didn't know what else to call him . . . came closer to her. "So," he said. "Emily Wood. From Marseguro."

She blinked. "How did you . . . ?"

Victor laughed. "Where else could Selkies have come from?"

A light went on in her head. *He doesn't know. He doesn't know about the Free Selkie Republic. He thinks all the Selkies he's seen came with us from Marseguro.*

She wished she could warn Shelby.

"Yes," she said. "From Marseguro . . . like Chris Keating," she added, watching to see if the name meant anything.

If it did, Victor didn't let on. Which was also very Richard-like: Richard had the best poker face Emily had ever seen, when he wanted to use it.

"Tell me, Miss Wood," Victor said, looking at her once more. "Life on Marseguro, before the Body so unfortunately managed to locate you . . . was it good?"

"Better than we knew," Emily said. Those days before the Holy Warriors announced their presence with blood and thunder seemed like a golden age from ancient history.

"My Kemonomimi, too, are working toward a world without the Body," Victor said. "So that they can enjoy, here on Earth, what you Selkies had for so long on Marseguro."

Emily said nothing.

"But there is a problem," Victor admitted. He looked from her to Shelby, who still sat with his head down, his breathing ragged. "You Selkies."

"Why is that a problem?" Emily said. "We're happy in the water, you're happy on land. We'll take the oceans, you can have everything else."

Victor laughed. "Miss Wood, are you trying to bargain with me? To negotiate?"

"There's no reason Kemonomimi and Selkies should be enemies," Emily said. "We're all moddies. Victor Hansen . . ." She hesitated. *Humor the insane,* her father used to say. *Just don't vote for them.* "*You* made us both."

"True, Miss Wood." Victor came close to her, uncomfortably close, and looked her in the eyes. "But there is one great distinction between you."

"They've got fur, we've got gills?" Emily said. It might have made Richard laugh. Victor only smiled.

"Besides that." He reached up and touched the side of

her neck, where the high collar of the landsuit hid her gills. She had to hold on to herself to keep from flinching, though when Richard had touched her naked gills just two nights before . . .

Another difference between them, she thought.

"You were my biggest mistake," he said softly. "I had already created the perfect race of moddies, and yet I created another. If I believed in sin, or believed in any god, I would say I suffered from hubris.

"But there is no sin, no God, and no such thing as hubris. There is only life, a brief stumble from nothingness to nothingness. What I did was not sin, but it was . . . unwise. I thought that since I had created one race, I should create another. But I was wrong."

He stepped back and put his arm affectionately around the white-furred Kemonomimi woman. Ubasti's eyes flicked from Emily to Victor as he did so, and Emily thought she didn't look pleased. "I had already created perfection. I could not create it twice. The Selkies were inferior in every way to the Kemonomimi. I kept thinking I could improve them, somehow raise them to the level of my first creation . . . but no. It wasn't to be.

"And then I made my second mistake—or so I presume, for I no longer remember making it. Nevertheless, it appears, from the evidence, that I felt pity for your kind, my flawed, water-breathing creation. And so I arranged for you to flee to Marseguro and escape the Body Purified. I even sent along an imposter who could pretend to be me, so that you would not be deprived of your Creator; then (so I surmise) used my new life extension techniques to make myself younger and put myself into suspended animation until the time was right to emerge and lead my Kemonomimi to their rightful place as rulers of this planet."

Emily's eyes widened. *Oh . . . kay,* she thought. *He's even crazier than I imagined. Good to know . . . I think.*

"I never dreamed you would one day return to Earth. But now that you have . . . well. There is no room on this planet for both my Kemonomimi and you Marseguroites. You will leave voluntarily, or I will drive you from this planet. And soon," he said in a perfectly matter-of-fact voice, "I will eradicate you. I should never have allowed you to live in the first place. Always clean up your messes:

that's one of the first things I learned in lab classes in university."

Emily didn't know what to say, because how *do* you respond to the clone of the scientist who created your entire race when he expresses his determination to wipe it out? She felt a bit like Noah, except she didn't think her version of God was going to tell her she would be spared if she only built an ark.

Shelby raised his head. Blood had run down the side of his neck and across his chest and belly, but his voice was clear. "The real Victor Hansen is dead," he snarled. "You're just a crazy clone." Ubasti made a move toward him and he flinched, but Victor raised his hand sharply and she stepped back again.

"I'm surprised to find," Victor said, "that the Selkies of Marseguro have so willingly accepted the Body's propaganda. Well, no matter. I know the truth, and so do the Kemonomimi." With the hand that wasn't wrapped around the woman's waist, he made a grand gesture, encompassing sea, sky, and mountains. "This world is theirs," he said. "The plague I engineered to kill the nonmodded humans has given it to them."

That was too much. "*You* didn't create any plague," Emily snapped. "My mother created it to protect Marseguro from the Body. Chris Keating brought it here by accident. We would have done anything to stop it reaching Earth, if we could have."

Victor shook his head. "You are deluded," he said. "The Selkies are inferior. They could never have engineered something like this perfect plague. I have examined the plague organism in detail, since it appeared and it became apparent I and my Kemonomimi were immune. I have taken it apart and put it back together again. It is clearly the work of a genius: clearly, in other words, mine. I don't know how you Selkies got your hands on it, I confess. Most likely I sent samples along with you and the man you falsely believed was Victor Hansen, back when you fled Earth seventy years ago, as insurance against the Body eventually finding you."

Emily was beginning to realize that arguing with Victor was a waste of breath. *Nothing I say will make the slightest dent in the self-centered fantasy world he's constructed*, she thought.

It's the gene-bomb. Victor Hansen's damned gene-bomb. He thought he could live forever through his clones. Instead, he just screwed them all up.

All except Richard . . . and that had been close.

Richard had told her what it had been like when the gene-bomb, partially defused in his case by the efforts of Body Security scientists, had gone off. He'd felt as if he were splitting in two, as if he had a new and unwanted personality in his head: the ghost, almost literally, of Victor Hansen.

All her life Emily had revered Victor Hansen as the creator of their race, the man who had, against all odds, successfully stolen, outfitted, and launched a starship with the first generation of Selkies on board in the very teeth of a Body assault and founded a new world where moddies and nonmods could live in peace.

And there was no doubt it was an amazing accomplishment, and he deserved to be honored for it.

But the great hero, the great founder of their world, the man whose statue she'd seen almost every day of her life growing up, had had more than one skeleton in his closet and quite possibly a few bats in his belfry. At the very least, he had been, without question, the biggest egomaniac old Earth had ever produced.

Unlike Richard, the clone in front of her seemed to have all of the original Victor Hansen's faults and none of his redeeming qualities. He had obviously filled in the gaps in his Victor Hansen-installed memories with an elaborate fantasy of his own devising so solid that it could not be shaken by mere facts . . . even the fact he couldn't actually remember creating the plague he now claimed as his own.

He's got all of Victor Hansen's genetically determined characteristics, untempered by the experiences of his later life, she thought. *He's like a teenager, so full of himself and his wants, so convinced that he's unique—not just unique, but superior—that he sees everything in black and white . . . and for him, the Kemonomimi are the good guys, and we, clearly, are the bad ones.*

She looked at the white-furred woman. She met Emily's eyes, opened her mouth—revealing alarmingly sharp teeth—and licked her lips with a long pink tongue. "What are you staring at, fishface?" she said.

"Now, now," said Victor. "Be polite, Cleo."

Cleo turned her head. "Why?" she said. "She's a Selkie. Subhuman. Why should I be polite to a subhuman?" She nuzzled his neck. "Ubasti got to blood the young one," she said, her voice almost a purr. "Let me try my claws on the female."

Victor's face went cold and he released her waist with a jerk. "No, Cleopatra," he said, his voice like ice. "You will obey me."

Cleopatra's own eyes narrowed, and she showed her teeth again. For a bare instant, claws flicked from the ends of her fingers. Then, suddenly, the tension evaporated from her body, and she flowed up against Victor again. "Of course, Creator," she said, her voice purring even more than before. "I'm sorry."

Ubasti watched the interplay with eyes narrowed and ears ever-so-slightly laid back.

It's not all sweetness and light between the Kemonomimi and their "Creator," Emily thought. *Or among themselves.*

Not that that knowledge did her the slightest bit of good at the moment.

"There's no reason for Kemonomimi and Selkies to be enemies," Emily said again, though she suspected an appeal to reason would do her no good either. "And there was no need to attack the sub."

"You landed here to spy on us," Victor said. "An act of war."

"I landed to talk," Emily said. "I would have walked into your town on my own within an hour."

"Really," Victor said dryly. "Pray tell me why?"

"I came to warn you."

"Warn me?" Victor's fingers ran up and down through the fur on Cleo's belly. "How unexpectedly . . . kind. . . . of you. Warn me about what?"

Emily nodded at Shelby. "Let the boy go, and I'll tell you."

Shelby's eyes flashed. "Emily, I—"

"Be quiet, Shelby." The boy subsided, his blood-streaked face sullen.

Victor smiled. "Well, even though he's a Selkie, I'll grant you I've no interest in seeing him hurt at the moment. It would be like kicking a puppy." He paused. "I'll make a deal. Give me your warning. If it is of any value to me, I'll let him go."

Emily hesitated. She didn't trust Victor, but she had no way to drive a harder bargain. "Very well." She took a deep breath. "The Avatar is still alive. He and a sizable army of Holy Warriors are marching through the mountains right now. They're coming to destroy you."

Victor's smile grew wider, as if he were delighted. "Really?" He looked at Cleo. "Did you hear that? The Avatar himself, coming to destroy us."

"Oooh," said Cleo, sounding bored. "Eeek."

Emily felt a sinking sensation. "You know."

"Of course we know," Victor said. "I've known for a long time about the Avatar's little hideaway on Paradise Island. That's why we came here: to kill the Avatar. We would have done it on the island, but then he chose to march toward us—which makes things even easier.

"When the time is right—very soon now—we will destroy him and all his forces . . . and that will be the end of the Body Purified, and the beginning of the reign of *Homo sapiens hanseni*: the Kemonomimi."

"And then you plan to launch a fleet and try to take Marseguro, do you?" Emily said. "We fought off the Holy Warriors. We can damn well fight off you."

Victor laughed. "We will not be attacking Marseguro."

"You said you would eradicate us."

"Soon, yes. Very soon."

"But how—"

Victor laughed again. "Now, why on Earth would I tell you that?"

Shelby's head suddenly snapped up. "You're crazy!" he snarled. "A fucking lunatic! You can't—"

Victor nodded to the Ubasti. She took two steps forward and kicked Shelby hard in the stomach. The blow drove the breath from the boy's body and he doubled up and fell onto his side, mouth stretched wide, gasping for breath.

"You should have listened to Miss Wood," Victor said, "and shut up." He looked up at her. "Now," he said. "I require some information from *you*."

Emily felt rage rising inside her, a fury she recognized, first cousin to the burning hunger for revenge that had set her soul aflame on Marseguro. She'd killed without a qualm then, on the ground and on board *Sanctification*, and she hadn't lost a moment's sleep over the horrors her mother's plague had visited on the Holy Warriors who had died at their posts, vomiting blood.

She'd thought she'd put her own warrior side behind her. She'd come here hoping for peace, not war. But at that moment, if she could have reached him, she would have snapped the grinning clone's neck in an instant, no matter how much he looked like Richard.

"I have nothing to tell you," she snarled.

"But you do," Victor said. "I need to know how many Marseguroites are on Earth, and how many more in orbit. I need to know what kind of weapons they have, and if they are likely to use them. And I need to know everything there is to know about Marseguro itself, and exactly how my pet plague was used to destroy the Holy Warriors who attacked it.

"I need to know so many things, Miss Wood." He smiled and pulled Cleopatra close; she put her arm around his shoulders and her tail around his waist, leaned in close, and nuzzled her head against his neck. "And you're going to tell them to me." His smile faded slightly. "One way or another."

Emily clenched her jaw, and said nothing.

Victor sighed. "You're going to make this difficult, aren't you? Well, no matter. The end will be the same." He nodded to Ubasti, who still stood over Shelby. The boy had finally managed to start breathing again but showed no signs of getting up. "Lock them up where I told you. Provide the boy with whatever first aid is required. I'll be along shortly to question them." With Cleo still clinging to him, he turned and walked away.

Ubasti nodded to one of the male Kemonomimi, who picked Shelby up like a sack of grain and slung him over his shoulder. The boy groaned and promptly threw up all down the back of the man's armored vest. The Kemonomimi grimaced and his tail twitched like an angry cat's, but he set off in the direction of the taller buildings Emily had seen earlier, the ones she thought marked the miniscule town's downtown core, such as it was. Her own guards grabbed her arm and propelled her in the same direction. Ubasti moved forward to once more take the lead.

"Downtown" seemed a little grand to describe a single street with a dozen storefronts, a restaurant/pub ("The Tipsy Sasquatch"), a Body Sanctuary, a town hall—and, next door to it, Newshore School, a two-story building of red brick trimmed with white limestone, with what looked like two classroom wings and a larger central section. The Kemonomimi dragged them up the broad flight of stairs at the front of the school, through the glass doors into a dark, musty-smelling lobby, and down the hallway to the right.

Doors opened on either side of the corridor, lit only by the light that made it down its length from the fire doors at the far end and the lobby behind them. Three doors down, they stopped. Ubasti pulled a keycard from her belt and opened the door. The Kemonomimi carrying Shelby disappeared inside with him. "Patch up his head," Ubasti ordered through the open door, then led the way one door closer to the lobby on the opposite side of the hall. Ubasti opened it, Emily was propelled through it, and then it slammed behind her.

She looked around. "You've got to be kidding me!"

They'd locked her in the girls' toilet. The walls were bare and a most unappealing shade of pink. High windows, far too small to climb through, let in a modicum of the morning light, while a recessed light ring in the ceiling provided a modicum more. Someone had set up a cot along the wall under the window, where it blocked one of the six stalls. *Well, after all,* Emily thought sardonically, *how many stalls do I really need?*

And that was that. She couldn't talk to Shelby. She'd had her chance to talk to Victor Hansen, and he wasn't buying what she was selling. Instead, he wanted information that would help him . . . what? Eradicate all the Selkies? But how, since he denied any plans to actually attack Marseguro?

He's crazy. You can't expect him to make sense.

But crazy or not, it sounded very much as if he intended to torture her to get her to answer his questions.

Emily had never been tortured, but she already knew one thing she would not—could not—let slip, no matter what: the fact that Selkies already lived beneath Earth's oceans. She hoped Shelby would have the presence of mind to keep that monumental secret.

She hoped *she* would.

She lay down on the bunk with her arms under her head, stared up at the pink ceiling, and waited.

Half an hour later, the door suddenly opened. Victor Hansen stepped inside the washroom. The same two Kemonomimi who had guarded her since she'd been first seized followed him, though there was no sign of Ubasti. "So," Victor said. "Ready to answer questions?"

"I won't betray my people," Emily said.

"Really?" Victor grinned, as though delighted by her refusal. "Oh, good, because I've been dying to try something, and now I have the perfect excuse." He nodded to the Kemonomimi accompanying him, who stepped forward. Emily drew back against the cot, but she had nowhere else to run.

"They won't hurt you," Victor said. "They just want your landsuit."

"What?" Emily felt as if she had just stepped into thin air from a thousand-foot cliff. "But I—"

"You'll gradually dehydrate without it," Hansen said conversationally. "Yes, I know. What I don't know—probably because of my unfortunate memory loss—is *how* gradually. Or what your reaction to the process will be. So this is the perfect opportunity for me to gather some solid data on Selkie physiology, potentially valuable should I find the need to question more Selkies in the future."

Emily felt cold. She'd had a taste of dehydration aboard the *Divine Will*, but that had been mitigated by her mother's sharing of her landsuit and the access to the shower. Here . . . she looked around. No shower. And simply wetting her gills from the sinks . . . wouldn't be enough. Not nearly enough.

"So," Victor said. "Will you remove your landsuit, or shall they?"

Emily's rage threatened to choke her, but she pulled off the landsuit and let it fall, heavy with water, to the ground, and stood there in her striped skinsuit, glaring at Victor.

"Now," he said. "I think we'll have the skinsuit off, too."

What? Her hands clenched. "No," she growled.

He sighed. "I'll have *them* do it, if you prefer. I'm sure they'd enjoy that."

Emily ground her teeth, but there was nothing for it. Defiantly she slipped the skinsuit off of one shoulder, then the other, then shoved it to the floor and stepped out of it.

The Kemonomimi's lips parted in toothy grins. Victor stepped closer. "Interesting," he said, running his eyes over her form.

"Is that why none of your Kemonomimi wear clothes, Hansen?" she snarled. "So you can ogle naked women?"

"They're not naked," he said. "They've got fur. And as for ogling naked women, my interest in your body is purely scientific, I assure you. I haven't had the opportunity to examine my handiwork before. Perhaps it will bring back some of my lost memories. Now stand still."

Emily's instinct was to fold her arms over her breasts, but instead she forced herself to stand proudly, arms at her side, glaring at Victor Hansen, imagining how his throat would feel in her grip, how it would sound as he choked for breath . . .

"Ah," he said. He walked back and forth as if examining a sculpture. "An extra layer of fat, I see; makes sense for an aquatic creature. And completely hairless." He looked up. "I wonder why I didn't get the hair off your head while I was at it? Seems useless for a sea creature." He stepped back. "Well. Very interesting. Inferior to the Kemonomimi, of course, but still, quite an amazing accomplishment on my part."

"May I get dressed now?" Emily grated.

Victor sighed. "Oh, every well. But no landsuit." He went to the door, then glanced back as she bent down and pulled up the skinsuit. "In eight hours, I will ask you some questions, and you will answer them; or if you do not, I will wait another eight hours and then ask them again. And then another eight."

"You'll have a long wait."

Victor shook his head sorrowfully. "Please, Miss Wood, spare me the bravado. You've been living a lie, all those years on Marseguro, convinced you were free. You have never been free. I am your creator, and I own you, as I own the Kemonomimi. And like all the creators in all the myths that have come down to us from Earth's ancient history, I play favorites. The Kemonomimi are my Chosen People, and the Selkies . . . the Selkies, in the words of the Christian Bible, 'I will spew out of my mouth.' " With that, he exited. The Kemonomimi followed, one carrying the landsuit. The door slammed shut behind them, and locked.

I won't tell him anything, Emily thought fiercely. *I won't.*

But as she sat down on the bed and wrapped its navy-blue blanket around her shoulders, she couldn't help thinking about his threat. Eight hours without water would be no problem; Selkies slept dry, after all. But they also went for a swim first thing in the morning, typically even before breakfast.

Sixteen hours without water . . . or more . . .

She remembered what she had gone through on the *Divine Will,* and her stomach roiled like a witches' cauldron at full boil.

He can't mean it, she thought.

But the way he had looked at her . . . the Kemonomimi had looked at her and seen a naked woman, an object of lust. She didn't like it, but she much preferred it to the way Victor had examined her, utterly coldly, as if she were simply an interesting scientific specimen.

He saw her whole race that way. And he would throw out any specimen in an instant if it no longer suited his purposes.

He would let her die, and not lift a finger, if she didn't answer his questions.

She sat and stared at the pink concrete floor. *Eight hours,* she thought. *A lot can happen in eight hours. The Free Republic knows we're here.* She looked up at the blue door, wishing she could see across the corridor, see how Shelby was doing. *He could have a concussion . . . or cracked ribs . . . or both!*

I was a fool. I didn't believe . . . the Kemonomimi, the Selkies, we're all moddies. The Body Purified is our enemy. We should have been able to help each other.

But we—I—didn't count on an insane clone of Victor Hansen.

The Free Republic had made it clear that they wouldn't rescue her if she were imprisoned by the Kemonomimi. But Shelby . . . Shelby, the son of the President . . .

Shelby was a different matter.

They would rescue *him*. And in the process, perhaps they would rescue her, too.

All she had to do was hold on . . . eight hours at a time.

She lay on the bed with the blanket up to her chin, put her hands behind her head, stared up at the ceiling, and resumed her wait.

Chapter 17

ANDY KING HAD HEARD Richard's order to forget the assault craft in Africa. He'd immediately gone to his station and begun issuing directives that would provide Richard with the force he needed to take the ex-Holy Warriors' shuttle down to the coast of British Columbia to attempt to rescue Emily and Shelby.

But those weren't the only directives he'd issued.

Andy had had plenty of time to sound out the crew on the journey to Earth and in the days since. He knew exactly how each member of that crew felt about the mission, and how they were pursuing it.

He knew several crew members who, while willing enough to distribute vaccine to innocent nonmods, had had something on their minds more than just a mission of mercy when they had signed on, no matter what they'd paid lip service to when asked.

They wanted revenge. They wanted to make the Body pay for what it had done on Marseguro. They had come to Earth because Earth was the only place where they could still find Holy Warriors to kill, the plague having ensured they were fresh out on Marseguro.

The Avatar had proved that his only interest in the vaccine was to enable him to attempt genocide once more: he'd made no effort—none—to distribute the vaccine to civilians anywhere on the planet. He had ordered an attack on the *Victor Hansen* that had led to several Marseguroite deaths.

Now, though—now he had assembled his remaining Holy Warriors and marched them out into the open; and down in Africa one of the same assault craft used to attack Marseguro lay waiting.

Richard had promised to rescue the President's son and
Emily, and Andy agreed wholeheartedly with that attempt;
so he gave the orders that would enable Richard to do what
he wanted to do: but at the same time, he gave a few additional orders.

He rode the shaft-transport with Richard and the fifteen
crew members they'd manage to scrape together to accompany him down to the hatch that gave access to the air lock
where the Holy Warriors' shuttle was still docked. As the
transport slowed, Simon Goodfellow emerged into the shaft.

"Hello, Simon," Richard said, holding up while the rest
of the crew launched themselves through the hatch with
varying degrees of zero-G aplomb. "What's our status?"

"You're good to go, sir," Simon said. "The shuttle's AI is
fully slaved to the ship AI. It'll help you fly the shuttle, no
questions asked. And if anything does go wrong, you can
disconnect the AI and fly manually."

"Well, *I* can't," Richard said. "But I hope Claude can."

"He can," Andy said. "Claude Maurois is the best pilot
we've got, since . . ." he realized what he was about to say,
and stopped.

"Since Melody and Pierre were killed," Richard said
quietly. "I'm sure he'll do fine." He held out his hand. "Take
good care of the ship, Andy," he said. "Not that I have any
doubt you will, after what you managed last time."

"Good luck, Captain," Andy said. He shook Richard's
hand, then did something he almost never did: he saluted.
"I hope you get Emily back."

"I will." Richard said it with grim certainty. "Count on
it." He returned the salute, then pushed himself off the
transport and disappeared through the hatch.

Andy turned to Simon. "Take the transport back to the
habitat ring," he said. "I need to check a couple of things
while I'm down here."

"All right," Simon said. "Um, I mean, aye-aye." He pulled
himself onto the transport; it slid away toward the bow.

Andy watched him go, then jumped across the central
shaft and began pulling himself further aft using the webbing. Shortly he came to another hatch—the one Richard,
Melody, Pierre, and Derryl Godard had come through
when they'd ridden to the rescue.

The crew members he had contacted surreptitiously

were waiting in the tiny shuttle. Derryl was one; he'd requested permission not to accompany Richard, and the captain, mindful of everything he'd been through, had agreed to let him stay behind. Sam Hallett, who had fought the Holy Warriors in the simulator room with Andy, was another. Annie Ash, a young Selkie, was the third. Andy made four.

"You don't have to do this," Andy told them. "Leave now, and no one will be the wiser. We're about to go against Captain Hansen's direct orders. That makes this the first mutiny in the history of the Marseguroite Space Navy."

"I volunteered my services to help get the *Victor Hansen* to Earth," Hallett said. "I never promised anything about what I'd do when I got here."

Annie looked nervous, but determined. "They killed my parents and my little brother," she said. "They'll kill the rest of us if they get the chance. We have to kill them first. I don't blame Captain Hansen for wanting to rescue Emily, but he's too softhearted to do what has to be done. He wants to save everyone. I don't think the Body Purified is worth saving. I'm with you."

Derryl just gave him a cold, flat look. "You're wasting time."

Andy nodded. "All right, then." He pulled himself into the cockpit and maneuvered himself into the pilot's seat. "I've given the shuttle computer the coordinates of the assault craft, as near as we can determine them, in Africa. Once we're almost down, I'll take over manual control and we'll see if we can spot it. There's no reason to think there'll be any humans around at all, due to the plague, but stay alert. We don't really know what we'll find."

He strapped himself in. Annie settled into the copilot's seat and pulled on her restraints, and behind him he heard the click of seat buckles as Sam and Derryl likewise secured themselves. "Computer," Andy said. "Execute program Andy 1."

"Executing," the shuttle's computer said. Andy had had Simon dumb it down so far it would answer anyone's commands, with no regard to their actual authority, if any. He looked out the cockpit windows at the vast silver bulk of the *Victor Hansen*, which his brain insisted was looming above them, threatening to fall.

The air lock door closed. There was a faint mechanical murmur, a bump, and then the *Victor Hansen*'s hull began to recede. The shuttle nose dipped, and the hull moved out of sight, replaced instead by the blue-green curve of the Earth.

As Andy had expected, the communications link snapped to life. "Shuttle! Report! Who's on board? Who gave you permission to launch?"

Andy powered up his end of the link. "Relax, Cordelia," he said. "It's me, Andy. I'm on board. I've got Hallett, Ash, and Godard with me."

"Andy?" Raum sounded bewildered. "I didn't know anything about this . . . where are you going?"

"Bit of a secret," Andy said. "You'll see soon enough. In the meantime, you have the bridge. Take good care of the ship until we get back."

"But, sir, I—"

"King out." Andy killed the link.

The Earth now filled more than half his field of view out the cockpit windows. They had nosed down.

They were heading to Africa.

"Message from *MSS Victor Hansen*," said the computer in the erstwhile Holy Warrior shuttle *Creator's Glory*.

"Computer, accept link," Richard said.

The screen lit up with Cordelia Raum's worried visage. "Sir? Andy King has left the ship."

Richard sat up. "What?"

"With Sam Hallett, Derryl Godard, and Annie Ash. He wouldn't tell me why. Sir, I'm concerned that we won't be able to hold the ship if the Holy Warriors try to take her again. We're down to about fifty crew."

"I don't think the Holy Warriors will be back," Richard said absently. His mind raced. "Are you tracking Andy's shuttle?"

Raum nodded. "Yes sir. They appear to be heading for Africa."

The assault craft. Damn! I should have guessed.

But there was nothing he could do about it. "Keep me posted," he said. "Hansen out."

He glanced at Claude Maurois in the pilot's chair; the young nonmod kept his eyes on his readouts. They'd reentered the atmosphere some time ago, and the ride was getting a little bumpy.

Then Richard looked back into the crew compartment. With the cockpit door open, everyone must have heard the message. How many secretly thought Andy was doing the right thing?

He looked back out the cockpit window as they plunged into thick clouds. He couldn't blame his crew for wanting revenge, after what the Body had done on Marseguro. But he didn't believe any of them would put that desire above the need to rescue Emily, hero of the resistance. She was the nearest thing to a princess Marseguro had, and they'd go through hell and . . . he smiled to himself . . . low water to free her.

The trick would be freeing her without turning the simmering conflict between Selkies and Kemonomimi into a full-scale war. And the first part of that trick involved being very careful to land where the Kemonomimi wouldn't see them. Richard and Andy had pored over satellite images and, with the computer's assistance, plotted an approach shielded by high mountain peaks, leading to a landing in a valley several hours' hike from Newshore.

At least the weather was cooperating: the whole valley was awash in clouds and rain. Richard looked at Claude's intent face and hoped he and Holy Warrior collision avoidance technology were up to the task.

They were. Half an hour after the message from the *Victor Hansen*, he and fourteen of his fifteen crewmembers (Claude would remain to guard the shuttle) stepped out of the shuttle's main hatch onto the lichen-stained rock of a very soggy alpine meadow.

"Everyone set?" Richard said, when the bustle of pulling equipment out of the shuttle and hoisting backpacks had subsided. There were ten Selkies—six men and four women—and five nonmods—three men and one woman, plus himself.

He hoped he could remember everyone's name, although just recognizing them might be the biggest challenge, since everyone looked the same in dappled green-and-gray Holy Warrior camouflage (though carefully stripped of its Holy Warrior insignia, of course). The Selkies wore it over their black landsuits.

"You know the plan," Richard said. "Stealthy approach, careful reconnaissance. When we've got a better idea of where Emily and Shelby are being held, then we can figure out how to get them out. But the important thing right now is not to be seen. If the Kemonomimi know we're out here, we don't know what they'll do to their hostages. Any questions?"

None. He didn't really expect any: they'd talked about this before they left the ship.

He glanced at the navcomp Simon Goodfellow had found, explained to him, and personally strapped to his wrist. It laid out his path for him in bright red, with simple written instructions. "Five kilometers due west to start," he said. "We'll be descending gradually, but the footing should be good and there's not much vegetation to slow us down." He readjusted his own pack. It hadn't felt that heavy when he'd first shouldered it, but it was already weighing him down. He'd never thought he'd miss zero gravity, occasional nausea and all.

"Let's go," he said, and the Marseguroites set off, single file, into the swirling mist.

Emily had had too little sleep for days. Prepared to wait, awake and alert, for eight hours, she instead woke with a start as the door to the washroom opened. She sat up. She could tell by the quality of light from the high windows that a great deal of time had passed. And since Ubasti was here . . .

"Eight hours already?" she said.

"I said get up!" Ubasti moved with blurring speed, grabbing Emily's arms, pulling her wrists behind her, binding them with strips of plastic, then propelling her into the corridor, where one of the men who had entered earlier with Victor waited. The door to the room they'd locked Shelby in was still closed, and Ubasti pushed Emily past it and on down the hall to a door near the very end. The man unlocked it with a swipe of a keycard, and Ubasti pushed Emily in, followed her, and locked the door behind them, leaving the male guard in the hall.

Emily found herself in a small room set up as a theater, with maybe twenty seats in four rows facing a screen, the windows blocked by metal shutters. And on the screen . . .

Shelby, his image obviously captured by a camera in one corner of his room. It was no more a prison cell than her washroom: its walls were pink and blue and had pictures of teddy bears playing among oversized flowers. It looked like a child-care facility, but whatever furniture and toys had been there in preplague days had been removed, replaced with a cot like the one in the washroom.

Shelby, still in his bloodstained white trunks and nothing else, lay on that cot, one arm thrown over his face. At some point someone had dressed his head wound with a large white bandage and cleaned the blood from his face and hair. A big purple bruise marked his right side where Ubasti had kicked him. His gill slits showed pink along the sides of his neck, pulsing slightly.

Emily's, she'd gradually become aware since waking, were doing the same. It was the first sign of dehydration. The pulsing would continue. Over the next few hours, it would become a tickle; then a burning pain. Eventually, the slight pulsing would evolve into throbbing agony, like someone slamming a hammer again and again on an already crushed finger.

Emily had been far along that road aboard the *Divine Will*. She didn't look forward to beginning that journey again. And Shelby didn't deserve to make it at all.

"Miss Wood," said Victor Hansen's voice. Emily jumped and looked around her, but except for Ubasti, she was alone. "I promised I would wait eight hours before I asked you any questions, and so I have. But it occurred to me I may have left you with the wrong impression.

"It is not my intention to deprive *you* of water, in order to get you tell me what I want to know. The school you are in has a swimming pool, your escort will take you there. It's filled and kept warm by a natural hot spring, so I think you'll find the water to your liking."

"That sounds like a carrot," Emily said. "What's the stick?"

Victor Hansen laughed. "I'm surprised you know that metaphor."

"I read a lot."

"I see. Well, the 'stick' is that while you may have free access to the pool . . . your young friend there may not."

Emily froze. "You bastard," she breathed after a moment.
Ubasti growled deep in her throat.

"Ubasti doesn't like it when you call her Creator names,"
Victor said; he'd obviously heard her reaction. He might
even be observing them as they observed Shelby, though
Emily hadn't spotted a camera anywhere. "Although I suppose an argument could be made that a clone, being father-
less, is indeed a bastard. In any event, I gather you
understand the situation."

"You're going to torture that poor boy until I tell you
what you want to know," Emily snarled.

"I'm not going to torture him at all. He's in a comfortable room, and will be provided with ample food and
water . . . but only for drinking, I'm afraid. That's not torture. At least, it wouldn't be for a normal human being, or
my Kemonomimi."

Bastard, Emily thought again, but didn't say. "He's already hurting," she said. "In eight hours he'll be in agony. In
twenty-four to thirty-six, he'll be dead. You'll be murdering
him in cold blood!"

"Not I," Victor said. "You. His fate is entirely in your
hands."

"And not in yours?"

"You should be thankful it is not," Victor said. "Since I
consider you both mistakes that by all rights shouldn't even
exist. Allowing you to live so I might learn from you is an
honor you do not deserve. Placing your friend's fate in your
hands is likewise." His voice hardened. "Eight more hours
until I come to call in person, Miss Wood. You are welcome
to use the pool for a period not to exceed twenty minutes,
once every two hours. The rest of the time you will remain
in that theater and observe what your stubbornness has
wrought.

"Hansen out."

Emily spun to face Ubasti. "Take me to the pool," she
snapped, wishing, as she followed the black-furred woman
out, that she could drown Victor Hansen in it.

Decorated with white-and-blue tile, lit by fluorescent
lights, the pool was purely utilitarian, but the water was as
wonderful as Victor had indicated. She'd been worried the
mineral content might irritate her gills, but in fact it seemed
to soothe them.

But nothing could soothe her spirit. She swam in clean water; Shelby tossed and turned on dry bedding. She could come back here every two hours; he could only continue to suffer, and the suffering had barely begun.

Would it be so bad if she answered Victor's questions? What difference could it make if he knew how many Marseguroites were on Earth? As long as she didn't tell him about the Free Selkie Republic . . .

Besides, she could lie. He'd never know the difference. And the other stuff he'd asked about . . . why *not* tell him about Marseguro? What could he do? He couldn't very well steal a Body starship and launch an attack.

But it was the fact she didn't *know* what he could do that concerned her. They'd already underestimated the Kemonomimi once. And Victor Hansen, either the original or any of his clones—and how many of them had there *been*, anyway?—wasn't stupid. His claim he would destroy the Selkies without attacking Marseguro seemed crazy, but . . .

Richard. President McLean. Between them, a rescue *would* be coming. Shelby only had to hold on until then. It couldn't be long . . .

It could be days, she told herself as she flipped over and began her fourth lap of the pool. *Days. Shelby won't survive.*

She stopped in the middle of the pool, let herself sink to the blue-tiled bottom, gills working, and stared up at the distorted images of the fluorescent lights. If Victor had only tortured *her,* she would have resisted as long as possible. But with Shelby involved . . .

Like a lead weight settling in her stomach, she knew Victor had beaten her.

She had to answer his questions. She had to buy time for the rescuers to find them.

And if they don't find you?

Then I'll think of something else.

Won't I?

She rolled over, swam as fast as she could toward the edge of the pool, leaped out, and landed on her broad, webbed feet, drenching Ubasti, who snarled and drew her sidearm. One of the pool room's big double doors swung open with a crash and the red-furred man leaped in, weapon in hand. He skidded to a stop when he took in the scene, then burst out laughing.

"Stuff it," Ubasti said. "And you, fishhead—" she pointed at Emily, "—do that again and I'll slice you into sushi."

"Well, what do you know, you can speak whole sentences," Emily said. "I was beginning to think all you Kemonomimi were really Victor Hansen's puppets and he was the only one who could actually talk."

The man's laugher ended instantly. "We are the Kemonomimi," he growled. "We are a free people. We follow the Creator of our own free will."

"Right," Emily said. "Whatever. Well, tell your glorious leader I'm ready to talk to him."

The two cat-people smiled, and with those teeth, the smiles weren't pleasant. "The Creator told you when he will return to see you."

"But that's hours away. The boy will be in agony by then. There's no need for it!"

"If the Creator feels there is need, then there is need," said Ubasti.

Emily felt the old rage burning inside her again. "Free people, my ass," she snarled. "Slaves, to let a boy suffer just because some nonmod says so."

The man's eyes narrowed and he hissed just like an angry cat. "We are not slaves!"

"Prove it."

Ubasti looked from Emily to the man. "Augustus—" she began warningly.

"I will pass your message to the Creator," Augustus said. "But it will do you no good." He turned and banged out through the double doors, snatching his tail clear just before they closed on it.

"Back to the theater," Ubasti snapped at Emily. "You've swum enough."

Emily picked up a towel from a table near the door and began wiping herself dry. "Indeed I have," she said. "Hadn't you better get one of these yourself?"

Ubasti hissed . . . but she picked up a towel just the same, and rubbed down her fur, which stood up in spiked tufts which might have been humorous on anyone less murderous.

They returned to the minitheater, where Ubasti forced Emily to sit in one of the chairs in the front row. In the other room, Shelby no longer slept. Instead he prowled the room, pacing along each wall over and over like a caged animal. Occasionally, he reached up as if to touch his gills, but then he snatched his hand away. Emily knew his predicament. They itched, but they were becoming inflamed, so touching them hurt. His skin must be feeling dry, too: he kept scratching, wincing when his fingers found his bruised side.

Around and around the room he went. And the second eight hours had just begun.

Augustus returned from wherever he had gone to contact Victor Hansen. He looked ... smaller. Emily and Ubasti turned toward him as he entered. "No," he said, looking at Emily. "The Creator will return when he has said he will return, and not a moment sooner."

Emily gripped the arms of her chair so hard her knuckles audibly cracked. She forced herself to look back into the room where Shelby paced.

"He's teaching you a lesson," Ubasti said. "Are you capable of learning it, I wonder?"

Emily didn't turn around. She kept watching the suffering Selkie boy.

She was learning a lesson, all right.

She was learning that she still knew how to hate.

Chapter 18

THE ASSAULT CRAFT GLEAMED in the South African sunlight two kilometers from where Andy and his crew lay on a tree-covered ridge. The shuttle had set itself down in a vineyard, tearing a huge gap through vines heavy with rotting grapes once intended to produce fine Pinotage for rich Body officials.

The winery and what had presumably been the owner's house and outbuildings lay about a hundred meters past the shuttle. Beyond that, a jagged mass of shining granite rose against the blue sky: Paarl Mountain, the computer had called it when Andy had asked on approach.

But Andy's attention now was entirely on the immediate vicinity of the shuttle. He was examining the scene with binoculars: Derryl, ever the pragmatist, was examining everything through the scope of the new sniper rifle he'd obtained from *Victor Hansen*'s armory. Sam and Annie had to make do with their own eyes.

"I don't see anyone," Andy said. "Derryl?"

Derryl lowered the rifle. "No," he said. "But that does not mean they are not there."

"Very Zen," Andy said. "But let's advance just the same." He got to his feet. "Single file. I'll go first. Tom, you follow me. Annie, you bring up the rear." He led the way down the slope and into the vineyard. The smell of rotting fruit was almost tangible.

They hadn't gone a dozen meters when Andy suddenly held up his hand and stopped. "Why aren't there any birds?" he said. "All this fruit, and no birds . . ."

"Birds carry the plague, don't they?" Annie said.

"Yes," Andy said. "But it doesn't kill them . . ."

He suddenly heard something moving nearby, something mechanical, turning toward them . . .

"Everyone down!" he yelled, flinging himself to the ground. Derryl acted instantly; Annie was close behind; Sam was a second slower . . .

. . . just enough slower that when the automated bird-killer fired, the load of birdshot slammed into his shoulder, twisting him around and throwing him against one of the wooden posts supporting the vines.

Sam screamed and writhed, trying to clamp his hand over every one of the dozens of tiny holes in his flesh as blood oozed out, soaking his shirt and the ground beneath him.

"Quiet," Andy snapped as he scrambled over to him, being careful to keep his head lower than the top of the grapevines, reasoning that the vineyard's defenses wouldn't be designed to unload buckshot directly into the vines. "At least you didn't get it in the face."

"It hurts," Sam moaned.

"I'm not surprised. Hold still." Andy unzipped Sam's shirt and eased it over the damaged shoulder. "They barely penetrated," he said. "You'll live. But getting all the shot out isn't going to be easy and we need to stop the bleeding." He looked toward the assault craft, out of sight now they were below the vines. "The assault craft has an autodoc. We need to get you there."

"But if we stand up, we'll get our heads blown off," Annie protested.

"So we crawl," Andy said.

Which they did, though it was a slow process, having to help Sam every inch of the way, one of them always supporting his good arm and thus taking most of his weight as well. The ground was sandy and stony and thoroughly unpleasant to crawl on, although the layer of water in their landsuits helped pad the Selkies' knees, at least.

They were only about halfway to the shuttle when they ran across the vineyard's ground-level defense. With a bloodcurdling chittering sound, something silvery bright rushed at them along the row, waving sharp-edged claws that glittered in the sun. Andy swore and tried to bring his laser pistol to bear. But the . . . thing . . . skittered almost comically to a halt a few meters away. Andy had the distinct feeling he was being stared at: then as suddenly as it had arrived, the bot spun around, raising a cloud of dust, and raced back toward the winery.

Andy blew the air out of his lungs. "Too big for it, I guess," he said. "It's probably designed to attack rodents."

Annie looked after it thoughtfully. "You don't suppose it's smart enough to come back with a swarm?"

Andy blinked. He hadn't thought of that. "I hope not," he said. "But let's pick up the pace just the same, shall we?"

Easy to say, hard to do, but at least they kept moving. Then, just when Andy had begun to allow himself to think that they might reach the assault craft with no more trouble, the vineyard sprang its last surprise on them.

"You're in our sights," a voice boomed. "Stop moving, or we'll open fire."

"Damn," Andy breathed. "Hold up."

They stopped. The bottom hatch of the assault craft dropped open and a man jumped out of it. He wore a white surgical mask and rubber gloves, carried a massive shotgun, and had the darkest skin Andy had ever seen. Victor Hansen had designed Selkies to express a wide range of skin pigmentation, and Andy himself was chocolate-brown, but this man's skin was more like ebony.

"Who are you and what do you want?" the man demanded in a strongly accented voice. He looked closer. "Let me rephrase that. *What* are you? And why aren't you dead?"

"Why aren't *you?*" Andy said. He pointed at Sam, lying panting on the ground next to Derryl. "He's hurt. We want to put him in the autodoc. We know there's one on that spacecraft."

"Yes?" The shotgun never wavered. "And how would you know that?"

Andy sighed. "Look, we're not attacking you. In fact, we came to this planet to help you."

"You're . . . aliens?"

Andy blinked at him. "What?" And then he realized that the man had never seen a Selkie before. "No. There aren't any aliens. Well, none that anybody has found, anyway. No. We're . . ." He hesitated. If the man were of the Body, admitting he, Derryl, and Annie were moddies might convince him to do a little freelance Purifying. ". . . just different." The man would be seeing their overlarge eyes, their tiny noses and ears . . . but he couldn't see their gills, which were safely tucked away in the cool embraces of the land-suits. "It's a birth defect. Runs in our family." He pointed at Sam. "He's the lucky one. Missed out."

"You must live a long way from any Body outposts," the man said. "People that look like you get sterilized when they run afoul of the Body."

"We do," Andy said. "Very isolated, our home. The Body's not in charge there."

The shotgun still didn't move. "Assuming I believe you, why did you come here?"

"We . . . heard about the plague." He paused. "And we have a vaccine."

At that, the man jumped to his feet, banging his head on the hull. He crouched again, rubbing his skull with one hand, finally letting the shotgun droop toward the ground. "You have a vaccine?" he said, eyes locked on Andy with burning intensity. "You're telling the truth?"

"Yes," Andy said. He glanced at Sam. "Unfortunately, it doesn't protect against buckshot."

"What? Oh . . ." The man looked up into the assault craft; down at Andy again. He took a deep breath. "Very well. He can come in. You, too. You others . . . stay put for now. But don't think you can try anything. There's been more than just this shotgun aimed at you for the past few minutes."

"Do what he says," Andy said. He went to Sam's side. Sam's eyes fluttered open, but it took them several seconds to focus on Andy. "Come on," Andy said. "Let's get you into the autodoc."

Sam nodded, and, with a groan, climbed back to his knees. Andy supported him on the side of his good arm and helped him shuffle toward the access hatch where the man waited, his eyes flicking between them and the other two Marseguroites waiting in the background.

Sam managed to climb up the ladder more or less on his own, with Andy supporting him from behind. Together they emerged into the main crew compartment of the assault craft, designed to hold maybe twenty Holy Warriors and their equipment. Andy immediately turned toward the rear of the compartment, knowing that was where he would find the autodoc, only to pull up short at the sight of a young woman and two small girls, one maybe six, the other no more than three, sitting in a kind of nest of mattresses, pillows, and blankets that was blocking his way. The children stared at him with wide brown eyes and held on tight to their mother, whose arms held them protectively.

"I'm sorry, I didn't . . ."

"Tseliso said you have a vaccine," the woman said. "Is that true?"

Andy smiled at the children. "It's true."

The woman's eyes suddenly glistened with tears. "Will you give it to us?" she said, voice choked with emotion. "Will you give it to my girls?"

Andy nodded, a lump suddenly forming in his own throat. "It's why we came. But . . . my friend . . . ?"

"Of course, of course," the woman said. She pulled the children aside. "Let the nice man through," she told them. The girls stared up at Andy as he picked his way through the family's belongings, Sam leaning heavily against him.

"That man's bleeding," said the older girl.

"Owie," the littler girl agreed.

"Yes, he has a bad owie," Andy said solemnly. "But he'll be all right." *And so will you,* he thought, and for the first time the importance of the *Victor Hansen*'s mission really struck home. All over the world survivors were living like rats, hiding, afraid that any gust of wind or passing bird or nighttime rodent might spell their death warrant.

The vaccine they had brought would end their fear, allow them to emerge into the light again, to rebuild their world.

Am I doing the right thing?

He settled Sam by the door to the autodoc. "Computer," he said. "Power up."

Like a beast awakening from sleep, the assault craft, long cut off from the AI on *Victor Hansen* and thus still recognizing Andy's authority without question, rumbled. Ventilation systems whispered, the interior lights flickered to life, controls lit in the cockpit. Andy heard the woman's gasp, but didn't turn around. "Computer," he said, "open autodoc."

The blank metal panel in front of him slid aside, revealing a chamber like a very small bedroom: so small it was all bed, no room. "In you go, Sam," Andy said, and helped his wounded crewman to his feet. "We'll need to get your shirt off."

"I was afraid of that," Sam said, but with Andy's help, he managed it, though his already pale face turned almost pure white during the process and at one point he staggered as though he would fall. Andy caught him, and helped him crawl into the autodoc.

"Autodoc," Andy said. "Examine and treat."

The door slid shut, cutting Sam off from his sight.

Andy turned around to see that the big man had climbed up into the passenger compartment—and had his shotgun aimed squarely at Andy. "Explain to me how you have voice control over a Body assault craft," he growled. "Explain it to me very carefully. Because if you are a Holy Warrior, I will shoot you down where you stand, before my own children."

Andy stood very still. "I'm not a Holy Warrior," he said. "Far from it." He very slowly raised his hands. "I'll show you, if you'll let me."

"Slowly," the man said. "Carefully."

Andy nodded. He touched the controls on his landsuit, and felt it sucking the water away from his skin, storing it for later use. Then he reached up and squeezed the collar release. The landsuit came apart down the front, and Andy let it slip down off his shoulders, feeling his gills tingle as the dry air hit them. The woman gasped. The older girl said, "Mommy, what—" and was hushed. The little girl stared at the pink slits on his neck. "Owie," she said again. And the man . . .

. . . laughed.

It was a deep, booming laugh, a laugh full of such pure joy and relief that Andy couldn't help but smile himself, though admittedly the smile would have been broader if the shotgun hadn't still been aimed at his head.

But a moment later it wasn't. The man threw it aside. "You're a Selkie! The planet you came from is Marseguro!"

"You've . . . heard of it?"

"Of course, of course," the man said. "The Body told us all about Its great victory over 'Victor Hansen's abominations,' how God's blessed Holy Warriors had Purified the last stronghold of his evil Selkies. But then they stopped talking about it, and we knew something had gone wrong . . . and I was glad. A lot of us were glad. A lot of us around here are . . ." he lowered his voice, as though by force of habit so strong changing circumstances couldn't break it ". . . Christians. We pray nightly to our God, the God of love, not their demon of hate and destruction. We pray for deliverance. And shortly after the Body stopped talking about Marseguro . . . our prayers were answered.

"We heard reports of a strange disease cropping up all over the world. Then those reports stopped coming, and we knew the disease must be worse than the Body was admitting.

"Shortly after that, the Body was telling us that the strange new disease was nothing to worry about, and we knew it must be very bad indeed. Shortly after that, the Body, still insisting the disease was nothing to worry about, was telling us to avoid crowds and stay away from animals. And then, shortly after *that*, the Body stopped telling us anything because the people who told us things were mostly all dead, like everyone else."

"But not you," Andy said.

"Not us," the man said. "And there are many other survivors scattered through the countryside. The cities . . . very bad. The plague liked crowds. But even in the cities, there are survivors. A few people are immune. A few . . . a very lucky few . . . even recovered.

"We didn't wait to find out if we were either immune or lucky. When we heard how the plague was coming closer and closer, even after the Body banned all travel, we fled here. We were fortunate, we had this place." He looked around the inside of the assault craft. "Well, not *this* place. But the vineyard. The winery. In my family since before Salvation Day. At first we lived in the house, but it was too hard to keep the birds away. And then, in the middle of the night, this thing came roaring down, planted itself in the middle of my best vines, turned itself off, and opened itself up."

I should have a word with Simon about how he programmed these things, Andy thought.

"And that's when I realized we could live in here. I modified the bird-bangers to fire something more than compressed air, left the ratbots to chase down the rodents, and moved us in. I go up to the winery, get food from the pantry, bring it back. So far I haven't been infected. But . . . it's no life. Not for me and my wife. Not for our little girls. It's like . . . waiting to die." His smile faded. "You really have a vaccine?"

"Yes," Andy said.

"Praise God!"

Andy didn't know how to reply to that. He'd never bothered with religion, even though religion, in the form of the Body, had certainly bothered with him.

Instead of saying anything, he refastened the landsuit, and felt the water flow over his skin and gills again. Then picked up his pack, opened it, and took out a hypospray. "Who gets it first?" he said.

"The girls," the man said.

Andy nodded, adjusted the dosage for the girls' small bodies, and stepped over to them. Both girls shrank back and the older one started to cry. The mother shushed her. "Give it to me, first," she said. "See, Asha, Mommy will go first so you can see it doesn't hurt." She pulled down the neck of her dress to bare her shoulder. "Go ahead," she said.

Andy adjusted the dosage upward again, then leaned forward and pressed the trigger. The hypospray hissed, and that was that. "It didn't hurt at all," the woman said to the girls. "Just a little cold, like someone put a dollop of ice cream on my arm."

That made the girls smile. "Now you, Asha," the woman said. "Show Ani how brave you are."

The older girl held out her arm. Andy adjusted the dose, sprayed her. Her arm jerked a little as the spray entered her skin, but then she held still. "See, Ani," she said to her little sister. "It's okay. It doesn't hurt."

Ani cried after she received her dose, but only for a moment.

Andy vaccinated the father next. As the big man rubbed his shoulder, the autodoc door opened, and Andy turned to look at Sam, sitting up now, his arm in a sling, his shoulder bandaged. "Autodoc, report," Andy said.

"Patient suffered multiple puncture wounds to his left upper arm," the autodoc said. "Blood loss was substantial but not life-threatening. Removed foreign objects from wounds, cleaned and dressed the shoulder, administered anti-shock medication and analgesics. Patient should make a full recovery with no residual physical ill effects and only moderate scarring."

Andy looked back at the family. "You're safe from the plague now," he said. "You can go anywhere you like."

"Praise God," the man said again. "And praise you, too . . . Andy, is it?"

Andy nodded. "Andy King."

"Andy King. My name is Tseliso Mathibeli. My wife is Letlotlo. My girls are Asha and Ani." He held out his hand. "I haven't shaken hands with anyone in months. I would like you to be the first."

Andy took the proffered hand. The man squeezed hard once, then released his fingers. He looked around the passenger compartment. "You came for this craft, didn't you," he said.

"Yes," Andy said. "And you don't need it now. You can go back to the winery."

The man nodded slowly. "There are other survivors in the area," he said. "How much vaccine do you have?"

"We can't stay and vaccinate everyone," Andy said.

The man's brow furrowed. "I thought that was why you came."

"Why we came to Earth, yes. But not why we came to your vineyard." Andy studied him. A Christian, persecuted by the Body, unfazed by the fact his prayed-for salvation came in the form of a moddie . . .

The truth, Andy thought. *He deserves it.* "The Avatar is still alive," he said. "He has an army of Holy Warriors. They stole vaccine from us—" *well, not* all *of the truth: effectively, Richard handed it to them on a silver platter,* "—and are on the move. They're planning to attack a community of moddies. After that, they will send vaccine around the world, but they will start with the survivors in the Body enclaves. It will mean the Body once more taking control of Earth, even more firmly than before, because it will decide who does and does not receive the vaccine. It will be able to wipe out its remaining enemies just by withholding the one thing that can save them from the plague.

"But we have a chance, now, while the Avatar and his men are on the march, on foot, to stop them once and for all." He looked at the man. "That's why I need this assault craft."

Mathibeli nodded gravely. "Then you may have it."

"You'll turn off the weapons targeting my other two crewmembers?"

Mathibeli smiled a slow smile. "I would, of course . . . but they don't exist." He shrugged. "I was bluffing."

Andy blinked, then burst out laughing. "After the birdblasters and the ratbots, it was a very good bluff."

"Thank you," Mathibeli said. His smile faded. "If you cannot stay to vaccinate the other survivors in this area," he said, "then please, I beg you, let me have the vaccine. Show me how to administer it."

"We don't have very many doses with us," Andy said. "We didn't really expect to find survivors."

"Then give me what you have, or at least what you can spare. Please." He looked at Letlotlo, already rolling up their bedding, and Asha and Ani, who sat quietly holding hands, watching the men. "There are other children. Have you seen a child die of this plague, Andy King?"

"No," Andy said quietly. "I have seen victims of it, but they were all Holy Warriors."

"I have seen friends, and family, and children die," Mathibeli said. "It is only by the Grace of God that we still live. If you can give me the means to save even a dozen people . . . a dozen children . . . please. You must."

"You'll put yourself in danger," Andy said. "If you have the vaccine, word will get out. Desperate people will come looking for you. They won't believe you when you say you have no more . . ."

"I have friends, neighbors, who still live. We will band together. We will protect ourselves, and our families. We can do that. But no one can protect themselves indefinitely from the plague. Only this vaccine of your, this miracle from heaven, can do that." Mathibeli suddenly dropped to his knees and held up his arms. "Mr. King," he said, "I am begging you."

"Don't!" Andy said. "Don't." He held out his hands, pulled Mathibeli to his feet. "I'll give you the vaccine I have. And I will do my best to get you more. Somehow."

"Thank you, Mr. King," Mathibeli said, shaking his hand again. "Thank you. But . . . if I may ask . . . if you came to

Earth hoping to vaccinate the survivors, why is the supply so limited?"

"We intended to manufacture it here, using Earth's microfactories," Andy said. "But the Body controls those."

Mathibeli blinked. "But . . . I have a microfactory."

Andy stared at him. "What?"

"The winery. We make . . . made . . . our high-end wines using very traditional methods. But we also made lower-end wines—still high quality, I assure you, but far less expensive. And those are made by microfactory. It's an old model, one my grandparents installed when they bought the property more than seventy years ago . . ."

"It's a seventy-year-old microfactory?" Andy said.

"Yes . . ."

Andy laughed out loud. "Then, my friend, you're out of the wine business . . . and into the vaccine production business."

A vast smile split Mathibeli's face. "God has doubly blessed us this day!" he said. "Are you sure you aren't an angel?"

Andy's smile faded. "Oh, I'm sure, all right," he said. "Very, *very* sure." He turned to Sam, who had climbed out of the autodoc. "Get Annie and Derryl up here. And then . . ." he looked back at Mathibeli. "We'll get your microfactory set up and producing vaccine in no time." *Assuming Cordelia lets me download the programming,* Andy thought. "But before we head to the winery . . ."

"Yes?"

"Could you please turn those damn bird-blasters off?"

Mathibeli laughed. "With pleasure!"

Richard sat panting on a boulder beside the trail and looked at his navcomp again, hoping it would tell him something different. But its instructions remained stubbornly the same: leave the trail, a well-groomed hiking trail complete with occasional text panels highlighting geological or botanical points of interest, and climb the ridge to the south. Newshore lay on the far side of that ridge.

The problem was that the "ridge to the south" looked more like the "sheer cliff to the south."

A mess of boulders and dirt and tangled trees and a massive scar showed well enough what had happened:

some seismic shrug had brought the path the navcomp was cheerily pointing them toward sliding down the mountainside sometime since the navcomp's database had last been updated.

Richard instructed the navcomp to provide him with an alternative route. It took it a lot longer than he thought it should have, rather as if it were pouting, and while he waited, he looked around at the rest of the rescue party. None of them seemed to be breathing as hard as he was. The Selkies he could understand: even weighed down by their landsuits, they were stronger than he could ever hope to be. But he couldn't understand why the other nonmods weren't finding the going as tough as—

He sighed. Actually, he could understand it all too well: he just didn't want to admit it. He was in his mid-thirties, and despite the exertions of the last year, had led an essentially sedentary life: certainly sitting in front of computer screens in Body Security hadn't done much to buff him up. They were, in Earth years, barely past twenty. The youngest was probably more like eighteen.

I'm getting too old to save planets, Richard thought.

The navcomp buzzed to get his attention, and he looked down. A yellow route had appeared on the map, winding down to the ocean and along the shore. He frowned. It looked awfully exposed—

Richard's microcomm crackled. "Point One here," a voice whispered. "We've got company. Four Kemonomimi just came out of the woods. They're heading your way."

Richard jumped up. "Everyone off the trail!" he ordered. "Company's coming."

Ten seconds later the trail looked as deserted as it had before they'd come along half an hour before.

"Point One," the voice said again. "They'll be at your location in thirty seconds."

Crouched in the woods with the others, Richard waited. Right on schedule, the Kemonomimi came into sight. It was Richard's first glimpse of them in the flesh, at least since he'd seen one shot down in the House of the Body last Salvation Day.

They're just modified humans, he told himself. *That's all. Certainly no stranger than the Selkies.*

But human beings had no built-in fear of gilled water-apes, whereas millennia of life on the African veldt had hard-wired a fear of big cats into them. Despite his best mental efforts, Richard felt the hair on the back of his neck rise as he watched the four males—*men,* he corrected himself firmly—come into view. One was glossy black; another had leopard spots; another was all white except for black points on his face, ears, tail, hands, feet and groin; one boasted tiger stripes that reminded Richard of Emily's favorite skinsuit. All were naked except for belts hung with sidearms, what looked like short swords, and other equipment he couldn't identify. All carried Holy Warrior rifles. They moved with uncanny grace, ears flicking, eyes bright as they glanced this way and that.

A hunting party, Richard thought. *That's all. Keep on going. Keep on going . . .*

But they didn't. They stopped, right at the boulder where Richard had been sitting moments before. As Richard watched, they sniffed, mouths opening as they did so, revealing alarmingly white and alarmingly pointed teeth. And then their heads came up in unison and—

—they looked straight at him.

Crap, Richard thought, and dove for cover.

Bullets ripped apart the trunk of the tree he'd been kneeling behind moments before and the fallen tree he cowered behind now. A splinter stung his cheek.

"Don't kill—" Richard started to shout, but it was far too late for that. The Marseguroites' weapons chattered. One of the Kemonomimi fell, chest shattered, but the others, lightning fast, vanished behind the rocks.

"Damn it!" Richard crawled on his belly over to the line of boulders where the others had taken cover. "We're not trying to start a war here!"

"They fired first," said one of the Selkie women—Angela, that was her name.

"Anybody hurt?" Richard said

Nobody had time to reply before the Kemonomimi's weapons opened up again. Richard hugged the nearest rock.

"Point One here," said a voice in Richard's ear. "Point Two is with me. We're flanking them. We should be able to take them out with—"

"Negative," Richard said. "*Don't kill them.* Just drive them into cover."

"I can do that," said a new voice—Point Two. A moment later the Kemonomimi's fire stopped as a new weapon spoke from the other side of the valley. A bullet ricocheted, whining off into the distance.

"Captain," said Point One, a Selkie named Chang, "they've got communications equipment on their belts. If they tell the town—"

"They already have, unless they're idiots," Richard said. "But they don't know why we're here. They haven't even seen us. They probably think we're Holy Warriors. We don't have to kill any more of them. We fade away, leave them chasing phantoms, slip on toward the town while they're searching the woods."

"They sniffed us out once," Chang said. "They can probably track us wherever we go."

Should have thought of that, Richard thought. "So we split up. A decoy party to lead them on a wild goose chase. Another party to conduct the rescue." And, damn it, he knew which one he was going to have to be in, though he wanted with every fiber of his being to be part of the team that would enter Newshore to bring out Emily. "They can't smell in the water. So here's the plan. We nonmods keep this bunch pinned down while you Selkies slip away on down the valley. Get down to the sea . . . then swim someplace where you can land unobserved. Watch the town until you locate Emily and Shelby. When you're ready, go in and get them. Don't kill anyone if you can help it. We'll lead as many as we can away from the town."

Angela gave him a long look. "The Kemonomimi have been evading Holy Warriors in these mountains for decades. You think you can keep ahead of them?"

"I'm going to try," Richard said grimly. "Point One, Point Two, do you copy?"

"Yes, sir," Chang replied.

"Yes, sir," said Point Two.

"Wait where you are. The other Selkies will join you. Nonmods, you're with me."

"Good luck," Chang said.

"You, too," said Richard. "Covering fire," he told the

other four nonmods. "But try not to hit anything vital. On my mark . . . fire!"

As they raised up and sprayed the rocks below with bullets, the Selkies ran upslope, deeper into the woods.

When he was sure they were away, Richard looked at the other four nonmods, reinforcing their names in his mind. Eric. Tembe. Akim. Dominique. "Ready for a game of cat and mouse?" he said.

Dominique snorted. "I'd rather be the cat."

"Me, too," Richard said. "But I'm afraid that role is taken." He took a deep breath. "Okay. One more volley, and then we run . . . back up the valley, away from the town. On my mark . . . three, two, one . . . fire!"

They sprayed the rocks, then scrambled off into the woods in the opposite direction from that the Selkies had taken, every step taking them farther away from those they had come to rescue.

There goes my chance to play knight in shining armor, thought Richard; but then he heard a very cat-like yowl behind them, and put everything out of his mind except running.

Chapter 19

EMILY SAT IN VICTOR Hansen's office in the air terminal building. For once, Cleopatra wasn't with him, but Ubasti stood behind her, hardly blinking as she watched her, one hand always resting on the butt of her gun.

Victor poured himself a glass of ice water out of a metal pitcher beaded with sweat, then tapped the pitcher against a second glass. "Drink?"

Emily ignored him. "Let the boy go. I'll talk."

Victor sipped his water, then held it up so the light of the softly glowing floor lamp in the corner shone through it. Outside, it was pitch-black; past midnight. Shelby had been without water now since early that morning, more than eighteen hours in total. Victor had deliberately stayed away long past the time he had said he would return, leaving Emily to watch, hands gripping the arms of the observation room chair, as Shelby went from prowling the room to curled in a fetal position on the bed, arms locked around his knees, moaning. Twenty minutes before Victor finally showed up, the moaning had stopped and Shelby had fallen into a restless stupor.

It had taken all Emily's self-control to keep from leaping at Victor the moment he entered. She longed to feel his neck in her hands, fantasized about killing him with the wrist-mounted dart guns built into her landsuit on Marseguro. But attacking Hansen would only have gotten her shot by Ubasti, and would have accomplished nothing for Shelby. Instead, she had meekly accompanied Victor back to his office. Then Victor had left there for another hour, still guarded by the apparently tireless Ubasti. He'd only returned a few minutes ago. She watched as he considered her offer of cooperation.

"I think not," Victor said at last.

This time Emily did surge to her feet in fury—or tried to; clawed, furred hands gripped her shoulders and pushed her, hard, back down into the black leather chair. "Then kill him and be done with it," Emily snarled. "And me, too. Why put us through this?"

Victor contrived to look hurt. "I'm not a monster, Miss Wood," he said. "The boy has already been taken to the pool and is now resting comfortably."

Relief flooded Emily; relief, then confusion. "But you said—"

"You asked me to let the boy go. I can't do that," Victor said. "He's obviously the perfect lever and leash where you are concerned. To ensure your cooperation, he remains a prisoner, just as you do."

Emily closed her eyes. It enraged her to look at that face, almost identical to Richard's, attached to such a . . .

Well. Her rage vanished like air from a pricked balloon. Whatever she thought of him, he had her number, didn't he? He knew she wouldn't let Shelby suffer to placate her sense of honor, not when the information she could provide Hansen probably wouldn't do him any good anyway.

Probably.

Though if she could figure out exactly what he was up to, she'd feel more certain of that.

Praying to any God but the Body's that what she was about to do wouldn't hurt Richard or Marseguro, she said, "All right. Ask your questions." She took a deep breath. "And I'll have that drink now."

"Excellent." Victor poured her a glass and pushed it across the desktop. It left a shiny black comet's tail of moisture behind it that he swiped away with his sleeve. "Let's begin with the basics. Tell me how many are in the crew of the . . ." He grinned. "*MSS Victor Hansen*."

We're going to have to change the name after this, Emily thought, sipping her water. She put it down, cleared her throat. "I didn't arrive on the *Victor Hansen,* but if I remember right . . ."

Victor kept her talking for the next hour. What was the population? What weapons did they have? What ships? What were the principal towns? Describe the vegetation.

The weather. The style of architecture. The level of medical knowledge. The . . .

On and on the interrogation continued, until suddenly Victor held up a hand to stop her in the middle of her description of the Marseguro Planetary Museum and its (in his view) "laughably fraudulent" displays. He yawned hugely. She remembered Richard yawning just like that the morning after they'd . . .

She clenched her teeth.

"I think that's enough for now," Victor said. "We'll carry on in the morning." He stood and held out his hand to Ubasti, "Let me have your handgun. I'll escort Miss Wood back to her quarters myself."

Ubasti hesitated. "Sir—"

"Do as you're told!" Victor snapped.

A soft hiss, but, "Yes, sir," Ubasti said, and handed the gun to him.

"Good." Victor waved a hand at her. "You're dismissed. Get some sleep."

"Yes, sir." Back ramrod straight, Ubasti turned and disappeared down the hall.

Victor turned, gun held loosely, not even pointed at Emily. "Let's go," he said.

Emily didn't move. "Are you sure you want to risk taking me back to the school all by yourself?" she said. "Aren't you afraid I might jump you? I'm faster and stronger than you are."

"And I'm holding Shelby," Hansen said. "If you kill me, the Kemonomimi will tear him apart. And they're faster and stronger than *you* are, Miss Wood. They'll hunt you down and tear *you* apart, too. You're not stupid enough to risk it."

"Then why do you need the gun?"

"Just in case you *are* that stupid. Now come on." He motioned with the gun.

Emily walked past him, down the hall, and out of the terminal building into the night. Lights, blurred by fog, glowed here and there among the trees. Two yellow pole lights at the end of the pier shone like cat's eyes, watching her. *How appropriate,* she thought.

They trudged toward the school. "I want to see Shelby,"

Emily said suddenly. "I don't trust you. Prove to me he's been allowed to rehydrate, or I won't tell you another thing." She stopped so abruptly Victor's pistol jabbed her in the back. "And if you have lied to me, Victor Hansen," she said without turning around, "then *I* will tear *you* apart, gun or no gun, no matter what happens to me afterward."

Victor sighed. "Oh, very well," he said. "We can look in on him before you're locked up again."

They passed through the empty downtown. The school loomed ahead of them, dark except for a single light in the entryway. Augustus lounged there, but he jumped to his feet as Victor and Emily climbed the steps. "Sir?" he said.

"I've brought her back to be locked up," Victor said. "But I promised her she could look in on the boy." He glanced at Emily. "You'd better come with us," he told Augustus.

Good, she thought. *I rattled him. Just a little.*

A miniscule victory, but she savored it.

They walked through the darkened hallway to Shelby's prison room. Augustus unlocked the door. Emily put her head in, intending only to take a quick look, but Shelby rolled over as she did so and sat up. Only a small amount of light made it through the room's high windows from a streetlamp somewhere outside, but she could see him clearly with her Selkie eyes, bare-chested, blanket covering his legs. He stared at her. "Emily?" he said. "What—?"

"Just checking to see that you're all right," she said. "Have they let you swim?"

"Yes, thank God," Shelby said. He pulled his knees up and wrapped his arms around them. "It was . . . awful." He sounded very young. "I've never hurt like that in my life."

"I know," Emily said, anger flaring inside her again. "I know."

"Are you finished?" Victor said. "Because I'd really like to—"

Gunfire interrupted him. Victor swore, gave Emily a sharp shove that drove her into Shelby's room, then slammed the door on both of them. Before she turned around, she heard Victor's and Augustus' footsteps pounding down the hallway.

She turned back to Shelby. He stared at her. "What's going on?"

"I don't know," she said. "Holy Warriors, probably." She prowled the room, but there was no way out: the door was locked, the windows too small to fit through. She sat down on the bed next to Shelby.

"Did they torture you, too?" he asked.

"Not . . . directly," she said. "They were torturing *you* to get *me* to tell them about Marseguro. Hansen has some scheme to destroy us once he's somehow wiped out the Avatar's forces . . . although he also says he has no intention of actually attacking Marseguro. I don't know what he's thinking." She suddenly thought of something and leaned in very close to his ear. He tensed. She whispered as softly as she could, "He doesn't know about the Free Selkie Republic. Whatever you do, don't mention that you're from Earth."

Shelby nodded. Emily leaned back, and he visibly relaxed.

What . . . ? she wondered, and then it hit her. Teenage boy, in bed, girl sits next to him, she leans in close . . .

Oh, good grief, she thought. *Boys! You'd think a little thing like gunfire in the streets outside the prison where you've been tortured by the clone of your creator would cool your libido.*

Apparently not.

So she casually got up and went to sit in the chair instead.

"But then . . . why did they *stop* torturing me?" he said.

Emily met his gaze. "Because I told him what he wanted to know. I don't see what use the information will be to him, and . . . I've been through dehydration. I didn't want you to suffer because of some stupid sense of heroism on my part."

Silence. Shelby looked away. *Have I managed to destroy his hero worship?* she wondered. *My feet are as clay as they get.*

But then his gaze returned . . . and he smiled, a little. "Thank you," he said.

She did her best to smile back. "You're welcome."

The gunfire had continued intermittently since she'd been shoved into the room, and once she'd thought she heard shouts. Now footsteps raced down the corridor toward them.

Emily jumped to her feet just as the door slammed open to reveal Victor Hansen and Augustus, large packs on their backs. Augustus leveled his rifle at the two Selkies, while Victor tossed something onto the floor with a grunt. Emily recognized the black bundle at once: their landsuits.

"Put those on," Victor said. "We're leaving."

Emily grabbed one, tossed the other to Shelby, and pulled hers on as quickly as she could. She checked the readouts on her wrist. The water supply was still good, the batteries strong. She glanced at Shelby; he had his on, too. She turned back to Victor, who now held a pistol. "What's going—" she began, but Augustus, who had slung his rifle on his back alongside his pack, rushed in, grabbed her arm, and practically threw her out into the hallway, so hard she banged against the far wall. When she spun, furious, she found Victor's gun leveled at her stomach.

"No talking," he growled. "Just do what I say."

Augustus reemerged, hand wrapped around Shelby's upper arm. "That way," Victor said, and gestured down the corridor, away from the main entrance. Augustus shoved Shelby in that direction, and Emily caught him before he could fall. She gave another furious glare over her shoulder, but Augustus had his own pistol out now, and with two guns pointed at their backs, she had no choice but to follow orders.

The door marked EXIT at the end of the corridor took them into a stairwell. There was a door leading outside at their level, but they didn't take it, instead descending into the basement where there were two more doors, one to their left that probably led to the janitor's workspace, and one to their right, painted bright red and padlocked. Augustus stepped forward and hammered the lock open with the butt of his rifle, then kicked the door in.

Beyond stretched a long, straight corridor, lit at irregular intervals by ancient fluorescent bulbs. Pipes, some copper, some insulated with white foam, some plain black plastic, ran along the walls and ceiling. "Go," Victor said. Once they were all through the door, he closed it behind them. Then they hurried along the corridor for what Emily judged to be at least two hundred meters, maybe more; right under the soccer field, if she remembered the layout of the school grounds, and then well beyond it.

At the far end, the corridor ended in another red metal door, while the pipes turned and disappeared up and out through the ceiling and walls. This door was already open a crack; the guard pushed it the rest of the way, took a quick look inside, then led the way into what appeared to be some kind of heating plant. Other doors led off in other directions. *All the public buildings must get their heat from this one plant,* Emily thought. She didn't know enough about the technology to figure out the heat source. Big metal tanks and boxes, a bewildering maze of pipes . . . geothermal, maybe?

"Up," Victor said. They climbed stairs made of metal honeycomb and stepped off onto smooth concrete. Some of the pipes and tanks from the lower level extended into this level, as well. A room off to one side, enclosed in glass, glowed with vidscreens: presumably, the control room.

Prodded by Victor and Augustus, Emily and Shelby hurried past the control room to another door. This one led into a carpeted corridor, dark except for pale blue glowstrips in the ceiling every two meters or so. Doors to either side opened into pitch-black rooms. At the far end, glass double doors let them into a reception area. Its lights were off, too, but two stories of glass wrapped around it, and although it faced away from downtown, distant streetlights bleeding through the fog made it easy enough for Emily to see the furniture scattered around the big room, and, above the massive wooden slab of the reception desk, a sign: "Newshore Community Geothermal Plant." Beneath that, smaller letters proclaimed, "God is the One True Power."

A not-so-distant explosion shook the building. "Keep moving," Victor said. "If they're in the school, it won't take them long to find the door into the steam tunnel."

Augustus grunted and led the way to the main doors. They opened at his approach, and all four of them slipped into the fog.

Once outside, Emily could clearly hear shouts and shots. But she couldn't see anything of the town: on the other side of the driveway that curved around the front of the geothermal plant dark forest marched up a slope, fading away into the fog.

A moment later, they plunged in among the dripping trees.

         *   *   *

Chris Keating was getting very tired of his Kemonomimi escort.

At first he'd tried to talk to them, but they'd ignored his efforts. They didn't even talk to each other, at least not where he could hear them. Of course, he usually only had two of them in close proximity: the other four ranged through the woods ahead and behind and to either side, alert for Holy Warriors who might spoil the surprise they had planned for the Avatar before it could be delivered. For all he knew, they chatted up a storm out there in the trees, but whenever they were around him, grim silence prevailed.

The silence had finally been broken as they'd been setting up camp near the top of the ridge Victor Hansen had pointed him to, but none of the talk had been directed at him, and although he could hear low voices all around him as he lay alone in his tent that night, he couldn't understand a word. The Kemonomimi could murmur to each other at a far lower volume than a normal human would have found intelligible.

He wondered what they were saying, and how much of that low murmuring, just on the threshold of hearing, concerned him.

He sighed and looked up ahead along the steep, switchbacking path they were following in what seemed like yet another endless series of ridges between him and the pass where he was to allow himself to be captured by the Avatar. Not that he could see very far. It vanished into the fog that had descended with the night.

His back ached, his legs ached, and the warm/cold coat's supposedly hypoallergenic lining made his skin itch. He couldn't honestly say he'd never felt as miserable as he did right then—he'd lived through some pretty miserable times recently—but *just give me a couple of days*, he thought.

The path was too narrow for them to walk abreast, so he and his two Kemonomimi companions moved in single file. And then the one in front stopped, so suddenly Chris almost planted his nose in his body-armored back.

"What are you—" he began in irritation, but the big moddie whipped his head around and snarled at him, excessively sharp teeth bared. Chris bit off the rest of his question for fear of having it bitten off for him, along with his head.

He glanced back. The trailing Kemonomimi had stopped, too. Both of the moddies stood motionless, heads raised, nostrils flaring and ears flicking as they surveyed the surrounding trees.

And then two shots rang out almost simultaneously, and both Kemonomimi fell, squalling, the one in front clutching his arm, the one in back his leg. Chris felt something warm on his face and when he touched it his hand came away red: Kemonomimi blood. He stared at the scarlet stain, too shocked to move.

An instant later four men and a woman in hooded, camouflaged coats burst out of the trees and ran toward the fallen moddies. The Kemonomimi who'd been shot in the leg tried to bring his rifle around, but the lone woman kicked it out of his hands and then banged him firmly and expertly on the head. The Kemonomimi slumped.

The one at the front of the line had been similarly dealt with. But then, to Chris' bewilderment, one of the men knelt down and began treating the bullet wounds, flipping back the hood of his jacket as he did so. Chris stared. "I know you," he said. "You're . . . oh, God." He felt a cold chill that had nothing to do with the fog. "You're Eric Hingston. You're from Marseguro!"

"So are you," said a voice behind Chris, and he turned to see another man pushing back his hood, revealing the face of the man he hated more than any other.

Richard Hansen.

Chris couldn't speak. Richard Hansen had been his nemesis since the moment they'd met. Richard Hansen had derailed everything Chris had planned for himself, and for Marseguro. He'd fantasized about killing him so many times he'd almost convinced himself he must be dead. And yet . . .

Here he was.

How? *Why?*

To finish what he started, Chris thought. *He's here to kill the Avatar.*

He doesn't know he's on the same side as these Kemonomimi.

And Chris wasn't about to tell him.

"Richard Hansen!" he said. "Thank God."

Richard stood a mere two meters away from Chris Keating, and he still couldn't believe it.

So far, the day had been one of unpleasant weather and unpleasant news. They'd managed to stay ahead of, and eventually lose, the Kemonomimi patrol that had found them, without having to do any more fighting. Then, in the middle of the night, they'd heard from the Selkie party sent to rescue Emily and Shelby . . . the party that had failed.

They'd tried to sneak into town when they spotted Emily being escorted through the town by a single man. But they'd been detected—they weren't sure how—and a firefight had broken out. No one killed on either side, as far as they knew, but there'd certainly been some injuries.

When they'd finally reached the school where Emily had been taken, she was gone. Apparently, she and Shelby had been taken out through maintenance tunnels that led to the community's geothermal generating plant. By the time the Marseguroites had figured that out, Emily and Shelby and an unknown number of Kemonomimi with them had vanished into the fog-shrouded forest—and the Kemonomimi in the town were beginning to regroup. The Selkies had gotten out while they still could, swimming down the river into the bay, then landing far up the coast. Now they were hiking back toward the shuttle, where the nonmods would rendezvous with them.

But then, this morning, Richard and his companions had seen, in the distance, another nonmod, not one of theirs, who was apparently a prisoner of the Kemonomimi, and had doubled back to "rescue" him. Only to discover . . .

Richard shook his head. That Keating still lived seemed a not-so-minor miracle. But that he not only lived but was here, being escorted by Kemonomimi . . . that was a miracle on the order of raising the dead.

Yet here he was.

And being escorted . . . where, exactly?

"Thank God?" he said in response to Chris' greeting. "I'd have thought you'd have given up on your God by now, Keating. *It* certainly seems to have given up on the Body Purified."

"Oh, I have," Keating said. "I . . . you have no idea, Richard, what I've been through. The plague . . . when I realized that I had brought it back, what it was doing . . ." He looked at the ground. "It was more than I could bear, almost. It almost destroyed me."

Richard looked at the young man. "Did it?" he said. "How lucky for you it didn't. It certainly destroyed pretty much everyone else."

"I'm sorry," Keating said. "That's all I can say. If I could change things, I would. But I can't."

Richard glanced at the fallen Kemonomimi. "You have strange friends for such a staunch Believer."

"They're not my friends," Chris said, with such vehemence that Richard fully believed him for the first time. "They're my guards. I don't know where they were taking me." He hesitated. "Do you know who their leader is?"

Richard shook his head.

Keating smiled an odd smile. "It's you."

"What?"

"Another of you. Another clone. Only this one actually thinks he's Victor Hansen—the original, not a copy. And the Kemonomimi think he is, too. They call him 'Creator.' "

Richard blinked. "Another clone . . . like me?"

"*Exactly* like you. Even the same age, or close to it."

Only in him the gene-bomb worked . . . more or less, Richard thought. *Victor Hansen, you son of a bitch.*

"One of his scavenging parties found me in the City of God. They wanted to know why I was immune. They brought me back here. I didn't tell him about Marseguro, or the vaccine . . . I didn't tell him anything. So he ordered these Kemonomimi to take me . . . somewhere. I don't know where. Maybe a laboratory. I think 'Victor Hansen' is planning to . . . experiment on me." Chris looked Richard in the eye. "I know we've had our differences—"

"That's one way to put it."

"But I swear to you, Richard Hansen, I'm glad to see you now. I'll take my chances with you over these abominations any day."

Abominations. That sounded more like the Chris Keating Richard knew and loathed.

His crew had finished treating and tying up the Kemonomimi. Now they stood looking at Chris. Richard saw the hatred on their faces, and suddenly realized how much danger Chris was in . . . not from the Kemonomimi (if he were even telling the truth about that) but from the Marseguroites, all of whom had lost family and friends when the Body attacked.

Up until that moment Richard had been assuming he'd keep Chris with him as a prisoner. But now he realized that if he took Chris Keating prisoner, Chris Keating might very well be dead within hours—if not from a knife in the back or a stray bullet, then from falling off a cliff or being hit by a falling rock. And even if Richard kept him alive, he would be an unending source of tension and friction among Richard's already troubled crew.

"Keating," Richard said, "I don't believe a word you've told me. I don't know what you're really doing with the Kemonomimi, and I suspect I wouldn't like it if I did. But I've got other things to worry about. So here's my best offer: get lost."

Chris blinked at him. "What?"

"Get lost. Now." And looking at the scrawny, barely-bearded boy/man in front of him, Richard felt his own anger suddenly erupting to the surface. He barely stopped himself from raising his rifle: if he did, he suspected the others would shoot Chris in cold blood seconds later. But his fists clenched and he let the anger into his voice as he roared, "Now!"

Chris took one look at him, eyes wide, then turned and ran into the foggy woods. Dominique, standing next to Richard, made a move as if to follow him, but Richard put his arm out to stop her. "Let him go," he said.

"He's a bloody-handed traitor," the woman growled. "He should be executed."

"He should be tried and, if found guilty, punished according to the law," Richard said. "But we don't have time to try him, and we can't afford to lug him along with us back to the shuttle. And we've waited here long enough as it is. There are more Kemonomimi out here somewhere."

"We should have killed these two," Dominique said. "What's the point of winging them and knocking them out? If we end up in a fight with them—"

"We don't want to end up in a fight with them," Richard said. "We want to make friends with them." He looked down at the motionless Kemonomimi at his feet, arm wrapped in a blue field dressing whose nanobots were already hard at work repairing the damage. "Although I admit that's looking harder to achieve all the time."

Dominique looked after Chris again, still visible occasionally between tree trunks, toiling up the slope. "You're the captain," she said at last.

Richard let out a breath he hadn't realized he'd been holding. "Yes," he said firmly. "I am. Now let's get moving. We don't want to get to *Creator's Glory* only to find the Kemonomimi got there first. Besides, Claude must be lonely."

He looked up the slope one last time, but Keating had disappeared into the trees.

Richard hoped he hadn't just made a fatal mistake by letting him go.

Chapter 20

EMILY HAD BEEN EXHAUSTED even before Victor and Augustus forced her and Shelby into the woods. By the time the first gray light of morning began to seep through the unyielding fog, she could barely put one foot in front of the other. The landsuit she had welcomed when she'd first put it on now weighed her down like a suit of armor.

Shelby had at least had some sleep before being rousted out, but he'd also barely begun to recover from forced dehydration. He, too, began to stumble as the night wore on and still they didn't stop.

The Kemonomimi didn't seem fazed by their wearying midnight trek. Neither did Victor, which annoyed her. He was the only nonmod in the group; shouldn't he have been the first to flag?

When Shelby stumbled for the fifth time and dropped to his knees, she knelt down and helped him up, then glared at Victor, who had watched impassively. "Where are you taking us?" she demanded for the umpteenth time. Every other time her request had been met with a curt order to shut up, but this time, to her surprise, Hansen answered her. "There's an abandoned mine a few more kilometers up this ravine," he said. "It's where I set up my research lab. I had intended to bring you up here in a day or two, but last night's attack advanced my schedule."

"Who was attacking?" Emily demanded. If Victor were in a talkative mood, she wanted to get all the answers she could. "Holy Warriors?"

Victor laughed. "Not likely. They're still slogging through

the forest toward their doom, although they don't know it yet. No. Your kind. Selkies."

Richard? Emily thought. "Funny how your 'superior' Kemonomimi couldn't fight them off."

"I'm sure they did, in the end," Victor said. "But they were obviously after the two of you, and in the confusion, there was always the possibility they might find you. And as long as I held you in the town, I would be inviting more attacks. So I removed the temptation." He shrugged. "It doesn't make any difference. I can continue your interrogation just as easily at my lab. I still have the necessary leverage." He looked at Shelby, leaning most of his weight on Emily and oblivious, it seemed, to everything being said. "And as I said, I intended to bring you up here anyway."

"Why?"

Victor's lips quirked in the smile she knew so well from Richard. "Enough talk. Get him moving."

Emily pressed her lips together, put her arm more firmly around Shelby's chest to support him better, and waited silently for Victor to move on.

Fifteen minutes later they reached the edge of the forest. The trees resumed another hundred meters up the defile, but in between was nothing but lichen-covered boulders, some the size of houses, and scruffy grass. Victor called a halt. "Augustus, go ahead and check it out."

The Kemonomimi nodded once and slipped ahead, padded feet silent on the needle-strewn path. He disappeared around a rock.

"Cleopatra. Augustus. What's with these names?" Emily said to Hansen.

"The Kemonomimi are mostly named after figures from classical literature or ancient history, from a variety of cultures," Hansen said. "As befits superior beings."

Emily started to make a retort as befitted a smart-alecky Selkie, but it died on her lips as a single gunshot rang out from up the path, echoing in the ravine like thunder. Victor spun, lifting his own rifle. From around the rock that had hidden Augustus a moment before came half a dozen figures in blue uniforms.

Holy Warriors!

Victor turned and ran without a word, vanishing among

the trees. Emily stared after him, shocked by his sudden disappearance, then spun back to see the Holy Warriors moving down the slope toward her and Shelby, rifles leveled.

She very carefully raised her free arm.

Shelby looked up, blinked, and did the same.

Karl Rasmusson had had just about enough of God's tests.

Now it was fog. Rolling in two nights ago, it hadn't lifted yet, and it made his army's progress painfully slow. Slick rocks and slicker grass posed both a nuisance and a hazard, and visibility was so poor they were in constant danger of the rear of the column losing contact with the front.

All of which made it perfect weather for an ambush by the Kemonomimi, who presumably knew these mountains like the backs of their . . . paws . . . and could undoubtedly hear better, if not see better, in the fog than his men could. If he were in charge of the Kemonomimi and planning to attack, he would do it now.

Against that chance, he had triple the usual number of scouting parties ranging far and wide ahead, to either flank, and behind: and he had called a halt for the day and made camp, though it was barely noon, to await their reports.

The last thing he thought his scouts would bring him was two Selkies in black landsuits, a young woman and an even younger boy.

The woman had short hair died a deep violet and, like all the Selkies, emerald-green, oversized eyes. She didn't look cowed as the Holy Warriors brought her to the door of his tent, where he sat on a camp stool, leafing through *The Wisdom of the Avatar of God*. In fact, she looked angry. The black-haired boy simply looked exhausted. Exhausted to the point of collapse, in fact, leaning heavily on the woman, and when the Holy Warriors tugged them to a stop, he sank to the ground and sat with his head on his knees, arms folded around them. One of the Holy Warriors put a hand on the boy's shoulder as though to force him to his feet, but the Avatar waved him off. "Leave him," he said. "He obviously needs the rest."

He got to his feet, putting aside the book reader. "I'm Karl Rasmusson, Avatar of the One Just God, By Its Grace the Head of the Body Purified." *Even if I still can't believe half the time I have the right to say that.* "Who are you?"

The woman drew herself up to her full, and not inconsequential, height. "I'm Emily Wood. I don't believe in your God, and I don't accept your authority. Let me go."

The Avatar almost laughed out loud at the sheer gall. He settled for a smile. "I'm afraid I can't do that, Miss Wood. You're a genetically modified human, which immediately makes you subject to arrest. Furthermore, you've wandered into the middle of a military operation. Operational security demands—"

"I didn't wander into anything," Emily snapped. "I was *dragged*—dragged *up* the mountain by one man, dragged *here* by others. And there is no security about your operation, Avatar. You're marching to destroy the Kemonomimi. The Kemonomimi know you're coming."

The Avatar let his smile widen. "Of course they do," he said. "But if they were going to flee, they would have done so already. Now they can't. We're too close, and my scouts are everywhere. They've missed their opportunity. They've trapped themselves.

"But never mind that. You're obviously from Marseguro. I know your kind freed Richard Hansen from Paradise Island. I want to know what Hansen is up to. Is he going to betray his own kind again? Is he planning to help the Kemonomimi the way he helped you Selkies? He won't find it as easy this time. No miracle plague can save *this* race of moddies. They *will* be Purified."

Emily Wood looked at him for a long moment, her eyes drilling into his. He found the directness of her gaze uncomfortable: none of the Holy Warriors ever looked at him that directly, that long—but he'd be damned if he'd look away first.

"I have nothing to tell you," she said at last, and looked down.

I win, he thought with satisfaction. "Perhaps not yet. But you will." He looked at the Holy Warriors. "Take their landsuits. Both of them. And ask Right Hand Atnikov and Grand Deacon von Eschen to attend me." He turned his gaze back on Emily Wood. "In a few hours," he said, "we'll talk again."

He sat back down on his camp stool and picked up the book reader, and, as the Holy Warriors seized the two Selkies and hauled them away toward the middle of the camp,

said a silent apology to God Itself, which had obviously
used the fog to deliver the moddies into his hands.

All things work to God's purpose, he read on the first
page he looked at. He smiled.

With a familiar feeling of dread, Emily submitted to being
stripped of her landsuit. A Holy Warrior gave them both
standard-issue pale-blue jumpsuits to put on over her still-
wet skinsuit and Shelby's wet trunks. She pulled hers on,
then helped Shelby with his. "Emily . . ." he said as she
zipped it up. "What's going to happen?"

She gave him a quick hug. "It will be all right," she said.
"We have friends looking for us. It will be all right."

Shelby blinked around at the armed men moving among
the camp's fog-shrouded tents. "How?" he said.

Emily didn't have an answer.

Having taken away the landsuits—and not incidentally
left them barefoot—the Holy Warriors left the two of them
alone. The tent they'd been ushered to was half the size of
the Avatar's and contained two fold-up cots, a coldlight lan-
tern, and nothing else.

It also came equipped with two armed guards outside
the flap, as Emily discovered when she looked out. Two
pairs of cold eyes turned to glare at her, and she pulled her
head back inside.

Shelby lay on one of the cots, arm thrown over his eyes.
They were both well-hydrated for the moment, at least:
they had maybe eight hours before dehydration would
begin to make itself felt.

But this time, Emily wouldn't—*couldn't*—answer her in-
terrogator's questions. Not to save Shelby, and not to save
herself. She could not betray Richard, her fellow Marseguroites, or the hidden Free Selkie Republic. Not to the Avatar.

There had been one piece of information she'd almost
shared with the Avatar, though, one piece she still held
tight in her mind, worrying it like a dog with a bone.

Victor Hansen had told her he expected to destroy the
Avatar and his Holy Warriors when they reached the pass
providing the only ready access to Newhshore.

The pass they were in now.

He hadn't told her how.

If she warned the Avatar, she could save a lot of lives ... but they'd be Holy Warriors, vaccinated Holy Warriors, Holy Warriors who would then be available to hunt down the Earth Selkies, her fellow Marseguroites, and the Kemonomimi.

But if she didn't warn the Avatar ... and if Victor Hansen had been telling the truth ... then soon, possibly at any moment, the Avatar and all his Holy Warriors would be killed.

And presumably, if they were still imprisoned, so would she and Shelby.

She remembered her mother, just before they unleashed the plague, explaining to her on Marseguro that those nonmods whom they could not vaccinate would die along with the Holy Warriors.

Until now, she hadn't fully comprehended how difficult it had been for her mother to decide to deploy the plague anyway. But she didn't doubt that her mother had made the right decision.

And now ... so would she.

The Avatar would learn nothing about the Kemonomimi's plans from her. And as for dehydrating them ... well, if they were going to die tomorrow anyway, how bad could it get?

If there were any comfort in that thought, it was extremely cold, and did nothing to help her to sleep when she lay down on the second cot and closed her eyes.

Richard sat in the copilot's chair of *Creator's Glory* and stared at the blank communications vidscreen. Beside him, Claude Maurois slumped in the pilot's chair, eyes closed.

Richard didn't want to make the call, but he had no choice.

He keyed in the frequency he'd been given. For several moments there was no response, and Richard sat in silence broken only by the heavy breathing of the members of his crew, who were mostly collapsed in various stages of exhaustion in the body of the shuttle. When the screen finally lit with the image of President McLean, her appearance shocked him: she seemed to have aged years in the past couple of days.

It reminded him uncomfortably of one truth he'd done his best to ignore: Selkies didn't live as long as nonmods.

Emily . . .

Well, Emily was several years younger than he was. Maybe their life spans would even out over the long term.

If he ever found Emily.

If her life hadn't already ended.

"You have them?" McLean said.

It tore a hole in Richard's heart, but he had to shake his head. "No," he said. "We don't. And we don't even know where they've gone."

McLean's face stiffened into a grim mask. "Explain!"

Richard related the events of the past two days as baldly as he could. When he had finished, McLean looked even grimmer. "Your crew screwed up," she said. "They moved too soon."

"They seized their best moment," Richard retorted sharply. "They saw Emily being escorted by a lone man through empty streets in the middle of the night. They saw where he took her. It was reasonable to assume Shelby was being held there, too. They successfully reached and entered the school. They can't be blamed for being unaware that a network of tunnels ran under the town."

"Really?" McLean snapped. "They never saw a central geothermal plant before?"

"No," Richard snapped back. "They're from Marseguro, remember? There are no geothermal plants on Marseguro."

"You're from Earth."

"I wasn't there."

They glared at each other for a long moment. Finally, Richard took a deep breath. "I know it's hard for you. Shelby is your son."

McLean pressed her lips together for a moment, then said softly, "And I know it's hard for you, too. Emily is your lover."

It took Richard a moment to answer. "Yes," he said slowly. "I guess she is."

"And they're both still missing," McLean said. "So what next?"

Richard rubbed his temples. "We'll take to the sky. See if we can spot them from the air. They couldn't have gone far after they left the power plant. They were on foot. We'll do a search, and—"

A strange sound filled the cabin, a buzzing alarm Richard had never heard before. Claude jerked upright, then ran his hands over the control board. "Assault craft," he said. "Heading this way."

"Holy Warriors?" Had the Avatar found them?

"Yes," Claude said, then, "no. No, wait, it's . . ." He looked up from the controls. "It's one of ours," he said. "One of the assault craft jettisoned from *Victor Hansen*."

Richard sat up straight. "Andy!"

"What's happening?" Sarah McLean demanded.

"I don't know for sure," Richard said. "I'll get back to you." His hand reached out to disconnect, then he pulled it back. "Tell Emily's mother . . . I'm doing my best," he said.

The President looked at him a long moment. "I will," she said at last.

"Richard Hansen out." He killed the connection, and turned to Claude. "It's heading *here?*"

"Currently on course to . . . no, wait." Claude reached out, tapped controls. "Not quite here. Further inland." He looked up. "I think he's attacking the Avatar."

Richard looked out the cockpit window and into the fog, as though there were the slightest chance he could somehow peer through twenty or thirty kilometers of the stuff and a mountain range to boot. "Can you contact the assault craft?"

"If anyone's listening," Claude said, and tapped controls again. Then he nodded to Richard.

"Andy, can you hear me?" Richard said.

Silence.

"Andy, I know it's you in that assault craft. It must be."

A brief crackle of static.

"First Officer King, answer me!"

"Hello, Richard," came a reply at last. "No need to get testy. How's the rescue mission going?"

"Badly," Richard snapped. "Andy, what the hell do you think you're doing?"

"What we should have done the moment we knew where he was," Andy said. "Taking care of the Avatar."

"You've only got a single assault craft. You can't take out an entire army."

"I'm not so sure, Richard," Andy replied. "They're on foot. I think it will be like . . . mowing the grass."

"It's bloody murder, is what it is," Richard said. "Those aren't squigglefish you're clearing out of a habitat intake. They're men."

"Men who would cheerfully kill me," Andy said. "And you. And everyone on Marseguro. Men who are going to kill those other moddies, those Kemonomimi you're so anxious to protect. You're too soft, Richard. Too . . . squeamish. You don't want to kill anybody. But sometimes you have to."

"I've killed," Richard said. "When I had to. You know I have. But this—there's no need for it."

Andy laughed. "Yeah? Before you went on your rescue mission, you were planning to use this assault craft against the Avatar, too. Or did you have some other plan in mind?"

"I was going to use it stop their advance, force the Avatar to negotiate," Richard said. "And give the Kemonomimi time to escape."

"Even if it worked, and you saved the Kemonomimi, it would only be a temporary reprieve," Andy said. His voice hardened. "You handed the Avatar the vaccine, Richard. Maybe you didn't mean to, to start with, but you did. The plague crippled the Body Purified—the monstrous religion that decimated our population, killed my wife, killed my friends, destroyed our cities—but you personally gave the Avatar what it needed to get back on its feet. You thought the Body would start helping the survivors scattered all over the planet. But you were wrong, Richard.

"I've met some of those survivors. They don't need the Body. They don't want the Body. Down in South Africa they've already started manufacturing the vaccine themselves. Cordelia Raum can give you the details; she allowed me to download the programming for their microfactory. There are other microfactories available besides those that belong to the Body, all over the world.

"So with all due respect, Richard, I've decided not to take orders from you anymore. I'm going to do what we should have planned to do from the beginning, if we found the Earth in this state: finish the job the plague began, and finish the Body Purified forever."

Richard felt cold, then hot . . . then cold again. Marseguro military culture was ... nonexistent. He was captain and leader only because the *Victor Hansen* had obeyed him, and through whatever respect he had earned with his actions during the battle against the Body Purified.

Could he even call it mutiny? Because, God knew, Andy King was right. He *had* handed the Avatar what he needed to relaunch his campaign to Purify the Earth. He'd miscalculated every step of the way since they'd come to Earth. Andy had successfully driven the Body off of the *Victor Hansen*. Richard ... Richard hadn't even managed to rescue his lover, or the son of the Earth Selkies' president.

"Andy," Richard said. "I'm asking you to reconsider. I know I've made mistakes. But you promised, back on Marseguro. Everyone in the crew. You took an oath."

"An oath to protect Marseguro," Andy said. "An oath to serve our world. And that's what I'm doing."

"You promised to obey orders."

"Not blindly. Nor to follow a blind leader. And you've been leading blindly, Richard."

"Andy—"

"That's it," Andy said. "I've said what I have to say. Our attack run commences in thirty seconds. King out."

Another burst of static, and then silence.

Richard looked out into the fog again. Just tens of kilometers away, one of the very assault craft that had rained death and destruction on Marseguro was about to return the favor on the Body Purified.

And the truth was ... Richard didn't know whether anger or celebration was the appropriate response.

Andy King looked around at the rest of his team: Sam, looking pale and in pain, but composed; Derryl, implacable as always; Annie, mouth drawn into a tight, determined line.

"Anybody agree with him?" he said, nodding at the communications console.

Nobody said anything for a moment. "Let's do it," Annie said finally. "Now."

Andy nodded. "Now." And he leaned forward and took manual control of the assault craft. *This is for you, Tahirih,* he thought as he pointed the nose toward the glowing red triangle that marked their fog-shrouded target on the heads-up display. *And for everyone else these bastards murdered on Marseguro.*

Revenge might be a dish best eaten cold, as the old saying went, but he intended to serve it up piping hot.

He took a deep breath. The triangle flashed green: in range. "Commencing attack," he said to no one in particular, and pressed the firing button.

Chapter 21

EMILY, LYING IN THE PRISON tent with her eyes closed, not quite awake but not fully asleep, at first barely registered the approaching roar of an aircraft. As it swelled, she opened her eyes and sat up on her elbows, twitching her head irritably from side to side as she did so: already, her gills itched.

Richard! was her first thought.

Or was it the Kemonomimi?

Or—

Whump! She heard and felt the explosion at the same instant, like someone had pounded her on the back. Shelby jerked upright. "What's—"

WHUMP! Closer this time, the punch of air flapping the tent walls. She could hear shouts from Holy Warriors, running feet.

"An attack. I don't know—"

And then came the third explosion.

The tent ripped apart. Emily felt herself flying through the air in a rush of scorching heat, then hit the ground hard and rolled, mud and rocks and bits of torn grass fluttering down all around her, along with something much heavier. She had a half-second, horrifying glimpse of the legless torso of one of the Holy Warriors who had been guarding the tent, lying not two meters away, then something heavy crashed down on top of her so hard it drove the breath from her body, enveloping her in darkness at the same instant.

For a few seconds she simply struggled to breathe, the continuing thump of missile fire racing to the end of the camp almost fading from her hearing. At last she drew a shuddering, painful breath, and the noise rushed back: aerial cannon fire now, she thought, a deep, earth-shaking chattering. It thundered toward her, then past her.

She pushed desperately against whatever it was that held her down. Heavy canvas pushed back. Part of the tent, then, but something else, too, something lying across her legs. She pulled mightily, but couldn't free them. More explosions, more cannon fire: the attacker making another pass. She remembered the video she'd seen of the attack on Hansen's Harbor. She'd been safe in deep water at the time, but now she knew how terrified those left behind must have felt, helpless to do anything but wait, protected from the rain of death only by luck.

The cannon fire chattered past. It sounded closer this time, and she could hear men screaming even above its noise.

And then, suddenly, she could see. Someone had pulled the tent off her head.

Shelby.

Blood poured down his face from a scalp wound, but he didn't seem to notice. "There's a pole lying across your legs," he panted. "Just a second." He disappeared from her view: a moment later the weight was gone from her legs and she could scramble out from under the piece of tent that had held her captive . . .

. . . just in time to see the assault craft scream overhead once more, cannons chattering.

The missile fire seemed to be over, but she could see fire rippling from the leading edges of the assault craft's wings, and she could see the line of destruction racing through the camp. Tents and bodies burned. Holy Warriors ran to and fro, trying to pull their wounded to safety. A few stood their ground, firing up at the shuttle as it screamed past again, but they might as well have been using peashooters for all the good it did.

"Let's get out of here," Shelby pleaded, pulling on her arm.

"What?" She looked around. For the first time she realized they were alone. No one had time to bother with them, and the guards that had been put on the tent were dead . . . messily dead. The tent hadn't been much protection, but somehow it had been enough that they'd come through relatively unscathed.

The safety of the woods lay just fifty meters away. "Right," Emily said. "Let's run."

They did. But they weren't as unobserved as they'd hoped. As they reached the tree line, a single rifle shot cracked behind them ... and Shelby screamed and fell, clutching his leg, into the tall grass through which they were pushing their way through. Emily threw herself into the weeds on top of him, and peered back at the camp. A Holy Warrior lowered his rifle and started toward them ...

... and disappeared in blood-red mist as cannon fire stitched a fiery line right through him, and through the piece of tent Emily had been lying under not five minutes before.

She rolled off Shelby, and pulled his hand away from the wound in his leg. "Just a graze," she said. "No arteries or bones hit, thank God." But they had nothing to bind it with. She looked back. There was little left of the man who had shot Shelby, but she could see another body lying in the same area that looked reasonably intact—and, more importantly, fully clothed.

The fog had blended with the smoke from the attack to the point that the only other Holy Warriors she could see were indistinct shapes. Several of them seemed to be clustered around one of the few cargobots in the camp. She thought they were pulling something free from it; then smoke swirled and she couldn't see them at all.

The roar of the assault craft had faded away. It would surely be back any minute, though. Taking her chance, she dashed out into the open.

No one shouted at her, no one shot at her. In a moment she was kneeling by the body she had seen before, pulling off its heavy coat, then its shirt, trying not to look at the bloody mess below the waist. She was struggling to free the corpse's belt when she heard the assault craft coming back.

Abandoning the belt, she took what she had and ran for the woods.

Maybe the crew had been reloading in flight: the assault craft seemed to have missiles again.

She heard them as before, whump! *Whump! WHUMP!*,

the final one close enough to knock her to the ground. She thought the cargobot must have been hit, but when she rolled over, it was still there: and the explosions had cleared away the smoke so that she could see the Holy Warriors near it.

The assault craft's roar faded, changed pitched, started to swell again as it came in for another pass.

Two of the Holy Warriors held a long tube on their shoulders, with the one in back peering into a glowing screen. He said something, or probably shouted it, but her ears were ringing and she couldn't understand the words.

Their meaning became clear an instant later, though, as the tube roared and spat fire from one end and something leaped into and out of sight almost before she could register it, leaving behind a pencil-thin trace of white smoke.

An instant later there was a new explosion, sharper, more metallic, from somewhere in the clouds.

The roar of the assault craft changed, becoming ragged, shrill. The sound rose to a tortured scream, seemed to be rushing straight at her . . .

. . . and suddenly the assault craft burst into sight through the low-hanging cloud, a jagged hole in its wing, red flame and black smoke streaming from it. It rolled from side to side, its nose pitched up as though the pilot were making one final, desperate attempt to pull it out of its dive . . . but then the wing snapped off.

The assault craft swerved sharply, rolled over, and plunged upside down into the forest on the far side of the valley, exploding in a ball of fire.

As bits of hot metal crashed sizzling into the wet ground around her, Emily staggered back into the forest.

"The assault craft has vanished," Claude told Richard quietly. "I think it's down."

Richard closed his eyes. He almost wished he still Believed, so he could say a prayer for Andy King and the three who had ridden to death alongside him . . . belated victims, in a way, of the Body's attack on Marseguro.

He wondered how many Holy Warriors they had taken with them . . . and if it would be enough to halt the Avatar's advance. Somehow, he doubted it.

He sighed. "Let's get airborne ourselves," he said. "But

stay away from the Holy Warrior camp. We've got Emily and Shelby to find."

The Avatar stood on an upthrust, lichen-covered rock and surveyed the damage. For fear of an ambush by the Kemonomimi, he'd ordered the men to spread out the camp as thinly as possible when they'd camped. Now the wisdom of that decision was apparent. They'd taken casualties ... at least a hundred, by last count ... his Right Hand, Ilias Atnikov, among them ... and lost a lot of tents, half a dozen horses, and two cargobots, but the bulk of their equipment, and the majority of his men, remained unscathed.

This time the Purification of Earth would be complete. There was nothing the moddies could do to stop it.

At first he'd thought the attack must have come from the Kemonomimi, but enough of the assault craft and its crew had remained intact to prove the truth: the assault craft belonged to *BPS Sanctification.* It was, in fact, one of the very craft that had taken part in the failed attempt to Purify Marseguro.

God has a very black sense of humor, he thought.

Its crew had been Marseguroite, too: three Selkies, one nonmod, if they'd put the pieces together right.

So the attack hadn't come from the Kemonomimi, but from Richard Hansen. *Is that the best you can do, Hansen?* the Avatar thought, looking up into the sky, where the fog, at last, was beginning to thin.

He smiled, then. The enemies of God had taken their best shot. And God, in the person of Its Avatar, had laughed at them.

The Purification could not be halted. The world would be freed from the abominable pollution of genemodded humans, and God would bless it once more, and once more raise the Body Purified to hegemony over it.

The dead were already being buried. The wounded were being treated. The damage was being cleaned up. The fog was lifting.

In the morning, the Body Purified would resume its march on the Kemonomimi.

Nothing could stop it now.

Chris Keating spent the night shivering in his tent, surrounded by the constant dripping of fog-drenched foliage.

One of the wounded Kemonomimi had been carrying the camp heater; another had been carrying most of the food. At least he had his sleeping bag, but it wasn't as warm as it looked, and Chris spent part of the night thinking black thoughts about Victor Hansen, who surely knew what he was doing when he had the Kemonomimi pack it.

What Chris had come to realize, as he opened his pack that night, was that although it appeared to contain everything he needed to survive in the wild, it was in fact woefully inadequate—though surprisingly heavy for all of that. Victor, he suspected, had wanted to ensure that he remained dependent on his Kemonomimi escort right up until he reached the Avatar, and that if he did try to make a run for it, he'd have to slink back with his tail between his legs or die a lingering death in the woods.

Well. He couldn't be far from the Avatar now, and the Avatar couldn't be far from the deadly pass that Hansen had booby-trapped with his special bomb. In the morning he would reach the Holy Warriors and warn the Avatar about the trap. The Avatar would either disarm or remove the bomb, and then Victor Hansen would find that the force he intended to destroy was instead marching right down his throat.

Chris sneezed. He couldn't wait.

And then . . . then the Avatar could deal with the *other* Hansen.

A universe without multiple versions of Victor Hansen. If that wouldn't be a sign that God had once again blessed the Body Purified, Chris didn't know what would.

Richard Hansen spent the night in the shuttle; landed in another alpine meadow after a fruitless afternoon in the fog looking for some sign of Emily and Shelby. Reclining as best he could in the pilot seat, while sleep still eluded him, he stared up through the cockpit into the pitch-black sky. Beside him, Claude snored. In the cabin, the rest of the crew slept. A faint green glow from the nearly dimmed control panel readouts provided the only light.

As far as they knew, Andy, Sam, Derryl, and Annie were dead, and Richard . . . Richard couldn't help wondering if he were responsible. Like the refrain of a song that had become stuck in his head after endless repetitions, his bad decisions since coming to Earth paraded through his head, one after the other, in an endless cycle of second-guessing.

He shouldn't have landed on Paradise Island so willingly. But he had. He could have destroyed the contents of the vaccine chest. But he hadn't. He'd done it to save the lives of the crew of *Sawyer's Point* . . . and, to be honest, his own. But he'd also done it because, even then, he'd thought there might be some use in letting the Body have the vaccine, that the best way to get the most vaccine to the largest number of survivors as quickly as possible was to make use of the Body's resources.

It still *felt* like the right decision . . . but it had been, once again, the wrong one. All he had done was enable the Avatar to march on the Kemonomimi, and he had no doubt that after dealing with them, the Avatar, if he discovered they existed, would next destroy the Earth Selkies . . . and eventually, if he could muster the resources, the ones on Marseguro, as well.

In each case, he had made what seemed like the only possible decision.

In each case, disaster had followed.

Story of my life.

Story of my grandclone's *life.*

Victor Hansen had created two races of moddies . . . just because he could. Then he'd made other decisions, to leave clones of himself behind, to implant them with gene-bombs . . .

The results? Death, destruction, misery on a grand scale. The original Victor Hansen had even launched the program that had led to the development of the doomsday plague. Untold millions had died as a result—a fact Richard knew intellectually, though he suspected he'd been sheltered from a full understanding of it so far because all his time had been spent in this remote region of the planet.

He would remedy that, if he got the chance: if whatever decisions he had still to make, in the days ahead, did not finally bring disaster down on his own head, he would make a point of seeing what havoc his actions had helped wreak on Earth.

Of course, if disaster did find him personally, as it very well might, perhaps it would only be just.

He kept staring out into the darkness, searching for any hint of light.

He didn't find it.

Between the fog and the forest, Emily and Shelby were soon thoroughly lost, even at the slow pace Shelby could manage with his wounded leg. And though the saturated air clung to them like a cold, wet blanket, it wasn't saturated enough to halt the slow dehydration of their gills.

They needed water, a body of water large enough to submerge in, and as night was falling, the gray fog lifting a little just as the light began to fade, they literally stumbled into it, slipping down a muddy embankment into a shallow stream.

The thigh-deep water was cold, cold as ice, and Shelby gasped at it bit into his wound, which she had bound tight with strips of cloth from the dead Holy Warrior's shirt. But unpleasant though it was, it wasn't as completely unbearable as Emily suspected it would have been for a nonmod, and she welcomed its wintry embrace a moment later as she stripped down to her skinsuit and threw herself headlong into it. Shelby was close behind her.

With relief she felt her nostrils snap shut and her gills snap open, water at last flowing through them. Her lungs stilled and her heart beat faster to push more blood through her gills for oxygenation and then to the rest of her body.

The maddening itching faded away.

After five or six blissful minutes, though, the cold began to penetrate even through her insulating layer of subcutaneous fat, and she sat up. Shelby saw her motion and rose out of the water too, his gills wriggling like cilia for a moment to shake off the water, then closing tight against his neck. She felt her own do the same, and regretfully started breathing with her lungs again.

"We'll camp in that clearing we went through a few minutes ago," she said. "Then in the morning we'll follow the stream downhill. Eventually, it's bound to lead us to the sea."

Shelby nodded. His teeth were chattering, Emily noticed: she quickly got up and helped him up the embankment. They both pulled on their jumpsuits again, then she wrapped him in the Holy Warrior coat he'd been wearing

all day and led him back to the clearing. With no tools and
the light almost gone, the best she could manage for shelter
was a rough lean-to covered with branches, but it was better than nothing, and would at least capture some of their
body heat overnight.

Body heat. She looked at Shelby, huddled in the coat
under the lean-to she'd just finished, barely visible now in
the gloom. *This is going to make his day,* she thought, and
then got down on all fours and crawled into the lean-to
with him.

"Cuddle up," she said. She lay down on the damp leaves
she'd spread over the muddy ground. She patted the ground
next to her. He hesitated, then lay down, not quite touching
her. She sighed, rolled over, and pressed her body against
his side, pulling the coat over them both. "Body heat," she
said into his ear. "It's the only way to keep warm."

"Um," he said. She could feel how tense he was, and she
knew perfectly well *why,* but there wasn't anything she was
about to do about *that,* and as the warmth between them
gradually warded off the chill of the night and the ground
and the stream, she let her own eyes close.

Boys, she thought, and drifted into sleep.

Chapter 22

M ORNING.
   The fog had vanished during the night, blown away by a rising wind from sea. Dawn came clear and cold, turning the sky the color of fresh salmon behind the jagged black silhouettes of the inland mountains.

As birds began to sing in the trees, Chris Keating groaned, rolled over, and sat up. *Today*, he thought. *Today I meet the Avatar*.

Richard Hansen opened his eyes and blinked at the improbably pink light beginning to crawl down the mountain he was facing, though the valley was still shrouded in shadow. *Today*, he thought. *Today we'll find Emily ... and Shelby. We have to*.

The Avatar stood on a rock in the middle of the camp and watched his Holy Warriors dismantle tents and prepare for the day's march. *God has given us good weather at last*, he thought. *The tests have ended, all save the final one. Today or tomorrow, we attack*.

Emily Wood woke but didn't open her eyes at first, instead nuzzling closer to the warm body in her arms. "Richard ..." she murmured, then suddenly remembered. Her eyes opened wide.

Shelby still slept, face relaxed and childlike in the morning light now finding its way through the many openings in their shelter. She disentangled herself carefully. Shelby stirred, but didn't wake, as she got to her feet and crawled out into the clearing, then stood and stretched, trying to work out the kinks brought on by a night on the ground. *Today,* she thought. *Today we should make it back to the sea.*

All around, the birds chorused with joy as though there had never been a more beautiful morning in the history of the world.

Richard wanted to get back into the air almost as soon as he woke up, but of course it took longer than that, with more than a dozen men and women needing to wake, stretch, relieve themselves, wash, and eat. The pink light was long gone from the mountains on the west side of the valley, replaced by brilliant sunshine on gray rock and dark-green pine, before everyone was settled.

As he had the day before, Richard had routed every exterior camera on the shuttle to the vidscreens in the back: two at the front of the compartment, and one on the back of every seat. What one pair of eyes might miss, he hoped a dozen might find. "Take her up," he said to Claude, and took a deep breath as the lifters roared to life and the shuttle rose into the air, then moved off across the valley floor.

Today, he told himself again. *We'll find her today.*

It took longer for the Holy Warriors to get ready than Karl Rasmusson would have liked, too. You simply couldn't hurry hundreds of men on their way, especially after yesterday's attack. One of the cargobots they'd thought undamaged turned out to have thrown a tread, and they had to shift everything they could from it to another bot, and divvy up everything that wouldn't fit on the second bot among two dozen men and their surviving horses. Grand Deacon von Eschen moved among the men, shouting and cursing, but still, the sun had almost cleared the mountains before the column began to move, climbing up toward the final saddle-backed ridge blocking their access to the town where the Kemonomimi waited.

They'd been on the road for about an hour, Karl, as usual, walking near the head of the column, when he heard a shout off to the left. He turned, shading his eyes, and saw one of his scouting parties emerging from the forest with someone else, clearly not a Holy Warrior, in tow.

For a moment he thought the Warriors must have stumbled on one of the Selkies who had escaped during the attack, but as they came nearer, he realized that the young man with them was a normal human, and as they came nearer still he frowned. The youth's face seemed strangely familiar.

Karl Rasmusson hadn't become Right Hand without a prodigious memory for names and faces. As the Holy Warriors brought the prisoner to him, and the column continued its steady, trudging march behind him toward the ridge, he said, "Chris Keating, I presume." He motioned to the guards, and they released their grip on the youth. One of them was holding a backpack, presumably Keating's; he dropped it to the ground, then unslung his rifle and stepped back watchfully. The other guard opened the backpack and began looking through it.

The Avatar ignored them and waited to hear what the prisoner would say.

Chris had hoped to walk up to the column freely, but he'd been intercepted by the Holy Warriors well back in the woods: possibly just as well, he had to admit, since they'd taken him in an entirely different direction than he'd thought he needed to go, and yet emerged from the forest right on top of the army. Left to his own devices, he'd still be wandering through the forest, if he hadn't fallen off a cliff by now.

He'd been pleasantly surprised by the size of the Avatar's force. Hundreds of heavily armed Holy Warriors, a few cargobots, even horses. The Kemonomimi didn't stand a chance if the Holy Warriors got through.

Well, it was his mission to see that they did.

He'd known at once that the man the Holy Warriors were leading him to—perhaps a bit more firmly than was really warranted—was the Avatar. Alone of all the men on the field, he wore black, relieved only by a thin braid of gold at the neck and wrists.

At last, Chris thought as he was half-dragged across the muddy field. *At last!*

It wasn't the way he'd always dreamed of it, of course. He used to picture himself being presented to the Avatar in the House of the Body in the City of God Itself, in the main sanctuary, probably with thousands of cheering citizens on hand to see him receive his just reward for having revealed the long-concealed hiding place of Victor Hansen's abominable creatures.

Richard Hansen had screwed up those plans, helping the Selkies survive the Holy Warrior attack, helping them spread their plague not only across the face of Marseguro but back to Earth itself.

And since then, of course, there had been no opportunity for Chris to talk to anyone within the Body and explain just how much he had done in God's service.

But here was the Avatar, at last, and if this muddy valley was not exactly the soaring marble-floored chamber he had dreamed of, it would do.

He'd already opened his mouth to introduce himself when the Avatar took the wind out of his sails by addressing him by name.

"Chris Keating, I presume," the Avatar said.

Chris closed his mouth, stunned—and immensely pleased. "Yes, Your Holiness," he said. "But how . . . ?"

"I was not Avatar before *BPS Retribution* brought you and the rest of its deadly cargo to Earth," the Avatar said. "I was Right Hand. It was my business to know who was aboard that ship when it returned. Unfortunately, we weren't aware of its true passenger list until it was too late." He folded his arms. Karl Rasmusson wasn't a large man, but he held himself with a kind of strength and determination that made Chris feel like an awkward boy. "Before I have you executed, tell me: how did you come to be here?"

Executed? Chris' pleasure of a moment before vanished like a pricked balloon. *No,* he thought, *no, no, no . . . he doesn't understand . . .*

"Your Holiness," he burst out, "I have been a True Believer all my life! So were my parents! The Selkies on Marseguro *murdered* my father. They let my mother die an early death. But I kept my faith and my determination to serve God. I was the one who activated the distress signal that led the Body to Marseguro. You have no more loyal follower than—"

"My patience is limited," the Avatar said. "Answer my question. The last I heard, you were imprisoned in the Holy Compound. How did you come to be here?"

"I was released from prison during the . . . final days," Chris said. "I lived on my own, scavenging, for many weeks. Then the Kemonomimi came. They brought me here. They introduced me to their creator." And *here's* something I'll bet you don't know, Chris thought. "They introduced me to Victor Hansen."

The Avatar's eyes narrowed. "Another clone?"

Sharp, Chris thought with admiration. "Yes," he said. "Although he doesn't believe he's a clone. He thinks he's the real thing."

"Does he?" The Avatar smiled a little at that. "And he leads them?"

"Blasphemous though it might seem, they worship him."

The Avatar shrugged. "It's not blasphemous at all. They're not human, and he is their creator, or at least a reasonable facsimile thereof. Which was precisely why I had him secretly birthed at the same time as Richard Hansen."

"You . . . know about him?"

"Well, he didn't spring out of thin air," the Avatar said. "We hoped that Richard Hansen might be able to lead us to the Selkies, a hope that was fulfilled. It occurred to me that another clone might be able to lead us to the Kemonomimi . . . which he would have, if he hadn't managed to escape his incompetent guards a few years ago and vanish into the wilderness.

"But never mind that. So that's why you're here, in British Columbia. But why are you *here,* standing in front of me?"

"Because Victor Hansen has set a trap for you, Your Holiness," Chris said. He pointed up at the ridge. "Beyond that ridge is one last valley, the only way for your army to approach the town where the Kemonomimi lurk."

"I know that," the Avatar said impatiently. "Why do you think we're marching into it? But this Victor Hansen of yours has already sprung his trap—with the help of his fellow clone, Richard Hansen—and it failed. An assault craft attacked us yesterday. We lost a hundred men, but the craft was shot down. He's got nothing else."

"Yes, Your Holiness, he does," Chris said. He paused, enjoying the moment. How many times had he had information that, if only he could have gotten someone to listen, would have turned the tide in favor of the Body? Now, at last, he stood before the Avatar himself. Now, at last, no one would stop him from receiving the accolades he deserved.

"Well?" the Avatar snapped. There was a ripping sound behind Chris, and the Avatar's eyes flicked past him. Chris turned to see the man with his backpack tearing out its lining. *He won't find anything in there*, Chris thought. *There was barely enough stuff to keep me alive for a single night*.

Chris faced forward again. "There's a bomb," he said. "A massive bomb. A matter/antimatter device, Victor Hansen called it."

The Avatar frowned. "Massive?"

"Yes," Chris said. "They planted it in the valley. They're just waiting for all of you to be in there, and they'll set it off. It will kill you all.

"Victor Hansen's insane," he went on. *That should go without saying*. "He believes the Kemonomimi will inherit the Earth."

To Chris' surprise, the Avatar snorted with derision. "Hansen was lying to you. He might have some sort of bomb planted in the valley—but it certainly isn't a matter/antimatter bomb. They're tiny. You could hide one in a . . ." his eyes slid past Chris again, and his voice trailed off.

Chris turned around. The Holy Warrior, digging deep into the bottom of the backpack, had pulled out something the size and shape of a flattened grapefruit, made of silver metal, featureless except for three red lights on top.

No wonder the damn thing was so heavy, Chris thought. *I wonder what—*

It was his last thought, and it went unfinished.

The Avatar saw the flattened metal ovoid come out of the lining of Chris's backpack, and knew immediately what it was. He would have known even if he hadn't just been explaining it to Chris.

It was, indeed, a matter/antimatter bomb, its explosive force capable of being finely tuned, and designed for remote detonation. They were ideal for putting down insurrections on distant planets, where you might want to destroy a city or two but not poison the biosphere: they produced no fallout. As Right Hand but acting Avatar, Karl Rasmusson had personally signed off on their development and use against the insurrection on New Mars. He'd seen detailed images of them, read their specifications, studied their schematics. He'd also seen vids of the destruction of Burroughston by just such a device as he now, for the first time, saw close up.

It's another test, he thought, heart suddenly racing. *It must be. We'll have to disarm it, prove once and for all to God Itself that we are worthy to serve it. Perhaps God wants us to use it on the Kemonomimi. And after that—*

But there was no "after that."

Without even time to be astonished or disappointed that the God he had served all his life had utterly abandoned him, Karl Rasmusson, last Avatar of the Body Purified on Earth, vanished with all his remaining Holy Warriors in a fireball of pure energy brighter than the sun.

The flash came first. Fortunately *Creator's Glory* was facing away from the explosion, so Richard wasn't blinded by it, but even the reflection off the snow-covered peaks in front of them made him cry out and throw his arm up over his eyes. Claude, with his more sensitive Selkie eyes, screamed and ducked down behind the control panel. Surprised shouts echoed from the passenger compartment.

The blast wave hit them seconds later.

The shuttle groaned with the impact as it was hurled skyward, the sudden acceleration pressing Richard down into his couch twice as hard as he'd ever been stomped on by G-force at takeoff. Claude, half out of his chair, was smashed to the cockpit floor, his breath whooshing out in an explosive grunt. More shouts of surprise and pain sounded in the passenger compartment.

Then suddenly they were dropping, falling into turbulence that threatened to shake Richard's teeth from his jaw as he forced himself upright and reached for the controls.

"I think my arm is broken," Claude moaned. "What's happened?"

"An explosion. Big one. Nuclear, maybe." Richard's hands flicked over the controls. "Half our systems are down. Claude, I need you. You're the expert."

Claude hauled himself into his chair again, left arm cradled against his chest. His face had gone pale, but he reached out with his right and studied the controls. "Looks like I'm not the only one with a busted wing," he said. "I think something punched a hole in one. Compensating with main thrusters." He moved his hand across the board, and Richard felt himself pushed down into his chair again.

Their rate of descent slowed to something that almost looked controlled . . . but it didn't stop.

"We don't have full power. We don't have enough lift to gain altitude," Claude said.

"Can we reorient, head for space?"

"Ground-to-orbit engines are offline. Looks like they took a hit, too." He looked at Richard. "We're going down. The best we can hope for is a controlled crash."

Richard took a deep breath. "All right," he said. "Can we make the sea?"

Claude punched a control, called up a map. "Maybe."

"Go for it."

"Yes, sir." Claude took his own deep breath, one that caught on a moan, then leaned in to the controls.

Richard unsnapped himself and made his unsteady way back to the passenger compartment. Around him, *Creator's Glory* bucked and jumped. Beneath all the sharp, sudden motions, he could feel a deep, shuddering vibration.

Most of his crew seemed to be intact, although Dominique had a nasty cut on her forehead that Chang was tending. "What happened, sir?" she asked.

"I don't know," he said. "Someone set off a bomb. Maybe a nuclear one."

"The Avatar took out the town?" Chang said.

Richard shook his head. "It wasn't the town. It came from behind us, up in the mountains. I think someone just took out the Avatar."

"The Earth Selkies?"

"The Kemonomimi?"

Dominique and Chang spoke at once.

"I don't know," Richard said again. "But whoever it was almost took us out as well." He had to grab the back of one of the chairs as the shuttle lurched. "We're too damaged to keep flying and too damaged to make orbit. We're going down, and we may not have much choice as to where.

"We're going to try to make the sea for a water landing. Failing that, we'll look for somewhere flat. But, whatever happens, it's going to be rough.

"So secure everything that's loose and then secure yourselves. It won't be long."

As if to emphasize that fact, the shuttle lurched again.

Richard made his way back to the cockpit, trying not to think about the one thing he couldn't help but think about: where had Emily and Shelby been when that bomb went off?

If they'd been captured by the Avatar, they might have been in his camp. And if they were . . .

Not for the first time, Richard wished he still had a God to pray to.

Creator's Glory groaned and rolled left, throwing him hard against the wall of the short corridor between the cockpit and passenger compartment. It righted itself reluctantly.

If he had such a God, he just might be offering a prayer for himself, too.

Emily and Shelby were taking a break from their steady downhill trek, soaking in a relatively calm pool in the stream at a place where it wound through a small, flat-bottomed valley. Emily was underwater when the bright blue sky she could see above her through the rippled surface suddenly turned white, the ripples sparking cold and sharp as diamonds for a moment.

The light vanished. Emily surged upward. Shelby had been sitting on a rock on the shore, nursing his bandaged leg, but she found him standing now, staring back the way they had come, toward the high ridge that lay between them and the Avatar's camp. That ridge had been prickly with the tops of distant pine trees: now it was bare, and black smoke and dust boiled up from its far side, climbing high into the air to join a mushroom-shaped column that told Emily more than she wanted to know about what had just happened.

"The bastard did it," she breathed.

"What?" Shelby said.

"Victor Hansen. He blew up the Avatar. All those men . . . they're gone."

The ridge had protected them from the blast. It couldn't protect them for long from any radioactive fallout that—should the weapon have been nuclear, and it sure looked that way—might soon be coming down from those clouds of smoke and dust now stretching up high enough to blot out the bright sunshine of a few moments earlier.

"Let's get moving," she said. "The sooner we're under deep water the better."

Shelby nodded. He looked scared as he glanced over his shoulder one more time at the towering cloud, and Emily couldn't blame him. She was scared, too, and not just because of whatever risk the cloud might pose to the two of them.

If Victor Hansen had weapons like that at his disposal, what hope did the Selkies or nonmod survivors of Earth have against the Kemonomimi?

She splashed over to the shore and joined Shelby, and the two of them begin hurrying downhill. The little flat-bottomed valley petered away oddly at its western end, and as they got there Emily realized why: beyond it, the land fell away sharply down to the sea, which she could see now, calm and beautiful, looking so much like the ocean of Marseguro that she felt her breath catch in her throat and her gills tingled.

And the streambed they were following flowed right into the river that in turn flowed through Newshore, whose roofs and runway she could see not all that far below.

Flowed?

In fact, she suddenly realized, the stream had almost stopped flowing. She looked back up the valley. Water still glimmered in pools, but very little was coming down. *Debris from the blast must have dammed it*, she thought. *Well, we're almost to the sea. Plenty of water there*. She looked back out at it again, its sunlit waves so inviting, especially with the tower of smoke and dust looming to the west. At least the prevailing winds seemed to be pushing that ominous cloud inland.

Shelby joined her. "We're not going through the town, are we?" he said.

"Not if I can help it," Emily said. "We'll stick to the stream till it levels out down there, right where it joins the river." She pointed. "Then we'll head off through the woods. How's your leg?"

"It's . . ." Shelby's head jerked around. "What's that noise?"

Emily heard it, too, then, a growing, screaming roar. She spun around and looked up just in time to see a shuttle, trailing smoke, sky showing through a gaping hole in one wing, burst into view over the valley. It hurtled over their heads so close it almost looked like she should be able to touch it, then plunged onward, shuddering, rolling from side to side so violently she expected it to turn sideways and crash at any second, but somehow remaining under control.

It screamed low over the town, braking rockets thundering, and she thought she could see movement, Kemonomimi running for their lives: and then it hit.

It pancaked down onto the runway, hard, but not fatally hard, she thought, and slid along it in a shrieking shower of sparks, smoke and dust. The runway ended: the shuttle kept going, ripping through fencing, tearing through bushes, finally sliding onto the beach in a geyser of sand and stones and then, almost gracefully, turning sideways, slipping lengthwise into the ocean in a huge explosion of spray and steam, close by the mouth of the river.

"Who . . . ?" Shelby said.

"I don't know," Emily said, but her heart screamed, *Richard!* "Let's get down there."

They lost sight of the town and the crashed shuttle behind the trees almost as soon as they started to descend. Emily would have galloped down the slope, but she could move no faster than Shelby could hobble on his wounded leg.

About fifteen minutes along, she heard a new sound, a new roaring. For a moment she thought it must be another shuttle, but it had a different quality, more organic, somehow, like ocean waves, like—

She spun and stared back up the streambed to the mouth of the valley they'd just left, just in time to see the massive wave of muddy, tree-choked water explode over the edge and begin pouring down the slope toward them.

The impact, when it came, was harder than Richard expected. It drove the breath from his body and made him see stars, tossed him like a rag doll in his restraints until his teeth chattered. He bit his tongue hard, and tasted blood. But the shuttle didn't disintegrate, and the cockpit window, designed to withstand micrometeor impacts in orbit, didn't break, and when the thunderous roar and scream of tortured metal finally ceased, Richard found himself looking up through the cockpit at the rippled underside of waves, shaken, tongue sore—hell, *everything* sore—but essentially undamaged.

Then, of course, the water stared pouring in.

The wall of water hit Emily and Shelby like the proverbial ton of bricks, and there was nothing they could do about it. Emily lost sight of Shelby instantly, as she was plunged beneath the flood. Drowning didn't worry her, though the muddy water felt gritty and unpleasant in her gills. But trees and rocks and other debris rode the water with her, and she had no control. Tumbled end over end, she banged hard against something, felt something else smash her in the side so hard she thought she felt a rib crack, then finally got her head to the surface and was able to see where she was going, though she still wasn't strong enough to fight the current. Then the swollen stream shot her into the much wider river. She found herself more or less in the middle of it, away from the trees that bent, and in some cases broke and uprooted, in the muddy torrent carrying her faster than she could have run down toward the sea.

But before the sea came the town.

The water rose faster than Richard would have believed possible, pooling around his ankles, lapping at his knees, almost reaching his waist before he could even get his restraints unsnapped. It rushed in around the edges of the cockpit window, which had apparently sprung despite being uncracked, and bubbled in from under his feet. One of the last things Claude had done before the impact had been to kill all power systems; earlier, he had dumped the remaining fuel from the main tanks, leaving just enough for braking. If not, Richard suspected he would either now be electrocuting or they all would have gone up in a massive fireball.

Claude! He turned to help the pilot, and congratulate him on getting them down safely, but the words died on his lips. Claude's head hung at an unnatural angle, and blood stained his lips. His sightless eyes stared at Richard.

His neck was broken.

Richard felt a surge of black anger at the universe, or maybe the God he claimed no longer to believe in, but there was no time for grieving or cursing: the water had climbed above his waist and he couldn't breathe it like more than half his crew could.

With difficulty he pulled himself uphill into the passenger compartment. "Anyone hurt?" he said.

"I've felt better," someone said, but everyone was moving, though some were bloodied and bruised.

"Let's get out of here," he said.

"What about Claude?" Dominique called from the rear.

"Dead. Come on. Out the back hatch."

Manually undogging the inner air lock door, and then the outer one, took a good five minutes, but finally Richard pushed open the outside door and let a flood of cool, salt-smelling air into the shuttle's muggy, stale interior.

The first thing Richard saw, framed by the hatch, was the towering cloud of dust and smoke to the east, behind the first ridge of the mountains. Thankfully, it was being pushed away by a strong west wind, the same wind that slapped a steady surge of surf against the beach and the bow of the shuttle. Spray drenched the small portion of him not already wet as he at last emerged into the open.

He brought his gaze down from that vast gray tower to see the Kemonomimi waiting for them.

They ranged along the beach, fifteen men and women, unclothed, furred, armed with long knives and automatic rifles, their slit-pupiled eyes staring at him as he eased himself out, so that he felt rather like a mouse at a cat convention. They looked more inhuman and alien than ever.

But beyond the immediate welcoming committee, he could see other Kemonomimi: unarmed, most of them, among them many children of varying sizes. They'd come rushing down to the water's edge to see the wrecked shuttle, but now they hung back, on the wooden bridge that spanned the river and on either bank, watching.

Richard still remembered clearly the little girl he had seen in her mother's arms in the Holy Warriors' holding pen just off the pier in Hansen's Harbor, when he still imagined he served the Body Purified. Her frightened face had had as much to do with changing his allegiance, he sometimes thought, as anything else that had happened.

These people aren't our enemies, he thought. *They should be our allies. They're moddies, like the Selkies, but they're also still human, like all of us.*

There are no aliens here.

And then, from behind the front rank of cat-people, an ordinary human being stepped to the fore, an ordinary human whose face was as familiar to Richard as his own, because in most respects it *was* his own.

Richard stared. "You're—"

"Victor Hansen," the man said. "Creator and leader of the Kemonomimi. Creator, too, to my vast regret, of those fishy monstrosities I see behind you." He made a gesture with his free hand, and all the rifles in Kemonomimi hands rose and aimed at the air lock: at *him*. "Get everyone out here. Now."

Slowly, Richard climbed down onto the pebbled beach. Behind him, the shuttle hissed and popped as metal cooled. The long muddy gouge they had plowed on their way to the beach stretched away past the Kemonomimi, scattered with debris from smashed fences, bushes, and one unfortunate house. He hoped no one had been in it.

The rest of the crew climbed down as well, though a couple needed help to reach the beach and then had to lean against someone else for support.

"I know who you are," Victor Hansen said. "You are my clone, Richard Hansen."

"I'm not *your* clone," Richard said evenly. "I'm a clone of the original Victor Hansen. As are you."

Victor laughed. "I'm no clone. I remember creating the Selkies, and the Kemonomimi. I sent the Selkies away to safety—my biggest mistake, after creating them, but apparently I was sentimental, then. I rolled back my own aging and, young once more, went to find my *true* children. *Homo sapiens hanseni.* The Kemonomimi. The race that, thanks to the plague I engineered, thanks to my destruction of the last Avatar and his Holy Warriors—" he pointed at the towering black cloud, "—will now rule the world."

Richard looked at the Selkies and nonmods ranged on either side of him. "There are others on this world," he said. He didn't mention the Earth Selkies: didn't know if "Victor" knew they existed. "They deserve to live, too."

"They can live," Victor said dismissively. "If they ultimately survive my plague, which I doubt. But they cannot be allowed to rule: not themselves, and not my people."

Richard didn't speak for a moment. He remembered everything he had read about the real Victor Hansen, the one who had led the Selkies to safety on Marseguro. He'd been utterly dedicated to his new race, willing to do whatever was necessary to save them.

But he'd never even mentioned the Kemonomimi, never told his new race of moddies that they were his second creation. He had apparently utterly repudiated the cat-people, making no effort at all to rescue them from the Body Purified after the Day of Salvation.

This clone, the only one in which the gene-bomb Victor Hansen had designed to implant his memories and personality had apparently functioned as intended, had simply made the mirror-image decision of the original.

But he's not *the original,* Richard said. *No more than I am.*

"Anton," he called. "Will you step forward, please?"

A Selkie roughly the size of a small mountain detached himself from the rest of the crew and came to stand beside Richard. "Are you thinking what I'm thinking?" he growled to Richard. He had the most amazingly deep voice Richard had ever heard.

"Tell them," Richard said.

Anton raised his voice to a pretty good approximation of thunder. "When I was a small boy on Marseguro," he said, "I met Victor Hansen. He was almost ninety Earth years old at the time, frail and liver-spotted, but still alert. He shook my hand and told me to keep studying science. And two weeks later, he died." Anton pointed at the nonmod among the Kemonomimi. "This man is not Victor Hansen. He is a clone of the original."

Richard didn't know what kind of reaction he expected. Howls, maybe, or shaking fists. But the Kemonomimi barely reacted at all . . . although a few heads turned in "Victor's" direction. For his part, Victor only smiled. "You cannot turn my people against me with simple lies," he said. "They know who I am."

"How?" Richard said. "Because you told them?" He raised his own voice. "Look at me! Look at your so-called creator! We could be brothers—because we *are* brothers.

Identical twins, separated only by our birth dates. I'm a clone, too. I'm a clone of Victor Hansen, the *real* Victor Hansen. And so is your creator!"

Did Victor's smile slip a little? Richard couldn't be sure. He *was* sure, though, that the Kemonomimi were looking closely from him to their Victor, and though the front rank remained poised, the children and adults farther back along the river were murmuring among themselves.

"You cannot shake my people's faith in their creator," Victor said. "And if you continue to attempt to do so, I—"

"You'll shoot us all?" Richard said. He kept his voice loud, wanting everyone to hear him. "For making your people question their faith? You sound just like the Avatar."

That got through. Victor's face reddened. "The Avatar is dead," he said. He jabbed a finger again at the towering cloud. "His ashes lie beneath that cloud. The Body Purified is finished, thanks to me and my Kemonomimi. And now we will claim the Earth for our own, as is our right."

"The Avatar is dead," Richard said bitterly. "Long live the Avatar."

"I've heard enough," Victor snapped. "Take them to the ..."

But nobody was listening to him.

A rumble had suddenly made itself felt through the ground, and the air filled with a rushing, roaring sound like a great wind, or a forest fire, or ...

"Flood!" someone screamed. The Kemonomimi on the bridge, mostly children, started to scatter to either end of it. The Kemonomimi along the riverbank turned to run.

Most of them didn't make it.

A wall of brown water, debris swirling and tossing within it, swept down the riverbank and smashed into the bridge.

The bridge groaned, children screamed, and then the bridge collapsed, dumping everyone on it into the swirling water that had also sucked in dozens of Kemonomimi along its banks.

The Kemonomimi closest to Richard tossed down their weapons and ran toward the river. "Wait!" Victor shouted after them, but they ignored him.

"Come on," Richard shouted to his own crew, and those that could ran toward the flooded river.

Already the surge of water had subsided, but it had

done its damage. Here and there heads bobbed in the water. Children screamed as the current carried them farther out into the bay. Some of the Kemonomimi had splashed in after them, but it was obvious few among the cat-people were strong swimmers. Many simply stood on shore, weeping and shouting. Others ran for the boats, but they were a kilometer from the pier.

"Into the water!" he shouted to the Selkies. "Get as many as you can!"

The Selkies in his crew were already shimmying out of landsuits and hurling themselves into the river and the Bay. Almost at once they began hauling victims to the shore. Richard wished, not for the first time, that he had more in common with the Selkies than just the genetic sequence that protected him from the plague, but he was as helpless in the water as any nonmod. Nevertheless, he waded into the surf to help bring the victims up onto the shore as the Selkies retrieved them, and sent one of the nonmods from his crew back to the shuttle to bring all the first-aid and survival equipment they had down to help in the effort.

As the minutes past, the frantic effort slowed, then ceased. The Selkies continued to swim back and forth across the bay, searching for any remaining victims, but it soon became apparent any Kemonomimi who could be found had already been found.

Richard stood panting on the shore. Not far away, Chang ministered to a little Kemonomimi girl with a broken arm. Others from his crew were handing out blankets.

A few other blankets had been laid over bodies.

Richard became aware someone was standing behind him. He turned to find himself face-to-face with Victor.

"This doesn't change anything," Victor snarled. "The Kemonomimi will rule Earth." He held something in his hand; for a moment Richard thought it was a weapon, but it looked too small: it looked like a globe of glass.

Richard heard a strange sound in the Bay, and turned to look. Out between the headlands, something emerged from the water, a long, black, rounded shape: a submarine. And clinging to its sides as it rose were Selkies: twenty at least, maybe more.

"*They* might have something to say about that," Richard said.

Hansen's eyes had widened. "How many of those fishy devils did you bring with you from Marseguro?" he snarled.

"They're not from Marseguro," Richard said. "They're from Earth. The Selkies have been living here right alongside you since the Day of Salvation. And they're not going to hand the planet over to a new dictator just because he's a clone of their creator."

"I'm not a clone," Hansen snapped, then shouted, "Kemonomimi! To arms!"

The Kemonomimi looked out at the submarine. A few of them picked up rifles that were close at hand, but they held them pointed down, and looked at each other uncertainly.

One of Richard's crew had just emerged from the water a few feet away. Richard ran down to her. "Get out there," he said. "Tell them not to do anything aggressive."

She nodded, dove cleanly into the surf, and disappeared from sight.

Hansen was running up and down the beach, grabbing rifles and putting them into his people's hands. "We're being attacked!" he shouted. "What's wrong with you?"

He stopped in front of a white-furred Kemonomimi woman, picked up a rifle from the ground and shoved it into her hands. "Cleopatra, why aren't you armed?"

Cleopatra looked down at the rifle, then looked up at him. "I don't see any enemies," she said. "None of us do." She looked along the beach; the Kemonomimi stood silent, watching her and Hansen.

"I am ordering you—"

"I think we've had enough orders," Cleo said. "The Avatar is dead. The Body Purified is no more. We've fought and hidden for decades from both. Now that we've won, you want us to start a new war with a new enemy. But the first thing this new enemy of yours has done is help to rescue our friends and our children." She threw the rifle to one side. "I see no enemy."

Rifles clattered to the beach in all directions.

"They're watching us," Hansen growled then. "The Selkies. My worst mistake. They're watching us now for weakness. They've just seen you disarm yourselves. You think they're not your enemies. But that's not how they think about you. They'll try to take the world, now that we've killed the Avatar. They don't want to share it with you."

"We will fight if we must," Cleo said. "We always have. But we won't fight just because you say so. We won't kill just to kill." She looked him up and down, gave Richard a similarly searching look, then looked back at Hansen. "Clone."

Hansen's grip on the strange sphere he carried tightened. He glared at Cleopatra; but then his gaze slid further along the beach, and a strange smile flicked across his face. "We'll see." He strode past her.

Cleo didn't even turn around. But Richard, puzzled, looked past him. Further along the bank, he saw two figures, Selkies, one lying on the ground, one bending over the first. He blinked. That zebra-striped skinsuit looked just like the one that belonged to . . .

"Emily!" he shouted, and ran after Victor.

In the final mad rush through the town Emily twice came close to being crushed between tree trunks whirling like giant bludgeons through the foam, escaping only by plunging deep into the turbulent waters. But she didn't dare stay submerged either, because the water was so muddy she could see nothing down there, and didn't know when a rock or broken stump might suddenly appear to smash her.

The swollen river scoured its banks as it thundered through Newshore, collapsing piers, smashing boats against the sides of buildings. An entire boathouse collapsed as she swirled past, and she could see the water breaking against the sides of houses on either bank, knocking one off its foundation but not quite carrying it along.

And then . . . up ahead, the sea, but before the sea, a bridge, an ornamental wooden bridge, spanning the river, crowded with people . . . Kemonomimi, she realized . . . looking the other way, at the crashed shuttle . . . and then they were looking her way, and though she couldn't hear them above the sound of the river, she could see the round shapes of their mouths as they screamed, and then they ran, but they were too late.

The river was going to crush her against the side of the bridge like a bug, she suddenly realized, and she dove at the last possible moment, sweeping under the collapsing span. Suddenly she spilled out into the sea, the water going from fresh to salt in an instant, but she wasn't alone anymore, she was surrounded by struggling Kemonomimi, many of them children, screaming, flailing, sinking.

She plunged beneath the waves and found a small body she had seen disappear into the water an instant before, turned, and swam strongly toward the shore, ignoring as best she could the jabbing, fiery pain in her side from the cracked rib. She struggled out of the sea with the child, his fur soaked and bedraggled, coughing and choking in her arms, handed him to the waiting arms of a Kemonomimi on the shore, turned, and plunged back into the waves.

For a few moments all was chaos. She dove, peering through the water of the bay, muddied by the outflow of the river but still clear enough that she found two more children as they sank, kicking feebly, toward the bottom.

In the end, there were no more Kemonomimi to find. She'd been aware there were other Selkies in the Bay, assumed they must be from the crashed shuttle, but there'd been no time to talk to them, no time to find out what had happened, no time for anything but the frantic effort to save as many lives as she could.

At last she found herself on the beach, sucking air into her lungs as best she could, one hand pressed against her damaged side. She glanced down the beach, saw the crashed shuttle, but then saw something else on the pebbles much closer to it, a young Selkie lying there motionless, and ran to Shelby's side.

For a moment she was certain he was dead, but his eyes fluttered open as her shadow fell across his face. "Made it . . . to the sea," he said. "What a ride, huh?"

She smoothed her hand across his short black hair. "It sure was," she said, with a huge sense of relief. "It sure was."

"My leg . . . hurts . . ." he said, and when she looked she saw why: the same leg that had been shot now lay at an unnatural angle, clearly broken.

"Just a break," she said. "You'll be all right."

"Good," he said. He closed his eyes. "I'd really like to go home," he said faintly.

"Emily!" she heard someone shout, and her heart leaped.

"Richard!" She looked up at the familiar face on the man running toward her . . .

. . . on the *two* men running toward her . . .

She lunged to her feet, then froze, as Victor Hansen stopped not a meter away, pistol in one hand, something else in the other. Keeping the gun aimed at her, he circled up the beach so that he could watch Richard . . . God, it really was Richard! . . . running toward them.

"Stop or I'll shoot her," Victor said, almost conversationally, and Richard skidded to a halt, breathing heavily.

"This won't accomplish anything," Richard panted. "You've already lost the Kemonomimi. They won't follow you now."

"Won't they?" Victor looked out at the sea, where the Selkie sub was now just a hundred or so yards offshore. The Selkies on it were watching the beach. Atop the sail, a man with binoculars seemed focused on them; Emily heard him shout something. "So many Selkies close at hand. Good."

He looked at Richard. "My great flaw, as a young man, was too much compassion. That's why I helped the Selkies escape. But I have regretted it bitterly since. My Kemonomimi are young, they share that flaw. But I will not let it keep them from their destiny."

He held up the globe in his hand. "I pride myself on using the best tool for any task. To remove the Body from power, the plague. To remove the Avatar permanently, a matter/antimatter bomb of the Body's own design. And to remove the Selkies from the equation . . . this."

He held up the globe so that the sun shone on it. Its contents, the color of gold, glinted in the light. "I intended to give this its first test on Emily and the boy in my hidden lab, but the Avatar's scouts interrupted our journey there. No matter: I'm confident in my work." He lowered the sphere, smiled at Richard. "It's the plague," he said. "The same plague that has cleansed the Body from the Earth . . . but with two small alterations.

"One: your vaccine will not work against it. Two: Selkies are not immune to this version. Kemonomimi are." He gestured to Emily and Shelby. "When I smash this vial, the new version of the plague will begin to colonize Earth's biosphere, helped along by a rather clever set of self-replicating nanomachines. The plague will spread from this spot all over the world. These two—" he indicated Shelby and Emily, "—will be Case One and Case Two. But soon enough, every Selkie—and every remaining nonmod—will be dead.

And the Kemonomimi will finally have the world they deserve."

Emily stared at him, hating him. How could she hate him so much, she wondered, when just beyond him stood his identical twin, a man she loved more than she had ever loved anyone before?

"You'll die, too," Richard said. "If you've made the immunity specific to something in the Kemonomimi DNA . . ."

"Nonsense," Victor said. "I said *your* vaccine will not work against it. Mine, on the other hand, works just fine." He held up the vial again. "Enough talk. Welcome to your new world." He pulled his arm back to throw the vial—

A single shot rang out, and a neat hole appeared in Victor's chest, a hole that vanished a moment later in a gout of blood.

He dropped to his knees, and as the vial fell from his suddenly nerveless fingers, Emily leaped forward. She caught the glass globe in midair and cradled it to her like a child as she rolled over and over in the sand, the cracked rib stabbing her side like a red-hot knife.

Victor looked down at the sea of red spreading across his chest with a look of utter disbelief, then fell to his knees. He looked down toward the sea, where Cleopatra was just lowering her rifle.

"You . . ." Victor choked out. "You . . . I loved you . . . I created you . . . and you've betrayed me . . . you've betrayed your Creator . . ."

"I hear it's the human thing to do," Cleo whispered, and as Victor Hansen pitched forward onto the pebbles and died, she dropped her rifle, covered her face, and wept.

Emily heard horrific, wrenching sobs from somewhere else, and turned her head to look inland.

Just above the beach, on the road to Newshore, the black-furred Kemonomimi woman Ubasti knelt, mourning her Creator.

Chapter 23

TWO WEEKS LATER, Richard sat in the captain's chair on the bridge of *MSS Victor Hansen*, with Emily standing behind him, hands on his shoulders. The bridge crew were in place, the computer once more firmly under his command, thanks to Simon Goodfellow, and President McLean was on the main communications screen, her son visible behind her.

"It looks like there are more survivors than we'd estimated, scattered around the planet," McLean was saying. "And we're bringing more and more microfactories on line to produce vaccine, every one we can track down and program with Ann and Jerry's help. The South Africans Andy King contacted have been almost evangelical in their zeal to spread the vaccine around the globe. Cleo ... sorry, Prime Minister Cleopatra ... and her Kemonomimi have North America covered. And every time another microfactory goes on line, the supply increases and more people fan out to find still more survivors. We're still losing people, but we're reaching everyone we can."

"Any more trouble with the Body enclaves?" Richard asked. In the first week or so after the Avatar's death, they'd contacted all the Body outposts around the planet from the Avatar's old base at Paradise Island and told them of the new reality. Most had promptly agreed to help with the vaccine distribution, but a few had gone ominously silent, and in Gdansk a few Holy Warriors in pressure suits had raided a vaccine-producing microfactory in a former cheese plant, destroying the factory and taking the vaccine for themselves.

The remaining assault craft, recovered from the bottom

of the ocean—the third had been found wrecked in the Himalayas—had been sent into the area with a Kemono-mimi pilot at the controls, and, when the Holy Warriors emerged for a second raid, they'd found themselves seriously outgunned. A few had tried to fight, and those few had died. The others had surrendered.

"No," McLean said. "Though I'm sure they'll be more trouble in the future. True Believers can go underground for years."

Richard thought of Chris Keating. "I know," he said. "What about Victor's pet bug?"

"We haven't found his laboratory in the mountains yet; the Kemonomimi swear he never told any of them where it was. But the vial he had on the beach went into a plasma torch."

Richard heard Emily's breath catch. "There could be more of that Selkie-killing virus lurking somewhere?" she said.

"We'll find his lab," McLean said. "It's only a matter of time."

That troubled Richard, and he was sure Emily was no happier about it, but there was nothing to be done.

"How are you doing, Shelby?" Emily asked.

Shelby moved forward to come into better focus. "Pretty good," he said. "My leg's getting stronger all the time. I still have that gill rash from the dirty water, but it's clearing up."

"Mine, too," Emily said. "And I can breathe without it hurting now. So it looks like we're both on the mend."

Shelby looked like he was going to say something else, but then he looked at Richard; then at his mother; and finally cleared his throat and said, "Have a good trip back to Marseguro."

"Your mother is standing by, Emily," President McLean said. She reached out, and the camera panned left, revealing Dr. Christianson-Wood.

"Emily," she said. "Give my regards to Marseguro."

"It's not too late to come home with us," Emily said, with the tone of someone who had already lost an argument but was too stubborn to admit it.

"I'll come home some day, Emily. But not for a while. They need my help. The vaccine works, but it may not be a hundred percent effective—there's been some genetic drift between Earth and Marseguro over the years, you know. And it's taking a terrible toll among nonhuman primates, too." She spread her hands. "I created this monster, Emily. I never meant it to reach Earth, but it has. I let the genie out of the bottle, and now I've got to try to force it back in. I've got all the resources I need to create a countervirus, one even more infectious than the plague, but one that provides immunity rather than causes disease." Her eyes unfocused for a moment. "I can see exactly how to do it," she said. "If I . . ." She blinked, then looked right at the camera again. "Sorry," she said. "Short version: I can do it, but it might take a year or three. Then I'll see about coming home. Or who knows? Maybe you two will decide to live here."

"I daresay we'll be back and forth," Richard said, but he knew in his heart he would never live on Earth again. Marseguro was home now, with Emily. There was still so much to be rebuilt there, not just infrastructure, but trust between nonmods and Selkies. Plus, they had seventy years' worth of Earth's technological knowledge stored in their computers, and holds full of modern microfactories and raw materials with which to manufacture that technology. With it, they could spread humanity across Marseguro, free from the fear of discovery that had hampered their society's development for so long.

Free, at least, from the fear of discovery by Holy Warriors on Earth.

"President McLean," Richard said, and the camera panned back to her. "I know resources are limited, but you've got to get more manned ships into orbit. I don't imagine anyone will approach Earth right away, not with the stories of the deadliness of the plague spreading out among the colonies. But there are still Body Purified ships, and Holy Warriors, out there. And eventually, they're going to try to return."

"We'll be ready," President McLean said. "Will Marseguro?"

"We'll do our best." Among the microfactories aboard *Victor Hansen* were the seed factories for starship manufacture, but it would be months before they could bootstrap their way to full-scale dockyards, even assuming the minebots could find the resources needed on Marseguro's one landmass, deep in its ocean, or among its system's asteroids.

"I am not a Believer in the Body Purified," the president said, "but I believe in a God: a kind and loving God, not the monster created by the First Avatar in his own image. I'll be praying for Marseguro, Richard Hansen, and for Earth. We've both undergone our baptism by fire. I'm confident God has better things in store for us in the future."

Richard didn't know how to respond to that. He had believed in the First Avatar's God, and that belief had been shattered. He couldn't now—he doubted he *ever* could—put that shattered belief back together . . . and even if he could, after all the death and pain of the past few months the God he thought he would find would be anything but kind and loving.

So he said nothing.

Emily cleared her throat. "Thank you, Madame President," she said quietly. "I'm sure a great many people on both planets will join you in that prayer."

President McLean nodded, then said briskly, "I have a Provisional Planetary Council meeting with Prime Minister Cleopatra and our respective staffs in ten minutes," she said, "so I'd best cut this short. Have a safe trip home and . . ." She smiled suddenly. "Thank you. For everything."

"Thank you, Madame President," Richard said. "Goodbye, Shelby. Good-bye, Dr. Christianson-Wood."

" 'Bye, Shel," Emily said. " 'Bye, Mom. I love you."

"I love you, too, sweetie," her mother said. "Tell Amy I love her, too, and I'm sorry I missed her wedding. Oh, and tell John Duval that if he doesn't treat her properly, I'll design another plague, just for him, personally." She smiled, blinking back tears. "Good-bye."

The screen went blank.

Richard heard Emily's soft sob, even if no one else did. He reached up and took her hands, warm on his shoulders, and squeezed them, and felt her lean forward and kiss the top of his head. He smiled.

"All right, then," he said. "Let's go home."

Edward Willett

"Their moral dilemma is only on of the reasons this novel is so fascinating. The Selkie culture and infrastructure is very picturesque and easily pictured by readers who will want to visit his exotic world." —*Midwest Book Review*

"Willett is well able to keep all his juggling balls in the air at the same time....It's a good story, a great mate to the first volume." —Ian Randal Strock at *SF Scope*

The Helix War
Omnibus:
Marseguro *Terra Insegura*
978-0-7564-0738-4

And don't miss:

Lost in Translation
978-0-7564-0340-9

To Order Call: 1-800-788-6262
www.dawbooks.com

DAW 177

Tanya Huff

The *Confederation* Novels

"As a heroine, Kerr shines. She is cut from the same mold as Ellen Ripley of the Aliens films. Like her heroine, Huff delivers the goods." —*SF Weekly*

A CONFEDERATION OF VALOR
Omnibus Edition
(*Valor's Choice, The Better Part of Valor*)
978-0-7564-0399-7

THE HEART OF VALOR
978-0-7564-0481-9

VALOR'S TRIAL
978-0-7564-0557-1

THE TRUTH OF VALOR
978-0-7564-0684-4

To Order Call: 1-800-788-6262
www.dawbooks.com

RM Meluch

The Tour of the Merrimack

"An action-packed space opera. For readers who like romps through outer space, lots of battles with gooey horrific insects, and character sexplotation, *The Myriad* delivers..." —*SciFi.com*

"Like *The Myriad*, this one is grand space opera. You will enjoy it." —*Analog*

"This is grand old-fashioned space opera, so toss your disbelief out the nearest airlock and dive in."
  —*Publishers Weekly* (Starred Review)

THE MYRIAD   0-7564-0320-1
WOLF STAR   0-7564-0383-6
THE SAGITTARIUS COMMAND
                        978-0-7564-0490-1
STRENGTH AND HONOR
                        978-0-7564-0578-6

To Order Call: 1-800-788-6262

www.dawbooks.com